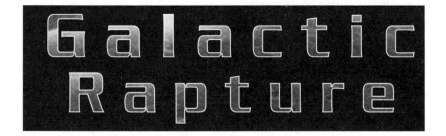

Prometheus Books

59 John Glenn Drive
Amherst, New York 14228-2197

Map illustrations by Chris Kolasny

Published 2000 by Prometheus Books

Inquiries should be addressed to
Prometheus Books, 59 John Glenn Drive, Amherst, New York 14228–2197.
VOICE: 716–691–0133, ext. 207.
FAX: 716–564–2711.
WWW.PROMETHEUSBOOKS.COM

04 03 02 01 00   5 4 3 2 1

Library of Congress Cataloging-in-Publication Data

Flynn, Tom, 1955–
    Galactic rapture / by Tom Flynn.
        p.   cm.
    ISBN 1–57392–754–6
    I. Title.

PS3556.L935 G35 2000
813'.54—dc21   99–051301
                                                                        CIP

Printed in the United States of America on acid-free paper

To Susan, who survived another book, and then some.

contents

Jaremi Four

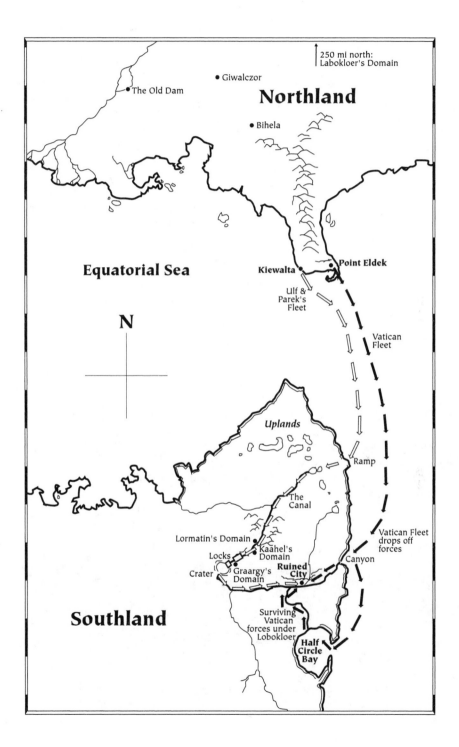

250 mi north:
Labokloer's Domain

• Giwalczor

•The Old Dam

Northland

• Bihela

Equatorial Sea

Point Eldek

Kiewalta •

Ulf &
Parek's
Fleet

N

Vatican
Fleet

Uplands

Ramp

The
Canal

Vatican Fleet
drops off
forces

Lormatin's Domain

Kaahel's
Domain

Locks

Canyon

Crater

Graargy's
Domain

Ruined
City

Southland

Surviving
Vatican
forces under
Lobokloer

Half
Circle
Bay

acknowledgments

Many people, places and ideas shaped this book. Special thanks are due to the Center for Inquiry and the Council for Secular Humanism; my years working for these organizations provided countless learning opportunities. In particular, my attendance at a 1993 Humanist-Mormon Dialogue, which the Council cosponsored, sharpened my fascination with the faith that remains one of America's fastest-growing in spite of the thoroughness and authority with which its claims have been debunked. Jim Cox, the late Greg Erwin, and Verle Muhrer shared Mormon history and lore. Steve Tryon and Richard Flynn consulted on military and naval matters. Tom Callahan revealed to me places that metamorphosed into key settings for this book. The late Gordon Stein and Tim Binga, past and present directors of the Center for Inquiry Libraries, put invaluable resources at my fingertips. The story of Arn Parek underwent two previous incarnations, as a one-act play (produced, ironically enough, at a Jesuit university) and as an independent video. I offer thanks to Dave Hayes and Ken Rowe (producer of the independent video), the first Dultavs; Paul Young and Bob Loblaw, the first Pareks; and Cindy Savage and Jode Edmunds, the first Ruths.

Credit is due to others whose explorations launched my own thought on new voyages. My debt to Richard Dawkins, for his idea of the spread of new religions as an epidemiological process, and to Fawn Brodie for her classic biography of Joseph Smith, should be clear. Also due thanks are John Schumaker, for his account of the roles of music and rhythm in religious experience; Mary Kilbourne

Matossian, for her speculations on molds, epidemics, and history; James-Charles Noonan Jr., for his encyclopedic survey of Vatican protocol and ceremonial; Malachi Martin, for his many riveting accounts of Vatican intrigue; Brent Lee Metcalfe, for his research into links between Freemasonry and early Mormonism; John K. Cannizzo and Ronald H. Kaitchuck, for their work on interacting binary stars; and Michael S. Triantafyllou and George S. Triantafyllou, for their provocative ideas about swimming watercraft. Happy Rhodes provided musical inspiration. In acknowledging these individuals, let me stress that they contributed through their published works and played no deliberate role in the development of this book.

Finally I must express gratitude to my volunteer review readers, who contributed prized input as the writing progressed: Tim Binga, Matt Cherry, Amanda Chesworth, Jim Cox, Michael Scott Earl, Greg Erwin, Gary Gerber, Scott Lohman, Tim Madigan, Ben Radford, Kathy Vaughn, and especially Ken Marsalek.

Of course, responsibility for the finished work is entirely my own. In the event that this novel provokes the first Mormon *fatwa*, those I have thanked will no doubt appreciate would-be assassins' best efforts to remember that.

Author's Notes

The epigraph at the head of Part Two is from John F. Schumaker, *The Corruption of Reality* (Amherst, N.Y.: Prometheus Books, 1995), pp. 237–38. Used with permission of the author.

The "Curse of Ernulphus" quoted in Part Three is an authentic Roman Catholic excommunication curse. See Henry C. Lea, *Studies in Church History* (Philadelphia: Henry C. Lea's Son and Co., 1883), pp. 343–45.

All quotes from the Book of Mormon are also genuine. With raw material like that, why make anything up?

Part One

To free a man from error is not to deprive him of anything but to give him something: for the knowledge that a thing is false is a piece of truth.

—Schopenhauer

1. Planet Jaremi Four—Northern Hemisphere

Ruth Griszam stood among the downstream ruins, breathing deeply. The morning air smelled of dew and moldering leaves. To her left, a hillside rose beyond the listless creek and its shell of fog. Ruth watched her companions lurch uphill. Ulf climbed surely, steamrifle slung across his back. Chagrin followed, looking like a blundering scarecrow in rags with an antique carbine over one shoulder. He pulled hard at his walking stick; one all-but-useless leg swung pointlessly as he climbed.

They search for food, Ruth thought. *So much the worse for whoever they find who has some.*

She squinted into a jaundiced sunrise. The implants tugged gently in her cheeks. To the north, pink aurora still swirled in the sky. She turned south, upstream. Toward the body.

13

The corpse bobbed face up. One foot had wedged in the crotch of a water-logged fallen tree; otherwise it would have just continued downstream. Ruth waded closer and prodded it with a long stick. Its arms quavered. Yellowed nails pulled free of the fingers and skittered away on the current like beetles' wings.

Dead for days, Ruth thought. *Must've gone over the spillway during the night.* Its face was black and distended. Someone had slit the throat. *Not Ulf's work. Just a passing corpse. No big story here.* Ruth shrugged. *Still, time to do some image-mongering.*

Ruth Griszam of Terra, undercover documentarian on assignment among the autochthonous peoples of the Enclave planet Jaremi Four, clocked in for the day.

She subvocalized a nonsense syllable, triggering the cascade of electronic and biological events that would put her online. It began with tingling in her cheeks. Biotech implants started to record the faintest movements of her eye, head, and neck muscles—each glint of neural traffic between her vestibular system and her parietal cortices—for later resynchronization to her visual field. Those who experienced, or *pov*ed, her recordings would need that data; uncompensated for, the flittings of her gaze might induce vertigo.

Deep in her skull, a tiny transceiver implant opened a channel to an OmNet satellite overhead. An instant later, Ruth knew the satellite was receiving her. It beamed back sync information and triggered alternate cortical pathways.

Ruth changed. Normally dormant areas of her cortex sparked into orderly action. In microseconds, the largest part of her cerebral capacity was devoted to fine-grained control of the muscles in her head, face, and neck. Nerve shunts routed potentially distracting somesthetic information out of her conscious awareness. Blood flow to sense organs increased. An artificial gland released a hormone that canceled her olfactory bulbs' adaptive capability. The smells of morning assaulted her anew, pungent as the day's first breath.

Subvocalizing one more nonsense syllable, she went fully into Mode.

Suck, rush, wrench!

For a moment her eyes danced unnaturally. With a familiar effort she drove the "senso shudder" beneath her muscular threshold. Others would see nothing odd about her, save perhaps the preternatural smoothness of her movements. More than anything else, it was this ability to suppress the reflex signs of Mode—to function as a Spectator without looking like one—that separated undercover documentarians like Ruth Griszam from less-accomplished practitioners.

Ruth squatted. The corpse's eyes were fogged over, the irises black with decay. If she peeked below the veneer of conscious awareness, she could hear the polyphasic *verify* signal softly humming, assuring her that aboard the relay satellite a senso recorder was registering it all—her visual field, the breeze brushing her neck, the chilly tug of the water at her calves, the body's stench. Later, she knew, the journal would be deep-beamed to OmNet Main on Terra, where it would be edited, catalogued, repackaged, and distributed to a Galaxy full of humans eager for vicarious adventure.

She was a Spectator. Her job was to observe.

With the smoothness of expanded muscle control, Ruth rose. Ahead of her, the crumbling dam stretched across the valley, its concrete wall honeycombed with cracks. Beside it loomed the six-story powerhouse, its empty doors and windows agape like toothless mouths, then the foaming spillway. Along its crest, pitted control wheels accused the brightening sky.

A shot rang out.

Another.

Forjel the artsy establishing pov! *Time this corpse disappeared. Then me, too.*

Ruth jammed her stick into the crotch of the fallen tree, freeing the body's foot. In what seemed a single motion, she was up on the bank. She glanced to make sure the body was moving downstream, rolled her trouser legs down over the boots she'd never removed, and pulled her fur wrap free of her ammo belt.

Another shot. *Closer! Definitely not from the direction Ulf and Chagrin went.* Her boots heavy with stream water, Ruth scrambled uphill from cover to cover. *Marauders!* Panting, she stopped below the twisted stairway that led up inside the powerhouse.

Thin voices could be heard now.

Ruth took the stairs two at a time and hurled herself through the yawning doorway and onto the powerhouse floor.

Kraa-ak! Steamrifle round. Really close.

"Get him!" a male voice shouted, no more than twenty meters away.

They're not shooting at me after all. Ruth scurried against a rust-pocked switching cabinet. She squinted back through the doorway.

Halfway up the hillside, a man in his late forties darted from the bushes. He wore fatigue pants and a bulky field jacket. A leather knapsack bounced on his right shoulder.

Another shot. The stranger lost his footing and tumbled downhill, half the distance to the dam. He came up cursing, clutching his left arm just below the shoulder. Red oozed between his fingers.

They winged him, she thought. *But who are they? Forjeler, who's he?*

The stranger staggered onto the spalled concrete of the dam. She lost sight of him. *Forjeler,* she cursed, *I should have strewn bugs!*

The stranger's footfalls slapped along the dam top. Ruth could see him again. He'd stopped dead, his body perfectly framed through a hole in the powerhouse roof. Frantic, he glanced about. With the spillway ahead of him, he had nowhere to go.

Ruth shriveled behind a turbine housing, watching intensely.

Another shot missed the stranger by centimeters. Recklessly, he hurled himself off the lip of the dam and landed heavily on the powerhouse roof. He tried to roll toward the opening.

Or would have.

The roof failed beneath under his weight. Rotten timbers squealed. In a shower of fragments, he crunched halfway through and got stuck.

Well, who says nothing ever happens in the Northland of Jaremi Four? Ruth climbed the turbine housing for a better view. The stranger's legs and right arm dangled inside. His wounded arm, shoulders, and head were still exposed above. After a moment, he pulled himself through. He clung to rusty trusswork beneath the roof, catching his breath, and cautiously lowered himself onto an ancient catwalk. It gave beneath his weight more than he liked, so he tossed away his knapsack. It smacked heavily to the powerhouse floor.

Ruth concealed herself again.

The stranger stared down into the powerhouse gallery. Ashen light faltered from empty doors and windows, illiuminating fissured stone walls and ruined turbines and transformers. Everywhere the floor was breached by irregular openings. Further inside, some crumbling stairways led down into darkness.

Silently, Ruth reached into a rusted cavity in the turbine housing and retrieved the steamrifle she'd hidden there.

The stranger stepped off the staircase onto the powerhouse floor. Squeezing his wounded arm, he began to look for cover.

Now!

Ruth clambered atop the turbine and bounded down the other side to the powerhouse floor. Water spewed from her boots.

Her steamrifle was centered on his chest.

The stranger frowned. "That doesn't work."

Ammunition hadn't been manufactured for decades; Jaremians often fired warning shots so strangers could know their weapons functioned. Ruth lowered the rifle barrel slightly. At least he could see all the winkies flashing green. "I'll fire a demo shot," she hissed, "if you don't mind whoever's chasing you knowing where you are."

The stranger decided not to call her bluff. Up went his hands—the right one all the way, the left one less so.

"You accept that this rifle works. I suggest you also accept that I know how to use it."

"No doubt."

She frowned toward the open doorway. "Why are they after you?"

"Why do people shoot at anyone? Maybe they liked my knapsack. Fucking marauders."

She peered at his wounded arm. "You're bleeding."

He gawked at her boots. Creek water puddled around them. "You're dripping."

Listen! They could hear hoarse shouts and quick footfalls along the dam top.

The stranger wanted to hide. He glanced nervously at Ruth's rifle.

"They can't see in," she told him. "It's too dark compared to outside."

"They might've seen me fall."

Ruth stood motionless.

"They'll come here looking," he warned.

She kept the steamrifle centered on him.

"Let me put this in perspective," the stranger hissed, exasperated. "Those are the bad guys. I'm a college professor."

"A . . . what?"

He shrugged. "All right, a former college professor."

Still she made no sign.

He dropped his hands in an imploring gesture. "Fucking hell, woman—"

She poked the steamrifle forward.

He stopped talking, but he didn't raise his hands again.

Through the yawning doorway, Ruth saw the first pursuer. He was clad in leather, improvised chain mail, and necklaces of teeth. Cracked-lensed goggles hung below his neck. The haggard marauder burst from cover halfway up the hillside. Seeing nothing, he melted back into the brush.

We can't face off here much longer, Ruth thought. *I have a feeling I can trust this stranger. And what the sfelb, maybe it's a story.* She waved with the steamrifle toward one of the openings in the powerhouse floor. "Okay. Go."

He smiled a little, bolted across the powerhouse, and came back with his knapsack.

Ruth had shouldered the rifle. Deftly she drew one pistol. With her fur wrap open, she knew he'd spot the butt of another gun jammed into her belt.

"Resourceful, you are," he said wryly.

"My prisoner, you are," she answered flatly.

A flight of dusty concrete stairs dropped away inside a floor aperture, heading deep into the powerhouse. Ruth gestured with the pistol. "Down you go. Hurry."

They descended into a warren of tunnels that once had serviced turbines. Circling a fractured column, she waved him down another flight of stairs.

"Stop here," she ordered at the next landing. She moved close to him and pressed the pistol into his chest. "Hold still," she grated. With her free hand, she reached up and found a dented metal sheet studded with nailed-on scraps of wood and electrical hardware.

The debris-dotted sheet metal was stuck on something.

Two floors up, boots clattered on the access stairway. *Marauders, following the stranger's trail.* She turned toward him, exasperated. "I can't get this cover loose with one hand. Help me pull it out."

Three-handed, they drew the camouflage hatch across the stairwell opening. It slid closed over their heads.

A casual searcher wouldn't know the lower levels of the staircase existed.

Below them, the stairs continued to a level that was clearly below the waterline. A lantern's glow cast weaving patterns on upcurled tiles. "What's this?" the stranger asked.

"I'm going to ask the questions. And I'll expect answers." She gestured with the pistol. "Go."

Well, well, she thought as she followed her strangely poised prisoner into the subcellar. *There's a definite tale in this somewhere. Today could be worthwhile after all.*

2. Aboard the Galactic Confetory Schooner *Bright Hope*

Glimmering spangles danced in the tactical display. The other ships were shifting to accommodate the new arrival, switching from a four-point to a five-point attack formation. Captain Laurien Eldridge scratched beside her eye with one of her six virtual arms. "Media and observer ships all properly behind the cordons," reported Detex Officer Lynn Wachieu. "At point zero-zero-zero, I show no readings."

"We're here already?" the Spectator asked. A registered documentarian of some repute, he'd come aboard just before *Bright Hope*'s departure.

"We are here already." Eldridge nodded. "Are you having any difficulty, um, seeing this environment?"

The interstellar schooner's virtual bridge resembled a ceramic desert that had run like fudge in a strong wind. Control pylons flowed upward from the featureless, glassy surface as crew members passed. "No difficulty, Fem Captain," the Spectator answered. "My experients will see and sense it just as you do."

"Your . . . what?"

"My *experients.*"

"The term is unfamiliar."

"Spectator jargon. Experients are my audience. You know, those who *pov* my work."

"Mm-hmm," said Eldridge blankly.

The Spectator smiled. "People say they 'watch' senso, but there's so much more to it than that."

Eldridge nodded dourly. Smiling was not on her agenda today.

"Um, about your appearance. . . ." the Spectator ventured.

"My extra arms? Or perhaps you mean. . . ." Eldridge nodded toward Detex officer Lynn Wachieu at her duty station. Wachieu had assumed the form of a hairless spider on a metallic web. Her abdomen was covered with eyes. Additional eyes sprouted from the joints of each limb. "Don't worry," Eldridge told the Spectator. "We're ordinary humans, stationed in locations widely removed about the ship so no single hostile strike would be likely to engulf us all. We work together inside this virtual environment."

"But why—" the Spectator blinked as Executive Officer Arla Gavisel passed by below him. She had the form of a cerulean otter.

"We take the forms we choose," Eldridge said. "The bridge software accommodates their characteristics. With these forms we enjoy more densely textured information—more options for manipulation and control—than natural bodies could accommodate." With her number-five arm, Eldridge pointed toward Wachieu's spider form. "Through her eyes and web, Fem Wachieu is processing the maximum information her brain can handle. Human senses no longer limit her. It's like that for each of us."

The Spectator nodded. "And you chose that goddess form? Nostalgic for Hinduslam?"

"Religion? Me? I'm Gwilyan." Eldridge shrugged her six arms. "I just have to run a lot of stuff."

Eldridge and the Spectator stood on an opalescent viewing platform. It arched like a frozen splash five meters above the bridge's glassy floor. Facing them from similar platforms several meters away were the other three observers assigned to this hastily organized mission. The folk singer wore uncured leather and clutched an Ordhian lute. The bridge maintained his actual appearance, as he would be performing shortly. On the next platform physicist Annek Panna appeared as a hovering nebula spangled with a dozen prominent stars. Virtual consoles surrounded her, the controls for the experimental stardrive that had been mated so hurriedly, so incompletely, with *Bright Hope*'s other systems.

Above the final platform floated the enigmatic presence known only as the VIP.

This mysterious personage had been whisked aboard at the last minute, under the highest security clearances and on the direct orders of the Privy High Council. It was mute testimony to the VIP's importance that he (or perhaps she or it) had been permitted to designate no virtual image at all. No one had the authority to assign one. The VIP appeared only as a formless, edgeless blob of purest black. To view the blob was to feel tugged to leap into its cheerless center. *There are good reasons,* Eldridge thought, *why few are permitted to enter a virtual bridge displaying nothing at all.*

"Message coming in," Wachieu called.

A small viewsphere opened before Eldridge. It showed the captain of the flagship *Alekko* which kept an oceanic theme on its bridge; the fleet commander appeared as an armored anglerfish with body plates the color of a ripe carrot. "Welcome to the anticipation fleet, Captain Eldridge," the anglerfish said.

"Thank you, fleet commander. Our systems are three-by-three greens."

"Very well. We will reduce our comm traffic to clear bandwidth for your transmission. *Alekko* out."

The Spectator nodded toward Eldridge. "Perhaps we could review once more what will happen."

"We're all feeling a bit under-briefed here," Eldridge rumbled. A tactical display rippled into the air in front of them. She pointed out the ships one by one. "That one's us. Here, the superdreadnought *Alekko*. There's the destroyer *Spindrift*, the weapons platform *AD-1601*, and the light cruiser *KC-1714*. The ships occupy the points of a tetrahedron at whose center the Tuezi will appear."

"Point zero-zero-zero," said the Spectator, indicating the center of the polygon. Eldridge nodded somberly.

A signal buzzed in the Spectator's mind. "We go live in one minute."

Eldridge gestured toward the VIP on the opposite platform. "A reminder—our VIP guest may not be seen."

"That's all arranged," said the Spectator. "I will just ignore him. . . . her?"

Eldridge shrugged.

"If, um, *it* gets into my field of view, the editors back at OmNet will just strip it out. You know, paste some background over it as though the VIP wasn't there."

Eldridge's eyebrows pricked up. "I thought this was a live 'cast."

"Oh, replacing part of the visual field in real time is no problem any more. It's done often."

Eldridge made a mental note never again to believe anything she saw on senso.

"T minus fifteen!" Executive Officer Gavisel brayed.

"Control crew!" Eldridge called. "This will be your last break before T minus zero. At ease, three minutes."

"*Stand by,*" the Spectator subvocalized to the folk singer. Her nod indicated that she was hearing the *verify* signal three-by-three greens. "*Three, two. . . .*"

The 'cast began with music. Plaintive chords cascaded from the folk singer's lute. He was the foremost interpreter of Ordhian ballads, and this was the saddest of them all:

Tuezi, Tuezi, Tuezi
Chant the haunted space folk

The handful who have heard one push through!
Hear that sound in your 'phones,
Bid farewell to your homes;
All their lands,
All their skies,
All you knew.

Below, Executive Officer Arla Gavisel bared blue teeth. Like every Arkhetil, she was a bitter atheist. "You know what he's singing, don't you?" she hissed to Wachieu. "It's a forjeling *hymn!* This is no place for that."

Wachieu frowned, to the degree a spider could. "Everyone knows where you stand, Arla. For me, religious feeling comes naturally at a time like this."

A moment before, the VIP hadn't been among them. Now he, she, or it was. "You seem profoundly distressed, Fem Wachieu," the VIP said.

"My people have feared the Tuezi for millennia," Wachieu explained. (She hailed from Ordh.) "Those things make my hair stand on end. Or would, if I had hair."

"You're seasoned officers," the VIP said measuredly, "yet the terror you experience at the approach of the Tuezi seems visceral and prerational—almost unfiltered by thought."

Our VIP must be a Terran, Gavisel realized. Their world had entered the Galactic Confetory only recently; Terrans often had difficulty in understanding how deep an imprint the Tuezi threat had left on Galactic culture. *Forjeling Terra should never have been let into the Confetory as a full memberworld!*

The folk singer continued:

The stars swim and shimmer
Where soon comes a'rippling
A platform devoid of all grace.
A vast grotesque island, swollen and quiet.
Now passes a moment.
Then soulless, it raises its shields,
Its pestilent errand begun.

Atop their shared platform, the Spectator gave Eldridge a subvocal cue. Linking several sets of fingers, the captain launched into the speech the High Privy Council's flacks had written for her. "Homs and fems across the Galaxy, this is Captain Laurien Eldridge, speaking to you from the bridge of the schooner *Bright Hope.* We are pleased to join this anticipation fleet. Our experimental Panna drive has enabled us to come from Pastrick Yards in just under six days—a journey that would take any other craft four weeks." As coached, Eldridge paused for an eight count. *Let those who wish to cheer enjoy this interval to do so.* "This new technology will soon cut interstellar transit times by more than a factor of four. The new ultrahigh-speed interstellar drive is the innovation of Dr. Annek Panna, who has joined us in the bridge today." Eldridge waved two or three hands toward Dr. Panna. With inhuman smoothness the Spectator twisted at neck and waist to regard Panna's nebular form. After a proper interval, he turreted back toward Eldridge. *"Bright Hope* was chosen as the Panna drive testbed because she is a medium-sized hull, far too large for earlier prototype high-speed drives. Though normally unarmed, *Bright Hope* was fitted with a standard weapons battery for this Tuezi anticipation mission."

Behind Eldridge, a tactical readout filled the sky. In it, a wireframe tetrahedron slowly wheeled, a ship at each of its five points. "Most of us know the story of the Tuezi too well. Uninhabited robot platforms, the Tuezi are interstellar genocide machines created by some unknown but advanced race. Though no one knows for certain, we presume the Tuezi were designed as weapons in some unimaginable war. Their makers may live in the past, the future, or simply very far away— another mystery. Nor does anyone know why the makers chose to scatter Tuezi, perhaps by the millions, across the Galaxy and throughout time."

The folk singer crooned:

No plan, no desire
No mercy, no pause.
No one knows where it came from, or when.

"But we know what happens when a Tuezi appears," Eldridge said grimly. "At the moment of transfer, it is vulnerable. Just a fraction of a second later, it raises almost impenetrable shields, proceeds to a nearby planetary system, and rains down destruction."

Choosing random its planet
Raining fire, denudes it
Unleashing hot fury below.
Some planets are sundered
Others just scorched.
When victims survive
They envy the dead.

Eldridge resumed her narrative as the folk singer strummed sadly. "As mysteriously as it came, having devastated a star system, the device destroys itself in an explosion so potent that not a scrap of wreckage remains for our scientists to learn from."

All at once it is over
Tuezi turns back its fire
Within its invuln'rable hull.
What naught else could harm
Explodes sudden in spasm
The blinding hot cruel light of hope.

The song ended on a prolonged high note. At its end the folk singer stood, spent. Tears trickled down his cheeks.

"The folk singer has performed a classic Ordhian ballad, rich in stoic resignation," Eldridge declared. "Until fifty-three years ago, that ballad captured human helplessness before the Tuezi. The hideous platforms came where and when they pleased. All anyone could do was console the survivors, if any, help in the cleanup, and hope against hope that the next time such a machine appeared, it would not be in the skies of one's own homeworld.

"Fifty-three years ago, at the age of eighteen, the child prodigy Fram Galbior solved the mathematics of how Tuezi strikes are distributed through space and time. Since then, his equilibrational calculus has enabled each of the eight known Tuezi emergences to be *predicted*. Knowing where and when a Tuezi will appear, we simply surround the spot with ships." Flickering green lines came alive in the display behind Eldridge. They indicated each ship's line of fire. "When the Tuezi comes through, we're waiting. Before it powers up and raises shields, we blow it to sfelb."

Eldridge stepped toward the Spectator for emphasis. "According to Galbior's calculations, today's appearance will be the only Tuezi strike many in my generation are likely to see. Of the trillions of humans in the Confetory, only the four thousand men and women of this anticipation fleet will participate in its destruction. We know the stakes. Let our aim be true."

The Spectator ended transmission. One could tell he was no field operative; he trembled visibly as he dropped out of Mode. "Very good, Fem Captain," he said.

"Have a moment, Captain?" the VIP purred, abruptly behind her.

"My orders are always to have time for you. Still, brevity would be appreciated."

"Understood. Now, Captain, do you mean to say that *every* Tuezi emergence since Fram Galbior published his equations has been correctly predicted?"

"Every *known* emergence," Eldridge corrected. "Perhaps Tuezi pop up every week in the Andromeda galaxy. But in the space patrolled by the Galactic Confetory PeaceForce, over fifty-three years we have never missed a Tuezi strike. And we've never had a false alarm. Galbior has predicted exactly when and where each would push through."

"That is impressive," the VIP agreed.

"Two minutes, thirty seconds," cried Wachieu from her crater.

"All personnel, maximum readiness," called Captain Eldridge.

"Contact!" cried Wachieu. "I have contact."

Shuddering, the Spectator signed back on.

"Let's hear it," Eldridge ordered.

There it was: the expected—but dreaded—sound of emergence. *Tuezi, tuezi, tuezi.* It was a sine wave of pulsing static flanging in and out, a waveform rolling endlessly over itself, an audio signature unlike any other.

Galactics had known and dreaded that sound for generations. The sound sparked a feeling like sharpened fingernails dragging along Eldridge's back—from the inside. *Tuezi, tuezi, tuezi.*

The folk singer launched into the final verse of his ballad, the one he'd saved for this moment:

> Like the indrawing, outrolling sea
> It sizzles, it whooshes
> With a rush slightly sibilant
> That sound signifies only death.

Tuezi, tuezi, tuezi. By means Galactic science had never unraveled, the robot marauder was being wrenched from its native time and place. It was being sent here, now.

"Optical disturbances!" Wachieu cried.

The tactical display transmuted into a visible-light view of starry space at point zero-zero-zero.

The starfield was swimming.

Tuezi, tuezi, tuezi. Whatever power it was that was forcing the Tuezi through, it bubbled space and profoundly refracted visible light.

"You are looking at a parcel of space twenty kilometers wide, centered on point zero-zero-zero," Eldridge told the Spectator. "If our Tuezi is of conventional design, it will just about fill the sphere."

Tuezi, tuezi, tuezi.

"Fem Wachieu, accuracy!" called Eldridge.

"Pre-emergence phenomena are on schedule to the picosecond. Position is exactly centered on point zero-zero-zero, to the nanometer. If there is *any* deviation from Hom Galbior's predictions, it's too small for ship's susceptors to register in real time."

On his platform, the VIP bobbed inscrutably. *Is he, she, or it nodding?* Eldridge wondered.

Tuezi, tuezi, tuezi.

Eldridge consulted a display that boiled from the bridge floor. *Our gunnery, such as it is, is three-by-three. To the mighty volleys of the real fighting ships,* Bright Hope *will add its few extra terawatts—all for politics' sake.* "Countdown, please, Hom Wachieu," Eldridge said aloud.

"Ten. Nine. Eight. Seven."

One by one, Wachieu shut down her susceptor arrays. Some of them were already useless, pegged by the phenomena attending the Tuezi's emergence. Others would be blinded by what was to follow. Only the susceptors required to probe the Tuezi or to record its destruction would be left operational.

"Six. Five. Four."

Others had urgent datacrawls to watch, or subsystems to monitor. Paradoxically, at this critical moment Executive Officer Gavisel found herself with no pressing tasks. So she fixed one otterly eye—and the gaze of about half the susceptors under her personal control—on the enigmatic blackness of the VIP. *Now we'll see.*

"Three. Two. One," Wachieu called. *"Emergence."*

One instant, the Spectator had been watching the stars swim; the next, the vision sphere was full from edge to edge with the threatening bulk of the Tuezi.

Complex, wholly without grace, it was a hodgepodge of modules and platforms and haphazard weapon tubes, a jagged-edged icosahedron sixteen kilometers across. All those impressions came to the Spectator in a gestalten flash. They had to, for the Tuezi was only there for a fiftieth of a second. His next impression, persisting maybe a half second, was of the Tuezi being riven by some two hundred weapon beams from the ships of the anticipation group. Explosions bloomed cancerously across its surface. The Spectator got a flash of a huge, V-shaped structure breaking free against a background of detonations. Then the attacking beams found the Tuezi's power core. The vision sphere overflowed with fierce radiance. That was the image that endured.

"Destruction complete," cried Wachieu.

"Weapons operated nominally," reported Gavisel. She broke away from the giddy round of celebration as soon as she could. She asked the bridge for privacy.

A sheath of bridge floor material obligingly arched over her and her "eyes-only" displays. Gavisel began reviewing the slow-motion recordings she'd made while the Tuezi died. Her probes had not focused out into space, but on the VIP.

Gavisel knew virtual imaging equipment like that in *Bright Hope*'s battle bridge was designed to respond to each user's rank and personality. Eminent individuals usually had inner logos. Virtual environments would display those logos by default unless commanded not to—as Gavisel herself had when she chose her otter *persona.*

In his, her, or its arrogance, the VIP had chosen to display nothing at all, an option the equipment was designed to discourage. *The VIP must concentrate continuously to keep that unfriendly empty blob on display.* Gavisel hoped that when the Tuezi died, if only for a moment, the VIP's guard might have wavered.

There! I was right. For about a tenth of a second, just as the Tuezi exploded, the VIP's obsidian shield had broken down. The bridge equipment almost had time to finish constructing the VIP's personal logo before he, she, or it had regained control and forced the blackness back.

Gavisel scrolled forward and back through the moment, selected the clearest freeze frame, and assigned a bank of thought engines to clarify the image.

Under their prodding, the logo became complete. There was a low red hat with an enormous brim, from which flowed coiled burgundy ropes, twin waterfalls of fabric tassels, and an elaborately decorated shield, behind which stood an ornamented, double-barred metallic cross. All on a field of red. Gavisel leaned closer and let out as soft a whistle as could reasonably be expected of a cerulean otter. *What the sfelb is this?* she wondered. "Art history module," she ordered the thought engine, "identify genre."

Quickly the thought engine threaded categories and subcategories. "Heraldry. Terran. Roman Catholic through Universal Catholic Church. Papal States through Vatican City through planet Vatican."

Of course, Gavisel thought. *I'd never recognize the trappings of a Terran church.* "Explicate imagery."

"The heraldic achievements—in plain language, the coat of arms—of a cardinal, an ecclesiastical officer second only to the pope. The hat is a *galero,* emblematic of what is called the cardinalatial dignity. The tassels, or *fiocchi,* are traditional adornments of the *galero.* Since the Church revived ecclesiastical heraldry about one hundred fifty years ago, each cardinal has been granted his own unique personal herald. The most personal elements appear on the shield."

Mystery solved, Gavisel exulted. Now all that stood between her and the VIP's identity was a quick scan of any public database of ecclesiastical logos. But even as Gavisel savored her glee, it turned sour. *By solving this mystery,* she recognized, *I have merely peeled back a single layer.* In so doing, she'd revealed a deeper conundrum. *A Catholic cardinal. On this ship. With a high security clearance. On such a crucial mission! In reason's name, why?*

"What the sfelb!" It was Eldridge.

Gavisel whirled. New banks of instruments stretched toward her from the bridge floor. They told her the same maddening thing her own eyes reported.

As if he, she, or it were never there, the VIP had vanished—not just from the virtual bridge, but from the ship altogether.

3. Jaremi Four—Northern Hemisphere

Ruth Griszam gestured with the pistol. The wounded stranger paced into the dingy chamber deep inside the dam. Aside from a guttering lantern, the only illumination was the muffled auroral light filtering through some vent shafts.

Ruth waved toward a bare wooden chair. "Sit there," she ordered.

The stranger sat and dropped his heavy knapsack.

Ruth checked again for the satellite's *verify* signal. *Three-by-three greens.* Her encounter with the stranger would be recorded for distribution across the Galaxy, repackaged to appeal to every possible audience.

Ruth sized him up. *He's healthy and lean, older, but still vigorous. His clothes are motley, but every piece came from somebody's very best line of survival gear back when there was manufactured clothing to be had.*

The man turned back and gazed squarely at Ruth.

Dark hair fell in gentle curls to frame her auburn skin. She had full lips and compelling dark eyes.

She shifted the pistol uneasily. "You tell me. Do I need this?"

"No."

"I'll trust you a little," Ruth said, stuffing the pistol into her belt. "If I regret it, you'll regret it more." From beneath a frayed sofa cushion she pulled an old but serviceable first aid kit. "Let's see that wound. Lose your jacket."

He tried to get the bulky jacket off, but the movement hurt too much. Ruth helped him off with it. With his good hand the stranger grabbed it and started rifling the pockets.

Ruth came around in front of him clutching a hungry-looking knife.

He froze. "I wasn't going for a weapon."

"Didn't think you were. I need to cut your shirt away from the wound."

"In a second." He resumed his rummaging and then produced an old metal flask—a big one, holding perhaps half a liter. He unscrewed the cap and took a gulp, grimacing. "All right, do it."

She cut away the fabric and spread the wound with her thumbs.

He yelped, raised the flask.

She plucked it from him, saying, "Let's pour this where it will do some good." She splashed liquor in the wound.

"Gzhaa-aaa-aah!"

Ruth passed the flask under her nose. *Where'd he come by this? This is a rare distillation, made only in a wealthy city four hundred kilometers away.* She pressed the heels of her hands all down his back. "Looks like you didn't get any new lacerations falling through that roof. Just the gunshot wound."

"That's not enough?"

She daubed the wound with liquor-soaked gauze. "It's a flesh wound."

"Oh?" he said, craning to examine it with new interest. She hunted in the kit for a roll of gauze. "Hold on," he said. He reached into his jacket again and handed

Ruth an old glass vial half-filled with some pasty substance. "Put this on before you dress it."

She opened the vial and sniffed. "Healing balm! From up north?"

He nodded rapidly. "Where the skies are more often pink than blue."

"But it's fresh. How did you—"

"Not the only resourceful one, you are," he said wryly.

"Full of surprises, you are." She spread a dab of balm over the wound. "You'll heal in no time."

The dressing completed, Ruth stepped back. The stranger stood and swung his left arm, cautiously at first, then in more sweeping gestures. "Not bad," he said, and smiled. She smiled back. "You live here?" he asked.

Invest in the story, Ruth told herself. "Just passing through. Looking for some old friends from the army."

"Which army?"

"Does it matter?" He'd offered her the flask; she drank. "Thought maybe we could band together if things get worse."

"Think your friends are alive?"

"I'd give them fifty-fifty." Ruth sipped again from the flask. "Why'd you ask if I lived here?"

"Infrastructure. You know, the sliding covers. This chamber."

"It was like this when I found it." She shrugged. "As for upstairs, I've been here a week. You know how things are. You deploy defenses quickly."

He nodded. "This is a great place. Complicated inside. Easy to defend."

She nodded noncommittally. *You're the documentarian, let him do the talking. Draw him out.*

"So where are we?" the stranger continued. "What is all this shit?"

"This dam made power once," she told him. "Pure power, like what the piezo devices put out, they say, only endless. And steam, of course. That's the story. Anyway, steamjacks used to live down here, tending the turbine reheaters. There's a whole complex of apartments carved into the base of the dam. This must have been their commons." She blinked. "Oh, I never introduced myself. I'm Ruth Griszam."

He stood. "Willim Dultav."

Auroral light from a skylight played in his hair. Feigning a local's pensive curiosity, she eyed his streaks of gray. "How old are you?"

"Forty-five."

What would an autochthon say? "Then you remember when things were okay."

"Things were never okay. I remember before they got worse."

"You're a college professor?"

"I was—for a while." He rose and circled the chair. "They say it's been three hundred years since the sky rained fire. So tell me why civilization lingered just long enough to raise my hopes for an academic career, and *then* collapsed."

"The Great Dismay," she said quietly.

"Don't you remember at all—how it used to be?" he asked. "From your child-hood?"

Time to let the outer self spin its story. "No. Up this far north, thirty-year-olds have dim memories of order. I grew up in the south where everything had already gone to hell. When my people died, I came north. Spent my teens thinking *I* was the one who brought devastation wherever I went."

He laughed bitterly. "Now there's no more golden north to seek. It's like this everywhere."

"You've been everywhere?"

"Close enough to know there's nowhere else to look."

She slipped the first aid kit back under the sofa cushion. "What did you teach, Willim?"

"Philosophy, sociology, religion. Subjects like that."

"Stuff with high survival value," she deadpanned. They laughed cynically. "So what do you do now?"

"I wallow in nostalgia." They laughed again. "No, seriously. I scavenge the old libraries."

"How do you eat?"

"Does it matter?" Dultav heaved his knapsack up on a fallen heat exchanger and drew out a pitted reel of datawire. "Ever see one of these?"

"No," Ruth lied.

"People could store information on these, once, and read it off, using the power that used to come from geysers and from dams like this one."

She took the wire reel, turning it over in mock wonderment. "Think anyone will read this again?" She looked up when she heard him draw a sudden breath.

He'd extricated an ancient book. Its cover was freshly split; presumably the damage had occurred when the knapsack fell to the powerhouse floor. Dultav cradled the binding tenderly, like an injured pet. "I thought I'd go back to campus and save the important works," he said sadly. "Instead I destroy them faster."

Ruth watched him test how tightly the cover's halves would rejoin. *Great, an engaging crank. Maybe I can sell a human interest piece out of this.*

He put down the wounded volume. "Think the marauders left?"

"Upstairs? Yeah. They don't stay long when they don't find anything." *And if they were still poking around, half a dozen bells would be ringing down here. But you don't need to know that yet.*

"I have a friend traveling with me," he said. "If you don't mind, I'd like to invite him here." He watched her eyes narrow. "He's okay. He was my student. We've stayed together since—"

"All right. This way." She stepped toward the portal leading upstairs only to realize that Dultav wasn't following. Instead he was hunting in the knapsack again.

She pursed her lips and watched him draw out another book. When he opened it, she gaped. A hole cut into its pages nestled a piezo-powered comm unit at least a century old. *Its value here is inestimable, if it works.*

Dultav had extended the antenna. He stepped over a fallen pipe. Daylight poured through closely spaced grilles in the adjacent wall. The spillway's roar could be heard outside. He angled the antenna between the slats, twirled the wheel to charge the piezo battery, and thumbed the call button. Half a minute passed; Dultav thumbed again. This time the unit squawked to life.

What do you know, she thought. *It does work. This is getting better.*

"Willim?" chirped a tinny voice. "Is that you?"

"Of course it's me," Dultav answered into the comm unit. "I had a little adventure. You should see the place I found."

"Should I join you?"

"Sure. You know the old dam in the creek valley? Go into the powerhouse. Find the stairway in the empty turbine bay. Work your way down. When the stairs run out, move the floor aside."

"Do what?"

"Move the floor. It slides. Um, to the right. We're two flights below the sliding cover."

"I'll be there in ten minutes," the tinny voice said.

"Watch for marauders. They're all around."

"No news there. Parek out."

"Dultav out." He collapsed the antenna, looking up into Ruth's feigned wide-eyed stare. "Never seen one of these, either?"

"Not one that worked."

"That was Arn Parek," Dultav was saying.

"Pardon?"

"The man I was talking to. His name is Arn Parek. My most promising student, once. You asked me how I eat. Arn's how."

"I don't understand."

"He supports my sentimental obsession. By day I sift the ruins; at night he puts food on the table."

"I see," she said. "Is Arn a soldier?"

This time Dultav laughed. "A soldier? Hardly."

A distant, male voice called, "Ruth!"

Ruth held up one finger and smiled at Dultav. "I'm in the common room," she called. "I have a friend."

Dultav hadn't realized that the darkness in the chamber's far corner concealed a lengthy corridor. Halfway down its length, silhouetted by auroral light playing on a distant wall, two threatening figures loomed.

"There's another way in," Ruth said.

"No shit."

The advancing figures emerged into full light and separated. One was stocky, paramilitary in his bearing; he cradled a steamrifle. Reedy, hunched, and somehow unwholesome, the other figure clutched a twisted walking stick in one hand, an ancient percussion carbine in the other.

"I'd hide the comm unit," Ruth whispered. Dultav jammed the comm unit into a pants pocket. The figures had drawn closer. "Meet Willim Dultav. Willim, meet Ulf and Chagrin."

"Gentlemen," Dultav declared with forced evenness.

Ulf stood by the lantern table. He was clean-shaven and had a crewcut. His face was aquiline and scarred, appearing stern and threatening. Like Dultav, Ulf looked old enough to remember life before the Great Dismay. "Ruth, you closed the covers upstairs." His voice was like rock salt on steel.

"When Willim dropped in," she explained, "some uninvited guests tried to follow."

"Willim was *invited?*" Chagrin demanded, hunched by the heat exchanger like a ravaged harlequin. His costume seemed to be assembled from rags from a dozen sources. Ringlets of dark greasy hair outlined his hollow cheeks. From skeletal sockets, reflectionless black eyes studied the newcomer.

"I said Willim was a friend," said Ruth coldly.

Ulf and Chagrin tipped their guns down.

Ulf crossed behind Ruth and Dultav and dropped a leather bag on the large table. Ruth joined him there, lighting a second lantern. From the bag she drew a chunk of fresh-roasted meat. *"Skraggel,"* she identified. "Still warm. Where'd this come from?"

"Some old fashioner in the woods."

Chagrin hobbled to the table. When no one tried to stop him, Dultav followed. The meat's aroma rose to meet him like an ocean wave; suddenly Dultav realized how hungry he was.

"How's the fashioner?" Ruth asked flatly.

"He was happy to share with us," Chagrin growled.

Dultav couldn't keep the disgust off his face.

Chagrin couldn't help seeing it. "Our visitor doesn't like the way we get our food," he rumbled, selecting a *skraggel* haunch.

Dultav reached for the bag. Chagrin threw it to Ulf, beyond Dultav's reach.

"Sure," Dultav husked. "Find some poor shit cooking the first meat he's found in three days, and stick a gun in his ear."

"People gotta eat," said Ulf around a mouthful. "Let me tell you something, Dultav, or whatever your name is. Before—you know, before the Great Dismay—I worked in a damn factory. I was nothing. When everything fell apart it was like chains sliding off. Now the only rules I follow are the ones I make."

"'Till someone gets the drop on you," Dultav said calmly.

"Then it ends." Ulf's eyes were flinty. "The ride'll have been worth it."

The three hadn't noticed Ruth glide to her feet. From her vantage point, the three men were arranged in a tight triangle. Behind them, the fallen heat exchanger brightened and darkened, lit by the lantern on the small table by the entrance. *This is one of the most intriguing first encounters anyone's had with Ulf and Chagrin,* she thought. *Why do I so hope it doesn't end the usual way?*

Intrusively, Chagrin grabbed his bum leg. Hooked it on the edge of Dultav's chair with a clatter. Dultav didn't flinch. "Sometimes there's a price," Chagrin growled, slapping the leg. *"This* happened in the food riots."

"What—sixteen, seventeen years ago?" Dultav asked cautiously.

"I was a kid," Chagrin confirmed. "When the emergency government sent steamwagons into our camp, I clambered onto the back of one. Put a shell through the driveline. Steamed the soldiers, four or five of 'em. Killed 'em almost instantly. *Almost.* I got to watch 'em squirm." He chuckled. "Then the wagon hit a wall. I was still on the back. Guess I pulled something important."

"He's had the limp ever since," Ruth supplied. "Or that's his story."

"I keep telling you, Chagrin," Ulf laughed, "there's nothing wrong with your leg. It's your head that's fucked up!"

Chagrin opened his mouth to respond. But no sound came out.

Instead, incongruously, a tiny bell tinkled.

Ulf and Chagrin dropped their food and checked their weapons.

"Tripwire four," Ulf barked. "Company's coming." He sprinted the length of the chamber and down the dark corridor. Moving more slowly, Chagrin tottered behind the fallen heat exchanger.

Dultav looked back at the table. The bag sat abandoned, still half full of *skraggel.* He had no more than touched it when Ruth pulled him away. She led them into cover behind a mound of debris at the back of the room.

Ruth liked this geometry, too: Dultav's anxious face filled the left edge of her visual field. At center she was looking over Chagrin's misshapen shoulders and across the heat exchanger, whose caved-in bulk split the composition pleasingly. At right, far in the background, she could just make out Ulf.

Between Ulf and Chagrin, still empty, yawned the doorway that led upstairs. Anyone who came down the stairway Ruth and Dultav had used would be walking into a crossfire.

A different bell rang. "Intruder coming down," Chagrin announced unnecessarily.

Ruth was surprised to notice that she was holding her breath.

4. Jaremi Four—Southern Hemisphere

P ain*pain*pain*PAIN***PAIN!**

First had come the heated prods. Then they took his fingernails. Next the flailing cudgel shattered joints. *Knuckle. Elbow. Ankle. Jaw.*

He felt bucketsful of icy water, though the day was frigid. Unstoppable shivering made his sundered joints shriek.

The scourge tore flesh and scattered blood. Now a rusty blade bobbed toward his right eye.

He hung from fetters at nightfall on a hilltop. He was Laz Kalistor, an undercover Spectator being tortured to death on Jaremi Four's southern landmass.

The blade pierced his cornea.

Anguish*torment*misery**gushing**SPURTING*deluging**PAIN!***

"Laz, you stand accused of sorcery," a hoarse voice chafed in his ear. It was Kaahel, the tribal elder.

He can end my pain, he thought. *So could she. But she won't.*

Kaahel bellowed now. "For the last time, how do you plead?"

The outer self gains little if I end the torture now, Kalistor thought. *My body's too damaged. On the other hand, the upper self has much to gain if this continues. Snuffers sell briskly, after all. When I'm dead they'll come for me. If they don't, my wife will be set for life on the snuffer revenues. Either way, I have no alternative,* he decided grimly. *Defy the elder!* "Kaahel, I will come for you," Laz Kalistor growled. "Afterward I will come in power. I will come for your daughters."

"You all heard that!" Kaahel circled, waving a hand missing two fingers.

Using his remaining eye, Kalistor fastened a piercing gaze on the woman. Her lithe carriage was complemented by an ample bust, a slender face, and a full, sharp nose. From such incongruities a compelling feral beauty sprang.

Linka Strasser was her name. Like Kalistor, she was a Spectator. Unlike him, no one had seen *her* eyes tremble as she was going into Mode. No one had decided she was a sorcerer.

Some fool villager had walked in on him just as he was logging on and saw him go through senso shudder. Kalistor's eyes had danced for only a second or so—if he took longer than that to suppress the reflex, he'd never have been cleared for duty on an Enclave world. But in a superstitious society, that second was enough to get Kalistor tied to the torturer's stakes.

"Why are you silent?" he demanded subvocally. Only Linka could hear him.

"You know I can't speak."

"You won't *speak."*

"I dare not," she retorted. *"If I told what I know, I'd have to tell how I knew it."*

"You might try a little creativity," he snapped. *"Would Enclave fall if you bent the rules this once?"*

She tugged at her jerkin. One finger traced the outline of a small, square glass lozenge sewn into the fabric. On the face of the lozenge, silhouettes of pearl-gray birds emerged from a gunmetal-gray background. Yet the background defined identical bird silhouettes. The contrast between the two grays was subtle, but to Kalistor's eye it produced a continual oscillation. *Figure becoming ground. Ground becoming figure.*

The others couldn't see it.

"Laz," she subvocalized to him, *"you know the Statutes. One rule can never be broken."*

"No matter the cost?"

Having circled behind the dying Spectator, the elder flung a cruel backhand against Kalistor's broken ribs. He screamed anew.

Linka tried to distance herself from her partner's agony. She focused on her own somesthetic matrix: Left calf dully aching from standing too long. Tongue probing stickily inside a dry mouth. Scratchy fabric creeping back and forth across her nipples each time she breathed.

She stood on the knob of a hill with six dozen others. They belonged there. She did not, though not in any way they'd recognize.

Slumping between crudely hewn poles, Laz Kalistor trembled, bleeding a river from one ruined eye. With the other, he stared at the woman.

Sewn into his own sodden doublet was another glass lozenge with the muted Escher pattern.

The elder whirled and raised his massive arms. "My people! Will any among you defend this foul wizard?"

"Please?" Kalistor asked Linka weakly.

"You really want that? Now?"

"No," he admitted after a moment. *"It's too late."*

"I couldn't have anyway," she said in his mind. *"Nothing personal."*

"I will never forgive this."

"I pronounce sentence!" the elder cried. "Newcomer, you are guilty of sorcery. The penalty is death!"

The witnesses hooted.

The elder grabbed a handful of Kalistor's matted hair and raised his shattered face. "I offer you one last choice," Kaahel growled. "Choose torture unto death or a coward's swift merciful end."

"No more pain," Kalistor sobbed. "I choose merciful death."

"You choose the coward's way." Kaahel paused. "Say it!"

Slurring, Kalistor said, "The coward's way."

Kaahel dropped Kalistor's head and circled to address the group. "He chose the coward's way." Stepping away, he gestured at two twisted figures in tattered robes. One was male, the other female, one gaunt, the other squatty.

One held a cudgel, the other held a scourge.

"You shall have your swift, merciful death," the elder shouted. "Soon. But first, the torture!"

The shambling figures closed in. Kalistor hadn't thought there could be a fiercer agony, but they managed to inflict it.

Heedless of his sundered mandible, his shattered ribcage, and his lungs that were slowly distending with lymph and blood, Laz Kalistor managed one final articulate shout: "Forjel you, Linka Strasser!"

Only she knew what he meant. Autochthons didn't curse that way.

With clinical intensity Linka Strasser documented her colleague's screaming death. She was a deep cover Spectator on an Enclave planet. Observing was her job.

When Kalistor was gone, Linka stepped closer. Doing that won her (and her Galactic experients) a gruesome vantage as the torturers tore the corpse apart. It also enabled her to confirm that when Laz died, his Escher lozenge clouded over. No autochthon would ever pick it up and be mistaken for a Galactic.

Linka glanced downhill when she smelled harsh fumes.

The elder had touched a firebrand to pitch-soaked tree limbs. Flames danced shoulder high. *Forjeler,* she realized. *Dismemberment. Immolation. Laz isn't going to make it back from this one.*

O/N-Two, it was called—Obliterated, Not recoverable, or Not sampleable. There wouldn't be enough left of Laz to recreate his body and charge his brain with memories up to the moment of his death. The best they'd be able to do would be to delve into the archives and revive him from the last antecedent sample-and-scan he'd left, restoring his memories as they'd existed only to that moment.

Who could've known that through oversight, so many years had passed since Laz last had himself sampled-and-scanned?

Helplessly, Linka reviewed her options. Was there anything, however contrived, she could do to sidetrack this? Anything that would trick the tribespeople into leaving enough of Laz so the recovery team, still ten minutes away, would have something to work with? *No,* she concluded after a terrible moment. *Nothing that might not give me away—or at least suggest to these barbarians the things they must never know.*

✦ ✦ ✦

Linka Strasser looked up from her washing. Inwardly she tried to shake off the unwanted memory. *That was three years ago, maybe more. Now I'm back on Jaremi Four. Another assignment. Another dismal settlement. I've got an identity to maintain.*

Across the laundry-pool, a Jaremian woman lay down the jerkin she'd been scrubbing. Her name was Verina. She tugged on a fabric shawl. It bulged over her pregnancy. Verina folded the jerkin and put it in her basket. She didn't take another.

To the far north, Linka could already make out the aurora. *The fires of the city of the gods, that's what they call it here. Dusk is coming.*

In a valley controlled by a shrewd but brutal chieftain, Linka knelt with five autochthonous women around a tiny cove off an ancient canal. At a grunt from Verina, the women gathered their wash baskets. Began trudging back to the settlement. Linka eyed Verina. Reviewed the story thread she represented in Linka's coverage.

Gap-toothed and pushing thirty, Verina had worked all day stripped to the waist, showing off. *Pregnancy comes harder for everyone each year; at Verina's age, here in Southland, she truly has something to boast about. Rather, she would.* Verina could not know that a serious fall some twenty months before had damaged her pelvis. She was all but guaranteed to die in childbirth. *And how could Verina dream that according to the saybacks, the fastest-growing segment of my Galactic audience hungrily anticipates her birth agonies?*

Out of Mode, but still in contact with her bird, Linka scanned her queues. A message from Tramir Duza was waiting. Duza was a fellow undercover Spectator who covered a neighboring tribe. He'd coded several windows of time when he'd accept a realtime callback. This was one of them. Linka subvocalized the *tap* command.

Duza was neither sleeping, recording, nor too busy to talk. The connection went through.

"*You buzzed, Tramir?*" she asked.

"*Yes,*" he subvocalized back. "*Is the execution still on?*"

"*Of course. The killer will be hanged at dawn on the next festival day, fifteen days hence.*"

"*You know he's no killer,*" Duza reminded her.

She sighed inwardly. "*And you know what you're asking, Tramir. So stop.*"

"*I'm not saying show your chieftain a senso playback,*" Duza protested. "*You witnessed it with your own eyes! You needn't betray anything Galactic to come forward with that.*"

"*But what would it accomplish?*"

"*Don't you care whether an innocent man hangs?*"

Linka sighed inwardly. "*Actually, no. If their system of justice hangs the wrong people, that's none of my business, or yours. That's why they call us Spectators, remember?*"

"*Sometimes I envy your detachment,*" Duza replied. "*Most times, it just makes me feel . . . I don't know, dirty.*"

"*You and your idealism. This one time, I could come forward and save an innocent native without compromising my outer self's credibility. I could make myself the center of the narrative. But what then? I'm without a partner here. There's no other Spectator to cover events from the outside."*

"Funny, isn't it? No one's eager to replace Laz Kalistor."

The trail ended at the water's edge. A collapsed truss bridge lay across the canal. Balancing their loads, the women minced across it toward the opposite bank.

"You know I was cleared," she spat back. *"Who imagined how much Laz would lose? Anyway, in that situation I couldn't have intervened without revealing myself. Letting Laz go took courage—you'd probably have started teaching the elders how to build stardrives."*

"Okay, foul shot. But this situation is nothing like that. You could do the right thing without risk. I can't understand why you refuse."

Passing between two lanky sentries, the washerwomen entered the main settlement. Haggard stone arches thrust uselessly among encroaching trees beside the ancient canal. Newer construction ran to log cabins and thatched huts. Linka scanned the camp. A handful of children played anemic guala ball, most favoring torn muscles or open sores. The camp was home to fifteen youngsters, not nearly enough for a village with a population of two hundred.

Smoke rose from cooking fires. At canalside, men and women hauled in nets heavy with fish. Older children threw back those with obvious tumors or malformations, perhaps half the catch.

The column of washerwomen gave a wide berth to smelly old Weldaey. The elderly man lay in a sodden litter, stinking of shit and decay. Linka knew he had a bowel obstruction; since this tribe knew nothing of surgery, Weldaey was doomed to die in agony. He was in agony already. Regurgitated stomach acids had eaten away his lips and much of the soft tissue on his chin. During the day he'd thrown up his own feces. *"I could tell them how to cure Weldaey,"* Linka suggested. *"I could cure him myself. Is that what you want?"*

"Of course not," Duza said tiredly. *"But that's the difference between us, Linka; I wish I could share my knowledge. You luxuriate in holding it back."*

"If one is obliged to do a thing," Linka aphorized, *"one does well to like it."*

"I can see I won't change your mind. So I'll get to the point. You might find it useful to know that on your tribe's festival day, the very day the innocent man is scheduled to hang, my tribe will attack yours."

"Chief Lormatin's last fiasco wasn't enough?" Linka snorted. *"He wants to sacrifice the rest of his young men?"*

"Lormatin found some old steamskiffs somewhere—forjeling things must be two centuries old. He can't repair the steamplants, of course, but they're still strong, fast hulls. He's going to load them up with oarsmen and attack straight down the upper level of the canal. They'll draw up at the locks and try to penetrate your settlement's defenses."

"They won't succeed," Linka said. *"The booby traps are as thick there as anywhere else."*

"Agreed. Don't worry, I won't run and tell Lormatin not to invade. Hey, here's an idea. Lormatin will strike at dawn, just as your guy hangs. If you find the right place to stand, you might be able to see the attack skiffs round the bend in the canal while the falsely accused twists artfully in the foreground."

"*Thanks for the compositional advice,*" she said dryly. "*Should be a good image. We'll speak again after my tribe whips your tribe. Strasser out.*"

Verina had led the washerwomen into a rounded hut. The heat inside made Linka's skin go taut. The women began arranging still-damp garments on a lattice of sticks over smoking coals. On impulse, Linka plunged her nose into the rough fabric of her own garment and sniffed. The tang of old smoke assailed her anew. Every garment was dried over such embers. *On which Confetory world has smoking one's clothing become popular, based on my coverage of this tribe? I can't remember.*

"There you are!" It was a crone's voice, worn rough with years. Hurriedly, Linka went into Mode. The Spectator systems snapped to life within her. Pushing down her eyes' demand to dance, she made herself a perfect camera once again. After less than two seconds, she turned to face the crone.

It was Sculfka, claspmate of the settlement's chieftain. At fifty, she was the oldest woman in camp—indeed, one of the oldest Jaremians Linka had ever met. A great damaged barge of a woman, she projected profound authority despite the palsy in her hands. She breathed in gasps. In one gnarled hand she held forth a colored stone. Mineral patterns swirled in its cut and polished face.

Sculfka held the geode out for Linka.

Reluctantly, Linka took it. "Again?" she asked resignedly.

"Graargy wishes it," said Scuflka, speaking of the chief, her mate. She led the way outside.

It was full dusk. To the west, the ruddy glow of sunset was failing. On the northern horizon, aurora would sparkle rosy throughout the night. Fires blazed. From a windowless hogan came endless muffled clacketing sounds of old blind women weaving nets. Since they needed no light, they worked round the clock in two twelve-hour shifts.

Mistaking Linka's watchfulness for reluctance, Sculfka grunted. "Don't dawdle, you've done this before."

Linka fell into step. Despite her apparent hurry, Sculfka had not chosen the most direct route to Graargy's compound. *She wants to talk.* "All-Mother, who visits?" Linka said aloud.

Sculfka sniggered at the honorific. "A minstrel from upriver. Graargy treats him like someone important."

"That's what he says of all of them."

Another party of women filed past. Each carried fifteen kilos of *fhlet* in a backpack, ten more in an ingenious headdress. Plentiful, nutritious, and easy to prepare, the breadfruitlike *fhlet* was a staple foodstuff here in ruined Southland. The women emptied their burdens before a line of stoop-backed cooks. Twin panels of ancient steel, perhaps the settlement's most prized possessions, had been laid flat over flickering embers. Cooks measured fish oil out onto the surface. They laid down slices of *fhlet* and slabs of fish. Smoke rose, bringing with it the savory aroma. Dinner would be good tonight.

With some surprise, Linka watched as the cooks sprinkled a fermented oil solution over *fhlet* and fish alike. *Anjhii,* the spicy mixture was called. It was precious, used only on very special occasions.

"See," purred Sculfka, "I told you it was an important visitor."

"For a tribe that values solitude, we have a lot of visitors."

"Not that many," Sculfka countered. "It's just that whenever Graargy lets one in, he wants you to play the welcome woman."

"Always me. It's unfair. Why?"

"You know," Sculfka said knowingly. She reached out with a clawlike hand and squeezed one of Linka's full breasts. "Remember, there are no young widows just now. There are only women clasped to men of influence. Children without experience. And you."

Linka allowed herself a sigh. *By now, I bet the promotions people at OmNet are already beaming word across the Galaxy: "Linka Strasser . . . the Terran Tart . . . she's at it again! On duty! On her back! Sweat with her, pump with her, gasp with her! Don't miss a pelvic thrust, a single moan! Coming soon, on channel three-five-A dot six-six-seven!"*

They rounded a bend. Graargy's command compound came into sight. "Don't worry," Sculfka said with sudden tenderness. "I've seen him. Did I tell you that?"

"No."

"He's young and pleasing to the eye. A good talker, too. This won't be so bad for you."

Soon enough, Linka thought, *I'll know for myself.*

5. Tridee Broadcast, Galaxy Wide • Origin: Terra—Wasatch Range, Usasector

A beefy white man addressed his audience with passion on one of the seedier Terran preaching channels. His sandy hair was shot through with gray. He wore a heavy muslin jumper adorned with dimestore mystic symbols. Innocent of tailoring, it bunched under his arms. Genuine sweat and fake sincerity oozed from the preacher in equal measure.

In a Galaxy that liked Terra's strange exports best, Mormon televangelist Alrue Latier was one of Terra's very strangest exports.

"The doubters, the snipers," Latier cried. "Those of little faith who have lost their way. They are the ones who deride me, who taunt my doctrines of the New Restoration. I have returned to the wearing of the sacred garments. For that they mock me. I have called out, as a shepherd in the forest, to reinstate the holy bond of plural marriage—no longer even a radical concept in today's Galactic society. Yet the naysayers ridicule me. They're offended when I revive olden forms; they're offended when I innovate. I am as he who faces the portals of hell on every side, who durst not turn right or left, damned whichever way I choose. But behold! Open your heart to the light of God and ask in all humility, why *not* a full-time, professional clergy? Do the spiritual hungers of a Galaxy allow us to make do with less?"

A false background assembled itself behind Latier's husky figure. It was an ocean, viewed from a great height, looking into some impossibly golden sunset. Cherubic voices sang an eerie background harmony.

"No, I say to you, no exceedingly. We cannot make do with less. We shall hold fast. We shall covenant to the ancient usages. Even so, it shall come to pass that we gird ourselves to minister to all those strewn across the starry deeps. Not just on Terra, oh no. Across the wide Galaxy! Inasmuch as these things are realized under my guidance as First Elder, we shall bring into the Galaxy the Mormon New Restoration of which I have dreamed for two scores of years and more."

Abruptly his manner changed. Latier broke into a smile as the image cut to a facial closeup. He leaned close to an orange accent light, like some drunken uncle by the fireside. "Perhaps you've wondered how you can prepare yourself for your own place in the New Restoration. If you're new to my church, you've probably thought, 'Oh, there's so much to learn.' Which ones were the Lamanites, which ones the Nephites? The prophet Abinadi's family tree. Who smote whom, when? And then, so many Scriptures to absorb! The Book of Mormon. The Doctrines and Covenants. The Pearl of Great Price. The Book of Abraham. *Elder Alrue's All-Purpose Anthology of Latter-day Imprecations.* Who can master all this? Yet, who can feel confident of resurrection if they do not?"

Latier turned away from the close-up pickup. Another cut: he was striding between workstations in some glittering electronics laboratory. "Brothers, sisters, now there's an answer! Double your tithing today and I'll send you, absolutely *free*, the very latest in rote learning technology." He raised two hands full of equipment. "That's right, a home-sized deep-brain didactic imposer. Press the disks to your temples and close your eyes. When you wake up, you'll know the Scriptures complete—chapter and verse, jot and tittle. Of course, when you wake up it'll be six hours later, so don't use the imposer just before it's time to go to some important appointment."

The image shimmered. Latier was standing before the golden ocean again. If anything, the cherub choir in the background was even more cloyingly sweet. "Look into your heart," he hectored. "Ask God's help in deciding what you can afford. Remember, double your tithe and the didactic imposer is yours. Act today." He smiled. Held two eyeball-sized metal disks toward the tridee pickup. "When you press these disks to your temples, you'll make your *brain* a temple. Don't delay, act today! Mine is a poor ministry, after all, and supplies are limited."

The image faded out, to be replaced by a canned documentary segment.

In a massive all-white studio outside of Salt Lake City, Alrue Latier stepped off the gimbaled treadmill from which he delivered his tridee preachments. Behind a broad window, artists, effects technicians, and affectational colorists labored at their tiered consoles. Formidably skillful, they could place Latier into any setting and apply any visual or auditory effect as rapidly as the tridee director could think of it.

An assistant rushed up with a bowl of water and a towel. Latier splashed water on his face, working it through his thinning hair with fingers as puffy as sausages. "The added tithes are already pouring in, First Elder," the assistant reported.

"Yeah, yeah. How many in Galactic currency?"

"Thirty-two percent, so far."

Latier grunted, clearly dissatisfied. "By the One Mighty and Strong, I'm ravenous," the aspiring religious leader bellowed. "When the sfelb is lunch?"

6. The Planet Vatican

P ain*pain***pain***PAIN***PAIN!**

In a genial hotel room he lay submerged in agony. Pain suffused him and overflowed his being.

First had come the heated prods. Then they took his fingernails. Next the flailing cudgel shattered joints. *Knuckle. Elbow. Ankle. Jaw.*

In a hotel room. . . .

He was there.

He was not there.

He hung from fetters at nightfall on a hilltop.

He lay on a soma disk under a hotel skylight. The sky was green and placid.

He was Laz.

He was Marnen.

Being tortured to death.

An avid experient, watching a senso and sharing the victim's agony.

On Jaremi Four's southern landmass.

On the Planet Vatican, ten minutes' walk from the Center. . . .

The blade pierced his cornea.
Anguish*torment*misery**gush**-**ing**SPURTING*deluging**PAIN!**
"Laz, you stand accused of sorcery," a hoarse voice chafed in his ear. It was Kaahel, the tribal elder. "For the last time, how do you plead?"
"Kaahel, I will come for you," Laz Kalistor growled. "Afterward I will come in power. I will come for your daughters."
"You all heard that!" Kaahel cried.
Using his remaining eye, Kalistor

focused on the woman. Her lithe carriage was complemented by an ample bust, slender face, and a full sharp nose. From such incongruities a compelling feral beauty sprang.

She is Galactic, Marnen Incavo thought deliciously in his Vatican hotel room. *She is Galactic, but I see her face unaltered.*

"*Why are you silent?*" Kalistor demanded subvocally.

"*You know I can't speak.*"

"*You* won't *speak.*"

They're Galactics, Incavo marveled again, *but I hear their subvocal conversations. Sometimes it feels like I can read their thoughts. How superbly vile this is!*

"*Laz, you know the Statutes. One rule can never be broken.*"

"*No matter the cost?*"

The elder flung a cruel backhand against Kalistor's broken ribs. He screamed anew. "I pronounce sentence!" the elder cried. "Newcomer, you are guilty of sorcery. The penalty is death! I offer you one last choice. Choose torture unto death or a coward's swift merciful end."

More agony? Unthinkable. Kalistor shuddered as he said, "No more pain. I choose merciful death."

"You choose the coward's way. Say it!"

Slurring, Kalistor said, "The coward's way."

"You shall have your swift, merciful death," the elder shouted. "Soon. But first, the torture!"

The shambling figures closed in. It hadn't seemed there could be a fiercer agony, but they managed to inflict it. They screwed Kalistor down to it with shafts of fire and twisted and twisted and twisted.

Laz Kalistor.

Marnen Incavo.

Jaremi Four.

Intolerable ordeal.

Vatican.

Hard-sought challenge.
In some high-walled mental preserve, Incavo still lay quivering in his guest room. Agonies raged, but he made himself hold his thumb off the cutoff switch. He knew what came next. This time he wanted to stay in to the finish.

Heedless of his sundered mandible, his shattered ribcage, and his lungs that were slowly distending with lymph and blood, Kalistor managed one final articulate shout: "Forjel you, Linka Strasser!"
Death was seconds away.

Like a swimmer under water too long, chest poised to explode, Incavo-on-Vatican gulped a majestic rush of air. He thumbed the cutoff switch.

Suck, rush, wrench. Wobble.

Being-thereness.
He was himself.

Trembling, soggy with sweat, he lay in tangled clothing on the soma disk. Under his left hand lay the cutoff switch. A cheap touchpad in a dented case, it resembled some inept teenager's entry in a science fair. By his knee was another small, featureless box.

On the night stand, a hotel-standard senso player the size of his hand winked its pause light, awaiting commands.

The man shifted his hips and felt a clammy wetness. While *poving* the torture, he had peed himself. Greedily he grabbed the module with the datacrawl display. *Two seconds longer,* he thought with grim satisfaction. *I stayed in Laz Kalistor's head two seconds longer than ever before.* He rolled to his feet. Laid the back of two fingers across the senso player. Obediently it expelled a program wafer. *If I can stand just three seconds more, I'll pov his death.*

His eyes swept the room with its marble desk, floating settee, glasteel beverage table (also floating), and an enormous chunk of spinel carved in the likeness of Saint Cyprian. Beyond that, arched windows stretched upward into a crystal dome. Outside, ornate hotels and office towers filigreed against the sky. Faint currents stirred the citron-colored algae that girdled the planet five kilometers above the surface and gave the sky its uncanny color.

His morning toughening exercise completed, private investigator Marnen Incavo set about stowing his apparatus.

He dropped the senso wafer casually on a keepit pad. *Doesn't matter who sees that.* With something like a million Spectators in the field living clandestine lives on forty thousand Enclave worlds, people died in Mode all the time. *Cross the chief. Fight the wrong battle. Dying's easy.* Plenty of Spectators had died with the recorders running, some as horribly as Laz Kalistor, or even worse. Many could be brought back, others could not. But that did not affect the quality of their terminal experiences.

Recordings of horrible death, called snuffers, were legal everywhere and openly sold, owned, and *pov*ed. They weren't for everybody. But then, in the vast Galaxy, nothing was.

Incavo turned the featureless box over and over in his hand. *Mere possession of this contraption means hard time anywhere humans walk,* he thought. Incavo should know; it had meant hard time for the couple he'd caught using the device on Ordh. (Never mind how he'd managed to board a starcruiser with it.) For its function was to defeat the firmware safeguards that kept senso within the bounds of Galactic society's rigid privacy standards.

When recording the entire contents of a Spectator's sensory field, everything wrote to the wafer: private subvocal conversations, the faces of other Spectators, if present, and sometimes, even a strong enough sense of the recording Spectator's somesthetic response that could allow a perceptive experient to puzzle out the Spectator's private thoughts. In a Galaxy where most people displayed a logo or a synthetic mask instead of their own faces when answering their comm, such profound disclosure was unthinkable. Trouble was, the senso signal was chaotically complex. To embargo the forbidden data at the source was impossible. So every senso player had mandatory circuitry that did the job each time a program was *pov*ed. *No hearing subvocal dialogue. No seeing the faces of Galactics. No guessing the Spectator's thoughts.*

The box defeated all of that. It made Incavo a voyeur without limits.

From under the desk Incavo hoisted a slender valise. He slid the box into its maw. The box literally disappeared. The kind of equipment cops and customs inspectors used could never detect the box inside a vanisher valise, but it was in there all the same. The thumb-tab cutoff device went in next, just for safety's sake.

Incavo drew a finger across the edge of his valise. The seam glowed scarlet. The valise would melt down now rather than open in someone else's hands.

Incavo shuffled back to the soma disk and shrugged his pee-soaked clothes off onto it. "Command. Dispose," he said quietly. The disk irised opened and sucked down both bedding and garments. Fresh bedclothes extruded across the disk as it closed.

Time for work. "Command. Music," Incavo said aloud. A twenty-second-century Gwilyan sonata filled the air. "Command. News. Voice only. Local."

Somewhere—not behind him, not in his head, but somewhere—an amiable voice murmured: "Merchants near Vatican Center say they will appeal to the Confetory Tribunal if Swiss Guards continue seizing establishments whose names include the term 'New Borgiaville.' In an apparent show of determination, Vatican officials closed a bistro whose soup-and-sandwich special was named 'Cesare and Lucrezia.'"

"Command," Incavo told the room. "Calendar. Today. With me."

An infosphere opened in midair, tracking him so as to be always steady in his gaze. "Ceremonies will be held tomorrow," prattled a news reader, "marking the

twentieth anniversary of Vatican as Terra's first sovereign planetary territory outside of the Sol system."

"Command," Incavo told the sphere. "Begin sort five."

The infosphere boiled. Today was busy. Every day was busy here. There were
conclaves, congresses, congregations, synods, subconsistories, major councils,
minor councils, petty councils.

"Despite strong growth in the senso industry," the news reader droned, "the
Universal Catholic Church remains Terra's most important cultural export, both
financially and in terms of social eminence. That from the Congregation for Pious
Statistics."

True enough, Incavo thought. When the Galactics had first stumbled across
Terra almost two centuries earlier, the little blue world had been so backward (relatively speaking) that it should've been made a Protectorate or even an Enclave
world, off limits to all save anthropologists and undercover documentarians. But
Terra turned out to be the long-sought "cradle world"; there and nowhere else had
arisen the tree of life whose fruits included humankind. And so Terra had been
admitted to the Galactic Confetory as a full memberworld, whether or not it was
ready for the honor.

Terra'd had little unique to offer at the banquet of Galactic culture. There was
senso, of course, instantly popular among Galactics. But Terran religions stirred
more excitement. Christianity in particular, with its patina of age and its air of
absurdity, took the Galaxy by storm. Of all Terran exports, only the institution now
known as the Universal Catholic Church had opened wide the taps of Galactic
wealth. Only the Vatican had so far managed to rate a planet of its own.

As he began to dress, Incavo scanned on. Here in rank order were the day's
schedules for the bureaus of incantation: indoctrination, indulgences, inspiration,
infiltration, instruction, inspection, intercession, invocation, *and these are just the
internal functions!*

"Aresino Y'Braga, Father General of the Jesuit order, will return to Vatican to
stand before an ecclesiastical court, which will consider his excommunication,"
the news reader intoned. "Y'Braga is known as a critic of church doctrine on
human consubstantiality."

The ecclesiastical tail-chasing gave way to a more important topic—in
Incavo's eyes, at least. *Lobbying!* Today Vatican Center was hosting fifty-six offplanet delegations. Each would compete for the attention of the *curia,* the pastoral
bureaucrats who controlled the floodgates of Vatican largesse. Incavo scanned
notices of formal balls, masked receptions, and command performances; peti-
tioners threw parties, flacks held fêtes, delegates gave *divertissements,* supplicants
staged soirees, and beseechers hosted breakfasts, brunches, banquets, and buffets.

Incavo deopacified the bathroom mirror. Vatican Center stood before him, not
a kilometer away, gargantuan and improbable. Three kilometers square at the base,
the structure rose in stepped rococo tiers studded with balconies and takeoff pads.
Scouts, flitters, and airyachts swarmed about it. Three hundred stories up, the
building tapered to a rod-straight cylinder of glasteel and plum marble five hundred meters across that rose another hundred stories. Craning, Incavo could make
out the building's crowning glory: colossal golden holoprojections of the papal keys,

tiara, and shield. Kilometers high, they counterrotated in the pistachio sky. Sometimes their tops brushed the algae layer. Those immense revolving emblems
dwarfed even the preposterous vastness of Vatican Center. Nothing else possibly
could.

"Command. Begin sort three," he told the sphere as he tugged on the last piece
of his formal costume.

"Authorities are probing an apparent case of food poisoning at a pilgrimage
hostel," said the news. "Sixty persons out of a party of five hundred from Scalbulia
Eight were hospitalized after a loaves-and-fishes supper at Sanctimony House in
New Tuscany. Spoiled fish is the most likely cause."

Incavo squinted into the sphere as a complex 3-D plot took form. The plot
ranked the delegations according to their size, spending habits, the length of time
spent on Vatican, and the value of the boon sought. "There," he said, locking his
eyes on a high bright spike in the data. "Command. Identify."

"Delegation from Khoren Four," a crisp metallic voice said in his head. *Them
again!* "Leader: Orgena Greder. Size of party: more than two thousand. Spending:
more than four billion per diem. Mission—"

"I know," Incavo told the hotel room impatiently. "Query. How many times in
the last two weeks have I requested identification of data anomalies that turned out
to be the Khoren Four delegation?"

"Fourteen."

"In other words, every forjeling morning." Incavo whistled. "Command. Display Fem Greder's social web."

A spidery tree chart formed, showing in schematic form whose parties the
leader from Khoren Four had attended, with whom she had exchanged invitations,
to whom she owed money, and who owed her money. In short order Incavo found a
familiar name, a delegate from Kalima Six who was owed a favor by Greder—and
who owed a favor to Incavo. *Of course, in Fem Greder's case, the indebtedness may
have come about honestly.*

As always, throngs jammed the streets of Lobbyist's Quarter outside Incavo's hotel.
Merchants hawked relics. Tourhosts walking in step with powered rickshaws jostled solo tourists listening to their guidemechs. Vendors shouted the foods they
offered, ranging from inspirational foodstuffs to cheap practical sandwiches.

Few lobbyists walked these streets. They usually preferred to pass overhead in
hermetic opulence. Incavo could have taken the aerial slidewalk, too, but today it
appealed to him to walk to Vatican Center at ground level, to drink in the menda-
cious energy of the streets. *New Borgiaville,* he thought. *They'll never kill that
name. It's too good a fit.*

He shouldered into one dark stall to buy something called a Jesuit's Horror. A
fat white man slick with sweat handed him the snack across a wooden counter
flecked with crumbs. The vendor smiled, counting out Incavo's change. Green
motes rimmed the vendor's chipped teeth.

The Jesuit's Horror looked like a fat breadstick wrapped in a scrap of cloth.
Incavo bit into it. He was surprised there was no filling. He'd expected meat paste,
maybe a fruit compote. No, it was just a breadstick—fresh, with a subtle herbal

flavor, but a breadstick all the same. "This is just bread," he shouted to the vendor as a party of acolytes crowded into the stand. "What makes it a Jesuit's Horror?"

The vendor flashed Incavo a toothy grin. "See, it is all of one substance."

Some day I'll understand this flap over human consubstantiality, Incavo thought as he pressed back onto the sidewalk. *Then again, why bother?*

Ahead, the improbable mulberry vastness of Vatican Center already filled the sky, though Incavo was less than halfway there. Incavo chewed the last of the breadstick and discarded the wrapper. When he looked up, he was staring at the neck of a donkey crossing his path. The odor of its sweaty hide was unmistakable. *That's no projection. It's a genuine forjeling donkey!* Incavo stepped backward, watching the beast pass, led by a gaunt, long-haired man in a tattered saffron robe. "Hey, watch where you go with that thing!" Incavo shouted at the man's back. With preternatural grace the herdsman turned. He was at least eighty, with sallow golden skin, sunken cheeks, and eyes that pierced as if through fog. His expression suggested infinite sufferings patiently borne. In a gesture of peace, he held up a slender hand. Through the palm had been driven a convincing and bloody spike. *Hey pal,* Incavo thought, *you should have had my morning.*

Snorting, Incavo pressed back into the throng toward Vatican Center. *Ahh, New Borgiaville. Keep your treasures warm, Fem Greder. Your Cesare draws near.*

7. On Board the Schooner *Bright Hope*

"I't's confirmed," Detex Officer Lynn Wachieu called from her metallic spider's web. "The VIP is nowhere on the ship." She frowned. "The more deeply I scan the guest quarters, the more it seems he, she, or it was never really aboard."

Captain Laurien Eldridge pressed six strong black hands together. She'd hustled the Spectator and the folk singer out of the virtual bridge right after the VIP disappeared. Now the command crew members were alone. "Forjel it all," Eldridge complained, "the VIP came aboard cloaked in such mystery."

"There's less mystery now." Executive Officer Arla Gavisel preened her guard hairs with a blue paw. "I know who the VIP is."

Eldridge leaned forward. "How?"

Gavisel explained how she'd monitored the VIP and captured a scrap of his personal logo. "Computer analysis said it was the herald of a Universal Catholic cardinal. But not *any* cardinal." She called up a portrait of a grossly heavy white man, balding, with full jowls and a weak chin. Puffy lips forming a mirthless grin, he measured the world through glossy black eyes pillowed behind swollen cheeks. "I give you our VIP," Gavisel said with mock grandeur. "Cardinal Ato Semuga of Terra."

"Semuga," Eldridge breathed. "I've heard the name."

"Semuga heads the Pontifical Council for Arcane Works," said Gavisel, consulting notes. "He's a conservative and controversial churchman. It's said he wields the pope's hatchet in the current controversy with the Jesuits."

"The Council for Arcane Works handles only the most sensitive projects," Wachieu agreed.

"Yet he spent five days aboard *Bright Hope*. Virtually, at least."

A viewsphere opened: the ship's intercom. Will Bickel, *Bright Hope*'s dogged Pragmatics Officer, stood at the center of a dormchamber that had been completely torn apart. Behind him, security techs scurried, repacking their equipment. "Bickel here, Captain," he said. "We've completed our physical search of the guest quarters. Neutron-activation and bioassay searches both agree: no living thing has occupied this suite since we launched."

Wachieu nodded. "Semuga was never aboard, except as a projection."

"Someone at High Command is going to get an earful of this," Eldridge growled.

Gavisel smiled. "Don't expect to hear much back."

"No?"

"Semuga's authority came from very high up. He came aboard having traded favors with someone powerful— someone who could issue him command codes capable of overriding our control over this ship."

"What?"

"How else could we *not* have known Semuga was a projection, not a passenger?"

"I see what you mean," Eldridge said. "Our susceptors would have recognized him as a projection unless they'd been overridden somehow."

"Was Semuga after the Panna drive?" Wachieu demanded.

"A cardinal wouldn't want a prototype stardrive," Gavisel argued. "No, I think he came aboard to see us kill the Tuezi."

"You could see the Tuezi destroyed on any street corner of any Confetory world. Our guest Spectator saw to that."

"But the only way to see it *in person* was to be aboard the anticipation fleet."

Wachieu nodded, finally convinced. "Those church prelates are a conservative lot. Being present in person—even if only as a projection—might seem important to them. The other four ships in the anticipation fleet launched long before us. With their conventional drives, they had to. *Bright Hope* offered the shortest voyage—by far the smallest bite out of Semuga's schedule."

Gavisel called up one more datasphere: a news clipping. "Here's the final piece of the puzzle. The last time Semuga was mentioned in the media was eleven days ago. He was hunting rogue Jesuits on Calluron Five."

"The closest world to our launch point," Wachieu observed.

"We have our answer," agreed Eldridge. "What we may never know is *why* the Universal Catholic Church's top troubleshooter needed so badly to see a Tuezi destroyed."

8. Jaremi Four—Northern Hemisphere

Ruth Griszam's Spectator gaze took in everything. In the far darkness Ulf lurked, steamrifle ready. Chagrin hunched behind the fallen heat exchanger with his carbine. Whoever came through the doorway Ruth and Willim Dultav had used would walk into the guerrillas' crossfire.

Dultav stood beside Ruth. His gaze kept darting toward the table four meters away, toward the bag of roasted *skraggel* meat. His craving was palpable. "Don't try it," she breathed.

With one finger, she traced the glassy lozenge sewed just below the neckline of the patchwork shift she wore. Galactics could see the subtle pattern it bore but Jaremians couldn't. Ruth searched for any sign that Dultav had noticed it. At the same time she scanned his clothing for a similar lozenge. *The exotic liquor he carried, the healing balm, the working two-way radio. Is Dultav a Spectator? If he was from offworld, he'd see the birds. The quirky figure-ground perception deficit, the inability to see the birds in the lozenge—the unique distinguishing mark of Jaremian autochthons. . . .* She astonished herself with the power of the yearning that rose in her. She'd been on assignment too long. She wanted Dultav so desperately to be a fellow Galactic voyeur. *"Can you hear this?"* she shouted to him subvocally. He did not.

Another bell chattered.

Ulf caught Chagrin's eye; pointing to the doorway, he raised his rifle.

Chagrin aimed, too, fingers wriggling nervously.

Metal scraped on cement. The sound arrived flanked by echoes. Two flights up, the access cover was being slid aside.

Ruth snared Dultav's eyes. "Is this your friend?" she whispered.

His confidence was incongruous. "Whatever happens, just watch."

They heard footfalls. From upstairs a tenor voice said, "Willim?"

A man strode through the doorway. He took two steps into the room and stopped.

He was light of frame with chestnut skin, high cheekbones, and a tiny mouth. Wholly relaxed, he projected the most compelling sense of innocence Ruth had ever seen.

Again he asked the air, "Willim?"

Waving Chagrin forward, Ulf strode out of the shadows. The guerrillas converged on the newcomer, rifles leveled at his chest.

Ruth studied the newcomer. Curly black hair gushed from his temples and cascaded down his back. His pate had been cropped to a dense stubble. Above his forehead, a triangle wide as two thumbs had been shaved clean. The apex, pointing downward, drew attention to his eyes.

He showed no alarm. Slowly he circled the lantern table.

"Stop!" Ulf hissed.

He stopped. "As you wish," he said equably.

Serene, the newcomer faced the guerrillas. He wore light-colored trousers, a pale tunic, and a gray poncho. Though made from local fabrics, the garments were intricately tailored. His boots were new and just as skillfully handmade. *He carries nothing,* Ruth thought. *No weapon, no rucksack, no tools.*

Her glanced flicked to Dultav. Clearly this was the former student he had summoned. *Yet Dultav is unworried,* she thought. *Plorg, his biggest problem seems to be controlling a smirk.*

Ulf and Chagrin moved closer. The newcomer stood with the lantern behind him. His face was in darkness. Golden backlight ignited his curls.

The stranger didn't move. Not really. He just shifted his weight. That was enough. Auroral light from an overhead vent lanced across his features. Suddenly he was a silhouette with a halo of blazing hair *and* a crimson streak across his eyes. Ruth marveled. *He's been here thirty seconds and he's figured out how to light himself like a god.*

The newcomer fixed his gaze on Ulf, opening his eyes wide like a cobra stretching its hood—the most masterful appropriation of command Ruth had ever seen.

Calming, irresistible, the newcomer's stare struck Ulf like a kick in the sternum.

The newcomer paused a half beat and pivoted before fastening his perforating gaze on Chagrin.

Chagrin became a statue of himself. His carbine barrel wobbled and dipped.

The newcomer turreted back and glowered again at Ulf.

With Spectator grace, Ruth drifted forward and then to her left. She stopped where she could regard Ulf, Chagrin, and the newcomer in turn.

None of them noticed her.

Ulf thumbed off the steamrifle. Its green winkies flickered red and died. The weapon clattered to the floor.

The newcomer swiveled and transfixed Chagrin again.

Chagrin's hands opened. His dropped carbine shattered floor tiles. The walking stick tumbled, too.

But the newcomer caught it.

Benignly he stepped toward Chagrin and held out the twisted rod.

Chagrin took it with something near reverence.

With that, the newcomer turned his back on the guerrillas as if he knew they posed no further danger.

They don't, Ruth realized with astonishment.

"Hello, Willim," the newcomer said.

Dultav stepped forward. The friends embraced.

Noticing Dultav's bandage, the newcomer touched it. He turned toward Ruth. "You did this," he said. His smile beamed thanks. Ruth found herself startled at the depth and authenticity of delight it called forth in her. *It's like walking into bath water shoulder-high.*

The newcomer astounded her once more. He turned back to face Ulf and Chagrin and said matter-of-factly, "Take your weapons."

They did.

He turned his back on them again.

"This is Arn Parek," announced Dultav. "Arn, meet Ruth Griszam."

"Pleased to meet you," Parek said.

Dultav continued, "You've met Ulf and Chagrin."

Parek bowed to them. Smiled that smile. Anxiety slaked off the guerrillas like snow down a warming roof. All at once they remembered how long it had been since they'd breathed.

"Who are you?" Chagrin croaked. "*What* are you?"

Parek chuckled disarmingly. "Some call me a holy man. I'm a wandering philosopher. I journey without plan, pursuing a revelation that is not yet complete to me."

Parek prowled back toward the guerrillas. He peered at Ulf. Ulf shrank back half a step.

"I know things," Parek murmured. "Things I shouldn't. Sometimes I don't know who to tell." Spinning, he faced Chagrin. "Should I tell you?"

Chagrin blinked. He swallowed and said, "Please."

Parek ran two fingers along Chagrin's walking stick. "I know you would give anything to cast aside this twisted branch and walk like a man."

Chagrin nodded and bit his lip. Parek turned away before he'd see Chagrin's tears. It was still too early for that.

To Ulf Parek said, "You know yourself. You don't need me to tell you who you are. To you I will reveal another kind of knowing." His eyes scanned the room. Crumpled in the corner lay a streaked old safety poster. He grabbed it. "Something to write with?" he asked no one in particular.

Dultav dug in his pockets and produced a mechanical pencil. Parek took it and led Ulf to the fallen heat exchanger, where he lay the poster down. Pressing the pencil into Ulf's hand he asked gently, "You write, no?"

Eagerly Ulf nodded.

"I want you to listen to all my instructions before you write," Parek intoned. "I will ask you to write down six names. One should be the name of someone you knew well, someone from your past. The other five should *not* be the names of anyone you know. They should be names picked at random. Names you make up." Parek lay an encouraging hand on Ulf's shoulder. "Have we ever met, Ulf, you and I?"

"No."

"You are sure?"

Ulf allowed himself a chuckle. "I'd know."

"Then I cannot know the names of anyone from your past."

"Of course not."

"Then write. Five fake names. One real one. Put the real name anywhere in the sequence you please. We shall see, then, if I can feel which name has meaning for you." Parek nodded imperceptibly. "Begin."

Parek watched Ulf write out the six names. Then he took the poster and pored over the list. He scanned the names once, then twice. "Ulf," he said abstractedly.

"Yes."

"Who is Gravelx?"

If someone tapped Ulf at that moment, he might have shattered like crystal before a scattergun blast.

"Who is Gravelx, Ulf?"

"He was my foreman, in the factory," Ulf stammered, "before—before—"

"Before the Great Dismay?" Parek asked.

Ulf nodded hollowly.

"Who was he to you?"

"The first man I killed."

Parek let the silence stretch. At length he put the poster back where Ulf had written on it and gestured for Dultav to retrieve the pencil.

When Dultav came forward, Ulf got out of his way.

"I can tell you this," announced Parek. All eyes snapped to him. "Once there was a prophet. A seer, a man of knowledge. He roamed the shattered countryside, speaking such truths as he knew to all who would listen. There dawned a day when he ventured into hostile lands. The people's hearts were barren. They trusted not the prophet. They would not clothe him, nor share with him their food and drink." Parek stood in near-darkness, letting auroral light from another vent caress his face. "And the prophet bore great anger against those people."

Parek trod unswervingly across the room, following a straight-line course that would compel each listener to step out of his way in turn. "Now the prophet knew of a great famine which lay ahead for that hostile land." Chagrin stumbled aside. "He might have prevented much death." Ulf backed away. The people could have laid up grain while yet the green things grew." Dultav sidestepped. "But the people had spurned the prophet." He stood before Ruth; she, too, retreated. "So the prophet kept his own counsel. Passed on his way." As though the least among them, Parek seated himself on a mound of fallen plaster. "And I tell you, it came to pass that the people of that region suffered greatly."

Parek sighed. It sounded final.

Ten seconds passed.

Twenty.

Comprehension bloomed.

Ulf bustled over to the large table and scooped up the bag of *skraggel* meat. He walked slowly toward Parek. Bending at the waist, he held forth the satchel.

Parek went on staring into a private space.

Ulf dropped to one knee and presented the meat again. "We will feed the prophet," he said uncertainly.

Parek acknowledged Ulf's presence and selected a roasted haunch. Fleetingly, he glanced toward Dultav. "He is with me."

Wordlessly, Ulf replaced the bag of *skraggel* on the large table. He retreated as Dultav took a seat.

Dultav flashed Ruth that mischievous half-smile and snatched a slab of *skraggel* meat. He began to bolt it.

Ruth drifted across the room, her *pov* centered on Parek. Oddly dignified, he sat in the debris, nibbling *skraggel* with a refinement that conjured memories of better times. *So long ago.*

In time, Parek stood. "I must meditate."

Ulf and Chagrin all but scrambled to his side.

"No," he said to them gently. "I must be alone. Go yourselves by another way, just the two of you. Ponder what I have revealed."

Shouldering their weapons, the guerrillas trudged back toward their hidden entrance.

Parek nodded to Dultav and bowed to Ruth. Brushing dust from his trousers, he strode down the opposite hallway.

Ruth sat next to Dultav, shaking her head. "Does he have any idea where he's going?" she asked, grabbing some *skraggel*.

"Does it matter?" Dultav purloined his third piece. "You asked how Arn Parek put food on the table. Now you know."

Ruth leaned back in her chair. Her outer self seemed to be shedding the strain of a violent encounter averted. Inside, her upper self was checking to make sure everything had recorded. There were saybacks already. *Already!* They were good— actually, the highest rating she'd ever earned on this posting—and were still trending up like a mining tug on full boost, as OmNet editors repackaged and reindexed the material.

They ate together, each uncomfortably aware of the strong, if tentative, attraction the other had triggered.

"Look," Dultav said at last, "about Ulf and Chagrin. . . ."

"Yes?"

"Is one of them—hell, both of them—you know, your man?"

Ruth convulsed with laughter. "Ulf and Chagrin have a simple relationship with me. I think. They do. That's all."

Dultav watched her eat. He was torn between prudent caution and the unexpected intensity of his need to share a secret. "Look, I'm an old professor," he ventured at last. "I seldom trust my instincts."

Ruth arched an eyebrow.

"My instincts tell me that I can tell you something—and if you feel it's best for Ulf and Chagrin not to know about it, you'll keep it to yourself."

"Maybe."

He fidgeted. "Ruth—"

"Yes?"

"Look, you tell me. Is there something *you'd* like to know?"

"Damned straight. How does he do it?"

"Arn?"

She nodded.

"He's got enough charisma for a good-sized village," Dultav answered, "and the most infectious self-confidence you'll ever see."

"I could see that in the way he stared down Ulf and Chagrin. What I meant was, how did he do that thing with the names?"

Dultav drew out the liquor flask again. She swigged and passed it back. "All right, Ruth. Before I tell you what Arn did, you tell me what you saw."

"Arn asked Ulf to write out six names—five fake ones, one a name from his past. As soon as Arn read the list, he knew which was the real name. And he knew that the guy was Ulf's old foreman!"

Dultav half-smiled. "That's the way you recall it."

"Yes, exactly."

"Did you have any idea which name was real?"

"No."

"You could have."

"How?" She looked at him narrowly. "Did you?"

"Sure." He sipped and passed the flask back. "It takes more thinking to write down a fake name than to write the name of someone you know. Ulf had to stop and *choose* each phony name one by one. It was different with the one real person. If you knew to look for it, you would've seen Ulf's hand hesitate slightly before he wrote down five of the names. The one he wrote without faltering—that was the real name."

Ruth laughed a moment but then grew serious again. "But how did Arn know who the man was?"

"Easy. He asked."

"What?"

Dultav leaned forward. "A moment ago you said that as you recalled it, Arn knew—seemingly in the same magical way that he'd known which name was real—that the man whose name Ulf had written down was his old factory foreman."

"Well, sure." She thought a moment. "Didn't he?"

Dultav laughed. "That's human nature, Ruth—to remember an event as being more extraordinary than it was. I've seen Arn do that trick a hundred times. All he does is pick out the genuine name. Then he has the mark say who the person was." He took back the flask, screwing down the lid. "More often than not, somebody turns up a few hours later ready to swear that Arn divined not only the name but the identity too."

She played the moment over in her memory. *Forjeler, I could have sworn Parek knew* both *pieces of information without any prompting. Some professional observer I am!* "Willim . . . you called Ulf a mark. You called what Arn did a trick. That's all it is?"

Dultav nodded. "That's the secret I wanted to tell you."

"Your friend sounds less holy by the minute."

Dultav laughed like someone who'd found a comrade with whom he could share an immense burden. "Arn Parek is the only kind of holy man there is—or ever was—one hundred percent bogus."

Ruth laughed long and bitterly. "A fake holy man!"

Dultav shrugged. "It's a living."

"Where's that flask?"

He gave it to her. "These woods are full of country con artists," he observed. "Some earn their livings telling people they can make twenty-year-old canned goods safe to eat. Arn and I—we offer a more profound kind of belief."

"How did this start?"

"I told you, I used to teach sociology, philosophy, religion. Arn was my top graduate student. He had a grasp of the material—of what religion *meant* to people—like no one I'd ever known. When things fell apart, we lost touch. I stumbled into him again a few years later, quite coincidentally. By then, he'd been working on his scheme for, oh, maybe eight months. He'd been analyzing the refugees of the Great Dismay: their experiences, their fears, their dreams, the kinds of new societies they were piecing together while all the structures they'd known were collapsing. What do people need when they're scrambling to make sense of the fact that finally, after generations of false alarms, they really *have* lost everything? Arn put theology and social science together and, well, concocted a religion appropriate to the times."

She sent a bit of herself backward to check for the *verify* signal. *OmNet, I hope you're getting this.* "An . . . appropriate religion."

"Exactly. Arn figured out what sorts of things the refugees ought to hear, and started preaching it to them."

"What they wanted to hear."

"Not always. He was more concerned to get across what the refugees *needed* to hear in their despairing hearts—sometimes, the last things in the world they thought they wanted. A web of messages that, once heard, rang far truer than any of the explanations they'd ever thought to seek.

"See, Ruth, people everywhere are the same. They crave close relationships with others, a sense of belonging to an exclusive community . . . some certainty that their pain stands for something in a grand cosmic scheme that's bigger and more meaningful than the limited canvases of their individual lives. And on some level, people yearn to surrender themselves to a warm and commanding authority—to someone who'll tell them it's all right if they believe those *other* things without figuring it all out for themselves. I doubt if many people ever needed more of that kind of reassurance than today's survivors."

Ruth kneaded her face.

"Sorry," Dultav breathed. "I was lecturing again. An old professor's failing."

She gulped deeply from the flask and gave it back to him with an air of closure.

He weighed it in his hand. "You didn't leave much."

"Something tells me you'll get more. Now let me get this straight, Willim. Arn preaches this line of oh-so-carefully designed shit, and you—so just where *do* you fit in?"

Dultav chuckled. "Mediator, humble servant, advance man, sidekick. It depends. Arn's the traveling holy man. I'm his all-purpose acolyte. And once we've turned a band of refugees into believers, they'll provide us with most everything we need."

"Virgins," she said disapprovingly. "Canned goods."

"I told you, we don't do canned goods."

"You know, Willim . . . on one level, what you and Arn are doing is really sick."

"Sicker than anything else people do to survive after the Great Dismay? Sicker than Ulf and Chagrin taking that *skraggel* from some poor son of a bitch? At least Arn and I encourage our marks to hope."

9. Vatican

$\mathbf{M}$isusing the name of a mutual acquaintance, private investigator Marnen Incavo had wangled his way into Orgena Greder's latest Vatican Center soiree. Now he stood face to face with Greder herself, the tyrant of Khoren Four, who was spending so prodigally on entertainments for the curia. "My apologies for failing to remember you," Greder said with faint confusion. "What did you say your business is?"

"I deal in rare religious manuscripts," Incavo lied. "Scrolls of saints. Palimpsests of postulants. Diskettes of deacons. Wafers of witch-hunters." He knew this was a safe dodge. Though Incavo knew nothing about rare manuscripts, Greder would ask no question he couldn't answer. In matters of religion as in everything else, Greder's tastes were strictly pragmatic.

"You're welcome here," said Orgena Greder. Dredging up a thin smile, she pressed a chit into his hand. "Enjoy my hospitality. Everyone else does. And please, join us under the dragon's tail at the top of the hour. We'll have a presentation."

Incavo nodded. "In person?"

"I do everything in person."

Excusing herself, Greder pivoted to greet two ecclesiastical visitors. Incavo recognized the taller of the two. *Alois Cardinal Rybczynsky, Secretary of State of the planet Vatican. Closest confidante of the pope! Whatever Fem Greder is up to, it's big.* Subvocalizing a command, Incavo activated the implants that redirected his zone of maximum visual acuity. Though he appeared to look elsewhere, he could watch sharply out of the corners of his eyes.

"Ahh, Cardinal Rybczynsky," Greder gushed. Rybczynsky was lean and sallow, with thin salt-and-pepper hair, piercing eyes, and bloodless lips drawn tight in perpetual disapproval. "Most Eminent Lord, I am truly honored. And who is your companion?"

Rybczynsky presented an elderly friar in the rough brown alb of a Franciscan. "Fem Greder, this learned cleric sponsors a mission on Frommel Seven. He is an elector in your case."

Greder took the friar's hands in hers and beamed. At sixty, she was still a handsome woman. She wore a *serapé* of diamond foil trimmed in emerald tape. The ring emblematic of her world sparkled azure on her right index finger. "Always a pleasure to meet one of my electors. Do I understand that you sponsor a mission?"

"In truth," the friar said gravely. "One bishop, ten monsignors, a hundred priests, seventy novices, three transphotic launchers, and a Mark Six dry-dock. The Church's only outpost in the Frommel system."

Almost imperceptibly she opened her hand. With equal delicacy the old friar slipped a small card into it. "I, too, know the pressures of knowing a world depends on you," she chattered. With economical movements she examined both sides of the card. She pressed her signet ring against a gray patch and subvocalized a number.

"You govern Khoren Four, then," the friar said. "What drives your economy?"

Incavo almost missed Greder's deft movement, returning the old friar's card. The gray patch now glowed crimson. "Actually," she said, "I *own* Khoren Four. The economy centers on mining."

The old friar glanced down at the card. He fought down a double-take, as did Incavo. *The friar can run his mission for five years on that transfer,* the detective marveled.

"Of course," Greder was saying, "I could make the place so much more pleasant with a more diverse revenue stream. Fix up the atmosphere, improve cultural opportunities for my autochthons, you know."

"Fem Greder's autochthons are not under Enclave protection," Rybczynsky explained. The friar nodded knowingly.

"I could bring them so much," Greder amplified. "All it would take is a secondary industry, one whose business cycles are not linked to those that plague us in mining."

"Tourism, perhaps?"

"You understand perfectly. Perhaps after we rehabilitate its biosphere, you might establish a mission on Khoren Four. I know the perfect site."

"I'd be honored," said the old friar. "Please excuse me." He doddered away.

Greder's smile collapsed. Incavo thought she looked as tired as a spacebase whore ten hours into her shift. She drew a tall brandy from a nearby autobar. Turning back to Rybczynsky, she sked hollowly, "How many more?"

"You will meet another elector after the buffet, and one during the intermission at tonight's concert. I trust you will show them the same generosity."

Greder nodded tiredly.

Incavo almost felt sorry for her. *On Vatican, it's always Palm Sunday.* Incavo strolled, dodging a strolling Callurian brass septet on his way back to the autobar that had earlier refused him. He carried a chit now. When he said "Ouzo on slivers" the bar spat him out a double. *Meet the hostess, then visit the bar,* he thought. *See, I am learning the way of this.* Tugging at his formal jacket, he surveyed the room.

St. George's Hall was one of Vatican Center's most opulent reception galleries. Carved from a single immense crystal of *faux* amethyst, it held eight hundred with ease. Viewports planed to monomolecular thickness offered rose-colored vistas of the Lobbyist's Quarter two hundred floors below. The tint reduced Vatican's pistachio skies to a muddy gray. An immense figure worked into the crystalline ceiling in zones of varying refraction depicted Saint George slaying the traditional dragon. The dragon's tail, sculpted in fuller relief, depended from the ceiling. Defining three sides of a rectangle, it formed a valance over the main stage.

Incavo subvocalized a request for the time. *"Three minutes before the hour,"* an inner voice replied. *Almost time for Greder's presentation,* he thought.

Ul' Fze B'Khraa stood a head over two meters tall. His features, what one could see of them, were brutal. He gnawed at some greasy, half-raw scrap of animal flesh. His garment was a long mantle made from thousands of bird skulls knotted together with strips of gut. The skulls clacked unnervingly as B'Khraa mounted the stage. *He sounds like a barrelful of castanets set rolling down a hill.*

Incavo tried to imagine how Orgena Greder expected to advance her case—any case—by putting this savage on display. He failed.

Incavo tuned his auditory implants to eavesdrop on a nearby conversation. "You know," an intense young theology student told his escort, "after a military victory on his homeworld, B'Khraa ordered enemy tribesmen to slay their own families or be executed."

"Eee-ew," shrilled the young woman, "and they did it?"

"Most of them, yeah."

"What happened then?"

"He served them an obedience potion and ordered them to kill themselves."

"Even though they'd submitted to his terms and butchered their families?"

"Quite."

"That's loathsome," she proclaimed.

"But look deeper."

"Oh, please."

"No, think," said the student earnestly. "Remember the passage in Matthew 11: 'Think not that I am come to send peace on earth: I came not to send peace, but a sword. For I am come to set a man at variance against his father . . . and a man's foes shall be they of his own household.' Or recall Luke 14:26: 'If any one comes to me and does not hate his own father and mother and wife and children and brothers and sisters, yes, and even his own life, he cannot be my disciple.' Jesus said that. Well, B'Khraa said the same thing."

"Only more so," she replied with distaste.

"Exactly," breathed the student. "He didn't just say it, he *did* it. Is this a small Galaxy, or what?"

So this barbarian is Greder's candidate? Incavo thought. On stage, B'Khraa reached into the fur pouch lashed to his arm and drew out another scrap of bloody meat. *He seems an odd choice. Colorful, though. No question there.*

Several hundred people—half of them clerics, the other half professional lobbyists and social hangers-on—ringed the stage. They nibbled the grandest hors d'oeuvres of a hundred worlds and sipped the most elegant known malts and wines and essences and liqueurs. Orgena Greder joined B'Khraa on stage. She was not a short woman, but B'Khraa dwarfed her.

Polite applause greeted the planetary tycoon who was paying for it all.

"Friends," she called to the crowd. "For you are all my friends."

There might have been more clapping, but too many hands were filled with plates and goblets.

Greder nodded acknowledgment all the same. "It has been my greatest pleasure to extend my hospitality to you all during our three months on Vatican. I have enjoyed meeting the electors who will decide the merits of our case." She gestured with her right hand, flashing the signet ring with which she authorized transfers of funds. "And I have enjoyed supporting the many worthy causes they espouse." That drew nervous laughter. "Yet *I* have profited, too. I have profited because of the opportunities I have enjoyed to learn from one of the most remarkable autochthons my world of Khoren Four has produced. Twice each day we present our candidate so that you may experience, as I have, his gentle wisdom . . . his profound spirituality."

B'Khraa's mouth engulfed the last fatty morsel. Gore seeped between his lips and into his disheveled beard.

Greder cried: "I give you Ul' Fze B'Khraa, greatest of the autochthonous chieftains of Khoren Four. As to what else he may be—noble electors, that determination lies in your hands." In a flutter of diamond foil she dropped to her knees before B'Khraa.

A handful of people in the crowd knelt also. But only a handful.

Twenty-five drummers filed onstage wearing the rococo livery of Greder's personal guard. They formed a line behind B'Khraa. A powerfully muscled young woman stepped forward, clad in scanty Khorenian battle dress. The pouch on her hip contained six great throwing knives, the ornately sculpted handles arranged in a semicircle.

Drums rolled. Two male soldiers wheeled a door-sized slab of Khorenian hardwood onto the stage. The plank was as tall as a human, as wide as outstretched arms could span, and five centimeters thick.

The snares rolled to a crescendo. Fell silent.

The woman's arms windmilled. *Thwa-Thwa-Thwa-Thwa-Thwa-Thwack!* In less than two seconds, she had hurled all six of her knives, each with sufficient force to sunder the target's thick wood. The soldiers slowly rotated the slab. Everyone saw the knives quiver in perfect vertical rows. *Well, Greder's amazon can certainly throw knives,* thought Incavo. *Since Fem Greder is rich, I bet her spaceships are shiny, too. What's the point?* The knife thrower bowed to scattered applause while the soldiers hustled the target away.

Greder strode onstage with a fresh pouch of knives. The woman donned it. The drums tattooed again.

Throughout the performance, B'Khraa had stood impassively at center stage. Now the woman moved to face him, her back to the audience. B'Khraa was her target. The two drummers who stood directly behind the autochthonous chief seemed unconcerned to be in her line of fire.

Again the drums came to a crescendo and fell silent.

The woman hurled six whistling knives at B'Khraa and leapt off the stage.

When it was over, B'Khraa still stood. He'd caught the knives by their blades, three in each callused hand. He threw them away.

He caught them without injury? Incavo wondered, not sure what it would mean if he had.

B'Khraa stepped forward and held up his palms. *Hardly without injury!* The chief's big hands were slashed in four places. One wound split his left ring finger almost to the bone. Blood coursed down his wrists.

The drums sounded again. B'Khraa held out his hands for fifteen seconds. The blood stopped. "Behold," cried Greder, flouncing back onstage. "Behold the might and healing power of Ul' Fze B'Khraa!" This time the applause was genuine.

B'Khraa strode to the lip of the stage. The voice was gentler than Incavo expected, but still frightening. "People! I need seven volunteers."

Seven onlookers—four old clerics and three of the beautiful people—joined B'Khraa onstage. Greder went out into the audience and solicited a metallic token from a watching bishop. She handed the token to B'Khraa and left the stage once more. She returned with four more volunteers, traditionally costumed Swiss Guards who elaborately blindfolded B'Khraa and withdrew.

"You seven who remain," Greder announced, her back to the volunteers. "One of you should take that token. Don't let B'Khraa or myself know who has it. Those of you who hold no token, stand with your arms at your sides. Empty your minds. If you have the token, let your empty hand hang at your side also. The hand that holds the token—press that to your forehead and hold it there. And pray." The volunteers did as instructed. The audience knew who had the medallion—and in which hand. B'Khraa did not know nor could he know. "Pray, all of you! Pray that his Father grant him clarity of sight!"

After a hundred seconds, B'Khraa growled, "All right."

"You who have the token," Greder commanded, "lower the hand that holds it. Keep your hand closed, with the token in it. Now, all seven of you—hold both hands out straight, fists closed."

When the volunteers had complied, the Swiss Guards who had blindfolded B'Khraa began to remove the wrapping. Impatient with their clumsiness, B'Khraa growled and tore the blindfold off himself. The big warrior strode past the seven volunteers. Without hesitation he grasped an old monsignor's left wrist and raised it. "Open your hand!" he cried.

The medallion fell to the stage floor. Out of fourteen possible hands, B'Khraa had chosen the right one.

"Behold his mighty works!" Greder cried as B'Khraa shambled offstage. "We invite your tests. Prove to your own satisfaction that B'Khraa is the current Incarnation of the True Christ. Then so elect him!"

Three hours and countless toasts later, Incavo found himself in a buffet line behind Sfix Geruda and Xyrel Hjinn, senior members of the College of Theology. Burdened by drink, they struggled to spear rare foods from a dozen worlds onto their plates. Incavo only pretended to be similarly compromised—his implants countered the alcohol and other costly psychoactives he had consumed.

"I agree," Geruda was saying. "B'Khraa is off-putting."

"'Off-putting!'" Hjinn snorted. "Viscerally repulsive, if you want my opinion."

Geruda poked at a Gwilyan brine slug with his spearstick. He was too slow; the slug seized the stick and began to gnaw on it. "Forjel it, I hate food that eats back. Very well, Xyrel, I'll grant you that B'Khraa's disgusting, even coarse."

"Don't forget loathsome and repellent."

"What of that? The Christ of Vyrdis Ten was the equivalent of a leper. Stinking, necrotic tissue sloughing off, the whole package."

"True enough," Hjinn admitted, skewering his slug three or four times until it held still. "There have been physically hideous Incarnations whose legitimacy everyone accepts."

"Then there are the biographical similarities," Geruda pressed. "Too many Gospel echoes to be pure coincidence, don't you think?"

"What I think," said Hjinn around a hiccup, "is that you've had too much of Fem Greder's free liquor."

Incavo broke away from the tipsy theologians and threaded through the crowd. Jugglers and fire-eaters plied their trades while musicians performed works from half a dozen genres in scattered parts of the room.

"I don't know you."

The woman who had interposed herself in Incavo's path was young, jet black, startlingly buxom, and calculating in manner. "I am Bei Hanllei, a member of Fem Greder's retinue. And you are?"

"My name is Incavo. Fem Greder has received me."

"Of course. Otherwise you wouldn't have a drink." She turned sideways to flaunt her bust.

About as necessary as Fem Greder flashing her bankroll, he thought. *I haven't been forgotten after all.*

"I will be direct," she said. "Which elector do you scout for?"

Incavo's laugh was genuine. "What makes you think me a scout?"

"You're here."

"Fem Greder and I simply a share a mutual acquaintance. I am here on Vatican buying and selling historic documents, and—shall *I* be direct?"

"I'd advise it."

Incavo leaned forward, flickering a wicked grin. "I heard Fem Greder throws a great party."

Hanllei chuckled, disarmed. "That she does. So, what do you think of our Christ?"

"I think it's good for Fem Greder that I *am* no one's scout."

"I beg your pardon?"

"We were being direct." Incavo put a hand on the woman's shoulder and steered her toward an autobar. "The catching of the knives and the stopping of the blood was impressive. Of course, highly trained warriors on five hundred worlds, in and out of Enclave, have mastered that trick. Now, the miracle of the medallion—"

Hanllei brightened. "You admit that's a miracle."

"It'll be a miracle if I'm the only one here who recognized how the fakery was done."

Hanllei's reaction mixed equal parts of surprise and hostility. *But no embarrassment,* he thought. *She does not rank high enough to be privy to the inner mechanics.*

"Would you like to know how B'Khraa did it?" he asked.

"Please," she answered stiffly.

"The monsignor who held the medallion—he raised the hand with the medallion to his forehead for almost two minutes. During that time his free hand, like the hands of the other six volunteers, hung straight down. Blood pooled in the thirteen free hands. Gravity drained a bit of blood out of the lone upraised hand, the one holding the medallion. When the seven volunteers put out their fists, six of them presented left and right hands whose color and texture were identical. Only one displayed one hand that was a little paler—whose veins were less distended. He was the one who held the medallion, and he held it in the hand that was paler. That's a stage magician's trick known on many worlds."

"Not on Khoren Four!" she bristled.

"So you say," Incavo chuckled. "If you wish to keep your snug little position—to say nothing of your snug little half-million-credit cocktail dress—I'd advise you not to report this conversation to Fem Greder."

"No?" Hanllei arched an eyebrow.

"She'll know you know too much. Excuse me."

Incavo injected himself into a knot of diplomats and left Greder's spy behind. Before long, he'd spotted Greder herself again. He contrived to bump against her. She was so intent on persuading a brocaded Scalbulian businessman about something that the collision went unnoticed. After a moment, Incavo placed the businessman's face. *Oh yeah. He builds hotels.* He tuned his implants to listen to their conversation even as he edged away from them.

"If you front-load the package the way I've advised," she was telling him, "I think I can lock in my planet's top six scenic areas for your first half-dozen hotels."

Sipping *absinthe,* the hotelier shook his head. "With the advance you're asking for, I can't possibly commit to less than a sure thing. Call me after the smog's cleaned up, and after that barbarian of yours gets elected Son of God."

Incavo found an autobar and drew another ouzo. He mingled on, trying to take the pulse of the crowd. Two diplomats hunched over a cocktail table, conversing too loudly. "Can't blame her for trying," slurred the Ordhian attaché. "Look at Kfardasz. Their Christ really put *them* on the map—hotels, pilgrims, infrastructure bonds from the Institute of Pious Finance, metatheme parks, the works."

"Or Minga Four," the Ghelttian envoy agreed, "the last full-fledged Confetory world ravaged by a Tuezi. They had billions of dead and octillions in damage, but relief funds came in *so* slowly. Only after they got a Christ did the credits start to flow."

Incavo joined a mixed group of monsignors, students, and policy hacks, knotted in a circle around a contortionist nobody was watching. "We shouldn't lose sight of the spiritual side of this," said a fiftyish monsignor as he downed more spirits. "Having a Christ isn't just a quick solution for all of a planet's problems."

"No," agreed a policy hack, "though it surely helps."

A portly young student shouted to make herself heard over laughter. "Wait one minute. Look at Gwilya. Their Christ went nowhere."

"There's no religion on Gwilya," snickered the policy hack. "Of course nobody paid attention."

A stick-thin woman wearing mostly jewels waggled her finger and said piously, "Well, if anyone doubts that the Vatican hierarchy is sincere about authenticating Christs on other words, they need look no further. No one driven by venal motives would waste their time trying to get Gwilyans excited about a Christ. The only possible reason to undertake so transparently hopeless a task is that you take the theology seriously."

"Theology!" wailed a monsignor. "Oh, we're not going to talk about consubstantiality again, are we? *Homoousios. Homoiousios.* It makes my head spin."

Incavo mingled on. The Royal Gwilyan Philharmoneum was tuning up on stage in person. *Three hundred musicians and their hardware, transported halfway across the Galaxy,* Incavo thought. *Whole worlds have been developed for less than the cost of this performance.*

Once more Incavo stumbled across the theologians Geruda and Hjinn. Arguing *con brio* across a punch bowl, they'd attracted an eager audience. "Explain this!" Geruda demanded. "Didn't the savage chieftain B'Khraa *also* say, 'Take up your pallet and walk'?"

"More or less. Actually, he said, 'Take up your crutch and get out of here.' But he only said it after he'd kicked the poor bastard's crutch out from under him."

"What about this? As an early adolescent, B'Khraa was separated from his parents."

"Be serious!"

"He was! Then he turned up at a center of learning where he amazed the priests."

"It was an autochthonous astrologers' school. And he didn't amaze the priests, he robbed them."

"And you don't suppose the priests were amazed by that?"

"Oh, Sfix, give it up."

"But he *had* been separated from his parents," Geruda pressed. "That no one can deny."

"Separated? He cut their throats."

Incavo's glass was empty. He was scanning the room for a nearby autobar when Orgena Greder circled before him. She carried two drinks. One was an ouzo on slivers. "Your drink, Hom Incavo?"

Incavo accepted it with a twinkle. "I'm impressed."

"My associate Bei Hanllei did not take your advice. You see, I don't believe there is such a thing as knowing too much. Of course, that's not the problem you face."

"And I imagine you'll be good enough to tell me what my problem is."

"You could crash any party. You chose mine. There is something *you* don't know."

Incavo shrugged and displayed upturned palms. "You've found me out."

"What do you seek?"

Incavo tried to look meditative. "To satisfy my curiosity, a curiosity that has plagued me since I came to Vatican."

"Go on."

"You believe in B'Khraa? That he is really the Christ?"

"I do."

"Then you are a pious woman."

"I am."

"I'll tell that to the autochthons who live out their dismal truncated lives in your mines."

"Come now," Greder laughed. "Was that the extent of your curiosity? To see how I'd respond if you criticized my labor practices?"

"No, my question is . . . more substantial." He began to spin his tale. "You see, Fem Greder, I deal mostly in documents from autochthonous religious traditions— creeds that arise on a single planet, put down roots, and stay put. Galactics find many Terran religions fascinating. But only the Universal Catholic Church has ventured offplanet, spread from world to world, and found fertile soil around so many suns. Why do you think that is?"

Greder quoted a favorite Catholic litany. "Many worlds, one God. Many worlds, one humanity. Many worlds, many Christs."

"One per world, more or less. And how fortuitous that Vatican has authorized itself to determine which Christs are legitimate."

"Who better than Holy Mother Church, God's chosen vicar in the Galaxy?"

"But you see," Incavo strung her on, "it is all these cosmic Christs that I do not understand."

Greder eyed him quizzically. "You deal in religious documents."

Incavo shrugged. "I buy and sell texts that sometimes make little sense to me."

"Pardon me if I insult your intelligence, Hom Incavo, but it is so simple. Forty-two thousand worlds support human life. On each of them people are the same, descended from a single large sample plucked off Terra eighty thousand years ago by the unknown Harvesters and strewn across space."

"Science has known that for centuries," Incavo objected.

"In our time the Church has acknowledged it, too, however belatedly."

"Not the Jesuits."

"They still cling to an archaic theory of separate creations. But they are alone."

"There are the New Restorationists," Incavo parried.

"Which is the next best thing to being alone. May I continue?"

"Surely."

"On all these worlds live humans who are the same in their molecules—the same in the sight of God. Why is it so surprising that He sent His Son to so many of them? And now that those worlds are known to one another, why is it surprising that an authority should naturally arise to examine all these visitations and decide which are true?"

Incavo nodded darkly. "Yet there are worlds without Christs."

"Khoren Four is one—at least, until our Incarnation is recognized. Other worlds still await their Incarnations. History is not over yet."

"You believe that in time, Christ will visit all the human worlds."

"I hope so."

"And then what? The universe ends?"

"Your cynicism overcomes you," Greder sniffed. "You're out of your depth among us." Frowning, she turned away from Incavo to press her ring to an invoice presented by a Swiss Guard.

Augmented drums rolled. The sound seemed to circle the room before it drew into tight vortexes and descended on the stage. The Gwilyan Royal Philharmoneum was about to begin.

The sights and sounds and acrid smells of New Borgiaville at sunrise were somehow comforting when Incavo emerged from Vatican Center the next morning. He'd sipped and spied, pried and parried for another four hours until an insistent lethargy had overcome him. He hadn't been tired or drunk—not with all his implants. No, the sense of depletion had meant that his office was trying to reach him. They'd been instructed to attempt contact only in emergencies.

In Vatican Center there were always guest rooms—for a nap, for a tryst; no one cared so long as the lobbying whirled on. The chamberlain had honored his chit from St. George's Hall: *Greder will be charged for the room.* Chuckling, Incavo had stretched out on the cot and opened his mind. In that near-trance state he would spend the next half hour receiving a trans-space message. As media went, trans-space was frustratingly slow, its tiny bandwidth suited only to delivering brief texts and strings of somesthetic commands. Its only advantage was that it was absolutely secure.

Incavo had risen, pawed at his hair, and tugged at his garments to increase their dishevelment. He had stumbled into Vatican Center's manicured halls. Res-olutely, attendants had looked the other way as one more casualty of last night's revels made for the emerald glow of the street.

Shouldering into a vendor's hovel, he ordered a Jesuit's Horror. *Herb bread or not, the plorg-warming things grow on you.* Incavo chewed while shambling through thick crowds and reflected on the trans-space message he had received. One did not "hear" a trans-space message. One did not even wake up with a cre-ated memory of having heard it. One simply awoke with a certainty of knowing something one had not known before—with no idea where the knowledge came from, but also with no particular inclination to wonder. It was there, and that was enough.

What Marnen Incavo had awakened sure of knowing was this: *"Your client called. Stop fishing. Cardinals have been summoned to Vatican. Leaders of foreign faiths are gathering. Find out why."*

Intriguing, Incavo thought as he threaded the swarming hordes of New Bor-giaville's streets. *If that is happening, there may be more to gain by getting involved than even my client needs to know about.*

10. Jaremi Four—Southern Hemisphere

Old Sculfka did not lie, Linka Strasser thought. *This guest is altogether pleasant looking.* Dressed in leather and linen and brass, carrying a Jaremian lute in a fabric sack, the young minstrel would inflame the desires of countless Galactic women who *poved* Linka's 'casts for vicarious titillation. Still in Mode, Linka peered within, making sure the *verify* signal was strong. *Billions will witness tonight's feast through my eyes—to say nothing of what comes after.*

None but males attended this feast. There were two exceptions: First, Graargy never entertained without his beloved elder claspmate Sculfka at his side. Second, traditional hospitality forbade a chief to flaunt any emblem of rank or privilege that was denied an honored guest. So if Graargy would have a woman by his side, the guest must, too. If it happened that the guest had been traveling without a woman of his own—not an unusual state of affairs for a minstrel—Graargy's duty as host was to provide one.

Linka smiled at the minstrel. She sat beside him, wearing (more or less) the best seductive finery the little settlement owned.

"Food," Graargy growled. A fur-clad mountain of a man, he was well into his fifties—a fabulous age in Jaremi Four's shattered Southland. Nonetheless, his youthful musculature was just beginning to go soft. Graargy locked hands with Sculfka. Anyone could see the warmth there.

The minstrel locked eyes with Linka and smiled, casting his eyes down her body with frank delight. "I am Tarklan," he told her. Menservants traipsed into the room, bearing platters of *fhlet* and fish seasoned with *anjhii* and flagons of what passed in this valley for wine.

"Linka is my name," she said around a fast-rising bubble of fear. She struggled to conceal her response. She didn't want the minstrel to read it, or Sculfka, or Graargy.

Most of all, she wanted to keep it a secret from her experients.

Forjeler in plorg, she thought, *I know this man!* Eagerly she raised a goblet of harsh valley wine. Let the bitter grassy liquid flood her awareness.

She wasn't sure who he was, or where she'd met him. But he was a minstrel, one who had traveled the canals and rivers of the South. He visited tribes who otherwise communicated seldom, if at all. She knew she'd encountered him on a previous posting, among some other clan. But was it under circumstances that would enable him to recognize her as easily as she had him?

"Welcome to our hall, Tarklan," Graargy thundered.

"I am obliged to you, great chief," Tarklan said formally. "Obliged for your leave to enter your domain, and for the feasts you have provided. Feasts for the palate"—he waved a hand over the table—"and for other senses, too." He laid a gentle hand on Linka's forearm. *He doesn't seem to have recognized me yet,* Linka thought, *or is he being canny, too?* As the minstrel drained his cup, she subvocalized a command to her satellite: *Search my old 'casts! Find his face! Open a corner in my awareness and play back what is found!*

She was still in Mode. A Galactic audience expected to savor this dinner through her senses. She cut off a chunk of *anjhii*-seasoned fish and made herself concentrate on the flavor. The fish tasted like soft metal; the rare seasoning added notes not unlike ginger, curry, and anise. *Anjhii,* too, had its fans.

"What news do you bring, minstrel?" Graargy asked around a mouthful of *fhlet.*

"From downriver, a ballad of bravery and luck. A song of my own composition, presenting the valor of Jiafarrh's people in escaping from a forest fire triggered by bolts from the sky. Based on hazards I shared with them, might I add."

Graargy grunted. "That's from down the canal. Downcanal, they are harmless. Even your Linka—did you know our Linka came from there?"

"No, we've just met."

I hope you mean that, Linka reflected.

"Linka was not born here. Two years ago she came to us, and I knew it was safe to admit her because she came from downcanal. So, friend minstrel, you can see I know all I need to about affairs downcanal."

Tarklan savored a mouthful of *fhlet.* Locking eyes with Linka, he raised an eye-

brow in a way that suggested sensual delights to come. *Where's my playback?* she
flared inwardly.

"What would my mighty host seek to know, then?" Tarklan inquired.

"When you encountered my sentries, you came from *up* the canal," Graargy
rumbled. Now his amiability concealed menace. "You've been beyond Kaahel's
bottleneck, perhaps in the realm of the greedy Lormatin."

"Perhaps so, noble chief."

Around the corner of Linka's primary awareness, an echo bubble opened. Her
bird's thought engines had identified Tarklan and pinpointed his likeness in her
earlier 'casts. A single bubble opened: *I crossed paths with him only once.*

"What news from upcanal, then?" Graargy demanded.

Tarklan drained his chalice. "Men die in battle, women in childbirth.
Somehow babies erupt in numbers great enough to replace them all—though perhaps not as readily as they once did."

"You toy with me, minstrel. What did you see in Lormatin's realm? Preparations for war?"

"When does Lormatin not prepare for war?"

Withdrawing as much of her attention from the discussion as she dared, Linka
scrutinized the bubble that echoed one of her old 'casts:

Several dozen men and women sat around a capering bonfire. There was Laz
Kalistor in the shadows, still alive, an autochthonous woman tonguing his genitals.
Kaahel, the elder who would later direct Laz's death and ordain his immolation,
looked on approvingly. *Two postings ago,* Linka thought. *Four years ago. Happier
times.* Some distance away—*there he is!*—Tarklan held forth, wrenching sure chords
from his lute, singing in an affecting tenor. Linka's view of the visitor was suddenly
occluded by the face of a long-ago lover. A callused hand slid inside her leather
tunic and encircled one breast. She felt the bulge of his erection against her hip.

"I am a minstrel," Tarklan was saying at the banquet table. "I pass from tribe to
tribe with a freedom few enjoy, because everyone knows I keep certain confidences."

"I don't ask you to abuse a confidence," Graargy countered. "I ask only what
you saw upriver. Did you see smiths forging swords? Fashioners laboring over siege
engines?"

"It's the military secrets I never reveal," insisted Tarklan. "Anyway, why
should you worry? Here in the valley your grandfather settled, adversaries consider
you untouchable. You're protected by the valley crags, the ruined locks, and the
ingenuity of your own fashioners. Armies have come against your famous traps, and
have been swallowed as though they never lived."

Graargy clutched one of Sculfka's ropy hands in his. "My claspmate and I have
not lived to this ripe old age through want of vigilance."

In the corner of Linka's awareness, the playback bubble imploded and was
gone. *That was the only time I met Tarklan,* she thought with relief. *He came to
Kaahel's camp for only a few days. Never got too close to me.*

Linka found relief in that, because Kaahel's land lay *up* the canal. Two years before, when she'd appeared at Graargy's lower locks asking for asylum, she falsely claimed to hail from downcanal. In that direction the tribes were more peaceful. From there Graargy thought it less threatening to accept refugees.

Graargy and Tarklan had finished staring each other down. Tarklan won. "Very well, minstrel," Graargy said. "It shall be as it always is with minstrels. You sing what you want to, and we will listen between the lines."

"Noble and generous you are, great chief," responded Tarklan. With one hand he raised his cup, with the other he squeezed Linka's hip with playful desire—but without any sign of recognition.

Tarklan didn't have much contact with me while I lived among Kaahel's people, Linka thought, *which is fortunate, because we'll have plenty of contact here.*

11. Jaremi Four—Northern Hemisphere

Steamrifle on standby, Ruth Griszam stood watch atop the dam. Willim Dultav climbed the steep slope that flanked the powerhouse. His wave was part greeting, part request for permission to board. She just had time to slip into Mode before he drew beside her.

"How's the arm?" she asked.

"Itches a little. I think it's going to be fine." He sat beside her in the gathering dark. "I'd like to— Arn and I—we'd like to join you."

Well, here's a development. "What, live here?"

"Sure, for two or three weeks, anyway. This place is close to the campus. It offers lots of cover, and despite my misadventure the other morning, the area's not usually hot with marauders."

"What will you do for food?" she asked.

"I don't think Ulf and Chagrin will begrudge two extra mouths for a while."

"No, not if one of them is Arn's." *Nobody in the Galaxy gives a plorg about Ulf and Chagrin,* she thought. *The saybacks tell me that. So why not liven the stew?* "Sure, welcome aboard." She offered him her hand. He kept it a long time.

"So," she said at last. "That extraordinary spell Arn has cast over Ulf and Chagrin—"

"Something he's done before," Dultav said. "He's acquired countless disciples before. And let them go when the time was right."

"Having Ulf and Chagrin for followers may be more than even Arn Parek bargained for," Ruth warned. "If they get wind that Arn's a fake, they'll kill him."

He eyed her coolly. "Will you tell them?"

"Of course not."

Dultav smiled. "Then they won't find out."

"I . . . have . . . seen . . . so . . . much."

Arn Parek's eyes snapped open as if from a trance. Ulf and Chagrin reclined on mossy wooden pallets leaned up against a cannibalized control console. They faced Parek motionlessly, heads raised achingly, mouths agape. *I don't think they've moved since I entered my reverie,* Parek reflected. *That was two hours ago.*

The three had repaired to an ancient turbine pen deep within the dam. A steel shaft half a meter wide dropped from one of several openings in the ceiling. It impaled a mammoth impeller housing. The forces set loose when the machinery seized long ago had twisted the metal shaft like bread dough.

Two lanterns flickered at opposite ends of the pen. Their tangerine light quivered on mold-streaked walls. Parek sat atop the impeller housing. Reposing on their pallets at a shallow angle, Ulf and Chagrin echoed the traditional pose of spiritual seekers in Jaremi Four's Northland, where the vivid aurora had bent religious imaginations towards the sky. The position was meant for gazing toward the zenith; raising their heads so long to observe an earthbound teacher had exacted a physical price. The guerrillas massaged the backs of their necks.

"What have you seen?" Ulf asked hesitantly.

Parek shuddered. "So much suffering. So much misery—but also the reasons for it all." Parek lifted a half-meter section of metal pipe. On one end, it had been sawn through. The other end was stretched and ruptured by some long-ago steam explosion.

If he'd raised a steampistol to his head, Ulf and Chagrin would have followed his lead. They raised pipe fragments of their own.

Parek held a deep breath and closed his eyes. He slid his pipe between three closely spaced metal conduits. At intervals he tapped one. Then the second. Then the third. *Clang. Shang. Ralang.*

Then he repeated the round a little faster. *Clang shang ralang.*

Ulf and Chagrin fell into his rhythm, clanking their pipes against tubing and conduits that descended from the ceiling by their pallets. *Clang shang ralang.*

With each repetition, Parek sped the rhythm up a notch. He and Ulf and Chagrin filled the turbine pen with a glittering ocean of sound. Now Parek imposed a secondary rhythm, tolling an added emphasis at the head of every fifth series, then every third, then fifth and third again. ***Clang**-shang-ralang. Clang-shang-ralang. Clang-shang-ralang. Clang-shang-ralang. Clang-shang-ralang. **Clang**-shang-ralang. Clang-shang-ralang. Clang-shang-ralang. **Clang**-shang-ralang. Clang-shang-ralang. Clang-shang-ralang. Clang-shang-ralang. Clang-shang-ralang. **Clang**-shang-ralang. Clang-shang-ralang. Clang-shang-ralang.*

They chimed that way for ten minutes straight, Ulf and Chagrin occasionally punctuating the din with breathy moans. At last Parek rang out three savagely emphatic series. ***Clang**shangralang! **Clang**shangralang! **Clang**shangralang!*

As one they ceased their jangling. In a state near trance, Ulf and Chagrin lay down their pipes.

"Truly," Parek breathed, "I saw the reasons for it all."

Dreamily Chagrin asked, "Reasons? For the Great Dismay? Tell us."

"Yes, I must share it before I burst with it." He stood and paced. "Something came to me today. The *why* of all of this. Why all the agonies happened—the petty wars, the food riots, the massacres. All the private little hells of the Great Dismay."

He whirled and let the light of one lantern flood his eyes from below. "We were afraid."

Ulf raised an eyebrow. "Us?"

"Not you and Chagrin," Parek droned. "Not us three. *Humanity* was afraid. Always we held ourselves back from doing the wonderful things we might have done. Always we retreated from consequences—political consequences, moral consequences, environmental consequences, social consequences." Parek let the silence hang.

After a moment, Chagrin spoke. "What should we have done?"

"Do you know what brought down fire from the sky so long ago—what kept us from rallying after it struck? Men and women drew back from using their intelligence. That is why we suffer the Great Dismay. But it will not always be thus. In time. . . ."

"In time. . . ." murmured Ulf, his eyes screwed shut.

"In time we'll learn the lesson of our hardship," Parek breathed. "The Great Dismay will teach us that none can better defend our interests than we ourselves; that is its real lesson. We must not throw our wills away again."

Perched atop the ruined console, Chagrin stirred. "I don't think I understand."

"Nor do I." Parek stared down at his new disciples. "The revelation is not yet complete. It comes in bits and pieces. Perhaps it will be clear for us all—soon."

"Soon," Ulf rumbled in return.

For Ulf, one thing was already clear. He was tasting the first possibilities of real power—maybe enough power to take vengeance on a world that had treated him cruelly all his life.

In some corner of his being, Ulf realized he could no longer remember a time when he hadn't wanted such vengeance.

Parek lifted the pipe again. The two guerrillas followed his lead. *Clang-shang-ralang. Clang-shang-ralang. Clang-shang-ralang.*

Before he slipped back into trance, Chagrin experienced a moment in which he could feel Ulf's craving clearly.

Even to him it felt grotesque.

12. Tridee Broadcast, Galaxy Wide • Origin: Terra—Wasatch Range, Usasector

" 'And it came to pass,' wrote Nephi, 'that I saw among the nations of the gentiles the foundation of a great church. And the angel said unto me: Behold the foundation of a church which is most abominable above all other churches, which slayeth the saints of God, yea, and tortureth them and bindeth them down, and yoketh them with a yoke of iron, and bringeth them down into captivity.'" Alrue Latier abandoned the easy meandering of his usual preaching style. His monologue acquired momentum as if he had caught the trail of a familiar quarry.

Of course, he had.

"'I beheld this great and abominable church; and I saw the devil that he was the foundation of it. And I also saw gold, and silver, and silks, and scarlets, and fine-twined linen, and all manner of precious clothing; and I saw many harlots.'" Suddenly Latier was not alone in the tridee image. He shared the frame with stock Vatican streetscapes: the Lobbyist's Quarter, St. Peter's Megasilica, wretched street vendors, cardinals in their vestments surrounded by hangers-on. "'And the angel spake unto me, saying: Behold the gold, and the silver, and the silks, and the scarlets, and the fine-twined linen, and the precious clothing, and the harlots, are the desires of this great and abominable church. For behold,'" Latier read in a carnival barker's voice, "'they have taken away from the gospel of the Lamb many parts which are plain and most precious; and also many covenants of the Lord have they taken away. And all this they have done that they might pervert the right ways of the Lord, that they might blind the eyes and harden the hearts of the children of men.'"

Latier was alone in the tridee image. He closed his book. Stared fixedly into the pickup. "Words straight from the Book of Mormon, First Nephi, chapter thirteen. Words many of today's so-called sophisticated Latter-day Saints hide from. They find them—how can I disguise it?—inconvenient and embarrassing. But not Alrue Latier! No, brothers and sisters, not me. I know what those words plainly say. And I know of which enemy they speak." Latier leaned forward so sharply that the tridee distorted his face. "Nor am I loath to speak the enemy's name aloud. It is the Universal Catholic Church. And verily, it threatens us all with the stink of its iniquity."

Suddenly Latier was seen full length, standing astride the bowed blue limb of Terra as angels fluttered among the stars. "Behold, I condemn!" he thundered. "I stretch forth my hand and condemn. I stretch forth my hand and condemn the prosperity Vatican has amassed. I stretch forth my hand and condemn the entrée it has gained into Galactic life, before and above the other Terran faiths. Alone among them it has built embassies and cathedrals on every world. Alone it has received a planet of its own. And why? Behold, it presumes to license the man-gods of alien worlds as authentic Incarnations of the Christ."

Latier leaned away from the tridee pickup. His mood switched from strident hectoring to an air of grandfatherly solicitude. The switch came so abruptly one could almost hear its snap. "I know what you're thinking, my faithful. Alrue knows. You're thinking, 'Here I am, chit in hand, ready to reserve my place on Elder Latier's all-inclusive mission pilgrimage to Ordh, and all Elder Latier can talk about is the evils of Vatican.' Well, rest assured, brothers and sisters, if you slide your chit into your viewer this very minute, you can book your berth on my chartered starliner without missing a word—neither one jot, nor a single tittle—of what I'm about to impart about the sins of that grotesque church."

Latier switched back into angry-prophet mode. "And behold, I stretch forth my *other* hand and condemn! I stretch forth my other hand and condemn the Universal Catholic Church for upholding the blasphemous theory that all humans are one flesh. Even now, Jesuits—the intellectuals and gadflies of the Vatican establishment—are being rounded up by their own church. Why? Because even *they* recognize what is wrong with this abhorrent doctrine."

Latier's tridee image hurled itself into a corner as stock shots from Ordh and Arkhetil and Gwilya marched past. "If all humans are one flesh, then what are we Terrans? We who see *all* the colors, hear *all* the sounds—what portion is left for us? Our priceless blue planet is the sole cradle not only of humanity itself, but also of its true religion. Are we to accept that we are no different, not even in spirit, from others in this Galaxy? Have they no uniquenesses of their own, one from another? Shall we pretend that the distinctions between Ordhian and Arkhetil, Kharaggan and Calluran, do not exist? As Saints of the New Restoration," Latier continued, "we know that God Himself is a man like us, only more advanced."

Latier's avuncular face had filled the image again. A phony-looking night sky twinkled in the background. "Just as gods and men have similar—but not identical—natures, so do Terrans and the various Galactic races clearly occupy distinct planes, or 'fellowships.' That is a truth the Universal Catholic Church seeks to repress, the better to claim the saviors of hundreds of worlds as apparitions of the deity for whom it claims to speak." Latier turned away from the pickup. He began to mount a synthesized stairway whose steps shimmered into being just ahead of his feet. Puffing, he raised himself up among the stars. "Brothers and sisters, behold! Sin and apostasy have too long dominated this universe of ours. Yea, it is time for a new return to purity, a call proclaimed by the earliest Mormons. Join me in restoring the ancient covenants yet once more. Together we will stretch forth our hands and live in the authentic and venerable ways. And behold, it shall come to pass that you, my faithful, can achieve Exaltation and live among the stars of the spiritual universe just as men and women already do among the stars of this universe of matter."

He had reached the stairway's apex. The Galaxy spun below him, grand yet somehow corrupt (a third-level impression engineered by half a dozen affectational colorists). "Now, brothers and sisters, still have those chits in your hand? Now is the time to slip them into your universal communicators. Now is the time to let Brother Alrue understand the depth of your commitment. Give, my faithful. Give. Give. Give."

13. Jaremi Four—Northern Hemisphere

Auroral light flickered through shattered skylights, painting rows of library shelves a pallid green. Willim Dultav bent to inspect the entry turnstile. A thread he'd placed there on his last visit was still intact. "No one's been here."

"Good," said Arn Parek. Clipped to his belt was an old military-issue utility lantern. He cranked it up and thumbed the piezo. Saffron light bloomed.

Dultav produced a similar lantern from his knapsack and brought it to life. He glanced toward the skylights. They pierced the floor of a plaza above the underground library. The plaza was surrounded by slumping high-rises. Dultav knew they were abandoned; he and Parek could work all night by lantern light without attracting attention. "Last time, I was in history."

"Think you're pushing this?" Parek asked.

Dultav hefted the knapsack up and down, up and down. "No, my arm's fine. It's time." They clambered up one side of a fallen column and slithered down the other. "Time I got back to work. And time you got something into your life besides those depraved disciples of yours."

"Ulf and Chagrin are dangerous," Parek pointed out. "My power over them guarantees our safety."

"You've got power over them, all right," agreed Dultav. They had reached the section he wanted. He placed his lantern atop a rusty shelf to cast a general light.

Parek handed Dultav his own lantern for close work and squatted beside him. "It's an unusual division of labor for us," said Parek. "I hang with the bodyguards and you get the girl."

Dultav pulled down a volume and thrust it into his knapsack. "I'm nowhere near 'getting' that girl, Arn. She has a remarkable inner authority. I don't imagine Ulf or Chagrin have touched her."

"I know they haven't."

"By now, you must know everything about them. For two weeks now, you've spent every waking moment with Ulf and Chagrin—praying with them, meditating with them, preaching at them, ringing those fucking pipes."

"Chiming focuses awareness," Parek reminded him.

"It creates a fucking trance," Dultav spat back. "Just one more gimmick. You've never invested so much in just two people. What are you doing to them?"

"I'm sure it's been intense for them. But I haven't really been focusing on them, on where I might be leading their thoughts."

"Maybe you should."

"Maybe so." Parek stopped pacing and ran a hand through the ebony ringlets of his hair. "Know what I've been doing these last two weeks, Will? Reflecting things off them. I've been using Ulf and Chagrin as foils while I work through some problems that have preoccupied me for months."

"Such as?"

"The last few months, I've been having strange dreams. I'd almost call them . . . visions."

Dultav went back to his books, affecting a casualness Parek didn't quite believe. "I wouldn't worry about it," Dultav said abstractedly. "If I'd been playing holy man as long as you, I might start having holy dreams, too."

"What if the visions are true? Consider something: when I designed the doctrines that went into my holy-man act, I used the most advanced sociology, the latest theories about the psychology of faith—everything you taught me! Well, there's much more to it now. "

"Like what?" Dultav asked coldly.

"Remember four years ago, that camp of twenty thousand, the big tent?"

"I recall we've never eaten so well or amassed so much wealth since."

"I recall that you were the one who made us walk away from it," Parek countered. "But don't you remember how it felt? Thousands of voices chanting. Revivals lasting long into the morning. People rolling in mud, staring into empty skies, screaming with wonder and delight."

Genuine anger rumbled in Dultav's voice. "Remember what it took to create that effect—and the consequences."

"They believed in me, Will! I brought hope into their lives, and no, we didn't do a half-bad job of lining our pockets. But what matters is, I was *saying* something to them."

Dultav grabbed the younger man's forearms. "Saying what? You forget one trivial detail: your religion is a fake. You made it all up! No revelations, no choirs of sky-nymphs, just one very mortal bookworm shivering in a tent, figuring out ways to sweet-talk desperate peasants out of food and a place to sleep."

Parek withdrew from Dultav's grip. "Okay, so there's nothing supernatural about it," he said coldly. "But it *works!*" He began to pace. "Come on, Willim, this was your field. How many religions were ever what they claimed to be? And how many began when some charlatan stumbled down a mountainside screaming, 'The sky gods spoke to me'?"

"Doesn't say much for the mentality of the average believer."

"They get what they need."

"And you . . . what do you need?"

"I need the tent again," said Parek after a long interval. "I need the thousands. I need them to see visions and hear the sky gods."

"No!" Dultav surged out of his chair. "We will not go back to that! You don't still have that shit, do you?"

"Easy, Will, easy." Parek stepped back, showing his palms. "It's gone. I don't even remember where we left it." They started moving back toward their original work area, Parek in the lead. "It's not . . . not that *stuff* that I need anyway. What I need is the people and the power."

"For what?" Dultav demanded.

"As a tool to do something . . . you know, about what's happened to the world."

Dultav erupted in bitter laughter.

When he finished, Parek was staring coolly at him. "Will, are you going to tell me that an ordinary man can't find a little chunk of the truth, all by himself?"

"That's not what's happening here."

Parek lifted a book and made a show of blowing dust off the cover. "Look at us, Willim. Scavenging old knowledge, for what? To no purpose. If things keep going as they are, nobody will read this again—or even know how—that is, if anyone survives." He pointed at the wound in Dultav's arm with two fingers, almost touching the scar. "How many more times do you want to be shot at?"

Dultav pursed his lips. "And you think you can do something about it?"

Parek nodded. "Someone has to end the anarchy."

"You want to end the Great Dismay," Dultav mocked. "And it starts with the tent, with the crowds? With that fucking hallucinogenic stew of yours?"

"Whatever it takes."

Dultav turned his back on Parek and began drawing books from the shelves. "I don't understand you, Arn. One minute you think you're for real. The next you talk about going back to deceit—back to that poison."

"As I said, I'll do whatever it takes if I can—just maybe—bring people together. Yes, if I can end the Great Dismay."

Dultav frowned and then nodded. "Here's something you can do to end my dismay." Half-smiling, he held out a book and a lantern. "Check out section eighteen. Bring me back anything you find by this author."

"Ah, the professor has lost enough arguments for tonight," Parek said with sudden mischief.

"Just go." Tired finality sounded in Dultav's voice.

Shrugging, Parek took up book and lantern, trudged across the library, and drew himself onto a rickety table. The aurora was all pink now. Through the empty skylights he watched it swirl and stream and curtain. *Willim's not ready,* he thought. *But I am. I know what I must do. And Willim mustn't find out about it.* Parek drew a deep breath through his nose. He let it out again and again. Staring up into the auroral shrouds, Parek smiled. *I know what this is. It's another sign. The one I've been waiting for.*

14. Jaremi Four—Southern Hemisphere

Ordinarily one did not *tap* a colleague uninvited. But this was no ordinary situation. *"Tramir!"* Linka Strasser hissed subvocally. *"What are you doing?"*

At some deep level, she felt him blink and stretch. *"I was sleeping."*

"Sorry, I didn't think I'd coded that *level of urgency."*

"Sleep, Linka," said her fellow Spectator from his posting, two hostile tribes up the canal. *"A predictable choice, considering what time it is."*

"This is important. I need you to pov *something."*

"Why?"

"You'll know when you see it."

She lateraled him a clip from early that evening.

Auroral light flickered above the valley wall. Grimy men, squalid women, and gaunt children sat in clusters. Fires leapt from fractured millstones all along the canal. Linka sat on a mossy log, flanked by Graargy and Sculfka. All eyes rested on the magnetic figure of Tarklan. Accompanying himself on an ancient lute, the minstrel declaimed a traditional ballad in a warm, clear tenor.

Side by side with the clip of that night's performance, Linka had been feeding Tramir the archival clips from Kaahel's camp four years before—the last time she had encountered Tarklan.

"Same guy? You're certain?"

"No question," she responded. *"Here's more from tonight, an hour later."*

Suck, rush, wrench.

Discolored tapestries parted before their outstretched hands. Two torches twinkled, their reflections dancing on a flagon of local wine the servants had left. Tarklan shrugged off his jerkin and lay down his lute. Once more she admired the muscles of his bare back, knowing many of her experients would do the same. If she and Tarklan had never met before, Linka would have enjoyed this welcome assignment. As it was, for the last two nights she'd used sex to forestall almost all conversation between them. *Go for three,* she'd thought grimly. She discarded her wrap and encircled him in her arms. Her nipples swelled against his back. She knew he felt it. "Another triumphant performance," she purred. "How about one more?"

He turned around in her arms and pressed a palm gently to her cheek. With his free hand he grasped the flagon. "Soon, delicious one. First we drink and talk."

Hiding her apprehension, she lifted two dented goblets. He poured. At his gesture, she sat on the bedstead. "You know what I do," he began. "I go from settlement to settlement. I sing and tell stories. Always I look for new stories. After all, at my next stop I must have something new to sing about."

She drank uneasily.

"I look at life here," Tarklan went on. "I talk to people. I think there is a story here . . . about you."

"Me?"

He nodded. "You and Yelmir."

The falsely accused one. The one who soon will hang. "That's no story," she said, laying down her goblet. "Not one I want to talk about."

Tarklan's smile turned sharp. "We are not concerned with what you want to talk about." Anger must have glinted in her eyes. "Tell me again, Linka. What did Graargy instruct you to do with me?"

"What you desire."

Tarklan crossed his arms impatiently.

"What you command."

He gave her tunic back. "Later I may command love. For now, I command you to speak."

She downed more wine. "Yelmir is a fashioner who tends Graargy's traps. They say he killed another fashioner, a man named Blaupek. Thirteen days from now he will hang. Is that the story you want?"

Tarklan shook his head. "I talk to tribespeople. More important, I listen. Some of them think you know more than you say."

"People talk. In your travels have you not learned to suspect the wagging tongue?"

Tarklan sat beside her and took her hand. "I've learned when to doubt and when not to. Seemingly, Yelmir had no reason to kill Blaupek. Yelmir's own family members think it was an accident. They think Blaupek simply stumbled into one of his own traps. It could happen easily enough here."

"What else would Yelmir's family think?" Linka challenged. "And who would accuse Yelmir falsely?"

"His accuser, of course!" Tarklan barked. "Harapel, who claims she witnessed the murder from the woods while she was out foraging . . . with you as her companion."

"I saw nothing," Linka insisted. "Why doubt Harapel's word?"

Tarklan's eyes were like daggers. "You didn't grow up here. Perhaps no one told you. Years ago, Harapel and Yelmir were to be clasped. When Graargy named

Yelmir a senior fashioner, he offered him one boon. Yelmir asked for release from his arranged betrothal to Harapel. She's hated him ever since."

In three days, he's gleaned history from these people that's been closed to me for two years! Aloud, she said, "For that, she'd lie to get Yelmir put to death?"

He shrugged. "People have worked far harder, with lesser motivation, for revenge. Linka, tell me. What happened?"

"Harapel and I were some distance apart. I saw nothing."

"I'm told foragers stay close together when they work among the traps."

"Usually," she admitted. "We got sloppy."

Tarklan refilled their goblets. "A sad, sad story. Lovely Linka sees a man die by accident. Another woman leaps up to paint it as murder. Though not close to the accuser, Linka keeps her silence." He leaned forward, his face barely a hand's width from hers. "But there is one thing Linka doesn't know. Linka doesn't know how she will feel on festival day, when Yelmir twitches away his life for a crime he didn't commit. When Linka realizes that she alone is responsible for his death."

"Even if that's true, what does it matter to you?"

"You matter!" Tarklan husked.

"I'm a welcome woman," she mocked.

"You're more than that. I see depths in you. And that's why I know how bad it will be for you. I've known others who let someone die by their omission. The guilt hollows you out, haunts you forever. When Yelmir's dead, you'll realize that, too. But then it will be too late. Tell what you know now and spare yourself that suffering."

You can't begin to imagine how little you know of me. "Tarklan, I know nothing. When Yelmir hangs, all it will mean to me is justice done. Sing of that if you want to."

Tarklan clasped her shoulders with stinging power. He rose from the bedstead and hauled her after him. Face to face, their eyes locked. "No, I will sing of you. I know who you are. You are one of the ones whose eyes dance!"

"Forjeler," Duza breathed somewhere in Linka's awareness.

"There's more," she promised. The lateral playback continued.

Tarklan still clutched her. He tossed back his head, laughed in gales.

"Tell me why you laugh so!" Linka demanded.

"So many people live one place all their lives. They say you've lived in two, maybe more. Minstrels . . . we see dozens, scores, even hundreds of places. Can you imagine a hundred settlements, Linka? A hundred tribes, a hundred chiefs, a hundred different ways of life?" Tarklan released her and took up his wine again. "Many tribes have legends now of new arrivals—soft intruders with dancing eyes and an aloof manner. They present themselves at the gate, or the shoreline—" he eyed her over the rim of his goblet. "Or at the lower locks."

What do I do, stop recording? she had thought in sudden terror. *No, keep going. This material can't be released, but it might have training value.*

"They ingratiate themselves," Tarklan persisted, "and live out the roles expected of them. In time, they seem committed to their new communities. But all the while they have their own mysterious agendas. Some, it is said, even appear in one tribe after another." He laughed resonantly. "But that is legend." He dropped his empty goblet, pressed a brawny hand into her back and heaved her against him. Their mouths collided.

She ended the lateral. *"This raises genuine concern,"* she subvocalized to Duza. *"Do you agree?"*

"Let me see it again."

Linka subvocalized a command to replay the lateral. While it unspooled, she surrendered her upper self to reverie.

It was almost three years earlier. She was back on Terra, waiting out the inquiry that had followed Laz Kalistor's more-or-less death. Always short of instructors, the Spectator Academy had pressed her to lecture while she awaited judgment.

"How do you realize the newly perfected medium?" she challenged. She strode in circles in a deep conical amphitheater. Two hundred first-year students stared down at her. "How do you move from the sheer fact that senso existed—that its technology worked—to an authentic framework within which artistic expression could occur? Those were the questions confronting DiLeppert and his colleagues two centuries ago, a quarter-century before the Galactics found Terra, when senso was first developed."

She prowled the speaker's circle, her gaze striking at this blank face, then that in the tiered seating rings above her. "Early still photographers emulated painting. The primitive cinema parroted conventions of the stage. Naturally the first serious senso productions were firmly rooted in the tridee drama, with its artifice and contrived spectacle. What demands did that place on the senso pioneers?"

No response lamps lit. *Were my own classmates this dense? Was I?* With a sigh, Linka continued. "Come on, people. You've *pov*ed it all your forjeling lives. A big tridee with an ambitious soundtrack is impressive to watch. But you can still turn around and see the room you're standing in. Can you do that with *senso?*" Cadets were shaking their heads. "Of course not. You *can't* look over your own shoulder during a senso. And when the Spectator looks over *her* shoulder, you see what's behind *her*. Senso immerses the experient in the Spectator's whole perceptual field. Vision, hearing, smell, taste, touch, vestibular sensation—everything. Now what was the first thing DiLeppert learned about senso, the thing that made it clear that many of the conventions of the cinema and tridee would be forever off limits?"

Ring upon ring of faces stared back blankly. "Think, cadets," she wheedled. "What was the most personally expensive discovery of DiLeppert's career?" More blank faces. More immobile hands. "Come on, what was his *last* discovery?" *Finally I made it simple enough.* She chose from among a half-dozen response lamps.

An Ordhian cadet stood. "You can't cut."

"Exactly," replied Linka. "Having perfected senso by the age of fifty, DiLeppert spent his elder years trying to build a *pov* switcher. He succeeded, and after he used it for four months he went irretrievably insane. Most people can't accept sudden switches in their *being-thereness*. No jumping back and forth. So forget Eisenstein. Forget Godard. Forget Sarbynski. Forget everything the masters of cinema and tridee had learned to do with fluid cutting. Senso is like theater: you must watch the action through a single pair of eyes. It's unlike theater in that those eyes can be anywhere. They can be inside the action. They can move around. But you can't cut.

"For thirty years people tried to make senso dramas with a single Spectator dancing through choreographed action. Some very good works came out of this period—but also a great many disasters. Particularly disappointing were the spectaculars. Simply put, in those days there were no postproduction effects in senso. Sfelb, it's difficult enough today. Everyone's heard about the *King Kong* remake that sank the Australian economy and plunged the Pacific Rim into five years of war. It became clear that artifice—at least, artifice on any scale ambitious enough to be interesting—lay outside the new medium's scope.

"By the time of Terra's Galactic Encounter, senso had lost its luster. People had turned their backs on it, except for a handful who recognized its power as a platform for documentaries."

She resumed circling in long strides. "Then the Galactics came. And senso, this visionary Terran technology that had fallen short of its promise, became Terra's first major export. To Galactics, of course, the core technology held no surprises. But the idea of applying senso technology that way—of sending artists into the field to have experiences that could be packaged and distributed to consumers for private *pov*ing as a means of entertainment or learning—that was novel. And it captured the imagination of the Galaxy."

She whirled and clapped her open hands on the speaker circle's golden rail. "Best of all, the Galaxy offered a way to reconcile people's hunger for entertainment with senso's limits as a documentary form. The answer was, of course, the Enclave worlds. Of the Galaxy's forty-two thousand inhabited planets, forty thousand had been judged too primitive to participate as full members of the Confetory. Just knowing that the Confetory existed would warp the development of autochthonous peoples. Yet on many of those worlds, life was colorful and often violent, filled with rich experiences and alternative social, political, and sexual architectures. Protected by the Enclave Statute, these worlds would never be assimilated into Galactic culture. Rather, they could develop along their own paths—or destroy themselves, if it comes to that. In pursuing their unique destinies, the Enclave worlds provide raw material beyond imagination for a medium with a desperate need to entertain through the documentary form."

She stopped short and leaned straight-arm against a rail at the edge of the speaking circle. "We all know what the solution turned out to be. Specially equipped senso artists—Spectators—would be trained and if necessary surgically altered to pass for autochthons. They'd be injected into the lives of Enclave peoples under deep cover, participating in events yet allowing them to unfold as they will, while a Galaxy watches through their eyes. Varied support networks would be put into place, again relying on Galactic technology to install what are often quite impressive infrastructures on Enclave worlds without the autochthons suspecting a thing. Spectators . . . that is what you seek to become."

She stepped under a harsh shaft of light and let her pain show through. "Occasionally, Spectators must make terrible choices to protect Enclave. Sometimes the Spectator must witness ghastly atrocities, or even commit them, without betraying any sign that a higher inner morality recoils from it. And at times, one must sacrifice a colleague's life, or one's own, to keep the secret secure.

"How far is too far? What pain must one endure—what pain may one inflict—in defense of Enclave? The reason I'm on Terra, not in deep cover among the tribespeople of Jaremi Four, is that a board of inquiry is weighing the nuances of one such horrible choice. The one I had to make four months ago that led to the essentially permanent demise of my colleague and friend Laz Kalistor."

Behind her, a tweeting sound. She turned. A cadet eight rows up had triggered his response lamp. "Speak, cadet."

The young man stood. "Fem Strasser, I'd like your personal opinion. After the loss you experienced, do you still agree with quarantining the Enclave worlds? True, free intercourse with Galactic culture might erode much of their rustic charm. But don't the Enclave peoples stand to gain so much more from modern cultural patterns, technologies, medicine . . ."

"*Silence!*" roared the Proctor, far overhead. "Fem Strasser, you may disregard the question."

"Thank you," she replied to the unseen monitor, "but I choose to reply. The question addresses a real issue." She whirled back to face the questioner. "First item. No, my personal views on the necessity of Enclave have not changed. Now let's put the issue in a larger perspective. Cadet, you may be interested to know that some opinion makers raised arguments like yours—not when the decision was being made to send Spectators to the Enclave worlds, but centuries earlier, when Enclave itself first took shape. Forty thousand inhabited worlds, so many peoples—could they be integrated into Galactic life? Most observers believed that to force a knowledge of Galactic culture on peoples not prepared for it by their own development would trigger a crippling culture shock lasting five to seven generations. Though the participants in that debate had no knowledge of it—and wouldn't for centuries, not until Terra was discovered—it might pay *you* to reflect on what befell the autochthons on North America of Terra."

Her finger stabbed the air. "Beyond that, cadet, our psych specialists tell us that sentiments like yours, benevolent as they seem, are actually rationalizations for selfish impulses. Don't be offended; it's just human nature for 'haves' to view 'have nots' as children who need to be assisted—often compelled—to become clones of the 'haves.' It's a dangerous paternalism. We must beware the primordial urge to do good." She paused. "What's your name, Cadet?"

"I am Tramir Duza."

"I look forward to working with you one day, Tramir Duza."

Linka swam back from reverie. Of course she'd gotten to work with Tramir Duza. She'd pulled strings to bring him to Jaremi Four. His way of viewing the people he lived among as ends in themselves continually challenged her. *Some say it keeps me honest.*

"*Linka.*" It was Duza; the repeat playback had ended.

"*Your analysis?*" she asked.

"*Your cover among Graargy's people is in danger,*" Duza subvocalized. "*Both from Tarklan and from gossips in your own community.*"

"*Tarklan's quite a sleuth. I never suspected half the things he uncovered. Now he's fomenting suspicions about transient newcomers—that is, us Spectators—in the scattered villages. I imagine OmNet will escalate our cover routines. Do you perceive a danger to Enclave if Tarklan lets villagers know that people of other tribes share their suspicions?*"

"*I suppose so. But if you want to call down a snuff, I won't participate.*"

"*You don't need to,*" she assured him. "*I'm senior here. No one need join in my call. I just needed another Spectator to corroborate my judgment that danger to Enclave might exist. You've done that, thank you.*"

"*Forjel you, Linka Strasser. Don't you ever worry about body count?*"

"*I demand his removal, Tramir. It's my decision.*"

"*Let the record show that. I'll fulfill my obligation and log that I concurred with you that danger to Enclave was at least conceivable. Then I wash my hands of this. Duza out.*"

Signing off that abruptly was rude—though no ruder than *tapping* someone out of a sound sleep. Linka logged an emergency alert and placed her snuff call. Tarklan's relentless curiosity would be quelled before he got much further toward discovering the existence of underground Galactics on Jaremi Four.

That done, she went out of Mode. The pleasing sights and smells and feelings of drowsing in the sleeping Tarklan's arms filled her awareness. *Tramir's idea about running away with him is not without merit,* she admitted. *But it seems far too risky to me.*

Her arms enfolded Tarklan. Silently Linka said her goodbyes to him. *Tomorrow,* she thought. *It all ends for you tomorrow.*

15. Vatican

Like flies teeming a dead elk, Marnen Incavo thought. That's what Vatican Center reminded him of. Always busy with yachts and flitters, today the airspace around the mulberry tower boiled with activity. Thanks to the hotel's soundproofing, Incavo felt but did not hear the rippling thunder of a big starliner screaming in on rapid descent. *That's what, the eighth or ninth big ship in this hour alone? A week's worth of traffic since dawn.*

Incavo stood alone in his suite, surrounded by dataspheres. An unprecedented assortment of dignitaries was gathering: divines and theologians, cardinals and archbishops, ecumenical delegates from far-flung worlds. Eight days ago someone in the Vatican hierarchy had sounded the alarm that triggered this vast infalling of prelates. Incavo had deduced that much by reverse-engineering the visitors' itineraries. Yet the media hadn't picked up a breath of it. *The trend analyst who tipped me to all this two full days ago—the tip concerning which my office sent me that trans-space message—he earned whatever extortionate amount he's going to charge me.*

Something buzzed in his ear. It was one of his informants. "Answer incoming," he said into the air. "Scramble."

Another sphere opened in the center of his vision, abroil with random pixels. It resolved into the haggard face of a concierge in one of the nearby hotels. Someone he'd bribed. "Talk to me," he told her.

"Fem Greder is leaving the day after tomorrow."

"Just like that?"

"She cleared her lobbying calendar this morning, canceled all her function room and entertainment reservations, and called back the members of her entourage who'd wandered elsewhere on the planet. B'Khraa's confined to his room. And she found berths for everyone on a starliner shipping out in just two days."

Incavo was incredulous. "There are more than two thousand people in her entourage."

"And they've all got private suites. It's a buyer's market for outbound volume now. With all those starliners coming in, they're ordering ships offplanet empty just to clear the pads."

"Your account will be credited as agreed," Incavo told the informant. "Wipe this link from your scheduler." He rang off and drained his snifter of ouzo. *A four-billion-per-diem lobbying campaign, over like that. I must look into this.*

"Oh, it's you." Orgena Greder's pneumatic subordinate Bei Hanllei blinked eyes whose irises were black as coal. She looked decidedly less glamorous today than she had in St. George's Hall.

"I'm here to see Fem Greder," Incavo said unctuously.

"Fem Greder sees no one today."

Incavo showed Hanllei what he had in his hand. "She'll see me."

"This brooch has been in my line for generations," Orgena Greder choked. She wore an austere cosmo, a simple hairdo, and elegant silken kimono. She looked far younger than her sixty years in her reception parlor, a room with transilluminated sulfur-colored crystals for walls. "Hom Incavo, how ever did you find it?"

"I found it at St. George's Hall, the night B'Khraa caught the knives." That much was true. Spotting Greder in the swirling crowds, Incavo had contrived to bump against her. She had been schmoozing that Scalbulian hotelier so intently that she barely registered the collision—much less noticed Incavo palming her brooch. "I stayed late," Incavo lied. "I noticed the brooch on the floor on my way out."

"It was the morning after that reception that I realized the brooch was missing."

No plorg, Incavo thought. "I was unsure what to do next," he continued aloud. "For a mere manuscript dealer to pop up with an object of such evident value— some might think I'd stolen it."

"I quite understand."

"Yesterday evening as I was turning the brooch over in my hand, I recognized the design as Khorenian. At once I thought of you. And here I am."

"Much to my delight," beamed Greder. Bei Hanllei stood two meters away, where she'd been ever since she led Incavo and the brooch through the confusion of Greder's suite. "Bei, get our guest a—don't tell me—an ouzo on slivers, is it not?"

Incavo smiled. "I'm impressed."

"And dinner for two, Bei, if you will."

Hanllei spread her hands in consternation. "Fem Greder, there is so much to pack—"

For a split second, Greder flashed her subaltern a cruel glare that in any language meant *Do as I said!* Her features softened into a motherly smile. "There will be time enough. I shall have a civilized dinner with my friend Hom Incavo." When she turned her smile toward Incavo, it had become . . . less motherly. "You can stay, can you not?"

"This is most unexpected," said Incavo affably. His wave encompassed his daycoat and casual jumper. "I'm not dressed for dinner."

Smiling mischievously, Greder settled into an overstuffed chair. "Never fear, Hom Incavo," she told him, "neither am I." She leaned forward just so. Her kimono parted, revealing half the curvature of one breast. Belying her age, its was full, generous, and all but girlish.

This is one angry woman, Incavo realized. *Determined to bury her hurt in a random indulgence. Perhaps to empty her heart into an understanding ear.*

Hanllei bustled back, bearing two thick crystal tumblers on a platinum tray. Somehow she had found time not only to draw the drinks, but to pull a crimson server's ribbon through her hair. Incavo took his ouzo; Greder accepted a fizzing concoction with a rich golden color. Incavo recognized it as Rikubian sparkling whisky, a rare and ostentatious beverage even on Vatican. Greder gulped five fingers of it and handed the empty tumbler back to Hanllei for a refill. "Drink up," Greder told Incavo. "We can be honest about our implants here."

Incavo drained his glass and gave Hanllei the empty. "You noticed."

"You drank four liters of ouzo that night," Greder said obligingly. "Like me, you take steps to enjoy strong drink without clouding your judgment." Her face was lightly lined and the skin leathery in a subtle way that almost disappeared in the parlor's diffuse golden light.

Hanllei returned with refills. She had managed to pull on a formal diamond-foil blouse and a server's red shoulder wrap. Her skin was perfect, an almost blue-black that threw back bronze highlights even in the chamber's indirect light.

"Thank you, Bei," said Greder. Leaning forward to show Incavo more of her improbably youthful cleavage, she raised her tumbler and asked, "You like Gwilyan brine slug, Marnen, do you not?"

He clinked her glass. "Among other things."

I must have intimate dinners with people who own their own worlds more often, Incavo instructed himself. *They make fascinating conversation.*

"Sealing the caverns was perhaps a radical decision," Greder was saying, chasing the last slug around her platter with an ivory spearstick. "But viewed in a certain way, the lives of a few thousand rebels. . . ." She shrugged and drove her spearstick into the slug. It was still struggling as she popped it into her mouth.

"Had the insurrection spread, it could have compromised my ore shipments. Without revenue, how would I do even what little I can for my cheerless autochthons?"

Incavo nodded. "With authority comes the duty of hard choices." Half-empty bottles of ouzo and sparkling whisky stood among the dinner dishes. Incavo had tuned his implants to allow a warm glow within him. He suspected she was doing the same.

"To bring back my brooch," she said, a wistful slur in her voice. "That was a hard choice."

Yep. He flashed a toothy smile. "But the right thing to do."

She fingered her azure signet ring, the one with which she had used to leave so much of her people's wealth on Vatican. "You must allow me to repay you."

"No, no, I would not hear of it," he said insincerely.

Greder regarded her ring hand with a disapproving sigh. "For the things that matter most, this is of so little use." With sudden anger she tore the signet from her finger and flung it into the parlor's far corner. "So little good it has done me here!"

"I couldn't help noticing the commotion outside," Incavo began, hoping he concealed his eagerness. "Is your work here complete?"

Greder frowned as she poured herself another tumbler of whisky and downed half of it. "We will talk of that later." With visible effort, she relaxed. "We were discussing the means of your repayment."

Forjeler, thought Incavo. *For a while I thought she was poised to spill some secrets. Well, let's see if I can't rescue the evening and backjockey her into bestowing a fat reward.* With mock humility he cast down his eyes. "No, please, Fem Greder. I couldn't take your money."

"Screw my money," Greder said breathily.

Incavo snapped his eyes back up. She had shrugged the kimono off her shoulders. She leaned toward him, eyes closed. *All right, then. Plan B,* he thought, and kissed her.

When their lips parted, his hands had followed a circuitous path to her shoulder blades. Her kimono lay on the gilded floor. Her face and hands were in keeping with her age, but her upper body suggested that of a much younger woman. "About your reward," she breathed.

He leaned backward, feigned hesitation. "But aren't you—you and B'Khraa—"

She let out an astonished snort, steering his hands back to her breasts. "Get serious," Orgena Greder said.

And fell on him.

Incavo and Greder floated in the orbit of a nulgrav sphere, damp and spent. He'd never had sex in a nulgrav before—some luxuries had yet remained beyond his grasp. "So," she said at last, "you don't mind an older woman."

"I hadn't noticed." It was Incavo's first altogether truthful statement of the night.

Greder rolled away from him. Exiting a nulgrav field was like sliding over a puffy cylinder rotating in two directions at once; she did it expertly. She padded back to the parlor and returned with their bottles. "Come on, get out of there," she ordered. "Drinking is *not* better in nulgrav." At her subvocal command, a frothy whirlpool for two rose out of the marble floor.

I could learn to like this, Incavo thought. Greder reached into a compartment along the whirlpool's edge and produced a crystalline cylinder one centimeter in diameter and about eight centimeters tall. It was utterly clear except for a lozenge of matte gray mesh at its base. By its refraction Incavo could just tell that the cylinder was filled with some clear liquid. Greder clutched the cylinder's base with both hands and raised it toward her eyes. Coils of bubbles came out of nowhere and organized themselves into sinuous ribbons and sheets. Obviously Greder was controlling them. When she created three stable ripple-edged sheets of foam whirling through each other, she grinned at him.

"Remarkable," Incavo said. "A vice about which I know nothing."

"That mesh projects a field I manipulate with my will," she said dreamily. "As I massage it, it governs the creation and momentum of the bubbles." She narrowed her eyes. One of the counter-rotating sheets bent at the waist and executed a seeming somersault while still interpenetrating its companions. "It's incredibly relaxing."

"May I?" He held out a hand flecked with suds.

She tapped a finger to her temple. "To guide the mesh's field, you need the proper implants." The three ribbons puffed into a froth of microscopic bubbles, which coalesced into one. "On Wikkel Four this is a child's pastime. I never outgrew it." The three bubbles looped and danced in synchrony. Incavo resolved to pass the time watching her breasts. "You asked if I was leaving," Greder said at last.

"Yes, I saw all the packing outside. Was B'Khraa elected a Christ?"

Greder dropped the cylinder into the water. "Watch yourself here, Marnen. The scoffers are right: Vatican is this Galaxy's blackest nest of deceivers."

He nodded grimly. "So B'Khraa was *not* elected."

"To lose an election would at least be dignified," she growled. "Due process. The correct forms followed. I've lingered here for months. I've spent billions, funded missions, raised offworld cathedrals—you'd think the least they owe me is an election to lose."

Incavo eyed her levelly.

"No one's supposed to know this yet," she declared. "Yesterday Cardinal Rybczynsky, the Secretary of State, summoned me to his office. All at once it ended."

"Your campaign to have B'Khraa proclaimed a Christ?" Incavo asked incredulously.

"In an instant. Defunct. Beyond discussion."

Incavo was stupefied. *Patrons of would-be messiahs as magnanimous as Greder has been are not abruptly turned away. Marginalized, yes, if their candidate is ludicrous, but thrown offworld? Not while they have a credit in their accounts.*

"For months we dickered," she recounted sullenly. "They were aloof, but there was a leisurely malleability. They would always endure one more demonstration for a price. Yesterday Rybczynsky was immovable. B'Khraa was not a Christ, nor could he ever be, he told me flatly. Just like that!"

"I never heard of such a thing."

"It has never happened in the history of Vatican. I checked."

"Of course you did."

She downed another glass of sparkling whisky. Her eyes seemed suddenly older. She mocked Rybczynsky's famous sing-song tones. "'And by the way, Fem Greder, how soon can you leave?' Forjel it all, it just is not done!"

Much, much later, Marnen Incavo made his way into the swollen streets of Vatican. Two hours prior to dawn, they still churned with pilgrims and mendicants and pretenders working their swindles. Ravenously hungry, Incavo pressed into the now-familiar stall for a Jesuit's Horror. He wolfed it down and then bought another for the road. He had an angle. He knew what to do, what he had to learn. *Time to play my trump card within the Papal palace,* he decided. *And then it will be time for me to leave Vatican.*

16. Jaremi Four—Northern Hemisphere

Ruth Griszam stood watch. Her steamrifle lay in one of the gaping powerhouse windows. Below, the creek meandered among ruins and scrub trees. To her left rushed the spillway, its whitewater blinding in the afternoon sun. Ruth glanced behind her, into the powerhouse. Ulf had improvised a table by laying an old door between two turbine housings. He, Parek, and Dultav sat together there.

Ruth's thoughts were trapped in an uncomfortable groove: the trick with names that Parek had played on Ulf at their first encounter. *I'm a professional observer,* she grumbled to herself. *But I remembered it wrong. I still do.* At the Academy, she'd known skeptics who insisted history was unknowable before the advent of objective recording media, that eyewitness testimony was useless, because human memory was so flawed. *They whispered about unexpected events that twenty or thirty Spectators happened to pov simultaneously: when the journals were compared, two or three of them would contain perfectly clear experiences of actions that never happened. Those individuals' brains had made some error during preliminary sensory processing that sent all their further experiences down the wrong chute. Then there's what I did—experience the event accurately, but remember it all wrong!* She shook her head, freshly astonished at the elegance of Parek's technique. *If you're poised to recognize and exploit errors of that sort and do it consistently, you can accumulate enormous power.*

She returned her attention to the table below her. "I need to get back to the library tonight," Dultav was saying.

"Not tonight," said Ulf. "Chagrin and me, we're planning a little raid. Won't be safe out there."

"Actually, I had ideas of my own about tonight," Parek breathed. He didn't need to look up. He knew Ulf's and Dultav's eyes would be on him. He knew they'd wait for him to say what the evening's plans would be. "By the way, where is Chagrin?"

"We scouted a long way this morning," Ulf growled. "With his leg, Chagrin'll need time to limp back."

One of Ruth's Spectator perceptual enhancements yanked her attention toward a movement through the open doorway.

Lurking forms on the hillside above! She'd seen one of them before: Leather. Imitation chain mail. Necklaces of teeth. Ruined goggles hanging from his neck.

"Marauders!" Ruth screamed.

She rolled and flattened. Two rounds slammed into concrete beside her.

The men were already under the table. "Everyone all right?" Dultav yelled.

Ulf was immobile until Parek said "I'm unhurt." Then the seasoned guerrilla took charge. "Ruth!" Ulf called. He pitched his voice loud enough to carry, but thin enough not to carry far.

She'd scuttled into cover behind a turbine housing. "I'm all right."

"Got your rifle?"

It lay on the window ledge, out of reach. "Shit!"

"Never mind," Ulf called. "What did you see?"

"Three, four marauders high up the hill. No one on the opposite bank, though; we'd hear the bells. Think Chagrin's close?"

A shell thwacked into the tabletop. Another ricocheted off metal nearby. "Not yet. You carrying anything?"

She checked her belt and the holster in her bandoleer. "Three pistols."

"Okay. Stay put," Ulf ordered. His steamrifle lay on the floor near Dultav. Ulf thumbed it on. Still hunched beneath the table, he slung it over his shoulder. He gripped Parek's hands and barked urgently at the prophet. "Those are marauders up there! Ruthless bastards. They want to kill us and take our shit."

"You'd know about that," Dultav said thinly.

Ulf ignored him. "No matter what you hear, don't *move* from under here till the shooting stops," he told Parek. Then he rolled out from under the table and dove behind a rusty switch box. A tracer shell screamed into it and broke up in a shower of sparks.

Ruth subvocalized an urgent call for Spectator backup—this was getting too hectic to cover from a single *pov*, especially that of a combatant.

"Spectator Cassandra Wiplien here," a voice buzzed in her head. *"I'm flying no-vis, altitude two thousand, about a hundred seventy klicks southeast of your present position."*

"Care to help cover a firefight?" Ruth squirted her the coordinates.

"Sure, Ruth. Be there in forty seconds."

Ruth subvocalized the command to put her implants into battle mode. For the third or fourth time, she cursed herself for not having strewn bugs. *At least there'll be aerial coverage.* She raised her head and peered outside. A marauder was weaving downhill toward the dam. Ruth squeezed off two pistol shots. Both missed, but the marauder stopped advancing.

"Wiplien here," buzzed a voice in her head. *"I'm on station."*

"What are we up against?"

"Six marauders clustered within about fifty meters. Armed with rifles and carbines, nothing heavier."

"Six!" Ruth echoed.

"Ruth!" Ulf barked behind her. She whirled. Ulf had scuttled behind the switchbox near the window that looked out on the spillway. He'd snatched a big antiarmor rifle and a knapsack full of dangerous toys. "Ready to cover me?" he called.

She nodded. "The plan is 'make like an army,' right?"

"You got it." Ulf tensed his muscles. "Now!"

Ruth pumped seven or eight shots through the open doorway. A sniper fell. *Hit? Diving for cover?* Ruth wasn't sure. Then the sniper tumbled into the open. The hands at his throat shone red.

"One down, five to go," Wiplien buzzed.

Uphill, a skinny woman wearing a poncho of mismatched animal hides screamed. She sprinted toward the fallen marauder. Ruth couldn't hit her, but by emptying her pistols she drove the woman back.

Ruth was empty. She started reloading. When she glanced back toward the spillway window, Ulf was gone.

A bubble opened in her consciousness. *Wiplien's pov. She's lateraling it to me.* It was a spectacular looping aerial: Wiplien was hurtling toward the dam from the north, five meters above the creek. She neared the spillway, gained altitude, and panned left. There was Ulf, climbing the powerhouse wall on the side the marauders couldn't see, a big gun over each shoulder, the knapsack on his back. Wiplien edged backward, closer to the wall. She delivered a dramatic facial closeup. Gritting his teeth, Ulf searched for handholds. The spillway was a luminous curtain behind him. *"You know about this guy?"*

"He's with me," Ruth assured her invisible colleague. *"Stay on him. I want to see how he does."*

The surviving marauders poured fire into the powerhouse. Tracers whizzed. Cement flakes and chips of wood leapt through the air.

After half a minute, it died down.

"They're reloading," Wiplien told her.

Ruth dashed across the concrete floor; rolling, she came up on her elbows next to Dultav and Parek. "Isn't this fun?" she panted.

A series of shots rang out from Ruth's former position. "What the fuck?" Dultav hissed.

"Fooler rack," she explained. "A stack of shells on a mechanical timer. Makes 'em think there's more of us." She diverted partial attention to Wiplien's bubble. Ulf was almost to the powerhouse roof. Lashed to the brickwork were several war-surplus shell racks like the one Ruth had just used, a routine defensive measure. Ulf activated one rack. It started firing simulated rifle bursts. Ulf sidled two meters to his right and poked his head above the roof line. He got off a shot, ducked, and then scrambled three meters further along a masonry ledge, head out of sight. He popped up again and fired.

Gunfire crackled from the hillside. "They're shooting at Ulf now," Ruth told Dultav. "He's got fooler racks and a mortar up there. It'll lob shells for about three minutes." As if to illustrate, one of Ulf's shells fell halfway up the hillside. Clods of earth soared. The marauders faded further uphill.

Wood creaked overhead. A glance into the bubble confirmed it: Ulf had rolled onto the roof. He took the big antiarmor rifle off his shoulder.

Ruth raised both pistols and laid down covering fire.

Ulf's first antiarmor shot struck high up the hill. Parek and Dultav couldn't see the impact, but they heard the explosion. They saw smoke and a rain of pebble-sized debris.

"Ulf did that?" Dultav cried.

"Antiarmor weapon," Ruth confirmed. "He got it from some old survivalist."

"Don't tell me. He was happy to share."

"I don't believe this," Wiplien reported. *"They're retreating."* Ruth checked Wiplien's bubble. Marauders were backing toward the tree line.

In the bubble, she saw Ulf clamber up onto the dam. "Run, you shits!" he screamed.

"They're falling back." Ruth told Dultav. "See you!" She rolled from under the table.

"Crazy bitch!" Dultav yelled. There was no cover between the table and the doorway. Ruth zigzagged with feline grace, hoping the marauders would be too confused to take advantage of the opportunity she presented.

They weren't. A shot sounded from outside. Ruth crumpled. Dultav screamed, "No!" He snapped upright and slammed his head into the underside of the table.

Astonishment lanced through the pain. *What the fuck was that?* he thought. Ruth uncoiled and resumed her run for the door. *She rippled,* Dultav thought. *Not a movement—her* image *rippled. As though I was viewing her through a flame!* Open-mouthed, Dultav glanced to Parek for confirmation, but Parek's eyes were closed. He was drawn up fetally, mumbling prayers.

For a split second, Dultav caught himself thinking Parek had brought Ruth back to life.

Hope they didn't get too good a look at that, Ruth thought, throwing herself through the doorway. Her feet touched only two of the six steps; she hit the ground on her shoulder and came up shooting. She *had* been hit on her way out of the power-erhouse, but in battle mode, her Spectator implants threw up a flash-stasis field that automatically repulsed the shell. *The field saved my life. But autochthons find it so forjeling unsettling to watch!*

Atop the ridge, marauders melted into the woods. Hysterical over the man Ruth had shot, the woman in hides was refusing to leave; a skinny guy in a leather jerkin shouted at her.

Ruth snapped her gaze over her shoulder. Ulf sprinted along the dam top, screaming a battle cry.

Up above, Leather Jerkin finally pushed the woman into the forest.

Ulf lifted the antiarmor gun. It had finally recharged.

The explosion sundered a man-thick tree trunk. Riddled with wooden shards, Leather Jerkin went down.

Ulf surged uphill. *This battle is not over,* Ruth realized. She chose an alternate route up the hillside.

Ulf paused over Leather Jerkin. The man lay in a pool of blood, his face and chest bristling with wood. Ulf drove his knife into each of the man's eyes and across his windpipe. He plunged into the woods while the dead man's back was still arching.

The forest was thick; Wiplien's aerial perspective was of little help. Ruth subvocalized a command to close the lateral bubble in her mind. She crab-walked between tree boles with Spectator precision. Her challenge now was to keep both Ulf and the four retreating marauders in sight. Ruth listened for the *verify* signal. *Three-by-three greens.*

Five meters ahead of her, Ulf scanned angrily. He'd lost the marauders' trail.

One of them shot at him and missed. It was a tracer. With a fresh fix on his quarries, Ulf skulked toward their position. Tree by tree, Ruth crept behind him.

"The marauders holed up in an outbuilding," Spectator Wiplien told her. *"There."* Wiplien squirted her the data. Ruth simply *knew* the coordinates, and a well-covered route to the spot to boot. She'd reach it before Ulf.

She hunkered behind bushes. An old stone pumphouse slumped in a clearing. Rifle barrels swaggered from its windows. Ruth's gaze snapped right. She could see Ulf approaching; the marauders couldn't. Ulf stopped; kneeling, he drew something from his knapsack. *"Can you see what he's doing?"* Ruth asked Wiplien.

"I'm looking over his shoulder," came the answer in her head. *"He tossed half a dozen old steamcartridges on the ground. Now he's balancing a piece of shale over them, leaning it against a tree trunk. Look sharp!"*

His task complete, Ulf was crawling straight toward Ruth. Only amplified motor control enabled her to slither into the bushes without making a telltale rustling. A meter and a half from Ruth, still unaware of her presence, Ulf stopped. From the knapsack he drew his last fooler rack. he pointed it toward the pumphouse and set the timer for one minute.

Ulf sidled off in a new direction. Ruth followed him as closely as she dared. *He's circling the pumphouse.* She could hear him whisper, counting off seconds. "Thirty-four, thirty-five, thirty-six. . . ."

When he reached forty, Ulf stopped crawling. Through the foliage he could see the pumphouse's gaping front doorway. Framed in it stood one of the marauders. It was the woman in the hide poncho. She had appalling skin, missing teeth, and a face streaked with tears. She stared out, keening like an animal. "Shut the fuck up," another marauder shouted. "Your guy's dead. It happens."

The woman was looking straight at Ulf's position, but she couldn't see him. Ulf could've dropped her on the spot, but that wasn't his plan. "Forty-three, forty-four, forty-five. . . ." he breathed.

Ruth watched Ulf unsling his rifles. He lay one to either side of him and pulled a slingshot from his knapsack. He fitted a stone into the sling. "Forty-nine, fifty, fifty-one. . . ." He aimed across the clearing. From here, his arrangement of steamcartridges and shale was just visible.

"What's going on?" Wiplien asked from the air.

"You'll love it," Ruth subvocalized back. *"Be ready to cover fast action."*

Ulf was intent. Only his lips moved, counting off seconds. "Fifty-eight, fifty-nine, sixty, sixty-one."

Twenty meters away, the fooler rack opened up. A few rounds hit the pump-house. Marauders scrambled to the right-hand wall, pouring out return fire at nobody.

Ulf fired the slingshot toward the improvised booby trap. The stone flew wide. Without wasted movement he loaded another stone. Drew back. Let it fly. This stone struck the shale slab, which fell onto the steamcartridges. Three fired in quick succession, followed seconds later by a fourth.

Predictable as a herd, the marauders rushed in the direction of this new "assault." They lined the rear wall of the pumphouse, firing shot after shot where Ulf wasn't, leaving their backs to the doorway.

Grabbing his rifles, Ulf simply walked into the pumphouse. "Hi there!" he yelled.

As Ruth watched through a window, the marauders turned. A round from the antiarmor rifle dismembered one and flung another against the wall, bloody and smoking. The skinny woman took a steamrifle round in the face. "Join your man!" Ulf snarled. Bone chips and teeth peppered off the stone walls.

The fourth marauder's steampistol was level with Ulf's chest.

Ulf stopped.

It was the leader, clad in leather, mail, and necklaces of teeth. The fractured goggles were on his forehead. Wild-eyed, he inspected Ulf's rifles. He smiled hungrily. "Your fuckin' winkies are red," he growled.

Ulf threw away both rifles to his right. They clattered on the pumphouse floor. The leader's eyes darted after them. He didn't see Ulf's right hand flick inside his left sleeve. He never saw the knife.

The leader's pistol clattered to the stones. Pierced through the larynx, he collapsed bubbling against the far wall.

"Knives don't have fuckin' winkies," Ulf spat. He started going through the marauders' effects.

"You get that?" Ruth asked Wiplien.

"Yeah," she replied. *"Son of a bitch."*

"Actually, I've never met his mother." Ruth sidled into the trees. She wanted to get back to the dam before Ulf did; ideally, he'd never know she'd followed him.

"Hey," Wiplien buzzed. *"Two hundred meters due west. Skinny guy. Carbine, ragged furs, long curly hair. Walking stick, a terrible limp. He one of yours?"*

"Yeah, that's Chagrin," Ruth answered.

"He heard the shooting. He's making for the pumphouse as fast as he can. Which isn't all that fast."

"Give me a fix on them both," Ruth replied. Knowledge rippled. She knew where Ulf and Chagrin would meet up, halfway toward the dam. *Don't want to miss that!*

"There you are!" Ruth came into a sun-dappled clearing, into Ulf's view, smiling broadly. "I guess you won."

Ulf grunted. He motioned with his head for Ruth to take some of the weapons he cradled in his arms. "I got five," he said. "One on the ridge top, four at their base."

Ruth smiled at his bravado, calling that sorry pumphouse a *base*. "I nailed one too."

"I saw. Yeah, we got 'em all." Leaves rustled.

Gasping, streaked with sweat, Chagrin lurched into view. "I heard guns," he said dully. "Sounded like a war."

"It was," Ruth said. "We won."

Ulf snorted, "No thanks to you, shufflin' shit."

Glaring but knowing he dared not speak, Chagrin shouldered a few rifles from Ulf's haul.

"Any more we need to worry about?" Ruth asked Wiplien.

"The woods are clear," the no-vis flyer replied.

"Then I release you. Thanks for your help." Ruth's account would be debited slightly to pay Wiplien for her trouble. Ruth could afford it; her saybacks had been stellar already, and this firefight couldn't help but give it an extra boost.

"There they come." Following Parek's pointing finger, Dultav watched Ruth, Ulf, and Chagrin emerge from the woods at the ridge top, laden with weapons. Dultav leaned on the ancient broom he held and scowled.

I couldn't have seen that, he mused. *I couldn't have seen her shot. She just tripped. That must be it.* Ignoring the ache in his head, Dultav went back to sweeping up wood and concrete chips.

As they tramped up the metal steps, Chagrin was still protesting his good intentions. "You'd see, Ulf. I woulda helped."

"You weren't there," Ulf snarled. "You weren't fucking there because you can't fucking walk!"

"You're all right," Dultav said to Ruth, beaming.

"We're safe now," she said, smiling back. "I think those were the marauders who shot you."

"Now the forest has nothing to fear except Ulf and Chagrin."

"Nobody needs to fear Chagrin," Ulf mocked. He emptied his arms onto the shell-scarred table, starting a pile of booty weapons. Ruth added her burden to the heap. Ulf unslung his steamrifle and the antiarmor weapon from over his shoulders. Setting the big gun aside, he sat atop a turbine housing with the steamrifle in his lap.

Sullenly, Chagrin shambled to the table and set down his armload of guns. "Stand guard, useless," Ulf rasped.

Chagrin glared at Ulf, his face a mask of rage. It collapsed the second Ulf met his eyes. Head down, Chagrin shambled toward the entrance door with his carbine.

Still cradling his steamrifle across his legs, Ulf drew a knife. He worked the blade back and forth across the wooden stock. Dultav wedged closer and stared openly. Ulf was adding to a phalanx of parallel incisions—surely no less than forty. They ran a third of the way up the stock.

Ulf looked up and eyed Dultav with primitive intensity. "Yes, professor," he chafed. "Savages like me, we notch our guns when we make a kill." He held out the rifle so Dultav could see the marks more clearly. "I've had this steamrifle less than a year."

Dultav growled in disgust and turned away—into an unexpected but delightful hug from Ruth. "I was so worried about you," she breathed in his ear.

"*You* were worried?" Side by side they wandered to one of the downstream windows. They lay their chins over crossed arms. After a moment Parek drifted into a similar pose at the next window, four meters to Dultav's left.

Who is this Ruth? Dultav wondered. *How can this lone woman dominate two powerful killers without a hint of sexual involvement? They're cunning bastards. Why don't they question her unaccountable departures, her mysterious actions, her ghostly grace?* He shook his head. *And why, despite my growing misgivings about Arn—why can't I make up my mind what to ask her for?*

At the next window, Parek cleared his throat. "Willim."

"What now?" Dultav half-whispered.

Parek tried to pitch his voice low but failed. "While we were under the table, during the battle, a vision came to me."

"Let's talk downstairs," Dultav hissed.

It was too late. Ulf put away his knife. Chagrin abandoned his watch. Like corpses rolling down a hillside, they drew closer to their sage.

Though it no longer served a purpose, the trip downstairs was inevitable. Dultav tried to hurry Parek, but Ulf and Chagrin were never more than a step behind. It fell to Ruth to drag back the access cover, yet even she managed to stay within a meter or two in her ethereal way. "The shell hits and explosions set up a rhythm in my consciousness," Parek was saying. "Suddenly I was in a dream. I'm still trying to piece it together."

"What kind of dream?" Dultav asked tartly.

"I can't recall it all," Parek said absently. "Swirling colors, images . . . voices, new ideas, hailing just out of my reach."

Dultav was uncomfortably aware of Ulf and Chagrin—of their proximity and the looks of wonder in their eyes. "Don't try to tell me it's—"

"I don't know what it is!" Parek snapped. "There were voices. Surging, boiling clouds. And. . . ." He stepped off the stairs into the shattered common room. "I saw a dead man!"

The stairway fairly vomited Ulf and Chagrin into the chamber. Next came Ruth, gliding briskly around them without apparent purpose.

"That's what the dream was about," Parek said with sudden conviction. "A dead man. He lay sprawled, hollowed and dead, on a stairway. The stairway led to the stars, I remember that. The body was the old logic. The old rationalities. It was—it was—" Parek stepped beneath one of the ceiling vents where the light played in his hair. When he spoke he seemed to be articulating from a universe away, saying not his own words but proclaiming those of a text. "The corpse, the husk of the old guard. The butchered remains of all that once seemed right, and true, and meaningful, rendered barren by the fires from the skies."

Ruth pressed forward and to one side. She managed to include the dumbfounded Ulf and Chagrin in her vision while she pushed in on Parek. *He looks like a god,* she thought, *or like a man possessed by one.*

"See the body," Parek continued. "See how it lies mangled and dead on the stairway to the beyond. And pity its people, who have fallen from its grip." The withdrawn look ebbed from his features. He dropped his head and slowly sank to his knees.

Ruth drifted backward as Dultav drew close to his friend. Dultav laid a hand on Parek's shoulder. With sudden anger he shoved Parek away, shouting: *"Will* you stop acting like a starstruck child!"

It was all Dultav got to say. He found himself on the floor tiles, pinned, Ulf on top of him, a knife cold against Dultav's neck. "Don't treat him like that!" the guerrilla hissed through clenched teeth.

Parek was there. He took Ulf's knife hand in a gentle grip and pulled it away. As suddenly as Ulf's rage had risen, it drained away.

Unseen, Ruth circled, capturing everyone's expression.

"Release him," Parek said evenly.

Without a word, Ulf climbed off Dultav. He rose and stepped away.

"Professor Dultav is my confidant," Parek told Ulf almost hypnotically. "We are close. I allow him certain liberties." Chagrin had finally lumbered into position at Ulf's side. "Go and ponder," Parek said to both of them. "Contemplate all you saw today."

Ulf and Chagrin shuffled toward the far corridor, awe in their eyes. Ruth studied their faces as they passed her. Smoothly she raised her eyes to acquire Dultav. He had picked himself up and stumbled against the outside wall. Parek approached him. Ruth worked her way forward. Unobtrusive as she was, she missed nothing.

"You all right?" Parek asked.

"I could live without another day like today, ever," Dultav gasped.

"But did you see that?" Parek exulted. "Did you *see* it?" He grabbed Dultav's sleeve like a child eager to go fishing. "Ulf believes in me. Chagrin does, too. They both do!"

"Does that surprise you?"

"Didn't you see?" Parek insisted, eyes bright. "Ulf passed the ultimate test of faith. He's learned to hate the infidel."

Dultav yanked his arm free. "As the infidel, I'm happy beyond expression."

"But think, Willim," Parek urged. "After seeing this, I'm even more convinced that I'm onto something here."

Dultav bustled away. Parek made no attempt to follow. Dultav whirled. "You're onto something, all right. But if you ever want off, will they let you?"

Having slid into a far, dark doorway, Ruth watched Dultav collapse into a chair. Parek shuffled away toward the security of his turbine pen.

Ruth stopped recording and subvocalized commands to dump the journal onto Net. She appended a tag indicating moderate urgency and much higher than average audience interest. *I can't wait to see the saybacks after this hits,* she thought. *This backwater where nothing ever happens is looking more like the center of the universe every day.*

17. News Broadcast. Galaxy Wide •
Origin: Terra—OmNet Main

"In entertainment news, the unfolding chronicle of Arn Parek, accidental mes-siah of Jaremi Four, whose misadventures are being recorded by the Spectator Ruth Griszam, is growing wildly popular. Especially noteworthy is the diversity of its metademographics. It seems there's something in the Parek saga for everyone."

One by one, tridee clips flashed past. "Meanwhile, messianic movements with strange underpinnings have begun to stir on the more religion-prone Galactic worlds. Flagellants on Omalihk Seven. A healer of radiation damage on ravaged Minga Four. On Parctantis Two, a cult whose communicants claim the ability to live on a diet of autochthonous plant and animal tissue instead of the genetically mod-ified feed species left there for them by the Harvesters when they planted the human seed. On Calluron Five, a former dancing master who stops and restarts his heart at will, preaching all the while. On Zbaghiel Three, mystics who say they have learned to defeat the inherent defect in their vision in the 450-nanometer range—and try to prove it by wearing ruby spectacles everywhere they go. Yes, they do seem to fall down a lot. Across the Galaxy rising prophets tell futures. Thaumaturges work wonders. Disciples comport with poisonous creatures. Vision-aries mouth folly. Is it a pattern, or just one of the coincidences our vast Galaxy offers in such profusion? Only time will tell."

18. Tridee Broadcast. Galaxy Wide •
Origin: Terra—Wasatch Range, Usasector

"Hom Latier?" the journalist inquired doubtfully.

"You don't recognize me." The Mormon televangelist smoothed his awkward muslin jumper. He was square-jawed, stocky, and ill-proportioned, like a teen ath-lete gone to seed in middle life.

"You look different in person."

"It's that Galactic privacy fetish. Even though I appear on tridee voluntarily, my features are altered to mask my true appearance. On the plus side, I don't get mobbed when I go out for pink lemonade. Pleased to meet you, Fem . . ."

"Mayishimu." She nodded. Highlights from the reception room's floodlights danced on her chocolate skin. "Meryam Mayishimu."

"Meryam, eh? Call me Alrue."

He led her around an elaborately sculpted screen of solid jade. At once she realized it was there to delay the visitor's discovery of the breathtaking view from Latier's terrace. The westward vista sparkled in the preternaturally clear air of the

Wasatch Range. Below, mountains stumbled against the endless plain, which Salt
Lake City overspread like a vast snake of metal and light.

"Salt Lake City," he announced. "In many ways the old LDS Church's last gift
to humanity."

"How so?"

"It wasn't swallowed into some Galactic pleasure zone when the Galactics took
old Terra's choicest real estate for themselves. The Catholics gave away Paris and
Rome. The Budhindus surrendered the Ganges Valley. Of all the spots on Terra that
combined religious significance and natural allure, only the Salt Lake Basin was
saved. Saved by the Latter-day Saints—not because of what their church is, just
out of regard for what it was."

"You said a gift to humanity. You really meant a gift to Terrans."

Latier harrumphed.

"So, First Elder, can I describe you as the prophet of the Mormon New
Restoration?"

"Prophet, Seer, and Revelator. That's me." A functionary glided past and left
a serving tray bearing a gelid beehive-shaped mass. Its green translucency imprisoned stubby white morsels. "The beehive, symbol of Old Utah." He spooned green
stuff onto a dish. "Jello mold," he explained. "Lime, with little marshmallows. Care
for some?"

"No, thank you. But please, enjoy."

Latier needed no prompting. He was already spooning out a second helping.

"Let's begin, Hom Latier."

"Please, call me Alrue. And I will call you Meryam. It's a Mormon thing."

"Very well . . . Alrue. Tell me about this building."

"It's my aerie." Latier smiled, a green fleck glinting between two teeth. "I built
this tower five years ago, when my ministry began to attract interest among Galactics."

"You mean, when Galactic specie became a regular component of your revenue stream."

"Offworld support made things easier. My ministry's headquarters functions
are based here: publishing, research, the genealogy materials we picked up when
the LDS lost interest in them."

"Plus the tridee studios."

"Oh yes. My media preachments are assembled just downstairs." He smiled
oleaginously. "So tell me, Meryam. What do *you* believe?"

"I believe that when I'm interviewing someone, I ask the questions."

"I meant my question in a pastoral sense. How does Meryam Mayishimu feel
about this world, and the next?"

"Are you trying to convert me?"

"Why not? I possess truth." Two gray cats slipped around a service door. They
leapt onto Latier's lap. "Good daypart, Urim. Good daypart, Thummim. Where have
you been?"

Mayishimu crossed her arms. "Hom Latier—Alrue. You built your ministry on
an idea some call audacious and others call mad, the idea of reviving historic Mormonism at its quirkiest and most controversial. Why?"

"When Joseph Smith caused the Book of Mormon to be published in 1830, he proclaimed the restoration of Christianity. He cast away the errors of eighteen centuries of ecclesiastical domination."

"So he claimed."

"So it *was,*" insisted Latier, "for a time. Then, like every church, the Church of Jesus Christ of Latter-day Saints lost its way. The bright gold of God's truth cannot remain long in human hands. Shortly it must tarnish."

"So sooner or later, it must tarnish in your hands, too."

"Perhaps. Or in the hands of some successor of mine. But now is the time of its purity. The restoration Joseph Smith launched is to be renewed, and I am the vessel of the New Restoration."

She nodded toward a bombastic statue in the corner. "Is that Joseph Smith?"

"Truly." The five-meter bronze showed a hawk-nosed man with the sinews of an athlete bounding over a fallen log. A brigand lay crumpled over his ancient rifle amid brambles and leaves. Smith's other arm gripped a loose-leaf stack of inscribed plates perhaps fifteen by seventeen by twenty centimeters, bound with hammered rings. "In 1827, Joseph Smith brought home from Hill Cumorah the golden plates on which the Book of Mormon was inscribed. As he jumped over a fallen tree, he was set upon by a highwayman. He downed his attacker with one blow."

"Joseph's mother, Lucy Mack Smith, told that story. Other Mormon churches found it embarrassing. They try to minimize it. You celebrate it. Why?"

"Those of little faith," Latier shrugged. "The LDS let itself be cowed by the carpings of skeptics."

"Carpings?" Mayishimu countered. "Pure gold weighs twice as much per unit volume as lead, three times as much as iron. If the golden plates were the size that sculpture shows, they'd mass eighty to ninety kilograms. Isn't that about what you weigh?"

"Well, yes."

"Quite a burden for Joseph Smith to carry while bounding over logs and subduing a desperado. Yet you preach that the story is literally true."

"I do."

"And you mock longer-established Mormon churches for refusing to teach it."

Latier smiled. "The Lord showed Joseph Smith so much. Later He demanded so much from him. Is it incredible that Joseph was simply mighty in the Lord that day?"

"No more incredible than believing the Lord carries a grudge against Canadians."

"Oh, that."

"Indeed," Mayishimu replied. "Why do you teach that the other Mormon churches erred in proselytizing Canadasector? Why do you refuse converts, even contributions, from that region?"

Latier tugged at his temple garment. "In January 1830, Joseph Smith needed money to get the first edition of the Book of Mormon printed. Jesus Christ sent him a revelation, commanding that two of Joseph's associates, Oliver Cowdery and Hiram Page, travel to Toronto and sell the copyright in the Book of Mormon. 'And the first price shall be one hundred thousand dollars of the money of the United States,' Jesus said to Joseph Smith— 'and not of Canada.' " Latier scratched one of his cats behind the ears. "Now if Canadian money wasn't good enough for the Redeemer of the world, why should I allow His sole true church to accept it?"

"As I recall, Cowdery and Page failed in their Canadian mission, after which Martin Harris mortgaged his farm to get the first edition printed."

"You've done your homework."

"That story was told by David Whitmer, one of the original three witnesses who authenticated the Book of Mormon," Mayishimu recalled. "Later he split from Joseph Smith and was excommunicated. Only then did Whitmer publish that account."

Latier nodded. "You should join us, Meryam. Mine is the Terran faith with the most to offer Galactics hungry for solace of the heart."

"Let's talk about polygamy."

"That?" He sounded hurt.

"Surely today, polygamy is the least controversial among the early Mormon usages you've renewed."

"I did no such thing."

She was incredulous. "You *deny* that you practice plural marriage? Just last week, you attended the opening of a new temple with six of your wives. Three Spectators *poved* it!"

"I follow the early example of Joseph Smith."

"He practiced plural marriage!"

"And he denied it." Latier drained another pink lemonade. "Though he acquired many wives, to his dying day he never admitted having done so."

She was skeptical. "Few could follow his example with such fidelity."

" 'Do what is right, let the consequence follow.' So the old hymn goes. I care only about restoring the truth."

"Including restoring the original edition of the Book of Mormon with all its, shall we say, unique turns of expression?"

He sighed. "You want to talk about the errors."

"The first edition is famous for them. That's why the LDS and Reorganized churches bought up all the copies they could find. That's why, to this day, they keep them under glass where no one can read them."

"Yet it is the original form of our holy writ."

"You stand by passages like these?" Mayishimu demanded. "Book of Mormon, first edition, Book of Alma, chapter forty-four, verse twenty-four: 'And this ended the record of Alma which was *wrote* upon the plates of Nephi.' Book of Helaman, chapter thirteen: 'And this shall be your language in *them* days, but behold your days of probation *is* past.' "

Latier chuckled. "You forgot this one. Same book, same chapter: 'But a seer can know of things, which *has past,* and also things which *is* to come.' "

Mayishimu stood. "See and raise. Same book, same chapter: 'And hidden things shall come to light, and things which *is* not known shall be made known to them.' "

"You forgot my personal favorite, Meryam: 'teach baptism unto *they.' "

"You admit your scripture's faults, yet you join me in toying with them."

"Yet I believe. Such is my faith. Be careful, lest your impertinence anger the Lord."

"Good advice there. As Joseph Smith also said, 'with whom God is angry, he is not well pleased.'" She resumed her seat. One of Latier's cats had claimed it. It leapt away scrowling. "Sorry, Urim."

"That's Thummim."

"Whatever." She opened a new line of questioning. "Your church has enjoyed most of its growth off your homeworld."

"We'll be the second great Terran church to operate Galaxy-wide."

"So you've often said. But how can you expect your creed to play among the stars when one of the things you've 'restored' is Second Nephi, chapter five?"

Latier rolled his eyes, but quoted gamely: "'For behold, they had hardened their hearts against him, that they had become like unto a flint; wherefore, as they were white, and exceeding fair and delightsome, that they might not be enticing to my people the Lord God did cause a skin of blackness to come upon them.'"

"That has to be a tough sell in a Galaxy where—aside from perhaps a twelfth of the population of Terra itself—no one is white."

"Your interpretation is naïve."

"Oh? You've preached about converting Galactics to Mormonism, taking as your text Second Nephi, chapter thirty: 'And the gospel of Jesus Christ shall be declared among them . . . and their scales of darkness shall begin to fall from their eyes; and many generations shall not pass among them, save they shall be a white and delightsome people.' Am I naïve, or does this amount to teaching that in the event of a Mormon epiphany, all believers will turn white? White like a Swede, Alrue? White like you?"

Latier fidgeted. "Whether the Book of Mormon's promise to transform believers into 'white and delightsome people' applies to anyone other than the autochthons of Terra's Americas is unknown. Revelation has been silent on that. Of course, a new revelation could occur at any time."

"No doubt. Until then, what does Alrue Latier say? Will believing Galactics become white? Is white the color of holiness? Or does your theology teach that Terrans are closer to God than anyone else?"

"Is it coincidence that whites appear only on the planet that is the cradle of the species—the cradle of so many creeds that Galactics find irresistible?" He cringed inwardly before the sentence had escaped his lips.

"You say your preaching supersedes the LDS Church, the Reorganized Church, and half a hundred splinter sects. In your mind, the New Restoration eclipses them all. Why should someone believe that?"

"The old Mormons are dying. The denomination lost its spark a hundred and fifty years ago. The time is ripe for new blood, new energy."

"In other words you are the way, the truth, and the light."

He shrugged. "In matters of faith, compromise kills. New creeds are full of energy and jealous about doctrine. They're the ones that attract converts and build wealth. Believers *want* to satisfy a demanding God. Demand too little and they drift away."

"Which is what you say the LDS did."

"It *is* what the LDS did. Mob violence, exile, fratricidal conflict— the Mormon pioneers had it all. They built Zion, made the desert bloom, and sent missionaries everywhere. But compromise was inescapable. By 2000 there were more Mormons outside today's Usasector than inside it. Long before that, one could see the signs of loss of will. Polygamy was relinquished in 1890 Terran. In 1978 the priesthood opened to blacks. By 2056, women achieved functional equality. After 2102, dissenting intellectuals at Brigham Young Megaversity were no longer persecuted."

"Shameful," Mayishimu deadpanned.

"Don't judge hastily. What ceases to be worth fighting for soon ceases to be worth believing in. A church is dying when it stops punishing its intellectuals. Openness, rationality, free inquiry— they're poison to a living faith. The Catholics never forgot to discipline their thinkers. That's why perfidious as it is, Vatican has spread its cathedrals throughout the Galaxy."

"Does the Church of the New Restoration persecute its intellectuals?"

"We don't have any."

"Pardon?"

"We're too young a church. We don't have intellectuals. We have me."

She grasped her wand and subvocalized the shutoff command. "And I fear I have no more time. Thank you for the interview, Hom Latier. It's been enlightening."

Latier laughed. "If God is with me, who can be against me?"

19. Jaremi Four—Northern Hemisphere

Hours after the firefight, hours after Parek proclaimed his vision, Willim Dultav and Ruth Griszam sat side by side on the edge of her sleeping loft. The loft was tucked high inside a fallen turbine casing. Dultav had come upon her unexpectedly; she'd barely had time to go into Mode as he climbed up beside her. "You understand," he said without preamble, "Arn wasn't kidding."

"That vision stuff?"

"He's almost completely certain that his phony revelation is true."

"You don't think much of religion."

"I don't think much of much of anything." He proffered his ubiquitous flask.

New stock, she thought after sipping. *A different liqueur. Yet another city's most prestigious export.*

"Historically, there are two options of an intellectual in troubled times: you grab hold of some crazy impossible vision, like Arn did. Or you maintain your perspective and start to despair."

"You believe in the gods?" she asked.

"Only one. Arn's in his turbine pen."

"You know what I mean."

He shook his head sourly. "I believe in what I can see."

"I used to believe," she said softly, surrendering control to her outer self. "In something, anyway. But it's hard to keep believing in gods who'd permit the Great Dismay. So much pain, so many years—could kindly forces look down on all this and do nothing?" After that she smiled and changed her tone. "What you can see, huh?"

"Arn and I used to talk about this, back when I could talk to Arn about anything. Did you know, there was a faith once that worshipped *skraggels?* There've been thousands of creeds—sky-god creeds, earth-god creeds. And good reason to believe most of them were made up no less self-consciously than Arn's religion. Each one was invented by people who claimed a revelation they must have known they never had." Dultav shrugged. "Some did it out of avarice—"

"Like Arn."

He'd nodded harshly. "Or out of the best intentions in the world. Also like Arn." He swallowed deeply from the flask. "Know what? I can't decide which one scares me more."

They drew closer, their legs still dangling over the end of the loft. "Two, three years ago Arn and I wintered with a savage tribe in some foothills far from here. Their leader—their chief, I guess—had a daughter who was desperately sick. Nothing helped. The chief begged and begged. Finally Arn agreed to pray over her."

"Did the daughter recover?"

"Fuck, no. She puked bile and fell down dead while Arn was praying. We fled into hip-deep snow, but a posse tracked us down and brought us before the chief. He was furious, as you might expect. Said he'd shackle us outside to freeze unless we explained why his daughter died."

Ruth narrowed her eyes. "What did Arn say?"

"Arn said nothing. The chief's pain overwhelmed him. It was the only time I ever saw Arn speechless."

"You're not dead. What happened?"

"I made a sociological conjecture."

"You what?"

"I played a hunch." He chuckled. "I looked daggers at the bastard and roared, 'I'll tell you why your daughter died. It was because you did not share your best with us.' "

"Harsh stuff. What did he do?"

"Caved like a tent with the stakes pulled out. He signaled his men. A minute later up come two squads. One's wrestling up cases of rare sparkling liquor. The other has a box full of tins of *skraggel* in eight-spice sauce. Stuff they'd pretended not to have so they wouldn't have to share it with us."

"What then?"

"We ate and drank. They gave us more luxury items when we left. I assume the chief spent the rest of his life blaming himself for his daughter's death."

"How'd you know he was holding out?"

"A safe guess. Any group that size has a treasure—some collector's item, some rare morsel. The leaders hide it as long as they can."

She shook her head. "You greedy, acquisitive, *insightful* bastard." He offered the flask. She took a long draft. "So, you admit Arn's religion is phony. Are there any real religions? Would you know one if you found it?"

"I'm a sociologist, not a theologian. I guess if one day you wake up dead and the skyfields of forever aren't like you expected, you'll know you were wrong." He laughed somberly. "Believers in *this* act just like believers in *that*. Does the object of any of their beliefs actually exist? Does it matter? It's real for them."

He shifted his weight. *Is he edging closer?* she thought. *Yes, he is,* she judged.

"There might be one way to tell," Dultav continued. "Faith is powerful. Capture it, and you get a special title to people's hearts. Faith can inspire compassion, art, sublime self-knowledge—or butchery. It all depends on who's directing it."

"In this case, Arn."

"Unfortunately. Consider this: A real holy man would be able to keep control. He'd keep his disciples' weaknesses from running away with them."

"But Arn's not like that."

Dultav nodded grimly. "A real holy man remakes the faithful according to his teachings. A fake? The faithful make of him what they choose."

"Will they kill him?"

"Maybe. And why not? Someday his followers will need a god and they'll find he's just a man." He twisted his face into that sardonic half-grin of his and squeezed her hand. "That's all I am, too . . . a man. But I admit it."

At his touch she went soft inside. *Studying his face, I can see he feels the same,* she thought. *Or am I reading my own desires into this?* Uncertain how to respond, she parted her lips and locked her gaze with his.

Tentatively he raised a half-closed hand. Brushed knuckles along her cheek. Then the curve of her jaw. His hand opened and slid around the back of her neck. He pulled her toward him.

Their breaths mingled.

"Yes," she whispered.

Their lips collided. The progression was smooth and inevitable: lip on lip, tongues tracing teeth, his hand caressing neck, ribs, thigh, breasts, hers caressing stubbly cheek, shoulder, buttocks, hip, groin. His weight skidding onto her.

By the light of a flickering lantern, overspread by vaults of fissured concrete and ruined machinery whose purpose no autochthon remembered, they consummated their attraction atop rumpled canvas. Their fingers clawed at air, found each other, and clenched. She felt and ignored a scrape of pain as his grip forced her knuckles across an ammunition clip among the bedclothes. She ignored the odor of decay and the powdery feel at the back of her throat.

Ecstasy amid destruction, hopelessness and abandon, headlong redemption through sensual indulgence—it was what being a Spectator was all about. It was why Galactics paused from their sterile lives to *pov* the journals of Ruth and her ilk.

Their lovemaking was earnest and unhurried, perhaps the most satisfying she had known on Jaremi Four. Afterward, Ruth feigned moodiness and drove Dultav from her loft. To her astonishment he left smiling, apparently confident she just wanted time to digest what had unfolded between them.

In fact, she wanted to dump her journal. She had learned too much respect for Dultav's perceptiveness to imagine she could log off in his arms without his noticing. The advisory tag she appended was routine, but one she hadn't needed in recent months: "Sexual content: voluntary hetero two-person conventional."

She stretched out in the sleeping loft. The canvas crept across the smallness of her breasts and chafed her still-responsive nipples. She exulted in the way her body felt. *He was so intense,* she thought. *And for two hours before we made love we talked about ideas!*

Sighing, Ruth clambered down from the loft and padded across chip-strewn cement. Overhead, an ancient drain tube allowed a glimpse of the night's weather. Pink aurora swirled in cloudless indigo. She plucked up her trousers and yanked on her boots.

Glancing up and down the little-used corridor, she squirmed behind a pitted impeller casing. She subvocalized a command. A hole in the casing became visible. Ruth reached into the aperture and withdrew her Spectator carryall, a Galactic vanisher valise disguised as a timeworn carpetbag. Outside, it was sixty centimeters long. It weighed two kilos. Yet it contained eighty kilos of equipment, some quite bulky, all of it invisible unless one knew the vanisher codes.

She pulled out a double handful of what looked like cement chips. They were gray, sharp-edged, irregular. She jammed all but one of them into a trouser pocket. She centered the last chip in the palm of her hand, extended her arm, and subvocalized a command. Her hearing seemed to shimmer—interference between the sounds reaching her ears and those picked up by the Spectator bug in her hand. A bubble opened in her visual field. The apparent cement chip was sending her a tridee feed. Within the bubble, she looked up at herself from the palm of her hand.

The bugs work. She shut off the test bug and slipped it into her pocket with the others. She primed them all. The two dozen or so miniature probes were ready to be strewn about outside. They'd filter events in their vicinities and seize her attention with early warning of interesting or threatening developments. Equally important, they'd provide supporting coverage if anything like the afternoon's firefight erupted, without the expense and delay of engaging a no-vis flyer.

Son of a bitch! Working by auroral light, Ruth laughed as she placed the outdoor bugs. *The saybacks are in, and seventy percent of my experients wish I'd slept with Parek instead.* She trudged along the hill crest and found a notch in a great boulder that overlooked the dam. She nestled a bug there. It returned a panoramic image of the hydro complex. *Oh, well, the public's disappointment hasn't affected my saybacks. Plorg, I'll come away from this posting a wealthy woman.*

Her work complete, Ruth picked her way downtrail. The powerhouse was unguarded, which was unusual at this time of night. *Where are Ulf and Chagrin?*

She felt an inner nudging. One of the bugs she'd placed earlier, inside the dam, had the answer.

She sampled the datastream.

The bug's output was as detailed as tridee, but lacked the vivid *being-thereness* of full senso. But the content. . . . *Ulf and Chagrin—by themselves. Near Parek's holy turbine pen—but not too near. Talking about. . . . Oh, plorg!*

✦ ✦ ✦

"Wha-a-a-at?" Ruth brayed as she circled around a stand of pipes. Arms akimbo, she confronted Ulf and Chagrin. The guerrillas stood hunched in a maintenance tunnel, backlit by lantern light. They'd been facing each other. Now they stared bug-eyed at Ruth. Her smaller lantern's gentle radiance brought their faces out of shadow and added a dancing orange catchlight to their eyes. "Say that again," she rasped.

"Pass by, Ruth," Ulf ordered. "This is private."

"It's absurd," she countered. "Are you seriously proposing to—"

Chagrin spread his hands. "Why not?"

Whatever anger there'd been between the two guerrillas, it melted into solidarity before Ruth's skepticism. Ulf clutched one of Chagrin's wrists. "I ask you, Ruth—if Arn Parek can't, then who?"

With his free hand Chagrin seized his walking stick and flung it furiously behind him. It clattered down the damp tunnel. "I'm sick of being useless. There's only one answer."

Ruth raked her hands through her hair. She was in Mode. The *verify* signal was strong. *Draw this out—make it sharp and clear,* she thought. *This is a turning point some of my experients will repov a hundred times.* "I don't think I believe this."

"Then don't think," Chagrin hissed. "Feel." His eyes were like searchlights. "Feel and you can believe, too."

She shook her head. "This is wish fulfillment, nothing more."

"No," Ulf blared. Hands in fatigue pockets, he stepped out of the tunnel. Something suddenly seemed broken about him. "Look, Ruth. I never thought I was the believer type. Kill it, move on, don't think about it. That was me. But now—I believe. In Parek. And believing's wonderful. I used to have this anger all the time. Just bubbling and bubbling inside, you get it? When I listen to Parek, I feel, well, reconciled. Like I can start letting go of my fury. Like I can quit looking for revenge every day. Maybe start to build something." Ulf spread his palms. "Parek's brought me beyond the hate. No more worries, no more doubts. All my questions answered."

Clinging to a cable trough, Chagrin lurched toward the tunnel's mouth. "This is a religious thing, Ruth. If you don't believe, you can't understand it."

Ulf had ducked back into the tunnel to retrieve Chagrin's walking stick. He was almost gentle as he handed Chagrin the twisted rod. Yet when he turned to Ruth, his voice was flinty, even threatening. "If you can't accept it any other way, concentrate on this. It's a way to find out for sure."

"I thought you'd outgrown anger," Ruth said dryly. *Show time!* she thought. *I wonder if Arn Parek has the slightest idea what he's set into motion here.*

20. Planet Vatican

Pope Modest IV soared between serried arrays of information: his schedules, his addresses and sermons and encyclicals in progress, his public and private notes on a thousand subjects, memos from the curia on each of those subjects and more, all stretching away in endless matrices. His consciousness fluttered past ranked filaments of data and contingency schedules in neat hyperqueues. They trellised in every direction like pearls. Modest enjoyed a kaleidoscopic awareness of each item in its singularity, yet also he grasped the nested layers of relations between the countless items in a way far beyond the reach of an unaided human mind.

Modest checked the latest census of the faithful and smiled inwardly. He took pleasure not only in the swelling numbers of the baptized, but also in the growth of folk devotion among the church's new legions. Traditional observances long missing from Terran Catholicism—veneration of the saints, resurgent cults of the Virgin, of holy water, rosaries and scapulars—all were wildly popular among off-world converts. *On Terwiljla Eighteen, they've revived the blessing of throats,* he noted with wonder. *Actually the blessing of stoats, but the concept's the same. Truly, since Terra's Galactic Encounter Holy Mother Church has become more and more like her old self. Aside from ritual pederasty, if Pius X came back he'd recognize nearly everything.*

Surveying the webs of his concerns, he noted how many vortices glowed the angry magenta he'd assigned to the Jesuit dispute. Less than twenty kilometers away, the so-called "black pope"—Aresino Y'Braga, Father General of the Society of Jesus—abided in Santo Spiritu, the Jesuit headquarters city. Modest had exerted substantial influence to compel Y'Braga's return to Vatican. At two or three removes, he'd exercised deadly force to suppress rogue Jesuits on a dozen worlds. Yet now, with Y'Braga back on Vatican, Modest felt unsure what to do with him.

There was prudence in caution, of course. Among the options Modest weighed was dissolving the Jesuit order for the third time in church history. "At issue," said a briefing file prepared by one of Modest's secretaries, "is principally the refusal by the Society of Jesus to accept the judgment of the Sixteenth Vatican Council that all humans throughout the Galaxy are of one flesh. Instead, Father General Y'Braga and his theologians continue to defend the rejected view that the mitochondrial relatedness of all humans is illusory, at best God's subtle metaphor for hundreds or thousands of similar but distinct creations." Under highest security, Modest had written to himself: "What Clement XIV did to the Jesuits in 1773 local, and John XXV in 2088, We may need to do again."

The current crisis has gone unresolved for sixteen years, he reminded himself. *We are under no pressure to settle it today.* He drew comfort from an aphorism so old it had first entered the Church in Latin: "Who outwaits all, rules all."

A balance subtly shifted among the manifold of his attention.

Modest's scheduled visitors were about to be admitted to the papal chamber. With effort he opened his eyes.

"Your Holiness." It was Bishop Wleti Krammonz, obsequious Prefect of the Papal Household, Chamberlain of His Holiness and Majordomo of the Sacred Palace. "It is time."

"Admit them," said the pontiff.

Krammonz bowed stiffly. Under the circumstances, reverencing the pope's ring was out of the question.

The audience chamber was perfectly flat, two acres of solid-diamond flooring inlaid now and again in ruby with the papal tiara and keys. The vast chamber had been hollowed from a single colossal block of ruby-colored spinel. It had the form of the *triregno*, the beehivelike papal triple tiara. Audience galleries scalloped its upper tiers.

An aperture opened in the floor. The blade of a medieval halberd rose from it, followed by a Swiss Guard in leggings, knee breeches, and a belted balloon-sleeved tunic striped in yellow, blue, and red: the ancient Medici colors. He wore the *gorget*, a stiff white ruff collar about his neck, and the *morion*, an ornate metallic helmet upturned at bill and back. Topping it all was a red ostrich plume.

The guard ushered three visitors upchute into the papal presence.

Leftmost was Alois Cardinal Rybczynsky, the Vatican Secretary of State. Upon his head he wore the formal tri-cornered *biretta*. He was vested in scarlet choir cassock, crisp with knife-sharp pleats. His waist sash, or *fascia*, of moiré-streaked watered silk was worn properly, just below the breastbone. Its hand-knotted fringes hung near his left hip. His pectoral cross hung from an elaborate cord of red silk shot through with golden threads. It was virtual, a glittering fiction of light except at its vertex. There a diamond-glass reliquary held a blackened sliver of wood—a fragment of the True Cross of Terra. Once such a relic was bestowed on all bishops and cardinals. Today Popes vouchsafed it only to their favorites.

Beside Rybczynsky brooded the plump, uneasy Cardinal Ato Semuga. Semuga's rumpled black wool simar spanned his ample belly, stained with long-dried sauce. His pectoral cross was drearily actual, made of mere platinum—hardly appropriate for a papal audience. *Despite it all,* Pope Modest thought, *Semuga remains the one We rely on when the unspeakable must be done.*

Between the two cardinals, the best-loved man in the Galaxy struggled to conceal his astonishment. Fram Galbior had been eighteen when he'd solved the equations that predicted each Tuezi attack. At seventy-one, he was graceful and patrician. Graying hair swept straight up from a widow's peak, accentuating the slenderness of his jaw. His high-collared cassock was plain gray brocade, accented only by the midnight blue sash and gold-and-ruby medallion of a high-ranking lay Steward.

Modest stood above them on a topaz dais. A strategically placed skylight cast pistachio highlights on the shoulders of his impossibly white silk simar, a floor-length robe with integral shoulder cape. A snow-white sash girded his waist. Its ends trailed straight down, terminating near his knees in a golden fringe and embroidered coats of arms. A virtual pectoral cross dazzled upon his chest, hanging from a golden chain. Upon his head he wore a tiny, round silk headpiece, the *zuchetto*.

"His Holiness, Pope Modest the Fourth," the Swiss Guard announced as he sank into another floor aperture.

Galbior trembled, helpless to decide whether to guffaw or gape.

The Holy Father of the Universal Catholic Church, bishop of Rome, vicar of Jesus Christ, Successor of the Prince of the Apostles, Supreme Pontiff of the Universal Church, Once and Future Patriarch of the West, Once and Future Primate of Italy, Once and Future Archbishop and Metropolitan of the Roman province, Once and Future Sovereign of the State of Vatican City, Sovereign of the planet Vatican,

Galactic Servant of the Galactic Servants of God, loomed on the dais high above his guests clutching a spiny anteater.

Modest pressed the half-meter long creature's snout to his forehead. The animal shuddered.

Aside from the throne, the only furnishing on the dais was an ornate terrarium. Its gilt-framed crystal walls confined a meter of loose dry earth. With something approaching reverence Pope Modest deposited the anteater inside it. Burrowing feverishly, the creature slipped straight down into parting soil like a ship scuttled in calm seas. In moments nothing could be seen but the spines on its back.

The smile Modest turned on his visitors was disarming, warm and genuine. "Our children. Welcome to Vatican, to the Planet of God." In a breathtaking breach of protocol the pope descended from the dais and strode to Galbior. Flustered, the mathematician genuflected and kissed the pontiff's ring. "Three hundred days indulgence, soldier of Christ," Modest said automatically. When Galbior rose, the pope's greeting was less formal. "Fram Galbior, your elegant mathematics have saved so many lives. We are your humble servant."

Galbior wrinkled his nose. Had any of the anteater's smell transferred onto his own fingers, his lips? "I am honored, Your Holiness."

Modest nodded briefly in Rybczynsky's direction before returning his full attention to Galbior. "We assume our dearest Cardinal has attended to your comfort."

Galbior nodded. "I am quartered at the Saint John Salvi. It is lovely."

"The VIP suite, Holiness," Rybczynsky whispered.

The pope embraced Semuga. "Ato, so good to have you back."

"So good to be back," said Semuga insincerely. He plucked uncomfortably at his traveling garments. "I came straight here from the spaceport."

"We can tell," sniffed the pontiff. He jammed his thumbs in his surcingle and acknowledged Galbior's puzzlement. "Come," he said, bidding his visitors to join him atop the papal dais. Rybczynsky and Semuga hesitated. Not realizing how exceptional a boon was being granted, Galbior climbed the platform without a second thought.

The four gathered around the terrarium. "You were curious about the animal?" Modest asked Galbior.

"Frankly, yes, Your Holiness."

"Very well. It is an echidna, a spiny, hairless anteater from Australia of Terra. We believe the scientific designation is *Tachyglossus aculeatus*. It is a monotreme," Modest riddled, "a mammal that lays eggs."

Not the only such creature in this papacy, Semuga thought darkly.

"Is it . . . your pet?" asked Galbior as noncommittally as he could.

"It is Our calendar," the pope explained. He coaxed the reticent creature back to the surface. Hoisted it for their inspection. "Our calendar, Our scratch pad, Our organizer. Sweet Wleti, tell them."

"Simultaneity is the echidna's gift, you see," the Prefect of the Papal Household explained. "It is the most advanced mammal that doesn't dream. Lacking REM sleep during which to digest its experiences, it must attend to its environment and manage its long-term memory simultaneously in real time. Relative to body size, it has the largest brain weight and the largest prefrontal cortex of any mammal, humans included. When suitably enhanced with biotech implants, it enables a human user to form simultaneous understandings of a great many objects in complex interrelationships."

"His Holiness has compared communion with the echidna to a good senso of free-coursing between the worlds," Rybczynsky supplied. "Only more productive." The beast seemed grateful when Modest returned it to the terrarium. Once again it burrowed straight down.

Modest led the visitors out of the vast hall to an equally generous outdoor terrace. They took seats around an ornate golden table. At once the inner chamber was abuzz with servants, valets, and secretaries. Quiet men removed the terrarium. Others served beverages. Scurrying functionaries puttered everywhere. Modest nodded wistfully. "Time alone with Our guests is precious and short—one of the prices We pay for being Pope."

"Heavy hangs the head that wears the tiara," Rybczynsky agreed.

"Cardinal Semuga," the pope began, "We should like to hear your report." He gestured to encompass the four of them. "We should all like that—the group of us, that is—not just We myself."

"As you know," began Semuga, "I was in the battle bridge of *Bright Hope*— via sim, at least—when the Tuezi came through. It was like a training exercise. They preset their weapons for the spatial and temporal coordinates at which Hom Galbior's equilibrational calculus said the cursed platform would materialize."

"It materialized at the spatial coordinates predicted?" demanded the pope.

"It did," Semuga replied.

"At the exact time predicted?"

"Most certainly."

"Surely there was some tiny residual error."

"None," Semuga answered.

"They aimed, it came, they exploded it."

"Just so. Nothing could have been simpler." From a vanisher pocket in his cassock Semuga drew a report bound in gold. "The power and accuracy of Hom Galbior's mathematics have been proven before my eyes, as Your Holiness commanded."

Modest ran slender fingers over the report. He considered, then rejected, actually reading it.

As I thought, Semuga sulked. *I was sent on a fool's errand. But I am not the fool here.*

Modest turned to Galbior. "So, your formula is formidable. What of your soul?"

Galbior fingered his medallion. "Your Holiness, I converted to the Catholic faith six years ago. From that day forward, I have studied doctrine and attended to my spiritual exercises. It is my joy to report that last month I was created the highest-ranking lay Steward on Guerecht Six."

The Pope nodded gravely. "Cardinal Rybczynsky, We understand you have been evaluating Steward Galbior's new predictions."

"I have," said Rybczynsky, for the first time betraying signs of anxiety. "The math is phenomenally difficult. But Steward Galbior's new predictions appear no less robust than those having to do with predicting the Tuezi arrivals."

"Very well," breathed the pope.

I wonder what you overlooked, Semuga growled inwardly at Rybczynsky. *Do you ever doubt yourself, Alois? Do you ever worry what minute error your servants might commit while you perfect your toilet?*

Somberly Modest swiveled his gaze from Rybczynsky to Galbior. "Steward Galbior, you may brief Us now."

Galbior's eyes darted about the patio. Half a dozen valets and secretaries buzzed about within earshot. Inside labored scores more. "We trust them all," Modest assured him, "else they would not serve in this palace."

"It is your wish that I give my full report—explicitly, without concealment or euphemism—in their hearing?" Galbior demanded.

Modest laughed gently. "We are not the PeaceForce, Hom Galbior. We have no security officers. We depend on the oaths and confidences of all our servants."

"Forgive me, Holiness," said Galbior with evident discomfort. "This is most irregular."

"Of course," Modest agreed in even tones. "But is not Our condition as the Galactic Vicar of Christ 'irregular' with respect to the condition of other men?"

Galbior blinked. "Undeniably, Holiness."

"Then accept Our word that We do things differently here." Modest flipped an encouraging hand at Galbior; to the mathematician he seemed like an ancient patriarch urging wedding guests to join an unfamiliar dance. "Please, Hom Galbior. Say in open language what you have come here to say to Us. In whatever words you choose, begin."

21. Jaremi Four—Northern Hemisphere

Arn Parek started at the sound of heavy footfalls. "Yes?" he said blandly.

Ulf was first to enter the turbine pen. A moment later Chagrin came forth, body tottering over the walking stick. The guerrillas stood together, nervously fingering the pallets on which they'd so often reclined to hear Parek preach.

Parek stood atop an impeller housing. He stepped to its edge and gazed down at them. "Yes, my disciples?"

Chagrin smiled. "We were wondering. . . ."

"Chagrin was wondering," Ulf said. The correction was small but revealing.

Five meters above, Ruth Griszam lurked in shadow. She stared down from a hidden catwalk. She was in Mode. Trillions were *poving.*

"I heard the firefight," Chagrin said at last. "When you were ambushed at the dam. When Ulf killed the marauders." The bleak disciple's eyes widened. "I got close."

"Not close enough," Ulf rumbled.

Near Ruth, something scraped. Without diverting her principal attention, she deflected a scrap of awareness toward the sound. It was Willim Dultav, trying— but failing—to steal silently along the catwalk.

Urgently she waved him to be more quiet.

He crept beside her, all but tiptoeing.

Chagrin wobbled on his walking stick. "My leg slows me down," he told Parek. "Today I wasn't good for much. Ulf could have been killed."

"I sympathize," said Parek inadequately. "We all do."

Above, Ruth clasped one hand over Dultav's where it gripped the catwalk railing. "What are you doing here?" she whispered.

"Same as you," he murmured. "Ulf and Chagrin are no longer satisfied to follow."

Something clattered below. Chagrin had thrown away his walking stick. Like a felled tree, his gaunt form toppled forward. He caught himself on the edge of the impeller housing. "I'm a fighter," he rasped up at Parek. "A soldier for you."

"Thank you," Parek temporized.

"I'm tired of being a cripple."

Dultav drew a sharp breath. Ruth hoped the guerrillas wouldn't notice the catwalk creaking. They didn't.

Parek stared blankly at Chagrin.

"Chagrin's leg," Ulf growled. "Can you. . . ."

Finally Parek understood. "Oh no, I couldn't do that! I have no capacity for miracles."

"Why doubt yourself?" Ulf demanded.

Parek spread his hands helplessly above Chagrin. "I admire your trust," he said at last. "But healing is not my gift."

"I know you can do it," oozed Ulf. His voice was liquid with menace.

"What you ask is not my way." Desperately, Parek tapped at his skull with two angled fingers. "My gifts are . . . up here."

"I want to be your defender!" Chagrin keened.

"And you shall be, always. But within the limits of . . . well, you know, your limits."

"You taught us to burst beyond limits," Chagrin said.

"*No!*" Parek boomed. He took three commanding strides around the impeller housing and whirled to face the guerrillas. "You haven't understood anything, have you? All my teachings, to you they're window dressing. You want cheap miracles."

Silently, Ruth shifted her position on the catwalk. The result was a textbook composition, Parek and Ulf and Chagrin forming the vertexes of a triangle.

"Not cheap miracles," Chagrin chafed. He sidled along the impeller housing, hands always tight on its rim. "I've been lame for seventeen years."

"You are unworthy!" Parek bellowed. He hoped they wouldn't hear the desperation behind his bluster. Yet he knew they would. Or rather, he knew that Ulf would—which, in the end, was the same thing. "You belittle my parables," he spat at them. "You disgrace yourselves."

"What's so wrong in what he asks?" Ulf pressed.

"It is wrong to demand that of me in this defiant way!"

"We don't defy you!" Ulf shouted back.

"We worship you," Chagrin croaked. He was fighting back tears.

Parek leapt from the impeller housing. He plucked up Chagrin's walking stick and thrust it back into the guerrilla's gnarled hand. "You are unworthy!" he repeated. He strode to the canted pallets on which Ulf and Chagrin had so often reclined to receive his teachings. "I will teach no more here! Go. Both of you! Take up your pallets, and leave me."

Ulf scooped up Parek's tunic in huge fists and forced him against the impeller housing. Ulf's hands opened and darted to Parek's shoulders. If the new hold seemed gentler, it was no less controlling. "I *know* you can do it," Ulf hissed.

Chagrin knelt before the master. The walking stick rattled to the floor once more. "Lay your hands on me," Chagrin implored.

"I can't cure you," Parek almost whined.

"It can't harm me."

Ruth checked her *verify* signal—three by three greens. She tried not to think how wealthy this little scrap of senso was going to make her. *At any rate, not now.*

Parek drew a breath to protest again. Ulf grabbed Parek's wrists. Slowly he forced the prophet's reluctant hands to cup Chagrin's cheeks.

Without a sound, Ruth dropped prone on the catwalk, bringing herself as close to the action as she dared. She grimaced at the racket Dultav made in following her example. It went unheard.

Ulf stepped back, eyes lancing into Parek's. Parek felt transfixed, unable to lift his hands from Chagrin's head. Ulf reached behind himself and lifted one of the chiming pipes. He inched it between four closely spaced vertical conduits. Slowly he clattered it from conduit to conduit. *Clang. Shang. Ralang. Clang. Shang. Ralang.* Ulf whirled the pipe faster and faster. *Clang shang ralang. Clang shang ralang.* The pealing rolled and spun in their ears.

"Say the words," Chagrin called over the racket. Tears cut tiny rivulets down the grime on his cheeks. "Bless me."

Clang-shang-ralang. Clang-shang-ralang. Clang-shang-ralang. Clang-shang-ralang. Clang-shang-ralang. Ulf began to sound the secondary rhythm. Dissociation tugged at Parek's consciousness. *If I feel it this strongly, what must it be doing to Chagrin?* he wondered. **Clang**-shang-ralang. Clang-shang-ralang. Clang-shang-ralang. **Clang-shang-ralang.** Parek knew he was trapped.

Later, he might find a way to finesse his blessing's failure. But there was no avoiding the necessity of giving it—no way to avoid granting Chagrin and Ulf whatever he could of what they demanded.

*Clang-shang-ralang. **Clang**-shang-ralang. Clang-shang-ralang.* Chagrin's eyes shone, limpid and trusting.

***Clang**shangralang! **Clang**shangralang!*

Parek expelled a breath. Showmanship overcame caution. He thundered, "I bless you, Chagrin. Be healed."

For a good five seconds, nothing happened. There was no movement save Ulf's obsessive chiming. Presently Parek slipped his hands away from Chagrin's head. Chagrin didn't notice. He was a blank.

I face an editorial decision, Ruth realized. A meter away from her lay the only autochthon whose understanding of what had happened here complemented her own. Would she keep watching the frozen tableau, or risk flicking her gaze up to read Dultav's response? *That's why they issue us bugs,* she thought. *So the Spectator can be free to pursue the telling detail.*

She turreted her gaze.

Reactions were washing across Dultav's face like the surf, wave after wave. Fear gave way to revulsion, then disgust, then anger. Anger surrendered to alertness, and alertness to curiosity.

All at once, curiosity passed into slack-jawed wonder.

Clangshangralang! Clangshangralang! Clangshangralang!

Mouth agape, Dultav bolted upright without thinking where he was. When the back of his head hit the railing overhead, he merely blinked. He never stopped staring.

Enough teasing the experients, Ruth decided. She flicked her gaze back downward.

She went cold inside.

Without his walking stick, without using his hands, Chagrin had risen.

He stood straight. Stable.

By himself.

The chiming stopped.

Chagrin circled the turbine pen, testing his legs, gradually permitting himself to believe what he was feeling.

Parek looked like a man who'd seen the future and by some casual accident turned it inside out.

Chagrin walked, strode, leapt, danced.

Ulf shrank back with a queasy look and dropped the chiming pipe.

Ulf had expected to discredit the prophet, Ruth realized. *Instead he's proved him a god.*

Chagrin threw back his head and howled himself hoarse. Before the echoes died, he'd run from the turbine pen and sprinted up the stairs. He raced hooting through the dam. Cursing, Ulf snatched the antiarmor rifle and hurtled upstairs in pursuit.

Ruth lingered, prone on the catwalk, gathering a few quiet seconds of what Spectators termed the "terminal image": Alone, astounded, Arn Parek looked hauntedly at nothing in particular. At last he raised, and focused on, his hands—the hands that, to no one's astonishment more than his own, had seemingly healed Chagrin.

Ruth sprang to her feet in one Spectator-smooth movement. Dultav had gone. His footsteps clattered away to her left. She darted right. As she ran she polled her bugs. One rewarded her with an image of Ulf chasing Chagrin across the common room, making for the stairs. "Sky gods, Chagrin!" Ulf panted. "You goin' topside? Take a fucking weapon!" *Now to get there ahead of them,* she thought.

When Ruth burst into the powerhouse, she already knew from her bugs that Ulf and Chagrin were outside. Looking the motley jester in his costume of chains and rags and bandoleers, Chagrin capered along the hillside. "I'm healed! I'm healed!"

"Shit, Chagrin!" Ulf hissed. "What if there were marauders out here?"

"I'd run away!" Chagrin exulted. "Or kick the shit out of 'em!" He clasped scrawny hands on Ulf's shoulders. "Sky gods, Ulf! I can walk, I can run."

"You fucking can," Ulf agreed. His anger evaporated in the warmth of Chagrin's glee.

"He healed me!" Chagrin gloried. "Thanks be to Parek!"

"Thanks be to Parek," Ulf replied. He accepted his gaunt companion's embrace and returned it with gusto.

While neither man was watching the doorway, Ruth glided across it, adding the punctuation of movement to her *pov*. She stopped short.

Winded, Dultav lurched up beside her. *She steers herself with such uncanny precision*, thought Dultav. *As though her highest priority in life is having a good view. She moves—that's it!—as if she serves multitudes who watch through her eyes.* He snorted to himself. *Aah, that's ridiculous.*

"Shh," Ruth whispered. "Just watch."

"Think of all we can do together now," Chagrin told Ulf. "The raids we can make!"

Ulf nodded. "A real fighter needs a real weapon."

"I've got my carbine—" Chagrin blinked and realized for the first time that he was unarmed.

"Asshole," Ulf said gently. "You left it downstairs." Ulf released Chagrin's hands and bent down to retrieve the antiarmor rifle where he'd dumped it in tall grass. With a smile, he held it toward Chagrin.

"For me?" Chagrin blurted. "That's your most powerful—"

"Take it," he told Chagrin. "You're a new man today. You deserve a new weapon. New to you, anyway."

Chagrin hefted the big gun and aimed it at a few random targets. He was beaming.

"We better get inside," Ulf said finally.

The guerrillas paid Ruth and Willim Dultav no mind. They pushed between them without a word and strode side by side back down inside the dam.

Ruth had planned to follow them, but Dultav took her shoulders. She considered logging off and decided against it. *He might see something that raises his suspicions further.*

"What just happened?" Dultav demanded.

"I don't know either. Chagrin says he's had that limp since the food riots. As far north as we are, that was what, seventeen years ago? I always thought it was in his head. So did Ulf."

"Something to show off around the firestone."

Ruth nodded. "For years those riots were the central event of Chagrin's life. The limp was his badge of courage." Her voice had a desperate edge. "Now something else is more important to him."

Dultav scowled. "His faith in my former student." Helplessly they stared down the aperture through which the guerrillas had descended. "What do you think they're doing?" Dultav asked.

I could poll my bugs and find out, Ruth thought. *But I won't. Later I can spool back the bugs' journals and reconstruct whatever went on below. For now, let my experients be as much in the dark as Willim Dultav is.* When she replied to him, it felt authentic somehow to be guessing, not disguising secret knowledge. "I bet they're going back to thank Parek."

"Or to ensnare him further."

She sought his hand. "You're the scholar. What did we see?"

"There's a new religion spawning down there."

"A false religion," she said.

"But able to open all the usual emotional and social valves, all the same. When the Church of Parek gets rolling, no telling who it'll roll right over."

She squeezed his hand. "Better to be on the steamroller than under it."

"Pardon me?"

She turned toward Dultav with calculating eyes. "When the Church of Parek begins its journey, you'll stand at Arn's side—and I will stand at yours." She kissed him hard and melted her body against him. She pressed her tongue into his mouth.

He didn't respond.

"What's wrong?"

He broke from her embrace. "Ruth, I've been thinking what I might do if something like this happened. Wherever Parek, Ulf, and Chagrin are going, I want no part of it."

"You'd steal off alone?" Her outer self was astonished, for solid Spectatorly reasons. *He grounds Parek and acts as a foil to Ulf and Chagrin. He's my love interest. Without him Parek's story may lose none of its importance, but it gives up most of its narrative bite.* But her upper self was astonished, too, astonished at how profoundly she'd miss him.

"Not alone," Dultav smiled. "I'll steal off with you, if you'll have me." He took her hand again. "I just know that if we stay too close to this thing that's happening downstairs it will devour us. Dear Ruth, I need your strangeness."

"How would we live?" she breathed. "You just root around for books."

He encircled her in his arms. "There are more honest ways to make a living— slightly, anyway." When he kissed her, she responded urgently.

After their lips parted, his eyes kept probing hers. He wanted an answer.

"You and me," Dultav told her, "living quietly, eking out enough from the ruins to live on. No exploitation. No followers. No lies. Not too exciting, perhaps, but. . . ." He gestured helplessly. "Will you run with me?"

"When?"

"I'm not sure. But very soon."

"I need to think it through."

He squeezed her hands. "We have days, at most." He headed for the stairs but turned back. "I love you, Ruth."

"I love you too," Ruth thought. *That's what I should say, if only to keep the story moving. But I can't. Forjel it, where does this certainty come from—the certainty that whatever I say next will have moral and emotional consequences for me even though I'm just a Spectator here?*

She did not speak. After a moment, Dultav relinquished her gaze and turned back toward the floor aperture. His disappointment at her silence was clear. But there was something else, too—something smug, a hint of that half-smile of his. *I haven't said I love him yet,* she thought. *Forjel him, deep down inside he's sure I will.*

She strode to one of the powerhouse's gaping windows and propped her chin on her elbows. *If I say yes, I turn my back on a gigantic story. I leave Parek, Ulf, and Chagrin to convert the countryside, or enslave it, or burn it, or whatever the sfelb they're going to do with it when they decide what their new religion is about. It'll be just Willim and me, living invisibly in some burned-out steamwagon, growing veg-etables and screwing all the time.*

It occurred to her that few Galactics would care to *pov* a life like that.

It occurred to her that she didn't care.

Realizing *that* made her breath catch in her throat. *Forjeler, am I seriously thinking about going Inplanet? Tear off the Escher patch, become an outlaw, and just subsist among the ruins with this crazy kindly philosopher?*

In Spectator culture, going Inplanet was the ultimate apostasy. Ruth had undergone years of Academy conditioning to fortify her against that temptation. The Spectator philosophy of "outer self" and "upper self"—the yin-yang tension between the Spectator's Galactic *persona* and the local identity she assumed among the autochthons—had no other purpose. "When the Spectator assumes a temporary *persona*, that is not a submergence of the Spectator's true self, but rather an unfolding in several directions." That was just one of the litanies whose tortuous subtleties she'd spent her Academy years teasing apart.

What were coming apart now were her Galactic loyalties. *Sfelb, give the implants five years to ramp down and I could have a child here*, she thought. *No ordinary child, either. One with a 50-50 chance of being able to see things pure-Jaremian children can't, of decoding figure and ground the way Terrans do.* When the mysterious Harvesters planted humans on forty-two thousand worlds so long ago, they hadn't wasted much thought on the DNA changes that branded each planet's population with a unique sensory defect. The genetics was elementary: Ordhians couldn't see green and Augralians couldn't see yellow. Their children had a 50-50 chance to be blind to green *and* yellow. But the Harvesters hadn't branded Terrans, the ancestral stock. Terrans had no artificial sensory gaps. This made Terrans desirable as Spectators. It also meant that children of a union between a Terran and a non-Terran had an even chance of being born without sen-sory defect. *The child I'd bear here might be able to see the Escher lozenges, able to tell the Galactics without a scorecard. To have no one suspect that you possess that power . . . now there's an intriguing legacy.*

The Galactic life she had to look forward to after her fieldwork was so veiled and abstract, after all. *My greatest fear is that I'll follow all the rules, do everything right, make a fortune I never could've imagined—then spend my midlife and gero-mentorhood being bored out of my mind.* She shuddered. *Being the secret eyes and ears of such a cloistered people may have raised appetites in me that only direct expe-rience can satisfy.*

She stopped recording, scanned her financials, and whistled. A Spectator's pay was indexed to saybacks, and the Parek affair had become a Galactic *cause celebre*. But this. . . . *Forjeler, they've moved it to a Galactic Zone bank!* That could only mean her accumulated pay had exceeded the statutory maximum a native Terran bank was allowed to hold on deposit. *Girl, you're richer than ninety-nine point three percent of your fellow Terrans. But then again, Spectator pay has always been one of the most powerful reasons not to go Inplanet.*

Dusk was falling as Ruth picked her way across the powerhouse toward the stairs. She felt not one nanometer closer to making what would probably be the most important decision of her life.

22. Jaremi Four—Southern Hemisphere

Old Weldaey had finally died of his untreated bowel obstruction. His sickness managed a last cruelty. Spasming, fecal matter spraying through his eroded lips, he'd seized a knife from one of his attendants and slashed blindly at his distended belly. What twisted out through the wounds had been unspeakable. Now his fetid corpse lay in a half-rotten old barge. Graargy, the chieftain, set it afire and cast the floating pyre adrift on the canal's sluggish current. By tradition, relatives and close friends would line the fallen bridge as the barge passed. Those who'd known Weldaey more casually stood on a promontory that looked down upon the lower locks.

Linka Strasser stood puffing at the summit. Tarklan, the minstrel, came up behind her, unwinded, lute strapped across his back. "I followed your every footstep," he said.

"That's why you're alive. This cliff is thick with traps."

Others joined them, including saucy young Ixtlaca, haggard, pregnant Verina, soft-edged Muldowa, and Harapel, whose false allegation against the innocent Yelmir would soon mean his death. *But first,* Linka thought darkly, *another death must be attended to.*

The ancient locks huddled in a notch among high cliffs far below. A ribbon of water a half meter thick sluiced over the locks' corroded lip, falling into a vast, round-walled splash pool. *It's thought a direct hit from some Tuezi weapon hollowed out that pool,* Linka reflected. *The drop's so steep that there must have been a flight of three or four locks here. Now only the topmost lock remains. Then the abyss. Such natural barriers keep Graargy's little empire safe.*

"Look!" Muldowa keened. A flower of orange, the burning barge had passed the fallen bridge. In less than a minute it boat would enter the lower locks' constricted channel. Linka deflected her awareness briefly; *verify* was three-by-three greens.

"Chief Oezkiia and his tribe live just below the locks," Tarklan said. "What does he think of these flaming biers Graargy sends down?"

"They're not appreciated," Linka said. "Oezkiia blames our death barges for the barrenness of his women."

Verina bristled. "Then let him explain why birth comes so hard to us! So old and drawn I grew, I feared my husband would stop loving me before I ever came with child."

A male voice buzzed in Linka's awareness. *"Fem Strasser?"*

"Identify," Linka subvocalized.

"Operative delta-three eight nine four," came the scrambled voice. By Spectator tradition, no-vis flyers on killing missions identified themselves by number only. The number was specific to this assignment, recorded nowhere; none would ever know the assassin's identity.

"Stand by," Linka subvocalized. *"Lateral me."* A bubble opened in her awareness. She watched through the assassin's eyes as he dropped below the promontory.

Part of the cliff's edge had been hollowed out. Only rickety timbers supported it. One tug on a frayed rope would bring it down.

"There it goes!" Harapel cried.

Cocooned in flame, the barge scraped over the top of the ancient lock doors. Attended by showering sparks, it plunged into emptiness and struck the splash pool. A medallion of greasy fire spread. "It's perfect," Verina breathed, scrutinizing its pattern. "Weldaey will be welcomed into the city of the gods."

Tarklan strained forward to see. "Careful," Linka told him a bit too loudly. He stood directly over the operative's trap. *"Now!"* Linka ordered silently.

The invisible Spectator wrenched at the line. Timbers collapsed. Brittle earth dropped out under Tarklan's feet.

Giving what she hoped would be a convincing shriek, Linka lurched to the edge and watched Tarklan fall. Below lay half a dozen of Graargy's real traps. Bouncing down the seventy-degree slope, Tarklan triggered one after another. With snaps and clatters they discharged, tearing and slicing as his body passed. He stopped savagely when the last trap hurled a wooden pole through his chest.

The women scrambled down the cliffside. Tarklan had triggered every trap, so it was safe. "A breakaway trap at the cliff edge!" Muldowa huffed. "I never knew. . . ."

"Must date from Graargy's father's time," grunted Harapel. "Oh, Linka. . . ."

Linka feigned horror and levered herself to a stop next to Tarklan.

He sprawled, skewered, on a seventy-degree slope. Bits of rib and shattered lute bristled around the chest wound. Parallel lacerations from another trap slashed his face. Blood poured from his nostrils. The white of one eye was all red.

He was still conscious.

"Tarklan," Linka howled.

The other women stood behind her. None but Tarklan could see her eyes. Linka signed off. Struggling against her training, she managed to sign off like a novice, her eyes twitching manically as she broke off.

Tarklan's eyes saucered.

"You are one of the ones whose eyes dance," he'd once half-seriously accused her. Now he *saw* her eyes dancing, and he realized that the vague legends about "soft intruders with dancing eyes" that he'd carried from tribe to tribe along the blasted canals were true. *I owed him that moment of understanding,* thought Linka. The idea that she might simply enjoy flaunting her dual identity as this autochthon died never occurred to her.

Nor did it occur to her to finish what she'd started. *"End it,"* she subvocalized.

Standing above Tarklan, the no-vis assassin pressed an exoskeletonized leg against a meter-wide stone. Scattering gravel, the rock lurched free of the cliffside. Thudding into Tarklan's neck, it almost ripped the head from his body. Linka drew back screaming. Ixtlaca began to vomit.

The women will report that Tarklan died by accident, that I tried to help him, and that the fatal boulder came from a forgotten delayed-action booby trap. I'll be blameless, my cover secure. Linka jammed hands into her trouser pockets. *"I release you,"* she told the operative.

"I hope I never cross you, Fem Strasser," the anonymous assassin shot back.

A *tap* whirred in Linka's head. *"Yes, Tramir,"* she subvocalized tiredly.

She'd guessed right. Of course it was Tramir Duza. *"Forjel it all, I shouldn't be surprised you went through with it."*

"We do what we must, Tramir. We're Spectators."

"I'm a Spectator. You're . . . I don't know what you are. But I realize there's no changing you. You'll just keep staring into these people's twisted lives until your experients get their fill of pain—which I fear will never happen."

"Thanks for the inspiring sermon."

Duza snorted. *"See you at the invasion."*

"Don't blink," she warned him. *"It'll be over that quickly."*

23. Jaremi Four—Northern Hemisphere

Ruth's awareness was a mosaic. Polling half a dozen bugs simultaneously, she monitored the whole perimeter of the dam complex. *No sign of Ulf and Chagrin returning from their hunt—or of Willim coming back from the library.* The feed from an interior bug confirmed that Parek was alone in his turbine pen, chin in his hands. *He's got enough to think about.* An adjacent bubble displayed a schematic of the dam and powerhouse interior. A red dot flashed. *This is the spot!* The ancient door was crusted with filth, but dirt and mold had been scraped away around its archaic lock.

From a pocket in her fatigues she produced an openall, one of the Galactic tools she normally kept in her vanisher valise. She pressed it against the lock. Shaped force fields permeated the mechanism and massaged the tumblers open. The door swung wide. She thumbed a piezo lantern alight. In its sallow light the three trunks and the rack of cylinders stood as Parek and Ulf and Chagrin had left them.

A *nudge* had awakened her hours before, just past dawn. Dultav slumbered beside her. Again she felt a *nudge,* a blunt tugging in her mind. *One of my bugs spotted something interesting.*

The bugs outside had spotted Parek, Ulf, and Chagrin struggling down the hillside. Each of them had a heavy trunk lashed to his back. *Even Parek!* Between the two of them, Ulf and Chagrin also carried a rusted metal rack pregnant with dark translucent cylinders. All three men were sodden with sweat. Piezo lanterns, now extinguished, clattered from their belts. *They've carried their burdens a substantial distance,* she realized. *They may have been on forced march for several hours while it was still dark.*

Ruth had watched them, switching from bug to bug as they trudged into the powerhouse and down a little-used corridor deep inside the dam. With difficulty, Ulf had unlocked the reluctant door. They'd stacked their burdens in a remote storeroom. All the while Parek reminded them that Dultav must never know anything of what they had done that night. . . .

✦ ✦ ✦

But now it was mid-afternoon. Ruth was alone in the dam. She'd made it into the storeroom. *What merits so much effort to bring here—and why must it be kept secret from Willim?* She went into Mode and logged on. Her openall solved the first trunk's lock in half a second. Inside were rank upon rank of dull metallic vials. *When Dultav was still in school, Northlanders used these to hold biological specimens,* she thought.

She pulled on electrostatic gloves of Galactic manufacture so she could handle the vials without disturbing their thick coatings of dust. She lifted one and peered through its viewslot. A fine, dry whitish powder clumped inside. She inspected vials at random until she was satisfied they all contained the same powder.

The second trunk held identical vials of the same powder.

The third contained fewer, larger vials. *Double, even triple lined,* she thought. *That's the way they might have stored some powerful contaminant or pathogen, to whatever degree one encounters such things on this world.* Inside each vial was a dark, granular substance. The particles gleamed greasily, yet they rolled about freely as if dry. Crude labels on each vial read CAUTION: MOTHER MATTER.

"Mother matter," she muttered aloud. "What the sfelb is that?"

All that remained was to inspect the rack of cylinders. Padded liners cradled stacked rows of clear plastic specimen carriers. Each tube contained the dual-stemmed spike of some Jaremian grain plant, distended by a knobby black mass that seemed to have consumed the kernels within. She held the clearest of the cylinders as close as she could focus. Like its cousins it bore an ancient, machine-printed label, a relic of better times, crinkled and faded but still readable: RAW MATTER.

"Doesn't mean anything to me," she whispered to herself. She closed everything up and stole out of the hidden storeroom. She logged off. *Perhaps,* she thought, *someone, somewhere who povs this journal will be able to understand it.*

24. Terra—Utah Desert, Usasector

Fighting back claustrophobia, the Spectator pressed on. Elbow, knee, elbow, knee, he crawled. The safety rope dangled easily from its carabiner. The beam of his primary helmet light flickered across tile walls. At last the Spectator reached a sky-blue ribbon tied to a stake—the spot where he had stopped caulking the day before. Bathed in sweat, he lay prone on the tunnel floor a full kilometer below ground. He gulped from the water bottle attached to his helmet.

Deep inside the bowels of the mammoth public works project on which he and his fellow prisoners had been condemned to labor, the Spectator started work.

He reached toward his right hip and drew up the bulky caulking gun. From his left he pulled a paddle. The blue caulk shone unhealthily, bead after bead. His job was to seal the corners, choke them with caulk, and draw the edges clean with his paddle. *A half-klick a day.* If he didn't make quota, the inspector robots would discover his lassitude that night. What would happen the next morning was unspeakable.

The work was mind-deadening, but somehow satisfying. And he knew that between the claustrophobia and the sweet monotony of labor, his journals would find a lucrative—if bizarre—audience. So he crawled and caulked, day by day, endlessly postponing schemes of escape, worming ever deeper into the immense water project, trying not to think of the immensities of rock that encompassed him on every side.

Numbly he persevered, caulking, drawing down the edges, crawling forward, stopping now and then to take a furtive suck from his water bottle. He thought of the harsh salty lunch strapped to his fanny.

But he did not think of the percussion pistol strapped between his legs. Those who toiled deep within tried to ignore the pistol—tried not to dwell on the reason why no one, not even a prisoner, would be sent in this deep without one.

Today was like every other day. He fell into the hypnosis of his task. Part of him poked past the reverie to be sure the *Verify* signal still whirred. *Three-by-three greens.* At least he was stationed on a world that had state-of-the-art monitoring. Even a kilometer or two inside the cliffs, he could log on.

Suddenly he became aware of a crackling sound. A narrow fissure black as vacuum opened in the tile. It raced behind him. He only had time to crane his neck.

Then all he could hear was the roaring of the planet's entrails.

It was rocketing bedlam, a cannonade without end. Everywhere. Irresistible. Unendurable! Some sequestered part of his consciousness mustered up the focus to think *Quake!*

Then he had all he could do to ride the bucking snake deep underground. His ears pounded. His chest pulsed. Thunder overwhelmed. His hands clawed at nothing, his eyes screwed shut. The din clamored, vast tsunamis of sound endlessly refreshed.

At once he felt something foreign, out of sync with the mountain's bucking.

About him, the tunnel was collapsing. *No!* Arm-thick tiles sundered like hard candy. Compressed soils flowed like fudge. Great coils of dust curdled over him, obliterated his sight. Dread clutched. *Nooooooo!*

Was it seconds? minutes? After some interval he could not gauge, the thunder was past.

His ears rang harshly. Eventually it occurred to him that he was alive. Awareness bobbed back in fragments.

One helmet lamp still worked. He willed his eyes to pierce the dust.

When the conduit caved in, the slab above him had caught on other debris. That was why it hadn't crushed his shoulders. He tried to move his legs. He couldn't. He could feel his legs, without pain, but they wouldn't move. Twisting his head as far back as he could, he glimpsed fragments of sidewalls protruding from a smooth flow of loam.

His legs were buried.

As the dust settled out, he could see more. The tunnel ahead had collapsed, much as it had behind him. He was impounded in a mocking little air pocket more than a kilometer inside a cliff. Solid rock in all directions. It occurred to him that this must have been a major quake. Hundreds, thousands of prisoners must be fused with rock in what remained of the parallel tunnels.

No doubt topside, the keepers lay stunned amid the rubble of their barracks, impaled on stockades, or crushed under watchtowers. Those who'd survived would rescue only themselves. None would think of the men and women trapped inside. Not that rescue would be possible, even if someone wanted to try.

The Spectator had only one hope. *The percussion pistol! At least I can end this.* . . .

Then he realized he couldn't reach the gun. However hard he pushed, he couldn't force a hand below his chest. He tried to rock his hips. He felt nothing except the spongy, irresistible hug of the gravel that enfolded him below the waist.

No, not like this. Unable to kill himself, he would lay pinned, conscious until he starved, dehydrated, or bled to death, in case he'd suffered lower-body injuries he was unaware of.

Or until I go mad.

Stifling adjacency congealed. Became bottomless horror. Hideous compacting bondage. *"Not like th i i i i i i i i i i i i i i s!"* He shrieked himself hoarse.

Panic heaved up his throat, arched back, and crashed down on him. It sluiced in through all the open places in his psyche. Aghast, he yearned to shudder and roar, to deny the world, to howl until the gods changed his fate.

But there were no gods.

This can't be happening, he obsessed. *I cannot bear it.* Yet it *was* happening. Inconceivable confinement was all he would know. *And on the other side.* . . .

"Noooooo, noooooooooooo!"

Then he *was* on the other side.

How many times had he thus plunged fully into terror, risen through exhaustion back to consciousness? It was happening again. Panic ebbed, unable to sustain its fury.

And nothing was different.

He still lay in his tomb of rock and loam and gravel and shattered tile. Still the rocks pressed his back, confined his limbs, loomed before his face, closer *It's starting again* and closer *It can't get worse* and closer *Nothing more than this* and . . .

"NOOOOOOOOOOOOOOOOOOOOOOOOOOOOOOOO!"

Flicker. Buzz.

His last sane thought was the realization that his trap, which he could not imagine growing more horrific, was doing exactly that.

His helmet light was going out. . . .

Suck, rush, wrench.

"Marnen. Marnen!"

What the sfelb? Someone was shaking him.

"Gather yourself, you degenerate."

Marnen Incavo remembered where he was. *The desert. Waiting for.* . . .

Drenched in sweat, he lay in a hammock next to his rented flitter. It was well past dusk. He whirled.

Alrue Latier stood beside him, eyeing the program wafer he had plucked from Incavo's senso player. The evangelist screwed up his features in disapproval. "Snuffers, Marnen? Hardly edifying."

"They make me strong," Incavo said. He eyed Latier curiously. The Mormon gadfly's trademark muslin jumper was flecked with red desert dust. "You know, the real Mormons wore those *under* their clothes," Incavo said as he strode around the front of his flitter. "Anyway, I thought I'd set up my senso player to shut off at the approach of your flitter—oh."

The workmanship on the reproduction eighteenth-century (local) phaeton was exquisite. The carriage's tall, wood-spoked wheels were enameled green and detailed in gold lead. Matched strawberry roans stood yoked, their breath cloudy in the chill air. "I don't believe you, Latier. A horse and carriage."

"Call me Alrue. It's a Mormon thing."

"The forjeling horse and carriage?"

"No, using first names. And don't curse."

Incavo circled the coach. "You came out here by buggy. Some new revelation?"

"No, camouflage."

"You call this glittering coach camouflage?"

"Most Detex doesn't pick it up." Latier twirled Incavo's snuffer wafer between thumb and forefinger. "Yours didn't."

Incavo finally felt at home in his body again. "In about five minutes, Hom La—pardon me, *Alrue*—you will be profoundly grateful for my fascination with senso."

"Which has, I hope, some bearing on why you so urgently solicited my clandestine presence out here."

"And I thought you only talked that way from the pulpit." Incavo gestured toward the hammock he'd so recently occupied.

Latier hoisted himself in. "So, Marnen, am I at last to see what I've been paying you for so grandly?"

Incavo fiddled with the senso player. "My fees have been reasonable."

"Granted. It's your expenses."

"Vatican's an expensive world." Incavo pulled up a camp stool and sat beside Latier. Their faces were a meter apart. "I hope you're prepared for something extraordinary. You may find it offensive."

"I sent you to spy on the pope," Latier said dismissively. "I'm prepared to hear of every deadly sin."

"It's not what you'll hear," Incavo gloated. "It's what you're going to *pov.* Ready?"

Latier nodded and closed his eyes. Incavo thumbed the senso player. It hijacked Latier into another *being-thereness.*

An experient's face was usually calm while *poving*—unless the senso was tremendously intense like one of Incavo's snuffers. Or like what Latier was *poving.* His eyelids fluttered, breaking senso contact. He sat bolt upright. "Hom Incavo, what the sfelb are you showing me?"

"Alrue, please don't curse. You wanted to know what the pope was up to."

"I didn't want to feel like I raped him! Him, and Ato Semuga and Alois Rybczynsky, and . . . who was the fourth man? He looked familiar, but somehow out of place."

"Him?" Incavo smirked. "Fram Galbior."

"Galbior? At a papal audience!" Latier twisted around in the hammock and reached toward the senso player. Incavo pulled it away. "For the love of Christ, Marnen, is this real?"

Incavo replaced the player on its stand. He stood and smiled. "Altogether real. I was able to find an undocumented rogue Spectator on Vatican, and secure him a secretarial position in the Papal chambers."

Latier gaped. "You did . . . *what?*" The evangelist howled with laughter. "Those expenses of yours suddenly seem reasonable." He settled back in the hammock. "Bootleg senso of a confidential Papal audience."

"Exactly."

"But I saw their faces. No logos, no heralds." Latier shuddered. *"I saw Galactics' faces!"*

"I told you it might offend," Incavo said evenly.

"But how did you—I mean, doesn't the senso player automatically protect Galactics' privacy?"

Incavo chuckled. "Not after certain modifications."

"They would disinto us both for that," he whispered.

"If they knew," Incavo agreed.

"I see why you wanted to do this in person," Latier mused, "and in such secrecy." He stifled another shudder. *Indecent as the recording may be,* he thought, *it is surely revealing.* He said aloud, "Continue, then. Let me see it all, then let me get the sfelb out of here."

Incavo thumbed *Play.*

There they were again: Sallow Rybczynsky. Fleshy, rumpled Semuga. Beloved Galbior. Pope Modest IV. Latier observed them through the eyes and ears and nostrils of Incavo's spy.

Somberly Modest swiveled his gaze from Rybczynsky to Galbior. "Steward Galbior, you may brief Us now."

Galbior's eyes darted about the patio. "We trust them all," Modest had assured him, "else they would not serve in this palace."

"It is your wish that I give my full report—explicitly, without concealment or euphemism—in their hearing?" Galbior had demanded.

Modest laughed gently. "We are not the PeaceForce, Hom Galbior. We have no security officers. We depend on the faith and confidences of all our servants."

Latier could not help laughing.

"Forgive me, Holiness," said Galbior with evident discomfort. "This is most irregular."

"Of course," Modest agreed in even tones. "But is not Our condition as the Galactic Vicar of Christ 'irregular' with respect to the condition of other men?"

Galbior blinked. "Undeniably, Holiness."

"Then accept Our word that We do things differently here." Modest flipped an encouraging hand at Galbior; to the mathematician he seemed like an ancient patriarch urging wedding guests to join an unfamiliar dance. "Please, Hom Galbior. Say in open language what you have come here to say to Us. In whatever words you choose, begin."

Galbior began.

When the playback ended, a minute passed. Latier sat up. He looked simultaneously drained and exhilarated. "Jesus Christ," he breathed.

"One could say that," Incavo agreed.

Latier heaved himself out of the hammock. The stand where the senso player had been was empty. "Where is it?" he demanded.

"In a vanisher valise," Incavo said. "Inside another vanisher valise."

"I paid for that data, and for that abhorrent machine you played it on," Latier snapped. "Shouldn't I have them?"

Incavo cocked an eyebrow at him. "Do you really want them, Alrue?" Latier dropped his eyes. "Do you want to take the *slightest* chance of being caught with a privacy-noncompliant senso deck? There, I didn't think so."

Latier felt less the triumphant spymaster than like an incompetent schemer caught in his own intrigues. "You have more than fulfilled the demands of your commission," he said quietly.

Incavo only smiled.

"I suppose some bonus is in order—to acknowledge your masterful work and, um, to compensate you for your silence."

Incavo only smiled.

"I shall transfer half a million Terran credits to your account tonight."

Incavo snickered.

Latier frowned inside, thinking, *I made myself no less vulnerable for having commissioned that hideous recording than Incavo is for having created it.*

"Very well, five million Terran," the evangelist spat.

Incavo merely grinned.

"Forjel it, fifty million Terran!" Latier blustered.

"I like it," Incavo said quietly. "Except the last word."

"The last. . . . You want fifty million *Galactic?*"

Incavo was not smiling.

"Marnen, no," Latier temporized. "Explosive as it is, you can't think your little senso is worth. . . ."

"Oh, but I do. And so do you . . . don't you?" Incavo dug a hand into his jumper pocket. "You realize as well as I do that you haven't any other choice. Isn't that so . . . Alrue?" The hands came out of the pocket holding a transfer card.

Scowling, Latier took the card, pressed his signet to it, and subvocalized a command. The fund transfer was immediate. *Good thing I've begun attracting Galactic contributions in earnest,* he thought. Still clutching the card, Latier rumbled, "Be relieved that I choose to reward your initiative, and not to punish your audacity in daring to blackmail an elder of the Mormon church."

"Daring, my ass," said Incavo oleaginously as he plucked back his transfer card. "A pleasure doing business with you, Hom Latier. Hire me again sometime."

Latier waddled back to his phaeton brimming with fury. But as he set the twin steeds cantering back toward the distant lights of Salt Lake City, rage was replaced by excitement—and a fever of calculation. *So I paid that unprincipled weasel more than I made in the first twenty years of my ministry on Terra,* he thought. *Information like this is worth far more than that. It's worth a world!*

25. Jaremi Four—Northern Hemisphere

"Wildfire," said Willim Dultav as he scowled over the valley downstream. "Big one, moving this way."

Arn Parek stood atop the dam beside his onetime mentor. He squinted at the angry red horizon. "How close?"

"We'll have tonight and the morning. Tomorrow afternoon, it'll be raining embers."

"In the morning," Parek said distantly, "I'll have to decide what to do."

"We should go deep," Dultav nodded. "Bottom level of the dam, way in back, under the reservoir. We'll stay cool, breathe air drawn from the surface of the lower impoundment. The smoke will be thin down there. After a day or two, we can come out."

Parek's mouth scrunched in disagreement. "I've been thinking of going into expansion again. You know, with the ministry."

"Tomorrow morning? You, Ulf, and Chagrin?"

"All of us," he said placidly.

Dultav snorted. "Running ahead of a wildfire?"

"One can do worse than move on the gods' schedule."

Dultav grunted and ran a hand through his graying hair. "And the gods want you to do big public revivals again, with Ulf as your sergeant at arms and Chagrin to lick your boots. Pump five, ten thousand brains full of your dream poison. Mumble nonsense. Take all they have."

Parek sat down on the dam's edge with his back against a control wheel. "You don't understand, Willim. You haven't for weeks now. This time I spent here with Ulf and Chagrin has been invaluable. Time to regroup, to think—to open myself to revelation."

Dultav said nothing. He kicked angrily at a cement chip. It landed chattering on the powerhouse roof. In the semidarkness of the wildfire night it sounded incredibly far away.

"Ulf and Chagrin and me, we've shared a spiritual voyage," Parek said brightly. "I've been paring away parts of my creed that I composed long ago, when I didn't take seriously what was happening to me. I'm more confident than ever of the message I *really* offer to roll back the Great Dismay. Willim, it disturbs me that you've kept yourself so distant from this. You've clung to your books, and your cynicism, to the hopelessness of this blasted world—and to Ruth."

"And what's wrong with Ruth?"

"Nothing, as women go. If we'd encountered her six months ago, she'd have been mine."

"A comforting thought." Grinning wryly, Dultav offered his flask. Parek refused with a look of distaste.

"I need no drugs where I travel."

Dultav drank deeply. "Where you're going, *I* need all the drugs I can get."

Parek spoke in a monotone voice with a thudding emphasis on every word. "The problem with Ruth is, she keeps you rooted here. We're more than con men now, Willim. I've learned new ways with the chiming. I'vd had new visions. I have a new message now. You keep denying it."

Dultav took his former student by one forearm. "Do you have any idea where this will go, Arn? You think you're some great true prophet? You'll be god for a day—or a week. A few months, tops." Parek pulled away. Dultav continued in even tones. "You know your history. You know what comes next. Your little faith will sprout a self-appointed college of theologians, and they'll start telling you what kind of god you're allowed to be." He drew a *bohtti* sprout from one of the pockets of his field jacket. He rolled it in his fingers until he was sure Parek had identified it in the half-light, then crushed it as he would into hot cider. The sprout puffed and collapsed into a drizzle of sweet powder. "You'll be their *bohtti* sprout. They'll squeeze you and sprinkle divine approval on whatever ghastly thing they'd been going to do all along."

"It might turn out like that," Parek allowed, "if I didn't know my message were real."

"Are you the same person who studied philosophy under me? What good's subjective certainty? Didn't we get rich half a dozen times manipulating the certainties of others? You've just caught yourself in your own snare."

"I'm ready to go out again, Willim. To go big. To draw thousands. To . . . to help."

Dultav shrugged. "If you go on that agenda, you go alone."

"You don't mean that."

"Yes, I do."

Parek spoke with real concern. "How will you live?"

"I'm not helpless."

"That's not what I meant. You'll find ways to survive. You—" Parek arched an eyebrow. "You and Ruth?"

"Probably."

Parek shook his head. "But you'll spend all your time *working* on surviving. You'll have to go where the pickings are good, never mind where the campuses are." Parek touched slender fingers to Dultav's forearms. "How will you make time for your books? Without me, you lose the luxury of your obsession."

Dultav stepped away from Parek's touch. "That's *my* problem. You have problems enough! Think about what you're creating here—no, think about what's using you to create *itself.* A giant, blundering machine that will focus all the survivors' hatred and fear and rage, set them on fire with it all over again—then turn them loose, with the grateful sanction of the sky gods stamped across their foreheads.

Then," Dultav threatened, "it really *will* be too late for you. Try to lead your faithful somewhere they don't care to follow, and they'll dispose of you outright—pausing only to invent some theological double-talk that explains it all away."

Parek's face was ashen with recognition of dire possibilities. "In the morning," he asked, "when my disciples ask me where to go, whom to kill—what do I tell them?"

Dultav nodded bitterly. "Only one of us speaks for the sky gods. You must decide."

When Dultav found Ruth, he had the oddest feeling she'd been expecting him. She stood naked in the bottom-most basement of the powerhouse, wading in a knee-deep holding pool, wringing out her shift and trousers. A single lantern flickered on a fractured concrete pedestal. Her boots and weapons lay next to it. Wordlessly Dultav removed his clothing and waded out to her. The water was nearly warm. He clasped his hands over her buttocks and drew her close. Her hands explored his chest, his flanks, his thighs, while his advanced along her ribs. He twisted her nipples between his thumbs and forefingers. Their tongues writhed together. Laughing, they fell back into the brackish water. For minutes they swam, groped. At last she guided him to a canted slab that had fallen only a forearm's length below the water. She motioned for him to lay down on it. She straddled him and impaled herself.

She rocked above him, her hair swaying in dark ringlets. Black water lapped with their movements. He clutched her thighs, her breasts. He drew her mouth onto his.

She was recording it all.

"Got your flask?" she said afterward.

"I'm out." His face was silhouetted against the lantern's light. He thought nothing of it when she rolled across him to regard him with the wan glow playing on his face. "I drank the last of it upstairs."

"Too bad," she said and kissed him again.

"I need your decision," he said at last.

With her own features in shadow, she knew she could log off without his noticing. She did. "So soon?"

"I think Arn's a lost cause," Dultav said gravidly. "I'll know for sure in the morning."

"And if you don't like what you hear, you're leaving."

"I hope *we're* leaving."

She rose to a crouch and leapt out into deeper water. She swam a few strokes. Thrust her head under. She came up slicking black hair back against her skull. "I need to think."

He gestured at the ruined immensity of the powerhouse. "I hope I'm not right. But if I am, after the morning this place won't be an option for either of us."

"Wake up!" The voice was Ruth's. "It's not dawn yet. But the wind shifted. The fire got here early!" As she rushed on toward the turbine pen, Dultav collected his things.

Lifting one of Parek's chiming pipes, she clattered it against bowed conduits. "Wake up, assholes! Wildfire, on top of us!"

"What the fuck—" Chagrin grunted as he flung himself from his bedroll. He slipped on his bandoleers and grasped the big steamrifle in a single motion. *He is so graceful now,* she thought.

"The wildfire!" she spluttered. "It snuck up on us. Sky gods, isn't one of you supposed to be on watch?"

Pulling on his weapons, Ulf spoke of Parek in a tone that mingled love with awe. *"He* sent us down. He wanted to be alone."

Chagrin's eyes went wide with horror. "Where is he?"

A fruitless search of the dam behind them, Ulf and Chagrin jostled for position in the powerhouse door. Breathless, Dultav and Ruth were but a half step behind them. The four negotiated the metal staircase and scattered onto the hillside.

"Shit," Chagrin cried.

The night air was alive with drifting embers. Behind them, across the spillway, small fires had already ignited. Flames bristled all across the valley floor downstream, less than a kilometer away. The air was rich with the smell of smoke.

Pitted girders erupted from the hillside three meters above where they stood. Arn Parek stood impassive on the widest girder. Ruddy light played on his dark features. He regarded the creeping inferno almost serenely. Obviously, he had been out here all night.

Am I recording? Ruth wondered with a start—for what she knew was probably the last time. *Three-by-three greens. I don't even remember logging on!* She'd never reached a conscious resolution, but she felt certain what her decision would be. *Inplanet. There'll be so little for me back home. Why not?* She clambered over to Dultav and grasped one of his hands with feral strength.

Parek had finally recognized their presence. "Morning comes early," he called with a trace of irony.

"Do we go . . . or dig in?" Chagrin called from a hillock a few meters away. Ruth's reflex was to answer. At once she remembered: such decisions were no longer hers. Chagrin and Ulf had fixed their gazes on Parek. He would decide. And Parek had focused his attention half a meter to Ruth's right.

On Dultav.

"What shall we do?" Ulf called to Parek.

Ruth drifted two steps away with Spectator grace. She panned her vision from Parek on the girders to Dultav by the staircase. They'd locked eyes with an intensity that summed up all their disputes.

The future of Parek's ministry, of Ruth's career, would be settled by the next words anyone spoke.

26.   Jaremi Four—Southern Hemisphere

Linka Strasser moved along the drowsy canal, stepping around debris of the festival eve bacchanal the night before. *Festival day. Time for an execution—and a
brief invasion.* The sentry, Tarbyl, struck the morning gong. By ones and twos
Graargy's people shambled out of their hogans.

Water lingered in a little catch barter. The oily film atop it caught sunlight,
throwing back rainbow hues. A pitted bucket broke the surface. Pregnant Verina
hauled up the morning's water using an old block-and-tackle someone had
mounted there so she wouldn't have to pull too hard. One of Graargy's junior wives
accepted the bucket and took it to the cooks, who'd rekindled fires below the
ancient steel cooking plates.

From the windowless hogan came the sounds of the blind women's weaving.
That sound never stopped.

Linka found Sydeno, as close to a lover she'd cared to affect among the tribespeople. He embraced her. "I'll never forget last night," he said intensely. Linka
said nothing.

Sydeno never questioned her moods or her watchful silences.

Tarbyl drew back the gate from a corroded metal culvert that led up into the
hillside. Abruptly it spat out Yelmir, the condemned fashioner. He thudded heavily
onto a bowed wooden platform, trembling uncontrollably. *The fruits of innocence,*
Linka thought as she inventoried his cuts and bruises. As tradition provided, he'd
spent the night at the mercy of the relatives of the dead man. *Blaupek's kin went
easy on him,* Linka thought. *Last hanging was a formality after the murderer's night
in the caves.*

Fifteen meters away, guards blocked the doorway of the hogan where
Yelmir'd lived. His claspmate and daughters crowded behind them, howling
their anguish.

Linka polled her bugs. There were thirty. She'd strewn some herself and
engaged a no-vis flyer to plant the rest within the upper locks, where she dared
never to be seen venturing. Everything was ready.

"*Show time,*" she subvocalized. "*Linka here, in Mode and recording. Tramir,
you there?*"

"*On station. I'm in the cliffs above the locks.*"

"*How'd you get away?*" Like Linka, he had an identity to maintain among Lormatin's people.

"*Believe it or not, Lormatin assigned me to infiltrate through Kaahel's territory
and observe the progress of the attack.*"

One's upper self and outer self seldom got the same assignment. She chuckled.
"*Nice work if you can get it, Spectator.*"

Duza wasn't laughing. "*You're going to let Yelmir die.*"

Linka ignored him. "*Who's no-vis?*"

A bubble opened unbidden in her consciousness. She saw herself from a

sweeping vantage ten meters above her head. *"Neuri Kalistor here. It'll be my privilege to provide aerial coverage for the latest display of Linka Strasser's cold detachment."*

Linka scowled inwardly even as she admired the graceful shot Kalistor was
creating.

Kalistor wheeled in mid-air over the fallen bridge, then swooped upstream toward
the upper locks. *Perhaps Linka will fall in this invasion,* she thought cruelly.
Wouldn't there be justice in that!

Neuri Kalistor was Laz Kalistor's widow—as much as a woman could be widow
to a man who wasn't dead. For years they'd been passionate lifepartners and successful Spectators. Over vacations they'd toured as old-fashioned stage magicians,
Laz teaching her the skills of the career he'd pursued single-mindedly before he'd
chosen a Spectator's life.

Of course, this was the same Laz Kalistor whose torture and hideous death
Linka had watched impassively three years before. Laz having died O/N-Two,
OmNet had followed procedure and revived him from the antecedent sample-and-
scan he'd left in the banks. By some oversight, Laz had failed to update for several
years. The antecedent from which they revived him dated from two years before he
met his wife.

The reunion had been wrenchingly unsuccessful. She was not the woman
who'd first enchanted him; now she bore the imprint of five-plus years of shared
experience he no longer remembered. *Was that why we couldn't click?* she thought
bitterly. *Was his younger self that different? Or was it that I'd matured?* Whatever
the reason, no lightning had crackled between them. Laz-as-he'd-been-five-years-
ago couldn't muster even strong interest in her.

After that debacle Neuri Kalistor had hidden in her work. Bound for promotion,
she would only remain in deep cover a few more months. *I've dreamed of how I'd hurt
Linka once I outranked her. But if today breaks right, I won't need to worry about that.*

As for the revived Laz Kalistor, he'd changed his name and disappeared in fury
and shame. Dying on Jaremi Four had shouldered his life into a new path—which
was to say, it had made him someone other than the person he'd been before. Under
Galactic values about privacy and the inviolability of the self, what Linka had caused
to befall Laz Kalistor was widely considered worse than death. Of course, it wasn't
Linka's fault that Laz had gone so long without a sample-and-scan, but still. . . .

Linka stared up into the empty sky where Neuri Kalistor's lateral suggested she was
flying. She, too, mulled over the tragedy yet again. *I'm not among friends today,*
Linka thought. *Well, no matter. We're all Spectators.*

Verina shuffled by, proffering a bowl of sour porridge to everyone. She raised
an eyebrow when Linka took it; usually Linka passed on the harsh gruel. *This stuff
goes beyond even my cultural flexibilities,* Linka thought. She joined her lover on a
fallen tree. *Today, let my experients pov all there is to life—and death—here.* She
gathered a greasy dollop onto her fingers amd shoveled it into her mouth. The
flavor was unexpectedly delightful. *Skhaar!*

More precious even than *anjhii, skhaar* was a fiery seasoning used only on the most special occasions—and at that, only when available. It came from two hundred kilometers north, on the shores of the Equatorial Sea. *Skhaar* was one of only half a dozen autochthonous spices in the Galaxy that provided the heat of a Terran chili pepper but with a different flavor palette. Since it was a seasoning, not a foodstuff, the fact that humans could not metabolize it made no difference. *If the first Confetory survey teams had stumbled across this stuff, Jaremi Four might never have been Enclaved.* Now, of course, gourmands enamored of *skhaar*'s gingery bite could only experience it by senso. *The taste of this spice will double my saybacks, no matter what else happens. I guess this is my lucky day.*

On the platform, innocent Yelmir vomited up his porridge, veined with blood. It was not his lucky day.

"You can still stop this," Tramir Duza buzzed in her head.

"Forjel off."

A shower of muddy clods sprayed down the cliffside as Linka's foothold failed. She thrust her knee into the damp cavity where the loose clay had been. She managed to keep her balance. Below her, the engineer Freydiin cursed. He clung to his staff and a protruding vine as the debris stung him. Linka called an apology over her shoulder and resumed her climb.

Neuri Kalistor floated no-vis, *pov*ing intently as the tribespeople labored up the safe path to the killing knoll. Descending against the party's motion, she inspected each climber. The cliff below the killing knoll was treacherous, the safe path narrow—all but invisible to an outsider which, of course, was the idea. Reaching the canal bank, Kalistor drifted over the canal and ascended once more.

Linka was just hauling herself onto the summit. Knots of men and women gossiped. A crude noose swayed in the breeze. With sinister playfulness, Kalistor maneuvered so that she saw Linka's head through the noose. After a few moments she circled behind the tribespeople, looking over their shoulders.

From the killing knoll, one could see the whole of Graargy's basin. Directly below, water shimmered azure in the further of the two parallel locks. The nearer lock lay empty, an ancient freighter slumped on her side at its bottom. It was typical of Graargy's haughty confidence in his defenseworks that the killing knoll, a perfect sentry point, was never occupied except for executions. The cliffs, the locks, the myriad booby traps—those were Graargy's sentries.

Tramir Duza stood among trees on the opposing clifftop, looking across the locks toward the killing knoll. Magnifying implants enabled him to distinguish Linka among the tribespeople. *"I see you,"* he subvocalized. She looked up, scanned the rugged cliffs across the canal. *"You won't see me."*

"By the way," Linka responded, *"I suppose the invasion is still on."*

"Just wait."

"Here comes Yelmir," Linka husked.

Linka edged to her right for a better angle. Two of Graargy's strong sons hauled up on a handmade rope. Yelmir rose, trussed, gyrating, terrified.

No member of Yelmir's family had been allowed on the knoll. The claspmate and two daughters of Blaupek, the "murder victim," were present. So was blowsy Harapel, whose false charge against Yelmir Linka had declined to contradict. Among the two-score tribespeople atop the killing knoll, many had sharp glances for Harapel, or Linka, or both. They suspected part of the truth, but so long as Linka and Harapel kept their silence, nothing could be proved.

Linka made her way to the front of the crowd. With smooth turns of her head and precise deflections of glance, she gave form to her narrative. Graargy stood commandingly, arms akimbo, his two-meter staff leaned against a tree. Dzettko, the settlement's tribune, recited the murder charge in a rheumy voice. Some in the camp believed Dzettko had actually lived since the days of yore when fires crackled from the sky. That was impossible, of course. Linka assumed his long, impromptu historical anecdotes sprang from schizophrenia. Whatever his inspiration, in minutes Dzettko had painted Yelmir as the vilest malfeasor ever to foul Graargy's little valley.

"I've acquired the invasion force," Neuri Kalistor crackled in Linka's head. The bubble opened; Neuri was hurtling just above the water, flanking an ancient steam-skiff rowed by six young men. Having established that skiff, Neuri lofted up and dropped back. In all, three hulls approached Graargy's upper locks. The soldiers wore stiff leather armor on their upper bodies and simple helmets of found metal. Each bristled with knives and slings and bags of rocks. Each had a spear or a pike or sword at hand. *Eighteen, twenty men,* Linka thought. *A tiny force. But enough to do real damage if they get through.*

His imprecation complete, Dzettko snatched down the noose. He held it before him like a victory wreath. Graargy's sons pressed Yelmir forward. Solemnly Dzettko worked the rope over Yelmir's head.

Dark delight blazed in Linka as the condemned man swept his face around, sobbing. He made eye contact with each witness—and for a brief instant, directly with Linka. Not for the first time, Linka found herself wishing she *could* let Yelmir know. She lusted to tell him she could spare his life with a word, to glory in her power to let him die by keeping silence. Of course, she didn't. She was a Spectator!

Graargy's sons led Yelmir to the promontory's newly spaded lip.

They backed away. Yelmir was alone on the scarp.

Linka devoted two seconds to lightning glances. She perfectly anticipated the moment when Dzettko looked up at Graargy for permission to proceed. Her eyes flicked to Graargy just as he gave an ursine nod of approval. She was on target again when Dzettko's papery hand threw a rough-hewn lever forward.

Concealed lines rigged after the manner of half a thousand of Graargy's hillside booby traps undermined the promontory's lip. Rocks and clay and grit collapsed under Yelmir's feet. Yelmir dropped about a meter and a half. Stopped hard.

Save for the creaking of a tree limb under its new burden, all was silent.

Linka realized she'd been prepared for a pang of guilt when Yelmir died. She was relieved, though by no means surprised, when none came. She watched a darkening patch spread across Yelmir's trousers with utter calm. *Tarklan was wrong.*

Behind the twisting body, the first of Lormatin's skiffs scudded into sight. They surged across still water toward the flooded lock. *"Thank you, Tramir,"* Linka subvocalized. *"You were right. It is a forjeling great shot."*

Hurriedly Graargy's son Jaekdyr climbed a tree for a better view.

"Three boats. Perhaps twenty soldiers," Jaekdyr called down. "Everyone rows. They come fast."

"Soon they must stop," Freydiin observed.

Graargy nodded and laughed. The laughter spread from person to person. This invasion force, like all the others, would be compelled to abandon its craft and assault the locks on foot—whereupon the locks would swallow them.

Harapel mustered a party of women that included Linka. They'd follow clifftop paths to the locks, where they would slaughter the wounded and loot the dead.

The first skiff entered the flooded lock and drifted to a stop behind its doors. The second and third skiffs pulled up alongside.

"Let's go, women," Harapel commanded.

In single file they strode carefully into the brush, avoiding traps: Harapel, Verina, Blorach, Blaupek's widow, Ixtlaca, Linka, and Blaupek's daughters. A dozen others. *"Tramir, Neuri, you've got the action,"* Linka announced.

Invisible, Neuri Kalistor overflew the line of women. She rose and then feathered to a stop four meters above the water of the flooded lock. Lormatin's sleek old craft had tied up. Troopers surged up onto the lock doors and split up. Some took to the concrete gangway, others made for the more primitive stairways. Aghast at the carnage, Kalistor stared as one by one, sometimes three or four at once, the attackers died in Graargy's traps.

There was movement, off to the left. Linka and the other women emerged from thick woods. *"So,"* Linka said to her. *"What you expected?"*

Kalistor shrugged. *"So far."*

So far? Linka wondered. The women spread out onto catwalks, weaving along paths they knew to be safe. They'd drawn knives. Expertly they checked the invaders for life, slashing throats or piercing hearts as necessary. They set about the grisly but rewarding task of rifling the corpses.

One bubble *nudged* for Linka's attention. She bid it open. It was a lateral from Kalistor. She floated directly overhead. Linka watched herself and Ixtlaca kick hidden releases. Mobile granite blocks slid backward, freeing the bodies they had pulped. Suddenly the picture in the bubble receded. Kalistor had jetted away.

Kalistor flew upstream, only a meter above the still water. *"Linka?"* she called over a private channel.

"What, Neuri?" Linka replied.

"You like the unpredictability of native life."

"So?"

She laughed. *"So, there's something I didn't tell you."* The canal meandered. She flew straight, lifting just high enough to clear the treetops. She burst back out over water.

Six more steamskiff hulls, each rowed by a dozen troopers, sped toward the upper locks and toward the women.

From his position on the opposite cliff, Tramir Duza glimpsed the approaching skiffs. He panned with Spectator precision, sliding his gaze downcanal to the lock catwalks. Linka and her tribeswomen were exposed and helpless. *"Remember, you're a Spectator,"* Duza said cruelly. *"You can't warn anyone till you see the boats yourself."*

"You knew there was a second wave!" Linka sputtered.

"Sfelb, yes. But no reason you needed to."

Invisible, Neuri Kalistor flung herself ahead of the approaching skiffs. She wheeled close over the catwalks, vividly establishing the tribeswomen's peril. *"Know what galls me, Linka?"* she subvocalized. *"If you die here, you're sure to be recovered and revived."*

Kalistor gazed upcanal. The second wave of skiffs rounded a final bend. Looting a corpse atop the lock doors, Harapel saw the attackers first. She leaned over the rail and screamed down, "More boats! Lots of them!"

Kalistor felt a certain glee as Linka, Verina, Ixtlaca, Selwaga, and the others looked up from their grisly work.

Harapel was icy calm. "Remember where we are," she called. "Everyone, up to me."

Puzzled, Kalistor circled. With incongruous composure twenty tribeswomen picked their way *up* the catwalks—closer to the attackers. They spread out across the cement gangway, just a meter and a half below the lip of the great doors. *What the sfelb can they be thinking?*

Harapel was moving purposefully along the gangway, crouching low, speaking to each group of women in turn. Kalistor drifted closer.

The second wave of skiffs pulled up to the lock doors, one by one. Seventy troopers stowed their oars and took up weapons, awaiting the order to strike.

"We've drilled this," Harapel told three young women, tearing at their wraps to expose more of their flesh. "Remember, stay low. Older women first. And act scared!"

"Act scared?" Kalistor said incredulously.

"What the plorg?" That was Duza.

Linka laughed up at them. *"Your turn to sample the unpredictability of native life."*

Unbidden, a new bubble opened in Kalistor's mind. On some level she knew Duza was receiving it, too. Linka was lateraling them the output from one of her bugs. A schematic formed in Kalistor's awareness, showing her that this bug was located on the killing knoll.

She saw the backs of Graargy and Tsretmak, the chieftain's eldest son, as they stared toward the locks. Their body language told her that Tsretmak was frantic. Graargy, on the other hand, seemed oddly relaxed. "Years ago, before you were born," Graargy said, "when Lormatin's father ruled his domain upstream, I caught an entire family hoarding ancient weapons."

"You hanged them, like Yelmir?" asked the son.

"No, I spared them," Graargy rumbled, "on condition that they turn over their youngest daughter. Dzettko and Sculfka and I, we raised the girl in isolation. We taught her everything she knew. Some of what we taught her was true, some wasn't. She believed that I *had* executed her family. She believed that if she escaped one day and made her way to Lormatin's father, he'd raise an army and kill us all. One day we guarded her laxly and let her make her escape."

"She told Lormatin's father our secrets?"

"She told him what she believed. For instance, she believed that when the

locks swallow an invading force, before we send the women out to rifle the bodies
we disarm the booby traps that haven't yet gone off."

Tsretmak gawked out at the women on the locks and stared back at his father,
his face a mask of stricken terror.

"Relax, Tsretmak," Graargy laughed. "We don't."

Tsretmak began to laugh. Graargy joined him, louder and louder.

Kalistor's heart sank as she watched troopers from the second wave peer over
the edge of the lock doors. They looked down onto the gangway and spotted half-
clad women. They hooted to their companions. *I am a Spectator,* she told herself
grimly, *all I can do now is watch.* Two troopers charged down a seemingly ancient
wooden stairway toward the women. The fake stairway collapsed beneath their
weight. They dropped screaming onto rusty spikes in the lower pool.

Four troopers, still lying in their skiff gathering weapons, looked up in puzzlement when they heard a powerful grating noise. Paving blocks between the two
parallel locks yawned apart, opening a channel two meters wide. Water rushed out
of the filled lock and sprayed into the empty one alongside. The current caught
their skiff. It lurched, scattering troopers to the deck. Kalistor floated centimeters
above their heads as their boat bobbed through the new channel. *I will follow the
action because I must,* she thought. *I cling to this: the difference between Linka and
me is I don't* like *doing this.* The skiff spewed into emptiness. Troopers screamed
as the skiff spun them free, riding a rope of whitewater onto—then *through*—the
hull of the freighter below.

Kalistor whirled. She stared back toward the flooded lock and watched three
other troopers from another skiff lose their lives to the lock-wall trap. One was
tossed overboard and hurled into the empty lock. Two others leapt needlessly from
their skiff into waterline traps.

As quickly as the paving blocks had parted they slid back into place,
stanching the torrent.

Kalistor darted downcanal, stopping above the catwalks. Graargy's women
scattered purposefully down stairways and chutes. The invaders split into squads
and followed. Always older women led the fleeing groups. Young women brought
up the rear, to draw the attackers on.

Verina, lame Selwaga, and one of Blaupek's daughters led three attackers
around a slumping pumphouse. The women rounded a fallen column, panting
troopers just a bodylength behind. Abruptly the squad leader shot forward. A lattice of wooden spikes had snapped from a hollow in the pumphouse wall. Impaled,
arms milling helplessly, the leader arched through open air. His two companions
retreated a step or two. They yanked a tripwire. A rack of bows powered by
stretched vines discharged. Crude, barbed shafts riddled them.

Linka and Blorach sprinted down a broad stone stairway, four troopers at their
heels. The women leapt over a certain step. The troopers didn't. Linka peeked over
her shoulder as two troopers rained into an abattoir amid sharp-pointed logs and
moldy skeletons.

The third and fourth troopers remained. A deadfall rig scattered garden tools
across the stairs, tripping trooper number three. He rolled down the stairs, tum-

bling between—then past— the fleeing women. A metal staff spewed up between paving stones and impaled him. He could still feel the kick Blorach hurled into his groin as the women passed. *One trooper left,* Linka thought. *Oh, there he is!* An ankle snare had whisked the fourth pursuer up and swung him against a watch-tower wall. Ancient stucco failed, revealing barbed blades. He stayed put.

Linka and Blorach split up. Three more troopers spotted Linka. She leapt through a gaping window into an ancient pumphouse. Two meters from the window, an empty doorway beckoned. The troopers lunged toward it, but one threw out his arms. "Don't follow!" he cried. "Could be a trap inside!" *No, the trap's just where you are,* Linka thought. With a sucking sound the eaves above the troopers' heads disgorged their burdens of spikes. The men fell quavering, heads, necks, and shoulders pierced by thumb-thick skewers.

Unbelieving, Duza stared at the slaughter, his vision magnified as high as it would go. He *pov*ed Linka lunge out the other side of the pumphouse—right in front of two more troopers. She knew where to step. They didn't. A hidden mecha-nism sent long, slender whips of oiled metal whirling in a savage arc. Sliced almost through in half a dozen places, the troopers fell heavily. *These are men I lived with,* he thought helplessly. *My people!*

Furious, Neuri Kalistor rotated three meters above the action. Young Ixtlaca, half-naked, seemed cornered on a blind ledge. Behind her yawned an eight-meter drop into greasy water.

Six leering troopers clumped on the stairway above her. One was already unbuckling his body armor.

Ixtlaca stepped onto a visibly loose stone, her back to the abyss. Suddenly she looked down. Bringing her face back up, she flashed her pursuers a look of terror. She pitched backward screaming. Kalistor *pov*ed her hitting the water, then looked back at the troopers.

"Shit, we lost her," hissed one.

"But we learned something," the squad leader roared. "Step *anywhere* but where she stood."

The soldiers minced onto the ledge, avoiding the stone from which Ixtlaca had fallen. Of course that was the wrong move. One trooper hit a trigger block. A barbed shaft leapt upward through his body. Reflex jerked his head back, so the shaft exploded through his right eye.

Two more troopers huddled under the eaves of a slouching pumphouse. It dropped its spikes on them.

Another pair trod breakaway pavement. Anticlimactically, they landed in a soft-bottomed pit just one meter deep. Before they could relish their fortune— much less step out of the pit—a replacement stone lurched into the gap. Sliding on greased ways, propelled by hidden weights, the heavy block severed them at their waists.

Sickened and astonished, Kalistor focused on the squad leader, who was now alone on the ledge. Eight meters below, Ixtlaca was very much alive, swimming energetically toward the bank. "The bitch fooled us," he huffed. He bounded onto the very stone from which Ixtlaca had leapt. "That's the *safe* spot," he grunted. Which it was for waiflike Ixtlaca, who'd taken care to step lightly. When the heavy, armored trooper thudded onto it, its mechanism came alive. The man went airborne. Kalistor followed him down.

The tribeswomen had reached the lower banks. They ran back toward the village, only four of the original seventy attackers still pursuing. Before Kalistor's eyes, they fell one after another to traps along the path.

Disgusted, she lofted up toward the killing knoll. Invisible, she floated a bodylength from Graargy as he boasted to his sons. "Between the first wave and this one, ninety attackers went down! Surely that's a third of Lormatin's able-bodied males. Add in the casualties from that raid last year, and Lormatin's lost more than half his young men. He'll be a blunted threat for at least a generation."

Stunned, Neuri Kalistor drifted back over the lower bank. Harapel was reassembling the women. None had been injured. Linka and Verina helped Ixtlaca from the water, to a chorus of cheers. The men picked their way down from the promontory to embrace their victorious women. The sight of Linka hugging Sydeno triggered a cold, impotent rage.

Linka broke the clinch as quickly as she could, then threaded though the group to capture the jubilation in detail. *Tramir and Neuri didn't get what they wanted. Instead, they spent this morning helping me document a one-sided battle that's sure to be astoundingly popular. I can just imagine the saybacks—the bonuses—from this.*

Linka stared at the sky where Kalistor flew. *"Neuri, I release you,"* she subvocalized. *"Tramir, you, too, I guess. Thanks for the support."* She chuckled cynically. *"I'll see that you get your full shares for backing me up."*

"I don't forjeling believe this," Neuri said to no one in particular.

"Sorry to disappoint you, Neuri. Say, Tramir?"

"What?"

"Told you my tribe would whip your tribe. Strasser out."

"Linka. *Linka!* Dammit!" It was Harapel.

"Sorry, Harapel," said Linka. "My mind wandered."

"Get moving." Harapel jerked her thumb back toward the locks. "We've got seventy more bodies to rifle."

27. Khoren Four

Tarpaper skies pouted slatily as the VIP transport lurched to a stop before Orgena Greder's palace. *VIP transport, my ass,* thought Marnen Incavo resentfully. *More like a prison crawler with the waste oil scraped off and disinfectant masking the stench of plorg.* "We arrive," grated the nearest of four centurions. "Offworlder, don't breathe the air unfiltered." Amid rancid steam the hatch lurched open. Despite lashing rain, the ground was cracked. Raindrops beaded up beneath sickly rainbow coats of oil. One or two stunted trees clawed at life. Otherwise the entry court—*the front garden of, bar none, the planet's grandest mansion,* Incavo reminded himself—was barren of living things.

Incavo clutched the rebreather to his face and sucked air with hard effort. *I can imagine how much material this filter screens out. And the autochthons breathe this hideous stuff their whole lives?* Twenty meters away, blue arcs danced between the tines of a electrified fence. Beyond it, gray men stooped and women trudged, all wheezing. Some led draft animals whose nasal areas bloomed with cancers.

Massive doors opened. Golden light and color blazed their welcome. With a final glance at the sky's gunmetal umbrage, Incavo hurried into the palace.

Bei Hanllei all but coruscated behind a transilluminated desk. Her face was blue-black, her eyes an arresting green. *Had they been that color before?* Incavo couldn't recall. A scanty plaid gown accented Hanllei's curves. "Hom Incavo!" she said with honest surprise.

Incavo shed his caked oilcloth greatcoat to reveal a formal costume. "Tell your employer her friend from Vatican is here with something delightful."

"So I was told," said Orgena Greder. She swirled from a scarlet doorway, ablaze in swoopings of sapphire lamé. One hand held her crystalline cylinder; the ladders of bubbles were just now starting to dissipate. She embraced him. "Welcome to Khoren Four, such as it is."

The storm bayed somberly beyond the great windows of Greder's office suite. *Ahh, backwater planets,* thought Incavo. *Armored limousines. Centurions plated head to toe. Plasteel gates with force generators. And nobody thought to pat me down for weapons!*

Greder plopped next to Incavo on a fur-covered settee. Hanllei served drinks. Greder drained a great draft of Aurhenian gin. "It's always gray here," she said, eyeing the windows with distaste. "Except when it's brown. So, Marnen, what brings you to Khoren Four? Few come here unless they have to."

"Unless one wants to reestablish contact with a valued friend," Incavo replied with an oily smile.

"Not even then," countered Greder. "I admit it, I've made a ruin of this world. Eleven days out of twelve, I'm not here myself. Too much pollution. Too many twisted autochthons who want my life. I stay at my terraformed resort on the sunward moon of Khoren Five."

"Yes," Incavo agreed. "But you're here today."

Greder took another gulp of the churning liquor. Her implants would neutralize its soporific effect. "You came onplanet yesterday and checked into a hotel," she said after a moment. "You arrived the same day I did. But no one knows my schedule."

Incavo drained three fingers of ouzo in a searing gulp, reminding her that he, too, possessed the costly implants. "I knew."

"You're more than a dealer in rare books. I knew that even on Vatican."

"I deal in something more universal than rare books. I trade information."

"I see." Greder smiled thinly. "The first piece of information you can give me is why you came."

Incavo nodded. "Very well, and it's the last piece of information I will *give*. If you're still curious why the Universal Catholic Church so abruptly ceased to entertain your claims for the godhead of Ul' Fze B'Khraa, I have the answer. I will share it, for a price."

She clutched his hand. "Dear friend, can you not simply tell me?"

"Orgena, friendship is friendship." He looked at her harshly. "And a great screw in nulgrav is a great screw in nulgrav. But what I have to offer is something else. *Electrifying* information. You must be prepared to pay richly. And even then, you must summon the courage to witness something many Galactics would find unsavory."

She regarded him closely. "I shall put your bravado to the test. *Bei!*"

Hanllei emerged from nowhere with a tray. Theatrically, Greder pulled off her signet ring and deposited it there. "Four hundred million Galactic to Hom Incavo, *if* I am satisfied with what he reveals." She swiveled her gaze back to Incavo. "Satisfactory?"

Incavo raised an eyebrow. He made no reply.

"Very well," she said to punish his silence. "*Three* hundred million."

Incavo smiled bloodlessly. "Four is accepted."

"Four, then," Greder murmured. "If it takes my breath away."

Hanllei marched out of the chamber with the ring. Incavo didn't notice Greder subvocalize a command that locked the office doors.

Incavo reached inside his tunic. Impossibly, he pulled out a valise half a meter tall by more than a meter wide. "Vanisher," he said unnecessarily. He ran his thumb along its edge. The lip glowed crimson. It opened to reveal another valise almost as big as a man. Incavo thumbed *that* open . . .

. . . and withdrew a simple senso player.

"You could have brought just the wafer," Greder protested. "Life is crude on Khoren Four, but not savage. We have senso players."

"Not like this one." Incavo circled from the settee and bid her stretch out there.

"Oh, I haven't laid flat on my back to *pov* a senso in . . . well, never mind how long."

Incavo completed his adjustments. "You won't wish to miss a nuance of this. Though as I said, you must be prepared to witness something offensive." He thumbed *Play.*

Being-thereness claimed Greder.

She *pov*ed the playback for about a minute before she shot bolt upright.

Incavo was getting used to the pattern.

"Rybczynsky!" she spat. "And . . . Ato Semuga?"

Incavo nodded. "You never met Semuga."

"But I did my research." Only then did it occur to Greder to wonder how Incavo knew that she and Semuga had never met.

"And His Holiness, of course," Incavo pointed out.

"Unfiltered," said Greder with admiration. "No logos, no heralds—the actual faces of these powerful people. You may well earn your pay this day, Hom Incavo. Who's the Steward?"

Incavo almost leered. "Fram Galbior."

Greder nodded in wonderment. *What could the Galaxy's greatest mathematician have to do with these Vatican toads—much less with the costly failure of my bid to authenticate B'Khraa?* "Someone else paid for this," she said darkly. "You betray your original patron by bringing this here."

Incavo shrugged. "Seldom does one develop information of such quality—to satisfy a taste as specialized as my original employer's—and then realize one knows someone else to whom the same information will be valuable—in another way, of course." He smiled hollowly. "Fear not, your purposes will not conflict with his."

"Bold turncoat." Greder smiled. She lay back again. "Resume your playback."

There they were: Rybczynsky, Semuga, Galbior, and the pope, all seated at a gilded table under pistachio skies. Greder watched through the senses of Incavo's spy.

Modest flipped an encouraging hand at Galbior; to the mathematician he seemed like an ancient patriarch urging wedding guests to join an unfamiliar dance. "Please, Hom Galbior. Say in open language what you have come here to say to Us. In whatever words you choose, begin."

Galbior began: "When I was eighteen, I perfected the equilibrational calculus. I learned to predict when and where the Tuezi would break through into our universe. Much of my manhood went to waste as I reveled in a hero's pleasures. By some miracle, my dissipations did not blunt my intellect. Late in life I tired of being a perpetual guest of honor. I trained my sights on spiritual things." He waved a deprecating hand at his Steward's garb. "You see one result. Cardinal Rybczynsky has asked me here to share with you another."

The Pope nodded, fascinated. "Go on."

"We Galactics take our Catholic faith seriously once it claims us, Holiness."

"A fact that brings Us joy, Steward Galbior."

"The mathematician in me grew obsessed with the idea of how God sends His Son from world to world, Incarnation to Incarnation, now to one side of the Galaxy, next to another, now five Incarnations in sixty years, then none for three centuries. Why? Surely the author of Creation does not discharge so meaningful an office capriciously."

The pope nodded.

"In a way they are so much alike," Galbior continued. "The unknown warriors dispatch their Tuezis; God dispatches His Son." Galbior leaned forward and eyed the scuttling servants again. "Your Holiness is certain I should continue?"

"We are," Modest replied.

"Pardon my phrasing it this way, Holiness, but the question of the order of the Incarnations was so much like the Tuezi problem I solved in my youth. In each, an ineffable, transcendently powerful entity dispatches emissaries through space and time."

The pope tilted his head toward Galbior. "A problem you have solved?"

Galbior nodded. "I believe so, Holiness."

"As do I," Rybczynsky added. "Steward Galbior has mapped all known Incarnations of the Cosmic Christ, and made sense of their distribution."

The Pope nodded. "So we—that is, not only We Ourself, but all humankind—are vouchsafed a new glimpse into the mind of the Almighty."

Galbior smiled. "Such, apparently, is His Will."

"Steward Galbior. According to your mathematics, how has the Church done in separating the true Incarnations of Christ from the craven imitators?"

"Fairly well, Holiness," Galbior replied. "My calculations confirm all the Incarnations recognized by Holy Mother Church, except for two."

The pope raised an eyebrow at Galbior. Glanced toward Rybczynsky. "Your calculations *disconfirm* two Incarnations that the Church has recognized?"

"Unfortunately so," Rybczynsky answered. "That leper on Vyrdis Ten, and—"

Modest raised a slender hand. "Let them stand. Say no more about them. Expunge any mention of their disconfirmations from these reports."

"A wise decision, Holiness," Semuga bubbled. "One I would have advised had you not already reached it."

"But Holiness!" Galbior exclaimed. "They are not true Christs! The Catholics of two worlds will misdirect their prayers."

The Pope smiled thinly, as if to say, *Oh, these literal-minded offworld converts can be cloying at times.* "Fear not, Steward. God will recognize their good intentions." Seeing that Galbior still doubted, the pope waggled a knowing hand. "We will talk to Him about it."

Galbior blinked. He relaxed in his seat.

Fighting a grin, Modest lifted another document from the table. "Now, Steward Galbior. What about this loathsome rustic from, where is it, Khoren Six?"

"Son of a bitch!" Greder cried aloud from her senso trance. Incavo smirked, knowing exactly where she was in the playback.

Rybczynsky spoke up. "Khoren Four, actually, Holiness. That vile industrialist Orgena Greder." He peered at his own notes. "Advocating for the godhead of one Ul' Fze B'Khraa."

"Ah, yes," breathed the pope. "And what do Hom Galbior's calculations tell us about this B'Khraa?"

"For certain," said Galbior, "he is no Christ."

"That is well. We always thought him a buffoon." Modest thought a moment. "Alois, what has Fem Greder spent at Vatican Center in the course of her lobbying?"

"Five hundred thirty-two billion," Rybczynsky reported. "Give or take."

Modest cradled his hands. "That's enough. Protract this no further. Tell her We have decided."

Rybczynsky matched the pope's cradled-hand pose and smiled through lips drawn tight. "I already have."

"Very good," breathed the pope. He eyed Semuga, then Galbior. "We gather there is more."

Galbior stood. He smoothed the brocade of his robe. "Your Holiness, it is one thing to separate the true from the false footprints of Divinity." He pulled in a deep breath. "It is another to say where—and when—the Divine Foot will tread next."

The pope blinked. He glanced at Rybczynsky and Semuga. Both cardinals seemed ready to burst with hidden knowledge. The pope stared at Galbior. Galbior stared back leadenly. *The learning that so delights the cardinals is a burden to him,* Modest realized.

Modest rose from his own chair and rushed forward to clasp Galbior's hands in his own. "Steward Galbior," he whispered, "you have *predicted* the next Incarnation?"

Galbior nodded somberly. "I have."

✦ ✦ ✦

Orgena Greder half-rose from the settee, still in senso trance. Gently Incavo brushed his hand across her brow. She relaxed and surrendered herself anew to the astounding playback.

Incavo had defeated the thumbpad lock on Greder's liquor cabinet. *Screw ouzo*, he thought. Instead he filled his tumbler with Guerechtian *aqua vitae*—so valuable that a single bottle would purchase some planets—and drank deep.

View on, dear Orgena, he thought. *As a Terran bard once said, you ain't seen nothing yet.*

28. Jaremi Four—Northern Hemisphere

G o . . . or dig in? The decision was Parek's. It would have to be made quickly. Sparks swarmed the predawn sky, drowning out the aurora. Ruth, Dultav, Ulf, and Chagrin clustered in a crescent below the powerhouse steps. From their position half a dozen pockets of wildfire were already visible. From his higher vantage atop the girders, Parek saw most clearly how little time remained.

Yet his eyes were riveted on Dultav's. Ruth flickered her gaze from one man to the other. Through her eyes the Galaxy *poved* their battle of wills.

At last Parek dropped his eyelids. His features formed a mask of calm purpose. "Ulf!" Parek called in a booming voice.

"Yes?" Ulf replied.

Parek's voice rang, empty of doubt. "You asked what we must do." He raised an arm. Pointed downstream. "We go. We will run before the fire. We shall *be* like the fire in the way we spread my word."

"That is a pail of shit!" Dultav shouted. He stood commandingly in the powerhouse doorway. "It's self-indulgent, nonsensical garbage," he raged. "The Arn Parek I knew would have been the first to recognize it! This must stop *now!*"

Parek crossed his arms. "You can't see it, can you? I can't stop it anymore. I don't have the right."

"You've given yourself over to power. It'll be the most fleeting power you can imagine." Dultav extended one fist and pantomimed a crushing movement. "You'll be the *bohtti* sprout."

"I pursue something real here."

"It pursues *you*. Only you've stopped running. You were just a scrawny grad student with no future, no tools for survival. Those who survived the Great Dismay"—he gestured toward Ulf and Chagrin—"did it through strength and ruthlessness, treachery and violence. But not you!"

Ruth scuttled from one side of the staircase to the other, staring up at Dultav, listening for the *verify* signal. Dultav strode one, then two steps down the stairway.

"No, not you," he snarled. "Arn Parek would survive with an *idea.*" The next tread squeaked sourly beneath his weight. "In a time when ideas were worthless Arn Parek took one and made it work."

Ruth risked a flicker-glance: Parek stood impassive on the girder, seemingly waiting for the storm of Dultav's rage to pass.

Dultav descended a fourth step and raised tight fists toward his onetime student. "Your *religion*, Arn! That was your idea. That was the thing *you made up*. Built from first foundations, each doctrine precisely calculated for its effect on the poor hapless victims you needed to fool—"

Later, when Ruth restudied her journals of this moment, she would wonder why she hadn't heard the steamrifle's report. The first instant contained no sound, just the blue-white flare of the explosive round's detonation. The sickening *thump* came an instant later, in step with the image of Willim Dultav's chest exploding in a miasma of blood and bone flecks and bits of meat.

Next came Ruth's own scream.

Hollowed, Dultav's body skidded up the stairs. The head struck the powerhouse floor and bounced twice. Flames danced from a chest wound as wide and tall as a laborer's splayed hands. Dultav's extremities trembled briefly and then fell limp.

Somehow Ruth forced herself to *pov* the others. Parek stood immobile. The clean-shaven triangle above his forehead emphasized the horrified bulging of his eyes. Ulf stared at Dultav's body and then back at Chagrin.

Smiling, Chagrin lowered the antiarmor rifle. Two graceful steps brought him to Parek's feet. He arranged himself on a low girder and lay the weapon across his lap. He drew his knife, found a bit of wooden trim on the gun, and began to cut a notch.

Working the knife, he raised idyllic eyes toward Parek. "I'm sorry, lord." His voice was serene. "You were saying?"

Parek looked back toward Dultav's smoldering remains. Later, Ruth would wonder that it never occurred to Parek to quote his own vision speech from the day of the powerhouse firefight. "A dead man. He lay sprawled, hollowed and dead, on a stairway," the text had run. "The corpse, the husk of the old guard." *Those words mean nothing,* she would think. *Cruel coincidence, nothing more.* "The butchered remains of all that once seemed right, and true, and meaningful." *How strange that amid all the folly and pain that lay ahead, no Jaremian ever contrived to find a prophecy in those words.* No, that dishonor would wait for others.

Parek folded up on himself and began to weep.

Ruth studied Chagrin's face. The disciple shouldered his freshly notched weapon. He climbed pitted steel to sit beside Parek. Reverently he took the crumpled messiah in his arms.

Ruth's vision clouded with tears. *Why does it surprise me how terribly this hurts?* Chagrin rocked Parek for minutes until both Parek and Ruth had wept themselves out.

When Chagrin spoke it was half a plea, half a command. "Lead us."

Parek chuckled darkly. "So soon am I the *bohtti* sprout? No, Chagrin. I lead no one."

Chagrin snapped his eyes to Ulf, as though for confirmation. Slowly the gaunt killer pressed his gun barrel against Parek's neck. It was still warm. Parek watched the winkies flicker down the barrel's length. They pulsed a solid line of green.

Silently Ulf climbed opposite Chagrin. He swept his rifle barrel into Parek's cheek.

"Lead us, lord," Ulf hissed.

Trapped between the guerrillas' guns, Parek shuddered.

He rose and cast his eyes about.

Listlessly he nodded in a direction that lay roughly downstream. Ulf and Chagrin stood. They escorted Parek off the steelwork and onto the hillside.

The air swirled not only with sparks, now, but flickering chips thick as a finger. Ruth had sidestepped halfway to the dam top. Wan light brightened the sky above the clifftop to her right. Her conscious mind was trying to decide what to do next, but her movement suggested the decision was already partly made.

Below her, Parek, Ulf, and Chagrin were moving out, taking their first hesitant steps down—*what had Parek called it?*—"a new trail."

Parek took point. The guerrillas flanked him a pace or two behind, their weapons trained casually but unmistakably at his back. Though Parek walked first, there could be no question who was actually in charge.

Twenty meters away, Ulf stopped the group with a grunt. As one the trio spun back to face Ruth. "Coming with us?" Ulf called.

Ruth recalled a snippet of Spectator philosophy the Academy professors so loved to roll between their lips. "If one has an option that benefits one's upper self, the outer self is wise to take it." Her upper self—Ruth Griszam, OmNet artisan, Terran and Spectator—was better off not following these three into whatever awaited them. For her outer self—for Ruth in fatigues and shift and fur wrap, Ruth the scrabbler among the ruins of Jaremi Four—the choice was clear.

"No," she shouted back. "I don't. . . ." She clenched her fists. "I don't believe."

Ulf raised an eyebrow. "You will. Someday." He gestured. The little group about-faced and continued on its way.

Ruth watched the swaying branches where the group vanished from sight. She felt a sudden wash of hatred—not just for Ulf and Chagrin, but for Parek, too—for Parek and the psychological strings he'd pulled so carelessly, and for all he'd let himself become.

Still unsure what she wanted next, Ruth sprinted back downhill. It rained flaming chips two fingers thick now. Some had ignited dry shrubs near the powerhouse. She climbed the stairs and squatted in the doorway above Dultav's body. An ember had lodged in his boot, the fatigue pants smoldered. She gripped his left hand. It was cold and heavy.

"I loved you, Willim," she rasped. *I would have run with you,* she added silently.

Grimly Ruth plundered what remained of the corpse. In one pants pocket, she found a small book. *He must have found it on his last trip to the library.* It was useless now. She flipped it away without bothering to see where it landed.

Time to go, Ruth thought. Before she could leave, no fewer than three bugs *nudged* her. Ulf and Chagrin and Parek were coming back! *Are they crazy?* She scrambled into cover and watched through bugs as the trio sprinted a third of the way back up the hillside. Ulf pointed to the powerhouse's exterior wall, five levels below Ruth's position. Chagrin selected his most powerful shell and chambered it. He fired the antiarmor rifle. A meter-and-a-half wide breach thundered open in the wall. All three vanished inside.

What can justify such risk? Ruth wondered. *Why just there?* She called up her powerhouse schematic: Ulf had selected the point closest to the storeroom where Parek had them hide those mysterious biologicals. MOTHER MATTER. *It must be important. I wonder who made the decision to come back for it.*

Less than a minute later, the trio emerged. Each man carried a dented trunk on his back. Between them, Ulf and Chagrin lugged the rack of cylinders. They melted back into the trees.

She discontinued her journal and posted a notice that this storyline was at an end—at least, for her. She appended a routine request for new assignments to bid on. *If they send me any, will I bid?*

Ruth sprinted out, down the stairs around Dultav's smoking body, and up the hill. At one subvocalized command, her vanisher valise self-destructed in its hiding place deep inside the dam. Another command obliterated her scattered bugs. Nothing remained that might tell other autochthons that Galactic voyeurs shared their world.

No doubt, she thought, *this final installment is even now being processed into nine thousand-odd editions geared to each of the Galaxy's conventional—and, for that matter, not so conventional—interest groups. What was it they used to say about old Chicago? Only the squeal goes to waste.*

Atop the dam, Ruth looked back. Ulf, Chagrin, and Parek's route through the trees was now aflame. *No matter,* she thought. *I meant to go any way but that.* She chose a direction based on two requirements. Her path had to be safe, and it had to lead *away* from the trio's last-seen bearing.

Crying again, she plunged into the woods.

29. Khoren Four

Marnen Incavo lolled in an overstuffed chair, savoring Guerechtian *aqua vitae* and watching Orgena Greder *pov* the rest of the papal meeting.

"You predicted the next Incarnation," Pope Modest stammered, slowly resuming his seat.

Citron highlights from the Vatican sky danced in Fram Galbior's graying hair. "The next several, actually, Holiness."

"Confine yourself to the next one. When?"

"I believe it has already occurred."

Modest was silent half a minute. "Tell Us more."

"If I interpret the calculations properly, this Christ has taken flesh, but has not begun His public ministry." Galbior ran a hand through his hair. "There is some uncertainty."

"It was the same with the Tuezi," Semuga explained. "Galbior predicted the arrival of his first Tuezi only within a week, the second within a day, the third within four hours. Now he calls them to within a picosecond."

"As each predicted event occurs, I conform the higher-order terms of my formulae to the actual outcome," Galbior explained. "Accuracy rises exponentially. That is how the equilibrational calculus works."

"I see," breathed Modest. He was not sure he really understood at all. "Today, you cannot say this Christ's age. But after a few of your predicted Incarnations have come to pass—"

Galbior's eyes blazed. "By the fourth one, Holiness, I will predict the time of birth to within three hundred thousandths of a second. Accuracy will continue to improve thereafter, but. . . ." Galbior shrugged.

Modest nodded sagely. "For the purpose, that seems all the accuracy one is likely to need." He leaned back in his chair, cradling his index fingers before pursed lips. "So, Steward Galbior, with what accuracy have you predicted *where* our Lord has sent His son?"

"I know the planet," said Galbior.

"Holiness," Rybczynsky hissed. He had set up a data display unit.

"Brief Us," commanded the pope.

Over the gilded table a three-dimensional image took form. It was a world, mottled white at each pole, brown and green between. A jagged strip of ocean girdled the whole equator. "This," intoned Rybczynsky, "is Jaremi Four, an Enclave world in Sector Upsilon."

"Sector Upsilon," breathed the pope. "So distant."

"Exploration of Sector Upsilon only began in earnest sixty years ago," Rybczynsky confirmed. "Even today, less than half of it has been catalogued. The Jaremi system was discovered about twenty-five years ago. The star bears the name by which most of the autochthons on the fourth planet refer to their homeworld." Datacrawls unfurled around the planet's image. "The vital statistics are earthlike, like most worlds where the Harvesters planted humans. There are two principal continents, one in the north and one in the south. Each subtends more than three hundred degrees of longitude. Between them an equatorial sea encircles the planet. Its width varies from a maximum of forty degrees of latitude to a minimum of eighteen . . . *here.*" Twin highlights flickered at the tips of two opposing points of land. They reached for each other like the halves of a sundered isthmus. "And there are also polar seas."

Rybczynsky's fingers danced on controls. The tridee view receded to show Jaremi Four and its sun in their celestial neighborhood. "The Jaremi system's closest neighbor is Cohller 5114, a cataclysmic binary star given to exceptionally energetic outbursts at irregular intervals. It lies just four hundred thirty-six light days above the planet's north pole."

"The people see the outbursts?" Modest asked. "Like novae?"

"No," Rybczynsky replied. "The events consist mostly of hard ultraviolet and gamma radiation. Invisible themselves, they trigger spectacular polar auroras. At the height of a typical discharge, the aurora can extend well south of the equator. To inhabitants of Jaremi Four's northern continent, aurora is a nightly companion. To inhabitants of the southern continent, it is usually a brilliant flicker on the horizon. The effect on patterns of religious belief is about as you might expect."

Modest nodded. "In the north, aerial or celestial deities. In the south, fire gods who live beyond the northern horizon."

"Exactly. Regarding the planet's history, until about three hundred years ago Jaremi Four supported a vibrant culture based primarily on hydropower, steam technology, and very elementary electronics. There were sophisticated agriculture and husbandry, frequent surface travel between the continents, rudimentary mass communications, and well-developed arts, in addition to basic understandings of physics and astronomy. A little aviation, also, if memory serves. If PeaceForce scouts had discovered the planet then, it surely would have qualified for full membership in the Confetory."

"Yet today Jaremi Four is Enclaved."

Rybczynsky called up tactical displays that simulated the events he described. "Three centuries ago, Jaremi system suffered a Tuezi strike. Planets six and seven were turned to cinders. Jaremi Four was not hit too harshly, as such things go. Nonetheless, the southern landmass absorbed several trains of medium-power volleys—not enough to compromise climate or atmospheric chemistry, but sufficient to devastate the human infrastructure. Civilization collapsed quickly across the south. The food chain was contaminated with toxic agents whose impact on health and fertility magnifies in each generation."

"Then with the passage of time the south must become a lifeless place?" Modest asked.

"Not necessarily. Just before the culture fell, agricultural researchers in the south perfected a food plant ideal for the trying times ahead. Known as *fhlet,* it provides nearly complete human nutrition. It has few parasites and grows prolifically almost anywhere with little tending. Without *fhlet,* the southern landmass would already be depopulated."

Modest pursed his lips. "What of the north?"

"It has *fhlet* too."

Modest scowled. "The damage, Alois. The damage."

Rybczynsky called up new sims. "Tuezi damage to the northern landmass was lighter. The further north one went, the less noticeable it was that anything had happened. For a period, most northern societies remained relatively intact. Relief missions were sent south for a century. But the devastation was too great for full recovery. Inexorably, the stable polities collapsed, the last of them just fifteen years ago. Still, many northerners older than age thirty still remember living under civilized conditions."

Modest raised one eyebrow. "You're saying that at the moment of its first Galactic encounter, Jaremi Four still supported pockets of civilization."

Rybczynsky nodded grimly. "Scattered precincts, impossible to preserve even at the Protectorate level without immediate and massive intervention. The majority of the population was already savage—in the words of the Enclave criterion, 'manifestly unready, technologically, culturally, and economically, to encounter Galactic culture.' So the decision was made. The last sparks of Jaremian civilization were allowed to flicker out. The planet was quarantined under Enclave. Today, all is savagery on both continents, the principal difference being that the ruins on the northern landmass are more recent."

Modest shook his head with exquisite slowness, pondering the implications of Enclave. "It is forbidden for any Jaremian to be told of the existence of Galactic civilization. No Galactic may interfere in autochthonous developments on Jaremi Four, however wonderful or hideous those events may be."

"Precisely," Rybczynsky replied.

"But if they are officially sanctioned and discreet, Galactics may go to Jaremi Four and observe."

Rybczynsky nodded. "And some do. Like most Enclave worlds, Jaremi Four has a scientific station at a location inaccessible to autochthons. I believe it's at the bottom of the north polar sea. Its staff of approximately two hundred is dominated by astronomers and anthropologists—the former studying the binary star, the latter studying native populations."

"Is that the only category of sanctioned observers?"

"No," Rybczynsky replied. "OmNet deploys some forty Spectators on Jaremi Four. About half fly about no-vis from tribe to tribe. The rest pass as autochthons, and have insinuated themselves into various communities on both continents."

Ato Semuga spoke. "Your Holiness may remember Jaremi Four. It was there, three years ago, that the hardline Spectator Linka Strasser declined to intercede to save her colleague Laz Kalistor from torture, death, and the irreparable destruction of his body."

"Ah, yes," said the pope. "The incident sparked theological discourse regarding the moral rectitude of the Enclave Statute."

"Indeed," confirmed Semuga. "It is now the problem scenario most frequently cited in applied ethics courseware."

Rybczynsky shut off the data display unit. The Pope swung back to face Galbior. "And you believe that Christ has even now taken flesh upon that world?"

Galbior nodded gravely.

"An Enclave world," Modest mused, "a place where Galactics cannot go." The Pope cast piercing glances first at Rybczynsky, then at Semuga. Each nodded his confirmation of Galbior's conclusion.

Semuga ended his own gesture with something more: a raised eyebrow, a shrug, a faint one-sided smile—as if to say, *Regarding our inability to go there, Holiness, I have some ideas.* . . .

Pope Modest stood and shivered. He made a leisurely sign of the cross. "Into such a maelstrom our Lord has chosen to send His Son? Ah, well, He has done no less before."

Orgena Greder opened her eyes. She sat up facing Incavo. "Who knows these things?"

"The Catholics, of course. And the Mormons."

"The *Mormons?*" Greder was incredulous.

"You're paying me for truth. They're the ones who paid me first."

"The Mormons are brain-dead," said Greder, rising. "It's been seventy-five years since the LDS had a shred of vigor."

Incavo frowned. "Some Mormons are different."

"What concerns me most, dear Marnen, is that no one *else* come to know it. You betrayed your Mormon employer. Why not betray me?" From the folds of her lamé dress she produced a slim, exotic-looking blaster and leveled it at Incavo's chest.

Incavo had maintained his battle reflexes. A few centimeters of Guerechtian *aqua vitae* remained in his tumbler. He hurled it at Greder's eyes and leapt from the chair. He rolled up on one knee, his own mini blaster drawn. Before she'd even turned to track his movement, he put a blaster beam through her left ear.

Literally.

The beam passed unimpeded through Greder's head. It struck a mirror behind her. Glass clattered across the marble floor.

Orgena Greder was unharmed. Not only was she unmarked by the blaster bolt, she showed no sign of having been distressed by the eyeful of harsh liquor. In fact, her face wasn't wet.

"Displacers," she said dryly. "Great technology." Her image shimmered away and reappeared in another part of the room. "I'm over here."

Incavo fired again. Another direct hit. An ornate chair behind her leapt across the room, trailing draperies of sparks. Greder laughed. Her image flickered out, only to reappear elsewhere. Incavo fired again, destroying a richly filigreed armoire. "Oh, too bad," she pouted. "I liked that piece."

Greder sauntered across the room, clutching her peculiar weapon casually. Incavo tracked her with his blaster, darting from cover to cover with increasing desperation. "I know what you're thinking," she said liltingly. "You're thinking that Khoren Four is a relatively poor planet, about as low on the development spectrum as a world can be and still be a Confetory Affiliate. You're thinking that displacers are not an appropriate technology for my little domain."

"Right," he mumbled, thinking feverishly. *She never looks at me,* he thought. *The direction in which she looks most frequently—the direction in which she usually points her weapon—that must be where I actually am relative to her. If I do the geometry right, I can figure out her position. . . .*

"Khoren Four could never afford displacers in every police station or mine foreman's office." Greder laughed. "But you see, Khoren Four is not a progressive world. It's a tyranny, and I'm the tyrant. Khoren Four can easily afford *just one* displacer."

Incavo solved the geometry problem. He whirled and fired toward where he thought she was. Flames lashed uselessly against the room's far wall.

Greder still stood before him, untouched.

"Nice try," she purred. "But you know what? I looked at my finances and decided I could afford *two* displacers." Incavo stared straight ahead. He watched Greder's finger tighten on the trigger of the pistol that so deceptively pointed to his left. An angry purple beam erupted *from* the empty air to Incavo's left, encasing him in mantles of lightning.

Incavo had an instant to recognize that if Greder had used *two* displacers in series, reconstructing her position based on her direction of gaze would have led him to fire in exactly the wrong direction.

He had the same instant to recognize that Greder had shot him with a ravisher beam.

Like displacers, the ravisher was wildly inappropriate technology for Khoren Four. It was also one of the most agonizing ways ever developed to kill a human being. At handgun power, the energy cocoon took almost a second to coalesce around him, after which Incavo would never recognize anything again.

He jerked and writhed as the cocoon spat out platoons of violet lightning to ravage his body. It wouldn't let him fall. Even more, it kept him excruciatingly conscious. He felt every static discharge, every explosion of his flesh, with extraordinary vividness. Pain*pain***pain***PAIN***PAIN!** His left knee vaporized. His skin bubbled and peeled back in a dozen places. His jaws fragmented. The shards blasted through his cheeks. At last his ribcage blew sideways, scattering gouts of flesh and internal organs on which independent traceries of purple lightning danced.

Anguish*torment*misery**gushing**SPURTING*deluging****PAIN!*** The agony lasted thirty seconds. It seemed longer. When the cocoon twinkled out, what remained of Incavo fell in pieces.

Orgena Greder shimmered into visibility at the place from which the ravisher bolt had erupted. She looked down, frowning. Incavo's right arm and hand were still connected. Greder never understood why he died with the index finger of that hand making stabbing motions, as though it searched for some invisible switch.

When the time came for Marnen Incavo to *pov* his own death, there was no way to toggle off the agony.

Someone was ringing the entry buzzer. Greder drew another pistol from her gown; this one was a PeaceForce-issue disinto. The gun projected a slender greenish beam. It struck one of Incavo's legs, sampling his physical composition. Next came a whitish flash. Then everything in the room pertaining to Marnen Incavo—including, she realized with a brief pang of regret, his senso player and that wafer of the Papal meeting—simultaneously disappeared in swirls of gray-white haze. The swirls marked the boundaries of force fields, Greder knew, which protected her from the radiation produced by loosing all the subatomic bonds within Incavo's body and effects. *I've learned what I need from Marnen's senso,* she rationalized. *And this way, no one else will ever see it.* When the haze glimmered out, there was no trace of Incavo and his property, nor any forensic clues such as char marks to betoken the manner of his disposal.

Precisely because it was so useful for committing—or concealing—perfect crimes, there was no weapon the PeaceForce worked more diligently to keep out of civilian hands than the disinto. *But of course,* she chuckled to herself, *tyrant that I am, I only needed one.*

The door buzzer pealed continuously now. Greder holstered her weapons. From an end table she retrieved her bubble cylinder. She clutched its base in thumbs and forefingers and raised it toward her face. She willed fans of bubbles into motion. Their dance filled her vision with shimmering synthetic movement, her mind with childlike joy. Smiling noncommittally, she subvocalized a command.

At last the portal opened. Bei Hanllei rustled in. She took in the smoky air, the damage, and Greder, standing placidly, absorbed in her cylinder.

"Hom Incavo had to leave us," Greder said at last, holding out her free hand for the signet ring. "You have seen none of this."

"Of course," said Hanllei, which didn't keep her from looking behind sofas for Incavo's body.

Greder strode to the panoramic windows. She surveyed her putrid capital with satisfaction. *The greatest prize in human history,* she thought, *on an Enclave world. So messy that will be!*

One of the problems with opening a door is that one never knows who will come in. Hanllei had stopped searching for Incavo and started picking up drink glasses instead, when Ul' Fze B'Khraa entered, his mantle of bird skulls clattering. Greder's claims for his godhood shattered, B'Khraa was in some ways valueless to her. But many miners were of his clan; killing him would spark riots. On the other hand, B'Khraa had seen too much on Vatican to be returned to his people. So he remained in Greder's palace, barely tolerated, a perpetual boarder without portfolio. In one hand B'Khraa held some greasy bit of animal tissue. In the other, a senso wafer. "Acch, Orgena," he growled, "You must see this!"

Greder scowled. "Pigeon meat?"

"No, the wafer!"

She took it. "And it is?"

"An entertainment feed from OmNet," B'Khraa grunted.

Greder snorted. "Entertainment? Why would I want to *pov* that?"

"You like this god-man stuff." B'Khraa smiled ruthlessly. "Wait till you see what just happened on Jaremi Four."

Part Two

. . . there is plenty of evidence that new religions are not difficult to concoct and that followers are not difficult to find.

—John F. Schumaker

30. Senso Broadcast, Galaxy Wide • Origin: Jaremi Four—Northern Hemisphere

The Spectator had assumed deep cover as a foot soldier. His *pov* clattered through cancered woodlands. It was just past dusk. Beyond the treetops, the aurora swirled. Several paces ahead ran a slender figure: the commander. *Ulf.* He wore body armor festooned with shriveled heads and hands and genitals. Behind him the Spectator felt (rather than saw) a presence drawing close. It was the prophet—*The Word Among Us.*

Few Spectators had gotten this close to Arn Parek in the year and a half since Ruth Griszam had walked away from the Galaxy's biggest story.

Ulf drew up behind a gnarled tree. A hundred soldiers scuttled into ranks behind him: the new "church militant."

149

Beyond a final line of trees, a clearing could be seen. A dozen ancient landing craft had been converted into a crude settlement. White plumes betrayed the location of crude cook stoves.

The Spectator's legs and back ached. His exhaustion was palpable.

Arn Parek edged around the Spectator. Disguising resignation as composure, Parek gave the order Ulf expected. "Like the fire, spread my word."

A steamrifle shell found a cook stove's fuel tank. Fire bloomed. A woman zigzagged, sheeted in flame.

The other soldiers drew their weapons—steamrifles, carbines, clubs, blades. Those with guns fired a single volley from cover. Three running villagers fell gouting blood.

Four musicians swaggered forward. They wore frame-and-harness contraptions on their chests. The frames were studded with irregular lengths of metal pipe. The musicians drew thin metal tubes from holsters on their hips and struck them against their improvised bell lyres. They chimed the five-then-three cadence Parek taught all his followers. *Clang-shang-ralang. Clang-shang-ralang. Clang-shang-ralang. Clang-shang-ralang. Clang-shang-ralang. Clang-shang-ralang. Clang-shang-ralang. Clang-shang-ralang.*

The chiming told the villagers which army this was. Panic bloomed.

Ulf chopped at the air with one hand. "Attack!"

Howling, the little army sprinted forward. The Spectator willed tiredness away and hurled himself into the clearing. His *pov* presented staccato glimpses of carnage.

Ahead, another soldier swung his carbine as a club. A village teen caromed to the dirt, hands cupped over a pulped knee.

The Spectator ran across the body of a fallen villager. She'd been shot in the face. Her jaw gave way under his boot. The Spectator twisted, kept his balance, and ran on.

A grimy youth charged forward waving a club. The Spectator fired. The youth jerked backward. Tumbled shrieking into a campfire.

Ahead, to the right, a soldier sprawled, screaming, clawing at his thigh. A *whizz* fled past the Spectator's right ear. "Take cover!" Ulf called. The Spectator flattened in high grass. Poor protection. All there was.

Fifteen yards away, three youths with hunting rifles hid behind a tree trunk as thick as a man stood tall. They were the source of the hostile fire.

To the Spectator's right, a soldier chambered a high-yield shell. Explosive rounds were precious; he aimed carefully. Fired. The bole that had been the youths' cover became a killing storm. They fell jointless, streaming blood.

The soldiers rose and resumed their charge. There was little further resistance.

The Spectator followed two other soldiers into a hovel. Lanterns flickered dimly. A scrawny tradesman bawled for mercy. To the left, a thatched screen leaned against a wall at an unnatural angle. *Someone behind it?* The sergeant rammed his rifle butt through the screen.

A rag-clad boy spewed out, six or seven years old.

"Hide from me, boy?" The sergeant snapped his rifle butt down once. *Hip.* Twice. *Left cheek.* The child pulled in on himself like a worm stepped on after morning rain.

"My son!" Howling, the tradesman lunged toward a nearby table. He sought a knife. Before he could clutch it, a soldier plunged his gun barrel into the tradesman's mouth. The tradesman crumpled, headless, fountaining.

The soldiers searched for loot. Overturned a small stove. Found nothing. Crouching, they scuttled out, leaving the ruined boy to the flames.

Outside, the encampment was a maelstrom of screams and smoke. Parek strode regally among the corpses, his ivory body armor spattered with blood. "We acted because we must," Parek boomed. "We must spread the word, spread our reach. That's the only way."

Most soldiers ignored him. Already they'd lined up at the posts to which the few surviving women had been lashed.

The Spectator had set about rifling the dead. He pretended not to look, yet attended closely as Ulf trod by. Parek dogged his steps. "I keep telling you, Ulf. Pillage first, *then* burn. We're supposed to be spreading my Word."

"We need safety, too," Ulf rasped.

"Safety! You can't make converts when everyone's dead."

Ulf and Parek continued on their way. The Spectator shrugged and went back to rifling a corpse.

Metal on metal. A different sound behind him.

The Spectator whirled and rose to his feet.

A wounded villager's eyes burned a hand's breadth away. Metal flashed. A hot line drew itself across the Spectator's neck. The Spectator's chest felt warm. Inside his throat, it was cold. The villager's knife came away crimson. Cold earth slammed into the Spectator's back. He heard two shots. His killer fell beside him, left shoulder gone, eyes and nose obliterated. It was the last thing he'd see. Like shutters dropping in sequence: Vision. Smell. Hearing. Consciousness of pain. All slipped away.

Darkness. An OmNet logo. Soft music.

An unctuous voice announced, "Spectator Laerl Q'Flehg was recovered and revived. He awaits reassignment. Thirty-nine Spectators remain active on Jaremi Four."

Ulf's unimaginative frontal assault took only minutes. In those minutes a village had ceased to be. It was a sorry beginning for a new religion. But such fare had attracted a loyal following of Galactic experients. However brutal it got, they never looked away.

31. Jaremi Four: High Orbit

Energy poured into the Jaremi system from the cataclysmic binary Cohller 5114. The electromagnetic noise crippled conventional susceptors. Not even high-end Detex could see far.

The cargo pod fell into the system disguised as a rogue meteor. If an obs module on an outer planet spotted it, no suspicions would be raised. Deeper inside the system, the noise was heavier. Stealth would matter less.

The pod broke up above the fourth planet. Twenty small satellites moved into obscure orbits. Though new inside, their bodies were pocked and corroded—artificially aged. They would disappear among decades' accumulation of abandoned, untrackable orbital detritus. Twelve satellites ringed the equator, thirty degrees apart; the others clumped in polar orbits. No part of the surface would lay outside their coverage.

The scientists at North Polar Station noticed nothing, suspected nothing.

As Enclave violations go, this was a small one. Then again, no Enclave violation was small.

32. Tridee Broadcast, Galaxy Wide • Origin: Jaremi Four—Northern Hemisphere

"Like the fire, spread my word." Delivered without conviction, Parek's command wafted thinly. The Spectator posed as a village woman. She cowered amid brambles, watching Parek's army advance. If *advance* was the word.

Troops shuffled into a settlement of huts fashioned from rusty metal. Two exhausted percussionists chimed indifferently. It made no difference. Whoever lived here had evacuated. They'd left everything behind. They'd hardly needed bother.

Listless soldiers squatted groaning on rocks and stumps. "The commander comes!" cried a voice heavy with lassitude.

No one responded.

Six soldiers labored into the clearing, bearing Ulf in an improvised sedan chair. Ulf's head lolled. His thin lips hung open. His stare seemed blank.

Arn Parek strode unevenly into the clearing. His flaxen robe was stained. Twigs, leaves, and muddy clumps clung to it. His body armor hung open, brown with dust. "Spread my word, that's what we'll do," he singsonged. "We'll spread my word, and my word is death. We bring death. That's all we can do, so it must be what we do." The prophet leaned trembling against a bridge pier. "Something like that."

The *pov* began to pull away. This Spectator had decided not to give away her outer self just yet. The senso feed retreated into a two-dee bubble. A commentator strode on beneath it. "Like most planets other than Terra, Jaremi Four's native microbes are of the wrong chirality to attack humans. Therefore disease is rare—but not unheard of. After raping its way across the Jaremian Northland for seventeen months, Ulf and Parek's army provides a setting where even a modestly virulent venereal disease can establish itself.

"Barring some new development, we may soon have heard the last of the so-called Word Among Us."

33. Tridee Broadcast, Galaxy Wide • Origin: Terra—Wasatch Range, Usasector

Damp and tousled in his ill-tailored jumper, Alrue Latier stalked a synthesized mountaintop. "As it is written!" he thundered. "As it is written in The Book of Mormon, sixteenth chapter of Second Nephi: 'Wo unto them'— and for those of you who receive this with surtitles, yes, that's 'wo,' spelled just *w-o*—'Wo unto them that draw iniquity with cords of vanity, and sin as it were with a cart rope.' "

The viewpoint surged into a sweaty closeup. "So there. None of that sinning with cart ropes for you Saints of the New Restoration. Don't even think about it."

Another cut: Latier strode over cloud tops. Sunbeams wheeled behind him. "And another thing: the words of King Benjamin, as recorded in the book of Mosiah, chapter three: 'And even at this time, when thou shalt have taught thy people the things which the Lord thy God hath commanded thee, even then are they found no more blameless in the sight of God, only according to the words which I have spoken unto thee.' Think about that, you who would be Saints. Even when you've learned all God has commanded, you are not blameless—except ye have hearkened to *my* words. Revelation is made anew each day." He smiled disingenuously. "Now, this is God's revelation to me for today."

Trumpets shrilled. In an explosion of fairy dust, Latier materialized behind his desk. The office was gaudy, decorated with golden finials, crimson damask, and white leopard-skin. "Friends," Latier oozed, "what I must speak today troubles me. Do you know? Some have said that I have denied God could have incarnated His Son on other worlds. Surely that's a lie, for who am I to say what God can or cannot do?"

On those full memberworlds whose laws encouraged such things, a government warning bleated into a sideband. "No comment on the religious content of this program is intended. Still, the viewer should know that the preceding statement was factually incorrect. In the past First Elder Latier has consistently denied that Christ visited worlds other than Terra. It has been the principal grounds for his attacks on the Universal Catholic Church."

Latier held up empty palms. "Once the evidence for non-Terran Christs seemed unconvincing." He looked poised, confident—not at all like someone reversing a long-stated conviction. "Today, by the power of God, the case for Christs on other worlds seems strong. Which is *not* to say the harlots of Vatican have been correct in the specific Incarnation claims they've sanctioned.

"Behold!" Latier rose, grunting, from his desk. "I announce a new revelation. The time is meet when God's true church should begin the *real* business of authenticating messiahs on other worlds. I announce the great and holy word of God. This day the historic doctrine of celestial marriage is extended. Once our church has certified authentic Christs from other worlds, contributors will be able to receive temple ordinations through the good offices of these so-called 'echo Redeemers.' The Old Order Mormons baptized Saint Francis of Assisi, Joan of Arc, Charles Chaplin, Hitler, and the Jews of the Holocaust. Why can't we extend that impulse

into today? For the first time men and women from across the Galaxy will be sealed
to the great community of New Restoration Mormons and be saved!

"Does this sound audacious, brothers and sisters? Well, that's how things go
when God speaks new rules for living. But it *is* audacious." Latier leaned close to the
pickup. His face looked as if mapped onto a tomato. "And it's *really* expensive."

Abruptly Latier was prowling a balcony in the mountains, a Book of Mormon
in his meaty hands. "I read from the Book of Helaman, Chapter 13: 'For I will, saith
the Lord, that they shall hide up their treasures up to me; and cursed be they who
hide not up their treasures unto me; for none hideth up their treasures unto me save
it be the righteous; and he that hideth not up his treasures unto me, cursed is he,
and also the treasure.' Think on that, once and future Saints . . . and give."

34. Jaremi Four—Northern Hemisphere

The soldier was insistent. "Please, High Commander Ulf says he cannot begin
without you."

"Of course he can." With trembling fingers the Arn Parek lifted a fallen leaf
to shield his eyes. "He's never sought my approval. When he needs it, he
announces it."

"Great Prophet, High Commander Ulf said I must bring you."

"Yes, surely so," Parek almost whispered, studying the leaf intensely. "Come.
Get off your knees. Sit beside me."

Obviously favoring aching joints, the soldier joined Parek atop a boulder. He
peered at the leaf Parek held before the sun. It was gray-green, but golden backlight revealed overlapping traceries of structure within.

"See, the leaf has two stems," Parek said. "It's from one of the trees whose fruit
gives no nourishment. A child knows that. But what else do you see here?"

The soldier squinted. "The leaf is full of forms. Tiny channels, some reddish,
some more blue."

"But what do they do?" Parek asked.

The man coughed convulsively, peered again at the leaf. "They . . . they branch."

Parek dropped the leaf. Behind it stood a gnarled tree, the setting sun blazing
through its limbs. "They branch indeed. The branching of the veins in that leaf—the
branching of limbs in that tree. Are they not the same—one small, one large, each
expressing the same pattern?" Parek coughed, once, twice, endlessly. When he reopened his watering eyes, the soldier had moved away. "You've seen enough of leaves."

"The meeting," the soldier said helplessly.

Parek picked up another leaf. "Ulf will meet without me. Tell him the sky gods
would not have me come." Parek began to chuckle. He stopped when it became
apparent that laughter would bring on more coughing. "First, tell me a thing. I
showed you a mystery just now. But it wasn't the mystery you sought, I could tell
that. What mystery preoccupies you?"

The soldier squeezed his eyes shut. Tears traced through the grime on his cheeks. "Oh, great prophet," the man sobbed, "what is wrong with us?"

"Now there's a mystery."

"First Disciple Chagrin speaks of how you healed him."

Parek raised the leaf before the sun. "It took time. I had to find the way." He glanced at the soldier and then stared back at the leaf. "What do you think? Might I not find the way—in here?"

Sadly, the soldier turned. He marched back toward the meeting tent as best he could.

Parek's boulder lay on a knoll at one edge of the main camp. Motley tents spread across a broad field. Here and there an existing building had been converted to the army's purposes. Fifty or sixty uniformed fighters trudged about. They hacked indifferently at chores or mostly rested. It wasn't the way a military camp was supposed to look. Young men serve in armies. These young men shambled and ached and complained as if in their dotage.

"Tell Ulf I mean it!" Parek called to the soldier's receding back. "I'm not coming. He should send no more soldiers!" Parek couldn't tell whether the man had heard him. *He thinks I've failed him,* Parek thought. *Well, I have. We're all so sick now, and I have no answers.* He twirled the leaf by one of its stems, then the other. *Who knows,* he thought, *maybe the answer is in here. One thing is sure, there are no answers in that meeting tent while Ulf's mind fades in and out. Ironic—once I hated Ulf for dominating me. Now I hate him for being useless.*

After a while Parek couldn't see the veins any more. He wasn't sure whether it was because the light was failing, or because he could no longer hold the leaf steady enough. He was so tired . . .

. . . woke with a start. Aurora swirled mockingly in a star-speckled sky. It had rained. Parek's clothes were wet. They felt like ice against his fever-heated skin. His body ached even more than usual from hours without movement in the dampness. Ignoring the pain, Parek surged to his feet.

He'd awakened filled with certainty—a sense of pure calm purpose he couldn't explain. He felt no less ill. But no time for that now! He was decoupled from his body and its complaints. Seemingly his real self stood on some isolated platform within—a platform from which, focused and alert, he could confidently drive his ailing limbs.

Arn Parek had no idea where he was going. And yet, he did. He'd awakened not imbued with knowledge, but rather filled with an overpowering awareness of *having known.* So far, the memories had resurfaced shard by shard, just in time to guide his next step toward a destination about which he—so far—remembered nothing. *I used to feign visions,* he thought. Parek maintained his manic speed through what were now dense woods, seeing by auroral light only. *Then I interpreted my best ideas as visions.* A tree root tripped him. He landed clumsily. The impact would have taken his breath away even if he weren't sick. Yet he sprung to his feet. *Then I dignified my fantasies by calling them visions.* Heedlessly he pressed his body forward. He thrust branches aside. One snapped back. A branch raked his right cheek. Parek pressed on. *But this is different from any of those.*

He burst into a broad clearing. Stars and aurora sparkled. Of course, he remembered: this was where he'd been heading all along. Parek stood still for three minutes. Gradually he became aware of his body's protests. Drying blood puckered the angry cut on his cheek.

The doubts began. *I had some idiot fever-dream,* he thought. *That's all.* For the first time it occurred to him that his prophetic career might end here on the heath—that perhaps the chain of events that had shaped his entire adult life was nothing but a cruel joke. *What if Willim was right? What if I'm nothing, what if it's all lies? An army raised, a few thousands killed, a few hundred people's view of the world changed—for better or worse, who can tell? And then I'm gone, and my prophecy with me. In a dozen years will people laugh at the suggestion that they should still remember me?* From somewhere, memory resurfaced and nudged him. *I'm to look at the sky now.*

Doubt vanished.

Overhead, a single star waxed incredibly fast. It grew brighter. *Brighter!* Its white turned luminous green. Its point became a disk. Now Parek could resolve green fire along its edge. *Whatever it is, it is falling on me,* he realized. Just then, it jinked to the south. The fireball slammed into the other side of the broad clearing, perhaps a hundred meters away. Thunder battered at Parek's ears. Only after the noise began did it seem odd to him that the object's *approach* had been silent.

Heat washed across him and drew the skin of his face tight. *I remember I'm to wait,* Parek thought. *Wait for what?*

The crater belched fog. The dense mist clung to the ground. Small fires dancing along the crater rim or on the bark of nearby trees flickered out as the fog touched them. A wave of cold washed across Parek's feet. He had no way to recognize an automated fire suppression system in action. When he recalled that the cooling interval had passed, he strode across the clearing. The crater's ring was a meter high, three in diameter. Though steam rose from its depths, its surface was glazed with ice.

Inside the crater lay a metallic cylinder half a meter long, perhaps as big around as Parek's wrist. Immediately he remembered knowing what to do with it. He grabbed the cylinder. Its temperature was neutral.

Again Parek found the energy to run across the clearing and back into the forest.

An ancient stone pumphouse contained the camp's kitchen. The cooks had been up for an hour already. Gruel simmered in great pots. The cooks moved slowly, coughing into their work. They gaped when The Word Among Us bustled in. His right cheek bore a cruel diagonal scrape. He held high a shiny canister. "Behold!" Parek cried. "Behold the means of healing!"

The head chef stumbled toward Parek, gesturing with a large cup. "Great prophet, are you feeling well?"

"No, I'm not," said Parek, snatching the chef's cup. "Nor are you. Nor does anyone in camp." Parek glanced about the kitchen. "There are five pots of gruel?"

"Yes," answered the head chef blankly.

"Then I need four more measuring cups. Quickly!" Parek set his hand to the cylinder's cap. It no longer surprised him when, just as he needed to know, he remembered how to open the container.

Now, it seemed he'd known all along what was in it. He poured out equal quantities of a blue-gray powder into the five measuring cups. "Mark this day!" Parek cried. "The day will come when your grandchildren will demand to hear how The Word Among Us healed you all!" He recapped the empty cylinder and tossed it away.

He held a cup of powder out over one gruel pot and emptied it. He plunged a wooden paddle into the gruel. Stirred with manic energy. "Hurry!" he shouted to the cooks. "Stir powder into the other pots." Four junior cooks scrambled to comply. In the steam and choking heat they labored alongside The Word Among Us.

The head chef pulled his gaze away from the astonishing tableau long enough to search for the cast-off cylinder. It was no longer shiny. Though Parek had discarded it less than a minute before, its surface was brown-gray, pitted with corrosion that suggested not seconds but decades of abandonment. The cook picked up the cylinder and opened it. To all appearances it was just another war surplus metal container.

"Keep it if you like," Parek rasped from above. "But give me a ladle!"

Without thinking, the head chef responded as he would to a fellow cook. He threw Parek a ladle. Before he could think what disrespect that might represent, The Word Among Us caught it. Parek drove the ladle deep into half-cooked gruel. With one hand he forced a dollop of the grainy paste into his mouth. His cheeks puffed out, pulling the wound on his cheek open again. Parek made himself chew. Half a dozen cooks pressed around, wide-eyed. He swallowed with effort.

"It'll be better when it is cooked through," the head chef said hesitantly.

"Of course," nodded Parek. "You may want to wait until it is done. But you all must eat. Today at breakfast, every man is to eat a full bowl." He stabbed his finger at the head chef. "Force it on the sick. Keep forcing it on them until they stop throwing it up. Gruel for everyone. *No* exceptions! See to it!"

With that, Arn Parek drew up his robe and trudged to his residence. The two healthiest sentries—which was to say, men able to hang onto rifles and keep their eyes open—flanked the door. Fist-on-chest they saluted Parek and dropped to one knee.

"We are saved," Parek told them. "This day the sickness shall be lifted from us all."

Three hours later dawn flooded the sky. Parek hadn't slept. He'd lain in bed, thinking furiously as his fever broke and as the lassitude drained from his joints. He hadn't noticed the wound on his cheek healing with prodigious speed, forming as a result an odd, permanent gray furrow across the blackness of his face.

Parek never knew he'd suffered from Jaremi Four's only indigenous sexually transmitted disease, that he and an eighth of his troops had contracted it sacking a brothel eleven months before, or that those originally infected had shared their illness during subsequent gang rapes until almost every man in the camp had the disease in some stage of its progression.

Nor could Parek know that the antibiotic powder from the sky would not only cure but as a side effect *immunize* him, his men, and anyone with whom they'd share women in the future against their world's only venereal disease. In this way Ulf and Parek's army would acquire an immunological advantage no armed force in recent Jaremian history had enjoyed.

Parek knew none of that. What kept him awake and his thoughts awhirl was the very first thing he'd remembered in the vision's maddening way. *"Do what is asked,"* he'd awoken on the boulder remembering. *"Do what is asked today. Do what may be asked tomorrow. The tomorrow after that. Obey consistently."*

And the incentive? Parek had forgotten how badly he had yearned for that. Now, tantalized, he hungered for freedom as he had in the first weeks of his public ministry, just after Dultav had died.

"Do what is asked," the message had promised, *"and in time, you will free yourself of Ulf."*

35.   Jaremi Four—
Elsewhere in the Northern Hemisphere

This far north, aurora hung in the sky like planar slabs of spun fire. With its salmon, sea-green, and silver colors, the auroral light frolicked on the snowpack blanketing the valley below. Distant bonfires and scattered lighted windows speckled the panorama. Here, in Jaremi Four's inhospitable arctic precincts, order had prevailed the longest. For its inhabitants the wealth of civilization's leavings made up for nearly perpetual winter.

Their sleigh climbed a cliffside turnpike. Through crackling air they gazed down at the squat stone fortress they'd so recently departed.

Friz Labokloer's heavy fingers twisted her nipples.

Ruth Griszam gasped.

Their bodies flowed together. His tongue leapt into her mouth. Ruth checked quickly for the *verify* signal as she surrendered herself to the sensations of the moment.

When next she looked out, the sleigh had stopped. The *sturruh* stood two by two in their yokes. Steam rose from their matted flanks. Ruth reclined in the arms of Friz Labokloer, a muscular, ebony bear of a man, the local noble with whom she now lived.

"Fantastic," she breathed. "This is my first chance to really see the northern aurora—you know, clearly, away from the sentry fires at the castle."

"Enjoy, my beauty. Absorb it all in that weird way of yours."

Lucky for you I'm not Linka Strasser. She'd think you'd figured out about OmNet and have you killed. I prefer to think you're intrigued by my intensity. The sleigh's sculpted design deflected frigid winds from their faces and everything else they exposed to the night. Within, behind layers of resilient fabric they lounged nude, blissfully warm beneath furs. Labokloer tugged a plush glove onto his right arm elbow high and reached outside. He jerked at the reins. The *sturruh* snorted and broke into an effortless canter. The beasts knew the way; the reins would not be needed again for some time.

Labokloer withdrew his arm and tugged a cord. Elastic straps pulled the face shield closed, shutting out the night. He slid his large hand along Ruth's flank. They slid down a short upholstered ramp into the main body of the sleigh. They faced each other in a fur-lined enclosure just big enough for two. Hot coals arranged in metal troughs below the sleigh's belly kept the chamber warm. Chemically luminous panels shed cool light.

The two removed tight-fitting fur caps, their only garments.

Labokloer reached beneath a pillow and produced a small transparent box. "The *fhlet* in the thermal caves fruited twice since I took you to my bed."

About as clumsy a way to say we've been together five months as one could ask for, she thought. "Is that . . . is that for me?"

She took the proffered box and pried it open. Within, nestled on a scrap of velvet, a triangular object of glass glittered. She turned it over between her fingers, hoping she wouldn't look as if she knew what a prism was. "It is . . . beautiful," she deadpanned.

"Look," said Labokloer. Childlike, he lifted the prism from her grasp. He arranged a scrap of pale leather beneath one of the luminous plates. Held the prism before the plate. He turned it slightly. A gappy spectrum could be seen on the leather. "See, from white light it makes colors."

"Not all of them," Ruth said. "The black stripes, are there colors missing there?"

"Only with the cold light plates. Daylight's different. They say when my father was young, everyone knew the reason why. Today. . . ." He shrugged.

From beneath another fur he drew a necklace chain. Tiny iron claws dangled beneath it. Labokloer seated the prism within their grip. With something like solemnity he draped the prism necklace across Ruth's shoulders. "My life has never had such wonderful as now: power, success, and you—you crown my bliss."

Quickly she reviewed what she'd learned of far northern folkways. *Is this a proposal? Will I be cast into some dungeon if in six months I'm not big with his child?*

Labokloer cleared his throat. Kneeling on his haunches, he regarded her. The prism bangled between the dark smallnesses of her breasts. "You're dear to me. I hope you'll choose to remain with me a while longer."

Oh, is that all? She flashed him the warmest smile at her command. "That would delight me."

They kissed. At length he held out her fur cap, grabbing his own with his other hand. "Let's enjoy the night again."

They donned the headgear and reached for the straps. They pulled themselves back up into the sleigh's seat. The storm shield opened just enough to pass their heads. Frigid air snapped at their cheeks. Fur baffles at their necks locked in the warmth below.

Huffing sourly, the *sturruh* had pulled them several kilometers along the road for another hundred meters up the mountainside. The valley sparkled, surreal in the raw night. "When I traveled north, I didn't know what to expect," Ruth said. "Certainly not this."

"When we met, neither did I," whispered Labokloer. "We all live at the whims of the sky gods."

There's truth in that, Ruth silently admitted. When Willim Dultav died, so had Ruth's musings about going Inplanet. Instead she'd wandered the forest, taking up with another band of highwaymen. She filed journals only when she felt like it. When living there meant compulsory attachment to the army of physical and spiritual conquest Ulf was building with Parek as his talisman, she'd decided to head north—the far north, the land least ravaged by that long-ago Tuezi strike, the land where autochthonous culture had only recently succumbed. Perhaps it was her way of honoring Dultav's memory. He'd sifted libraries for remnants of Jaremi's lost civilization; she'd journeyed where its corpse was warmest.

She and Labokloer'd met eight months before. Three months later, she'd moved into his castle. *I came north without plans, expecting to log dull journals about being a scullery maid. Instead I catch the eye of the region's fastest-rising young mikado. Okay, the man's an idiot. He still leads a storybook existence. Jousts. Feasts. Palace intrigues. Baroque revivals of forgotten technologies. A smorgasbord of sex. And my saybacks?* She shrugged inwardly. *They're not even a hundredth of what I got hanging around a forjeling dam with some guy who thought he was God.*

A cloud drifted before the aurora, casting color-edged shadows on the valley floor. "Ruth?" Labokloer said quietly. "There's something I want to tell you."

"Yes."

"Promise to tell no one."

"I do." After a few silent seconds, she said, "If it weighs on you so, perhaps you're better off not telling me."

Labokloer chuckled. "No. My growing wealth and power—where do you think they come from?"

Ruth frowned. "Craft and cunning. Perhaps some luck. The caves, of course." She frowned. "I expect you left some bodies along the way." *Basically, I just figured you were the biggest son-of-a-bitch in the valley.*

"As I thought." Labokloer laid his huge hands on her shoulders. "Ruth, I don't like when you admire me for something I'm not."

"You're too modest."

"No, I have a cruel secret. Much of my good fortune—perhaps half my political influence, most of my wealth—has nothing to do with my own virtues."

"That's no secret. Every great fortune begins in happenstance."

"With me it is more than that. *My* luck was handed to me out of the sky—by an oracle."

"Wha-a-at?" Ruth drew out the word while her awareness darted within. *Still recording three-by-three greens.*

"You must realize, Ruth," Labokloer said hesitantly, "I'm not as smart as I look."

"No?" she said tonelessly.

"When we met I was a very minor noble. I was close to losing my castle. Then the oracle sent me a scroll filled with prophecies."

"How?"

"If I told you, you'd think me mad. Just accept that I received the scroll, in most dramatic fashion. It bore political and economic predictions—which way the price of *fhlet* would move against the price of cold light plates, who'd win a certain battle. With the abandon of a desperate man, I wagered on all the predictions."

"So you bet a little risk capital."

He shook his head. "I bet heavily. Every prediction came true. From that day my wealth was secure. A few months later, I received a second scroll. I staked everything on those predictions, too, and won again."

"That was when you brought me to your castle—about when you completed those nonaggression pacts with your neighboring warlords."

Labokloer nodded. "They look like nonaggression pacts. Really, they're just a way for the others to save face—to continue their reigns though their wealth and power had passed to me. I've received one more scroll since then. I owe it my success in ousting the Lord of Cranh and defeating the turnpike marauders. The scroll also contained some um, more spiritual advice."

Ruth pursed her lips. "Were there more scrolls?"

"Just those three. Though I never know when another may come." He looked at her with something verging on anguish. "There, you think less of me now."

She reached for his hands. "Not at all. You've had great windfalls. Instead of just enjoying them, you thought to ask why." *Actually a surprise, there.* "You have no idea who sends them?"

"None. Who *could* know such things? I tell you, Ruth, it's like they come from the sky gods."

I could tell you a thing or two about knowledge from the sky. "But why?" she asked aloud. "Why channel such wealth and power to a random stranger?"

"I wish I knew." Withdrawing his hands from her, Labokloer began tracing with his fingers along her arms. "It must serve someone's purpose. And I suppose the day will come on which I must pay for my good fortune. Someone, or something, will appear in the midst of all my wonderful and hand me a bill." His hands had inched up her arms. Now they encircled her breasts. "Until then, Ruth, so long as we *know* we are someone else's pawns, the ride is worth its price, no?"

Yes, she thought, melting once more into the ride within the ride that invariably beckoned when Labokloer was around. *Right now, it is worth the price indeed.*

36. Tridee Broadcast, OmNet Terran Service

"**M**ysteries keep piling up about Arn Parek," the editorialist intoned. "Why does he so fascinate Galactics when there's been so little direct coverage of him? How does he manage to stay out of sight now that there are sixty-five Spectators on Jaremi Four?"

Graphics sprouted like mushrooms after rain. "The less Galactics see of Arn Parek, the *more* inclined they become to obsess about him, argue about him, or even to worship him. For us on Terra, there's an ironic upside. For the first time in years, there's a religious leader who's popular across the Galaxy but who *doesn't* hail from our world."

More bubbles emerged; they presented aerial images of a primitive walled settlement. "General Ulf displayed uncharacteristic ingenuity in taking this town. Though he had close to eight hundred troops, he sent just seventy-five men to charge the city's wooden gates. This plainly inadequate assault force retreated in disarray under defensive fire, losing twelve fighters in the process. Two hundred men and women—most of the settlement's militia—streamed out to pursue them. The pursuers picked off another half-dozen attackers. By now, the defenders had charged some six hundred meters beyond their gates. They couldn't know they'd rushed *between* two of Ulf's detachments until crossfire mowed them down." Enfilading fire ravaged the long column of defenders. Men and women screamed, spun, convulsed. Some tried to run. That only changed the directions their riddled bodies faced when they fell.

"Meanwhile," the editorialist commented, "Ulf had detailed riflemen to mark the locations of the settlement's artillery. They held their fire as the village's three cannon spewed death at Ulf's advance force. Meanwhile the militia surged out through the gates. Only then did they open up on the artillery emplacements, killing the gun crews while leaving the cannon intact.

"Only after that did Ulf deploy his main force, some four hundred and fifty strong. They quickly toppled the town gates and encountered no further resistance." Grisly images of plunder and rapine followed. One bubble grew to dominate the visual field: it was a tridee squeezedown from a Spectator attached to Ulf's army. Entering an undefended granary, the Spectator died when his sergeant accidentally jostled him from a catwalk. The news reader reemerged in the foreground. "Spectator Nevrol Andervek of Novasovietsector lost his life in the assault—amazingly, the *fifth* Spectator to die while covering Ulf and Parek. He was recovered and revived.

"Still, what's most remarkable about this action is that by means of inventive, well-executed strategy Ulf utterly reduced a village of six hundred inhabitants and seized its artillery, yet lost fewer than thirty troops—this from a man who displayed strategic skill only when plotting guerrilla actions involving fewer than half a dozen fighters, whose signature when commanding larger forces had always been dull, costly, uninspired frontal assaults. What changed? Some wonder whether Ulf has a divine coach on his general staff.

"Others wonder what all this Enclave bloodshed can have to do with a new religion. We Terrans know that answer. Think of the violence during the original expansions of Islam, the millions killed in the Crusades, the Inquisition, the Holocaust, and even the twenty-first-century Hindu-Islamic wars. Clearly, in the budding Church of Parek the generals are far ahead of the chaplains. But it's not outside the envelope for a faith in its infancy."

Another bubble opened. Beneath the red skies of Buerala Six, elegant Galactics gathered round a tridee set, cheering the bloody conquest. "And yes, Parek's Galactic admirers have seen these images. Those who take Parek most seriously as a religious figure know just how deeply his movement is drenched in blood. It doesn't faze them. Some say the body count simply confirms Parek's significance."

The image shifted to file footage from weeks before: Ulf's sick, exhausted army struggling just to walk across an empty village. Ulf himself raving in his sedan chair. "Two larger questions," the editorialist declared. First, how did this army, which so recently seemed ready to collapse into sickbeds, regain its health? And second, why do 32 percent of all Galactics tell saybackers they *accept* Arn Parek's claim that he cured his troops—more properly, Ulf's troops—by miraculous means?"

37. Jaremi Four— North Polar Research Station

Still sweating, the newly assigned Spectator bustled into the station commander's office. It had slanted walls and a low ceiling swarming with apparatus. Three faces crowded a tiny conference table. A haggard man with almond eyes spoke. "Spectator, your presence aboard Jaremi Station is noted. I'm Commander Rikhard Allihern."

"Thank you for the welcome," the Spectator replied.

"I said only that your presence was noted." Allihern nodded toward a middle-aged man whose demeanor said *cop*. "This is Lieutenant Lor Ye'Uhz, our Enclave Compliance Officer." The third face belonged to a severe, almost shapeless woman. She slouched in a polychair, her black hair and pale clothing imperceptibly awry. "And this is our chief scientist, Dr. Moreyn Dorga."

"How was your trip?" Dorga asked without real interest.

The Spectator bristled. "It almost terminated in your upper atmosphere."

Dorga's look suggested she wished it had.

"Forjel it," the Spectator snapped, "I'm a fellow professional, here on business like any of you. My lander almost collided with some defunct satellite."

Allihern laughed. "Our guidance systems are crude. It's impossible to monitor traffic in Jaremi space anyway with all that radiation from the binary. We might as well bring Spectators in blind."

"That's the way they should leave," Dorga sniffed. "You senso people swagger through here by the dozens. You wink at Enclave law, corrupt the autochthons with Galactic this, Ordhian that, and Terran the other thing. What's important here is the behavior of that most exceptional binary star and the needs of our handful of astronomers and the engineers whose machinery pushes air and noise out of the way while the astronomers observe." She turned toward Commander Allihern. "All right, Rikhard, I've met the latest cultural buccaneer. Can I go?"

Allihern nodded. She left noisily. "None of us are overjoyed to see you gawkers pass through," Allihern admitted. "Lately OmNet's been shoving Spectators down our throats as fast as they can get them here, which gives some of us our first reason to be grateful Jaremi Four is so remote. As it is, the burdens of processing you people in reduce the already minimal services we provide to our astronomical community. Lieutenant Ye'Uhz, please brief the new Spectator."

Ye'Uhz stood pugnaciously. *Makes you wonder where he left his riding crop*, the Spectator thought.

"It may be that somewhere in this Galaxy, there are worlds whose compliance officers wink at breaches of Enclave," Ye'Uhz rumbled. "Jaremi Four is not such a world. You'll find autochthons puzzling over the function and purpose of trinkets from their planet's golden age, almost always guessing wrong. You'll watch men and women dying painful unnecessary deaths, surrounded by implements that could save them if they understood their use. You'll live among people who ache to know more about their past, to get past the twisted legends and grab some little nugget of truth." Pacing close to the Spectator, Ye'Uhz leaned forward. "And you know what? *You will tell them nothing.*"

Ye'Uhz stabbed a control. A tridee bubble opened, showing Linka Strasser, grime-caked, hollow eyed, her face drawn tight.

The new Spectator recognized the clip, of course. It was his own last view of her before the torturers took his eyes.

Laz Kalistor shifted in the polychair, forcing his features to betray no reaction.

"Do you know who this woman is?" Ye'Uhz barked.

"Sure, that's—"

"Don't interrupt! Of course you know who Linka Strasser is. Some Spectators think she's a heroine. To others she's a maniac. Know what I think? I think she's a paragon of forjeling principle."

Kalistor said nothing.

Ye' Uhz pitched his voice low. "I want you to be just like Linka Strasser. No matter what assignment you draw, no matter what identity you assume, your *first* obligation is to keep the secret of Enclave. And I mean at any cost. If you must let someone die, even another Spectator, you do it. If you must order the death of an autochthon or even commit the murder yourself, you do it. If you must acquiesce in your own death—even under circumstances that might preclude your being recovered—you do it."

You bastard, Kalistor thought. *If only you knew. If only you had the tiniest forjeling idea.* But Ye'Uhz didn't. Once again Kalistor was impressed with the power wielded by those who'd made themselves his patrons. *My cover fooled the compliance officer, just as they said it would.*

Ye'Uhz stepped back. "End of lecture. I'm not going to ask you whether everything was clear; you're responsible for it all in any event." He jerked a thumb toward a hatchway that irised open in the gritty wall. "Tech support's down that hall. They'll link you up with your bird and set up your accounts. Go."

"By the way," Allihern interjected as Kalistor started for the hatchway. "Good luck on Jaremi Four, Spectator."

Kalistor permitted himself an inward chuckle as the hatchway irised shut behind him. *I remember my control's words when he gave me my* real *assignment. "Humor the Compliance Officer once, and you'll never have to deal with him or her again." But then, every Spectator on every Enclave world knows that.* Silently Kalistor made his way from kiosk to kiosk in the tech support area, collecting his satellite channel assignments and appropriate clothing. He kept his own counsel as chatty cosmo techs added permanent dirt to his nails and fingertips and chipped two of his teeth.

The final clause of Kalistor's remembered instructions was more personal, more unique. *"Don't let them suspect you're not just another Spectator."* Wise counsel indeed, he thought. *No one must know that Laz Kalistor's come back.*

He entered a surgical theater. A plump woman in a physician's uniform approached him silently. She punched commands into a touchpad. Kalistor felt, rather than heard, a subtle hum—as if all the air in the room had turned sideways. "Shields up," she said. "We can't be monitored. Thank vacuum you're here. How bad was it?"

"No worse than I was told to expect." He passed her a data wafer. "My cover assignment."

The woman slid the wafer into a box, removed it, and handed it back. "Duly altered."

"When do I leave?"

"Go straight to departure bay. Something will become of your baggage. But first—" She pulled an improvised tool from a holster and touched it to his chest. The Escher patch sealed into his Jaremian-style tunic popped into her free hand. "Give me the rest of your planetside clothing." Efficiently she worked her way through a duffel full of costumes.

"I didn't think those came off."

"Not usually," she said, scooping dislodged lozenges into her pockets. "This is the new wrinkle. You'll wear no Escher patches. And none of your journals will go out onto Net."

"I'll be the little Spectator who isn't there. Why?"

"Unlikely as it sounds, there's conjecture he's found some way to identify Spectators. Things keep happening to them." She was done. Hastily he repacked. They clasped hands. "Be careful."

Careful? Kalistor thought. *How can I be anything but careful when my mission is to get close to Arn Parek?*

38. Near Jaremi Space

*W*hen the Holy Father sent me here, I demanded to travel first class. Now they say this is first class. Vatican Secretary of State Alois Cardinal Rybczynsky fought to control his stomach as the stealth capsule shook. He floated under zero gravity in a compartment barely larger than the inside of a casket. He could avoid claustrophobia only by immersing himself in virtual work. *Ah well, no shortage of that.*

Rybczynsky knew the commotion had to do with his craft's being launched from a private transport, well outside Jaremi space. The capsule he occupied was embedded in millions of tons of igneous rock. With the contramagnetic braking engines retracted, the entire vehicle's resemblance to a four-by-ten-kilometer asteroid was perfect.

Except that asteroids didn't normally jet toward the Jaremi system at half a dozen times the speed of light. *At this stage of the journey, speed matters more than a natural appearance. Or so they tell me.* Rybczynsky sighed. *Ah, they know their business. And if they don't, God's will be done.*

The cardinal settled into composing a confidential memorandum for the pope. "Are all human beings the fruit of a single act of Creation?" Rybczynsky dictated. "Or does each known planet's population result from a distinct Creation, one of as many as forty thousand such Divine acts? At last cognizant of the folly of considering such matters by the illumination of theology alone, the bishops of the Sixteenth Vatican Council consulted eminent biologists before settling their minds on this question. The vocabulary was familiar from Terra's fourth-century Arian heresy: Are human beings *homoousios* (of one substance) or merely *homoiousios* (of like substance)? Resoundingly the Council declared the former. Alone, the Society of Jesus clung to the latter. For seventeen years the accustomed sober pace of Vatican machinery seemed sufficient to guarantee eventual resolution. But today the Church must take quick action to purge Herself of heresy on this question. She must speak with one voice regarding human nature. For in each of His historic Incarnations the Cosmic Christ has partaken fully of human nature. So we see in the light of faith that to speak of human nature is also to speak of the nature of Christ. Hence the urgency of settling this matter of consubstantiality, of ending the long altercation with the Society of Jesus."

Through kilometers of rock Rybczynsky heard the braking engines deploy. Fire. *My craft enters Jaremi system.* Its course would keep the fake asteroid behind the third planet, hidden from possible observation from planet four while it decelerated to sublight speed. Its prodigious Cerenkov radiation would go undetected.

Rybczynsky paused, uncertain what to recommend next. The Jesuit leader Y'Braga was as set on his interpretation as Pope Modest and his theologians were on theirs. Moreover, the controversy had up to now unfolded according to a languid Vatican choreography. All parties assumed that resolution lay generations distant. On that timetable, this was not the time for bargaining. It was time to harden positions, to build foundations from which future divines might conduct the final battles a century or two hence. *It's unlikely Y'Braga will see the need to reach middle ground quickly,* Rybczynsky admitted to himself, *especially since Modest has ruled out telling the Jesuits that an Incarnation is predicted.*

More roaring. Flailing. Pitching. The pod had circled the third planet. Its gravity spat the imitation asteroid toward Jaremi Four. From the viewpoint of any planetside observer it would approach out of the sun, a further hedge against detection.

Rybczynsky knew this two-hour span would be the longest quiet interval of the trip. "If it is important to achieve unanimity on the question of human nature, it is no less important to clarify our expectations regarding the current Christ," he dictated. "Yet the information required remains ever elusive. Is this Christ yet to take flesh? Is He already an infant, wrapped in whatever some Jaremian tribe regards as swaddling clothes? Might He be an adult, embarked even now upon a public ministry?" It was this uncertainty, not the controversy with the Jesuits, that Rybczynsky found most disturbing. Never far from Rybczynsky's thoughts swirled the nightmare vision that the Church might fail to locate the Christ Incarnate on Jaremi Four until after His Sacrifice. *What's the point of one more empty tomb? We have enough of those.*

"Holy Mother Church must turn the prodigious intellects of her scholars toward solving these problems of Christology," Rybczynsky concluded. "The answers will be needed in weeks or months—surely, on no time scale more generous than a handful of years. It follows that Vatican preoccupation with the Society of Jesus over consubstantiality represents a distraction. If the Society can be conformed to the teachings of the Sixteenth Vatican Council without punitive action, so much the better. If this settlement cannot be brought about at once, I urge you, Holy Father: Dissolve the Society of Jesus quickly and decisively. Put this issue of heresy behind us."

Rybczynsky sighed and closed the memorandum file. He muttered prayers against what he knew was to come—the real fireworks. Alarms sounded. Straps deployed. *G*-membranes extruded and inflated. An annunciator sounded: "Collision in five, four, three, two, one. . . ."

A stasis field threw its protective fuzziness between Rybczynsky's already-tethered body and the capsule interior. In spite of it, the impact was deafening.

Looking like nothing more than a fast-moving rogue from beyond Jaremi space, the craft slammed into a natural asteroid at some three thousand miles per second. The speed had been chosen because the energy it released would mask the power signature when disintos obliterated the braking engines.

The target asteroid absorbed most of the kinetic energy. As the engineers predicted, the rock containing Rybczynsky shattered. More than forty dozen larger shards tumbled into Jaremi Four's gravity well—among them the jagged two-hundred-by-ninety-meter chunk accommodating Rybczynsky's capsule.

It was a meteor now, ablating with burning fury. Previous disturbances had been sharp but brief; penetrating the atmosphere meant a full minute of din. Rybczynsky wished the capsule allowed him room to raise his hands over his ears.

The stasis field fired again.

Splashdown!

A fountain of spray marked where the rocky envelope slammed into Jaremi Four's Equatorial Sea. Ninety degrees of latitude and ninety degrees of longitude would keep it out of view from the North Polar research station.

Throughout the descent, Rybczynsky had seen no sign of the island on any of his virtual instruments. But then, he wasn't supposed to.

The cardinal reopened his memorandum and made final refinements.

He barely noticed the thuds and jerks as divers captured his capsule.

39. Office of the Terran Delegate to the Privy High Council • Confidential Memo

[EMBEDDED SENSO JOURNAL: *NUDGE* HERE TO PLAY]

A Spectator who'd been unable to get into a Parek sermon was interviewing an autochthon who'd heard it. "One thing he said that astonished me," the autochthon was saying. He was gaunt and clad mainly in chains. He rattled when he breathed. "He said, he said. . . ."

"What?" the interviewer pressed.

"I don't remember, quite." The autochthon raised a sullied tumbler. "Got any more of that shit? It's really good." The tumbler dropped out of *pov.* Liquid burbled. "Mm, that even *looks* delicious. Damn straight. Anyway, back to your question. What's his name—oh yeah, The Word Among Us. You just call him Parek. Don't let *them* hear you talk that way."

"Yeah, yeah, what did Parek say?"

"I'm getting to that. Parek stood on top of this ruined pillar and preached for hours. He has the strangest fucking scar—"

"Stay on subject, if you would."

"One thing really stuck with me: He said that spirit and matter are one. The idea that our souls are made from something different than what rocks and trees and aurora are made out of . . . he said that's wrong. He said matter and spirit are the same. Almost the same, anyway. Spirit is just—how'd he say it? spirit is just more pure. Does that make any sense to you? 'Cause it doesn't mean a fucking thing to me, and the more of your liquor I put away the less sense it makes."

[JOURNAL ENDS]

[EMBEDDED SENSO JOURNAL: *NUDGE* HERE TO PLAY]

Night in a Jaremian refugee camp. Mud everywhere, punctuated only by islands of flat rock on which fires guttered. Filthy women squatted about a tall bon-fire built on a platform of shale plates. In the foreground knelt a teenager, thick in the arms and thighs. She'd been crying a long time. "I lost count how many times I was raped. That's how it's been for girls since the army moved through. It drew us together. We help each other when we're pregnant, so we won't bring children of theirs into the world. And now this—this *man* comes before us. Strange hair. Scarred face. He's worshipped by the men who rape us."

"That was Parek?" asked the Spectator.

"Parek? The Word Among Us, they called him. That shit told us we have a *duty* to bear children." She hugged herself. Tears staggered down her full cheeks. "He says we must have as many as we can. He says spirits are all lined up, just waiting to enter the world. Why anyone would line up to come live here I don't understand."

[JOURNAL ENDS]

Lord Councilor, I apologize for the casual structure of this memo. The results of my research have surprised even me, and you need to know that those two teachings— the doctrine that spirit and matter are of one kind, and the doctrine that fertility is important because spirits are waiting to enter the world—coexisted in primeval Mormonism. Joseph Smith, the founder of the Mormon Church, developed those tenets at the dawn of his career. He'd already stopped emphasizing them by the time the Mormons left what was then the state of Ohio. Today, few Latter-day Saints know the teachings existed. Nevertheless, Smith's early writings are the only place those doctrines previously occurred together.

I must respectfully urge Lord Councilor to consider your options in the event that this is not a coincidence.

[MEMO ENDS]

40. Jaremi Four—Equatorial Sea

D aylight flooded the capsule when its side panel was removed. An ample face with eyes like black beans beamed in. "Most Reverend and Most Eminent Lord Cardinal, good daypart."

"My brother in Christs," Alois Rybczynsky answered. He stepped through the opening and pretended to cherish the welcoming hug he received from Ato Cardinal Semuga.

"It is good to see you, Alois," Semuga oozed with what may have been real wonder. Despite Rybczynsky's arduous journey, the Cardinal-Secretary of State's black woolen simar was unwrinkled. It hung perfectly over his spare frame, pleats sharp and straight as the facets of a gem. "You look so . . . so fresh."

"I elected to make the journey without gravity," Rybczynsky said. "Less comfortable, but it keeps the vestments crisp."

"I'm sorry, Excellency," said Semuga of his own disheveled appearance. His simar was rumpled and stained. "It's been so busy here."

Yes, thought Rybczynsky dryly, eyeing the stains. *Vichyssoise* and *bouillabaisse. A busy day indeed.* "So, Ato, let me see what Holy Mother Church has wrought on this forbidden globe."

The cardinals stood on a crowded dock. To Rybczynsky's left stretched a turquoise harbor dappled with white. Fifteen surface ships, half a dozen flitters, and a profusion of amphibian vehicles lay at anchor. Beyond were enormous sub pens and founding docks. To the right rose office blocks, dormitories, manufactories, warehouses, and gantries, all emblazoned with the Papal tiara and keys. Beyond the buildings rose ranks of antenna arrays; shield cones; and, incongruously, a traditional stone cathedral steeple. A holoprojected tiara and keys spun lazily above its apex.

"Industrial installation" is too meek a phrase, Rybczynsky realized. *Semuga has truly raised a city on this hidden island.* "All this, in defiance of Enclave, utterly unsuspected. How many shipments from offworld?"

"Only four hundred. We were able to manufacture a surprising amount here."

Rybczynsky gaped. "You got four hundred freighters on and off this world and no one noticed?"

"We have our ways," Semuga replied. "Your Excellency has experienced several of them. Of course, the electromagnetic flux from that binary next door complicates others' observations."

Rybczynsky fell to his knees. "Praise be to God."

"Come now, Cardinal," Semuga drawled. "Surely you've seen cityscapes more magnificent than this."

"But I know how quickly *this* city was assembled . . . at what terrible risk . . . and for what purpose." Crossing himself, Rybczynsky rose. "I also know what it cost." He drove wonder from his countenance and donned the critical scowl of the Lord High Inspector, for that was the role the Cardinal-Secretary of State had voyaged to Jaremi Four to fulfill. "Come, Ato," he said, waggling a patrician hand. "Reveal to me what God's true church has to show for its clandestine hundreds of trillions."

Semuga gestured. A personnel carrier floated toward them, a standard armored transport aside from the side-mounted external seats and Medici bunting. It wafted to a stop. Its armored side opened in clamshell fashion. Footmen in medieval Terran livery leapt from the external seats and guided the cardinals inside.

Semuga and Rybczynsky eased into Louis XIV chairs with red damask cushions. Gold leaf and silver and crystal glinted in the light of gently tinkling chandeliers. A vivid *pietà* in blue spinel rotated on an alabaster pedestal. A rich tapestry adorned the fixed side wall.

"All reproductions, I assume," Rybczynsky said.

"Except for the sculpture," said Semuga.

Rybczynsky laughed. "Very droll, Ato. That's Valatu Brouhkin ve Greneil's *Pietà in Sapphire.*"

"Indeed. I used a contingency account to buy up the Greneil estate last year."

"*You* were the mystery buyer?" Rybczynsky reached for the translucent statue. "Doesn't that seem an unorthodox use for black-budget construction funds?"

Semuga shrugged. "We have twenty-eight Greneils here. They've appreciated three hundred percent since purchase. So far, that's paid an eighteenth of the construction cost. Just don't break the statue."

Gingerly, Rybczynsky replaced the sculpture on its rotating keepit pad.

The vehicle eased into motion. Snifters of cognac rose by the cardinals' hands. Semuga raised his in a toast. "Welcome to Vatican Island. God bless you on your visit."

"God bless."

Semuga drew in the cognac's bouquet and drank deep. At last he fixed his button eyes on his superior. "You'll like what I wrought here. I wish only that I better understood why we have done it."

Rybczynsky chuckled. "You seek a better reason than the next Incarnation of Christ?"

"Surely not," responded Semuga. "But we have built so much, and not just here."

Rybczynsky raised an eyebrow. "Where else?"

"You must read my reports more carefully, Excellency. In moments you will see. My point is that so often, we spent *extra* trillions for versatility—for miscellaneous capabilities we might need simply because we do not yet know to what ultimate use the force we are building will be put." He swirled his snifter. "Has there been progress in deciding what to do next?"

We have the same doubts, Rybczynsky thought. He elected to project false confidence. "Not yet, but don't concern yourself. Your charge was to build a mighty tool for Holy Mother Church." He drained his snifter. "First the toolmaker creates a tool. Then it is used."

"It's easier when one knows whether one is creating a hammer or a meathook."

The transport slowed. Rybczynsky glimpsed a cathedral square outside. "So much depends on developments. Pray for patience."

He feigns confidence, Semuga told himself. *But he is as disturbed as I by all these unknowns.*

The carriage clattered to a halt. The sidewall yawned open. Before them, a broad stone staircase six meters high lofted toward the entrance of a classic Gothic cathedral. "Based on Amiens?" Rybczynsky asked.

"Indeed. Don't worry, this *is* a reproduction. In fact, it's mostly sim." Semuga lay his right hand on Rybczynsky's arm. "Walk straight forward. Expect level ground." The cardinals strode not up, but *into* the cathedral's stone staircase. "Nice holoprojection, don't you agree?"

The security station was antiseptic. Lumipanels blazed in every wall, the ceiling, and the floor. Rybczynsky counted ten armed guards, with indications of at least six more in concealment. Still holding Rybczynsky's arm, Semuga thumbed an ID pad. A downchute dilated beneath their feet and eased them through the floor.

"Magnificent," Rybczynsky exclaimed. The control hall was sixty meters long, fifteen wide, and ten high. Consoles glittered. At least forty technicians worked here: uniformed cadets; robed monks; black-cassocked priests; costumed Swiss guards on floating watch platforms, clutching traditional halberds, contemporary antipersonnel weapons gleaming on their hips. Rybczynsky couldn't help smiling. "Ato, do you mean to take this planet?"

Semuga smiled back. "I thought we meant to take more than that."

Their downchute settled onto polished plasteel decking. Puffing, Semuga led Rybczynsky down the length of the hall. As best he could, Rybczynsky inspected the clustered readouts. One set displayed more than two dozen telescopic and spectroscopic views of Jaremi Four's surface, obviously taken from a single point in low orbit. Some jittered with static while others were clear. "You've built in space as well?" Rybczynsky asked.

"Indeed," Semuga confirmed.

"A surveillance platform?"

"That and more. You'll see."

Rybczynsky's brow furrowed. "In orbit? How do you avoid detection?"

"You will see," Semuga singsonged. "You will see."

A duty officer strode toward Semuga, clicked his heels. "Dispatch day today," said the officer in clipped tones.

"You'll enjoy this, Excellency," Semuga told Rybczynsky. The duty officer led them both inside a ring-shaped control console. On the backlighted surface of a central table, two small message scrolls lay side by side. Bubbles opened displaying a datacrawl of each scroll's meaning. They were identical, except that one scroll predicted that a well-known Northern-hemisphere satrapy would fall in a coming battle. The other predicted it would prevail.

"Which shall it be?" asked Rybczynsky.

"Both, Excellency," explained Semuga. "Half the recipients get the victory prediction. The other half get the prophecy of defeat." The duty officer led them toward a workstation at which gaunt monks controlled high-power orbital sensor arrays. Static from the binary clouded the picture, but one could still make out an aerial view of a meadow. Along its fringes two large primitive armies had begun to muster. Battle was at most a day away. "Soon after our autochthons receive their scrolls, they—and we—will know which prediction is true," Semuga explained.

Rybczynsky scowled. "Half your list will get the wrong prophecy."

"Exactly," confirmed Semuga. "Each time we lose half our targets. This scroll will go to half as many as the one before—only to the ones who received the correct prediction last time around."

The duty officer thumbed a control.

Semuga guided Rybczynsky toward a tridee bubble. "Now, Excellency, you will see what our trillions have bought."

Mothers of God, Rybczynsky thought. *For once in his life Ato Semuga employed understatement in composing his reports.* The tridee pickup prowled immense vaulted spaces. *A sizable manufactory in orbit.* Passing a curved glasteel-walled bay, the pickup panned right. Supervised by a Capuchin monk, rows of electromechanical printers inscribed endless scrolls in what seemed ordinary Jaremian calligraphy.

"How fast can scrolls be produced?" Rybczynsky asked.

"Seventy thousand in an hour," Semuga replied. "Each one personalized."

As Rybczynsky watched, scrolls tumbled from the printers and traveled down a colloidal slipfield. Manipulator fields snatched scrolls one by one and dropped them into fat plasteel cylinders. Robotic devices capped the loaded cylinders before arranging them into ten-meter-long trays, each of which reeled down another slipfield conveyor. The trays were catapulted into space. Viewed from outside, the manufactory was another skillfully disguised asteroid. Hundreds of trays drifted away from it, a glittering cloud. The trays ejected their cargoes of cylinders.

Thousands of cylinders floated at uniform intervals in every direction. Below their swarm gleamed the sun-dazzled limb of Jaremi Four. "Soon they'll enter the atmosphere," Semuga explained. "Each scroll comes to ground as a meteorite in a secluded spot accessible to its targeted recipient."

"This would be easier if Jaremi Four still had a postal system," the duty officer observed.

Rybczynsky harrumphed. "That would do nothing to rectify the inherent wastefulness of this distribution scheme."

I knew it had to come, Semuga thought. *The mocking, critical voice. Well, Alois, I am ready for you!* "True," Semuga agreed aloud, "with each dispatch we lose half of our prospects. But that can't be helped. What matters will be the end result. The autochthons who chance to receive *five* accurate predictions in a row will comprise only one thirty-second of the population we started with—a half of a half of a half of a half of a half—perhaps four thousand persons in all. But having received five correct prophecies, these will be four thousand petty leaders who'll believe—and obey—anything else we tell them." Semuga drew close. Whispered in Rybczynsky's ear. "By then, Excellency, we *will* have to know what to tell them."

Rybczynsky laid hands on the console and began punching controls. "In time, dear Ato, in time. For now let us see if an old man can help you raise *eight* thousand officers, instead of four, for your army of the deceived." Rybczynsky peered into a datacrawl. Smiled. "Here, Ato," he said, pointing with a manicured finger.

Semuga squinted. "An ephemeris?"

"A quasiperiodic ephemeris," Rybczynsky explained. "The autochthons can't predict when that cataclysmic binary will flare up, when the aurora will peak. We can." Rybczynsky raised the magnification and pointed again. "Look at the second column, showing the dates when energy fronts from the binary reach Jaremi space."

"Here's a sizable cataclysm," Semuga said.

"Will its effects be visible from the surface?"

"Definitely."

"And the date coincides with what?"

"That's when we plan to distribute the fifth and last scroll—oh, I see."

Rybczynsky nodded grimly. "One less split prophecy that costs us half our targets. We will make one *genuine* prediction, an astronomical forecast that is sure to come true. On that final round we needn't lose a single prospective believer."

"Delivering twice as many autochthonous lords for the end phase," Semuga breathed.

Rybczynsky nodded severely. "Dear Ato. If you had consulted me earlier, we might have put sixteen thousand petty lords at your disposal. Speak to me no more about the cost of versatility."

Damn you, old badger, Semuga thought. His eyes narrowed. "I'll need more probes." Whispering, he said, "And when the army's mission is determined, twice as much of whatever that mission demands."

"If it is within the power of the Church, it will be yours," promised Rybczynsky. "And remember, if our plans bear fruit very, very little will be beyond the power of the Universal Catholic Church."

41. Jaremi Four—Northern Hemisphere, City of Bihela

*T*he advice I receive in my peculiar visions has been highly effective, Parek reflected. He adjusted his snow-white, jewel-studded poncho. He wore the rich garment over a newly woven pearl-colored sweater. He also wore ivory canvas pantaloons and gray calf-high boots. He stood among the stout timbers that supported the stage his fashioners had constructed. Though he couldn't see the crowd he could hear its chanting. *So many!* Someone had told him ten thousand could squeeze into Bihela's amphitheater. "Pa-rek! Pa-rek! Pa-*rek!*" they chanted. Beneath the stage, Parek pumped at the air with clenched fists. He felt the old excitement again—the way he used to feel at the outdoor revivals he'd done with Dultav.

The way he used to feel before Ulf had seized his destiny.

✦ ✦ ✦

Laz Kalistor listened for the *verify* signal. Calmly he *pov*ed the increasingly expectant crowd awaiting Parek's eighth great meeting at Bihela. Kalistor's journal would never be aired; its only experients would be a small cabal with extremely special interests. Yet the way a Spectator observed and laid down a journal didn't change.

Kalistor reclined in a litter that leaned against a retaining bar. To his left, several dozen people on litters lined the back row of the section. Many were strapped in. The air reeked of piss. To Kalistor's right, across a narrow aisle, swept a sea of ancient seats. Four-fifths were filled with ambulatory onlookers. None seemed to mind the smell.

He surveyed the chamber. The ancient amphitheater's ceiling was a half dome blackened by generations of torchlight. Was it natural or artificial? He couldn't tell. The audience faced a great flat half-moon vertical expanse of rock—marble?—before which stood the stage.

Most people had been here three hours already. They were singing, chanting, writing questions on little reed-paper squares, sealing them in pouches and handing them to Parek's roving pages. They threw trinkets into the baskets ushers always kept in sight. "Pa-rek! Pa-rek! Pa-*rek!*"

Parek no more knew *how* the visions came to him than he did when the first one spurred him into the forest to await the curing powder. Nonetheless, he'd grown used to obeying their advice. So far the results had been encouraging.

Vision counsel had prompted him to work independently of the army. "Where's the real wealth, the influential converts?" Parek had asked Ulf. "In the collapsing cities! Places like Giwalczor and Bihela. Full of cultured people just recently uprooted, the ones most likely to accept a new religion. The army can't take those cities by force."

"Not yet," Ulf had admitted.

"But I can seduce them. Let me try!"

Ulf had shrugged noncommittally. "What d'you have in mind?"

"We're near Bihela. Leave me there for a month with a few dozen retainers. Take the army, ravage the countryside. When you return with your spoils, I'll greet *you* with the booty of Bihela. But Bihela will still be intact, its kitchens and manufactories and brothels still open to serve us."

As the vision predicted—*Is "vision" the right word for something I never see, but just remember?*—Ulf hadn't been able to resist that logic. Today, Parek was ready once more to seize the people's faith with both hands. *Already today I've seized the attention of my entourage.*

Kalistor had arrived four hours before, limping in circles before the amphitheater's crumbling entrance. Praying in a loud voice: "Oh sky gods, through the power of The Word Among Us let me be healed this day! Oh sky gods, this day I would walk like any man!"

The woman who approached him had *staff* written all over her. "Good day, yeoman," she said.

"I am called Laz Kalistor." No reason not to use his name; none but the cabalists would ever *pov* this journal.

Her eyes roamed him appraisingly, from his shoulders to his waist and to his crotch. "You came for healing?"

"For my leg." He raised his voice. "Oh, sky gods—"

"Yes, yes. What's wrong with your leg?"

"A draft animal knocked me down three years ago," Kalistor lied. "Nothing was broken. Everyone thought I'd get better, but I didn't."

"Why not?"

"I don't know. My brothers say I enjoyed the women taking care of me too much. But that can't be it."

She arched an eyebrow. "Your wife cared for you?"

"Her sisters, too. They indulged me like a chieftain." He shrugged. "It's like I forgot how to walk right." *That should sound psychosomatic enough for them.*

"Why seek healing now?"

"The famine. My family abandoned me. Now I must support myself. I crave healing! Oh sky gods—"

The woman nodded. "We'll see what The Word Among Us can pluck from the aurora for you."

"But I haven't the price of a ticket—"

"No matter." Uniformed orderlies had appeared bearing a litter fabricated from crude fabric and tree branches. "Get on."

"I don't need this," Kalistor protested. "I only limp!"

The woman leaned forward, face clouded. "You want healing? Get on the litter. Walk when you're told, and not before."

Chagrin tapped Parek's shoulder. He wore a gray slant-bottomed tunic and dark leather leggings over heavy boots. Hesitantly, he handed Parek a handful of small square reed-paper pouches. "The questions." Parek nodded and slipped them into a pocket. "Two minutes to stage time." Chagrin's voice quaked.

"You all right, old friend?"

"You ask me that?"

Parek's waxy gray scar wrinkled as he smiled. *Chagrin can't be blamed for reacting this way,* the prophet thought. *After all, he's the one who found me dead this morning.*

"Do I remember rightly, lord?" Chagrin asked hesitantly. "This morning you were—"

Parek nodded. "I was . . . on other business."

"You weren't breathing. Your body was cold." He swallowed hard. "Does it happen often?"

Whenever I dissolve a pinch of "mother matter" under my tongue, Parek said to himself. To Chagrin, he said, "Whenever I need a thing from the sky gods. Should you come upon me that way again, it's not necessary to sound the general alarm." Opening his eyes after half an hour of torpor, Parek had found thirty people crowding the bedchamber.

"Sorry."

Parek clasped Chagrin's arm. The disciple shrank from his touch. "It's still me, Chagrin! Please, tell no one else of this." Having thus ensured that the garrulous Chagrin would go on telling everyone the story of how he'd found the prophet dead, Parek reshuffled the question pouches. *Useful as my visions have been,* he thought, *I don't want to depend on them completely. Word of my brush with "death" should help ground my own power farther from Ulf's.*

"Seeking a miracle?" A stooped rustic pushed close to Kalistor. His family followed him down the crowded aisle. *A family,* Kalistor thought with mixed excitement and distaste. *For all my ethno conditioning, families still swirl my plorg. I swear, if these savage peoples could learn to form good solid procreant cliques their other problems might take care of themselves.*

The rustic wore sordid rags and a tattered coat. The spices on his breath did little to mask the stench of decaying gums. He was at most twenty. "You, sir, you here for a miracle?" he called.

Kalistor nodded. "Just get here? It'll be a miracle if you find a seat."

"Jerl, look!" the rustic's woman keened. "Three together!" She'd been pretty once, perhaps when she was fourteen. The four or five years since had been cruel. A lightning scar lanced down her forehead and across one cheek. Several teeth were chipped, the rest a sickly brown. Her left eye was almost opaque. With slaps and kicks she shepherded three grimy children of uncertain gender toward open seats almost across the aisle from Kalistor. The man let his brood in before him and turned to take the outside seat. A tattered rucksack hung from his back. With a start Kalistor realized that the . . . the *thing* in the sack was human.

The man sat cradling the horribly deformed two-year-old on his lap. The child had no ears. Hand-length flippers instead of arms, goggle eyes, and a cleft palate. Its torso seemed warped—*some fusing of the hips,* Kalistor speculated. "Talk about your miracles," the rustic called across the aisle, bouncing the monstrosity on his knee. "Now *I'm* here for one." He brushed cracked lips across the creature's misshapen head. "I'm here to see my son made whole."

Oh, you need a miracle, Kalistor thought. *Of the suspend-the-laws-of-nature, make-time-run-backwards variety. Unfortunately, nobody's handing those out today.*

Ten percussionists strode onstage. They wore motley costumes, Chagrin's old regalia as interpreted by a lunatic. By new-minted tradition their bell lyres were just like those used in the army's first marauding days, fashioned crudely from found materials. *Probably mass produced now,* Kalistor thought, *but details, details.* . . . At first the musicians just stood, bodies gently rocking in the slow rhythm of the audience's chants. "Pa-rek! Pa-rek! Pa-*rek!* Pa-rek! Pa-rek! Pa-*rek!*" On a downbeat they began to chime. *Clang-shang-ralang. Clang-shang-ralang. Clang-shang-ralang. Clang-shang-ralang. Clang-shang-ralang. Clang-shang-ralang.* Their meter first echoed, then transformed the rhythm of the chants. Smoothly they slid into the five-and-three rhythm Parek had always found best for making minds pliable. *Clang-shang-ralang. Clang-shang-ralang. Clang-shang-ralang. Clang-shang-ralang. Clang-shang-ralang. Clang-shang-ralang. Clang-shang-ralang. Clang-shang-ralang. Clang-shang-ralang. Clang-shang-ralang.*

A theater page pushed up the aisle, glancing at scraps of paper and scanning the litters. With practiced grace she swept past the rustics and their monster child, zeroing in on Kalistor. She leaned close. "Be patient. You'll be called." Then she was gone. Thrusting a hip into the aisle, she charged up the stairs. Deliberately she failed to notice the rustics' frantic waves. The mother and father crumpled into their seats. *Sorry,* thought Kalistor. *Parek's people understand who can be healed. And who can't.*

Parek stepped onto a seesaw contraption under the stage. Above his head was a mechanical trap door, still tightly closed. Robed acolytes stood by the mechanisms, eyeing Parek with mixed awe and terror. "See you're timely with the trap door," Parek bantered. "I'd hate to die twice today."

Beads of sweat wobbled down the acolyte's faces.

From above, ***Clang**-shang-ralang. Clang-shang-ralang. Clang-shang-ralang. Clang-shang-ralang. Clang-shang-ralang. **Clang**-shang-ralang. Clang-shang-ralang. Clang-shang-ralang.*

The crowd was swaying. Parek could feel it through his feet. In moments it would be show time.

Clang shang shang! The bell lyres clashed a final tattoo and fell silent. Kalistor's gaze swept the auditorium from left to right.

"People of Bihela!" someone cried through a megaphone. "This morning he abandoned his body to commune with the sky gods in their auroral home. This night he comes back to us. Gird your souls for an experience like no other. Terror of the ruined lands . . . prophet now and forever . . . The Word Among Us . . . *Arn Parek!*"

The center-stage trapdoor sprang open. Incendiaries flared. The seesaw rig spewed Parek onstage. With his poncho billowing, he charged up onto a raised platform and stood there, his arms upraised. The percussionists chimed furiously, triggering renewed chanting. ***Clang**-shang-ralang. "**Pa-rek!** Pa-rek! Pa-rek!" **Clang**-shang-ralang. "**Pa-rek!** Pa-rek! Pa-rek!" **Clang**-shang-ralang. "**Pa-rek!** Pa-rek! Pa-rek!"*

"Hear me!" Parek cried.

Silence.

Forty rows back, somebody sniffled.

Everyone heard it.

"Many in this city attended last night's revival, or one of the six before that," Parek declaimed. "I am not the same person any of them saw. I stand here tonight changed by my adventure beyond the skies. This morning I deserted this husk"— he slapped his chest— "and went into the aurora."

Audacious, Kalistor thought. He studied the nearest pages and ushers. *Their body language—they think he really did it. They're horrified that he speaks of it in public.*

"While I was there," Parek proclaimed, "I learned that the sky gods are not that much unlike us . . . indeed, that we are much like them. I learned that we all are gods in embryo. While I was learning that, my body was dead. But I came back."

Thunder rose. People were slapping the arms of their chairs, the Jaremian equivalent of applause.

"Hear me!" Parek screamed, arms upraised.

The silence washed back.

"As we gather here in harmony—as I speak the Word, as you write it on your hearts—my army rampages on the heaths and in the barren places. Defenders crumple before it, afflicted because of their iniquities. Behold, my soldiers pile up bodies like cordwood and set them alight. A mere handful survive to hear and accept the Word. Only here in Bihela have I come among you in peace. Upon Bihela only do I have compassion. Only to you do I offer the chance to restore your lives without first passing through fire and the sword."

Kalistor surveyed the crowd. He noted how the pages and ushers had been stationed, watching the likely shills—one of whom, he realized, would be himself. *Let Parek use me*, he thought. *I'll return the favor.*

"Everlasting welfare unto Bihela," Parek shouted, "where the Word first came in peace!" Parek stood immobile, arms upraised. He let the applause flow.

He reached into his poncho. The house went silent.

Whispers rustled through the audience as he produced ten or fifteen reed pouches. Theatrically he fanned them. "Many of you filled out cards and sealed them in these pouches. You were invited to express your deepest troubles. My acolytes selected these." Parek pulled one pouch from the fan and held it at arm's length.

Don't tell me, Kalistor thought, all but dumbfounded. *Don't tell me he's going to. . . .*

"Some questions are too profound, too urgent to answer publicly," Parek said gently. He raised his eyes and sought a face in the crowd a few rows behind Kalistor. He raised a pointing finger. "We will speak after the service, privately."

Kalistor whirled. A woman in checkered robes leapt from her seat, clasping her hands and wailing in something close to ecstasy. "Oh yes, Word Among Us! Thank you!"

Before he'd become a Spectator, Laz Kalistor had been a professional illusionist. No doubt that was why the cabal had chosen him. *Forjeler, this Parek's every bit as good as he looked in the early sensos. Better. We've gone so long with spotty coverage, and he's learned new tricks.*

Almost arrogantly, Parek opened that first pouch. He scanned the card inside, as if to confirm he'd divined it correctly. He nodded and thrust the card back into his poncho. He flourished another sealed pouch.

On the other hand, Kalistor thought, *what Parek's doing right now is anything but a new trick.*

Parek regarded the second pouch narrowly. "A visitor from Giwalczor craves knowledge of long-lost relatives," he announced. "He inquires after three cousins who set off for the south and never returned." Parek scanned the audience. A man in varicolored rags stood up, arms pumping delightedly.

Parek nodded toward him and closed his eyes, as if listening to the gods. "The youngest and the eldest live," he said abstractedly. The crowd murmured. "As for Nafuto"—the standing man yelped in wonder when Parek *named* the middle cousin—"I am assured that his death was easier than most."

Parek let the applause thunder while he opened the pouch. He read the card and smiled slightly.

Altogether, Parek consumed half an hour reading twelve such pouches. When he was finished scarcely a person in the hall doubted his power. Scarcely a person except Laz Kalistor, who had avidly subvocalized comments on top of his senso coverage. *"What Parek has done—it's a classic bunco cheat known as the one-ahead. That method for appearing to read the contents of a sealed message has been discovered on countless worlds. One begins by circulating a number of identical cards and envelopes, on which onlookers write questions. Ushers or pages gather the cards, and the bunco artist—in this case, Parek—makes a great show of trying to read one while it's still sealed. Of course, he can't. Several work-arounds are available: if he'd placed a shill in the audience, Parek could say anything about the contents of the first pouch and let the shill authenticate it. Without a shill, one simply announces that the first card is unreadable, or that the question inside is not appropriate to answer in public. Parek did that, but he added a nice wrinkle. He singled out a woman in the audience and told her it was* her *question that had so affected him. Her rapturous authentication sealed the illusion that Parek had in fact read the first card while it was still sealed.*

"Was that woman a shill? Not if Parek is as brash as I think he is. Audience members had been prompted to write questions they considered meaningful. Who wouldn't want to believe her question was that profound? Parek could point anywhere, confident that someone *would jump up in ecstasy.*

"By now, Parek has the audience thinking he has magically read the card inside the first pouch—which, of course, he didn't. Now he opens the pouch and reads the card normally. People think he's checking his accuracy. He's actually seeing what it says for the first time. He pockets that card, takes up the next sealed pouch, and pretends to scan it with his mind. Then he simply answers the question from the first *pouch, the one he read normally in front of everyone. That's why they call it the 'one-ahead.' The victims always think the con artist is reading one pouch ahead of where he actually is in the series."*

Parek's head bowed in contemplation. A choir slipped onstage. While they sang, robed ushers fanned through the crowd. It was the night's fifth collection, but the first after a Parek "miracle." The giving was bountiful, even extravagant. When the basket passed him, Kalistor made a show of showering into it a handful of high-grade steamrifle shells.

The usher crossed the aisle, almost masking his repugnance toward the rustics with their twisted child. The father reached into his threadbare coat, produced a bauble. The usher stared. So did Kalistor: In the usher's basket gleamed a digital camera from before the Great Dismay, crusted with mold but undented. It was the best-preserved artifact of Jaremi Four before the Tuezi that Kalistor, at least, had ever heard of—a treasure whose value, if one knew how to sell it, could've supported the rustic family in comfort for years.

"Does it work?" the usher asked, impressed.

"Last time we saw it hooked to an inductor." The rustic lifted his monster child. "Can The Word Among Us help my son?"

"If the sky gods will it." Ashen-faced, the usher turned away. He scurried downstairs with his precious cargo, gesturing frantically to be relieved.

The rustic felt Kalistor's eyes upon him. "I found it, sir," he explained, "years ago. It's the only thing of value we've ever possessed—and of little enough value for feeding a family."

Kalistor went hollow inside. *You down-and-out bastard, if only you knew.*

"Perhaps it can buy our little one a real life," the mother said, voice close to breaking.

Kalistor looked away. The choir was retreating. Parek had called a woman on stage who complained of unpredictable headaches. He waved his hands in circles over her. He stiffened one arm and proclaimed, "I stretch forth my hand and manifest your healing. Headaches shall burden you no more." Consumed by emotion, the woman needed two pages to help her from the stage.

Very neat, thought Kalistor. *Dramatic, emotionally satisfying—and no way to tell whether the "healing" really worked.* Still, the crowd applauded wildly. At a nod from Parek, ushers with empty baskets fanned out into the hall once more. *"What you will see next,"* Kalistor advised his shadowy experients subvocally, *"is not Parek's doing."*

He leaned into the litter and let his head roll back. Using years-old ventriloquist skills, he projected his voice up into the vaulted ceiling. As sounds do beneath half domes, it channeled along the ceiling's curvature and dropped from above at the corresponding spot on the other side of the house.

"I hear you!" shrieked a stocky woman. She stood up, thirty meters to Kalistor's right. She wore leather and corduroy and steel, body armor as the wealthy sometimes affected it.

"Sit back down!" Kalistor hissed into the ceiling. "We will address you where you are."

The woman fell into her seat. "Who . . . who are you?" she wailed.

Kalistor glanced about. All eyes were on the woman on the other side of the house. Even Parek stood transfixed.

"Who are you?" she wailed again.

"We are the sky gods," Kalistor projected.

"I hear you! The sky gods! The sky gods speak to me!"

Chagrin had edged onto the stage with a squadron of guards. Parek caught his eye and nodded angrily toward the woman. There was no mistaking the prophet's body language. The only miracles tonight were supposed to be his own.

"Tell The Word Among You to stay his guards," Kalistor cast upward. "Tell him we have a message for him—a message from Ruth."

"The sky gods would speak to you, Word Among Us," the big woman called. The guards had sprinted offstage, heading up two adjacent aisles, intent on surrounding the woman. "Stay your guards."

Parek did nothing. The guards kept coming.

"The sky gods have a message for you," the woman shrieked. "From Ruth!"

"Hold!" Parek barked. Only meters from the woman, the guards stopped. Parek waved them back.

"Ruth . . . Griszam!" Kalistor supplied. "She is in the aurora. She regrets having doubted him before."

Quaking, the stocky woman shouted out the message.

Parek was working through astonishment. He struggled to convey the impression that this miracle, too, was the fruit of his power. "Ruth?" he called out. "Ruth is dead?"

Kalistor took a calculated risk. "Ruth says The Word Among Us should not be concerned. He was where she is, just this morning."

"Do not worry, Word Among Us," the woman intoned. "Ruth is in a place you know. You were there this morning."

Parek's brow furrowed. "I did not see Ruth there."

"See," Kalistor had the woman shout. "The sky gods keep their secrets even from The Word Among Us. But beware, humans, you have no secrets from him!"

Kalistor decided to play one last trump. "Woman, show your faith. The gift you had decided not to make—make it now!"

He'd guessed right about the woman's wealth. She reached below her breastplate and drew out a jeweled necklace. Shrieking, she threw it in a high arc. It landed between two ushers, who scrambled to snatch up stones the impact had cast loose from their settings.

"We release you," Kalistor stage-whispered.

Here and there people were following the wealthy woman's example—ripping off necklaces and jeweled ornaments and pitching them toward the stage.

Parek took a step back, striving for composure. Urgently he nodded to the choir. It burst into song as the ushers raked up the unexpected booty.

Parek reclaimed the momentum with two more showy healings. Then he stepped forward and scrutinized the right side of the house. "Where is Laz?" Parek demanded.

As though too much shouting and praising had rendered him mute, Kalistor leaned forward in his litter and waved his arms. *Wouldn't want anyone to hear the sky gods again.*

Chimes roiled. Ushers lifted Kalistor's pallet and carried him onstage. "Laz comes to us from the barren places," Parek announced. "He's been deeply lame, unable to work since a beast of burden made pulp of his leg three years ago." Parek turned to Kalistor. "Three years ago. Isn't that right?"

Kalistor nodded passionately. *That's right, ask me to confirm the only part of my own story you haven't exaggerated beyond recognition.*

At Parek's gesture, ushers set Kalistor's litter between two tall sawhorses. "Returning the power of locomotion to the lame and halt is among the most difficult of miracles," Parek told the crowd. "Be silent and pray with me. Let us call down a covenant that Laz be restored." For five minutes Parek stalked in circles around the litter and roared out nonsense syllables. He screwed shut his eyes and splayed his fingers so wide his hands trembled. He made mystic passes over Kalistor's body. Sweat rushed along his skin. "Laz," Parek said in a voice Kalistor alone could hear. "When I bid you, by the power of the sky gods you will rise and walk!"

Parek posed before the audience with his feet spread wide, his arms outstretched at his sides. He turreted one arm. Its fingers pointed straight out and over the onlookers' heads. "I stretch forth my hand and manifest your healing," Parek shouted in a commanding voice. "Rise. Walk!"

Kalistor sat up without effort. Before he could fling his legs over the edge of the litter, Parek's hand was on his shoulder. Pressing him back, hard. "Slowly, slowly," Parek whispered.

Kalistor played along. Gingerly he slid his buttocks off the litter and touched toes to the stage. He withdrew his hands from the litter and stood erect.

The audience exploded into screams and slapping applause.

Kalistor took two wobbly steps. He began with increasing confidence to stride about the stage.

Below, ushers scattered yet again through the crowd.

Kalistor looked into Parek's eyes. He watched shock and satisfaction bloom into delight. *If I'd just come off that litter with the limp I had this morning, it would have been miracle enough*, Kalistor thought. *And that's all Parek expected. Instead, The Word Among Us thinks he's brought me to full mobility. Another genuine miracle, like Chagrin.*

Kalistor stepped forward and clasped Parek's hands. "You will remember this," Parek husked. He scarcely noticed the folded paper Kalistor pressed between his fingers.

Two ushers flanked Kalistor as he cantered downstairs and off the stage. Onlookers pressed forward, some to congratulate the man who had been so spectacularly healed, others just to touch him. "Sky gods be praised!" cried one. "The power of The Word Among Us rests heavy on you!" bawled another. However false he knew it to be, not even Kalistor could resist the feeling.

Borne back to his seat on a torrent of joy, his heart jetted upward like some scrap of driftwood riding a flash flood.

Ushers had set a portable chair where his stretcher had been. The other cripples still languished in rows of litters. The excrement smell was sharper now. Kalistor struggled not to look to his right. Eventually he had to. Uncomprehending, accusing, the eyes of the rustic family drew his with siren power. Both adults and children gaped not in wonderment but in covetous hate—the father, his ruined woman, scarred and cloudy-eyed, the three healthy—if that was the word—children. Despair etching his features, the man clasped a trembling hand to the misshapen head of the two-year-old. The gesture was an indictment. There was no mistaking its message: "Why *you?*"

Onstage, Parek stood beside his warbling choir, concealing a quizzical expression.

He'd opened Kalistor's note.

"Remember the woman who heard the sky gods?" it read. "She was my gift to you. Do not seek me, I will come to you again in private. Laz."

The seed's been planted, Kalistor told himself. He had no illusion that Parek would heed the "do not seek me" passage, but hoped The Word Among Us wouldn't send guards to look for him until after the service. When the time seemed right Laz Kalistor lost himself in the crowd. He fled the hall into the aurora-streaked night.

42.   On Board the Schooner *Bright Hope*

The land stretched unspeakably flat in all directions. Even the vegetation was gunmetal gray. A faltering breeze did nothing to relieve the clammy humidity. Annek Panna and Captain Laurien Eldridge stood on a modest metal platform. Though it stood a scant meter and a half above the ashen flatland, the extra height significantly expanded their visual horizon. Not that there was anything to see.

This was a sim of Gwilya, after all.

"It even smells like home," Panna whispered, blinking puffy eyes. She was tall but sickly slender, with kinked hair and waxy olive skin. Her jumper was blazoned with the six-starred crest of Gwilyan Comprehensive Ultiversity.

Eldridge sipped a transparent intoxicant. She settled into an aluminum-colored chaise longue. "You said you missed it."

"True enough," said Panna, settling into a chaise longue of her own. "Too long we spend just racing across the Galaxy. Too bright. Too busy." She stared out at the barren horizon and sighed. "It was in a place like this—an actual place, of course, not an echo in some schooner's recreational sim chamber—that I designed my stardrive."

The drab panorama was as characteristic of Gwilya as oceans and jagged cliffs were of Ordh. Eldridge and Panna were both Gwilyans, and Gwilyans abroad seldom missed an opportunity to recenter themselves in such an ancestral milieu. "I should come here more often," Eldridge breathed. "I could stand more time to just think."

"Think about what?" Panna chuckled. "Watch and wait, that's what you do all day. At least it's your duty. I do the same, but for less reason."

"Something could go wrong with your drive."

"But it won't," said Panna. "That's not ego talking, I just know the math involved. So for me, this shakedown cruise is the quintessence of boredom." She tugged at her short-cropped hair. "The others—the ones who believe some religion—sometimes think there's a higher reason for everything in their lives."

Eldridge frowned. "I never accepted that."

"Few Gwilyans would. But have you ever wondered what it would be like? To believe, to suppose your every experience meshed into some matrix of hidden significance?" Panna stood, stepped to the rail of the low platform.

Eldridge drained her glass. "I can't imagine. I genuinely can't."

Panna turned toward Eldridge. "So why did you join the PeaceForce?"

"The procreant clique I grew up in had a tradition of sending every twentieth child into the military. I was it."

"You had no choice?"

Eldridge shrugged. "I could opt out. But no one had in over a century. Funny, while that never seemed onerous to me, I'm sure many people would think it as oppressive as anything that goes on in a natural family. The more things change . . ." She went to the autobar and refilled. "How about you, Annek? Where did your motivation come from?"

"What's the first question that any two Galactics who've achieved *anything* must ask each other?"

Eldridge frowned. "Um, 'why did you choose to do anything at all?'"

"Exactly," Panna said intensely. "We have such wealth. No real enemies. Why strive for anything? Why not just put the senso player on 'continuous' and never come back?"

Eldridge nodded somberly. "Why stand on the shoulders of giants when you can sleep there instead?"

In the middle distance, a sim shrike whirled over the plains on outstretched wings. A chubby sim rodent peered from a clay-ringed hole in the prairie. It never saw the predator. The shrike lurched skyward, wings pumping, the vole in its talons. It dove toward a thorned scrub bush and released its burden. Finger-length thorns impaled the vole in a dozen places. The shrike circled, waiting for the vole to stop twitching. Then it moved in to feed. Panna watched it all in silence. "You see, Captain, I never got around to answering that question."

"I don't follow."

Panna paced toward the autobar. "I never actually decided not to *pov* my life away. I never confronted the temptation; evading it isn't the same thing. At the ultiversity, I just dabbled around. Propulsion science happened to capture my interest, but it could have been anything else. And I never had the illusion that designing stardrives would be my reason for living." She refilled her goblet. "Like every student, I knew that someday I'd need to decide whether to just be an experient all my life. But I never did. I kept finding interesting research problems. I just lurched from one accomplishment to the next, but all the while I'd never really resolved whether engagement in the real world was the life I wanted."

"Could you go back now?" Eldridge asked. "Turn away from it all, become a senso hermit?"

"That's what terrifies me," hissed Panna. "I'm *sure* I could! All this time cruising without priorities—it's been enormously difficult. I've had nothing but time, and I spend most of it realizing how easy it would be to void my commitments and go live out my days back on Gwilya in comfortable gray ease, endlessly *pov*ing."

Eldridge regarded Panna helplessly.

"Forjeler, Laurien," Panna breathed. "You don't think you have a good enough reason for the sense of duty you feel. I'm not sure I have a duty. I can't put into words how it frightens me that out here, I may finally tackle the question I've spent my life evading."

"Captain?" The voice belonged to the X.O., Gavisel's. It echoed incongruously in the drabness.

"Eldridge here."

"I know you didn't want to be disturbed, but we are receiving new orders from High Command. Your eyes only."

"Be there presently." Eldridge emptied her glass. The intoxicant was sim, too; its effect would vanish when she exited the chamber. "I don't know what to say to you."

"You must say farewell," Panna said quietly.

Eldridge nodded. "Have a good daypart. Duty calls."

"I envy you."

Eldridge flickered away from the platform. Panna was alone at the center of ineluctable gray desert.

Empty without, empty within, Panna thought forlornly. *How I ache for the want of purpose. Any purpose.* She drained her glass in one gulp. The sim *aqua vitae* burned her mouth and throat most satisfyingly. *Yes,* she thought with grim self-knowledge. *Any purpose at all.*

43. Jaremi Four—Vatican Island

"**P**riority communication from Cardinal Rybczynsky," the comm unit trilled.

"Forjeler!" Ato Semuga flung his bulk toward the edge of the whirlpool tub. Soapy water splattered. Inattention earned the slave youth whose mouth had been at Semuga's crotch a bloody nose. "Sorry, child." Semuga thumbed the *vision protect answer* switch. Formally he answered: "At your service, Your Eminence."

The audio-only connection opened. Semuga could hear the hushed console noises of a ship's comm center. "I can't see anything," he heard Rybczynsky say testily to someone on his end. "Is the comm circuitry defective?"

"I am audio-only from this end," Semuga shouted. "Your excellency calls at . . . a private moment."

Hand over nose, the youth rose from the tub. Semuga cringed, frustrated; surely Rybczynsky had heard the water slap. "You're so circumspect, Ato," Rybczynsky said dryly. "No one expects the old celibacy any more."

"Where are you now?" Semuga asked, eager to change the subject.

"Returning to Vatican from Jaremi space, in transit aboard a Church-owned caravel. I call with urgent word from Vatican."

Semuga sat up straighter in the frothy water. Fat tottered on his chest and flanks. Waves slapped the big tub's sides. "Have they decided where we shall find the Christ?" Semuga demanded.

"Not yet," Rybczynsky answered, "but you must mobilize. Do it at once."

"Mobilize eight thousand petty lords and their troops to no purpose in particular?"

Rybczynsky sounded genuinely abashed. "I am sorry, my friend. The theologians still can't agree whether Christ is an adult or a newborn. But they say developments are unfolding faster than anticipated. They say that even though we know not why we need our weapon, it is time to withdraw it from its sheath."

Semuga stroked his chins. "The eruption of the binary, which our fifth prophecy so fortuitously predicts, will be electronically disruptive. I could dispatch general orders to our eight thousand at the height of the outburst without risk of detection."

"Good. Do so."

Semuga shifted his weight in the slick water. "It shall be done, Excellency. And

I can doubtless stretch out the mobilization to consume eight or ten weeks. After that, we must know what use we will make of our forces, lest they lose their edge."

"If that interval passes and the theologians still have not reached a decision, you will have to keep them sharp," Rybczynsky said with cold precision. "Until then, be kind to yourself. We are men. Today's Church allows us certain outlets for our passions. Be not self-conscious about enjoying the pleasures ritual pederasty puts within your reach."

"As you say, Excellency."

"After all, Ato, you know what Ignatius of Loyola said. 'Give me a boy until he is five, he is mine forever.' And you know what Pope Pius the Fifteenth said as he ratified the *Codex Pederasticus.*"

" 'Give me a boy until he is ten,' " Semuga quoted. " 'Then I lose interest.' "

"Words to live by, Ato."

"I take your meaning, Excellency. Semuga out." Semuga allowed himself a grin he knew his superior couldn't see. *If Alois knew which pleasure I was enjoying when he called, he would not have been so quick to encourage me.* The cardinal piloted his bulk out of the whirlpool. His fishbelly skin jostled with each step.

The youth sat hunched, slender fingers pressed over the bridge of the nose. "Ah, my beauty," Semuga said oleaginously, holding out his hand. "I'm sorry, I did not mean you pain." The youth's eyes widened in wonder—at his whiteness, or his corpulence? Semuga was never sure. Slim fingers wrapped around Semuga's meaty digits. The cardinal smiled. "When I mean you pain, you will know it. Come forward, be not ashamed."

The slender native child pressed against him. With a still-wet thumb Semuga brushed away a trace of blood beneath one nostril and stroked the youth's cheeks and lips. He fondled her spare young breasts. The girl pressed her cheek against his chest, alternately gasping and snuffling. Semuga stopped. He lifted her face toward his. She tried to speak but produced only faint gruntings.

"It is all right," he said gently. "Clear your head." She blinked, placed two fingers against one nostril, and exhaled explosively. A crimson rope of congealed blood and mucus slapped onto Semuga's chest. Its was as long as two fingernails were wide. Pink water rolled from it, wending between his chest hairs.

Semuga held the girl close and guided her hands where he wanted them. His flesh looked even whiter beneath her chocolate skin. He led the mute Jaremian waif back toward the whirlpool tub. "We must have our pleasure quickly," he whispered. "Then Uncle Ato must go and start a war."

44. Jaremi Four—Northern Hemisphere, Labokloer's Fortress

The auroral light cast lambent speckles on the bedchamber's flagstones. Through frost-rimmed dormers Ruth Griszam watched the aurora frolic. *So bright,* she thought. *And soon to become so much brighter.* She could see her breath. She clutched the layered fur and flannel comforters more tightly around her.

Beside her, Friz Labokloer grunted and stirred in his sleep. He was half in, half out of a rumpled fur comforter, with a small Jaremian kaleidoscope—a *n'dren*—chained round his neck. Ruth lay on her back, stretched straight out. *Logging on to do your housekeeping with your autochthonous lover snoring at your side is not generally recommended,* Ruth admitted to herself. *If he awakes and finds my attention completely elsewhere, I could have some explaining to do. Still, Friz Labokloer is no Willim Dultav. And if there's a danger of losing contact with the bird this morning, I'd better tidy things up.*

She plunged into Mode and prowled her saybacks. They were dismal, as they had been ever since she'd taken up with Labokloer. *No matter how good the sex is, these Arthur-and-Guinevere things never pull,* she thought dourly. *Not unless there's a good war on, and since Friz started following those plorg-warming prophecies he wins his battles hands down.* She shifted. Something jabbed her flank. *Another forjeling* n'dren, she thought. She frowned and swept the forgotten kaleidoscope out of bed. *Just another of the annoying qualities he's developed since that oracle came into his life.* Expecting more sour news, Ruth peeked at her financials.

Spectators of her experience weren't supposed to gasp and sit bolt upright when something surprised them. *But this!* Her worth had almost doubled. Literally overnight, she'd been credited with almost as much as she'd earned during her glory weeks with Parek at the dam. *"Explicate,"* she subvocalized.

Suck, rush, wrench.

A senso playback inhaled her awareness. *An echo of my own reportage,* she puzzled.

She was back inside the dam, sitting next to Dultav at the lantern table, eating *skraggel.*

"Arn Parek is the only kind of holy man there is—or ever was—one hundred percent bogus," Dultav told her.

Ruth laughed long and bitterly. "A fake holy man!"

"It's a living."

Ruth-in-the-bed thrust a part of her consciousness beneath the surface of the echo playback. As expected, her OmNet handlers had appended an explanatory subtext. *So let's see what this old journal has to do with that bolus infusion of cash.*

"How did this start?" Ruth-in-the-senso demanded.

"I told you, I used to teach sociology, philosophy, religion. Arn was my top graduate student. He had a grasp of the material—of what religion *meant* to people—like no one I'd ever known."

Forjeler in chains, Ruth-in-the-bed whistled inwardly. *So that's where the money came from.* OmNet's lawyers had patiently and discreetly unraveled layers of dummy conglomerates. It was the Universal Catholic Church which had demanded total rights to this journal: unlimited rights to rebroadcast, repackage, and issue sensos, tridees, twodees, audio-only, and print—anywhere, anytime they wanted. It was an unprecedented request.

"He'd been analyzing the refugees of the Great Dismay," Dultav was explaining, "their experiences, their fears, their dreams, the kinds of new societies they were piecing together while all the structures they'd known were collapsing. What do people need when they're scrambling to make sense of the fact that finally, after generations of false alarms, they really *have* lost everything? Arn put theology and social science together and, well, concocted a religion appropriate to the times."

Ruth's OmNet handlers had responded to Vatican's unprecedented request by striking an unprecedented bargain: the most lucrative residual contract any Spectator had ever received for a single journal. *I thought my stint with Parek had made me rich before. Now I'm flush beyond anything I dreamed.*

Ruth-in-the-bed logged off, shook her head ever so circumspectly. *The Universal Catholic Church is as permanent as an unsavory reputation. Arn Parek's a fad. Why should Vatican want to go to such expense to make Parek look bad? What the sfelb, that's not my problem.*

Bells seemed to sound in her mind. *Some new alarm from the bird?* she wondered. Her awareness twisted back into the real world. The bells were actual. *Slaves,* she realized. *Sounding bells in the antechamber. A wake-up call? Now?*

Labokloer regarded Ruth with bleary eyes. "Good morning, my beauty," he said tenderly.

Ruth scowled. She pretended to rub sleep from her eyes. "Morning's a while off."

"Dawn comes early today," Labokloer said blissfully. "You'll see." To the slaves outside he shouted, "We're awake! Leave breakfast. I'll tend the fire. Go." He kicked off the comforter and padded toward the bedchamber's man-high fireplace. Dull-red coals still flickered in the fire grate. Labokloer was a silhouette. Groaning as he squatted, his limbs stiff with cold and sleep, he thrust twigs and slender branches into the coals.

Ruth thumbed her bedside lantern alight. Her eyes flickered onto the mattress. Where Labokloer's legs had been, there was a bloody spot.

Ruth went fully into Mode. Suck, rush, wrench! Labokloer had his back to her; he couldn't have seen her eyes dance even if she'd let them, which of course she hadn't.

She stared again at the bloodstain so her experients could register it. *Okay, outer self, you're on.* Angrily Ruth surged out of bed. The cold of the bedchamber slapped against her. She stared down at Labokloer. He wore only his kaleidoscope and a band of dark gray fur, a hand's breadth high, wrapped around his right calf. At its top and bottom one could see tiny sharp-edged thorns that bit into his flesh. She knew the inner face of the band bristled with thorns. "Damn you," she hissed, "you're still wearing it! How long has it been on?"

She recalled their lovemaking the previous evening. He'd come to her in the bath, still wearing fur-lined leather trousers and outdoor boots. He'd caressed her in the water and drawn her up to sit on the big tub's tall edge. He'd worked his trousers down only to his knees and taken her. When they'd screwed again, in bed in the middle of the night, the fur comforter had swaddled his lower legs. The story had been similar the night before that, and the night before that. . . . Sudden realization further darkened her voice. "You've had that—that *thing* on for days!"

"I've told you what it's called," he said icily. "It's a *silish.* It belongs to my new spiritual discipline."

Ruth turned her back on him.

"You like all this well enough," he said, striding around to face her. "Wealth, prestige, security. You don't mind these things my oracles give. But they say more. They tell me to perform exercises. This morning, I'm to perform a new exercise. The *silish* is part of that, and I remove it for no one—not even for you, my love." He reached to brush a bent index finger along the underside of her breast.

She pushed the hand away and gestured toward the *silish*. "I thought I told you—"

He gripped her shoulders—gently enough, but with a firmness behind it that suggested the force he could wield if he chose to. "I don't do everything a woman tells me," he growled. "Anyway, you said you didn't want to see the *silish* when we made love. Did you see it? Then I kept my bargain." He squatted and turned back to the swelling fire.

Ruth paced the frigid chamber. *I meet a man and some forjeling religion comes between us. It's becoming a pattern. The only difference between Dultav and Labokloer is that whoever's behind Friz's oracles only wants to kill him slowly.*

The massive fireplace was flanked by man-high metal doors, one on each side of the hearth. Labokloer opened one. "Dress for outside."

The door on the opposite side of the hearth was Ruth's closet. "Where are we going?" she asked.

"Just the terrace. But we'll be there a while."

Ruth pulled on a thick woolen undergarment. Like everything in the metal closet, it was deliciously charged with the fire's warmth. "Why so early?"

Labokloer grimaced as he pulled a tight woven legging over the leg bound with the *silish*. "This is the appointed time."

"Your oracle?"

Labokloer nodded as he tugged on oversized fur trousers. "That fifth scroll I got. Its prediction will come true—or not—in minutes. Don't talk so much, dress."

Ruth reached for a fleece-lined leather parka. Its metal fittings sounded like ice when they bangled. They threw back reflections in all the colors of the aurora. *The aurora!* She couldn't help taking a breath. *Does he know what's going to happen in the sky? The cataclysmic binary spasmed four hundred thirty-six days ago. The radiation will hit the upper atmosphere in minutes. Friz's oracle knows* that?

The private terrace erupted from the castle's wall six stories up. Its view was magical. Even breathing through a scarf she felt the hairs in her nasal passage frost over. Labokloer took her double-gloved hand in his. His other hand held one of his ubiquitous kaleidoscopes. "Only the *n'dren* shows us greater beauty than the northern sky," he said. "Soon the sky's beauty will overtake any *n'dren*. That's the prophecy. The scroll predicted wings in the sky."

A crevasse began to open inside her. *Wings in the sky! The autochthons' term for an auroral formation associated with radiation storms of exceptional magnitude.* "How soon?"

"Minutes."

How can anyone know that here? She watched the northern sky. Another part of her awareness snaked into the bird. She appended an emergency *oboy-watch-this* code to her journal. According to her briefings, others on Jaremi Four had received oracle scrolls. But until now no Spectator had *pov*ed a recipient verifying a scroll prediction—assuming she didn't lose touch with her bird. *It all depends upon how much EM noise the radiation kicks up in the stratosphere. Even OmNet can't predict that.* "It's colder than shit out here," she said.

"Nah, shit's warm."

"You said this is another spiritual exercise?"

"The fifth scroll demands my unconditional commitment."

"To what?"

"The command was clear. If there are no wings in the sky—if the prophecy fails—I am free. If the wings appear, I must shout eternal loyalty to the sky gods."

"Be careful what you promise, Friz."

His voice was ecstatic. *"Look there!"*

A patch of northern sky frothed with light. Furrowed tongues of color explored a steadily growing span of sky. Iridescent cilia trembled and flowed. Like crystal order whisking across a film of freezing water, gossamer ligatures erupted throughout the auroral display. They blazed across at least twenty degrees of the northern sky.

Like God stepping out of his chrysalis, Ruth thought.

A hundred kilometers overhead, a central pillar took shape. Striated pinions boiled from it. The sheets of luminance rippled so far to the east and west that Ruth saw them as simultaneously flat *and* curved. Nested layers of internal structure blazed—channels, tendons, ligaments. And the colors—saffron, melon, tangerine—these were shades Ruth had never seen in the aurora before.

A brighter patch unfurled at the pillar's core, an actinic blue almost painful to watch. Like a sky-sized blister it swelled, forcing a pressure front throughout the display. For a terrible moment, there in the swirling radiance of the central pillar, Ruth thought she'd made out a sinister face with unfeeling eyes, an endlessly widening mouth, and teeth in ranks as thick as tweed. Then the pattern changed. It was a face no more. Green and salmon fluorescence billowed in meaningless tumbles.

"Look!" Labokloer whispered.

The pinions—the vast churning sheets of light that had overspread the whole of the northern sky—were undulating in a smooth, powerful movement.

Upstroke.

Downstroke.

The wings in the sky were flapping.

Has anyone pov*ed an aurora this fierce?* Ruth wondered. *The ionosphere must be seething.* From inward, an alarm tone . . . the *verify* signal grew scrappy and granular. It expired. Ruth had lost contact with her satellite.

"You see?" Labokloer howled. "See the power of my oracle!" He marched forward to the terrace's edge, raised his arms, and threw back his head. "The prophecy is fulfilled! I will follow you!" he bellowed. He pumped gloved fists toward the roiling sky. "I'll follow you forever!"

Ruth felt hollow. *What a time to be out of touch.*

Labokloer turned toward her. His face was bliss.

"The prediction came true," she said at last. "You gave your commitment. Now what will it want from you?"

"That hasn't been revealed," he said contentedly. "All I know is I'm supposed to think of this as the last pure demonstration of the oracle's power."

Ruth nodded grimly. "In other words, the next voice you hear will give orders." Disgusted, she rolled her eyes upward. She spotted something! "What's that?"

High in the western sky, a point of light utterly unlike the frothing meringues of aurora—steadier, warmer, unvarying—was coming their way. Reflexively, Ruth slide-stepped, turning her head to catch Labokloer's reaction.

He was terrified.

"There wasn't supposed to be a sixth scroll," he rasped.

"When the oracle sends you a scroll, it looks like *that?*" She subvocalized the most urgent override codes she knew. There was no response. Her bird was still down.

The meteor grew brighter, stationary in the sky. *It's coming straight for us!* Ruth couldn't break Labokloer's grip on her hand. *He's seen this before,* she reminded herself, *and he's not afraid.* The meteor jinked downward. It slammed into—*through*—the fortress wall just two stories below them. They felt the impact in their chests and feet.

Side by side, they stared over the balustrade. Two floors below them the broad patio was flecked with ice shards, slabs of stone, and flaming timbers. "Just a leatherworking shop down there," Labokloer said. "No one would be there this early." He reached under the lip of balustrade and twisted a hidden lever. A fire ladder dropped out of the terrace roof above them. It slid down toward the patio on oiled tracks. "Go!" he cried, clambering on.

Ruth followed. "Every scroll you get, *this* happens?" she cried.

"The other times I woke up knowing to go out to the woods. The scroll would land in a clearing."

"This time somebody skipped a step." Again she struggled to *tap* her bird. No response.

They dropped onto the debris-strewn patio. A jagged hole twice the width of a man's chest pierced the fortress wall. Light from a sizable fire danced within what had been the leatherworking shop. Labokloer drew beside the opening. He stopped and raised an arm. "Hold!"

Ruth stopped short.

There was a hissing sound from inside. The orange glow guttered and died. The fog wafting through the hole was so cold that even in this icy dawn it hugged the flagstones. *I don't forjeling believe this,* Ruth growled to herself. *Friz gets one of his oracles right in front of me—resembling nothing so much as a Galactic secured courier canister, right down to the fire suppression system—and I can't record a thing.*

Labokloer levered himself through the hole. He waved for Ruth to follow. The shop was a shambles. Foamy ice caked angled surfaces that seconds before had been afire. "I liked it better when they came down in the fields," Labokloer grunted, shouldering debris aside.

At the center of the room, a metallic cylinder lay half buried in frost.

Ruth let herself gasp out loud. Friz Labokloer found the reaction natural, though he could not suspect why she was so surprised. *Forjeler in plorg, that looks Galactic!* Grimly she tried again to punch through the static. *Just give me enough bandwidth to send tridee. Duplex voice. Anything. . . .*

Mockingly, the bird remained silent.

Labokloer squatted before the cylinder. He tugged off two sets of gloves and picked it up. Deftly he began to deactivate its nested locks.

"You know how to do that?" Ruth hissed.

"I . . . remember," Labokloer answered, puzzled. "Just before I need to do something, I feel like I've always known how."

Its seams glowing green, the cylinder yawned open. Labokloer withdrew a foolscap scroll and unrolled it. Ruth glimpsed what seemed like classical Jaremian script. "What does it say?" she asked.

Labokloer turned to face her. His face was flinty. "So soon. So soon. This is the bill for my good fortune." She snatched the scroll and tried to *tap* the satellite again. No reply.

The paper seemed ordinary enough. So was the calligraphy. *But the content. . . .*

Labokloer tugged his gloves back on. "It's full of allegory. To make sense of it, you must have grown up here with all the heroic poems and legends. But it's clear to me. I am called to war."

Ruth stepped backward. *Galactics fomenting war on an Enclave world? Or has some autochthon resurrected an ancient Jaremian messaging technology whose existence we never suspected?* Aloud she only said, "Oh, Friz, no."

Labokloer nodded heavily. "I must mobilize my fighters. We will journey ahead of them to Giwalczor. An expeditionary force will be assembled there. Our mission, it says, is to fight the false god."

"What's *that* mean?"

"I have no idea. Perhaps on the way to Giwalczor I'll remember." He caught her eye. "Watch the scroll."

Magenta filaments crackled across the foolscap. They seemed hot, but somehow their fury never left the plane of the paper. In seconds the scroll was gone. The metallic cylinder vanished in a confined haze of whitish glare.

Labokloer bulled the shop door open. Firefighters and security troops scrambled in. Ruth drifted back toward the scroll probe's entry hole. The wings in the sky were collapsing. Ruth's awareness blossomed into multiple levels in the old familiar way. A bubble opened in her consciousness. It was the bird's test pattern. *Wonderful, now I get my connection back.*

Back on the patio, she and Labokloer stared into a darkening dawn. She sucked in draughts of needle-cold air. *I may not be able to prove anything I saw,* she thought. *But I can forjeling well scream out a warning.*

45. Jaremi Four—Northern Hemisphere. City of Bihela

The ancient mortar clattered on the receiving table. "It's from before the food riots," its owner said. Although no more than thirty, he looked twice his age. "Issued by a government."

"So?" a bored adjutant drawled. "Does it shoot?"

"Far as I know. You have shells?"

"One government issue mortar, functionality uncertain," the adjutant recited as he wrote. "No shells." He lay down his pencil. He expected more.

A banner bearing a huge likeness of Parek rippled on the afternoon breeze. Lines of ragtag pilgrims snaked toward eight big tables in the square before Bihela's amphitheater. No mass healing was scheduled tonight, so access to The Word Among Us was doled out by Parek's guards. The price: what the market would bear.

The mortar man laid out more things. "Two cans, unknown meat product," the adjutant recited. "One jar of pickled *fhlet*. No visible decay. One compass, broken. . . ."

"Crystal's cracked, is all. Still works." The man put a gentle arm around his woman. For her part, she poked at a festering sore on her cheek. "Isn't that enough?" he demanded.

The adjutant eyed the woman. He shrugged. "She looks really sick."

The man fumbled inside his threadbare field jacket. He tossed a hypodermic needle onto the table.

"Still in the government package," said the adjutant. "Nice."

"Adequate," a cruel voice rasped. "Nothing more."

"Lord Chagrin!" the adjutant sprang to his feet and saluted fist-on-chest.

The First Disciple wore a brightly colored sash over layered leather garments in gray and black. He took the wrapped hypo and eyed the mortar man coldly. "You got anything to use with this?"

"Pardon?" the man asked.

"Drugs," Chagrin said impatiently.

"I have nothing more. Can The Word Among Us bless my wife?"

Chagrin stepped back. He signaled the adjutant to resume.

Lips drawn tight, the adjutant scrutinized the woman. "Just the facial sore?"

"My knees hurt, too," the woman blurted.

"I don't know." Finger on chin, the adjutant rocked from side to side.

"Robbery, that's what this is." The man reached into his waistband. Reluctantly he produced a pitted metallic telescope of obvious prewar manufacture.

"Not that," the woman moaned.

"I need you well, darling." The man held the instrument in trembling hands. The adjutant took it greedily. He remembered who was looking over his shoulder.

"Your tribute is appreciated," Chagrin husked, slipping the telescope into a his cape. "The healing entrance is on your right. Follow the signs." With a curt "Carry on!" to the adjutant Chagrin strode away.

"Next!"

A spindly young man stepped forward. He whispered furtively in the adjutant's ear.

The adjutant nodded. He bellowed, "Price check! How much for impotence?"

"Who, that scrawny guy?" a clerk shouted back.

"Hasn't gotten it up in two years," yelled the adjutant. People were staring.

"I'd take his boots," the clerk opined. "A boot a year."

"You heard him," the adjutant snapped. "Lose the boots."

Furious, the man gestured toward his knapsack. "They're the only boots I've got! Don't you want to see what I brought *intending* to offer?"

"No boots, no cure." The adjutant made a show of straightening intake forms. "You can walk or you can fuck. You decide. But don't dawdle."

"Next!" The votary in charge of the fourth intake desk lacked a right arm, a right eye, and two spoonfuls of tissue from his right cheek. Even so, he smiled at the two penitents who trudged before him. The man looked like a rancher. The girl was maybe fourteen. Under a layer of grime she was beautiful.

"I've done this before," the rancher said. He lay a bulky hand on the girl's shoulder. "This is my daughter. She's a virgin."

"One virgin, alleged," the votary recited, pencil dancing. "Height, ten and a half hands. Weight, forty *drajhms* . . ."

The girl bristled. "Thirty-seven!"

"Never fails." The votary stood. "Open your mouth."

"Hey, wait a minute," the rancher blared. Suddenly he had a trooper on each elbow.

A third trooper pried the girl's mouth open. "Full set of teeth," he reported.

"Very good," the votary said, scribbling. "Now open her tunic."

"She's not my offering!" The rancher tried to surge forward. "She's here to be blessed. I brought other things to pay with."

The votary nodded. "Show me." The troopers released the rancher's arms, but stayed close.

The rancher man emptied his knapsack. "I've had relatives blessed before. I brought quality stuff. An artillery rangefinder that works, canned *sqvelti* fish—from before the riots, but still tasty. I had some myself just last week. And look here. . . ."

"Excuse me," Chagrin thundered.

"First Disciple! I'm honored." The rancher saluted. "There's a misunderstanding."

Chagrin regarded the girl with desolate eyes. "No misunderstanding."

"But I brought her here to be blessed!" Troopers swarmed him.

Chagrin half-smiled. "She'll be blessed, all right."

"That's not why I—" A boot slammed into the rancher's stomach.

"We see canned fish twenty times a day," Chagrin told the rancher as he retched. "Know how often we see a virgin?"

"What have I done?" the rancher blubbered, laying doubled over in his vomit.

Chagrin opened a tin of *sqvelti* fish and smiled. "What you've done is, you've brought us some good fucking fish. Want some? It'll help you forget." He smiled to the disfigured votary and jerked a thumb toward the girl. "We'll be in my quarters."

The votary nodded. "Next!"

Laz Kalistor stepped around the rancher and his puke. *Too bad the general public will never see this journal. It should be required viewing for anyone who'd mistake Arn Parek for a holy man.*

"Afternoon, sir. What are you here to be healed of?"

"I've come to see the healer."

ʼThe votary guffawed. "No one sees the healer."

"Send word that the man from three nights ago is here. The one who gave The Word Among Us a certain note."

The votary's eyes widened. As Kalistor expected, standing orders had been given concerning him. "Wait here," the votary stammered.

"You changed your name. Falsified all your records," the agent had said after catching up with Kalistor. "Created a forbidden new identity. That is—"

"It's not forbidden. It's simply without precedent. There's a difference."

"A difference few tribunals will recognize." The agent spread his palms. "The way you modified your identity is so far beyond any acceptable standard. . . ."

"I lost more than five years after I died on Jaremi Four," Kalistor hissed. "I came out of the tanks to face a lifepartner I don't remember meeting, a woman I couldn't love. If nothing else, I owed it to her to disappear. Better Neuri think herself a widow than I cast some perpetual shadow over her life."

"Very noble," the agent mocked.

Kalistor shrugged. "Civilization lost its appeal. Can you blame me?"

"No. But if I fail to obtain your cooperation. . . ."

"I obey, or I fall on the privacy violation," Kalistor said hollowly. "Clearly you want something from me."

The agent said nothing.

"I'm listening," Kalistor sighed.

"Remember the sleight of hand from your younger days?"

"As far as my memory's concerned, I'm still in my younger days." He materialized a shower of pebbles between his fingers. "Prestidigitation. Mentalism. I remember everything."

"Good." The agent had nodded. "Since you've already vanished, the rest is simple. We need you back to Jaremi Four."

"Jaremi Four! Because of my past?"

"Because of what's happening there now. And because of your skills. I'm sorry if the place has bad memories for you. You will return to Jaremi Four as a Spectator—a *private* Spectator."

Kalistor scowled. "That's a greater violation than anything I did."

"Not for my sponsors."

"What, are they above the law?"

The agent's voice was toneless. "Hom Kalistor, they *are* the law."

I accepted that, Kalistor thought sourly, *not that I had any choice. Now here I am.* The votary returned with six acolytes, who let him in a stage door behind the amphitheater. They'd told him to crawl. They hadn't told him why.

A single lantern flickered. When he made out the objects that surrounded him, he had to fight down an impulse to laugh. The hallway was festooned with crutches, pallets, and bandages. From one splintered post hung two dozen eye patches. A bag of netting bulged with prefabricated leg casts. Split up the back, they clamshelled open on concealed hinges. *A healer's prop closet.* A notch in the wall held four shapeless flesh-colored objects with stained elastic straps. After a moment Kalistor recognized them: artificial stumps, designed to conceal healthy hands. *It's hard to imagine that a world as optimized for carnage as Jaremi Four could fail to provide enough disfigurements for a night's healing. Hom Parek must really hate to take chances.*

Around the corner, a ramp angled upward. Its ceiling sloped down. Kalistor had no choice but to crawl. The exit was barely a meter square. Thick curtains whisked open. White luminance dazzled.

On hands and knees, Kalistor entered a high-walled, whitewashed room with no apparent ceiling. Fresh white cloth was stretched overhead, diffusing sunlight.

Five meters away, Arn Parek stood on a meter-high platform. He wore a spotless white robe of generous cut. Long full sleeves concealed his hands. The only thing in the room that wasn't white was Parek's face.

Kalistor rose to one knee and attempted to stand.

"Creep to me!" Parek thundered.

Kalistor was surprised at how quickly he collapsed to his hands and knees.

He was even more surprised when two halberd blades whistled through the air above him. Had he finished rising, either would have cloven his neck.

He hadn't seen the white-clad guards who swung the halberds. They'd stood atop stone pediments on either side of the opening he'd crawled through.

"I seldom give second chances," Parek declared, stepping off his platform. "But you spared me the effort of finding you." At a nod from Parek, the guards hustled away. Parek thrust his left hand from its sleeve. He clutched the note Kalistor had passed him on the healing stage. "Stand, Laz. You will tell me how you gave me the woman who heard the sky gods." His voice more than merely anticipated obedience. "Then you'll tell me what you know of Ruth Griszam."

Slaves scattered when Parek emerged through the stage trapdoor. The prophet left the stage and strode up one aisle of the amphitheater. Kalistor watched Parek beeline for the right side of the house, rearmost row of the middle section—exactly where the wealthy woman sat when she received her sky god messages. Expectantly, Parek took her seat. "I assume position matters?" he shouted down to Kalistor.

"Oh yes."

"Very well, miracle maker. Make the sky gods address me."

"A moment, Word Among Us." Kalistor leapt from the stage and trotted up the opposite aisle. "I must take my own place. Where your ushers laid me on that pallet." He climbed to the corresponding position on the left side of the house.

For almost a minute, Parek watched Kalistor tug at his greatcoat. Kalistor stretched and relaxed the muscles of his arms and swept his hands through his hair. "Nothing's going to happen," Parek whispered to himself.

Thirty meters away, Kalistor smiled mischievously. He whispered, "Don't be such a skeptic."

Parek heard the whisper with a clean dry presence, as if Kalistor stood beside him. He stared.

"Hey there, Word Among Us," Kalistor whispered. "Sky gods here. You've done all right for yourself. Less than two years ago, you were hiding under a table in an abandoned dam and getting shot at."

Parek exploded from his seat.

Kalistor stood, too. "Today's your lucky day. Our close friend and general bottle-wiper Laz Kalistor is here to teach you some real knock-'em-dead miracles."

Parek moved toward the aisle. Kalistor mirrored his steps on the other side of the house. "How does it work?" he shouted.

"No need to shout," Kalistor whispered, pointing upward. "It's the ceiling. The half dome reflects sound. My voice hits the ceiling, follows along the curve, and comes down where you are."

"That's all there is to it? Ceilings with that shape just . . . do that?"

Kalistor smiled. "Where I'm from, several ancient public buildings have half domes. The effect is well known—and every bit as simple as that trick you did with the pouches."

Parek waved Kalistor to approach him. For what he had to say next, he did not care to trust the listening dome effect. When they were face to face again, he whispered, "My powers are real. But they wax and wane. To satisfy a fickle public, sometimes I must supplement the real miracles with, well, inspirational showmanship."

"But some of your miracles are real."

Parek raised an eyebrow. "Your leg, for one."

Kalistor said nothing.

"I expected you to rise from that litter with the same limp you had when you came here," Parek said urgently. "Instead you came up strutting like a soldier."

"Actually, I've always walked like this."

"You . . . feigned the limp?" Parek was aghast.

"Deception offends *you?*"

"I admit, it must seem droll. Still, why did you want to mislead me?"

Kalistor smiled. "I wanted to meet you." He drew rolls of gauze and a length of stained black silk from his greatcoat. "Others can practice inspirational showmanship. Here, blindfold me."

Parek took the cloths uncertainly. "How do you want me to—"

"As thoroughly as you can. Put balls of gauze over my eyes. Then wrap the silk around my head as tight as you like."

After several minutes, Parek was confident he'd rendered Kalistor blind. "Done," Parek proclaimed.

"Very good," Kalistor replied. "Now bring me something to read."

"Something to—?"

"Anything will do."

Parek located a urine-stained broadside the custodians had not yet swept off the theater floor. "Here," he said, pressing it into Kalistor's hand.

After thirty seconds of straining and hand gestures, Kalistor read the crumpled healing service program aloud—verbatim.

"You amaze me again." Parek crossed behind Kalistor, loosed the blindfold. "Can you show me the way of it?"

Kalistor nodded. "Again, it's simple." Turning toward Parek, he lay his right index finger beside his nose. "Look down your nose. No matter how carefully they blindfold you, you can almost always peek down alongside your nose."

"Laz," Parek said after a moment's thought. "Friend Laz. I see we have much to discuss."

✦ ✦ ✦

The private chamber was rich with polished woods, elegant tapestries, and sculpted metal. A stone mantelpiece dominated one wall, a broad earthen apron before it, logs flaming in its maw. Parek faced Kalistor across a cracked marble table. Between them glistened a decanter of rare Northern liqueur. "Let us drink."

Kalistor sipped. The flavor was complex, redolent of cinnamon and cloves. "Very good. A taste you acquired from Professor Dultav?"

Parek frowned. "You know more about me than some might think healthy."

Kalistor laughed. He set about removing his boots. "I don't think my health's in danger here."

"A barefoot instructor," Parek mused. "So how do you know so much about me? Why'd you make the wealthy woman say Ruth was dead?"

"To get your attention," Kalistor admitted, rising from the chair.

"You succeeded."

Kalistor took up poker and shovel and began prodding the fire. "Actually, I have no idea how Ruth Griszam is now," he lied. "I met her a few months after you, Ulf, and Chagrin walked out on her."

"She stayed behind while we pressed forward," Parek corrected.

"As you say," Kalistor agreed. "Until now, I'd heard the story only from her." Without seeming to try, he'd gathered a tall mound of luminous embers in the shovel. "In any event, I encountered her a few months after her time with you—a short while before the importance of your movement became apparent. She told me about you, about Willim Dultav—about how Willim died."

Parek's eyes flickered down.

"And she told me about Willim's fondness for exotic liquors." Kalistor spilled the shovelful of hot embers out onto the earthen apron. He scooped out another, then a third. Turning the shovel upside down, he smoothed the coals into an even carpet. "That's all."

"That is all," Parek said skeptically. "And on the strength of that alone, you journeyed to Bihela to seek me out."

Kalistor upended a wooden bench. He set it on its side between the fire and the carpet of embers he'd created. The bench cast a shadow across the coals. Their ruddy glow showed clearly. "Not for that alone. You're famed as a man who speaks for the sky gods. And, not coincidentally, one who lives well."

"We come to your actual business."

Kalistor replaced the fireplace tools. "I wish to join you."

"Tell me why."

"Everything lies in ruins. Each year there are fewer people. More suffering. Ahead I see nothing but poverty and despair." Kalistor sipped again from his glass. He threw the remaining liquor onto his embers. Blue fire danced translucent where the droplets had fallen, another proof that the embers were still hot. "Only here with you is there hope for prosperity."

Parek spread his hands and smiled. "They say I steal from the rich. And the poor."

"So be it," declared Kalistor, refilling his glass. "I'd rather be inside that enterprise looking out than on the outside looking in."

Parek refilled his glass. "But why should I invite you in?" He fixed Kalistor with an ironic stare and filled his mouth.

"Because of the things I can show you." Locking his eyes onto Parek's, Kalistor stepped barefoot onto the carpet of embers.

One step. Two steps. Three steps. Four. Unhurriedly he trod the bed of coals.

Parek spewed out his unswallowed liquor. The golden aerosol speckled his snow-white robe.

Kalistor stood at the opposite side of the fireplace, in no observable discomfort. He squinted at the carroty stains blooming across Parek's garment. "Think that'll come out?"

Parek stood, mouth agape. The embers bore fading gray footprints where Kalistor had stepped.

"Want to see it again?" Kalistor asked cheerily, making to double back.

"No!" Parek shouted. "That was quite enough."

Kalistor returned to his seat. He brought one foot up in order to replace his boot. The sole of his foot was unmarked.

"You can . . . you can teach me that?" Parek stammered at last.

"Certainly," Kalistor said. "But it will take time."

"Take time, my ass," Kalistor subvocalized to his select audience. *"If Parek pulled his boots off and marched across those coals right now, he'd be fine. Unless he got a coal stuck between his toes or stopped in the middle to reel off some forjeling prophecy! On world after world enterprising fakirs have astonished their marks by walking barefoot across coals. The trick never fails to impress, simply because most people would never dream of trying it. They forget, charcoal's a low-density material. The embers may be red hot, but because their specific heat is so low, they can't impart harmful amounts of heat to other objects—say, feet—during brief contact. No, it'll probably take several sessions of 'intensive training' before Parek will imagine he's 'learned enough' to walk the coals himself."*

"I'll be honored to join your organization," Kalistor said aloud, pulling on his other boot. "If you'll have me."

Parek stood, bowed gracefully. "I am honored to welcome you, Laz Kalistor."

Kalistor picked up the decanter. He topped off Parek's glass and his own. "Now, if I am to teach you all that I know, then when we're alone as we are now, we must be utterly candid with each other."

"Of course," Parek said cluelessly.

"So, no deception between us as to who and what you are. You admit you fabricate some of your miracles. You're pleased to learn new deceptions from me. Just between us, isn't it the truth that there *are* no real miracles, that there's really nothing to this god-man pose, just an enormous, successful pretense?"

"It's been a long time since anyone dared speak to me thus," Parek said levelly.

"Since Willim?"

Parek nodded stiffly. He stared intently at Kalistor's chest. *What does he search for?* Kalistor wondered.

"Let me be candid, then, Laz. When I started on the path that led me here, it's true that I considered myself a charlatan." Parek sipped thoughtfully. "Gradually it occurred to me that in trying to manufacture teachings that people yearned to believe, I was actually reflecting the higher reality *in which* people yearn to believe. I concluded that religion portrays a reality after all. Do I still use fakery? Of course. Because Ulf is a part of my movement, I use terror and brute force, too. I use whatever I can to transmit my Word. I'll do anything to make people listen."

Kalistor steepled his fingers. "And how do you know you might not simply be deluding yourself?"

Parek leaned forward. "I have visions."

Kalistor peered within for the *verify* signal.

"The sky gods speak to me," Parek continued. "Not out of some domed ceiling; they really speak to me. As my insight grows they address me more directly. They speak of many things—doctrine, tactical ideas for Ulf, ways to cure disease—many and wondrous things. They taught me the illusion of the pouches."

His visions taught him the one-ahead, Kalistor thought. It made him feel cold.

Parek paced the chamber. "At first the sly gods addressed me indirectly. I'd wake up and I'd remember knowing what they said. The night after I healed you— two days ago—all that changed. I commune with the sky gods more fully now. My contact appears before my eyes in a haze of auroral light. I converse with him, as naturally as you and I are speaking now."

Kalistor subvocalized to his sponsors, *"I hope to sfelb you're getting all this."* To Parek, he mockingly said, "You 'converse with him.' So your sky god has a gender?"

Parek smiled.

"Has he a name?"

Parek waggled a finger. "I cannot speak it, except to him. Even I have my obligations to the sky gods."

Citron aurora boiled in a blackened northern sky when Kalistor left Parek's sanctum. He tugged the stage door shut with difficulty. He hurried from shadow to shadow toward the main square. After so many hours in Mode, it was a relief to set polyphasic consciousness aside and simply exist in the here-and-now. *I've been most successful thus far,* he thought. *I've earned Parek's confidence. Already I've filed secret reportage in which Parek admits to subterfuge.* Those were his missions— missions that might seem unremarkable enough when viewed against the history of human espionage. Of course, that would not be the way most Galactics would view his exploits, if they learned of them. There'd be harsh outcry at the news that no lesser authority than the Privy High Council, Enclave's final warden, had wrenched a famous former Spectator from seclusion, cloaked his identity, and sent him onto an Enclave world to spy!

Parek reclined in the private chamber. He poured out the decanter's dregs. *Things had been getting dull,* he reflected. *Now this teacher appears with illusions that will revolutionize my stagecraft. And only two nights ago, I met a sky god face to face.* One more time, he replayed the latter incident in his mind.

He'd burst from sleep. In the way he knew so well, Parek *remembered* that he needed to slip out of bed—quietly, without disturbing the temple strumpet who snored beside him. He stole into the antechamber even as a whorl of feeble light began to coalesce a bodylength before him.

"Our blessings on you, Arn Parek," a sparkling voice proclaimed. "Everlasting welfare unto you."

The whorl intensified. At its heart an image took form—dimensional, magically sharp, internally alight in a way Parek had never imagined. He discerned a humanlike figure.

"Who . . . who are you?"

The figure was broad of build and silver-haired, its chubby arms were bare, its legs uncovered below the knee, and the body obscured beneath some formless off-white garment shimmering like a waterfall against the sun. "We believe you know who and what we are."

"Yes, yes," he stammered. "I know who you are."

The apparition continued to take on detail. Peculiar symbols adorned the shapeless garment at the breast, the navel, and the knee.

Parek swallowed. "What shall I call you?"

"You may call us . . . God." The figure, now obviously male, folded beefy arms. "In fact, do."

"Do what?"

"Do call me God!"

Parek massaged his eyes and reflected on what the phantasm had told him—the secrets vouchsafed, the promise to return, the promise to address him directly from then on, the promise that soon Parek would be entrusted with a charm by which he could summon the ghostly mentor whenever he might need to.

When next I face my God, Parek wondered, *shall I tell him about this remarkable Laz Kalistor? I think not,* he decided. He drained his glass. *A sky god should not depend on me for knowledge. And some things I should keep to myself.*

46. The *Bright Hope*

"Just a moment." Dr. Annek Panna plucked the wafer from her senso player. Labeled PAREK, WHAT THEY CAN FIND OF HIM, it disappeared beneath a pillow. "Enter."

The stateroom door dilated. Captain Laurien Eldridge and X.O. Arla Gavisel stepped in.

"Please sit down," said Panna. Polychairs bubbled from the stateroom walls. "A problem with the final performance analysis?"

Smiling, Eldridge shook her head. "We finished recompiling the performance data from our transit of the Galactic disk. It confirmed your own readings; after you made those final alterations, the drive performed at one hundred eighteen percent of original spec. Most impressive."

"As I knew. That completes the test series, no? I look forward to going home."

"We received new orders from High Command," Eldridge said slowly. "That's why we're here. We've been dispatched to Jaremi Four, an Enclave world in Sector Upsilon."

"You are of course aware of the religious disturbances there," Gavisel said.

Panna's heart leapt. *So the events that so fascinate me have been deemed worthy of closer scrutiny.* Yet she masked her joy. "Why must *Bright Hope* go on this errand?"

"To show the flag and patrol against any efforts to violate Enclave," Eldridge replied. "It happens there are no capital ships in or even near Sector Upsilon."

"And we are closest?"

"No, but because of your drive, *Bright Hope* can get there first all the same."

"Then you'll be putting me ashore somewhere."

"Unfortunately not," Eldridge said. "They want us to depart at once, and they want you aboard in the event of any problem with the drive."

Panna affected resignation. "How long will we remain in Jaremi space?"

"That's unknown," Eldridge said. "I can tell you that we'll arrive five weeks ahead of any other ship. I doubt we'll be permitted to stand down until we're relieved, perhaps not even then, depending on developments."

"Like that, my tour of duty on *Bright Hope* is extended, oh, another year. And I am a civilian!"

Eldridge shrugged. "You're a civilian who has something they want. We're sorry."

If it means a trip to Jaremi Four, I'm not sorry, Panna thought. *Though I feel more comfortable not revealing my newfound devotion to Arn Parek.* Aloud, she said, "Well, if I wanted to spend my life at home, perhaps I shouldn't have gone into designing stardrives. Thank you for informing me, Captain."

After Eldridge and Gavisel left, Panna reached under the pillows. She found the senso wafer, popped it into the player and thumbed PLAY.

Suck, rush, wrench.

For what seemed like the twentieth time Panna reviewed what senso there had been of or about Parek in the last six months. *Parek, Parek*—she thought. *O Word Among Us. I thought I must admire you from afar, but now I fly to you. Who are you? What are you? Perhaps I shall be the one to find out.*

47. Office of the Terran Delegate to the Privy High Council • Confidential Memo

Lord Councilor, I apologize for addressing you again in this most informal way, but the importance of what I have to say compels me to act, even though Your Lordship has not seen fit to reply to my previous memo.

The situation on Jaremi Four continues to look suspicious. Weeks ago I hesitated even to suggest that a single Enclave violation might be occurring there. Now I suspect there may be several.

Please note this recent journal filed by the Spectator Ruth Griszam. She and her consort Friz Labokloer have traveled to the northern city of Giwalczor, where Labokloer was told to wait for a prophecy meeting.

[EMBEDDED SENSO JOURNAL: *NUDGE* HERE TO PLAY]

Midday. The courtyard of a tavern. Lunch. Labokloer raised his favorite *n'dren* to his eye.

"Look at me when I talk to you," she sighed.

"You're just going to ask to attend the meeting again," said Labokloer. "I never should've told you that the meeting is tonight. No one is allowed who didn't receive scrolls addressed to them personally. No one who hasn't taken on the discipline. Those are the rules." A server set tankards of harsh cider before them. "We didn't order these."

"They're from the old squire," the server said.

A drunken man of forty slouched at a nearby table. Once his garments had been costly. Now they were stained and faded. Smiling almost toothlessly, he lifted a tankard. His fingers gripped its handle in a peculiar way. He looked into Labokloer's eyes. "Peace," he said.

Labokloer blinked, clearly surprised. The fingers of his right hand squirmed into a figure similar to the one that the old man had formed on the handle of his tankard. "For eternity," Labokloer replied uneasily.

[JOURNAL PAUSES]

Clearly, Lord Councilor, "peace" and "for eternity" are passwords. The finger movements serve a similar function, as ways for members of a secret society to recognize one another without drawing outsiders' attention. Pray continue *pov*ing, there is much more.

[JOURNAL RESUMES]

The old man shambled to Labokloer's table. The hitch in his step seemed familiar. "Welcome to Giwalczor, if that's necessary. I am Ileatz Quareg."

"Friz Labokloer. This is my companion, Ruth Griszam. We come from five days' journey west."

"Thermal caves, scrap mines," Quareg nodded, ticking off the principal features of Labokloer's territory. His eyes dropped toward Labokloer's calves. "And a strange way of cutting leather for a man's boots."

"A little extra room for a *silish.*" Labokloer nodded. "You wear one too?"

Quareg swigged from his tankard. "I did." He looked suspiciously at Ruth.

"She knows," Labokloer assured him. "She's seen my *silish.* Even seen a scroll arrive."

Quareg coughed violently. "Scrolls!"

Labokloer leaned forward, puzzled. "I thought you were of the discipline."

"I said I was. I left when the miracles stopped."

"You're mistaken," Labokloer laughed. "The miracles haven't stopped."

"I was not mistaken. It was the scroll, the damnable fourth scroll! Three scrolls I got, you know how they come. Each one was correct. I was already powerful in Giwalczor. The guidance of the scrolls made me the strongest of all."

Labokloer nodded. "It was the same for me."

Quareg swatted at the air. "The first three scrolls were true prophecy. I strove to master the disciplines they taught. Then came the fourth. False through and through. It ruined me."

"What did it say?" Labokloer demanded.

"It predicted the Lord of Cranh's faction would triumph."

Labokloer's eyes widened. "That can't be."

"The scroll told me in so many words to give Cranh unlimited credit. When he fell, I went down with him. Within three days, some rising noble had added my lands to his holdings. No one even remembered me."

"What did your fourth scroll say, Friz?" Ruth asked.

Labokloer shook his head. "It didn't just predict Cranh's downfall, it told me how to hurry it along."

"So you profited from Cranh's overthrow—and my ruin."

"I am sorry," Labokloer said, hands spread wide. "Whatever your fourth scroll said, *mine* was true prophecy. And the fifth. . . ."

"You got a fifth?"

"Didn't you?" The old man's look of defeat drew a sigh from Labokloer. "My fifth scroll was true also," said Labokloer. "It predicted the wings in the sky twenty days ago. And when the wings stretched widest, I received the sixth and final scroll—the one that brought me here."

Quareg rubbed his temples. "The final scroll . . . so the rumors are true. The sky gods ordained a prophecy meeting here in Giwalczor." Quareg chuckled darkly. "Beware, young baron. The sky gods can fling you down as senselessly as they raised you up."

[JOURNAL ENDS]

Lord Councilor, observers have been puzzled about the many minor nobles who say they've received prophecies from the sky. Often, those prophecies have been associated with significant changes in the balance of power. Still, this is the first solid indication that different nobles are receiving *different* prophecies. It's unclear what this means. If only we had better background information with which to interpret it. One problem, of course, is that 'peace' and 'eternity' are popular concepts. They often coincide in religious rhetoric, in utopian political tracts—for that matter, in love poetry. My investigations, however casual and of course nonfunded they may be, continue.

Now, Lord Councilor, I am sure you know about the journal I will cite next. When it is over I will tell you something about it that I'm sure you don't know.

[EMBEDDED SENSO JOURNAL: *NUDGE* HERE TO PLAY]

The journal began with an introduction by Ged Silbertak, the president of OmNet itself. Such was its importance. "Again, we apologize for the delay in bringing you this most extraordinary journal. It is a mystery to us, too, that something so eagerly sought after should have languished on a shelf for almost three weeks! You have my word, it is a mystery we shall solve. Let us turn now to consider the journal itself. For technical reasons we are unsure which of our Spectators on Jaremi Four filed this journal. Nonetheless we are satisfied with its authenticity."

Silbertak stood and linked hands behind his back. "What you're about to *pov* is the lengthiest continuous observation of Arn Parek since Ruth Griszam was covering him. The complete journal runs some three hours. It documents almost in its entirety a public healing service in the ruined city of Bihela. The journal is sure to be controversial. Not only does it clearly show that Arn Parek continues to employ deceptive methods, but that similar methods are also used by the Spectator who recorded it. In the event it is not clear when you *pov* it, know that the Spectator feigned his limp." Silbertak took his seat. "Fems and homs, OmNet proudly presents the closest scrutiny yet of the public ministry of Arn Parek." His voice took the tone of a midway barker: "The Word Among Us! God-man or charlatan?"

*Being-there*ness rippled. A nameless Spectator approached a decrepit amphitheater, making a great show of dragging one leg. "Oh sky gods, through the power of The Word Among Us let me be healed this day! Oh sky gods, this day I would walk like any man!"

The woman who approached him had *staff* written all over her. "Good day, yeoman," she said.

"I am here for a miracle." It was subtle, but somehow the somesthetics felt wrong when he said that.

Her eyes roamed him appraisingly, from his shoulders to his waist and to his crotch. "You came for healing?"

"For my leg." He raised his voice. "Oh, sky gods—"

[JOURNAL ENDS]

I am sure you know what follows, Lord Councilor. The Spectator is borne inside on a litter. Parek reads question cards sealed in pouches. He cures headaches. And in the Spectator's own case, he seemingly makes the lame walk.

What I am about to reveal may seem extreme. My senso tech friends tell me this journal has been carefully, but not perfectly, edited. The changes are significant. The Spectator never said, "I'm here for a miracle." Instead he spoke his name. That's a difficult manipulation, and if you review that moment you'll notice that the perceived mouth movements don't match the Spectator's words.

Here's an even stranger one. We know the Spectator deceived Parek by faking a limp. Apparently he went much further, but the journal was edited to conceal it. Remember when that wealthy woman across the theater thought the sky gods were speaking to her—just as the Spectator was struggling so hard to hold back a sneeze? That powerful sensation was crudely superimposed to conceal what the Spectator was actually doing: *feeding* the woman her sky god talk with some ventriloquist trick! In vacuum's name, why? Why did the Spectator behave as he did? Why was the journal aired at all? Why now? Why with these edits and not others?

I mentioned that the Spectator's name was imperfectly covered over. You can edit audio, but the *feel* of speaking the name is still there. I was able to reconstruct it. The unknown Spectator called himself *Laz Kalistor*. As you may recall, Lord

Councilor, that's the name of the famous Spectator who died on Jaremi Four a few
years ago—the one Linka Strasser allowed to die—the one who came back with no
memory of having married his wife. The real Kalistor went underground shortly
after all that. Why use *his* name? And having used it, why cover it over?

The meaning of this is clear—and frightening. We've already seen Parek
preaching ancient Mormon doctrines. We still don't know the meaning of all those
prophecy scrolls in Northland. Finally, we have a Spectator going after Parek with
some kind of hidden agenda.

Lord Councilor, something terribly peculiar is happening on Jaremi Four. Certain that you will give my confidential report the attention it deserves and act
accordingly, I remain your obedient servant.

[MEMO ENDS]

48. Jaremi Four—Northern Hemisphere, City of Bihela

For the occasion of Ulf's return with the army, Parek had a reviewing raised in
the square before the amphitheater. He and Ulf and Chagrin stood atop it. Ulf had
arranged a parade of the booty he'd taken from his marauding in the countryside,
while Parek had arranged a parade of the renewable booty he'd persuaded the
Bihelians to volunteer. "They say you died and came back," Ulf grunted.

"They say truth," Parek responded.

"I saw it," Chagrin volunteered. "His body was cold."

"But where his soul went? For that we have to take his word." Ulf scowled
toward Parek. "And what was that parlor trick you did before you mounted the
reviewing stand?"

Parek raised an eyebrow. "Parlor trick indeed. Your face went beige when I
walked across those coals. Later I'll read your mind, and show you wonders you
never imagined."

"Hah! Now look there." Ulf stretched a hand toward an approaching platoon.
"There are wonders *you* never imagined." The soldiers pushed three great carts
across which had been spread the twisted but recognizable framework of some
simple, ancient flying craft. "Well to the north, it was said that men still lived who
could remember when people flew through the air in devices like that."

"Have you brought those men?" asked Parek.

Ulf's gaze flickered briefly downward. "They died."

"Men tend to, around you. Women and children also. Now, here is life!"
Cheers went up from the soldiers as the delegation assembled by Bihela's guild of
brothel-keepers pranced into the square. Clad in garish scraps, girls, women, and
boys gamboled among Ulf's fighters. "Tonight there shall be love enough for every
man," Parek laughed. "And tomorrow night, instead of being shattered or dead,
they'll be smilingly ready for more."

A new platoon marched into the square, dragging four trudging men clad in furs and metal netting. Dried blood matted their hair. "All that remains of a savage backwoods people," Ulf said thinly. "They will never threaten us again."

"Did they before?"

Ulf shrugged. "So how'd you learn these new miracles?"

"You mean like this?" Smiling, Parek produced fireballs from his upturned palms.

Ulf jumped backward. He yelled at Chagrin, "You didn't tell me he did that!"

Chagrin shrugged. "Can't remember everything."

"My visions taught me," Parek explained. "But now, they come more vividly."

"I must tell you a thing," Ulf said tonelessly. "I doubted your visions, your doctrines, the advice you gave in battle." Ulf inhaled and swallowed. "Sometimes I'd wonder whether it was the sky gods speaking or simply you. At any rate, I doubt no longer."

Parek pursed his lips. "What changed?"

"Now I have visions, too," Ulf said matter-of-factly.

"Visions?" Parek asked as neutrally as he could. "Um, what do they concern?"

"Strategy, at first," Ulf replied. "Ways to win battles."

Parek placed a hand on Ulf's shoulder. "Sometimes ideas occur to me with vividness and power and urgency. But they're not true visions."

"I know that," Ulf chuckled. "The true visions—they're the ones with the swirling lights and the little sky god speaking out of the auroral glow."

Parek pulled back his hand and stepped away.

"The ones that, before they come, I wake up knowing I need to sneak off to a special place and await the god." Ulf's narrowed eyes locked with Parek's. "Now you believe me." He pushed his fingers through the stubble of his gunmetal hair. "This morning I received a vision unlike any other."

"What was its content?" Parek breathed.

"A single, blunt message. A command. 'Laz . . . must . . . die.'"

Parek was unable to cloak his astonishment.

Ulf spread his hands. "Who the fuck is Laz?"

Bihelan constables—men now pledged to serve as Parek's personal guards—pushed a large raised platform on a wagon chassis into the square. At its rear, a large fire roared in a metal grate. At the platform's center stood a stout log three meters high. A man stood lashed to that pole with strips of animal hide.

"Come down with me," Parek told Ulf. "We will meet Laz, if only briefly."

The straps were of fresh hide. Drying, they shrunk, cutting into Laz Kalistor's flesh. He thought of logging off—a final defiance, denying his betrayers whatever knowledge they might glean from *poving* his death. Finally he decided that unwise: *Now that OmNet numbers me among its assets, by staying in Mode I might attract some rescuers.*

Parek, Ulf, and Chagrin strode onto the execution stage. "Laz Kalistor," Parek proclaimed. "Meet High Commander Ulf. So great is your treachery, Laz, that he, too, received a vision commanding your death."

"What treachery?" Kalistor bluffed. "What have I done?"

Parek shrugged. "The gods alone know that."

"But they've told us what to do about it," said Chagrin with a sadistic leer.

"Come, disciples." Parek led Ulf and Chagrin off the platform.

Kalistor realized that the three leaders' departure was probably the signal for the execution to begin. *Stasis is out of the question*, he thought; *too many witnesses.* Were there Spectators hovering no-vis overhead, ordered not to contact him, but there to deliver him all the same? *I can't imagine how, there must be fifteen thousand autochthons here.* Bleakly, Kalistor's thoughts centered on a single recollection from his cultural orientation briefing: "The autochthons of Jaremi Four have relatively unsophisticated ideas about death. Often they'll leave for dead a Galactic who is only badly wounded—one well within Galactic medicine's power to revive." *So it all comes down to the speedy retrieval of my body*, Kalistor realized. *A retrieval which I have no idea whether anyone intends.*

In other words, Kalistor's only hope of outfoxing these autochthons bent on his death lay in letting them kill him.

As if I could stop them. Six marksmen leveled steamrifles at him. Parek, Ulf, and Chagrin stood behind them. Parek raised a gleaming sword.

I'm going to die again on Jaremi Four, Laz Kalistor admitted despondently. *I'm going to die forjeling O/N-Two again.* Grimly, he maxed his autonomic functions. *Plorg, you know what? This time I hope I don't come back.*

Parek gave the order to fire.

Fifteen thousand voices raised a mighty cheer. The soldiers had killed someone. The crowd had no idea why. But the Word Among Us had ordained it. That was enough.

Climbing back onto the blood-spattered stage, Parek reflected that he had no idea why this death was necessary either. Kalistor lay sprawled, one hand still suspended by a strap, blood and organs oozing from half a dozen fist-sized wounds.

"We have acted on our visions," Parek said grimly.

Ulf nodded joylessly. "This is not enough."

"I don't think he can get much deader."

"You acted on your vision, Word Among Us," Ulf rumbled. "Not mine." He held out one hand. "I need your sword."

"You wear an arsenal."

"The vision said I must use a sword. Like you, I'm under commandment."

I worried that when Ulf came back this day at the head of his troops, he might dream of deposing me, thought Parek. *No matter now. Ulf's visions give him a new agenda. As long as he feels threatened by their mysteries, he'll know he needs me.* Half smiling, Parek handed Ulf his sword.

With a battle whoop, Ulf hacked at Kalistor's neck. After two, three, four terrible strokes, the head finally came free. Ulf strode holding it high, blood raining on him. After a moment he tossed it into the fire grate. Its skin bubbled and blackened. "To me!" Ulf shouted to his personal guard. "Bring swords." Ten men doubletimed onto the platform brandishing blades. Grimly, they chopped Kalistor's body apart. The fire took it all.

No Galactics had schemed to recover Laz Kalistor. If any had, what Ulf had done would foil them. Dismembered and immolated, Kalistor was again beyond the power of any world's medical science to bring back.

"Why do this?" Parek asked eventually.

"I don't know," Ulf panted. "After he was shot, I just . . . *remembered* needing to do it."

"I know," Parek said quietly. "It's of the visions."

Satisfied at last, Ulf stepped back. "Your vision said nothing about disposing of the body?"

"No," Parek replied. "Perhaps the sky gods knew their word to you would be sufficient."

The percussionists had resumed their places on the first tier of the reviewing stand. Pipe sections whirled within their bell lyres. ***Clang****-shang-ralang. Clang-shang-ralang. Clang-shang-ralang. **Clang**-shang-ralang. Clang-shang-ralang. Clang-shang-ralang.*

"Pa-rek! Pa-rek! Pa-*rek!*" the crowd shouted in rhythm. Parek stepped between Ulf and Chagrin. He clasped his hands around theirs and raised them high. Together, bound by rhythm and grim accomplishment—more than ever, by wonder—they felt as they had in those glorious days of discovery in the turbine pen at the old dam. The three comrades drank in the adulation of the crowd. Their crowd. Their army. Their city.

Parek couldn't know whether Ulf's enjoyment was tempered, like his, by a pang of uncertainty. *It's strange enough that I have these visions,* thought Parek. *But why Ulf, too? And why should one of his visions convey a detail absent from my own?*

49. Vatican

Near the apex of the towering Papal Palace, the Universal Catholic Church's most powerful leaders met her most learned scholars for lunch. It was not a happy occasion.

Aresino Y'Braga, Father General of the Society of Jesus, strove to govern his rage. His fingers trembled as he speared the single chunk of shellfish Florentine on his plate. After the Jesuit manner he was clad *in nigris,* the black cassock of a simple priest. "Am I to understand that this matter of a possible Incarnation on Jaremi Four has been under discussion for . . . *some time?*"

Smiling weakly as he chewed, the pope could only nod. He wore the classic simar and *zuchetto,* both dazzling white. He ignored the servers who whisked away his empty plate, depositing before him another gleaming platter bearing a fresh golden spoon and a tiny scoop of paté.

"And the Society of Jesus was not told!" Y'Braga's black eyes flashed. Muscles twisted in his slender face. An arm reached around him and set down a small dish containing one miniature red potato sprinkled with Callurian fennel.

The Cardinal-Prefect of the Council for Devout Protocol blanched. "Let the Father General be assured that due deliberation was given, in the fullness of grace, as to revealing this sensitive matter."

Y'Braga's eyes fixed on the pope. "Am I to be managed by your lackey?"

Pope Modest IV scowled. "You forget your vow of humility, Father General."

Y'Braga bowed his head. "Your Holiness is correct, of course." His insincerity was palpable.

The exchange had disrupted the measured pace of the pontiff's eating. Deftly, a server withdrew unused chopsticks from the pope's hand. Another plucked away the plate, an untouched cube of Minganese rice dusted with *chuli* at its center. A third scooped the rice into a golden chalice. Two others set a fresh portion, a new fork, before His Holiness.

Theologian Xyrel Hjinn picked languidly at his own plate, a large platter piled with delicacies enough for three men. He shot a meaningful glance toward his colleague, Sfix Geruda. Geruda, too, ate from a single plate, as did the other half-dozen academics clustered near them. They all sweltered in formal academic dress: ample purple silken robes, their full sleeves striped with parallel rows of puffy velour.

Romanitá, churchmen still called it. Though Rome was a fading memory, the old term endured to label the swirl of intrigue that had ever orbited the seat of papal power. Thoughtfully Hjinn strove to gauge the feints and thrusts on the other side of the table. Actually, *other side* was a poor description; the luncheon table was an enormous ring of ivy-green tourmaline.

"Profound as our differences have been, this may be a time to set them aside," suggested Alois Cardinal Rybczynsky in silken tones. Rybczynsky's jet-black simar was crisply perfect as always, its scarlet piping self-luminous. Still returning from Jaremi Four, he attended the meeting via sim. Another difference: of all the high churchmen there gathered, Rybczynsky alone ate from a single plate that bore his entire meal.

"I'm curious," Hjinn said to Rybczynsky. "I look behind His Holiness, behind the Father General, behind the other Cardinals, and I see platoons of servers. Cardinal Rybczynsky has no waiters, a single platter." Hjinn smiled at Rybczynsky. "Your Eminence eats as we theologians do."

"Cardinal Rybczynsky is in space," Devout Protocol puffed.

"So?" asked the Cardinal-Prefect of the Congregation for the Evangelization of the Worlds. "At home, in transit, here at Vatican—I dare never set aside this damnable fashion."

"Doctor Hjinn makes an interesting observation," said the pontiff. "Alois, have you abandoned the benefice?"

"Hardly, Your Holiness. I have streamlined it."

The Dean of the Stewards rotated a chunk of curried pheasant on a silver fork before him. "None of us is too good for the benefice," he said jovially. "Each plate we eat from, each utensil—on some planet there's always a new devotional society eager for such relics."

Sfix Geruda snorted with a theologian's disdain. "Once, *relic* meant an object pertaining to a saint."

"No longer," countered the Cardinal-Prefect of the Congregation for Institutes of Consecrated Life and Societies of Apostolic Life. "The saints are dead. We are still eating."

"Supply and demand," Y'Braga mocked ever so gently.

"Once it was a badge of status to have risen so high in the Church that bump-kins coveted your dishware," chuckled Congregation for the Evangelization of the Worlds. He raised an artichoke heart to his mouth and bit off half. He couldn't put down the remaining half; his plate was gone. "Now?" The spearstick was whisked from his fingers. He sighed. "One more onerous duty."

"Yet I'm told that Cardinal Rybczynsky generates more revenue from the benefice than the rest of us combined," said the Dean of the Stewards. "Tell us, Alois. What is your secret?"

Rybczynsky chuckled. "No secret. They want my plates, my forks, my spear-sticks. I send them."

"Really?" asked the Cardinal-Prefect of the Congregation for Institutes of Consecrated Life and Societies of Apostolic Life.

"I send them," Rybczynsky smiled. "By the tens of thousands."

"But how can you eat from so many—" Devout Protocol stopped in mid-sentence. Geruda was astonished. "Your Eminence does not *use* the implements?"

"A riddle: When is a dinner plate not a dinner plate? Apparently, never," said Rybczynsky. "Here is my dinner plate. I eat my lunch from it, it remains a dinner plate. If I eat nothing from it, it is no less a dinner plate. The faithful never know."

"But they think—" Geruda stammered.

"That is their conceit, good doctor."

Devout Protocol pursed his lips. "Actually, Alois, tradition at least *implies* the promise that the dishware has been used."

Rybczynsky spread his palms. "What is tradition? Assumptions grown stale. They ask for a dinner plate, I send a dinner plate. I do not promise that I *ate* my dinner from it."

The pope honored Rybczynsky with muted applause and said, "We hope you've been as innovative in your machinations on Jaremi Four."

And so the wily fox steers this luncheon onto its intended business, thought Hjinn.

Geruda swallowed hard. Less cynical than Hjinn, he had not already sus-pected that Holy Mother Church might be hip deep into Enclave outlawry. *We're marked men now,* he thought despairingly. *At the least suspicion of our loyalty, His Holiness will destroy the College of Theologians entire, rather than risk one of us taking this knowledge outside.*

"Cardinal Semuga astonished me," Rybczynsky said evenly. "On Jaremi Four he's raised a city, founding docks, a manufacturing center—all in secret. He's launched a great orbital manufactory. His engineers have hewn auditoriums from the living rock across the far north, every thirty degrees of longitude. He's about to mobilize an army raised and led by eight thousand autochthons of fierce unques-tioning faith. And the Confetory knows nothing."

"We are impressed," Pope Modest said. To judge from his expression, *flabber-gasted* was the better word. "What are Our options for action?"

"We can enforce our will on Jaremi Four." Rybczynsky nibbled glazed sweet-breads. "Now we must decide what our will is. *Your* will, Holiness."

"Never mind Our will." The Pope flickered patrician fingers skyward. "What is *His* will?" He speared a candied mollusk from its shell and swallowed it whole. "Doctor Hjinn, learned theologian! Explicate God's will for Us."

Hjinn dropped his fork. "Holiness, I hardly. . . ."

"We are not mincing words here, Doctor." The pope stared icily. "What says the College of Theologians? Is Arn Parek the Christ, or not?"

Hjinn and Geruda exchanged nervous glances with their half-dozen colleagues. Geruda began. "Holiness, it is the considered position of your theologians that Arn Parek of Jaremi Four is not the Christ."

"Summarize your thinking for Us."

Geruda began. "First, there is the matter of Parek himself. He's clearly a fraud. His preachments contain little that is recognizable in terms of any known Christian tradition. He spreads his word by the sword with a ferocity unparalleled in the annals of the sanctioned Incarnations. Granted, the Almighty has occasionally chosen unusual ways to accouter His Son for a given world. But this case seems to go far beyond the previously known boundaries, even taking into account conditions on Jaremi Four."

"We also conducted an exegetical search of all known inspired texts," Hjinn added. "No prophecy hints at an Incarnation of so extraordinarily profane a character."

Pope Modest steepled his fingers, under the circumstances a most papal thing to do. "Is Parek a precursor, then?"

Hjinn swallowed. "It is the unanimous position of the College of Theologians that Arn Parek is no Coblasta. No John the Baptizer. No Bentito Ynez."

The pope leaned forward. His eyes turned cold. "If Parek be not the Christ, and if he be no straightener of the way, then what is he?"

"Yes, learned doctors," Rybczynsky added urgently. "Who do you say that he is?"

"Simply an unfortunate coincidence." Hjinn said grimly. "A mountebank who, by mischance, gained visibility just as the Galaxy turned expectant eyes upon his world."

Pope Modest scanned the delegation of academics. "You all concur in this?"

Some of the learned heads nodded strongly, others almost imperceptibly. But all nodded.

"You're certain?" the pontiff demanded.

Hjinn spread his hands. "As certain as theologians can be."

"We are to take comfort from that?" Pope Modest leaned back and gestured for wine. A single swallow was handed to him in a diamond goblet that was snatched back the moment the claret was gone. "So, then. For the first time it is given to Holy Mother Church to enter into the Incarnation narrative. It is Her lot to play Bentito Ynez, to make straight the way. Is that the interpretation Our theologians make?"

Eight gray heads nodded.

"Then We know His will." The Pope frowned and raised a commanding index finger. "Cardinal Rybczynsky!"

"Yes, Holiness."

"Command Cardinal Semuga to send this army of his against Parek and smite the false god."

Rybczynsky nodded. "As you ordain, Holiness."

Unsettled silence gripped the chamber. Never slow to thrust himself into a vacuum, the Dean of the Stewards spoke first. "Parek must be exposed to the Galaxy as a charlatan, lest more of the faithful be deceived."

"Your Holiness must issue some statement," agreed Y'Braga.

"Truly," nodded Evangelization of the Worlds. "We need some bull."

Before Pope Modest could answer, Rybczynsky spoke sharply. "Tread carefully, Holiness. Few in the Galaxy yet know that we expect an Incarnation at all, let alone on Jaremi Four."

"There's truth in that," said Y'Braga with dark sarcasm.

"For Holy Mother Church to issue a document stating that Parek is *not* the Christ is to admit that we once thought he might be," argued Rybczynsky. "Why license a category of speculation that has been inactive among the general public until now? Why dignify Parek even to that limited extent?"

"We see your logic," mused Modest. "Still then, how shall he be resisted?"

"We have Semuga's army," Devout Protocol observed.

Modest shook his head. "The army will check his influence on Jaremi Four and smooth the way for the real Christ to come. But what of Galactic believers? Billions, perhaps trillions, already obsess over Arn Parek. How do we draw them back?"

From an unseen vanisher valise Rybczynsky drew a gilded senso player. He lay it on the silvery tabletop before him. "We have this. Is everyone prepared to *pov?*" A Swiss Guard entered at the far end of the room. He wheeled up a large multiuser sensocasting unit. "My senso player will link to the relay player where you are. Ready?"

In his stateroom on a caravel thousands of light-years away from Vatican, Rybczynsky waved a thumb past a control surface. It claimed the consciousness of all around the tourmaline ring.

Suck, rush, wrench.

A man now dead aimed lively eyes straight into Ruth Griszam's as he ate *skraggel.* "Arn Parek is the only kind of holy man there is—or ever was—one hundred percent bogus," Willim Dultav said.

Ruth laughed long and bitterly. "A fake holy man!"

"It's a living."

"Where's that flask?"

He gave it to her. "These woods are full of country con artists. Some earn their livings telling people they can make twenty-year-old canned goods safe to eat. Arn and I—we offer a more profound kind of belief." . . .

"Devastating," breathed the Dean of the Stewards when the playback was over. "It will go far to discredit Parek among thoughtful Galactics. But it must be *pov*ed and *pov*ed and *pov*ed again."

Rybczynsky nodded. "Exactly my view, which is why I made sure that Holy Mother Church has unlimited rights to this journal. Any medium, any form, as part of any program."

Y'Braga was aghast. "Unlimited rights to an important clip about someone so popular as Parek? What did OmNet charge us for that?"

"Truly, you do not wish such knowledge," Rybczynsky smiled. "Just praise God that Cardinal Semuga is a lucky art speculator."

"To make straight the way, no price is too high," counseled Pope Modest.

With a bitter smile Y'Braga said, "I trust Your Holiness will remember having said that when you see Cardinal Rybczynsky's financials. And we thought the Patrimony of the Church was overextended before!"

Modest ignored the Jesuit and turned toward the theologians. "Doctor Hjinn, you and your College will attach the highest priority to exploiting this senso journal. Make it ubiquitous."

"I understand," Hjinn replied.

"Do you?" Abandoning the manner of a pastor, Modest hissed orders as harshly as any general or business baron. "Hjinn, inside of two weeks We want mouthy teenagers on every Confetory world to be driving their gero-mentors, peer counselors, parents, or ward captains *crazy* with the phrase, 'It's a living.' We want to see saybacks showing that sixty percent of Galactic adults rank Arn Parek among the greatest frauds the Confetory has ever known."

Hjinn smiled thinly. "That was my plan, Holiness. Fear not. We shall brandish this journal *con brio.*"

Across the table's ring, eleven of the Universal Catholic Church's most powerful leaders stared back blankly.

"*Con brio,*" Hjinn repeated after a clumsy moment. "It's Latin."

"Yes," prodded Rybczynsky with vague memory.

"Sorry," said Hjinn at last, flustered. "It means that we will exploit the journal with great energy."

"But with subtlety, too," warned Rybczynsky.

"Indeed," added the pope. "We want every Galactic to know this bit of senso. But We would prefer if most did not know—at least, not for certain—that Holy Mother Church was responsible for its pervasiveness."

"A great challenge," Hjinn breathed. He and Geruda exchanged nervous glances. "But as you say, Holy Father. To make straight the way, no price is too great."

50. Jaremi Four—Northern Hemisphere, City of Giwalczor

"**P**eace," a robed sentry growled.

"For eternity," Labokloer answered. They exchanged hand signals. "I am Friz Labokloer, from—"

"I know your origin. Enter."

The underground hall had been hewn from rock. It was immense. Its fixtures were mismatched, clearly temporary. Cold-light plates nestled in random niches in the wall. The granite surfaces were smoothly rounded and gleamingly clean.

Lying in bed in an inn three kilometers away, Ruth Griszam studied the images that streamed into her awareness from the Spectator bugs Labokloer wore. *No mold, no rock chips, no dust. As though the room had been hollowed out by magic only yesterday, just for this event.* She snorted. *That's impossible. This is Jaremi Four, everything's a hand-me-down.*

Labokloer had given her drugged wine just to make sure she wouldn't try to follow him to the prophecy meeting. No matter; she'd already loaded his clothing with Spectator bugs. When the drug entered her system, her implants had recognized it. She'd told them when to wake her up. She was in Mode now, seeing what Labokloer saw, hearing what he heard, and recording it all.

At least two thousand thronged the hall, all men, all richly clothed. On a world where most groveled for their bread, each man radiated power and wealth.

Yet they seemed as children compared to the black-robed figure who ascended a tall stage at the hall's far end. A graceless block of a man, he bore his bulk with commanding haughtiness. A generous cowl shrouded his face. Yet none could doubt that this was the man on whose behalf they had all been showered with scrolls. This was the man who sent the prophecies that had raised them to undreamed-of power. This was the man they'd journeyed so far to hear.

"Men of the north!" the robed figure boomed. His voice came from everywhere, crystal clear in every ear. *Impossible in a hall that large,* Ruth thought. *Unless the acoustics are extraordinary. Or unless. . . .* She squinted away irrelevant thoughts and concentrated on the robed master and his message.

"In your own lives," he began, "you've seen all that is good slide out of reach. Purposes your grandfathers knew how to achieve, machines your fathers knew how to make work, medicines your mothers could once compound—all mysteries now. The grim contagion gnaws at your cities, your trading halls, your castles, your mines and farms. Each day ignorance gains precious ground—ground it seems likely never to surrender. You are worldly men. You've heard of the agonies that consumed Southland generations ago. You've watched the Great Dismay creep closer to our blessed auroral domains. Your grandfathers dreamed that the sky gods might spare the north the worst of this, that somehow our lands might abide until the mysteries of 'steam' and 'hydro' and—what did your great-grandparents call it, 'metallurgy'?—might be reclaimed. You men, you are the generation that has seen that dim candle of hope gutter out."

The robed figure paused. He gave his hearers a moment to turn to their neighbors and voice affirmation of what they'd heard. "Where is it written that decay must triumph?" he cried at last. "Where is it proclaimed that we shall bequeath only savagery to our children? I say to you, there is another way. I will speak to you this night about a grand commission. Accept it, pledge your lives and honor to the cause I will announce, and we can yet turn back the forces of ruin. We and we alone can end the Great Dismay! Who is with me?"

Friz Labokloer had never heard a sound so loud, nor had Ruth—not on Jaremi Four, at least. The cheer that tore itself from two thousand throats was a shriek, a snarl, a war cry, a victory howl.

It hailed redemption.

When the men had shouted themselves out, robed minions appeared. They threaded through the crowd pushing carts laden with flagons and cups. Each man gratefully swallowed a delicious concoction that soothed the pain in his throat.

The robed seducer continued for more than an hour, alternating proclamations of despair with guarantees of power and renewal. He wove rhythm into metarhythm and metarhythm into tidal surges of meaning and emotion. Six times the men cheered themselves hoarse. Six times the minions distributed the soothing elixir.

And when they were ready to do anything he wanted, he told them what he wanted.

"Men of the north! A great evil gathers strength. As we have pledged our very lives this night to oppose the forces of decay on our continent's sourthern reaches, further from the blessed aurora, schemes are laid to complete our world's final plunge to destruction.

"At the head of this abominable horde strides an odious charlatan, one whom some have hailed as a god-man. Hear his name. It is Arn Parek."

By reflex, Ruth checked the *verify* signal. She raised her journal's priority to the highest level a field Spectator could assign. While her body shivered, her mind balanced two simultaneous thoughts. *Will I never be rid of Parek?* mingled with *Well, this ought to pump up my saybacks.*

"Parek is false," the robed priest blared. "But I tell you, a true god-man comes. And who am I to offer such a warrant? Hear my name. I, Samu, pledge that the sky gods will answer your sacrifice by sending a true deliverer. You men have been brought here to perform a great work: *to prepare our world for a true god!* A god not of violence, but of grace. A god not of the sword, but of the spirit. A god who does not belong to this tainted day, but who is yet to come. Who is with this god?"

Again the listeners cheered; again the minions nudged carts among them.

The men had stood raptly listening, shoulder to shoulder, for three hours. Few noticed the film of cool water that swept across the hall's vast floor, carrying away the urine they'd unthinkingly released. Few discerned the streams of frosty air that relieved the chamber's heat and helped them stay alert. *The water barely ripples as it crosses that vast floor,* Ruth thought. *How was it polished so incredibly flat? What moves that air?* She shrugged. *What makes me think I'll ever get answers to such questions?*

"Men of the north!" the hooded teacher intoned. "Among all men, you were selected for this great work—for good reason. You were entrusted with the prophecies of the scrolls. For good reason! You were endowed with treasure and might beyond your desert. *For good reason!* So very much has been given to you. Soon so very much will be expected. You will be called to fight. Some of you, and no doubt many among those you conscript, will taste death on the field of battle. But fear not! Be uncompromising, for to compromise is a sure sign of not possessing the truth. Do not shirk the demands that soon will be made upon you. Remember this: the god who is to come is like a stone mason. With his mighty chisel he chips away at the rough edges of your souls. Hesitate to become what he demands when he demands it and you will be reduced to rubble. I seek mighty men of spirit, men who will not hesitate. Who is among those?"

More shouting. More soothing libation. Three more times Samu's pulsing voice thrust them into deep chasms of fear. Atop intoxicating summits of deliverance. At length, he approached his summation.

"Tonight we have learned who we are. To whom we are pledged. And now our lot is to return to the world—presenting unchanged faces to those around us, yet clutching inside the priceless realization of how we've been changed. Men of the north! I give you the sign you shall await." Samu raised one robed arm. His fingers danced in a simple but unforgettable pattern. Across the hall, scattered minions parroted the sign. No man was more than ten meters from a minion. None failed to impress the sign on his memory. "I bid you, return to your cities, your trading halls, your castles, your mines and farms. Pursue your interests. Exercise the power that has been granted you. But remember the sign. Be prepared at any moment to receive the instruction that—when it comes—will overturn your lives like the wind. Most important, speak to no one about what has been revealed this night."

Samu touched a chubby finger to his robe above his right knee. At the touch it opened, revealing a meaty leg with a *silish* around the calf. He lifted his sandaled foot onto a stool.

"As a token of your new estate," Samu proclaimed, "I release us all from the discipline of the *silish.*" He unstrapped his own torture band, revealing angry red flesh. "We who have pledged this covenant have no further need of mortification. When you return to your lodgings, remove your *silish*es. Grant yourselves slumber. The elixir you drank here contains medicines imbued with the power of our work. You will awaken with the skin of your calves unblemished."

Another cheer rose, the only one Samu cut off with an impatient gesture. "Men of the north, our prophecy meeting is at an end. The minions will give each of you a nutritious ration. Chew it as you return. Go. Be strong. Be just. Be ready."

Ready, Ruth wondered as she released her recording to the Net. *Ready for what?*

51. Office of the Terran Delegate to the Privy High Council • Confidential Memo

Your Lordship was silent to my warnings and entreaties even as I lost my position. Some might think my firing a punishment for having shared my misgivings with you before. But I know better. You had to stand aloof as I was discharged; to do otherwise would reveal the link between us. I understand the need for you to maintain appearances, Lord Councilor, and so I will be brief.

After Ruth Griszam's most recent journal, there can be no further doubt. The senders of the prophecy scrolls—the backers of this robed giant Samu—they are Terran. Or at the very least, they have chosen to base their organization and doctrines on a Terran model.

Samu's speech was filled with echoes of a Terran religious organization called Opus Dei. That means *God's Work.* It was a secret society that flourished within the twentieth- and twenty-first century Roman Catholic Church. In the guise of a spiritual fellowship it mobilized influential laypeople for a variety of political and economic manipulations. You remember that pass code: "Peace." "For eternity." In Latin, it was "Pax." "In aeternum," a password exchange often used by Opus Dei. When Samu ordered the men to go back to their homes, continue their businesses and political intrigues, and let no one see how they've changed, that's exactly what Opus Dei initiates, or *numeraries*, used to be told after their initial indoctrination.

Samu's metaphor of God as a stone mason and his continual references to "the work" reflect the Opus Dei vocabulary. "Be uncompromising, for to compromise is a sure sign of not possessing the truth," Samu said. That comes verbatim from Maxim 394 in the *Camino*, a book of adages by Opus Dei founder Jose Maria Escrivá de Balaguer. With Opus Dei as our key, we can even solve the mystery of the *silish*. Opus Dei used to encourage its members to practice private mortification, often employing a band of thorns bound around the calf. In Spanish this was called a *cilicio*.

I anticipate your skepticism, Lord Councilor. You are probably thinking, "It's too neat. With the penalties for breaking Enclave so high, why would a Galactic choose a single, historically decipherable model and follow it so slavishly? Why not change a few details, just to throw observers off the track?" The original Opus Dei *worked*, Lordship. Dilute it too much, camouflage its essence behind too many irrelevancies, and you may take away its power. At least, it might seem that way to schemers who never expected a Spectator to happen along and expose their scheme to the Galaxy. It seems clear to me, if not to others, that Arn Parek has at least one Galactic handler—maybe two, depending on what that Spectator who used Laz Kalistor's name was up to. Judging from the recent improvements in his generalship, Ulf may have one also. Now Samu's backers employ the imagery of Opus Dei to raise a native army to be hurled against Parek. Fems and homs, it's getting crowded down there.

Lord Councilor, you need not restore my position. You need send nothing to comfort me. I know that to show me gratitude would cause uncomfortable questions to be asked. I ask no acknowledgment save that you *act* on the warnings I have sent you. Enclave may be crumbling, Lordship, and only you have received the information required to save it!

[MEMO ENDS]

52. Terra—Wasatch Range, Usasector

"Three, two, one," the head of the affectational colorists called.

"First Elder," Heber Beaman called into the studio intercom, "we roll the intro." Beaman eyed the nearest monitor sphere. In a burst of choir harmonies, the image of Terra in space assembled itself. Written to wafer by the sim artists weeks before, the two hundred second establishing shot dropped into Terra's atmosphere. It swept east to west. Crossing the Greenwich meridian, the *pov* bled off altitude and broke south. It screamed across the Atlantic just ten kilometers above the surface. Coming ashore in Brazilsector, the *pov* skimmed an imaginary pristine Amazon at treetop level. It climbed once more as it neared the Andes. The choir

lurched into its final triumphal chord backed by three vast organs and rank upon
rank of bells. The *pov* relinquished momentum. Languidly it circled the first human
artifact it had revealed: the ruins of Sacsahuaman, an ancient Inca defenseworks
and ceremonial center overlooking Cuzco, Andesector.

Rubble veneered the zigzag walls. This was Sacsahuaman as it had looked
before its mid-twenty-second-century restoration.

"Ready with the tridee matte," called the head colorist. "Match moves programmed on gimbal pickup two."

"Stand by, First Elder," Beaman whispered.

At the apex of the fortress lay a ruined circular structure, its floor crisscrossed
by ancient weirs and flumes. There, apparently, stood Alrue Latier, hands clasped
behind his broad back.

"Cue the First Elder!" Beaman snapped.

Alrue Latier smiled warmly up at the rotating camera. "A reading from Third
Nephi, Chapter Eleven: 'And it came to pass that while they were thus conversing
one with another, they heard a voice as if it came out of heaven; and they cast their
eyes about, for they understood not the voice which they heard; and it was not a
harsh voice, nor was it a loud voice; nevertheless, and notwithstanding it being a
small voice it did pierce them that did hear to the center, insomuch that there was
no part of their frame that it did not cause to quake; yea, it did pierce them to the
very soul, and did cause their hearts to burn.' " Latier leaned on one corner of a
rampart. He favored the tridee pickup with a casual pose. "In such a voice spake
the Eternal Father to the Nephites, that ancient righteous people of Terra's western
hemisphere, before he presented to them the risen Christ. For all we know, Christ
may have come out of skies at this very locality."

The subvocal monitor crackled. Even while preaching, Latier could bark a
command into the control room. *"Any day, Heber."*

Beaman stepped to his console. *"Lookatme* away," he reported.

A well-written *lookatme* would scatter in seconds throughout every level of the
Galaxy's vast communications infrastructure. Essentially a benign virus, it would
force each autoattendant and intelligent filter it encountered to examine the program description embedded in Latier's 'cast, and make an *extremely* liberal esti-
mation of the program's interest level. Across the Galaxy, data-sift modules at
major news organizations flagged Latier's 'cast for priority evaluation. Billions of
individuals casually *pov*ing senso or tridee found their personal entertainment
matrices tuning spontaneously to the gaudy preachment.

Strictly speaking, *lookatme*s were illegal. But they were tolerated so long as
they were not employed too frequently—and so long as they were generally used to
call attention to 'casts that genuinely were of extraordinary importance.

In the years that followed, no one would ever suggest that this 'cast of Latier's
was not important.

Beaman eyed the monitor. Latier appeared to stride the ancient rampart's
crumbling edge, exuding authority. Beaman looked out the studio window. In
reality, the gangly evangelist walked his gimbaled treadmill in a featureless white
studio, tridee pickups weaving near him on robot arms. All the rest was sim.

"The time has come again," Latier rumbled. "Time to speak the words which were earlier proclaimed by the Eternal Father, that as the scripture demands, they might 'hiss forth from generation to generation.' " The *pov* twisted up to gaze into featureless blue sky. In the distance a point of white radiance shimmered. " 'Behold my Beloved Son,' " Latier quoted in a voice like thunder, " 'in whom I am well pleased, in whom I have glorified my name—hear ye him.' " The point of radiance had drawn closer. It resolved into a luminescent human figure. Organ chords and keening voices and overflowings of bells washed in from every direction.

Mouth agape, Beaman leaned as close to the monitor bubble as he dared. "My Lord and my God," he gasped.

Just when the music crescendoed, it became possible to discern the identity of the luminous figure.

He was a man of light frame with chestnut skin, high cheekbones, a tiny mouth. He was wholly relaxed, possessing a compelling sense of innocence. Curly black hair gushed from his temples, cascaded down his back. His pate was cropped to dense stubble. Above his forehead, a two-centimeter triangle had been shaved clean, the apex pointing downward, drawing attention to his eyes.

"Hear me!" cried Alrue Latier.

"Effects sequence eighty-two," called a sim tech. "Stand by. Take it!"

"Adding vertigo and exultation," said an affectational colorist, writhing in her full-body waldo.

In the finished image, Latier floated from his rampart to join the glowing figure in the clouds. "I give you Arn Parek, prophet of the shattered Enclave planet Jaremi Four. It has come to pass that Arn Parek *is* the next incarnation of the true Christ."

The image had shifted again. Now Latier seemed to be in formal dress, pacing his terrace overlooking the Great Salt Lake. " 'Beloved brethren, I have spoken these words unto you according to the Spirit which testifieth in me; and my soul doth exceedingly rejoice, because of the exceeding diligence and heed which ye have given unto my word.' " He crooked an elbow on the balustrade. Unseen hands pressed a pink lemonade into his grip. "Arn Parek is the true Christ—a truth which the Universal Catholic Church has striven to conceal for its own dark purposes."

The pickup pushed closer. "The decadent hierarchs of Vatican can thunder denials as they may. We have heard the truth. At long last Christ has truly come again. He has taken the flesh of a contradictory, charismatic warrior prophet on a richly tragic world. Arn Parek is the Christ. Arn Parek is the One Mighty and Strong prophesied in the Mormon scriptures. Brothers and sisters, God the Eternal Father has honored our New Restoration with a New Incarnation! I quote again from the Book of Alma, chapter seven: 'And now, may the peace of God rest upon you, and upon your houses and lands, and upon your flocks and herds, and all that you possess, your women and your children, according to your faith and good works, from this time forth and forever. And thus I have spoken. Amen.' "

The image faded to black. The revolving 3-D bust of Latier which normally closed his 'casts had a partner now. Beside it floated a matching bust of Parek. As the music rose, a *basso* voice proclaimed: "The Son of God toils once more in this vale of suffering. Exceeding great will be his agonies. When he calls out to us, we—we Saints—will know what to do."

53. Jaremi—Northern Hemisphere

The army had grown huge. The officer corps alone numbered five thousand. Somehow Parek's sky god—or Ulf's—had always dispensed the wisdom prophet and general needed to keep them all fed. But now The Word Among Us and his High Commander were at loggerheads.

"My sky god spoke to me," Arn Parek said coldly. "Today when we assemble the officers, I shall teach that *the universe* is everything. It contains our land, the fabled lands to the south, even the aurora and all that may exist beyond it. The universe was not created. It has always been. It is eternal."

Ulf threw up his hands. "What's the point of teaching that?" Knowing nothing of Terra, Ulf could hardly be expected to recognize an idiosyncratic Mormon teaching borrowed from early nineteenth-century (local) Terran Freemasonry.

Parek ignored him. "There are two more things I must teach tonight. When I traveled beyond the aurora I learned that after death we journey to another world. There, each one of us will be patriarch over a world of our own. What riches will we enjoy there? That is determined by how fiercely each man fought for me in this life. To those who die fighting for my Word I pledge eternal ecstasy."

Ulf shook his head. "Are you finished?"

"No. My final teaching is that in the fullness of time I shall give to each of my officers a secret name. Should they die in battle, when they cross over into the world after death, if they shout out their secret name I will be there. I will pull them through to the other side."

Ulf pushed callused hands through his graying hair, befuddled. He could scarcely hope to recognize a fragment plucked from the secret Mormon temple marriage ceremony. "Word Among Us," Ulf grated, "When I assemble the officer corps for the afternoon preachment, that is *not* what we'll teach."

Parek folded his hands so tight the knuckles went beige. "What are you saying?"

"I am saying what *my* sky god said I should teach today. It is of the visions."

Parek nodded, lips pursed. "The gods speak to you also. Let's hear your proposed teaching."

Ulf struck a commanding pose, as if speaking before thousands. "The Word Among Us speaks of battles yet to come. As High Commander it falls to me to announce our army's next glorious mission. Many of you heard stories on your grandfather's knees—stories of a land beyond the southern ocean, a hapless land where the anger of the sky gods burned hotter than here. I tell you the real secret behind the Great Dismay. The sky gods never meant to smite us! We suffered just collateral damage—damage even the gods couldn't help inflicting as they rained down judgment on heathen Southland."

Parek knitted his brow. "Your sky god told you that?"

"Not now, I'm on a roll." Ulf's voice took on tones of command Parek had never heard in it before. "You fighters know that if conditions here deteriorate much further, we cannot survive. Fortunately, now we have the power to finish the sky gods' work in Southland and turn the gods' rage away from us. We will journey across the Equatorial Sea. There, we shall do what we do best." Ulf raised his arms in a gesture of triumph. "Like the fire, spread His Word."

"What?" Parek said too quietly.

"When we redeem the South, the sky gods will reverse the Great Dismay," Ulf cried. "Our sons and grandsons will know Steam again. Soon we sail. Go and dream of a better world."

Parek stood. "Are you mad?"

"This is of the sky gods," Ulf said with conviction. "You think I could make a speech like that without help?"

Ulf had a point. Parek had to admit that. "All right. Just for the sake of argument, let's suppose the sky gods gave you a commandment they didn't see fit to share with me. It concerns military matters, after all. But now you intend to pledge that our army—five thousand officers, ninety thousand men, half that many camp followers, artillery, cannon, and repair shops—all will go campaign across the Equatorial Sea." Parek spread his palms. "In three generations not so much as a canoe has cast off for Southland. Now we'll be disgraced as liars if we fail to land the largest army in memory on southern shores." Parek slammed his balled fists onto the table. "What are you doing?"

Ulf gestured. An aide stepped outside the council tent. He returned with Chagrin, clad in dusty traveling clothes.

"I know you've been dying to ask me where Chagrin was these last six weeks," Ulf said. "Well, here's the story. Six weeks ago I had a vision—a vision my sky god specifically asked me not to tell you about."

"What?" Parek gasped.

"That's what happened. The sky god said Chagrin should lead an expedition south to the Equatorial Sea."

Chagrin took up the story. "Ulf taught me the text of his vision. It seemed like nonsense, but as we went south, each verse turned out to identify a clear landmark. When we reached the ruins of a city called Kiewalta, we spent hours sifting through debris to find the access door the poem said was there. But it *was* there." His eyes widened. "We went down, and came out onto a catwalk. There they were."

"There what were?" Parek rasped.

Ulf said, "Show him."

Chagrin drew a lustrous object from beneath his cape. It was the digital camera—the invaluable artifact that the wretched petitioner with the shattered child had given up at that early revival in Bihela. Chagrin held the device a hand's breadth from Parek's eyes so the prophet could see its thumb-square monitor.

Fuzzy but decipherable, the images stuttered past in the tiny display.

Chagrin standing at the shore of the Equatorial Sea.

Chagrin directing platoons of soldiers in hammering through a long-concealed access doorway.

Chagrin standing on a catwalk, overlooking a line of ancient, roofed-over docks that seemed to stretch away forever. Moored at every dock was a stout metal ship, an incredible vision from the heady years before the Great Dismay.

Image by image, the monumental scope of Chagrin's find became more clear. Here were cruisers.

Destroyers.

Assault transports.

Fashioners' vessels studded with winches and cranes and scaffolds.

Scores of ships, hundreds of ships, all grime streaked, half-covered with cobwebs and fallen timbers, yet clearly seaworthy.

All lined up and waiting at the edge of the Equatorial Sea, waiting to sail south.

"Word Among Us, I never imagined that the ancients could have built anything so huge," Chagrin said breathlessly. "And under such a broad roof! My fastest runners needed fifteen minutes to sprint from one end to the other."

"You found a fleet," Parek breathed.

The camera's power cell expired. "If The Word Among Us would see more, I can get the inductor," Chagrin said.

"No need." Parek folded his hands. He looked up at Ulf. "I expected you would challenge my authority one day. I never thought the sky gods would send you such a sign. Very well, summon the officers. Make the announcement yourself." He folded his arms. "We sail south."

54. Jaremi Four—Vatican Island

Cardinal Ato Semuga threw the printouts at the trembling monk. "You call this courseware!" Semuga thundered. "It's *boring!*"

"These are autochthons," the monk stammered. "We can't herd them into a wardroom and show them a tridee."

"We'll show them a senso if I command it!" Semuga thundered. "We only have one chance to make Catholics of them. So make it a tridee, and make it *visceral!* When Christ dies on the cross, I want the bass rumble of the thunder to make the soles of their feet itch. When St. Hyacinth sails on the sea on his cloak, monstrance in one hand and statue of the Blessed Virgin in the other, I want them to notice the tiny cracks in the ancient statue's enamel. When the raven brings St. Paul the Hermit his daily loaf of bread, I want them to smell it."

"The raven?"

"The bread!"

"If you want them to smell things, you'll need senso. . . ."

"You know what I mean!" Semuga roared. "Drama. Immediacy. *I want converts!*"

As the monk retreated, Semuga scanned the control hall. Nearby technicians and Swiss Guards had glanced toward his outburst. Faced with his stare, they averted their eyes. To either side, walls packed with displays and instruments leaned inward as they rose. High overhead, two clerics stood on a nulgrav platform, anxiously tapping controls. *Still sifting for correspondences between autochthonous symbolism and the doctrines of the Church,* Semuga thought with grim satisfaction.

An alert tone pealed. "Priority secured communication from Cardinal Rybczynsky," a voice buzzed.

"Understood." Shields condensed around the desk, blocking sound and diffusing vision. A comm bubble twisted open. The hash of pixels resolved into the face of Rybczynsky. "Still in transit, Alois?" Semuga asked.

"I reach Vatican tomorrow. What is your status?"

"The army is as mobilized as it can be without orders," Semuga reported. "I've used most of the last week developing ways to look after the soldiers' spiritual welfare."

Rybczynsky blinked. "Their . . . what?"

Semuga smiled. "They will do the work of Holy Mother Church. If we can save their souls at the same time. . . ."

"Very thoughtful, Ato. All the same, after this call you may be thinking of other things." A secondary bubble popped open next to Rybczynsky's image. It displayed a map of Jaremi Four. The viewpoint tracked south—out of the far north, across the midlands, then down a broad isthmus projecting hundreds of kilometers into the Equatorial Sea. "We know now what the army must do."

"Yes?" Semuga said cautiously.

"Our army must become a navy." Rybczynsky ventured a brittle smile. "It must acquire and neutralize the fleet of Parek and Ulf on the high seas."

Semuga leaned forward, eyes wide. "Send eight thousand officers and two hundred thousand troops *to sea?*"

Rybczynsky smiled thinly. "I order it."

"How?"

"Were I in your shoes, I'd start building boats."

Semuga keyed a few parameters into a strategic modeling module. "Excellency, might this be an over-reaction to those rumors of naval action that circulate among Parek's fighters?"

"Parek's forces move south."

"The seashore will stop them."

Rybczynsky adjusted some control out of the tridee bubble's field of view. A third bubble swam into being. "You've been too busy playing the missionary, Ato." The third bubble resolved into a satellite image of ruined wharves and warehouses. "While you've been polishing homilies, Vatican analysts were sifting the truly wonderful surveillance data your orbital manufactory supplies when the binary is quietest. This is a ruined port known as Kiewalta." A series of enhancements rippled across the image. The fallen roofs became transparent. Beneath them were docks in perfect order. In most of the slips waited vessels.

They didn't just wait. They *floated.*

Cruisers, transports, trawlers, fashioners' ships—assembled from partly standardized modules after the style of Jaremian shipwrights in the days before the Tuezi.

A final enhancement revealed that aboard several of the larger vessels, the steamplants were already hot.

Working steamplants on Jaremi Four, Semuga thought. *Today!* Aloud, he said, "Holy Mothers of God, where'd they find those?"

"Where they float, I surmise," said Rybczynsky. "Not only are Ulf and Parek serious about 'liberating' the southern landmass, they have the means to go there."

Semuga's strategic modeler had churned out some results. "We could attack the dock complex."

"Our forces muster too far to the north," Rybczynsky objected. "Parek's troops will get to Kiewalta first and establish strong landside defenses. There'd be a protracted battle. That area's crawling with Spectators. We might attract coverage in, shall we say, embarrassing detail. As an alternative, consider this." A simulation showed Parek's fleet steaming south from its base near the tip of the great isthmus.

Another base flashed into view. Separated from Parek's facility by eighty kilometers and a line of mountains, it was no less advantageously located for mounting a naval expedition to the south. "This place is called Point Eldek," said Rybczynsky. "There you shall erect your docks."

Animated ships weighed anchor from the second shipyard.

Across the Equatorial Sea, Parek's fleet made for a huge half-circle bay hundreds of kilometers down the shore. "We are confident Parek will make beach head at this bay. It's the first break in the forbidding bluffs that otherwise dominate the coastline."

The second fleet—Semuga's—sailed faster. It intercepted Parek's fleet some five hundred kilometers out to sea. "Engaging the enemy offshore will minimize our exposure to unwelcome witnesses."

"And the sea swallows the evidence."

"*All* the evidence," Rybczynsky said darkly.

Semuga tapped pudgy fingers on the desktop. "If we don't destroy Parek's force at sea?"

"Then we follow Parek to the southern landmass and engage his forces there. In Southland, Spectators are few and far between." Rybczynsky smiled. "But I doubt our fleet will lose the naval engagement. We will have the luxury of configuring our vessels for ship-to-ship warfare. Intelligence data shows Parek's fleet optimally equipped for amphibious operations, only lightly armed for defense at sea."

"An understandable oversight," Semuga gloated. "After all, whom could they expect to send a fleet against them?"

Rybczynsky nodded. "Whom indeed?"

Semuga scanned his strategic modeler and scowled. "Unfortunately, my preliminary data suggest *we* can't send a fleet against them either."

"Indeed?" Rybczynsky said icily. "What are your assumptions?"

"I assume that Parek's fleet launches in two weeks," Semuga recited. "Equipping our ships with faster drives is not a problem. Even so, even with our manufacturing resources, there seems no timeline under which we could build, fuel, and stock a fleet able to carry two hundred and eight thousand fighters that quickly." Semuga's spatulate fingers stabbed control surfaces. He altered his modeler's assumptions. "Even if we project fifty percent casualties during the naval engagement—absurd in view of our tactical superiority—we can't create a fleet capable of engaging the enemy, possibly pursuing that enemy all the way to the southern landmass, then returning the survivors home."

Rybczynsky shrugged. "You assume too much. Reduce each ship's propulsion reserve by a third. Cut fuel bunkers forty percent. Halve food storage and galley reserves."

Semuga was suddenly, sharply conscious of a bead of sweat trapped in a fold of flesh between his belly and his chest. It felt cold. "They . . . don't come back?"

"After our fighters vanquish Parek's force, we have no further need of them."

"Scuttle the fleet? At sea, after its victory?" He swallowed. "With all hands?"

Rybczynsky nodded. "The reminiscences of returning veterans might later prove compromising."

"Your Excellency contemplates the murder of two hundred and eight thousand autochthons."

"Don't romanticize!" Rybczynsky snapped. "No doubt there will have been casualties from the sea battle."

Semuga shook his head. He tapped new patterns into the modeler. "Very well, Excellency. We can run Vatican Island's existing founding docks around the clock. We can fabricate additional hulls and equipment in orbit and aboard our two beached starfreighters. About eighty percent of the matériel for the isthmus ship-yard can be delivered by submarine freighters. The rest will require, um, three sub-orbital starfreighter runs. The binary star will give us adequate cover."

"As *we* knew, Ato." A fourth bubble ruffled open: it was strategic modeler output from Vatican, identical to Semuga's scorched-sea scenario in all but the tiniest detail. "Analysts on Vatican had worked it all out thirty hours before." Rybczynsky's gray eyes were desolate. "Indulge your dreams of saving souls later. Holy Mother Church calls you now to serve her as shipwright and wrangler."

"And ultimately, as her butcher."

"Yes. Butcher, too."

"Before I drown the soldiers," said Semuga, "let me be the architect of their salvation."

Rybczynsky nodded tiredly. "If time permits. But the mission comes first."

Semuga crossed himself. "God's will be done."

55. Jaremi—Northern Hemisphere, Point Eldek

F riz Labokloer had never seen the Equatorial Sea. It spread unbroken horizon to horizon as their tram surmounted the last coastal ridge. He didn't turn toward Ruth Griszam. Rather than share his impressions, he bowed his head and muttered a prayer.

"Not even here for you, I am," Ruth said sullenly. "It's just you and the view and your god."

"I see the beauty," said Labokloer in controlled tones. "It glorifies him who is to come."

Ruth squirmed in the tram seat so her back was to him. She hugged her knees. *Why do I keep on with Friz?* she wondered. *Do I need to see yet again what faith does to a man on this ghastly world?* The tram windows held no glass. Road dust clung to her shoulders and her neck. It mixed with pooled sweat and caked stickily inside her elbows. Sighing, she leaned back against Labokloer. His shoulder pressed against the place where Ruth's back met her neck.

"Don't," Labokloer said, shooing her gently. "It's too hot." He wiped his face with his hand. Left gray streaks.

"Welcome to the south," Ruth said irritably. A silent minute passed. "Dammit all, Friz—we were so good once."

"My life's no longer mine," Labokloer rumbled. "It belongs to the work." Ruth didn't recognize the Opus Dei reference. Others, far away, might have—if she'd been logged on. She wasn't.

After an interval, Labokloer held a kaleidoscope toward her. "Here, pass some time."

Ruth sighed. "Not everyone finds solace looking through a *n'dren.*"

"Finds what? Never mind." He smiled, waved the toy closer. "Come on, you'll feel better."

Exhaling through pursed lips, she took the kaleidoscope. Abstract forms succeeded each other, punctuated by shuffling noises as the glass shards tumbled into new arrangements.

Ruth lowered it as the tram thudded to a stop. Its fifty passengers, all fighters conscripted from Labokloer's domain, exchanged worried comments. They had reached the lip of an escarpment. Uniformed grooms unhitched the *sturruh* that had hauled the tram the last forty-odd kilometers. Others, soldiers by their look, guided stout metal hooks through steel eyes on the tram's exterior. Tied to the hooks were ropes thick as a man's arm. Half a dozen such ropes snaked along the ground, disappearing into wooden block-and-tackle rigs lashed to thick tree trunks.

Ruth stuck her head outside. She gaped. Samu's people had opted to create an immense incline. The roadway dropped into a ruler-straight one-in-three grade perhaps a kilometer long. Supported by unimaginable quantities of fill, it represented a brute-force solution to the problem of accessing the coastal plain from the escarpment. *Once again, this mysterious Samu impresses me with his logistical audacity,* thought Ruth. *If only I could cover this normally.* Shrugging inwardly, she worked one of the fingernail-sized bugs out of her palm and up between her thumb and forefinger. She dropped it to the ground outside the tram. It looked like any other gravel chip.

Shouting soldiers bunched behind the tram. They pushed it downgrade, ropes paying out behind it.

Keeping her face out the window, Ruth went into Mode. By now the procedure to trigger the bug while suppressing transmission of her own sensory field came automatically. She entered into the *pov* of the bug she'd dropped. She watched her own tram grumble downgrade.

Objects were moving at the bottom. Creeping up the greased plank tracks that paralleled the road at either side. But the bug could not yet resolve them. *Forjel this whole situation,* Ruth thought angrily. *It just keeps deteriorating! Sfelb, I can't even work the regular way any more.* Somberly she reviewed her predicament for what seemed the thirtieth time. Some eight thousand petty lords were streaming toward Point Eldek from every corner of the northern continent, leading an army of more than two hundred thousand fighters and techs and armorers and fashioners and personal companions like Ruth.

Perhaps another fifty thousand troops had guarded their path, facilitating the southward exodus.

Of the whole company, only three Spectators remained. Once there'd been seven. Two had attended Samu's prophecy meetings in person on successive nights, each dying within hours under mysterious circumstances. Ruth was the only Spectator to cover a prophecy meeting and survive; of course, she'd attended vicariously, *pov*ing through bugs she'd slipped into Labokloer's clothing.

Later, while the fighters began their southward trek, two more Spectators had died. One's first journal went onto the Net fourteen hours after she'd recorded it. She'd been felled by an accidental steamrifle discharge just an hour later. Another was trampled by a runaway *sturruh* while still in Mode; OmNet had been broadcasting his journal live.

For months, Spectators on Jaremi Four had known it was almost impossible to get into Parek's army without dying. Now Samu's military venture had acquired the same infuriating characteristic. A few Spectators—or their agents—rashly charged that both Parek and Samu must have Galactic contacts who let them know what OmNet revealed about them. Those charges were, of course, ignored by bureaucrats who knew perfectly well that Enclave violations on such a scale were inconceivable.

Nonetheless, Ruth and her two surviving colleagues had adopted the precaution of never posting their *pov*s direct to the satellite. Instead, they spread bugs. They squirted up journals when the bugs' owners were a safe distance away. So far, the stratagem had worked. Those three Spectators had covered the trip south in reasonable detail without additional losses. Then again, the whole idea that Samu's backers monitored OmNet might be so much paranoia.

Keeping her direct awareness veiled from the satellite, she peered downgrade. "Look," she told Labokloer. "As we descend, two empty trams are coming up. They use them as counterweights."

Labokloer stood up. He nodded. "Two-to-one gearing."

"The previous tram hauled them halfway up. Ours will finish the job."

Labokloer shook his head. "Two trams go down, two come up. They keep recycling them. How the hell many soldiers are there?"

Ruth knew that answer, but kept silent.

At last the tram dropped below the escarpment's dense canopy of trees, granting its passengers a view of the coastal plain. Ruth couldn't help staring. She hardly noticed when Labokloer wedged his muscular bulk beside her.

She pressed a bug into a spot of sticky residue on the tram's side. It clung just below the windowsill. *I hope with so many trams, they'll be unable to reconstruct which one this was taken from.* Ruth opened a third channel to her bird.

To the right, looking west along the great peninsula, tents peppered the coastal strip: bivouac tents, mess halls, artisans' enclosures, and tarped-over supply depots. They marched back in neat rows as far as Ruth could see, which was no further than two or three kilometers, with all the smoke. Ruth crossed the tram and leaned out the opposite window. She planted another bug.

Looking east, the view was clearer—and more astonishing. An archipelago of land arched out into the Equatorial Sea protecting a vast oval-shaped harbor. It was choked with ships—cruisers, troop ships, cutters, battle scows, nimble gunboats that seemed barely to displace enough to support the huge steam-cannon on their decks. Most were brown with rust from stem to stern. *They must be four hundred years old,* Ruth thought. A few were simply gutted hulls with new superstructures hewn from logs and greasy fabric. Yet all appeared seaworthy. All could float. All could fight.

Fifty minutes later, Ruth and Labokloer were riding across the coastal complex in a rickshawlike vehicle. Three soldiers pulled it, their uniforms sodden with sweat. Ruth looked behind. Workers had fastened a sling beneath the tram that had brought them here. Three *sturruh* drew it off the roadway. Soldiers lay down wooden skids. Twenty men maneuvered the tram into place on the greased planks so it could be hauled back up for more soldiers.

Ruth looked into broad tents where men and women toiled at looms making sailcloth. Elsewhere, vast forges and furnaces belched heat. Flame. Molders poured steamgun shells. Everywhere were messengers on foot and on *sturruh*back. Squads and platoons of fighting men trundled by in *sturruh*-drawn open buses. Quartermaster's troops guided traffic and directed lost pedestrians.

The flagship was unmistakable. Once she had been a pleasure ship, probably a liner that had traveled regularly between the northern and southern continents more than three centuries ago before the Tuezi struck—or such was her design. Now she was studded with medium-sized guns. Her silhouette was dominated by twin towers of wooden superstructure, fore and aft, each several decks high. Between them, the waist of the ship formed an open promenade a deck or two above the bulwarks. Perhaps it had once been a heliport. "Hey, you have that *n'dren?*" Labokloer asked.

Ruth's hand went to her pockets, then to the waistline of her fatigue pants. "I'm so sorry, Friz. I must have lost it!"

"What's it matter today?" Labokloer laughed. He clasped an arm around her. His thumb brushed the undercurve of her breast where it arched away from her abdomen. "In our stateroom, we'll see about your apology."

She settled against him. "You remember me again. Why now?"

"Today my god who is to come stands vindicated. And in what a way!" He turned to look full at her, his eyes roaming her body. "Life has its wonderful again."

That's your perspective, thought Ruth, surrendering to Labokloer's sweaty kisses.

56. Jaremi Four—Equatorial Sea—
Parek's Fleet

Arn Parek paced the tiny stateroom. He stopped behind the golden tube of the periscope and pressed his eyes to the viewing hood. *Amazing device,* he thought. *Remarkable that it survived the centuries in such good condition.* He swung the scope to port, then to starboard. Two hundred and eighty-three ships, Ulf had told him, ranging from rehabilitated old luxury liners and troop transports to fashioners' barges, trawlers, merchantmen, steamschooners, and amphibious skiffs. Somehow, despite their dissimilarities their skippers maintained tight formation. Parek twisted the scope to look ahead. Beyond the ships on point, nothing could be seen but brittle blue sky, sapphire water, and scattered clumps of floating mangroves.

Counting the camp followers, thought Parek, *almost a hundred and fifty thousand people ride aboard these ships. If only Willim could've lived to see so many set to sea in a single cause!* Parek tumbled into a lavishly cushioned berth and laughed bitterly. *Willim would have needed only a moment to see through the wonder of this fleet. He'd have eyes only for the wheel on my door. The wheel I cannot turn.*

Parek knew the scope tube ended amid a forest of pipes and tubes and flags atop the control platform three floors above. No one's attention would be drawn by its movement. No one would connect it with The Word Among Us and his inexplicable absence—not even now, as the fleet everyone still thought was Parek's began its greatest campaign.

With a metallic squeal, the wheel turned. Chagrin bustled in. Burly guards shut the hatch behind him. Chagrin eyed the tray he'd brought an hour before, still undisturbed on the stateroom's tiny desk. "You didn't touch your dinner."

"I'm not hungry. Other matters preoccupy me."

"Other matters?"

"I keep wondering how Ulf could have reconditioned all these ships. Where'd he find the artisans? How did he train so many in the arts of sailing—from running those ancient steamplants to knowing the codes those lanterns flash from ship to ship? Where did Ulf find enough fuel for all these steamplants?"

Chagrin made a gesture of helplessness. A deep *thrumming* in their feet rose in intensity and pitch. "We've made the open ocean," Chagrin announced, trying to change the subject. "Ulf ordered the throttles opened."

Parek spoke gently. "You're not my man any more. You're Ulf's. I don't disapprove. I only ask why."

Chagrin closed the clips that locked the serving tray closed and tucked it under one arm. "Ulf is strong with the sky god."

"Who died and came back?" Parek snorted. "Who transfixed the people night after night in Bihela?"

"Who brought us this fleet?"

Parek sighed.

He had the strangest sensation he was being nudged. But no one was there.

Chagrin's eyes narrowed. "What's happening?"

"I am not sure." Parek massaged his temples. "It's the sky god. He taps at me inside."

Awe and cynicism vied in Chagrin. Cynicism won. "You expect me to believe—"

"Sky god!" Parek blared. "Come to me as I have lately implored you so often! I need your wisdom!"

Chagrin stepped to the hatch. He raised his hand to rap for the guards outside to open it. He twisted and gave Parek a final dismissive glance.

And saw . . . it.

In midair, an arm's length before Parek's staring eyes, a luminous spiral coalesced. It was sourceless and semitransparent. But Chagrin knew nothing from his world could give rise to light like that.

"Blessings, Arn Parek." The voice came from everywhere. "Everlasting welfare unto you."

Chagrin sidled beside Parek. He tugged at Parke's sleeve. "This is how—"

"I know, this is how Ulf sees the sky god," Parek hissed. "Remember, I saw him first."

Chagrin peered forward. A human figure emerged within the whorling colors. "Blessings from the auroral sky of possibilities," the figure intoned. Involuntarily Chagrin shrank away from Parek's side, away from the spirit's gaze.

"Oh god named God, I've called to you and heard no reply," Parek said in a strong voice. "I feared you had turned your back on me."

"I feared you had run away from me," the sky god thundered. "Much affliction have I known, yea, and been sore aggrieved as I sought in all the lands for my prophet." The sky god seemed to redirect his gaze back into his own world, at something Parek and Chagrin could not see. His tone changed. "This can't be right."

Parek took advantage of the pause to signal for Chagrin's attention. "I must commune with the sky god alone."

Chagrin nodded, but made no move to leave. His eyes were riveted on the glowing presence. At the moment, the presence seemed to be ignoring them both. "Do it again," the god groused to entities unseen. "This says he's in the middle of a forjeling ocean."

"Go, Chagrin," Parek ordered.

"What do you mean that's where he is?" the god demanded.

"We're on a ship," Chagrin called. "That's why we're on the ocean."

The god looked up and pointed an angry finger at Parek. "You are not alone?"

"It's just Chagrin," Parek assured the god. Urgently he waved Chagrin away. "Go, go. Now. You must."

The sky god turned to face Chagrin. "You! Leave us."

Chagrin froze, mouth agape. He made no move; he couldn't.

The god muttered something; it sounded like "Effects sequence one-oh-six." Suddenly the glow surrounding the god's image turned inside out. Columns of orange flame boiled where the cheery color had been. "Scat!" the god raged. "Leave! Get thee hence!" Lightnings danced from the god's hands and around his eyes. He stared straight at Chagrin. "You! Fuck off!"

Chagrin leapt backward. He pounded a tattoo on the hatch. Ulf's troopers undogged it. With all possible speed and energy Chagrin fucked off.

The sky god's glow flickered back to its usual pattern. Smiling, yet with an air of command, the god turned back toward Parek. "Very well then," he said unctuously. "Where were we?"

57. Terra—Wasatch Range, Usasector

Alrue Latier composed himself. Smiling, yet with an air of command, he tapped the control that rotated the gimbaled treadmill in his studio a hundred and forty degrees. "Very well, then," he said unctuously. "Where were we?"

Urgently Latier hissed a subvocal command to his director. *"Crash priority. Find Heber. Get him here."*

Parek floated before Latier. Or rather, a crisp tridee image of Parek shimmered in the air of the Terran studio. It was an unimaginably illegal live feed from far-off Jaremi Four.

Parek dropped to his knees like a rag doll. "Oh sky god," he wailed, "you know my predicament. Why am I being punished?"

Latier blinked. He wished Beaman was there to stream analysis into his ear. "What makes you think you're being punished?" he hedged. "And what's this about being on a ship?"

"I abase myself before you. I've been less than candid, oh sky god, and you have found me out. Stripped of power, I suffer at your whim. Tell me what I must do to be restored to your warm bosom."

"I'll give the commands here," said Latier sternly. "And you will do such telling as is to be done. Tell me how it is that you are stripped of power."

Parek bent forward at the waist. He pressed his hands to the deck plates. Now Latier could see it. *A metal floor?* thought Latier. *Where the sfelb is he?* "I am covered with burns," Parek moaned, "yet you drag your toenails across my flesh. Such is your pleasure, but I beg you, toy with me no more. I'll do whatever you command. Only command *something!*"

"Who burned you?"

Parek's brows wrinkled. "No one. It's a figure of speech."

"So then you're not really on a ship, either."

"Of course I am," Parek sobbed. "Sky god, you know I sail with your own fleet."

"Surely," Latier temporized. "Gods know things like that." *Fleet?* he thought. *What do people on that ruined world consider a fleet? Two canoes and a dinghy?*

Parek struggled to hands and knees. He raised his eyes. "I was a fool to imagine I could conceal anything from you. When Laz Kalistor came to me in Bihela, I told you nothing of him. Yet you knew to command that 'Laz . . . must . . . die.' So you told me. So you told Ulf."

"*I* told Ulf?"

A tone burred in Latier's ear. *"Heber Beaman here,"* came a small voice. *"I'm in the control room."*

Latier subvocalized a reply. *"See if you can make sense of this. Parek's in the middle of the forjeling ocean, prattling about losing his power. He thinks I'm punishing him."*

"We've done so well keeping him out of the view of Spectators that we lost touch with him ourselves," Beaman observed. *"Our birds autosearched Jaremi Four for eighteen hours just to find him."*

"What do I tell him?"

"Whatever you do don't even hint that you don't know what he's talking about."

"How will I learn anything?" Latier demanded.

"You're his god," Beaman reminded him. *"He thinks you know everything. Don't wreck that."*

"Oh, plorg," Latier breathed down the subvocal channel. To Parek, he brayed, "So you ride in bondage aboard my ship."

"Truly," Parek sighed. "But I have insulted you enough."

"Help me here," Latier ordered Beaman. To Parek, he said imperiously, "Indeed you have. Let us speak of it."

Parek knelt prostrate in sullen silence.

"You may start," hinted Latier.

"I tried to hide things from you," whispered Parek. "Now shall I offend you again by repeating what you already know?"

"Try me."

"Surely you know my heart, oh god named God," Parek sobbed. "You know my contrition is real. What do you gain by protracting my agony?"

"Contrition!" Beaman hissed in Latier's ear.

"I heard it," Latier chortled. *"Now sit back and see why they call me First Elder."*

Latier transfixed Parek with an iron stare. His voice pealed like thunder in a canyon. "I gain nothing by protracting your agony, Arn Parek. How could I? I am the god of the sky and the aurora, the god who has chosen you out of a world filled with discontent to spread a great truth. A god of magnificence and fortitude such as few have the privilege to meet."

"That's thick enough," Beaman coached.

"I gain nothing from your suffering," Latier rumbled. "But you may gain something very important from it. You may gain my grace."

Parek straightened his back. He looked quizzically at Latier. "I don't understand."

"This day I institute a new form," Latier proclaimed. "Remember the doctrine of scandal?"

"Surely, oh sky god. You taught me to proclaim ridiculous tenets from time to time, because I'd know that if my followers kept on believing them, then that would mean they also continued believing the important teachings."

"Indeed. And you remember that I said scandal was a private doctrine, exclusively reserved for use between a prophet and his sky god—not one you should pass on to your faithful. Well, here's a new doctrine of the same sort, for just between us. I call it confession."

"Confession," Parek said woodenly.

"I know all, so it might seem I needn't hear you recite the manifold ways you have offended me. But *you* . . . you need to *speak* them. Inventory your heart, arrange your transgressions in order, and speak in plain language all the things we both know you've done to anger me. And I say to you, behold, that as you speak it, each transgression shall be lifted from your shoulders."

Parek's face brightened. "I see. I think."

"Be neither terse nor elliptical in your confessing," Latier instructed. "Explain the circumstances, set forth the context. In that way you will cleanse your heart. Your escutcheon will again be unblemished."

"Pardon me?"

"Your escutcheon. Trust me, you don't want blemishes on it. Now confess!"

Parek rose, collecting his memories. "May I sit to do this?" Taking the god's silence for assent, he pulled over the stateroom's lone chair. "I suppose I should begin at the very start. When I had been holding public meetings in Bihela for about a week, Laz Kalistor came to me. He taught me to see through blindfolds—"

"Not exactly," said Latier acidly.

"Well, no. Under the blindfold, actually, along my nose. He taught me to walk on fire."

"Not quite."

"All right, dying coals."

"What I mean is, you have not begun at the start."

"But I have," Parek said testily. Then he remembered to whom—to what—he was confessing. "Then, great sky god, I must begin by confessing that I do not know when I began to offend you."

Latier steepled his hands. "Was it Kalistor who inspired you to spread that rumor that you'd died and come back to life?"

Parek looked back in genuine puzzlement. "Rumor?" he asked.

"Careful," Beaman warned. *"You just expressed ignorance of something he regards as obvious fact."*

"Be not unclear, Arn Parek," Latier grated. "Confess to me!"

"It was a little before Kalistor visited me," said Parek in a rush. "A little after you first appeared to me in the form you do now. I consumed some plant matter. It makes one fall into a state like death. For an hour one breathes only intermittently. The flesh goes cold."

"You have not said who suggested this thing."

"No one, sky god," said Parek urgently. "It was something I've known about for years. I'd been planning to use it for months, even before you first spoke to me."

"Enterprising little cuss, isn't he?" Latier subvocalized. Aloud, he said nothing while he raked Parek with a steely stare.

"I see now, I should've confined myself to your teachings," Parek wailed. "I should have abandoned my own false devices. Please, I meant no disrespect."

"Continue."

"Later that day, Laz Kalistor visited my healing service. He caught my attention by causing a woman to hear voices that I did not send her. When I healed him, he slipped me a note so I'd recognize him later. After a few days he visited me. He began to teach some of the wonders I described. He taught me to read while blindfolded and to walk across coals—"

"Confession is good," Latier interrupted, "but not so good that you need confess anything more than once."

Parek nodded. "It was perhaps a week later that you appeared to me next. Forgive me, mighty god! In my arrogance I decided not to tell you of Kalistor. I didn't tell you I'd made him my closest confidant. I thought perhaps you didn't mind, because you said nothing against him—at least not then."

"Not then," Latier echoed. "Go on."

"The day Ulf led the army back to Bihela, on that day I should first have known that you were warning me. On that day I should have changed my path. I am so sorry!"

"What the sfelb is he talking about?" Beaman whispered to Latier.

"You heal yourself by speaking," Latier told Parek. "So speak already."

Parek jammed balled fists into his thighs. "That day, Ulf told me you had addressed *him.*"

"What?" Beaman spat.

Latier kept his composure. He phrased what he thought would be the right response. "And again, you did not tell me."

"Tell you what?" Parek sobbed. "Tell *you* that you appeared to Ulf in a vision?"

"Heber!" Latier subvocalized. *"Were we sending anything to Ulf—as part of some backup plan or something?"*

"Nothing," Beaman replied. *"Draw him out."*

Latier raised one arm in a grand gesture. "Today, Arn, you must tell everything."

"As you say, sky god." Parek ran a hand through his thick curls. "Ulf, too, had heard the words 'Laz . . . must . . . die.' He was surprised I'd heard them, and that I'd already arranged for Laz to be executed that day. But when Laz was dead, Ulf showed me you'd given him more detailed orders than the ones you gave me."

"In truth," Latier said neutrally.

"Ulf cut Laz apart and threw the pieces in the fire. You hadn't ordained that to me."

No, Latier admitted to himself, *but I should have. It's a foolproof, permanent way to dispose of a Spectator.*

"For months I heard nothing further about Ulf's visions," Parek resumed. "Then, on the day before I was to deliver your revelations about the universe and the secret names, I realized you'd been visiting Ulf often, telling him things he'd need to eclipse my power."

Struggling not to seem a nervous god, Latier commanded, "You must name them."

"You bade Ulf to send Chagrin south with an expedition. You sent Ulf a verse, which gave Chagrin directions as he journeyed. Finally Chagrin found the fleet."

Latier smiled. "Ah, that fleet again."

"That's why it was Ulf, not I, who spoke to the multitudes and proclaimed your mission to purify the southern continent."

"*My* mission to—" Latier's voice trailed off.

Surrounded by spheres and bubbles, Beaman keyed his pushtotalk. "*His position lies on a known shipping lane, one that was still in use when Confetory scouts first mapped Jaremi Four.*"

"*Where's it go?*" Latier subvocalized.

"*The southern continent. He's not kidding, he's really headed across the Equatorial Sea.*"

Latier addressed Parek tonelessly. "Now Ulf leads, um, the *fleet* you say his visions showed him. And your role in this?"

"A puppet," Parek confessed. "A puppet whose endorsement Ulf has so little need of, I don't know if he'll bother pulling my strings again."

"Confess more," Latier ordered. "Tell me about this fleet."

"You know," Parek said glumly. "Almost three hundred ships, carrying the whole of the army."

"Whaa-a-a-at?" The moment he emitted it, Latier knew that his astonished screech was, well, ungodly. *Bull it out*, Latier thought. *Just stare at him. Forjel it all, I'm a god. I can make any plorg-warming noise I want to.*

The ruse worked. Parek stood and massaged his cheekbones. "I understand, oh great sky god. My words do not suffice to describe your fleet."

"*I like this god thing,*" Latier cackled subvocally. "*If they believe hard enough that you can do no wrong, then you can't. No matter how deep you put your foot in something, they'll pull it out for you.*"

"*In this case, most fortunate,*" Beaman agreed. "*Wait, where's he going?*"

"Aspect rotation!" called the senior affectational colorist. "Forty degrees right!" From the corner of his eye, Beaman saw the sim artists writhing in their waldoes, struggling with arms, legs, fingers, and toes to modulate scores of control channels.

Latier's projection revolved and tracked Parek's movement across the tiny cabin.

Parek clacked down the periscope handles. "What I lack the eloquence to tell you, perhaps I can confess by showing you," he said. "Is it within your powers to look in here?"

"*Can I?*" Latier subvocalized.

Beaman's fingers skittered over control surfaces that redrew themselves beneath his fingers. "*I think so, First Elder.*"

"I am the god of the aurora and the winds," Latier-in-the-cabin blustered. "Of course I can look in a periscope."

"Aspect extrusion," Beaman called to the sim artists.

Parek leapt back from the scope, gaping. His back slammed the wall.

"*The effect of your movement must be disconcerting,*" Beaman warned Latier.

"*Can't be helped.*"

Beaman palmed controls. "*We'll see what you see, First Elder. Now call Parek back. He must aim the scope for you.*"

"Come, Arn," Latier beckoned. "Step close. Reach within the radiance."

Swallowing bile, Parek inched his fingers toward the scope. Tentatively he reached into the glowing halo that surrounded Latier's miniature figure. Feeling no discomfort, he clamped trembling fingers around the periscope's handles.

"It's your confession, boy," Latier rumbled. "Choose where I should look first."

Parek swung the handles a few tens of degrees. He nodded.

Beaman thumbed a control paddle, pushing Latier's *pov* forward.

Latier pressed his virtual eyes into the viewhood. "Secret works of darkness," he breathed.

"By the One Mighty and Strong!" cried Beaman. His hands went slack on the control surfaces.

It *was* a fleet.

The periscope looked aft. Row upon row of ships surged behind them. Directly behind was a fashioners' barge at least a hundred meters long, its deck a mad lattice of crane arms and scaffold modules and portable bridge sections. The men who strode its decks seemed dust-mote small. Two hundred meters to starboard a troop transport towered, its immense superstructure looming ten decks above the water. On its forecastle soldiers could be seen exercising in platoon-sized groups. To port of the fashioners' barge, an amphibious lander thrust its prow through a wave crest. Spray thudded over dozens of rafts and skiffs and motor launches strapped to her bulwarks. Parek twisted the scope to port, then to starboard, and finally ahead, as Latier requested. The vista was everywhere the same—ships, ships, ships.

At last Latier drew back from the viewhood. He floated once more before Parek in his chair. "You say Ulf found this fleet," he breathed.

"You gave it to him—and told him what to do with it," Parek said evenly. "Since I'm confessing, I may as well say it all. It disturbed me when you told Ulf things that you withheld from me. It disturbed me when you revealed the great marvel of this fleet to Ulf and not to me, further eroding my influence. But I thought you had your reasons."

"Perhaps I did," Latier waffled.

Thinking the god wanted more groveling, Parek fell to his knees. "I am your truest servant!" he all but shrieked. "I confessed. I beg you, forgive me. Return me to my place at the head of this army."

"*What now?*" Latier subvocalized.

Beaman had no answer.

"You have made a good confession, Arn Parek," Latier stalled.

Parek rose to his knees. Tears of relief streamed down his cheeks. "All praise and felicity to you, great sky god."

"I'll leave you alone to probe your heart for a few minutes. Then I shall return," Latier announced. "Do not move from this cabin!"

"A commandment I am certain to obey," Parek said with a trace of his accustomed wryness.

Latier stepped off the studio treadmill. His hair and his temple garment were soaked with sweat. Beaman sprinted in from the control room. "By the lusts of Corianton," Latier demanded. "Did you *see* that fleet?"

"No one just stumbled onto that, First Elder," Beaman advised. "Not even Ulf. It must have been built specifically for this purpose."

"On Jaremi Four? By *whom?*"

Beaman nodded urgently. "Must've been Galactics."

Latier sat straighter, lips agape. "Galactics? Who?"

"No way to know," said Beaman. "Someone who spent a great deal more than we did on remote manufacturing capabilities."

"Someone working through Ulf the way we work through Parek."

Beaman blinked his ferret eyes. "They want Ulf to replace Parek as the head man. To do it, they gave Ulf that fleet."

"So we're no longer alone on Jaremi Four." Latier leaned back. He laughed convulsively. "Let the games begin."

Beaman clasped nervous hands together. "Perhaps we should abort, First Elder. Our plans always assumed we'd be the only meddling Galactics. What if our opponent makes some error that attracts a blue-ribbon Enclave tribunal? Under that scrutiny our actions could hardly go undiscovered."

"Heber, I will never abandon Jaremi Four." Latier laughed. A servant brought him pink lemonade. "Arn Parek's my ticket to ultimate power over the Galaxy's trillions of souls. First my church will stand alongside Vatican as the second Terran faith to branch out into the Galaxy. Then I'll outstrip the Universal Catholic Church." He clasped meaty hands around the lemonade glass. "The dotards at the Tabernacle think me an embarrassment. They'll change their tune when I stand astride the Galaxy."

Beaman nodded. "I understand."

Latier sighed. "Speaking of remote manufacturing, what's the status on the satellite repairs?"

"No further progress," Beaman said, eyes downcast.

"We can't deploy more birds?"

"Not in time, not with the money you have left, and not with *Bright Hope* and her Detex systems screaming toward Jaremi space at Panna speed."

Latier spread his palms. "So what can we do with the satellite systems that remain operational?"

Beaman ticked items off on his fingers. "We can plant ideas in people's heads while they sleep."

"Like when we told Parek to go wait in the forest."

"Right. We can manufacture small objects and deliver them to the surface."

"Like the medicine we sent Parek to cure that venereal disease."

Beaman nodded. "Of course, I've repaired the modules that permits you to appear to Parek face-to-face, as you've just been doing. Parek can initiate contact with you, as well, now that we again know his position well enough to monitor him."

"Beyond that?" Latier asked.

"We can make pretty lights in the sky, visible to the autochthons but not detectable from orbit. You know, if the aurora's not giving us enough of a light show."

Latier grimaced. "Nothing more?"

"The heavy manufacturing module's a total loss," Beaman said grimly.

"So we won't be building any fleets of our own."

"We wouldn't be building a fleet like *that* even if everything were six-by-six greens. No one here imagined ever wanting to operate on that scale. But it *would* be nice to be able to slip Parek a set of body armor, a personal escape sub, or a few hundred enhanced artillery pieces. I doubt we'll ever restore the systems that could do that."

"Still, keep trying."

"Of course."

"So where do we stand now?" Latier rumbled. "It seems I'm left with the asset with which I began my ministry—a good line of sfelb."

Beaman smiled narrowly. "Your messiah awaits."

"I'm ready," said Latier. Grunting, he mounted the gimbaled treadmill.

Beaman's voice crackled in Latier's head. *"On station. Do you have a plan, First Elder?"*

"A corker," Latier subvocalized. *"Have the sim artists make this flashy."*

Parek had never seen fireworks. When the superposed finales of two dozen festive displays seemed to erupt in his cabin, they earned his undivided attention.

"I'm back," Latier said redundantly as The Word Among Us righted his chair and resumed his seat thereon. "Are you sitting down?"

"I am now, er, again—um, yes," stammered Parek.

"Behold, I must share a secret with you. A terrible secret no sky god has ever revealed to a mortal since the universe began." Latier linked his hands behind his back. Pushed his head forward conspiratorially. "In the sky and its aurora there are many gods, of whom I am but one."

Parek nodded. "As we've always surmised."

"The difference between us is this," Latier whispered. Parek leaned forward, straining to hear him. "Most of the other gods are evil."

Parek leaned further forward. "Their escutcheons," he said in a tone approaching horror. "They're blemished?"

"Blemished? Positively besmirched."

"But you," Parek said, calculating feverishly. "You're a good god."

"Exactly. Now here is the other part of the secret." Latier brought one hand forward and waggled a finger like a martinet. *"I have not been appearing to Ulf."*

Parek sat up straight in the chair. Comprehension bloomed. "One of the evil gods?"

Latier steepled his hands under his chin. "It is an evil god who counsels Ulf. That evil god sent Chagrin to find this fleet and conceived the mission to the southern continent. And it's that evil god who plots Ulf's elevation above"—Latier pointed both index fingers at Parek—"the rightful bearer of my Word."

In the control room, Beaman leaned forward, hands over his mouth. He could only hope his stifled laughter wouldn't distract the sim artists.

Parek stood. He poured himself a drink. "Does Ulf know?"

"No," Latier improvised. "He believes he's having visions of a good god, as you do."

Parek drank down a finger of rare nectar. He looked guiltily at Latier. "Once again I am sorry, oh great sky god." He held forth the bottle. "Can I offer you—"

Latier chuckled. "As a god, I drink only ambrosia."

"Ambro . . . what?"

"Ambrosia," said Latier hurriedly. "It is used all over the universe. For cleaning escutcheons, mostly. But never mind that now. What matters is that the evil god must be defeated."

Parek knitted his brow. "Not . . . not so fast."

"Eh?"

"You are a good god," reasoned Parek. "I know that because you told me so."

"Of course," Latier said blankly.

"You appear to me in a vision, and give me wisdom, and help me do impossible things. I worship you. And I . . . I proclaim you."

"Like the fire," Latier agreed, "you spread my word."

Parek gestured with both hands in a way that suggested stacking small boxes one on top of another. "Now Ulf has a god, too. Ulf thinks his god is also a good god. No doubt, if Ulf asked, Ulf's god would tell Ulf what a good god he is, in just the way you reassure me."

"I suppose so," Latier wavered.

"Ulf's god appears to him in a vision, and gives him wisdom, and helps him to do impossible things. Yet under your counsel, I have never achieved anything nearly as impossible as this fleet."

"What's your point?" sniffed Latier.

"How do I know *you're* the good god?"

"Excuse me?"

"How do I know Ulf's god is not the good god? What if *you're* the evil one?"

"Lightning," Latier subvocalized. The sim artists improvised. Parek stutter-stepped backward across the tiny stateroom. Aloud Latier thundered, "Don't be a fool, Arn Parek. Whom does Ulf's god want to elevate to supreme power?"

"Um, Ulf," Parek said quietly.

"If Ulf's god is victorious, where will you end up?"

"A figurehead, at best," Parek said defeatedly. "Probably dead."

"Now, you only get one shot at this. If Ulf's god wants Ulf on the throne and you in a compost heap . . . is that *good?*"

"I . . . I guess not."

"I rest my case."

Beaman rested his face in his hands.

"Despite his power, at some point Ulf will need you—if only for purposes of display. When the opportunity presents, you must be ready to exploit it."

Parek nodded grimly. "Then shall my escutcheon be unblemished. It shall shine like a universe to all the ambrosia."

Latier nodded vaguely. "Exceeding expert in many words as I am, I could not have said it better. This audience is at an end, Arn Parek. We shall speak again."

58. Vatican

"**D**o this in remembrance of me."

Pope Modest IV raised the disk of bread. Limned green beneath a skylight, the thin flat wafer trembled in his joined hands. He contemplated the newly consecrated host. *Our Lord and Our God,* he thought. *If only for a moment, We truly know where You are.* Bowing his head again, Modest drew back his arms. He brought the wafer to his mouth. Placing what he did not eat on a solid ruby tray, he reached for the diamond chalice that contained the wine.

One of the church traditions Modest had restored was the requirement that each priest celebrate the Eucharist once daily, in private if need be. The papal schedule contained no public Mass today. But it provided a quiet interval before his emergency broadcast. He'd hoped by performing this day's Eucharist alone to find some inward peace. Solitude was so rare for the pontiff. In his private chambers, solitude was—if briefly—guaranteed. Peace continued to elude him. The wine lingered bitter in his throat. Modest set the chalice on the tiny altar. He picked up the pall, a square of stiff crystal faced with cloth, and placed it over the chalice. Impatiently he tapped its edges until the cloth skirt hung properly, making of the chalice a little cube-shaped damask tent. *Stop fiddling,* he told himself. *It's far too late for fiddling.* Modest stepped away from the altar. Rang for a server to collect the liturgical accoutrements.

Hands folded before him, fingers knitted not in prayer but in misgiving, he shuffled to the window.

He did not turn when the chamber door whispered open, admitting Bishop Krammonz. Rather, Modest continued to scowl out over the city. It sprawled tastelessly under algae-burdened clouds the color of pistachio.

"Holy Father," Krammonz said quietly. "You have a visitor."

Modest turned. "Good daypart, Alois." Gracefully as always, Alois Cardinal Rybczynsky crossed the papal chamber. He bent to reverence the Fisherman's Ring, an ancient badge of office Modest had revived as an item of daily wear.

The two churchmen settled into baroque armchairs. Tea was waiting. Krammonz withdrew, latching the door noisily so the pope and the Cardinal-Secretary of State would know they were alone.

Rybczynsky sipped tea. "The die is cast, Your Holiness?"

Modest patted a fat leather-bound volume on a nearby table. "The theologians made their conclusions. The bull is complete. Billions of copies await distribution. All We do today is go on tridee and announce what others have thought and written."

"You are the Holy Father." Rybczynsky spread his hands. "You can reverse the church's course, even now, with a word."

Modest smiled. "A word We choose not to speak."

"You think the theologians are right?"

"They tell Us that Arn Parek is not—cannot be—the Christ," Modest said slowly. "They tell Us the true Incarnation is on Jaremi Four, but probably still in the womb—at most, a babe."

"So they tell you," Rybczynsky acknowledged. "But what does the Holy Father believe?"

Modest lowered his eyes. "We accept the theologians' judgment."

Rybczynsky leaned forward. "But what do *you* believe? I address now not Pope Modest, but the man Vitold Byrtoldi. The man at whose side I worked for so many years in the curia. Does Vitold believe it best serves the church to proclaim infallibly that Parek is not the Christ?"

"You always knew how to pierce Our defenses, old friend. Very well, let Us abandon the papal 'We.' The truth? My intellect is convinced by the theologians' arguments. My heart remains uncertain. After all, it is not the theologians who predicted this Incarnation. It was Fram Galbior. And his equations are consistent with a Christ not yet born *or* a Christ already well into public ministry."

Rybczynsky frowned. "Then how can you stand before a Galactic audience this day and pronounce, in the name of God and Holy Mother Church, a doctrine of which you are uncertain?"

"One does what one must," Modest said tiredly. "Even when one is Pope." He chuckled darkly. "Especially when one is Pope." He waved a slender hand. "The power, the spectacle—it's all hollow, didn't you know that, Alois? Ultimately it all comes down to one man, alone with his thoughts in the middle of the night, desperately struggling to decide which of his cascading ideas might embody a hoped-for answer to prayer—which ideas are just idle human maundering. Certainty in my heart? I can't wait for that."

"But what if the theologians are wrong?" Rybczynsky pressed. "What if Parek *is* Christ?"

Modest smiled gently. "In whom shall we believe? The Christ of whom it was said, 'He is the same yesterday and today and forever,' or this man Parek of whom it was said, 'It's a living'?"

Rybczynsky smiled. "Is that from your speech?"

"Indeed."

"Very arch."

"Doctor Hjinn did well," Modest said too jovially, sensing a chance to change the subject. "Willim Dultav's characterization of his former student's ministry has become a universal figure of speech."

"Yet Parek's popularity continues to grow." Rybczynsky picked at a fleck of dust on his robe. "On thirty-eight worlds there are hunger strikes. Perhaps three-quarters of a billion people are starving themselves in an almost surely futile effort to have Jaremi Four's Enclave status set aside. Each day that number grows. They yearn to go to Jaremi space as pilgrims and pillage at Parek's side."

Modest frowned. "If Parek is attracting such unseemly devotion, so much the better that the church speak out against him quickly."

Rybczynsky nodded darkly. "Perhaps. But consider also what the Church has to lose by defying popular opinion. Please, Holy Father. If your theologians are right that the Christ is just now taking flesh, another decade will be time enough to say who Arn Parek was or wasn't."

"Alois, I appreciate your sincerity." From nowhere, Krammonz had returned. His muted hand signal was all the pontiff needed to see. "The broadcast is nigh.

The true doctrine has been written. It falls to me—" He fingered his outsized ring. Even from two meters away Rybczynsky could see its engraving, an image of St. Peter casting his net into the sea. "It falls to Us to transmit that truth to the scattered sons and daughters of humankind."

The chamber door opened. A tridee crew awaited. They surrounded an elaborately carved chair on a balcony that looked out toward Vatican's synthetic Mount of Olives. Modest stood impassively as *monsignori* swarmed him, decking him with vestments. Over the simple papal simar went the alb; the surplice; the ornately embroidered golden chasuble; and the *camauro,* an archaic red velvet bonnet trimmed with ermine.

Krammonz lifted an ornate arm-length case of solid diamond. He thumbed it open. It was the first time Rybczynsky had ever seen the Prefect of the Papal Household do something with his own hands.

From the case Krammonz lifted a long, narrow strip of ceaselessly trembling white light. He touched his lips to it and stepped reverently behind the pontiff. He draped the luminous stole over the papal shoulders. Golden Maltese crosses flickered at its fringes, betraying the deepest and most seductive dimensionality Rybczynsky had ever beheld. No existent thing at all, this stole was wholly virtual, a variation on the classic vestment permitted only to the Holy Father.

Modest turned to Rybczynsky with compassion in his eyes. "Rest easy, Alois. You of all men should give thanks that Parek is not the Christ."

"Why is that?"

Modest glanced about to be sure no technicians were in earshot. "In less than ten days," he whispered with a predator's smile, "your man Semuga's navy will send Arn Parek and his messianic pretensions to the bottom of the sea. Were We in your shoes, rather than those of the Fisherman, We should welcome what is about to be proclaimed."

With that, Pope Modest bustled through the chamber door. Clerics and techs surrounded him. They adjusted his vestments and sprayed sparkle gel into his eyes. "Thirty seconds," someone called.

Rybczynsky left the studio. He took a chair in the papal chamber. "Tridee," he commanded the room. A bubble opened.

"Homs and fems of the Galaxy," intoned an announcer. "An urgent pastoral message from His Holiness, The Holy Father of the Universal Catholic Church, bishop of Rome, vicar of Jesus Christ, successor of the prince of the apostles, supreme pontiff of the universal Church, once and future sovereign of the state of Vatican City, sovereign of the planet Vatican, Galactic servant of the Galactic servants of God: Pope Modest the Fourth."

The image switched. Modest leaned paternally into the pickup, one hand on the leather-bound papal bull. Strategically placed accent lights gleamed off the sparkle gel in his eyes, producing the knowing twinkle that was this pontiff's public trademark.

Wishing he felt anywhere as certain as he knew he appeared, Modest set about pronouncing one of the most eagerly awaited statements of doctrine in the Church's Galactic history.

"Friends in Christs. . . ." he began.

59. Jaremi Four—Equatorial Sea— Samu's Fleet

Ruth Griszam stuffed hands into the central pocket of her pleated tunic. She breathed the cool sea air. This far south, there was no aurora; the tropical sky was pitch black. She could see perhaps sixty ships, the closest blazing with light from rigging, decks, and portholes. The farthest were little more than luminous points. Each glided atop a shattered mirror image of itself, chopped by the water into countless swaybacked fragments. Here and there, single yellow lantern lights pursued zigzag courses toward the flagship: the last few launches and dinghies were drawing close. A delegation from every ship in the fleet would board the flagship tonight to hear Lord Samu's speech. She rested her elbows on the rail. Gazed tiredly at her own crossed hands. The sea swept past behind them. Ruth caught herself mentally rehearsing a pan-tilt movement that would shift up from her hands, drift aft to survey the gathering crowd, and settle on Samu's balcony four decks above. *No need for beauty shots,* she thought with a bitter inward chuckle. *I can only record using bugs.* Samu's railed platform exuded from the superstructure one deck below bridge level. Already it blazed under the green-tinged luminance of more cold light plates than Ruth had ever seen used simultaneously on Jaremi Four.

She slouched against the rail. Early in the voyage, it had satisfied her to document the fleet's vast size, seeking ideal spots to plant bugs and capture the majesty of the ships sailing in close formation. Then she'd savored discovering the incredible abundance of functional baubles from Jaremi Four's technological past which Samu's artisans had managed to restore. By week two that thrill had faded, too—as had Labokloer's renewed ardor. Shipboard discipline and an ever-growing schedule of spiritual exercises had reopened the chasm between them.

Ruth expelled a sour breath. *I don't need to follow this story down to the destruction it seems headed for. I could call for a pickup. Leap over the side. In five or six months I'd be back on Terra wondering how to spend all my money.*

Motion tickled the corner of her eye. She glanced upward. From a platform near the peak of the forecastle, a shiny sphere rose. Half a person's height, it glistened in reflected ship-board light. Ruth watched the sphere vanish into the night. Every fifteen minutes the flagship released a weather balloon, one of the more remarkable ancient technologies she assumed Samu's engineers had stumbled on while restoring the fleet. *Mine should be next,* she thought. She laughed quietly. *How facilely I beguile myself to carry on.*

Ruth set her lips, went into Mode.

Suck, rush, wrench.

She polled her bugs; more than twenty were active, including the bug she'd attached to a weather balloon now being seated in its launcher. This balloon would be released two minutes into Samu's speech, assuming he began on time. He usually did. In spite of everything, Ruth nourished a childlike excitement about the *pov* that bug would deliver as the balloon lofted above the glittering fleet.

Ruth had some time. She scanned her mail queues. *An astronomical advisory, of all things,* she thought with mild annoyance.

A cannon fired. Ruth wrenched her attention back to the ship.

The forecastle deck was choked with cheering people. Visitors wore sashes marked with colored shapes that identified their home ships. At the signal cannon's peal, the cold light plates illuminating Samu's balcony had ratcheted their brightness even higher. Samu's speech would begin momentarily.

Ruth opened bubbles from each of her shipboard bugs. She prepared to subvocalize the command that would initiate the satellite's recording system. Then held back. *This secrecy makes everything so forjeling complicated.* Frowning inside, she issued a *self* command. She scrutinized the twenty-four bubbles one by one. Sure enough, two bugs' field of view covered the forecastle deck. She appeared in their images, her own figure flashing an angry red.

Under Galactic privacy conventions Spectators' images could not be reproduced unaltered—they *were* Galactics, after all. Legal senso players stripped away the Spectator's likeness and substituted the likeness of another: the experient, perhaps, or some real or imagined love object. But the technology that recognized Spectators and marked their images for replacement would also enable a determined Galactic to pick out a Spectator in any 'cast from an Enclave world: not to see his or her features, but to be absolutely certain which body in a crowd had been the Spectator's.

Under current circumstances, when Spectators who revealed themselves had a way of dying, Ruth had to be out of view of *all* her bugs. She squeezed toward a secluded area under a walkway and ordered *self* again. No red telltales. Now she subvocalized the *record* command and focused her concentration on observing.

Just in time, she thought. On Samu's balcony, the door slid open. Uniformed men strode out and took stations behind the signaling lanterns at either edge of the platform. They rotated their shuttered lanterns, one to port, one to starboard. A chamberlain strode onto the balcony. He wore a scarlet robe festooned with shiny chains and ingeniously mounted plates of colored glass. "Complement of the flagship!" he cried. "Visitors from throughout the fleet! You also who attend only by means of the signal lanterns!" The chamberlain paused and waited for the signalmen to chatter their shutters, sending an abridged account of his words to the other ships. "Hearken to the words of the holy and powerful Lord Commander Samu."

The signal cannon sounded again. Dwarfing the chamberlain—dwarfing forjeling near anyone—Samu lumbered onto the platform. *He does not carry his bulk like an average man wearing an unwieldy costume,* Ruth thought. *He moves as though he truly is that size.* Samu's robe, gloves, and boots were jet black. Every stitch and detail of their construction were visible because of the balcony's intense lighting. Yet within his generous cowl, where one might think to look for a face, there was only blackness. Ruth focused her primary awareness on her "hero" bug. She'd attached it four days earlier to a lifeboat. At that time the lifeboat had lain on deck being repaired; now it swayed at the top of its davit, roughly level with Samu's balcony. Of all Ruth's bugs, it was closest to the black-clad giant. Yet no matter how high she boosted the visual gain, she could resolve no details inside that cowl. *A Series Gamma bug can make the blackness of this tropical night look like noon. Why can't it see inside the commander's hood?*

"Servants of the god who is to come," Samu called in a deep, powerful voice. "We have voyaged long and uneventfully. Too uneventfully, perhaps. For it has come to my attention that many now wonder why the god who is to come makes so little use of his workstones. Some even question whether our commission is true."

Samu paused for the lanterns to catch up. *He certainly gets to the point,* Ruth thought with grudging respect.

"Doubt and misgiving are human things," Samu intoned. "When doubt gives way to faith, that is of the gods. Even in the face of boredom there can be heroism—glory—opportunities for manifesting deeper commitment to the Work."

Ruth's consciousness darted from bug to bug, reading faces in the crowd. *Samu's going down a blind alley with this one,* she told decided. *This is not what these people need to hear tonight.* She was surprised to find herself comparing Samu's technique with what she imagined Arn Parek would say in the same situation. *Parek wouldn't make this mistake. Samu's going to make matters worse. Unless he's building up to something else, something enormous. . . .*

Somewhere behind her awareness, parallel streams of thought converged into a single sturdy torrent. Her entire understanding shattered and reassembled itself like an image in one of Labokloer's *n'drens.* Suddenly Ruth's upper self could imagine no more urgent task than to dive into the mail queue and read that plorg-warming astronomical advisory.

On the balcony, Samu lifted heavy hands halfway to the sky. "We have pleased the god who is to come. He has bidden the sky gods to show us a token of his love."

This cannot be, Ruth told herself. She trifurcated her primary awareness, concentrating simultaneously on the astronomical advisory, the lifeboat bug's image of Samu, and the satellite's master clock. *For vacuum's sake, I hope I'm wrong.*

"The god who is to come has bidden the sky gods to show us a token of his covenant—his pledge that whatever sufferings await us, they will serve to make the world right for his coming!" Samu extended his arms fully, clawed at the sky with black-gloved fingers. He all but screeched: "He sends us his sign!"

Everything went dark.

The cold plates illuminating the balcony snapped off. The lights in the rigging had been extinguished, too. Scattered pools of light glinted behind portholes or in dim companionways, but nothing more. Ruth glanced over the rail; the other ships, too, had switched off all but their most essential running lights. Only the signal lanterns flickered, still relaying the last of Samu's words from ship to ship.

North, Ruth thought with mounting dread. *We're standing at the bow of a ship sailing south, looking aft. We're looking north.*

Behind the superstructure, across the horizon in the direction from which the fleet had come, the sky began to writhe with green fire.

It was an aurora such as only those from the far north were accustomed to. An aurora of such strength was seen in the tropics only a time or two each decade.

Sweeping halfway across the bowl of the sky, it resolved into green curtains swirling overhead and rushed southward. Irrationally, Ruth yearned to feel the wind of their passing brush her cheeks.

The sea glowed green. Every ship of the fleet was clearly visible. One could see horizon to horizon. Nothing cast shadows.

The whole sky glowed now. Bands of pink and soft-edged bars of white whirled among the verdant draperies in the sky.

Ruth returned her gaze to the deck. Here a guard stared slack-jawed at the coruscation in the sky. Two young privates laughed, marveling at the chalky gray tone the almost-monochromatic green light brought to their flesh. Everywhere Ruth looked, men and women marveled.

Yet another element demanded Ruth's attention. The automated mechanism atop the flagship's forward superstructure had released the weather balloon that carried Ruth's bug. It sent an astonishing crane-up shot. At first it was an image of the people on deck. Then it was a shot of the flagship. Even the flagship seemed suddenly tiny under the aurora's sourceless light. Moments later, it was a picture of the fleet, twenty score ships transfixed in a sea coruscating with salmon and green.

Ruth concentrated on the image until the fleet itself was barely a dot on an endless green ocean. She felt a grim satisfaction. *It's the most intensely beautiful visual of my career. Being a Spectator hasn't lost its thrill after all.*

Hearty cheers rose from every ship's deck. Ruth's own feeling was closer to horror—the dread that had filled her mind before the aurora came. *How could Samu fail with a light show like this?* she thought. *But how could he know it was coming?*

Ruth reread the astronomical advisory she'd found waiting in her mail queue. Four hundred thirty-six days ago, the cataclysmic binary Cohller 5114 had spasmed, a discharge of unusual power and extremely rapid onset. When it reached Jaremi Four, the planet's auroral hood would expand south of the equator in a matter of minutes. *It happened right to the second, Ruth realized. And Samu had to know that; otherwise he couldn't have timed his speech the way he did.*

Of course, to know a thing like that Samu had to be a Galactic—hence Ruth's sense of horror.

I've been so stupid, she thought. *I should have recognized this days ago. There were so many independent chains of evidence: The nature of those probes Labokloer received. The way one of them predicted the "wings in the sky" aurora. The pristine perfection of that cavern Samu used for his recruiting oration. The sheer logistics of mobilizing so many soldiers and getting them to Point Eldek from all over the northern continent. That gigantic incline railway leading down to the harbor city. The existence of this fleet—which was probably built new, after the style of ancient Jaremian craft, not restored from ancient hulks. Even Samu's forjeling cowl—on Confetory worlds, any adolescent studying fashion design knows how to incorporate light sinks into a garment.*

That recognition changed everything for her. First of all, it set onto firm foundations her commitment to continue covering the voyage. *You've got yourself an Enclave violation here,* she told herself. *Maybe the first in history—surely the first on this scale. Talk about saybacks! Sensible people ought to find this much more exciting than some backwoods con man who thinks he's God.* She chuckled to herself. *Then again, if people were sensible there'd be no senso industry.*

She turned to the rail once more and gazed out at her crossed hands. As before, the sea whisked by beneath them. But she could see it horizon to horizon, an endless dappled plain reflecting auroral color, studded with ships. *I chided myself for not figuring out about Samu sooner,* Ruth thought. *But enforcement officers must have been monitoring my stuff. They're the experts! Why haven't they realized what all this adds up to?* She shook her head. *Then again, maybe they solved the puzzle but chose not to let us planetside grunts know about it.*

Ruth shut down the bubbles from her bugs. She subvocalized the commands to condense all the bugs' outputs into a single data structure and ran a final check to make sure none of her primary sensory experience had crept into the journal. That done, she subvocalized the most urgent tag she could think of. *"Flash flash flash! Higher than average plot development interest! Critical critical critical security interest! In my opinion this journal proves that the leader Samu is a renegade Galactic. Probable massive Enclave violation, I say again probable massive Enclave violation. Maximum priority, crash precedence. Examine immediately upon receipt."* Flushed with renewed purpose, she subvocalized the *send* command and signed off.

White and gold glinted beside her. It was Labokloer, resplendent in dress whites. "Ruth," he said neutrally. "I'm glad I ran into you."

"You missed everything."

"No. I was with my scripture study group."

She kept her distance. "Are you done with them?"

"I must get back. Spiritual exercises." He leaned forward and planted a lustless kiss on her forehead. "God's chisel would do more work on me."

She shouldn't have been surprised at her anger, but she was. "Will I see you at all?" she demanded coldly.

He drew back and looked through her. "I sleep with the men tonight."

She stepped toward the rail with a finality that told him he shouldn't follow.

Facing the sea, she blinked back tears. At the same time another part of her wondered why she had let this cultbound yokel affect her so profoundly.

I can't bring Friz back—any more than I could've kept him very long under any conditions, she thought sullenly. *I must be the Spectator here. Whatever happens to Friz, I did the right thing sending my warning. Whoever you are, Lord Samu, when Galactic justice comes down on you I hope its wheels turn across you very, very slowly.*

60. Jaremi—Equatorial Sea—Parek's Fleet— That Night

"**A**rn! Wake up."

"Go away." His back to the visitor, covers over his head, Parek curled into a fetal position.

"I prod at thee, Arn Parek. Awake!" The glowing sky god planted fists on his broad hips and looked about impatiently. "I said, I prod at thee."

"Owwww!" The "prod" felt more like a sharp rabbit punch in Parek's kidney.

Parek sprang upright in the stateroom bunk, pressing a hand to his flank. "Oh, it's you," Parek sputtered.

"I beg your pardon?"

Parek blinked fully awake. He bowed his head. "Hail, mighty sky god!"

"That's better," said the sky god. Clad in his stained and symbol-studded temple garment, the meter-tall image of Alrue Latier floated at the center of a shimmering radiance. Petulantly he demanded of someone Parek could not see, "What the sfelb time is it down there?" He turned back toward Parek. "Rather early to be asleep, is it not, man child?"

Parek swung his legs out of bed. He sat on its edge facing the sky god. "It's been raining for a day and a half. My periscope fogged up. I got bored and went to sleep. Ghaaa." He grimaced and massaged his back. "Great and powerful is thy prod, oh sky god."

"Sorry," said the god. "I suppose you're wondering why I have manifested myself to you in glory."

Parek's expression made clear that he hadn't been wondering that at all.

"I have come to witness the fulfillment of my plans for you," the sky god grandly proclaimed. "When we spoke this morning, I predicted that the rain would end half an hour after sunset."

Parek nodded absently, fingering the scar on his cheek.

"You slept through the fulfillment of that prophecy!" the god blustered. "Sunset was more than two hours ago. Were you watching? No, you had a blanket over your head. The periscope should be clear now. Go see if it's still raining."

Stammering apologies, Parek bolted toward the golden scope. Slapped down the handles. "The rain has stopped," he reported. "Looks like a beautiful night."

"Very well," said the sky god. "Now I don't suppose you remember what I prophesied next."

Parek looked up from the scope. "Oh, yes. Aurora. You predicted a huge aurora, moving over very quickly and lighting up the whole sky."

"And when did I say it would occur?"

Parek thought for a moment. Awe overspread his features. "Oh sky god, you came down here just to wake me so I can see the aurora!"

"Precisely. With all those evil gods making mischief, you might think I'd have better uses for my time. Nonetheless, here I am." The sky god gestured impatiently at Parek. "Well, plant your eyes on that scope. The aurora will begin any second."

"Of course." Parek pressed his face to the eyepiece. He began rotating the scope slowly. "There! It comes from the north."

"It always comes from the north. Let me see," ordered the sky god, extruding his luminous presence toward the periscope in the way Parek found so unnerving.

Parek stepped away from the scope. He successfully fought the urge to retreat across the stateroom. "You are a god," Parek stammered. "What need have you of a periscope?"

"Other mortals would feel fortunate that a god even *desired* to share their view of a miracle," snapped the sky god. "Hell, they would feel so blessed that they would willingly prostrate themselves in hot stinking shit. Never mind that, just turn me ten degrees to the right."

61. Terra—Wasatch Range, Usasector

Alrue Latier whistled inwardly at the image that was being relayed to him from Parek's periscope. *The Galaxy offers few spectacles more grand than a big auroral storm on Jaremi Four,* he thought. *If Enclave ever lifts there, I should like to go and see one in person.* *"Pull me back,"* he commanded subvocally. Aloud, he said, "You may use the scope, Arn Parek." Forgetting his discomfort with the sky god's method of movement, Parek rushed to the eyepiece.

"Listen," Parek said after a while. The sound of the ship had changed. There were distant alarm bells and the clatter of running feet on metal. "Ulf's stopped the engines." Parek moved the scope through a lazy circle. "The aurora's everywhere. It looks like a cloudy day out there, a day without shadows."

"Only green," Latier pointed out.

"Yes," said Parek abstractedly. "A green and cloudy day."

Latier stood on the studio treadmill, arms akimbo, for what seemed ten minutes as Parek stared at the aurora. "Now, Arn Parek," he thundered at last. "Did you do as I commanded?"

Parek looked up from the scope. "Yes. Yesterday I asked Chagrin to tell Ulf that the aurora would rage tonight."

"And did he tell anyone besides Ulf?"

"If I know Chagrin, he told everyone."

"Then Ulf will visit in the morning. You'll have one chance to seize back the initiative."

62. Jaremi Four—Somewhere

Midnight winds keened across the barrens. Hollow-eyed villagers crowded the tiny hovel. "Window" was too formal a word, but through an irregular gap in the crumbling stonework one could discern, if one cared to, a reddish halo flickering beyond the horizon to the north. Few bothered. Instead they fastened their eyes on the torn, discolored blanket the midwife had suspended across the single room.

How will we pay her? a haggard, palsied woman beseeched herself. No point in looking to the father. Had he died? Fled? No one knew. No one even knew his name.

Behind the blanket, there was hoarse rhythmic screaming: it came from the haggard woman's daughter, a girl of fifteen.

The shrieks stopped. Terrible silence.

Then a slap. A piercing yowl in another register altogether. Those assembled on the other side jostled and whispered. None dared lift the makeshift curtain.

Two endless minutes later, wizened bloody fingers pulled back a corner of the blanket. Pallid, her rheumy eyes serene, the midwife faced them.

"Yes?" the haggard woman croaked.

The midwife broke into an almost toothless smile. "A child is born."

63. The *Bright Hope*

T hey stared at the flattened luminescent spiral. Within it flared a harsh blue-white disk, an achingly bright white pinpoint at its center. Beside the disk and almost matching its diameter, there floated a plump, dim red dwarf. "Cohller 5114," X.O. Arla Gavisel breathed. "Jaremi system's next-door neighbor."

"I don't believe it," called Detex Officer Lynn Wachieu. From her metallic web she monitored all the ship's nav systems. "*Bright Hope* braked from flank speed within eight kilometers of her planned position."

"Once again I salute you, Dr. Panna," Eldridge said. "Most impressive."

The virtual nebula that was Dr. Annek Panna rippled. "It was nothing, Captain." The starry cloud rotated, more or less. "It's the binary that's impressive."

Crossing three pairs of arms, Eldridge grimaced toward the main tactical display. "Fem Gavisel, you've been reading up on that thing. Care to brief the rest of us?"

Gavisel nodded. A bank of graphics controls morphed up from the bridge's glassy floor. "The dwarf nova Cohller 5114 is the celestial object whose radiation drives the famous aurora on Jaremi Four. It comprises two dwarf stars crammed into an area no larger than a class G star—say, Calluron or Terra's Sol." Gavisel's paws stuttered over controls. The image zoomed in toward the smaller and brighter of the spiral's two points of light. "Cohller A, the primary star, is a shrunken white dwarf with the mass of a G-type star but the diameter of an average inhabited planet. You can imagine the core density." The image zoomed out, swung again to survey the larger, dimmer secondary star. "Cohller B is a pale red dwarf. It's hundreds of times larger than Cohller A, but much less massive."

The display rebuilt itself, switching from visible light imagery to a schematic time-lapse simulation. As if hanging from an invisible hoop, the two stars chased one another around a point in empty space. "Like dervishes, Cohller A and B orbit their shared center of mass in a screaming binary embrace, completing a revolution every two and a half hours." The *pov* pushed in on Cohller B. The big ruddy star was far from spherical. "Cohller B is distorted by the primary's gravity," Gavisel said. "As you can see, it's teardrop-shaped, with the tail facing Cohller A. It continually loses mass to the primary star." Starstuff leapt from the red star's surface, tumbling toward the primary.

Now the *pov* coursed back toward the white dwarf. Radiant ejecta spewed overhead, hurtling toward it. More detail became visible: the stream of matter from Cohller B did not strike Cohller A; instead it hurtled into a vast glowing disk.

"Material from Cohller B piles up in an accretion disk, a flat shell orbiting the primary at relativistic speed."

Gavisel's paws danced on her console. On the tactical display spindly arrows flickered within the streamer and disk, interpreting their internal dynamics. "Cohller 5114's a cataclysmic variable. From time to time density fluctuations in the disk lead to local temperature increases, and ultimately to a chain reaction of disturbances that liberates material from the disk. The freed material falls in on the dwarf star, triggering an outburst event: an abrupt rise in output that begins in the ultraviolet and quickly spreads across the entire electromagnetic spectrum. In visible light alone, the system's luminance can grow a hundredfold in under an hour."

"How long do the outbursts last?" Panna asked.

"Usually a few days," said Gavisel. "Then the cycle begins again."

Gavisel punched controls. In compound movements the *pov* retreated from the Cohller system and curled through space to acquire the Jaremi system nearby. "Now, Cohller 5114 lies four hundred thirty-six light-days above the plane of the ecliptic of the Jaremi system. To an observer at Jaremi Four's north pole, the binary lies straight up. Fourteen months after each binary outburst, colossal energies rain down on the planet's northern hemisphere. Fortunately, Jaremi Four has an active magnetosphere. So instead of frying all life, the radiation drives huge auroral displays. The strongest ones blanket the northern hemisphere and extend well past the equator. To the autochthons, the auroral outbursts are unpredictable. Of course, with our quasi-periodic ephemeri we can predict them to within fractions of a second."

"Most thorough," Panna said sincerely. "But Captain, one thing I do not understand. Why did we stop at the binary? Why not go straight to Jaremi space?"

"The truth?" Eldridge smiled thinly. "In case there was any navigation error or problem shutting down the drive, High Command wanted to make sure we wouldn't slam into Jaremi Four."

Gavisel chuckled. "It wouldn't do for us to become a visual effect just while Arn Parek was calling down fire from the skies."

Panna said nothing.

Eldridge's voice sounded too matter-of-fact. "Fem Gavisel, lay in a medium-speed hop to Jaremi Four. Our next stop will be our patrol orbit."

Sullenly, Panna quit the bridge.

Suck, rush, wrench.

After a moment her *being-thereness* rebuilt itself. Panna was back in her quarters. "Back" was not the word; her body had been there all along. *This stardrive is a trifle,* she thought somberly. *They've tested it thoroughly and yet they still don't trust it. Don't they realize that my math is foolproof—that if my equations weren't right in every detail, the forjeling drive wouldn't work at all?* Cursing, she stretched out on a polysofa and planted her thumb on the "play" button of her senso player. *Real life,* she muttered inwardly. *Its satisfactions are so inconstant. By now I should know where my real friend is to be found.*

She punched "play."

Suck, rush, wrench.

She was with Parek.

64. Terra—Wasatch Range, Usasector

"**B**y the Gadianton bands, look at the size of *that* fleet." Alrue Latier and Heber Beaman sat clustered in Latier's gaudy private office. Several tridee bubbles floated in the middle of the room. The largest displayed a frozen image: an overhead view of Ulf's fleet, taken by Ruth Griszam's bug as it had ridden the weather balloon into the sky at the height of the auroral eruption. "Heber, do we know its position?"

Beaman brought up a map. Red pointers sparkled at the locations of the two fleets. "Samu's fleet is closing rapidly on Ulf and Parek's," Beaman interpreted. "Intercept in four or five days, max."

"What then?"

"Slaughter at sea. Samu's fleet is equipped for naval combat, Ulf's isn't."

Latier fingered the leopard skin rug that covered his desk. "It does us no good for Parek to become a martyr so early."

"None," Beaman agreed.

"This would be a wonderful time for our primary satellite's heavy manufacturing module to work, even once."

"It's almost ready," Beaman replied. "At least, as ready as it will ever get."

Latier beamed. "What will it do?"

"I think we can persuade it to run once," Beaman reported, "perhaps for half an hour."

"Then what?"

"Then it'll melt down. So we'd better use it for something important."

Latier frowned. "Half an hour, you say."

"I know," Beaman said. "If we could run it for a week we couldn't manufacture enough hardware to defeat Samu."

Latier rolled fingertips over his desktop. A luminous pointer lit up and darted across the projected map. "Parek needn't defeat anyone. Escape will suffice." Latier sent the pointer toward the half-moon-shaped inlet, still ten days' voyage south. "This is where we assume Ulf means to establish his beach head."

"The nearest easy landing site," Beaman agreed.

"Now let's see the *closest* land," Latier growled. Fidgeting with controls, he pulled the pointer back north. "The fleet can reach here in two days."

"But it can't land," Beaman objected. "An oceanic plate's being subducted beneath the continent. Look at that coastal upthrust."

Latier nodded. "Bluffs a kilometer high, lining more than two thousand kilometers of shoreline."

"That half-moon bay is the first break in the cliffs."

Latier leaned forward, grinning ferally. "We don't need a break in the cliffs. Now where is that spot? I found it yesterday." He greatly increased the magnification and scrolled a short distance south along the seacoast. "There, what's that?"

Beaman leaned forward. The bluff was set in from the shoreline, creating a sea

level beach maybe four hundred meters deep. Latier spooled the magnification
even higher.

"What the sfelb?" Beaman breathed.

Latier had exceeded the map's resolution. Nonetheless, the shifting pixels
seemed to depict some unnatural formation, a nearly straight bar of land running
east to west.

"I need better imagery of this area," Latier said unnecessarily.

Beaman's fingers danced on controls. "There's not much. Meteorological conditions there produce almost constant cloud cover. Still, it must clear up sometime—here we are!"

"Son of a bitch," rumbled Latier. "I mean, jeepers." The structure was clearly
artificial—an immense stone-paved ramp rose from beach to clifftops at a seventy-
degree angle. "Like Samu's incline at Point Eldek, only paved—and much
steeper."

"The bed of an old funicular."

"An old what?"

"Incline railway." Beaman overlaid archaeological survey data. A radial pattern of streets emerged on the plateau at the head of the incline. At its foot, structures like docks wove themselves across the beach. "Apparently before the Tuezi
struck, there was a commercial center on the bluff here. It used the funicular to
communicate with its seaport."

"This is even better than I'd hoped," Latier said, smiling. "Now suppose we
could get Parek and, oh, just a few of Ulf's divisions up that incline." Latier
reclaimed control of the map display. He scrolled to the west, further inland. "If the
troops cross this sixty kilometers of marshy upland, they'll reach the headwaters of
a navigable river. They could build rafts and ride the current into the interior,
making converts as they go. Samu would be alone in the ocean trying to figure out
what happened."

"The pursuit fleet has Galactic support," Beaman noted.

"That's good," Latier gloated. "There are Spectators aboard the flagship, so
we'll know Samu's movements. On the other hand, we seem to have succeeded in
ridding Ulf and Parek's force of Spectators. So whoever's handling Samu won't
know where Parek and Ulf went." One of Latier's cats hopped into his lap. He
stroked it thoughtfully. "If our manufacturing module will only run for half an hour,
what can we build, and what fraction of Parek and Ulf's forces can we get up that
incline?"

Beaman tapped calculations into a small thought engine. He scowled and then
smiled. Handed the unit to Latier.

Latier dropped the cat.

"The ships, too?" His chuckling built into raucous laughter. "Sorry,
Thummim." Gasping, he returned Beaman's thought engine. "Heber, this will
work?"

"The numbers say it will."

"Ulf's not going to take this scheme lying down." Latier steepled thick fingers.
"It's not enough for him and Parek to be equals. We must make Parek the unequiv-
ocal commander of his fleet."

65. Jaremi Four—Equatorial Sea— The Next Day

*C*lang-*shang-ralang. Clang-shang-ralang. Clang-shang-ralang.* Parek last heard that chiming the day Ulf deposed him. *Today, I steal back my place.*

A revival stage sprawled the width of the flagship's forecastle deck, hastily built from spare hull plates according to sketches Parek had given Ulf. The stage rode a wood and metal framework two meters above the deck. Men could pass beneath it if they had to. The fleet's business could go forward. Additional hull plates had been arranged to either side of the main stage, standing upright, defining a proscenium of sorts, and creating wings where VIPs could cluster out of view of the audience. Behind one such row of plates stood Arn Parek, Ulf at his side.

Ulf wore plain tropical fatigues. He stood scowling, arms crossed. Plainly he disapproved of all that was to happen today. But after Parek's successful—and widely known—prophecy of the aurora storm, Ulf had had no choice but to humor his former master. *This once, at least.* Parek rolled the plan over in his mind.

Of course, it was God's plan, actually.

Parek could see no flaw in the scheme. But since he might get only one chance to play for the crew's allegiance, he would've preferred a more flamboyant miracle.

Parek paced backstage. He wore all white: leather tunic, leggings, gloves, and cape. The costume was beastly hot, but few in the audience would be close enough to see him sweat.

***Clang**-shang-ralang. Clang-shang-ralang. Clang-shang-ralang.* Mind-numbing rhythm had claimed the watching crewmen. They slapped hands on the bulkheads. Stamped feet on the deck. Twice already Parek had signaled the percussionists to play longer. *It's time,* he thought at last. "Ready," he breathed to his guards.

The percussionists' clangor shattered into silence. The players spun smartly and marched off stage right.

"I predicted the aurora!" Parek shouted, walking on stage left. "I return with more hidden knowledge!"

As Parek expected, Chagrin had told many people about Parek's predicting the aurora. Because of that, and because he'd been out of sight for so long, the resulting cheer roared on for seven minutes.

"My soldiers. My artisans. My defenders. My worshippers!" he cried when at last he could make himself heard. "I regret the time I have spent away from you. But I cannot regret what I learned. Behold, the sky gods have shared with me another of the hidden secrets of death itself."

From the corner of his eye, Parek watched Ulf in the wings stage left. Furious, the High Commander stormed as close to the stage as he dared. He had to stop, lest any in the audience see him behind the proscenium. *He begins to realize the trap I have laid,* Parek thought.

"The sky gods told me that this noontide there should be a terrible accident," Parek boomed aloud. "Let the word go out! Let the victim be brought to me."

The word didn't need to go far. With great commotion a rescue party blustered out of the superstructure. Shooing away enraptured soldiers, the cursing medics pressed toward the stage carrying a litter. "Word Among Us! Word Among Us!" The man on the litter was one Fzel Harisjen, a weapons master well known on the flagship. Though he bore no wounds, he lay still in a way every man recognized.

In the wings, Ulf clasped his arms around himself. He trembled with rage. Harisjen was one of Ulf's personal loyals, a gifted armorer and assassin who'd insisted on remaining bound to Ulf when Ulf had surrendered the rest of his personal guards. *If Harisjen is dead, I've lost one of my most reliable enforcers,* Ulf thought. *If Parek brings him back, can I trust him again?*

The medics wrestled the litter up onto the stage. "What happened here?" Parek demanded regally.

"Fzel Harisjen was inspecting piezo detonators," explained the medic leader. "One went off. He took the spark."

"How is he now?" Parek asked for effect.

"He's dead," moaned the medic leader. Any fool could see that. Harisjen's normally jet-black skin was nearer the color of stale porridge.

"Set him here." Parek waved the medics off stage right—the side opposite Ulf. He'd be unable to question them right away.

Parek tugged off his white leather gloves. He lay one hand on the dead man's head. *So cold,* he thought. *Can this possibly work?* The man's lips were gray, as were his fingernails. *Just start,* Parek told himself. *No time for doubt. Trust the god named God's teaching.*

Lacking any conscious idea of what he'd do next, Parek pressed his hands against the victim's forehead. He tilted the head back. In the familiar way, he suddenly remembered knowing what to do next. His free hand lifted Harisjen's chin and probed the dead man's mouth for obstructions. There were none. "By the sky gods, Fzel Harisjen, I breathe life back into you!" Parek bellowed. He pinched Harisjen's nose shut and locked his mouth over that of the corpse. He forced two deep breaths in. The chest rose and fell. Rose, fell.

Now Parek remembered knowing that he should check for a pulse in the man's neck. He didn't remember knowing why. No matter; no pulse. "I press life back into you!" Parek cried. He slapped the palm of one hand low on the dead man's breastbone and dug the heel of his other hand into the tendons of the first. *What now?* he thought. *Oh yeah, I knew that.* Elbows locked, pumping with his shoulders and back, Parek pressed Harisjen's chest down, then released. Down, release. Down, release. Down, release. Fifteen thrusts in all, less than a second apart.

Back to the head, he recalled. He tilted back the man's head and locked mouths. He forced in two more breaths. The chest rose and fell. Rose. Fell.

Somewhere near the back of his mind, he could feel the sky god watching him. The open channel could be sensed, much as someone walking at night might sense an open well and so avoid walking into it. *"CPR, Alrue?"* a garbled voice seemed to say from the other side.

"Shush," shushed the voice Parek recognized as that of the god named God. *"It was all I could think of."*

Parek forced his attention from the ghostly exchange. *Thrust again.* He moved back to Harisjen's chest and positioned his hands. He locked his elbows. Bore down with shoulders and back. One, two, three, four, five, six, seven, eight, nine, ten, eleven, twelve, thirteen, fourteen, fifteen. *Back to the head.* Tilt, lock lips. Breathe. Breathe. Thrust again. Position hands. Lock elbows. Bear down. Again, three, four, five. . . .

After the fifth breathe-thrust cycle, Parek remembered knowing he should check for a carotid pulse. It wasn't there. Tilt, lock. Breathe. Rise. Fall. Breathe. Rise. Fall. Hand on breastbone. Hand on hand. Lock elbows. Shoulders and back, shoulders and back, shoulders and back. . . .

By the fourth time Parek felt for that nonexistent pulse, he was drenched in sweat. His hair hung in shining curls. He'd long since discarded the cape. Inside his jerkin and leggings, salty rivulets pooled where folds of leather touched his skin. Parek's wrists, his shoulders, the muscles of his back buzzed with agony. "I call on the sky god of sky gods!" he bellowed. "Help me force life into this cold, stiff body. I call you, sky god!"

"You're doing fine," buzzed a familiar voice inside his head. *"It's supposed to be like this. Just keep pumping."*

Droplets arched against the clear tropical sky when Parek tossed his head. He hoped the percussionists would recognize it as a command to return to the stage. Grimly he pressed his palm to the dead man's breastbone. Hand on hand. Lock elbows. Shoulders and back, shoulders and back, shoulders and back. . . .

Clang-*shang-ralang. Clang-shang-ralang. Clang-shang-ralang.* **Clang**-*shang-ralang.* The percussionists had taken the hint. The audience fell back into the rhythm. They stamped and clapped. "*Pa*-a-rek! Pa-a-rek! Pa-a-rek! *Pa*-a-rek!" soldiers chanted in time with the clashing chimes.

Shoulders and back, shoulders and back, *fifteen.* To the head. Tilt. Lock. Breathe. Breathe.

"Pa-a-rek! Pa-a-rek! Pa-a-rek!"

Clang-shang-ralang. Clang-shang-ralang. **Clang**-*shang-ralang.*

Breastbone. Hand on hand. Lock elbows. Shoulders and back . . .

Clang-shang-ralang. "Pa-a-rek! *Pa*-a-rek! Pa-a-rek! Pa-a-rek! *Pa*-a-rek!"

Breathe. Breathe. Feel for pulse.

No pulse.

Parek panted. The dry gasps rasped his throat. Fatigue seared his muscles. Awareness had narrowed to a tunnel useful only for observing breastbones and lips and rising chests.

And necks without a pulse.

"It isn't working," the strange voice piped in his head. *"Parek's dying out there. Which is more than I can say for the victim."*

"Keep pumping, boy!" exhorted the god named God. "*I am with you. You cannot fail.*"

Shoulders and back, shoulders and back, shoulders and back, shoulders and back. . . . "Pa-a-rek! *Pa*-a-rek! Pa-a-rek! Pa-a-rek! Pa-a-rek!" **Clang**-*shang-ralang. Clang-shang-ralang. Clang-shang-ralang.*

Breathe. Breathe. Feel for pulse.

No pulse.

No pulse.

No pulse.

When Parek's body could continue no longer, the prophet turned away from the corpse of Fzel Harisjen and toward the suddenly silent crowd. He stood trembling, his head hanging forward.

The chiming stopped.

Parek's arms were tingling logs. He didn't notice when his hands dropped to his sides. He pitched forward onto his knees. "Sky god!" he moaned. "Sky god. . . ."

Parek heard laughter. He stared into the wings stage left. It was Ulf, guffawing derisively. The sight filled Parek with a rage that cut through his exhaustion. But Ulf was not its target—not yet. Teeth clenched, Parek strode off stage right, away from Ulf, toward the rescue party.

As Parek left the stage, the chiming resumed, more frantic than ever.

Backstage onlookers heard only Parek's backhanded slap across the medic leader's face. "How long was he dead!" Parek shrieked. He brought the heel of his hand up hard against the man's nose. Better aimed, the blow could have killed. As it was, the medic leader collapsed, blood pooling in his doubled hands. "How long was he dead!" Parek shrieked. No one dared restrain him. The Word Among Us snatched up a stagehand's forgotten prybar. He swung it against the medic leader's head. Howling, the man pitched sideways like some ancient tower.

Parek took the prybar in both hands. Holding it horizontally, he lunged past the fallen medic leader and toward the other man who'd borne Harisjen's litter onto the stage. The prybar caught the litter bearer below the shoulders and heaved him back against metal.

"Speak or die!" Parek roared in the litter bearer's face. "How long was Harisjen dead?"

"Half an hour, Word Among Us!" the litter bearer squeaked.

"How long?"

"Forty minutes!" the man blubbered.

"That's too long!" Latier sputtered in Parek's head.

Parek released the litter bearer. He slid out from behind the prybar and stuttered down the wall. Spreading urine badged his trousers. Parek dropped the prybar. He squatted. His face was less than a hand's breadth from the terrified litter bearer's. "The sky god speaks to me," Parek hissed, tapping his own head. "Do you know what he says? The sky god speaks to me from the aurora to tell me forty minutes is too long!"

"We're sorry, Word Among Us!" the man sobbed.

"Did you just snatch up some cooling corpse from sick bay?"

"No, no, we followed your instructions! We came up behind Harisjen with the piezo and gave him the spark, just as you commanded—just *when* you commanded."

"He was supposed to be fresher!" Parek spat.

The litter bearer coughed and grimaced. He clawed below his left shoulder with his right hand. "We brought him into the passageway where you said. But the chiming went on too long. Then the men cheered you for so long. Harisjen grew colder. . . ."

Parek sighed, stood erect. He raked blood-stained fingers through his sodden hair. *I've failed,* he thought emptily. *My god named God has failed.* Parek picked up the prybar again. He raised it in a hand whose knuckles paled with rage.

The litter bearer gasped. He strove to draw away, but he was not Parek's target.

Two meters away, the medic leader had risen to hands and knees. He clutched his pulped right ear. "The Word Among Us is not done with *you!*" Parek snarled. He whirled. He brought up the prybar under the medic leader's chin. Bone snapped. "Don't try to stop me!" Parek shouted.

No one had been about to.

Parek raised the prybar overhead. He brought it down on the medic leader's spine, the back of his neck, and the bony ridge of his left shoulder blade, which sundered agreeably.

On his skull *on his skull* **on his skull.**

In all his ministry, Arn Parek had never killed. He'd ordered deaths, to be sure, sometimes while staring into the victims' eyes. His visions had caused hundreds of thousands to die. No small portion of that carnage had occurred in his sight. But his soldiers and officers had pulled the triggers, swung the cudgels, and set the fires. Panting, flushed with a feral delight unlike anything he'd known, Parek looked down on the shattered mess that had been the medic leader's head. He laughed. *No longer am I a bystander,* he gloated. *Now Arn Parek is a soldier, too.*

He raised his eyes and turreted to regard each of the stagehands, soldiers, and hangers-on. Their expressions mixed terror and disgust with a new, more fearful kind of worship.

The litter bearer, whose collarbone Parek abruptly realized he'd broken, prostrated himself painfully at Parek's blood-specked boots. "Great are you, Word Among Us!" he sobbed.

"You are forgiven," Parek said with a gentleness that bewildered his onlookers. He set the prybar down softly. "Go, get that looked at."

Only then did Parek's mind register what his ears had been hearing for almost a minute.

The crowd was louder than ever. They were stamping, slapping, chanting, and hooting.

Fear struck cold into Parek's chest. *Has Ulf seized the momentum again?* Parek stared stageward. He expected to see the general working the crowd and roaring in pestilent triumph.

No, Ulf skulked behind the opposite proscenium, staring at the audience in sick disbelief.

Now Parek could hear what the crowd was chanting. "Pa-a-rek! Pa-rek! Parek! Parek!"

A hand touched his shoulder. Parek whirled.

With hollow cheeks, stringy hair, dark deep-set sockets with coal-fire eyes, Chagrin smiled. He shouted, "They are yours."

Parek peered outward. He knew how to read a crowd. This one couldn't have been more committed to him if Fzel Harisjen had stood up and danced.

"How?" Parek demanded of Chagrin. "How?"

"After the chiming restarted, a captain mounted the stage. He made the musicians pause and shouted, 'Who else would wrestle with the sky gods for one of us?'"

"I am with you, you cannot fail." That is what the sky god said to me, Parek thought. *His words came true, though not in any way I'd dreamed.*

Parek raised his arms in a gesture of triumph—*how they ache!* He strode back onstage. Ignoring Harisjen's body, Parek pumped at the air with clenched fists and absorbed the adulation of the crowd. *Let them wonder where all this blood on me came from,* he thought.

The cheers rolled endlessly. It was enough time for Arn Parek the student of religious behavior to emerge from behind Parek the messiah, from beneath Parek the exultant killer, to wonder on his own at the marvel he had so unwittingly wrought. *The miracle my sky god taught me failed, yet they believe. The outcome wasn't what mattered. I sanctified the event just by the ferocity of my effort.*

"Hear me!" he cried four or five times before his exultant listeners fell quiet. "I am your prophet and you are my army. I have spoken to the sky gods! Our fleet faces danger from an unexpected quarter. We planned to sail ten more days and seek a bay protected by walls of high rock. Instead, we must divert to the southwest and make for the first land we find. Your faith was tested today. You recognize that being powerful in the sky gods doesn't guarantee triumph over each of life's adversities. But I say to you, when we make this new landfall it shall be your blessing to behold the mightiest miracle that ever the hands of gods and men have joined to work. Who is with me?"

The cheering and howling and stamping and slapping erupted anew. Magnanimously, Parek looked into the wings stage left. He held out his hand to Ulf.

Parek watched Ulf wrestle with himself. *Ultimately he has no choice but accept what power I choose to share.* Cheerlessly, the High Commander walked center stage and locked his fingers inside Parek's. They thrust joined hands skyward. It was a gesture of victory only one of them felt.

None could hear the words they exchanged. "Where you take the fleet there are only cliffs a kilometer high," Ulf grated.

Parek replied with easy confidence. "When we reach the top, we'll ride a mighty river into a land of wealth and spiritual conquest."

"Reach the top!" Ulf cried. "That miracle had better work."

Parek tilted his head toward the cheering crowd. "And this one failed?" He flashed his vanquished general a predatory smile. "Believe in me, and whether things go well or ill you will know that everything unfolds as it should. The most genuine thing I offer is certainty. That is the true gift of a prophet, friend Ulf. All the rest is ornamentation."

66. Terra—Wasatch Range, Usasector

"'The Lord hath made bare his holy arm in the eyes of all the nations,' " Alrue Latier quoted. "'And all the ends of the earth shall see the salvation of our God.' "

"Pardon?" Beaman rasped.

"We lucked out," Latier interpreted, planting his palms on his legs. "By which means our rustic god-man has saved his neck—and ours—yet once more." At a gesture from Latier, the waldo artists cut the satellite-mediated link to Parek's consciousness through which they'd been monitoring events on Jaremi Four. It was three A.M. local. Technicians powered down their consoles and filed out. Scattered panels remained alight: automated systems beaming Latier's routine religious programming to the Galaxy.

Beaman shook his head. "Who'd think he'd get so much mileage out of a miracle that failed?"

Latier and Beaman were alone in the semidarkened heart of the communications center. "You were right, Heber, the CPR thing was too subtle. I should've opted for something flashier, something that relied on more effects work from here. All the same, who'll be giving the orders on that flagship now?"

"Parek's back on top," Beaman admitted. "I just can't see how."

Latier shrugged. "Sometimes a failed miracle's as powerful as a successful one. Consider your Terran religious history. Recognize the name of William Miller?"

Beaman frowned. "American millenarian, middle nineteenth century."

"Very good. Miller prophesied three successive dates on which the world would end. Each deadline passed, the world declining to end on schedule. Each time Miller lost some of his followers. But others stayed beside him. Astonishingly, they grew stronger in their faith for the very wonder their leader had failed to work. After the world didn't end on Miller's third predicted date, those who still believed in him had moved beyond the power of any worldly defeat to shake their commitment."

"The beginning of the Seventh Day Adventists," Beaman supplied.

Latier smiled. "Then there were the nineteenth-century spirit mediums—the Fox sisters, Eusapia Palladino, a dozen others. With crude, often self-discovered magicians' tricks they convinced millions they spoke to the dead. As they gained experience, they learned *not* to produce an apparition at every séance. Onlookers took the occasional failure as proof that the mediums were up to something genuine and difficult."

Beaman leaned forward. "I seem to recall that Joseph Smith had a few such experiences as well."

Latier chuckled. "While leading the Mormons from Ohio to Independence, Missouri, Smith prophesied that on arrival they'd find that Oliver Cowdery, who'd gone west ahead of them, had raised a great church. When they arrived, Cowdery had built no church. Upbraided for this failure of prophecy, Smith coolly told Edward Partridge, 'I see it, and it will be so.'

"Years later, a mighty church *was* raised on that site. Of course, neither Smith nor Cowdery played any role in building it." Latier rubbed his eyes. "Then there were the accidental miracles. At the very beginning, when Smith was living on David Whitmer's farm and translating the golden plates, Whitmer's wife was the household's only skeptic. One day she announced she'd had a vision of an old man with a white beard who showed her the plates. Her opposition within the family circle ended then and there. Not having lifted a finger to bring about Mrs. Whitmer's vision, Smith was no doubt astonished by her sudden conversion."

Beaman punched a code into a food synthesizer. He withdrew a tall tumbler of bourbon. "I gather I need no longer fear your knowing I like this."

Latier chuckled. "I suppose not."

Beaman sipped and sighed. "Alrue, I always assumed that on some level you took yourself and your religion seriously. But that's getting harder to square with the deception here."

"Deception!" Latier swept open his arms, a theatrical gesture. "Don't think small, Heber. Cunning! Artifice! Chicanery! They're as necessary in the religion business as in any other line of human endeavor." He settled back and rested his chin on one fist. "They seem to be the way God *wants* us to make our way in the universe."

"You're saying this?"

Latier spread his hands. "It's late. It pleases me to unburden myself. So I will tell you something I've never admitted to anyone before. All the things that used to be said of Mormonism by its enemies—back when Mormonism mattered enough to *have* enemies—they're all true."

Beaman stared silently, astonished.

"The Mormon religion *is* a fraud. Joseph Smith and Oliver Cowdery and David Whitmer and Martin Harris and Sidney Rigdon and, in his time, Brigham Young— they made it all up."

"You believe that?" Beaman whispered. "You *can* believe that?"

"I'll tell you another thing. Of the eleven major religions to emerge on Terra after the rise of Mormonism, all are known frauds, which does nothing to quell the ardor they spark among their believers, nor to reduce their value as social and emotional glue. Now, if all the major Terran faiths to emerge since 1830 are fraudulent, then there's no powerful reason to surmise any *ancient* religion began less falsely." Latier pushed himself out of the chair. He paced with his hands locked behind him. "Was there a Terran Christ? Was there ever even an actual man named Jesus about whom all those legends accumulated? Even today, lay scholars remain divided."

"What does Alrue Latier think?"

"I'm undecided. But because I know Mormon history, I understand that Jesus *need* not have existed in order for Christianity to arise." Latier pressed his palms together. "Joseph Smith preached an outrageously counterfeit creed. His enemies had the forensic skills to untangle his deceptions. They had enough access to communication technology to disseminate their findings. Yet despite its transparently ridiculous character, despite mountains of disproof, Mormonism flourished. If that could happen in nineteenth century America, by ancient standards a fairly sophisticated place, why should anyone imagine that in more naïve times Christianity or Judaism or Theravada Buddhism must have begun the way their founding documents claim?" Latier drew another pink lemonade from the autobar. "Humans have such a vast capacity to believe manifest nonsense, one never needs to assume that a great religion has any basis in truth. Don't you see, Heber?" He drained half the glass. "Religions don't have to be true to work. Mormonism is the proof!"

Beaman stood. "After that, what are we left with?"

"We're left with creeds that function because of the untrue but reassuring things they say about the cosmos and humanity's place in it. They touch people where the hurt is. Maybe that's not what you grew up thinking that religion was, but that *is* what it is, and that's all it is. No one can expect my church to aim higher."

"Alrue, are you an atheist?"

"Literally, yes." He rose and rounded the low table. Raising Heber's glass of whiskey, he drank deeply from its opposite side. "And I'm also the truest Mormon there ever was. If that's contradictory, so be it."

67. Jaremi Four—Off the Southern Continent

D riven from his former quarters when Parek claimed them, Ulf had had the ancient liner's aft lounge converted for his use. Man-high windows in the fantail gave an expansive view of the sea. Like faerie islands the following ships of the fleet bobbed, their nocturnal signatures twinkling when masts and rigging occluded onboard lights. *How could anyone—even the ancients—cast windows so colorless, so free of ripples?* he thought. *And so huge!* Open golden staircases led to a marble-floored saloon a manheight below.

The darkened saloon contained a single command chair, high-backed, uphol-stered in cracked leather. Slowly, alert for obstacles unseen in the half-darkness, Ulf wheeled the chair to the head of the banquet table and seated himself. He closed his eyes. He centered his awareness as he had been taught.

"Oh sky god," Ulf moaned. "Now I am alone. Come to me after your way. Come, as you have ordained me to expect."

His eyes snapped open, staring *through* a point an arm's length above the table. Empty air seemed to be rippling, distorting the images of objects faintly per-ceived behind it.

The motion sharpened. A clear circle—actually a sphere—resolved. Within it, air twisted on itself, color flickered. Cyan and yellow sparks and muted crimson lightnings flickered.

Then the image.

The woman wore a floor-length gown. The fabric wasn't merely white, it glowed. She stood with her bare back to Ulf, the skin black as the night outside the fantail windows. Her buttocks were generous. The woman turned. Her feet didn't shift; she simply revolved. In profile the fullness of her bust was arresting. The front of her gown was open down to the pubic area. Varicolored highlights defined her belly and her breasts. Ulf's eyes followed the undercurves where they vanished into the gown, forming shadows of deeper ebony. Catchlights flickered in the cleavage and the double dome of her midriff. Her face was symmetrical, her expression impish. Her earrings, too, glowed by their own light. Endless corkscrews of vermilion and prim-rose and cerulean twisted inside the crystal bangles.

Tonight, her eyes were reddish-brown.

"Ulf," she said simply. Her voice was like music. Behind it wind chimes tin-kled. Brittle surf rushed onto some unseen pebble beach.

"My worship to you, Host Nymph," Ulf said in ritual monotone. "And to your mistress."

Host Nymph curtsied, revealing still more cleavage. "My mistress will speak with you. Love and power unto you, faithful Ulf." A sheath of fuchsia radiance closed above her head. With a sound like a crystal goblets shattering, the radiance puffed away.

Bei Hanllei had disappeared.

In her place stood an august presence. She was clad from neck to floor in a generous cape of the same luminous white fabric that had composed the Host Nymph's gown. Its folds muted but could not fully mask a mature, earthly sensuality. *Part grandmother, part seductress,* that was how Ulf had come to think of her. The woman stood motionless, hands touching palm to palm, their joined fingers tucked under her chin. Her deep brown face and hands were vaguely leathery. Abruptly the cape disappeared in a helix of sparks. Her glowing gown revealed less than the Host Nymph's, yet it revealed enough. Her figure was without the thickness of middle age. Her breasts were supple with incongruous youth. As he always did, Ulf remarked to himself that her body seemed too young for her face and hands.

Colored lights made a halo of her hair. "You summoned your sky god," she said imperiously. With the sound of her voice rushed the ringing of bells, the keening of prairie winds, the chatter of glass shards skittering over marble. "I have come."

Ulf bowed his head and recited the litany. "God and goddess, life and death, initiator and destroyer."

"Yes, yes," said the goddess impatiently. "Now report."

Ulf swallowed, spoke. "In the morning we land at the bluffs. Parek commands the fleet. He thinks I am powerless."

The goddess cocked her head knowingly. "All is prepared?"

"I have gathered several officers loyal to me. Their men will obey them. We have a plan."

"When does it begin?"

"When everyone sees that Parek cannot defeat the bluffs."

"And not a moment before." The goddess clasped her hands together. "Remember, not until he fails. There is more, loyal Ulf: Parek must not be killed. If possible, he should not suffer injury. He is not evil. The gods who seduce him— it is with them that the evil lies."

"Vast is your power and wisdom, oh sky god," Ulf intoned. "And yet. . . ."

The goddess frowned. "What now?"

Ulf spread his hands. "You have such power. Why wait for Parek to fail? Can't you just order the evil gods to surrender?"

"Of course I could," the goddess answered with something like annoyance. "But. . . ." Her eyes flickered away toward someone or something off to Ulf's right that he couldn't see. She seemed to listen, then nod. When she turned back to him, her voice rang with fresh assurance. "That's not the way of the gods," she said archly. "It pleases us to work out our struggles among you humans. Fear not, Ulf. Your victory is guaranteed." She looked away again, briefly. "It is late for you, is it not?"

Ulf blinked. "The middle of the night, yes."

"Take to your bed, then. Be sharp tomorrow and you will conquer The Word Among Us. Till then, dream of me and Host Nymph." The shower of sparks that enveloped Orgena Greder was the blue of a morning sky. It rippled into cold fire and disappeared.

The air above the banquet table was empty.

Ulf stirred in the chair. He became conscious of his erection. It always seemed to follow his visits with the celestial messengers. Unbuttoning his jacket, he swaggered toward the double doors. Three sculpted metal weights hung from the ceiling on chains. *Gold for emergencies, brass for food . . .* Ulf closed scarred fingers around the third weight and tugged sharply. *Steel for a woman.* He stripped, leaving only weapons—a sheathed blade strapped to his left forearm, a blackjack hidden in a velvet pouch on his right bicep. *Just in case.* He pulled a bottle of liqueur from a sideboard and swigged deeply. He flattened himself beside the double metal doors.

One door unlatched and squeaked open. He could hear guards guffawing outside.

She spewed through the door, falling to knees and elbows on the deck. The door slammed shut. The woman hadn't noticed Ulf. She was naked. Ulf stepped up behind her. He threw his right arm under her torso. The hand slapped over her left breast. His fingers clamped. Ulf pulled the woman yelping to her feet and spun her to face him.

Disgust. Ulf was surprised by the strength of his reaction. Though the woman was under twenty, her skin bristled with pockmarks, moles, and tiny scars. Her breasts were different sizes. The skin of her stomach puckered in odd ways. Her hair was stringy and dull. One eye was startlingly higher than the other. *Shit,* he thought hollowly, *and I'm sure she was the best they had.*

Her hands were raised to fend off a blow. Recognizing Ulf, she relaxed. Unlike some of the officers, Ulf was known for using his pleasure-women without inflicting harm. "High Commander," she said and bowed her head. She peered up at him mischievously. She glanced down at his crotch and back into his eyes. She grinned crookedly, revealing gray chipped teeth.

Afraid of losing his erection, Ulf lunged at her. He moiled her breasts and thrust his tongue into her mouth. *Compared to Host Nymph and the sky goddess, real women are . . . so shabby,* he thought, *so flawed.* He blustered her onto her back atop the banquet table. Vellum ripped where her elbows and heels scraped a priceless ancient map. Ulf threw half of it aside and clambered onto the table. He fell into her. *What the fuck,* he thought, abandoning himself to the animal rhythm. *Real women, flaws and all . . . they're all there is. Real women . . . cliffs that don't kneel down . . . cruel surprises for messiahs whose prophecies fail.*

"High Commander. Commander." The flagship's captain saluted crisply as Ulf and his lieutenant Akkad Felegu stepped onto the flagship's bridge. While his power had seemed secure, Ulf had chosen to dress simply. Today his fatigues sprouted a forest of medals and ribbons. Fabric braid festooned with teeth and tiny skulls covered his shoulders. Over it all he wore a deep blue cloak joined around his neck by a golden clasp.

Felegu was less formal. His combat poncho hung in expressionless folds. Shiny as a leaf, skin stretched over the cavity where some long-ago gunshot had claimed a few teeth and part of his jaw. He batted black and gray hair from his eyes with a two-fingered hand.

Two Brethren—Ulf's men once, now pledged to Parek as members of Parek's elite squad—harried Felegu. They took the digital camera he carried and passed it quizzically back and forth. Ulf blustered forward. "You know perfectly well what that is! Give it back."

"With respect," a scarfaced guardsman sneered, "I no longer report to the High Commander."

"Let him have his magic box." Parek strode onto the bridge. He wore his trademark white leather tunic, leggings, and boots. Over one arm he carried a chalk-white silken cape.

"Word Among Us!" The guards, the captain, the bridge crew, Felegu—all saluted fist-on-chest.

Silently Parek eyed Ulf until he saluted, too.

Felegu took the digital camera. Parek clapped Felegu's shoulder. "I'm glad you brought your device. Use it to record what the gods will work through me this day."

Or what they won't, Ulf thought. He leaned on the binnacle. Beside the steersman, a bell began to jangle. "Lookout's signal," the captain said. "Land is in sight."

A ruddy gray strip violated the horizon. Above it swelled towering gray-black clouds aflicker with lightning. Here, trade winds came off the sea. Colliding with the coastal bluffs, they rose quickly. Adiabatic cooling triggered prodigious condensation. The cliffs were under almost perpetual cloud cover.

"Come," Parek commanded. The captain, Ulf, and Felegu followed the prophet and three of his guardsmen onto the outer promenade. They lined up along the balcony's pitted bronze rail. Ulf dropped his eyes and surveyed the deck. *What the fuck?* he thought. Every movable object had been lashed down. Ropes and webbing dangled everywhere. A jury-rigged contrivance of black tubing stood empty on the forecastle deck, tied down like everything else. Six meters on a side, it had been subdivided into rows of perhaps fifty cells, each defined by tubing and cagework, each sized to contain a single man. Inside each cell hung safety harnesses, ropes, and webbing. Puffy gray pads had been affixed to the pipework.

The captain produced an ancient telescope. He scrutinized the distant bluffs.

"Well, Captain?" Parek asked.

"Just as Ulf said. Nothing but cliffs." He handed Parek the scope. "We can't land there."

"As I expected, too." Parek raised the spyglass, unsure what came next. With the usual irresistibility he remembered always having known what he was looking for. He scanned to the south. *Further . . . further. . . .* He lowered the scope and squinted into the morning glare. He sighted through the tube once more. "Captain, what's my bearing?"

"Twelve units to port, I'd say."

"That is our course." With mingled relief and satisfaction Parek held the captain's scope out to him.

Ulf snatched it away. "Let me see!" Parek's Brethren inched forward. With a jerk of his head Parek bid them stay back. Ulf aimed the scope twelve units to port.

He saw a section of sea-level beach a few kilometers wide. *Four, five hundred meters deep. Looks like clean sand.* A gap in the clouds transfixed the vertical cliff with sunlight. A vast triangular shadow emblazoned its face.

Terrified, Ulf lowered the scope. "A ramp," he breathed.

"What?" hissed Felegu.

Ulf handed Felegu the scope. "He found a fucking ramp."

"The sky gods showed me the way," Parek explained. "A gift from the ancients to us."

Mouth agape, Felegu let the scope drop from his face. He held it out. The captain grabbed it away and sighted for himself. "I don't see anything."

"Wait until sunlight plays on the bluff again," Felegu advised morosely.

The scudding of sea clouds bathed the bluff face briefly in sunlight. The triangular shadow returned.

"By the aurora," the captain breathed. He lowered the scope and regarded Parek with saucering eyes. "Great indeed is The Word Among Us." He shouted, "Steersman! Twelve units left rudder."

"Twelve units left," came the reply from inside.

"Word Among Us," Ulf croaked. "We will abandon the ships and march up the ramp?"

Parek smiled. "Abandon the ships? We take them with us." To the captain. "All has been prepared as I directed?"

"Aye," the captain said uncertainly. "We are rigged as for a gale. Hatches battened. Loose objects lashed down. Watertight doors closed and dogged. All fiddles deployed. Safety restraints at every duty station."

"Very good." Parek knitted his fingers together. "Here are your orders, Captain. Instruct the fleet to proceed without us. The other ships should anchor line abreast a kilometer out, facing the beach. In line with the ancient incline, they should leave a substantial gap at the center. As for the flagship, we will assume a position three kilometers out, lined up on the ancient incline. Order all hands to make themselves secure. Call general quarters, then make for the beach at maximum speed."

The captain nodded. "Pray continue."

Parek smiled. "That is all."

The captain looked nervously toward Ulf. He sidled closer to the prophet. "Um, Word Among Us. . . ."

"Yes, captain."

"When do I slow down?"

"You don't."

"Word Among Us, those orders would cause me to beach the flagship."

Parek nodded.

Ulf reached into his pants pocket. He thumbed the piezo transmitter. Again. Again. Elsewhere, across the flagship, the squad leaders among his conspirators would hear three bursts of static. The *stand by* signal.

The captain stepped backward, hands beginning to tremble. "Forgive me, Word Among Us, but I—I cannot obey those orders."

"Of course you can," Parek said casually. "Believe, Captain. Just believe."

Frantic, the captain locked eyes with Ulf. *I could end this,* Ulf thought. *I could say The Word Among Us had taken leave of his senses. Some of the old guards would obey me. I'd lock Parek in that blind stateroom and take his place.* His fingers massaged the piezo transmitter. *But the goddess said not to act until everyone has seen Parek fail.* It never occurred to Ulf that by acting now and deposing the prophet in front of a tiny audience hours before anyone could see his prophecy founder, he would create a martyr. Banishment would do that almost as effectively as death.

Though Ulf was not capable of so subtle an interpretation, Orgena Greder was. *The goddess said wait.*

And so Ulf returned the captain's frantic look noncommittally. He flicked his eyes toward Parek's Brethren as if to say, *What can we do while all of them are here?*

The captain's shoulders slumped. Eyes blank, he whirled toward Parek and saluted fist-on-chest. "It will be as you say, Word Among Us."

Goddess most captivating, Ulf thought desperately, *I hope you know what the fuck you're doing.*

68. The *Bright Hope*

"Captain," called Gavisel. "Patrol orbit achieved."

"Acknowledged, X.O.," said Eldridge.

From the corner of her eye she watched Dr. Panna's nebula form above a vacant viewing platform. "Permission to enter the bridge, Captain?" Panna asked.

"Granted," Eldridge said automatically. *What made her want to come out now? She's been practically a recluse.* "Fem Wachieu. Maximum susceptor scan."

"Max scan," Wachieu called. Her legs trembled on the metallic web.

"Trouble?" Eldridge asked.

"Noise from the binary, Captain," Wachieu said with annoyance. "Even from this orbit, fine monitoring of surface events will be extremely difficult." A forest of viewspheres bloomed around her. One showed a forest fire burning out of control. A second overflew the central square of a small town, stoop-backed men and women shambling through the streets. Another bubble flickered with an unstable view of some ancient factory ruins, its collapsing roofs riddled with stout trees themselves plainly centuries old. None of the images remained stable for long. After a few seconds each would submerge into static. "There!" Wachieu coalesced half the spheres into one outsized display. An enormous fleet of warships, inching across the Equatorial Sea.

"Parek's fleet or Samu's?" breathed Gavisel.

"Samu's, of course," Panna bristled. "The flagship's dual superstructure is unmistakable."

Dr. Panna has a new interest, Eldridge thought with surprise.

The image sundered into static and collapsed. "That's the best I can do," Wachieu said sourly. "Observing from orbit is going to be an off-again, on-again thing."

"And the binary's quiet now," Gavisel observed. "It'll get worse."

"Can we get a fix on Parek's fleet?" Eldridge demanded.

Wachieu's wings stuttered. Luminous control banks swam into being at her wingtips. "I'll try for it," she said. "They should be almost adjacent."

Bubbles opened and flashed with noisy images. They imploded one by one— savage settlements, deserted ruins, treeless gouges in the southern continent where Tuezi rounds had struck centuries ago—but no hint of Parek's fleet. "I can't resolve it," Wachieu husked.

"Both fleets have been staying within the ancient shipping lanes," Panna suggested.

"There could be a dozen fleets down there," Wachieu said with annoyance. "The susceptors just aren't punching through."

"Analysis, please." Eldridge leaned with four of her arms on a rail that flowed up from the bridge floor for the purpose. "Fem Gavisel, Fem Wachieu. Have we anything that can image the surface reliably?" Eldridge asked.

Gavisel peered at readouts. "A high-power satellite in a lower orbit—say, geostationary or below—would get through more often than not. Nothing would be nine-by-nine reliable."

"Subdelta band would come close," Wachieu suggested.

Gavisel frowned. "That's what OmNet uses for its Spectators."

"Exactly," Wachieu husked. "Of course, subdelta's no good for remote monitoring. You've got to have a Spectator with implants at the observing end."

"In other words," Eldridge interrupted, "we've flown all the way out here to Sector Upsilon, and our primary source of information about events on the surface will continue to be sensos from OmNet, just as it was before we left."

The otter and the spider exchanged anxious looks.

"In other words," Eldridge continued, "we came out here to enforce Enclave— yet a fleet of speedsters could cruise within a thousand kilometers of us and we might not notice them. Half a dozen transports could land on open terrain down below and days could pass before we happened to glimpse them down there."

Wachieu shrugged. "Correct on all counts. In my opinion, Fem Captain."

Eldridge rested her chin in three hands. She seemed spent. "There's an old spacefaring tradition," she said tiredly. "A tradition that at each new planetfall, the commanding officer shall say a few words to set the tone for the encounter to come."

The otter, the spider, the other bridge officers in their diverse *personae*, and even Panna turned their full attention on Eldridge. While massaging her eyes, she crossed two hands behind her back.

"Well, then," Eldridge said by way of invocation. "Here we are."

69. Jaremi Four—
Off the Southern Continent

"Brace for crash!"

The call leapt from man to man, barely audible over the bells and sirens and whistles of general quarters. Throttles maxed, the flagship's drives roared like wounded animals.

Ulf and Felegu exchanged glances. They glimpsed nervously forward, upward. The bluff towered impossibly high. *It's so close!*

An hour before, Ulf had looked down from the bridge promenade and wondered at this improvised framework. Now he, Felegu, Parek, and forty-seven others were locked into the safety frame's cells. It would enclose them, there on the forecastle deck, as they rode out the flagship's beaching.

From forward, there was an immense rumbling. "Contact!" someone yelled unnecessarily. Doing close to thirty knots, the flagship's prow left the water. Momentum hurled her ahead. Ulf pitched forward against the safety webbing. In the cell to Ulf's left Felegu tumbled about, holding out one forearm to protect the digital camera. To aft, the drive sound lurched from maddened howl to something more like shrieking.

Ulf glanced to his right. Eerily composed, Parek watched the incline shudder closer.

With an immense, hollow thud, the bow punched into the incline. It pierced the veneer of paving stones. Dust fell in cataracts. Rocks peppered the deck.

Forward motion stopped.

There was a moment of terrible calm. Then sand began to shift beneath the hull's weight. The flagship groaned as if some monstrous choir lay dying in her hold. She was listing to port. "No! No! No!" Ulf heard someone shrieking. The port bow dug in further. Its rotation scooped stones from the incline's surface. They crashed to the deck, escorted by billows of soil.

It was the most terrifying ninety seconds of Ulf's life as the flagship heeled a third of the way over.

Finally the tilting stopped.

Silence.

Ulf heard distant breakers, wind whistling over indifferent blufftops, the chittering of circling birds.

Then he heard cheering from twenty-five hundred throats. Parek had wanted the flagship beached. Now it was, and nobody was dead.

The tilted deck made walking and working difficult, but not impossible. Inside ten minutes laborers had the safety frame suspended from chains. A jib swung it over the side. Through gaps in the expanded metal floor Ulf watched the beach spin lazily, twenty-five meters below. While its fifty occupants clung to straps and posts, the entire contrivance lurched toward the sand. Fighting vertigo, Ulf watched porthole after porthole slide upward. The hull plates were streaked with grime and rain-loosened paint. Below the waterline, metal glistened though caked with rust. Seashells clung in shapeless clumps.

The safety frame thudded down. Parek and his seven Brethren did something with the doors of their cells. Their cages swung open. After a moment Ulf figured how to open his own cell. His boots found sand.

He walked backwards and then ran. His breaths came in gasps that scraped at the inside of his chest. He stopped when he could see the flagship whole.

She was the largest manufactured object he'd ever seen out of its element— surely the most helpless. The forward two-thirds of her hull lay beached. The prow had driven into the ancient ramp three meters deep. Still, the hull seemed intact. Above, Ulf could see men crabwalking across canted decks. Panting, Felegu appeared next to Ulf, clutching the digital camera. "That thing still work?" Ulf demanded.

"I think so."

Ulf wagged his hand toward the beached liner. "Do whatever the fuck you do. You know, little pictures."

Felegu snapped away. At length he pointed and began laughing. "Look!"

Unaccustomed to humans, slow-flying seabirds with wingspans the length of a man's arm wafted low overhead. Soldiers broke out sidearms. They fired round after round, bringing birds thudding to the decks. "The downside is, the flagship may never sail again," Ulf said sardonically. "On the upside, there'll be something novel for dinner tonight."

By the time Ulf trudged back to the safety frame, Parek was gone. He'd donned his white silk cape and sprinted up the incline. "What did he say he would do?" Ulf demanded of a Brethren officer.

"He said he didn't know," the man replied. "He thought he'd remember on the way up."

"Why didn't you follow?"

"He said he'd already remembered he was to climb alone."

Ulf stared upward, sucking his teeth. Already Parek had had to slow down, picking his way among sinkholes and dislodged stones. *The Word Among Us can't even haul himself up that slope,* he thought.

Frowning, Ulf sized up the others Parek had hand-picked to ride down to the beach in the safety frame—the seven Brethren and ten uniformed percussionists, hauling their bell lyres free of padded cases. *They'll be a big help.* The other thirty were a ragtag assortment of cooks, stevedores, tailors, and steamrifle techs. *What was he thinking?*

Ten minutes later, Felegu pressed a spyglass into Ulf's hand. "The captain won't miss this."

Chuckling, Ulf raised the scope to his eye. "Crazy fucker's still wearing the cape and everything."

"Where is he?"

"Almost all the way up." Ten meters above Parek, two pitted stone columns flanked the crest of the incline. The ancient steles were as tall as five men, their surfaces cluttered with carvings in some forgotten language. Ulf handed Felegu back the scope. He thumbed the piezo transmitter four times. To his coconspirators, four bursts of static meant *Be in full readiness.*

"He's at the top," Felegu reported.

"What's he doing?"

"Waving his arms." Felegu refocused. "Like he's shouting at the sky gods."

Ulf nodded. "No doubt demanding to know why they don't answer."

Felegu laughed. " 'Demanding to know why they don't answer.' That's a good one."

Ulf's eyes narrowed. Then they widened. "Felegu," he hissed, "lower the scope."

Felegu did. Now that his field of view was larger, his jaw dropped as far as Ulf's had.

In the air, scant meters above Parek's head, a glowing cyclone of light had begun to form. Petals of white and green and salmon—auroral colors—counterrotated between the ancient stone pillars. The seabirds feared it. Flocks wheeled away in every direction.

Ulf stared through the spyglass. Parek had seen the cyclone. He stood in a pose of exaltation, legs spread wide, arms straight skyward. He turned to gaze downslope. The land breeze caught his cape. It billowed forward around him.

His voice boomed like a sky god's. "Hear me!"

"Fuck," Ulf breathed.

On the beach, within the flagship, Parek's voice blared from everywhere. It was impossibly loud and impossibly clear. "And now we only wait to hear the joyful news declared unto us, for the time cometh, we know not how soon. Would to the gods that it might be in my day; but let it be sooner or later, in it I will rejoice. Soldiers of righteousness, behold! The works of the sky gods are come to pass on this day!"

Aghast, Ulf tapped Felegu's arm. "Little pictures! Little pictures!"

Felegu raised the camera. He shook it in sudden anger. The winkies along its side flickered dull red. "Damned power cell," he growled.

"Fuck it," Ulf croaked. "Look!"

The cyclone had swelled. It floated high above the stone columns. Jagged lightnings raced around its perimeter. The bolts gathered strength. Fork after fork fell thundering against the stone pillars. The columns erupted in sheets of soft green fire. Their surfaces crumbled. Torso-sized fragments sloughed away like chalk beneath a chisel.

Heedless of it all, Parek stood motionless between the disintegrating columns, arms upraised, cape flapping madly.

As suddenly as they'd come, the cyclone, lightning, and green fires vanished. The pillars, too, were gone.

In their place stood gleaming metallic columns, lustrous sentinels that had apparently always waited inside those stony sheaths. The columns were as tall as the stone pillars had been and as thick as a strong man's shoulders. Ulf took the spyglass. It resolved elaborate detail on the columns' brassy surfaces. There were raised polygons of complex shape, and incised trenches pregnant with light, and conduits of unguessable purpose.

Between the columns' tips, violet lightning danced.

Between their bases stood The Word Among Us. Slowly Parek lowered his right arm and extended his fingers toward the flagship.

The lightning between the columns' tips winked out.

A green ribbon appeared at Parek's feet. *Not an object,* Ulf realized. *A ribbon of . . . light!*

Perhaps two meters wide, partly transparent, it unrolled like some impossible carpet, coursing down the incline as fast as a man could run.

Parek stepped atop it. He spread his feet and crossed his arms. He began to drift down the incline. "His legs don't move," Ulf said with a shudder.

Parek was gliding downslope faster. But something else was faster still.

"Jump!" Felegu yanked Ulf aside. The green ribbon had reached the bottom of the incline. It shot across the beach and through the spot where Ulf had stood. It rushed forward to the water's edge.

There, it stopped. Steam hissed. Surf puckered from the ribbon's edge.

Ulf dropped to hands and knees. He stared *under* the flickering ribbon. It floated a hand's width above the sand.

"Is it the aurora?" Felegu demanded.

"How the fuck would I know?" Ulf rolled onto his back. Hesitantly he extended his hand beneath the ribbon. "It feels cold," he reported.

"Can you touch it?" Felegu asked.

"No." At first it felt spongy. As he pressed harder, it went firm. "I can't touch the light," he reported. "The closer I get, the harder it pushes me away."

"High Commander! High Commander!" It was one of the cooks, part of Parek's mysterious complement of thirty. The man gestured frantically upslope.

Ulf lurched to his feet and looked about. Hundreds of men thronged the decks of the flagship above, looking up the incline, pointing and shouting. Ulf raised the spyglass.

Parek was halfway down the incline. His cape and his dense curly hair billowed violently behind him. Knees bent, arms extended, mouth agape, he raced down the ramp. He was already moving faster than a *sturruh* at full gallop. Whatever the ribbon was, it made motion effortless.

Apparently it also made stopping impossible.

"He's shouting something," Ulf reported.

Felegu scowled. "I don't hear anything."

"Maybe the gods only strengthen his voice at the top." Through the glass, Ulf watched Parek wave his arms and shout with obvious desperation. "What the fuck is he saying?"

A shift in the wind let Parek's unamplified voice reach them thinly. "Get . . . out . . . of . . . my . . . way!"

"Oh, shit!" Ulf spat. Though he didn't notice, he was in command again. "Everybody scatter! Away from the ribbon of light!"

Screaming, Parek rocketed down the incline and onto the flat straightaway of the beach. From a safe distance, Ulf and the men watched Parek pitch by. Just before he reached the end of the glowing ribbon, his speed dropped to almost nothing. He didn't seem to feel any impact or deceleration.

When the ribbon ended, Parek was unprepared. He pitched forward into waist-deep water, about as gracefully as a candlestick falling off a table.

Shaken but intact, Arn Parek rolled over. He sat up in the water. Rescuers surrounded him. He raised his arms. "Stand back!"

They did.

Arms still upraised, Parek stood. The silk cape clung to him in rumples as if he had been newly baptized. He waded toward the beach. "Music!" he cried.

The percussionists exchanged puzzled glances.

"I said music!" Parek screamed.

The evocative rhythm rolled forth. *Clang-shang-ralang. Clang-shang-ralang. Clang-shang-ralang. Clang-shang-ralang. Clang-shang-ralang. Clang-shang-ralang.* Above, on shipboard, others sounded the miracle cadence.

"Behold," Parek cried, "I stretch forth my hand!" Gravely he dropped his left arm from vertical to horizontal and pointed dead ahead. "Behold, I stretch forth my other hand!" With equal dignity his right hand settled beside the left. "This day our swords are made bright against the unrighteous of Southland!"

"What swords?" a trooper asked, staring down at his steamcarbine.

Slowly, slowly, as if leveraging immense forces, Parek spread his arms.

Clang-shang-ralang. Clang-shang-ralang. Clang-shang-ralang. Clang-shang-ralang. Hissing, the ribbon widened. It spread to the full width of the ancient funicular bed and rose to waist height above the sand. It floated a like distance from the incline's angled face. The ribbon spread out as wide as the flagship. Steaming and sparking, it extended out over the water to embrace the stern. Its brightness increased until one could no longer see through it.

Felegu stammered incoherently and pointed downward.

The sand was writhing. It boiled away from the keel as if alive and in pain.

Ulf closed a useless hand around the piezo transmitter. He had no idea what instruction to send.

From above, there were shouts of surprise. Within the keel, steel moaned. Felegu shook seawater from the ancient camera in frustration.

The flagship was rising.

Clang-shang-ralang. Clang-shang-ralang.

Slowly, reluctantly, Ulf waded toward Parek. He raised his hands and let the piezo transmitter drop into ankle-deep water. Blue light briefly flickered from it.

At a gesture from Parek, the Brethren guards let Ulf pass.

Ulf met Parek's eyes. He collapsed to his knees, his thoughts of conspiracy forgotten. With both hands he gripped one of the prophet's legs. "Forgive me!" Ulf pleaded. "I doubted you. Word Among Us, forgive me!"

Clang-shang-ralang. Clang-shang-ralang. Clang-shang-ralang. Tenderly Parek lay a hand on Ulf's head. He nodded toward the ship with gentle irony. "Turn around, you're missing it."

Ulf turned around. The immense hull was free of sand and sea. Whitewater poured from its impellers. Where the bow had pierced the incline's slope, soil slithered away from it, like a viscous brown liquid. The bow was twisting back to starboard. Paving stones split, wobbled, and skittered out of its way.

The flagship's deck was level again.

Clang-shang-ralang. Clang-shang-ralang.

"Stop!" Parek cried.

The percussionists fell silent.

The immense hull floated, motionless, almost a meter above the flickering ribbon. From Felegu to the lowliest cook, everyone stood speechlessly and stared.

It need hardly be added that no Spectator was present to record this miracle—for that is what it would later be called.

Parek clapped Ulf's shoulder. "Ulf. Ulf. Take your eyes off the ship, Ulf."

"Y-yes?" Ulf stammered.

"Who rules?"

Ulf's lip trembled. "You rule, Word Among Us."

Parek withdrew his hands. He turned toward the levitating flagship. "Come on, people!" he called. "We have a lot of ships to get up the hill." Pressing past the dumbfounded he leapt onto the ribbon. He wobbled from side to side for a moment, then stood confidently. "There, see?" he cried. "You can stand on it—just over it, actually. It's all right. Just don't work up too much momentum. Do I have everyone's attention?"

Parek reached up. Caked with barnacles, streaked with rust, the flagship's rudder stood at least a dozen meters tall. It weighed tons. Parek clasped hands on its tip and pushed.

The ship slid forward. Only a few centimeters, but *it moved.*

"Fuck. Fuck." Ulf breathed. "Fuck, fuck, fuck."

Leaning into his work, Parek moved the immense hull forward several manlengths. Panting, he withdrew. "It's easy with more people. Come, my thirty," he urged. "Fifteen on the port side, fifteen to starboard."

Afraid to approach the ribbon, afraid to disobey, one by one the cooks and fashioners and artillery techs edged toward the ship. They split up and formed two lines. They pressed against the sides of the keel with their hands.

Parek gestured encouragingly to the thirty. "Go on, men," he said casually. "Haul it to the top of the bluff. *Music!*"

Clang-shang-ralang. **Clang**-*shang-ralang.* *Clang-shang-ralang. Clang-shang-ralang. Clang-shang-ralang.* **Clang**-*shang-ralang. Clang-shang-ralang.*

Parek approached Ulf. "Ride the safety frame back up to the deck. Take my orders to the captain. He should signal the fleet. As soon as the beach is clear, ships should power themselves ashore at ten-minute intervals. A supply ship first, then all the fashioners' barges, then the rest. The captains need not secure their cargo and crew as we did. With the ribbon established, beaching will be smooth. Each craft will disgorge from ten to thirty men, depending on its size, and they will walk their craft up the incline."

Ulf blinked. "That's what you want me to tell him."

"It will make sense after they've seen the flagship do it. Now go." Already the ship's movement was dragging the safety frame across the beach. Ulf jumped aboard it. He clung desperately as the jib crane lofted the frame from the sand.

Ulf gaped helplessly. Even while the crane hauled him up, the flagship's bow was rising. At one point the hull touched the ribbon only at the forward edge of the keel, which lay on the incline, and at the rudder, still on the beach. Ten men tugged at the bow. Twenty more pressed against the rudder. The rest of the keel was too high above the ribbon for hands to reach it. No matter. The flagship moved smoothly. Inconceivably, the hull gave no protest. Every rivet held.

By the time Ulf and the safety frame had reached the deck, the entire hull was on the incline. The deck was tilted seventy degrees, almost vertical.

No one minded.

When the framework touched down, Ulf felt a moment of vertigo. Something twisted inside him. All at once the canted deck felt level. It was the *world* that was at a crazy angle.

Ulf had no astonishment left. He simply walked down the seventy-degree incline as though it were level ground. Climbed the underside of a ladder that was nearly horizontal. Stepped into a gangway at whose end he could see the ocean—from above.

Ulf strode toward the bridge with Parek's orders.

70. Khoren Four

B ei Hanllei burst into the tridee control room. Smoke stung her eyes. They were hazel today.

Artists and operators' stations swept in half-circles on four descending levels. Said artists and operators—those not dead or wounded—cowered beneath their consoles. At bottom, the studio lay in shambles. Greder's multigimbaled "goddess platform" lay on its side. Chairs, prop tables, and lumoprojectors lay overturned. Smoke roiled from an electrical distribution panel into which someone had emptied a percussion pistol. In two, no, three places, there were streaks or spatters of blood.

The architect of the destruction was no mystery. With bestial snarls Orgena Greder, planet owner and tyrant, raged through the control center. A senior tech crawled away from her, trailing blood. "You need more, riffraff," Greder growled. Her next shot pitched the man onto his back, screaming. Where his left shoulder had been was a smoking pulp the size of two joined fists. "No medcare for this one!" Greder screamed to no one in particular. "Take its number. Anyone who doctors it dies."

There was an opening in the circle of guards around Hanllei. She edged through it and clamped her fingers on the wrist of Greder's gun hand. "Enough, Orgena," she shouted. "Forjeling *enough*. Now what happened?"

Greder stared at Hanllei. "You stay," she whispered. She dropped her percussion pistol and shouted, "Everybody else, out!"

Techs and artisans uncoiled from their hiding places and scrambled for the exits. None spared a thought for the wounded.

Hanllei counted five people down. She found herself torn between distaste at the needless carnage and the recognition that she was Khorenian gentry herself. If she'd become enraged and shot a few autochthons on impulse, she'd expect no one to object.

She and Greder were alone in the control room. Nervously the younger woman edged downstairs toward the open space of the studio, for whatever benefit that might confer. Greder followed. "All right," Hanllei asked, striving to keep her voice level. "What the sfelb happened?"

"*Sit down, traitor!*" Greder roared. Hanllei sat heavily on a half-ruined console. "Who do you work for?"

"You!" Hanllei said, her voice quaking.

"You always wondered what became of that Incavo fellow. If you're less than truthful, you'll find out."

Hanllei stood slowly. "I never lied to you. Now what are you talking about?"

In a lightning motion Greder brought up her palms. They caught Hanllei under the chin and caromed into her cheekbones. Hanllei howled with the pain of biting her tongue. Greder pushed the younger woman backward once, then again. Hanllei tumbled out onto the studio floor.

"You know perfectly well what I'm talking about," Greder spat. "You gave Parek back the fleet!"

Hanllei uncoiled and stood. "I did *what?*"

Greder swung again. The palm blow could have broken Hanllei's nose, but the younger woman blocked it.

"Stop this!" Hanllei screamed.

"No one else knew," Greder snarled through clamped teeth.

"Knew *what?*" Hanllei backed away. She circled behind a still-upright prop stand. "I did nothing, Orgena! Tell me what happened. Maybe we can determine together who's to blame."

Greder picked up the prop stand and overturned it. Trays of Host Nymph crystal earrings scattered. The flimsy console flew apart when it struck the floor.

But Greder flung it away from me, Hanllei realized.

Massaging her cheeks, she struggled to read her employer's eyes. "Okay. Okay," Hanllei said tentatively. "Can we approach this as a shared problem?"

"A shared problem?" Greder backed up a step into the control area. Grunting, she cleared debris off a console. She stabbed at a still-functional control tab. "Solve *this.*" At the center of the studio, haloed by residual smoke, a tridee bubble blossomed. It was Ulf. "The journal of Ulf's most recent encounter with his glorious goddess," Greder explained.

The Jaremian commander stood in his saloon. His clothes were in disarray. He was very drunk. "Ye'r the evil god," he slurred. "Fr'm now on I side with the god named God. Parek's god. There's a god of pow'r. Ye'r just a deceiver. I kill liars like you before bre'fass."

Ulf lurched backward, blinking. *Greder must have sheathed her goddess image in crimson fire. Or something.* "I am your celestial sponsor!" Greder-in-the-tridee shrilled. "Through my power you got this fleet."

"An' through the power of Parek's god the fleet's been lifted inna the fuckin' sky!" Wavering, Ulf swept a hand back toward the fantail windows. "Look for y'rself!"

The image was optimized for Ulf's shadowed face, making the windows featureless blooms of white. Some nervous tech dialed down the exposure. Ulf became a silhouette. The view outside grew clear.

The ocean and sky looked wrong somehow.

"Out of my way," Greder-in-the-tridee rumbled. The *pov* lifted and surged in jerks toward the windows.

"Don' do that!" Ulf cried. "At leass, warn me first."

"We've got to figure how to move the image around a room without inducing vertigo," Greder-in-the-control-center whispered to Hanllei.

Ignoring Ulf's puking, the *pov* lumbered up the golden staircase.

"Oh, plorg . . ." Hanllei whispered.

At the far horizon sea still met sky. Closer to the ship, there was only . . .

Grass.

Thick reeds spread left and right without limit. The *pov* snapped straight aft and peered down. Receding from the ship's centerline was a brilliant green ribbon. A quarter kilometer behind, a light cruiser followed. *A light cruiser.* Impossibly it balanced above the same pulsing band on the knife edge of its keel. *Completely out of the water!*

The *pov* glimmered back onto the light cruiser. Greder-in-the-tridee had invoked artificial magnification: Hanllei reared back by reflex as the image swelled.

What had seemed like incongruous movement beneath the cruiser stood revealed as stark absurdity. A handful of soldiers—surely no more than fifteen— strode along the ribbon, each pressing a single hand to the keel. *They're walking the cruiser,* Hanllei thought. Aloud: "Looks like a colloidal slipfield. A big one."

"Basic technology in any Galactic warehouse, dry dock, or mine," Greder agreed.

"Except yours."

Greder ignored the comment. "But what's a colloidal slipfield doing on Jaremi Four?"

Hanllei shook her head. "How'd this happen?"

"If Ulf's account can be believed, Parek ordered the flagship beached. Then lights came down from heaven and created the slipfield." Greder paced down into the studio. "Obviously it's Galactic technology. Now, there's only one place Galactic technology could have come from—here. On all of Khoren Four, only two people know what I'm up to in Jaremi space." Greder drew another pistol.

Hanllei screamed inside. *Forjel on plorg, it's a ravisher!*

"You and I, Bei—we're the only ones who understand. Now *I* didn't go behind Ulf's back and give Parek a forjeling slipfield."

Hanllei forced strength into her voice. "Neither did I."

"You didn't do it, I didn't do it." Greder smiled thinly. "That exhausts the possibilities. Tell me, Bei, have you any idea how terrible a way this is to die?"

Hanllei's mind raced. "Orgena, before you kill me—think."

"I have." Greder tapped open the ravisher's safety. "That's why I've decided to kill you."

Hanllei struggled to keep her tone casual. "What if there's someone else?"

"There's no one else."

"For vacuum's sake!" Hanllei shouted. "What if we have competition down there? Other Galactics, also operating on Jaremi Four?"

Greder paused. Two beats. Three. The pistol tilted downward. "You still live," she said quietly.

Hanllei struggled to compose her thoughts. "We never worried much about the mysteries that surround some of the other people down there. Who's Samu? Where did he get his fleet?"

Greder shrugged. "Maybe he actually *did* find his in mothballs somewhere."

Hanllei shook her head. "We scanned Jaremi Four for usable derelict craft, remember? We didn't make the decision to fabricate Ulf's fleet until we were satisfied no suitable autochthonous hulls existed."

Greder waggled the pistol. "Scanning's chancy down there. Maybe we missed something."

"Maybe," Hanllei admitted. "But that leaves other mysteries. Was Samu behind those prophecies that peppered Northland from out of the sky? How did he handle the logistics of moving people to Point Eldek from all over the northern continent? How'd he throw that port city together almost overnight?"

"Have you any answers, or just questions?" The ravisher barrel was drifting back toward Hanllei's chest.

Hanllei nodded. "I've had all kinds of answers proposed to me, most of them asinine."

"By whom?"

"Trendriders, mostly, looking for backing so they could run down some crazy theory or other."

"Freelance policy wonks?" Greder snorted. "Looking for contracts from Khoren Four?"

"Desperate wonks," Hanllei conceded. "This Parek thing's brought them all out of their hollows. But some of them asked intriguing questions. For instance, where does Parek get his doctrines? Does he make them all up?"

"He did just that for years before Ruth Griszam encountered him. Anyway, we considered contacting Parek directly and ruled it out. He's too visible."

"Others might have decided differently. Parek always says the sky gods speak to him in visions. We assumed he was lying or hallucinating. But what if some other Galactic is wrangling Parek the same way we do Ulf, with satellites and projected visions and gifts of hardware?" Feeling almost confident, Hanllei circled. "So many theories! One wonk thought Parek was regurgitating Kfardaszian utopian philosophy, another said transcendental hagionomy—you know, from Ordh. Two claimed they spotted the influence of that Terran seer Nostradamus." Hanllei dared a chuckle. "Another wonk tried to convince me she'd found echoes of The Book of Mormon. When I didn't buy that, she suggested Scalbulian metempsychotic calculus instead. . . ."

"The Book of Mormon?" Greder croaked. The ravisher's maw staggered downward. Hanllei trailed off. *Shut your mouth, girl,* she told herself. *You said the magic word.*

Greder slid the ravisher back into her sleeve. As if nothing had happened, she stepped around fallen objects to the control room's second level. *I'm not dead,* Hanllei realized. *Nothing has happened.*

Greder was all business. "If we wanted to test this theory that Parek draws his doctrines from Mormon sources, how would we do it?"

Hanllei forced herself to center. "I could run a conceptual matching series. We've got every word Parek ever uttered on senso, and I'm sure I can call up that Mormon scripture from somewhere." She moved toward a console, trying to stop her hands from shaking. Greder brought her a chair. "Does this thought engine still work?" Hanllei tabbed controls. Flickering schematics documented the system's progress in finding ways around the damage Greder had inflicted. Greder pulled up a second chair and sat silently.

After a moment the panel projected a circle of virtual controls centered on Hanllei's fingers. Hanllei locked eyes with her employer. She smiled. "We can do this."

"Bei, I'm sorry I doubted you."

Hanllei shrugged. "It's a living." She massaged projected data structures. "Here's Parek's collected statements of doctrine," she said abstractedly. "Okay, I'm through to Terra, the LDS archives in . . ." She scowled at the display and wrinkled her nose. Outside, a thunderclap clattered so loudly above Khoren Four's perpetual teratogenic squalls that the sound punched through to the heavily insulated tridee center. "Yuck, who'd want to live on a salt lake?" Her hands danced again. "Cross-checking—" The results painted across the console. "The correlation's better than chance, but not overwhelming."

Greder edged closer. She scowled at the readouts. "But there's something there. What's this?"

"Some other body of concepts that correlated to Parek's doctrines almost as strongly as the Book of Mormon," Hanllei said. She tapped the panel, furrowed her brow. "What are masons?"

"Bricklayers," Greder supplied. "What, Parek preaches to bricklayers? Oh, that must be Freemasons!"

Hanllei shrugged. "This explains something?"

"A charitable and social organization organized into lodges with colorful rituals. A Terran thing, popular today on a handful of worlds."

Hanllei gave Greder a look of utter perplexity. "How do you know these things?"

"The Catholics hate them. So I joined—or tried to."

"They turned you down?"

"Of all the half-witted old Terran conventions to revive! Their lodges don't accept women."

The laughter Greder and Hanllei shared was as unforced as it was genuine. *Five minutes ago my life was in peril,* Hanllei thought. *Now we're cronies again. Some day I'll be less lucky. Yet I stay. Sfelb, I can't imagine being elsewhere.*

Greder steepled her fingers. "If memory serves, Freemasonry was popular on Terra when Mormonism originated. Scholars say Masonic influence colored the primordial Mormon creeds."

Hanllei traced the contour of her upper lip with a fingertip. "Mormons and Masons. Masons and Mormons."

"'Some Mormons are different,'" Greder quoted absently.

"Pardon?"

"The last thing Marnen Incavo said, before the shooting started. 'Some Mormons are different.'" She stood, smiling sardonically. "In any case, we know Parek has a Galactic wrangler."

Hanllei nodded. "We contend with someone like us for control of Ulf's fleet."

"For control of *my* fleet," Greder corrected. She began to laugh. "It seems so obvious now. While we guided Ulf on campaign, our rival taught Parek to run those grand and lucrative healing services."

"The rival ordered Parek to kill that rogue Spectator on his inner council," Hanllei continued, "just as we did."

"We gave Ulf a fleet, and with it the prestige to slap Parek under house arrest. The rival told Parek when the next auroral storm was due, and on the strength of that prophecy Parek reclaimed the top spot."

Greder nodded. She walked to the console controlling the satellites that beamed images to the Jaremian surface. "Can you run this, Bei?" she asked.

"After a fashion."

Greder tabbed the console's RESTART key. "Ulf," she said at last. "We need to win him back."

Hanllei seated herself before the master vision mixer. Most of it worked. "Parek's handler mounted one enormous miracle."

"So we must top it."

"When you and I both appear to Ulf, we usually rely on a staff of eight."

Greder waved toward the empty control center and the shattered consoles. "What we have is us. Sfelb, go to the image banks."

Hanllei raised her eyebrows. "Direct transmission of Galactic imagery?"

Greder's gesture encompassed the mauled tridee center. "What's one more Enclave violation? It's all we can do by ourselves, and who knows? Ulf might find stock shots of Galactic life more impressive than some old broad in a glowing dinner gown." Greder threw over a few controls. "I'm online to our satellites."

"Image banks are hot," Hanllei reported. "I can *tap* Ulf whenever you're ready. How old's that tridee you showed me?"

"Less than an hour. He'll still be drunk."

Hanllei rubbed her cheek. "What do you want to do?"

Greder reached over Hanllei's shoulder. She invoked the sequence to beckon Ulf. "Forjel it. Show him the Ice Capades, anything."

71.   Jaremi Four—Southern Continent

All along the shore of the shallow lake, manmade glare beat back the night. The mainmasts of four dozen ships had been removed and rooted in gravel. Their lights, so gaudy at sea, cast daylike radiance onto the beach. Ships lay in pieces everywhere. Hundreds, no, thousands of men moved about purposefully. A hundred other ships bobbed glittering at anchor.

This was where the slipfield ribbon ended: at a shallow lake sixty kilometers inland from the bluff. And still ships came. A former destroyer laden with nested racks of landing craft slid into the lake. She cast a swell of water two manheights before her. The soldiers who'd pushed her leapt into the surf. They clawed at net ladders and climbed toward her bulwarks. The destroyer's engines coughed, then growled. Onboard lights winked on, bank after bank. She steamed outward just in time for two dozen men to walk the next mammoth craft off the slipfield ribbon.

Chagrin rode up on *sturruh*-back. The flagship's conversion was complete, he realized. She'd been fissioned into, among other things, six daughter craft. The big black attack boats floated in slings above the water, suspended by scaffolds that extended between two fashioners' barges. Crews stood in hip-deep water, maneuvering steam drives and impellers into narrow slots in the boats' hulls. Ancient Jaremian naval architecture had always been modular, a fact of which the fashioners had taken maximum advantage. Bits of the flagship's prow and fantail had been pieced together to give the boats a sharp keel with a shallow draft, ideal for fast cruising in inland waters.

Three of the attack boats differed from their sisters. For one thing, they'd been fitted with great clear sidewalls all along their bulwarks. "Son of a bitch," Chagrin laughed, "they turned the fantail windows into shields." In addition, rugged fan assemblies had been bolted to the hero boats' foredecks. Their fabrication was crude; they must have crafted in secret during the sea voyage, even while Ulf's power was at its peak—even while the High Commander thought he'd found and aborted all the prophet's hidden projects.

The Word Among Us paced the deck of the boat most nearly completed. Beneath the worklights his white leather uniform seemed to glow. Brethren guardsmen melted back as Chagrin climbed a ladder onto the deck of the elevated boat. He watched Parek stride between the fan assemblies, asking questions of his fashioners, barking orders to laborers. Ulf dogged the prophet's every step, his manner deferential.

Parek squatted to inspect one of the improvised fans. It was as big around as a man, shielded in a hammered metal fairing a meter and a half wide. The fairing lay open, revealing complex mechanical linkages inside. "Word Among Us," Ulf truckled, "I still can't believe your artisans completed these while I held sway over the fleet."

"What was that, friend Ulf?" Parek asked, menace climbing a trellis of whimsy in his tone.

"While I *thought* I held sway," Ulf corrected without a trace of hidden anger.

"Does your sky god still try to win you back?" Parek inquired.

Ulf shrugged. "So far, I'm not impressed. Though if we ever make it back up north where the lakes can freeze, there's something I want to try with strips of metal anchored to my feet."

"My prophet." Chagrin called attention to himself. He saluted fist-on-chest.

"Ahh, Chagrin!" Parek smiled grandly. "What is your report?"

"It was all as you prophesied. After the last ship climbed the incline, the green ribbon plowed the beach flat and destroyed the ramp. Then the two metal towers disappeared in a flash of greenish light. No one will follow us, or even be able to tell where we went. As for the last ship, it should reach here tomorrow."

Parek spun to Ulf, grinning exultantly. "You see?"

"Great are you, Word Among Us," Ulf intoned.

Chagrin wondered at the transformation that had overcome the High Commander. Clearly the Miracle of the Ships—for that was what the men already called it—had collapsed Ulf's ambitions. *For now,* Chagrin thought darkly.

A wooden dory drew up, puffing steam. Crewmen hurled up ropes. Parek himself plucked one from the attack boat's deck. "Hurry! Hurry!" the prophet called. Fashioners, laborers, techs, even Ulf and Chagrin hastened to the starboard bulwark to collect bulky wooden crates handed up by the dory's crew.

"What are these, anyway?" Chagrin asked.

"Aboard the flagship," Parek panted, "I had two secret workshops Ulf's sky god never showed him. One was the fashioners' shop, where the fans were made. The other was a laboratory."

A pockmarked lackey pried a crate open. Inside nestled two dozen metallic cylinders, each long as a hand and thick as a wrist.

"Ulf, Chagrin, you're both a part of this." Parek plucked one cylinder free. The metal was dull, near-bronze in color. It bore signs of hammering. "Remember just before we left the dam, when I insisted on going back for some containers?"

"I thought the fire would catch us while we struggled with those things," Ulf said.

Parek smiled. "I'd saved them for years. I used to use them in my preaching." His voice turned bitter. "Until Dultav made me stop."

"You . . . took them into this secret laboratory?" Chagrin reasoned dimly.

Parek fed the cylinder into the big fan's loading mechanism and swung the fairing shut. "I taught the chemists how to revive the mother matter, how to grow and harvest it. This is the result." He stepped on a deadman's pedal. Twin handles snapped up, each topped with a bulky red thumbswitch. Parek grasped the handles. Holding his thumbs clear of the switches, he demonstrated how easily the fan unit could be swiveled and aimed. When Ulf and Chagrin had grasped the principle, Parek stepped off the deadman's switch. The handles leapt back beneath the fairing. "When we cruise downriver with the wind from the sea at our backs, the lead boats will run these fans at maximum speed."

Ulf nodded obediently. Chagrin asked, "What will that do?"

"The sky gods will conquer our enemies before we reach them. You'll see."

Whistle bleating, a water taxi pulled alongside. Half a dozen gray-caped scribes filed aboard. "Gather round," Parek called. "I shall prophesy the sky god's first words since we poised ourselves to bring righteousness to Southland."

"Hear The Word Among Us!" a scribe called in a wheezy voice.

"Silence!" Ulf bellowed. Laborers stopped in midstep. Fashioners looked up, stricken, from their work. "Lay down your tools!" Ulf snarled. "We have all night for work. Now The Word Among Us speaks."

Parek reached into his cape and held up an ovoid woody husk the size of a child's head.

"*Fhlet*," someone whispered. "He will prophesy about *fhlet?*"

Parek displayed the hairy gourd in outstretched fingers. "As we journey we will often take food from onshore. It's a different world in Southland. You'll find exotic things to eat. You'll also find that *fhlet*—dull, nutritious *fhlet*—grows here in a profusion you never imagined. All the same, my word to you"—he flashed sharp eyes at the scribes, who redoubled their scribbling on small pads—"the word that shall be copied down this night and proclaimed with utmost urgency to every ship, every soldier of the fleet—is this: You may freely eat of every good thing you will find in this shattered land." He held the *fhlet* forward and stared at it with an electric gaze no man could have withstood. "But of the *fhlet* you shall not eat." Snarling, he pitched the gourd over the side. "For in the day that you eat of it you shall die. So speaks The Word Among Us."

72. Vatican

P ope Modest IV pressed the echidna's snout to his forehead.

Suck, rush, wrench.

The hyperqueues yawned before him. He knew where he must go. First, the Jesuits. Magenta was their color. New magenta event vortices had spread like mushrooms overnight. Drawing on the echidna's gifts, Modest multiplexed his awareness. He absorbed the tangled totality.

"It's a gesture of defiance unparalleled in recent Church history," a lay commentator yammered. "After a year of virtual house arrest Aresino Y'Braga, Father General of the Society of Jesus, released an omnigraph sure to touch off harsh new controversy in the Church. Y'Braga, the first non-Terran to lead a major Catholic religious order, strikes directly at the Church's Terran roots."

Modest found the for-his-eyes-only briefing from the Congregation for Pious Statistics. "Y'Braga cites the Church's increasingly strict mechanisms for verifying the truth of Incarnations on other worlds. He argues that by contemporary standards, the Incarnation on which the Church was built—that of Jesus of Terra—is so poorly substantiated that if it occurred today, it might not command acceptance.

"In metachapters whose insights reviewers reluctantly term 'magisterial,' Y'Braga marshals powerful evidence," the summary continued. "Y'Braga observes that none of the Terran Gospels were written by eyewitnesses, and indeed, that no writings survive from anyone who actually encountered Christ during His Terran life. Y'Braga demonstrates that when the extant writings are arranged in their most likely order of composition, the figure of Jesus first appears as a thoroughly mortal teacher of mysteries, to whom messianic characteristics are ascribed ever more freely as one moves into documents written later. In other contexts this would be prima facie evidence of myth-making. Further, Y'Braga raises devastating objections to Terran Christianity's reliance on Saint Paul, a convert who never met the religion's founder save in a vision of unknowable veracity—a fact that is doubly suspicious because the authentically Pauline teachings are so different in spirit from those attributed to Jesus."

Modest shifted his attention to another commentator, a lay analyst from Gwilya. *Now We shall see what the unbelievers make of this,* Modest thought.

"Y'Braga—who, never forget, is Ordhian rather than Terran—stops short of asking the crucial question," the Gwilyan pundit complained. "But no thoughtful person can come away from the Father General's omnigraph without asking oneself: If the Incarnation that gave rise to Terra's Catholic Church no longer meets that Church's own standards, whither Vatican? Whither Terran humanity's most important, not to say lucrative, cultural export?"

Perhaps We should've followed Rybczynsky's counsel and dissolved the Jesuits, Modest thought. Shuttling his consciousness into an area where Galactic responses to Y'Braga's publication were indexed, he abandoned his fears. *Events have overtaken Y'Braga,* the pope realized with ironic satisfaction. *He did his best to shake the Church to her foundations; as little as two years ago, he might have had a devastating impact. Today, few are interested in Y'Braga's iconoclasm.* Each time the magenta vertices—representing the impact of the Jesuits—approached critical levels, an outcropping of cyan would thrust in, disrupting their aggregation.

Cyan, Modest laughed inwardly. *How well We know that color!* Cyan was reserved for nodes related to activist Parekism. There were a sea of them. Bracing himself, the pope began cherry-picking.

Shimmer.

On Vyrdis Ten, mobs lofting holoprojections of Arn Parek danced before a cathedral in flames.

Shimmer.

A wizened bishop stood behind a desolate crystal pulpit. His cathedral was all but empty. No more than forty worshipers huddled in pews that could seat six thousand. "Some say I should not speak against the false messiah!" he thundered. "But the Holy Father dared to speak truth, devil take those who disagree! Dare I do less? Dare you, the legions"—he squinted into the unpeopled dimness—"well, the vanguard . . . um, the righteous remnant? Not for us the fashions of the day! Arn Parek, that Jaremian fraud, he is no Christ. He is unworthy of our attention, unworthy of our worship." The bishop intended his pause to be compelling. Instead it showcased the barren echoes as thirty-six of his forty listeners closed their kneelers and made for the cathedral's tall sculpted doors.

Shimmer.

"It's the greatest, and by far the most unexpected, challenge to Vatican's conquest of Galactic culture," the news reader said. "Galactics have been eager to embrace the Church—eager to relive Terra's past, to prostrate themselves in glorious obeisance to the Papacy's most trivial promulgations. But with one voice they say they will not stomach *this*. The charisma of Jaremi Four's genocidal messiah Arn Parek has undercut their faith. Some call Parek a fraud, a butcher, and worse—but believers have found in him a Cosmic Christ for whom they willingly cashier Catholic tradition. Modest IV's declaration that Parek is no Christ has divided the Church like nothing since Vatican Council Fourteen institutionalized ritual pederasty."

Shimmer.

On Guerecht Six, an orderly but nonetheless wrathful crowd of two hundred thousand Catholics thronged a public square. Catholics, yes—but Catholics united in their hatred of Modest and Vatican. "Betrayer of the Cosmic Christ," read the caption beneath Modest's likeness on most of the holoplacards he could read. Other placards bore the face of Parek.

Shimmer.

On Buerala Six, Parekists swarmed through the streets. Anti-Catholic rioting had swept the capital. Columns of smoke snaked into algae-red skies. Parekists swarmed, wearing white synleather in imitation of their prophet. The *pov* jerked to the left. Rioters had surrounded a knot of cringing Catholics. Male and female gero-mentors shoved half a dozen children into a blind alcove at the base of a flaming commercial structure. The man uncapped a metal vial of holy water. Tenderly he pressed it to the woman's head, the children's, and his own. With a snarl, he flung the vial forward, asperging the crowd. He seemed genuinely surprised that when the droplets struck them, the rioters didn't break ranks and run away screaming. Instead they . . . instead they. . . .

Horrified, Modest replaced the echidna in its terrarium.

"Holiness!" a voice called. It was Krammonz, of course, followed by Rybczynsky, resplendent in scarlet choir dress. "We tried to reach you through the event nodes," Krammonz said.

"We lay down the echidna," Modest explained. "It was too painful." Rybczynsky scuttled forward. He reverenced the Fisherman's Ring with only the most cursory bending of his knee. "Three hundred days indulgence, soldier of Christ," Modest said absently.

"Holiness," Rybczynsky snapped without preamble, "there has been an urgent development."

"More urgent than—" Modest waved toward the terrarium.

"The story breaks just now," Rybczynsky explained. "A wealthy lay Steward on Ordh has just made a terrible announcement."

"Someone We know?"

"Doubtful," Krammonz said. "His name is Stenoda Gerris, an Ordhian shipping magnate who took Steward's vows about six years ago. Aside from his wealth, he had no remarkable characteristics."

"Until now," Rybczynsky added darkly. "Gerris announced his conviction that Parek is the Christ."

"Thousands have done that," the pope scoffed, "quite a few high-ranking religious among them."

"Gerris went further," Rybczynsky said grimly. "He says he converted an enormous cargo trawler for passenger service and filled it with forty thousand pilgrims—all religious extremists who share his view that Parek is Christ."

Krammonz folded his hands. "Steward Garris says the trawler is already seven-eighths of the way to Jaremi space, and that once it arrives it will take any action necessary to break Enclave on Jaremi Four. He says 'the pilgrims will not rest until they can tread the soil of Jaremi Four at the side of the Son of God.'"

Modest tugged his upper lip. "Is there reason to believe what he says?"

"He furnished tridee footage of the converted trawler—about twenty kilometers long and bristling with inhabited pods—as well as vitae of the highly experienced mercenaries he retained to be her crew," Rybczynsky said.

Modest slumped in his throne. The bright-eyed face once loved by trillions fell into his slender hands. "Mothers of God, intercede for Us," Modest whispered. "What transpires on Jaremi Four, Alois? What, Wleti? The newest coming of Christ, or some hideous mid-orbit collision that We may watch in slow motion, but lack the power to stop?"

73. Jaremi Four—Equatorial Sea— Samu's Fleet

"**H**e went *where?*"

Ruth Griszam sprang upright in her berth.

It was happenstance that the flagship commander had encountered Samu outside, happenstance that Samu received the news in the open, on the upper deck, where Ruth had so many bugs.

They spoke of Parek, which was why Ruth's implants had wrenched her awake.

She rubbed her eyes. The stateroom porthole showed the blackness of auroraless sky. Labokloer wasn't there. *More forjeling spiritual exercises. Just as well.* She maxed her vision instead of risking a light. She yanked on boots, fatigue pants, and a silken jacket. Each jacket cuff contained an Escher lozenge. The seductive alternation—figure and ground, ground and figure—tugged at her eyes as she laced the jacket shut.

She stole outside, monitoring Samu and the flagship commander through a bubble in her awareness. "Parek and his forces are a hundred klicks inland," the flagship commander reported. "Somehow they converted their fleet into shallow-draft attack boats. They follow canals and rivers into Southland."

Samu was enormous, robed and cowled, all in black. "You're certain?"

"OmNet just released the senso. Parek's reconfigured fleet reduced a river-bank settlement to ruin in only minutes."

The flagship commander is a Galactic, Ruth realized.

"There's no mistake?" Samu demanded.

"He came ashore less than five meters from the Spectator. I know Parek when I *pov* him."

"Where did this occur?"

Samu's no pawn of his handlers, Ruth thought. *He must be Galactic himself.*

Reluctant to brandish Galactic devices on deck, even at this late hour, the flagship commander cautiously drew a small display module from his doublet and held it toward Samu. "The senso was recorded at a village located . . . here."

"Parek must have surmounted the coastal bluffs," Samu growled. "How?"

"Unknown, Excellency."

Ruth emerged onto the first surdeck, a crude wooden structure that overspread the flagship's original upper deck. Samu and the flagship commander were directly below her. Silently she peered through the latticework floor. "The binary's too noisy tonight," Samu said. "We won't be able to establish a good enough link to the island."

The island? Ruth wondered.

"To reconstruct what Parek has done, I'll need access to my most powerful strategic modelers," Samu continued. "I must go to the island at once."

The commander was aghast. "We reach the half-circle bay in less than ten days."

Samu nodded. "Understood. Unless you receive other orders from me, here is what you'll do when you get there." He grabbed the display module and twitched gloved thumbs on its controls. "Two days' sail north of the half-circular bay—*here*—there's a dry riverbed whose canyon pierces the coastal wall. See it?" The flagship commander nodded. "If I'm not back by the time you reach the canyon, land there. Send half the army ashore. Then sail with your remaining forces to the half-circle bay and make beachhead as planned."

"What's the plan?"

Samu pocketed the display. "By ducking inland, Parek's escaped slaughter at sea. But now he must travel and conquer downriver, down a canal: an impossible strategy. He is sure to bog down. When he does, we'll surround him." Samu made a hurried sign of the cross. "You've been briefed. Command is yours. God be with you." He whirled and scrambled into the aft superstructure.

Ruth followed. The surdeck narrowed to a catwalk that clung to the superstructure's exterior like webbing to a cliff. There was nothing below but sea. Ruth pressed aft, using her Spectator grace to move silently. Through open portholes she could sometimes hear the clap-clap of Samu's boots and the wheezing of his breaths. Lighter footfalls sounded, pursuing him. *The flagship commander,* she thought.

Behind the aft superstructure, the surdeck opened again into a broad wood-latticed esplanade. It was unoccupied. Darting from shadow to shadow, Ruth kept Samu in sight below her as he emerged from the aft superstructure.

Breathing heavily, he tore off his gloves. His hands were fishbelly white.

Forjeler, he's Terran, Ruth thought.

Next Samu discarded his massive robe. His face still cowled, he spoke urgently into one sleeve. "Jonah Three, this is Redfriar. I declare condition five-by-five reds. Emergency surface, position theta-alpha-epsilon. Execute in sixty, I say again six-zero, seconds."

The flagship commander burst out of the aft superstructure, scooping up Samu's cast-off clothing and snapping orders into his own sleeve. "Ahoy the bridge! Lord Samu wishes to debark aft. Clear the poop deck. Feather any lights that play aft of our stern."

Peering down through the surdeck lattice, Ruth waited for Samu to pass under a light. *Let's see what he looks like under the robe.*

Robed or not, he was enormous.

With each stride his torso bobbled like balloons angry beneath silk. His scarlet cassock was soaked with sweat. A sapphire cross bounced against his chest on a silken cord. Ruth assigned a thought engine on her bird to identify Samu's costume.

The answer came back on one of her data channels. She hadn't gone live in weeks, but this. . . .

Ruth's previous report of possible Enclave violation had been ignored. *Let them ignore this one,* she thought angrily. "*Flash flash flash!*" she subvocalized. "*This journal contains proof that the Jaremian leader Samu is a Terran and a Cardinal of the Universal Catholic Church. Confirmed massive Enclave violation, I say again, confirmed massive Enclave violation! Absolute priority, topmost precedence. Go live, go live, go live with this!*"

Below her, Samu removed his cowl. Ruth stared. He was almost bald. He had a weak chin and puffy jowls. His lips were drawn tight. Glossy black eyes were cushioned among bulging cheeks. Ruth tasked her bird with identifying his face.

Samu lumbered up a companionway. Huffing, he lunged out onto the empty poop deck. "Jonah Three, this is Redfriar," he gasped into his sleeve. "Execute."

Ruth crept onto a broad apron one level above the poop deck. It was floored with wood planking. *I'll have to watch Samu using bugs.* She shut her eyes and ran across the apron relying on her tactical sims. In her mind's eye, she followed a glowing blue line that would keep her feet above the apron's supporting beams, clear of resonant areas that might make her steps audible below.

The facial ident routine *tapped* with its report. Ruth scanned it and whistled inwardly. *"Positive ident,"* she subvocalized over the subdelta-band link. *"Positive ident! 'Lord Samu' is Ato Cardinal Semuga of the Universal Catholic Church, Terran by birth and head of the Pontifical Council for Arcane Works."*

Now that the ident routine knew to look for churchmen, it flashed her an ID on the flagship commander, too. He was Oriel Spibbert, an Ordhian and a deacon assigned to Vatican.

The apron ended short of the stern, overlooking the poop deck. As Spibbert had ordered, the poop deck was empty and dark. Ruth maxed the visual gain of the bug she was using. She saw Semuga stoop, panting spasmodically, hands on his knees.

Which was when the submarine came up.

It pierced the sea three hundred meters behind the flagship, silently and without lights. *Unamplified human vision wouldn't detect her unless you knew just where to look.*

Semuga did. "Closer, Jonah Three!" he grumbled into his sleeve.

Ruth drew an involuntary breath. The submarine's tail . . . *flexed.*

The trailing third of her hull swept to port and back to starboard. All at once, she lurched to within fifteen meters of the flagship's tail. *Piscine sub,* Ruth thought with amazement. *Swims like a fish.*

A dorsal hatch irised open in the sub's hull. A faint blue beam leapt from it, striking the poop deck a meter from Samu. It widened into a shimmering bar of light. *Tractor-beam gangplank,* thought Ruth. *Absolutely Galactic.* Ruth knew a little about piscine subs. *You need hyperplasteel for the flexible hull and Peace-Force-surplus gravity generators to isolate the crew from the hull's movements. For your trouble you get a fast and nimble vessel, able to cruise in deep ocean at five hundred klicks an hour without leaving a signature detectable from space. What the sfelb's one of those doing here?*

Grunting, Samu swung his bulk over the aft rail. He stepped onto the luminous gangplank and waddled toward the sub, the flagship's wake churning below him. Ruth smiled grimly at the image. *About the only way this could be more incriminating is if a hundred white priests jumped out of the sub and started singing "Kumbaya."*

A blond head popped up through the hatch. Below it, Ruth saw the telltale white square of a clerical collar. "Excellency! You are being *poved*. Hurry!"

Then again, Ruth realized, *a single white priest might do.*

Another bug *tapped* and squirted Ruth an image. Spibbert and an engineering

officer were sprinting aft—toward her. "The bitch's on the first surdeck!" the
officer called. He scurried up a ladder and waved Spibbert to continue ahead at
poop deck level.

Ruth frowned. *How can they know where I am? . . . Oh forjel, I'm live!* In the
excitement she'd forgotten that trivial detail. Trillions of Galactics were *poving*
OmNet and seeing what she saw as it happened. Clearly, there'd been one such
experient on the flagship's bridge and at least one more aboard the sub.

My only chance is that my eyes are still closed. Ruth had been relying on her
bugs and her tactical sims. The sims entered her awareness at a level that would
not register on her senso output; she shunted the bugs' visuals down there, too.
Anyone pov*ing me is working blind now.*

That didn't bother the engineering officer. He'd already found her. "Halt!" He
emerged from a hatchway not two meters from Ruth.

She watched him through a bug. He was black with short, straight white hair.
The facial ident came back almost instantly. *Garren Wehrman, a monsignor from
Frensa Six, assigned last year as Cardinal Semuga's engineering attaché.*

Wehrman pointed a ravisher at her. *Galactic, of course.*

"Monsignor Wehrman," Ruth said confidently. His eyes widened. "You're a
long way from Frensa Six. I'm Ruth Griszam. Yes, the one from OmNet." She held
out her arms and showed him the Escher lozenges in her cuffs. "Welcome to my no
doubt highly saybacked live feed."

The flagship commander—Spibbert—bustled up a stairway. "Labokloer's
woman?" he husked, raising his needler uncertainly.

"This is the mystery Spectator we've been searching for," Wehrman husked.

Ruth smiled. She snapped her sightless face from man to man. "A needler,
Deacon Spibbert? And Monsignor Wehrman has his ravisher." She waved aft. "And
a piscine sub. Brought out all the Galactic toys tonight, you have."

A Spectator staring at her assailants with eyes scrunched shut. Armed Galactics staring back, unable to exploit the advantage of their weapons. Trillions *poving*
it all in real time. Essayists would spend generations untangling the dynamics of
this brief stalemate. Not having the benefit of those as yet unwritten essays,
Wehrman and Spibbert could only exchange anxious glances.

Resolution came quickly.

Another bug *tap*ped for Ruth's attention. This bubble looked aft, toward the
submarine. Semuga stood behind the sub's dorsal hatch. Three black-cassocked
priests boiled up through the opening and sprinted down the invisible gangplank
toward the flagship. "Where's that Spectator?" one shouted.

"Still working blind," yelled another.

"Forjel it!" cried the priest in the lead. "She's up there somewhere!" He raised
a big military-issue stunner and maxed its angle.

"She's *poving*, you idiot!" Semuga shouted from the sub. "The Galaxy will
see."

Too late. The weapon bathed the flagship's whole aft section, diffuse but ultimately irresistible. Above, a sentry on the topmost surdeck collapsed. His steamrifle pinwheeled through the night air. Ruth maxed her autonomics. Through a bug
she watched Spibbert drop his needler. He tumbled face down onto the apron.

Wehrman groaned. His eyes rolling back in his head and he crumpled across Spibbert's back.

Despite her implants, Ruth could endure the soporific field only seconds longer.

The priests reached the flagship and vaulted onto the poop deck. *Did I see that through a bug, or are my eyes open?* She didn't know.

Subvocalizing a final command, she tottered unconscious to the planking.

At which point, of course, her live feed flickered off.

Ruth had triggered a subroutine designed for use when a Spectator died or lost consciousness in the middle of battle. It caused her satellite's thought engines to remove her from the loop and forge direct connections with her bugs instead. Without Ruth, the links between bird and bugs would be unstable. When they broke down, the bird would automatically post whatever it had recorded for Galactic distribution.

For that reason, about an hour passed before experients across the Galaxy could watch the priests scramble up to the apron, scoop up the sleeping Ruth, and carry her aboard their plainly Galactic submarine; about an hour before they *poved* the sub rotating in her own radius after one snap of her flexible tail; about an hour before they watched the dark craft slide beneath the waves with Ruth and Semuga in her belly.

About an hour before the Galaxy realized that the story of Arn Parek, his enemies on Jaremi Four, and of all their handlers had lurched in a startling new direction.

Oblivious to all that, the navy the Universal Catholic Church had built held course. Ruthlessly it steamed into the Jaremian night.

74. Jaremi Four—Somewhere

N ot yet sixteen, the young mother already trembled with the beginnings of the palsy that had struck down so many women of her line. Her son had crawled further than she approved of. She scampered after him. She noticed her right foot turning inward more markedly than before.

Seven months old, the half-naked babe crawled giggling across the barrens. A cracked earthen clod collapsed beneath him. He spilled into loose dirt. Some got in his mouth. He began to cry.

Fear dissolved into fond relief. *No damage done,* the mother noted. She reached for the child. Missed on the first try. Finally she scooped him up. She looked into the babe's eyes and smiled broadly. A chill wind passed her parted lips and struck her abcessed canine tooth. She did her best not to show the pain. Infection was rare on Jaremi Four, but when it came it brought all its accustomed terrors. Even the slightest pressure against the tooth drenched her in misery. Still, she maintained her smile and cooed at the child. She stroked grit from his hair.

She shuffled toward a rust-ribbed girder, a relic of some ancient machine whose function none had guessed at for generations. She didn't wonder, she just sat down. She exposed a pitted breast. Cold wind prodded the nipple erect even before the babe locked his mouth over it.

She gave herself over to the dim pleasure of nursing. She stared toward the northern horizon. Beyond the barrens jagged hills rose purple with distance. Beyond them, the glare of the earth gods' fires danced brighter, closer than she'd ever seen it. *An omen?* she wondered. *Mother would have thought so.* Before dying six months earlier, days after going blind, the woman's mother had fastened trembling hands about her wrists and pulled her close. "Care for your baby," the dying woman had wheezed. "He's not like us. Not just one more weary scrabbler in this dying land." She'd paused and drawn a convulsive breath. It bubbled. "Not like us. He's special."

Blinking back tears, the young mother shifted the child's weight in her arms and teased her aching tooth with her tongue. *Can that be?* she wondered dimly. *Can he be something different? How could my mother know?* She tossed her head to whisk matted hair from her eyes. The movement called a hot sensation from the roots of her bad tooth. It humped cruelly behind her eye. She did her best to ignore it. *How could my mother be wrong?* Cradling her son, the young mother nurtured an unfamiliar emotion.

She had no word for it. But it was hope.

Part Three

It is with pious fraud as with a bad action; it begets a calamitous necessity of going on.

—Thomas Paine

75. Jaremi Four—Southern Hemisphere— The Inland Canal

In the fleet's conversion for river warfare, comfort had been the first casualty. Even Arn Parek rated just two cramped compartments belowdecks in one of the lead attack boats. He sat sweating, stripped to the waist. The soles of his white boots rested on the sill of the forward cabin's broad window.

"The First Disciple," a Brethren guardsman announced.

"This cabin is so tiny," Chagrin marveled. He shrugged. "Going up the cliff in liners and down the river in smaller craft—so the god named God ordained."

"The stateroom where Ulf held me prisoner was more comfortable," Parek admitted. "Sit, sit."

Chagrin maneuvered himself beside his prophet. "Why stay down here?"

293

"The privacy is worth the heat." With one hand Parek stroked the waist of the only strumpet space allowed. A girl of thirteen at most, she lay in a fetal position. Even in sleep her naked body was beaded with droplets. He nodded toward the window. It had come as a unit from the original flagship. With its glass locked down it would be as impervious to native weapons as any metal. "This stretch of river is uninhabited, so they let me keep it open." The breeze that sighed through offered no comfort.

"You asked to see me, Word Among Us?"

"No hurry. No hurry." They watched the riverbank edge past. Through frequent gaps in the forest canopy dead trunks fingered like accusations. "The river imposes its rhythm on us," Parek mused. "It makes us take time to really see the country we're conquering. But not all of us will look."

Chagrin glanced up strickenly.

"I don't mean you." Parek drew a palm down his face. He tried uselessly to wipe off the sweat onto his leather breeches. "It's Ulf and his shallowness, his impatience. Think of it, Chagrin! It's been generations since people crossed the Equatorial Sea. We're on a different continent, a different world, really, with new plants and animals, new societies. Ulf sees none of it. He sees only obstacles—or targets."

Chagrin nodded. "Maybe that's not so bad for a general."

Parek laughed. "You and I, we're not generals. That's why I summoned you." He stared forlornly toward the riverbank. "I can't convert them."

"You make many converts!"

Parek shook his head. "I drive many villagers to their knees. Not because they accept my word, but because I blow up their chiefs."

Chagrin shrugged. "That impresses people."

"Why can't I convert one chief?" Parek chopped the air with rigid hands. "We've taken, what, eleven settlements now? In each one I try to spark some curiosity, touch some spiritual hunger in them. Each time I fail."

Chagrin rested his chin on his hands. "People don't buy what you sell. They seek what they need."

Parek's head jerked up. "Come again?"

"Just something I learned in school."

"School? You?"

"For a while, before everything fell apart," Chagrin reminisced. "Come to think of it, when order broke down I was sitting in school. I was the one who reached the teacher first. You should have seen her face. . . ."

"Chagrin. . . ."

" 'I thought it would hurt more.' That was the last thing she. . . ."

"*Chagrin!*"

"Yes, lord—" He leaned forward, his head tilted. From above there was shouting and clattering.

Guardsmen burst in. They pulled Parek away from the window.

Chagrin bustled out. In seconds he was back. "You'll want to see this," he said.

"Hail, Word Among Us!" The lieutenant was new to the Brethren. His white silk tunic all but fluoresced in the tropical sunlight. "Conqueror in the north and south, master of life and death, traveler in the aurora, architect of the Miracle of the Ships, the all-high arbiter of—"

"Thank you, Lieutenant Diazlam, but Ulf's met me before." Parek clambered onto the attack boat's foredeck, buttoning his jerkin. "What's up?"

"Intruders," Ulf growled, saluting fist-on-chest.

"You don't say. I imagine they think the same of us."

"They came by canoe," Ulf explained, glancing to starboard. A bark canoe lay upside down in a lifeboat. "These were the oarsmen." At the center of the foredeck, four young savages hunkered inside a cagework left over from the Miracle of the Ships.

"And this?"

"Their chief." Beside the cage, one autochthon stood surrounded by rifle-toting Brethren. He might have been forty. He looked older, in the Jaremian way, but he carried himself like a master all the same. Chevron tattoos adorned his cheeks. In a hand missing two fingers he clutched a scroll of partially cured animal hide.

"Kneel before The Word Among Us!" roared Diazlam.

The old chief knelt.

"They approached from astern, but he says they come from upriver," Ulf reported.

Parek lifted the chief's face toward him. "Eyes are clear," he said to no one in particular. *If he really came from upriver, he should be drugged.* "Why did you come?" Parek demanded.

The chief looked up at him without blinking. "To plead for the lives of my people."

"Why should I spare your people?"

"Because I can tell you what lies ahead." The old chief waved his hide scroll. "There are surprises."

At a gesture from Parek, Chagrin took the scroll.

"What's your name?" Parek demanded.

"I am Kaahel, chief of a domain that lies along your path."

Parek laced his fingers behind his back. "You say you come from the direction we're going. Yet you rowed up on us from behind."

"I can explain."

"Let him go," Parek told the Brethren.

Kaahel—the tribal elder who, six years before, had presided over the torture-death of Spectator Laz Kalistor—stepped tentatively forward. "Days ago a minstrel came to my domain. He sang of a mighty conqueror." Ulf and Parek exchanged startled glances. "The minstrel said when the conqueror came, first there were sickness and visions of the gods. Two days later a navy would fill the river from bank to bank. The ships would call down thunder to destroy everything. Only a handful would survive, and they only if they accepted some foolish teaching about gods in the sky."

"Silence!" Diazlam shouted. He raised a pistol.

"Hold," Parek commanded, exchanging a knowing glance with Ulf. "Continue, Chief Kaahel."

Realizing it was probably unwise to share so freely his opinion of the mighty conqueror's religion, Kaahel expelled a held breath. "Because I'd heard the minstrel's story, when my people became sick and started having visions I knew what it meant." He edged toward the fan housing across which Chagrin had spread his scroll. No one stopped him; he stepped forward confidently. "Come, mighty one. I will show you."

The scroll was a crude map. It depicted the meandering path of a waterway that was sometimes a river, sometimes a canal. "I came from here," said Kaahel, tapping a spot where the water choked its way between cliffs. "The sickness tore at us, too, but I took my strongest warriors. We forced ourselves to row." His index and pinky fingers edged upstream. The river turned a bend that opened into a broad cove. "By night we rowed through the domain of my old enemy Lormatin. They did not see us. Despite the visions, we rowed upstream all through the night, until we came upon your mighty force."

"And then?" Ulf demanded.

"We kept rowing."

"You rowed *past* us?"

Kaahel nodded. "We hugged one bank, rowing from mangrove to mangrove in the darkness. As your countless boats passed behind us, our heads began to clear. With the dawn we felt strong again. We rowed back to overtake you."

"I will see that our night sentries are more vigilant," Ulf grumbled.

Parek smiled at the old chief. "Speak no more of the visions. I call now to my sky god, that he may test the truthfulness of the knowledge you offer."

Parek prodded with his mind in the way his god named God had taught him. *"Oh god named God, hear your servant!"* he silently beseeched. *"Forgive my disturbance, but a native offers us intelligence whose value only you in your wisdom can assess."*

76. Terra—Wasatch Range, Usasector

Alrue Latier and Heber Beaman hurried to seats before the communications center's master modeling console. "We're positioning your apparent *pov* just over Parek's shoulder," a sim artist explained. "You'll see more or less what he sees." A bubble swam together in midair. The depth kept sputtering in and out. Colors looked wrong. But unquestionably, it was Kaahel's map. "Parek will hear you but not see you."

Kaahel's mangled hand swooped above the chart like a disfigured bird. "Lormatin rules this cove. He lost most of his young men a few years ago. He'll put up little resistance. But here, past Lormatin's domain, past mine—here even *your* forces may be put to rout, mighty conqueror, if you know not what lies ahead."

"That's the settlement where Linka Strasser lives," Beaman whispered.

Latier nodded. Years ago when her journals were exciting, he'd been a Linka Strasser enthusiast. "Arn, hear your god!" he called. "If this Kaahel is honest, he will tell you of ruined locks side by side that bristle with deadly traps, of a village whose defenses no one can breach, and of truss bridge fallen across the canal. Finally he will tell you of another, subsequent lock, one whose doors open onto a deep, rounded canyon."

"This is all true?" came Parek's subvocal query.

"Unfortunately yes," said Latier.

"Can the fleet overcome it?"

"Certainly," Latier boomed, ignoring Beaman's pointed shrug.

Parek jabbed an accusing finger at Kaahel. "Great is the power of my sky god," he shouted. "Through him I already know all you came to tell me: the twin locks and their traps, the deadly village, the fallen bridge, the lower lock that opens onto rocky emptiness."

Kaahel stepped backward, his face ashen. Parek's glance flicked aside, toward Ulf, Chagrin, and Diazlam. They exchanged astonished looks.

"Still, I came to help you!" Kaahel stammered. "Um, about sparing my people. . . ."

Parek sighed. "You don't understand, Kaahel. I don't need your information. I don't need you. The only way—"

A pistol barked. His face and chest imploded, Kaahel's ruined body thudded to the deck. Rifles thundered; Parek whirled. The Brethren guards had taken Kaahel's death as their cue to empty their guns into the caged oarsmen. They spewed against the bars at the back of their cage, convulsing. The deck ran crimson.

Parek stared at Diazlam. The lieutenant stood wide-eyed, his pistol still steaming, still aimed where Kaahel had stood. "I wasn't done with Kaahel!" Parek rasped.

Diazlam dropped to one knee. "So sorry, Word Among Us! I thought you said you were."

"Your zeal will undo you one day. Talk to him, Ulf."

Ulf smiled thinly. His pistol, too, was drawn and steaming. "I thought you wanted them dead, too."

"I have to be so *careful* around you!" Parek sighed. "Rise, Diazlam. You've done no real damage. Soon enough we'll meet this chief Lormatin." Parek stalked aft. He scowled down into the brown water.

Ulf joined him. "You see the obstacles ahead?" he whispered.

"Just now I am told of them," Parek replied. "Next the god named God will tell me how to master them."

"In good time, Arn Parek," Latier commanded in a voice that he hoped would mask his nervousness. "In good time. I will reestablish contact. You know, when the answer is to be revealed. Everlasting welfare unto you." He drew a finger across his broad throat.

Contact was broken.

Beaman called up maps. "Graargy's valley, where Fem Strasser lives. It must be the best-defended territory on the whole forjeling planet."

Latier nodded. "Why didn't it occur to any of us that we were sending him there?"

Beaman tapped at his tactical modeler. His ferret eyes sparkled. "If the fleet can get over the first locks, I think we can get them over the second. It will demand some ingenuity in using the equipment on the fashioners' barges, nothing more."

"By the javelin of Teancum!" Latier spat in sudden frustration.

Beaman stared up at him.

Shaking his head, Latier raised a pink lemonade to his lips. "I meant to ask Parek about those visions that afflict the tribespeople each time he strikes."

77. Jaremi Four—Southern Hemisphere— Graargy's Domain

"**D**isclaspment?" Linka Strasser breathed.

Sydeno crouched. He retrieved the three polished obsidian pebbles from the footpath where she'd dropped them and returned them one by one to a wine-stained fabric pouch. "Disclaspment," he said neutrally. "That's what the pebbles mean." Behind him, weary sunlight spangled off the oil that filmed the water of the old canal.

"Nice image," a woman drawled subvocally. *"Really plays to the pathos of the moment."*

Sydeno held out the pouch. Tradition demanded that Linka take it. She opened her jerkin and slipped the bag into her waistband. The afternoon was hot; the resulting glimpse of her sweat-beaded neck, generous breasts, and a shadowed wedge of her belly drew his eyes like a flash of fire. *Even now.* "Why disclaspment?" she asked.

Tenderly he reached inside her jerkin and flattened his palms against the subtle arch of her midriff. "We have been clasped for more than two years, and you do not come with child."

Among Graargy's people either partner could cry disclaspment after two years of barren wedlock. But few acted so quickly after the deadline passed. What could Linka say? Field Spectators were immune to pregnancy.

"I do believe I'll cry," the woman said.

Three years had passed since that festival day when the innocent fashioner Yelmir was hanged, a sacrifice to Linka's principled silence. It was at that same day that a failed invasion had cost the rival chieftain, Lormatin, most of his village's young males. Since then Linka and Sydeno had clasped and made a home behind the locks and cliffs and booby traps of Graargy's basin.

The pubescent waif Ixtlaca had come of age; sometimes Graargy chose her instead of Linka when visitors were to be entertained. Life had settled into a soft declining sameness. Linka's saybacks reflected that decline. Now and then she thought her assignment here had run its course. She thought of leaving, but never did.

"Moving on is easy. Disappear by night. Make it look like you fell into the canal." The woman laughed. *"You're the purist, Linka. Actually die! Throw yourself into one of Graargy's countless traps. That way there's no mystery, no hint of the unresolved to nourish speculation among the tribespeople."*

"Coming with child is so hard now," Linka told Sydeno. "The All-Mother says it was easier when she was a girl."

Sydeno pressed scarred hands together. "I visited Dzettko and paid for his magic. He mixed my semen with herbs and cast his runes. He declares me fertile."

"Dzettko's a doddering fool."

"Dzettko is wise."

"If he said you were infertile you'd call him crazy, too."

The morning was hot, the air choked with mist brazed white by the sun.

"Yes, please, a scenic. This is getting cloying," the woman said.

Sydeno and Linka plodded past the fallen truss bridge. Moss and rust competed to dominate its surfaces. "Linka, I want children."

She jammed balled fists into her breeches pockets. "Verina's husband stayed with her fourteen years before she came with child."

"Mm, low blow! Hit him again."

Sydeno sneered. "Freydiin was a fool. Verina's barrenness was a warning."

"A warning of what?"

"That she wasn't right inside. Freydiin should have recognized it. He should've disclasped her years ago and taken up with someone fruitful."

"Verina gave her life trying to give Freydiin a child!"

"And now Freydiin has nothing." Sydeno stepped past her and continued toward the village. She had to follow. "When Verina conceived, we all thought she and Freydiin beat the odds. But her defect had its way. It took her *and* the babe." Sydeno turned, showed her his haunted eyes. "Now Freydiin is old. No fertile woman will have him. When he dies, his line will end."

"So that's your fear?" She sidled toward him, held out an open hand.

He did not take it. Then again, he didn't pull away. "Linka, *I* want to be an ancestor."

They passed a quintet of children—more than a third of the basin's progeny, Linka realized with a start. The tykes lunged toward a fishing net some adults had just hauled onto shore. Bantering, they separated healthy fish from the tumor-ridden and deformed. One little girl held up a ghastly creature two hands long. It bifurcated just forward of the pectoral fin. Its twin heads writhed. The child hooted laughter and threw the monster back.

"See that?" Sydeno said emptily. "This isn't just my fear. Death is everywhere. When we clasped, two hundred lived in this basin. Now? A hundred and eighty-seven. Why the loss?" He gestured angrily. "Look! Just thirteen children. Not one healthy baby since Verina died two years ago. At this rate we'll disappear!"

"Where'd you get this guy? He can't write his name but he thinks he's a demographer."

Linka shrugged. "Coming with child is hard for others, too. You don't see them disclasping."

"They don't see the danger," Sydeno rumbled. He eyed Linka sadly. "The fertile must seek each other."

Realization flared into anger. "You've already picked your next claspmate," Linka snapped. "Who?"

"I've spoken to Graargy about Ixtlaca."

✦ ✦ ✦

The journal ended. After a few seconds of stiff silence the woman said, *"You've got to be kidding, Linka. You want a transfer because your native lover is jilting you?"*

Linka bit back what she felt like saying. It was night; she and Sydeno lay with their backs to each other on a thatched slumber pad. He was asleep. Linka was in Mode, conferring subvocally with her new section boss.

Linak and her new superior didn't get along; then again, they never had. Her new section boss was Neuri Kalistor.

"Answer the question," Kalistor demanded. *"Why did you lateral me this journal? Why do you want a transfer?"*

"Not because Sydeno jilted me," Linka said measuredly.

"Because that little trollop Ixtlaca gets all the best assignations, then. Now she gets your clapsmate, too." Kalistor sighed. *"Age stalks us all, darling."*

"Look, can't we put our history aside?" Linka asked. *"You're my section boss, I'm a senior field operative, and I've made a simple request for transfer."*

"Request denied. Really, Linka, if we were meeting face to face I would raise a glass to you—a widow's toast. Now we've both lost a man on this hideous planet."

"For vacuum's sake, Neuri—you of all people should know that Sydeno is nothing to me. What's one autochthon in the hay more or less? I lie back and think of Enclave."

"With you it's always Enclave," Kalistor sneered.

"Exactly. And that's why I'm through in Graargy's basin. Sydeno's grown obsessed with my inability to conceive."

"Lots of women can't. Southland is poisoned."

"But that's not the reason why I can't conceive," Linka explained. *"It's my implants."*

"And I know that you of all people will never tell him that. It won't endanger your cover." Kalistor paused to make sure her next barbed statement would sink deep. *"Then again, if it does, you can always call down a snuff."*

"This is a simple request," Linka insisted. *"I'm entitled to this, even from you."*

"Actually, you're not."

"Perhaps I should take this over your head," Linka threatened. *"Do you think the higher-ups will find your management style irregular?"*

"Not when the complaint comes from a Spectator whose saybacks are a dismal as yours have been. This is OmNet, Linka—you know fairness isn't even an abstraction here." Kalistor chuckled. *"Anyway, none of this is my doing. The block on your transfer came from the higher-ups."*

Linka was nonplussed. *"Someone told you not to allow me a transfer?"*

"Paranoia ill becomes you," Kalistor said harshly. *"It isn't just you, all deep cover assignments along the canal have been frozen pending future developments."*

"What future developments?"

"You'll know soon enough. Kalistor out."

78. Jaremi Four—Southern Hemisphere— Lormatin's Domain

F uture developments weren't long in coming.

Lormatin's subjects had staggered from their huts into the dawn. Dreams had jangled their nerves and thrust them from slumber. Some complained of hearing voices or music. One teenage boy said everything he looked at was fringed by multiple shimmering boundaries. As the day wore on, some experienced visions of the gods. Others simply took ill; retching, sweating, they clung to their slumber pads.

By noon fewer than a dozen of the settlement's hundred and forty people could function. Spectator Tramir Duza only feigned disability. His implants reported neutralizing some psychotoxin they could not identify.

Duza realized this might be his last day covering Lormatin's domain, two settlements up the canal from Graargy's valley.

A woman hunkered on hands and knees, snarling "I see it! Don't you see it?" to no one at all. A one-armed man lay on sodden leaves staring into the sky. His expression was beatific though his wrist rested on the firestone, his only hand a finger's width from flame. The skin bubbled and peeled back, exposing bone. He didn't notice.

Duza stepped toward the wooded shoreline. He reached the canal shore just as the first attack boat cruised into sight. She was twenty-five meters long. Enormous windows ran the length of her bulwark. Behind their protection, redundantly armored figures regarded the shore. The boat's foredeck bristled with cannons, fans, and searchlights. No villager could guess the composition or purpose of such objects; until now, none of them had seen a metal object bigger than two splayed hands.

"No rowers. No oars," said a trembling old villager huddled against a tree trunk.

"The gods move it with their breath," explained a palsied woman. She sounded like she was watching them do it.

The attack boat drifted to a stop.

Nothing happened.

Affecting aimlessness, Duza zigzagged toward the shore. Freshwater mangrove trees floated in dense colonies. The Spectator leapt aboard one. Squeezing forward among the clustered boles, he peered upriver. The first boat was followed by armored speedsters, graceless barges packed with troops, artillery boats with their gunners contemptuously in the open, enclosed transports, small fashioners' barges laden with gridwork and hidden riflemen, victualing scows, and boxy ordnance ships. All the craft moved without oars. They formed lines, three or four abreast. The naval column extended the length of the village's shoreline—not dozens of boats nor scores, but hundreds.

And thousands of soldiers as well.

From the fleet came rhythmic chiming. *Clang-shang-ralang. Clang-shang-*

ralang. *Clang-shang-ralang.* *Clang-shang-ralang.* *Clang-shang-ralang.* **Clang-***shang-ralang.*

Duza drew back behind a mangrove trunk, glancing back toward the village. His stomach went hollow. Too addled to take cover, the villagers were all shambling *toward* the river. Some walked, others crawled, but most swayed drunkenly. Drawn by the sound of the chiming, they converged, clotting the bank. *What is this for-jeling psychotoxin?* Duza wondered, sick inside. *Did it come from the boats?*

Clang-*shang-ralang.* The chiming ceased. From the fleet, a voice cried: "Like the fire, spread His Word!"

Duza leapt ashore. He sprinted inland and leapt into a gully.

No one else moved.

Rifles crackled from the boats. Classic Jaremian weapons: all power, no finesse. Villagers' chests and abdomens burst open, faces exploded, arms and legs blew free. Men and women fell amid clouds of gore. Teeth and fingers and toes tumbled in air. Bodies rotated, spewing away parts, slapping onto now-sodden ground.

Bullets disintegrated a serving table piled high with *fhlet,* spewing chunks of wood. Earthenware shards. Those near it fell seizing, riddled by fragments.

Explosive rounds poured into the mangrove trees, clearing additional lines of fire. Half a dozen more villagers fell amid whistling bark and wood chips. Sundered, branches slashed down. One snapped a woman's legs in two. Another crushed a boy of eight.

Repeater rifle fire slashed into a knee-high ridge; the shells burst through the other side in showers of clay. Those behind the grassy crest collapsed, blood spewing from pulped shins and severed ankles.

All that was missing were reactions on the part of those so brutally slaughtered. None of the villagers made the connection between the strange boats, the river, and this hail of fire, noise, and death. *Psychotoxin aside, they've never seen anything fiercer than a fire arrow.*

Mortars *whoomp*ed. Huts dilated in blooms of yellow flame. A stray round landed among four men not far from Duza. Heat drew his cheeks taut. Shock pressed him back. The flash left a lingering afterimage of bodies spouting skyward, limbs distended at crazy angles.

Finally grasping a threat, Lormatin's people stared in every wrong direction. Up at the sky. Toward an inland ridge.

Finally a handful recognized the need to run. Duza joined them. He leapt over bodies and fallen branches. He passed a hunch-backed village woman. A round struck her from behind. The impact spun her and thrust her into Duza face-first, her body ruptured from sternum to navel. Duza dashed on.

He glanced down at himself. His collision with the dying woman had left him painted with her blood. Deliberately, he sprawled headlong and came to rest sitting upright, his back against a boulder. He looked like he'd been shot. Now he could lay in the open, yet *pov* in safety—if safety was the word.

Nearer the water, an elderly archer had figured out where the enemy was. He stepped from behind a rock and let fly. A gunner aboard an open-decked boat fell grabbing for the arrow in his neck. On deck, marksman brought up his rifle. The defiant archer pushed forward a wood and leather shield, thinking it would protect him. The marskman's rifle barked. The archer tumbled back in a cloud of his own fluids. His shield arm was gone below the elbow. His face was a mask of astonishment.

"Enough!" blared an amplified voice from the river. "Everlasting welfare unto those who remain. Gather them."

The survivors exchanged wide-eyed glances. The din and carnage were beyond their ability to process. But this enormous voice that boomed back from nearby cliffs—that could excite their sense of wonder.

Through thickening smoke Duza watched an ungainly transport power itself onto the bank. Troops in leather body armor surged ashore. Some gripped nets, some lassos, others truncheons. The only lethal weapons they carried were holstered pistols. All along the bank, transports and landing craft and attack vessels sliced through wet clay and thudded to rest. They disgorged their human cargoes.

"Do not resist and you won't be harmed," boomed the amplified voice.

The first of the black attack boats scraped onto the muddy bank. A cluster of men on deck strode toward her bow. Riflemen ringed the group's periphery. At its center were two figures: one was a hawk-nosed general wearing ornamented fatigues beneath a white fabric cape, the other a tall ebony man clad head to toe in snowy white leather. An upside-down triangle was shaven into his close-cropped pate. A gray scar lanced across his right cheek.

Ulf and Parek, Duza realized. He appended a special-handling notice to the journal he was recording. *I'll make a fortune today. Let's hope I don't die, I hate that.*

"Find the chief!" Parek called out, booming. The amplified voice was his. Parek descended a ladder from the deck of the beached attack boat. He stepped ashore, clutching a bulky but functional wireless microphone. "Bring me the chief!" he commanded. Troopers and Brethren fanned out across the settlement.

Microphones? Public address systems? Duza thought. *On Jaremi Four?*

Duza tugged off the blood-soaked tunic and rose to his feet as clumsily as he could.

A small fashioners' barge scraped ashore behind Parek. A dozen men debarked. Two by two, they hauled ashore sections of metal trusswork. Parek waved his hand toward a modest knoll where the fashioners commenced to assemble a prefabricated stage.

"Where's the chieftain?" Brethren guards barked. They spun passing villagers around and hauled up the fallen to inspect their faces. "The chieftain!" Following the Brethren came a wave of troops. With glinting knives they dispatched the seriously wounded. A single slash across the throat and on to the next. With lassos and prodsticks, still other Brethren gathered those who could stand, herding them toward the stage.

They found Lormatin, Duza realized. Three prod-wielding Brethren drove Lormatin forward, cloak swirling. He was a riot of hues: golden feathers, green enameled found-metal shingles, and scraps of red and blue fabric. Blood gave one arm a morbid sheen. "The chieftain! The chieftain!" shouted the troopers.

Parek and Ulf had mounted the prefab stage. "Bring him here," Parek called. Hands pushed Lormatin forward. He fell onto both knees.

Troopers arrayed the remaining villagers facing the stage in a half-ring around their leader. Fewer than twenty had survived.

"Greetings," Parek rumbled into his microphone.

Villagers lurched backward at the giant sound. Blows from the troopers returned them to their places.

Parek leaned close to the chieftain. "I am the conflagration who has come for you," he said.

Lormatin raised one bushy eyebrow. He said, "Mm-hmm." Parek's microphone picked up his voice, too. It thundered from the fleet's loudspeakers. Lormatin's eyes widened.

"I am Arn Parek."

Diazlam rushed to the chieftain's side. "Worship The Word Among Us!" he screamed. Eyes wide with zeal, he kicked Lormatin in his wounded bicep. Lormatin fell writhing. Troopers pulled him back to his knees. Diazlam swung a mailed hand across Lormatin's mouth. Blood streaked down the chieftain's chin.

"Yes, yes," Parek said impatiently. "The necklace."

Diazlam turned. A sergeant sprinted up, clutching an ornately sculpted wooden box. Diazlam swung the box open and drew out an outsized necklace made from small metal plates. "Behold!" Diazlam shouted. "The Amulet of Truth."

Parek nodded anxiously. "On his neck, today, please."

Two troopers steadied the groaning Lormatin as the lieutenant lowered the bulky necklace onto his shoulders. From beneath its back clasp, the lieutenant drew a slim metal cylinder with a shiny red button on one end. A long twisted wire connected it to the necklace. *A piezo detonator,* Duza realized. *Must be explosives in the amulet. Clever, these Parekists.* Diazlam stepped forward and handed Ulf the cylinder with the red button.

Parek hopped offstage and swaggered before Lormatin. "We come from the north with boats that propel themselves and weapons that thunder death from great distances. Tell me, whom do you worship?"

"The gods beyond the hills. Doesn't everybody?" Lormatin blinked to hear his own voice again cast back, louder than thunder.

"They are false gods!" Parek husked.

"At night we see their council fires on the horizon," Lormatin objected.

Parek squatted. Snarled at Lormatin. "I am come to proclaim a new truth. The gods beyond the hills are an illusion, a lie. The true gods live high in the sky, further north than you can imagine." He swept the air with a gloved hand. "I proclaim the sky gods whose fires illuminate my homeland—from above. Accept my teachings or die." He raised his head toward the tiny audience. "That choice faces you all."

Lormatin spat out a tooth. He said nothing.

"You've heard the truth," Parek cried. "I command you, convert!" The last word echoed once, twice from the cliffs. Rising, Parek circled Lormatin. His voice grew hypnotic. "And when you shall receive these things, I would exhort you to ask the great sky god if these things are not true; and if you shall ask with a sincere heart, with real intent and faith, then he will manifest the truth into you through his power."

Sfelb, that sounds familiar, Duza thought.

"Will you convert?" Parek demanded.

It occurred to Lormatin that he could use Parek's microphone to make a final defiant gesture before what remained of his people. "You say you are from the north," he called. "Legend says you live beyond the sea, beneath a sky filled with fire. Us, we only know four lights in the sky. There's the light of the sun, the mocking light of the stars, the council fires of the gods." His face contorted into a mask of hate. "Finally there is the light that long ago ravaged our lands, bringing fire and death. Is that what you're made of, foul intruder?"

Parek withdrew the microphone. He stepped back onstage. The troopers clasping Lormatin's arms released him and trotted away.

"Sky gods!" Parek cried. "Revenge yourself upon this savage for his disrespect!" Abruptly Parek spread his feet, thrust his arms skyward. It was the pose he'd struck when he called down the Miracle of the Ships.

Ulf squeezed the red button. The necklace detonated. Lormatin's head and shoulders vanished in greasy flame. His body pitched forward; the explosion had scooped it open from the sternum up. The villagers retreated until they felt the troopers' prodsticks.

Parek let the moment decay. Gradually he lowered his arms. "Now who will accept my Word?" he demanded.

One by one, survivors came forward. They dropped to their knees.

After a moment, Duza did too.

"The prophet has spoken," shouted Lieutenant Diazlam. "The thinking is done."

The Brethren wrestled the kneeling survivors into a ragged line. Parek and Ulf and Diazlam moved down the line. Parek would lay a hand on each villager's head and pronounce some mumbled absolution.

Parek came to Duza. He eyed the Spectator up and down. "This one dies," he told Ulf.

Duza never had time to be surprised, much less to feel the percussion round sunder his brain.

79. The *Bright Hope*

To be precise, it was fifty-three minutes after Ruth Griszam collapsed on the surdeck of Samu's flagship when OmNet received the journal her satellite had assembled from the output of her bugs. The network expended just nine minutes in legal vetting and promo, then rushed the journal into release. It hit the program queues precisely sixty-two minutes after the event it documented.

Galaxy-wide, trillions set aside their activities to learn what had happened to Ruth. They *poved* the three white priests from the piscine sub scrambling aboard Samu's flagship, carrying the unconscious Ruth over the aft rail, crossing a plainly Galactic tractor-beam gangplank to a plainly Galactic submarine which already contained an unmasked Cardinal.

"Fem Wachieu," Eldridge called after a minute, "how's the comm traffic running?"

"No change," said Wachieu's many-eyed spider. "Continuous communiqués. Trial balloons. Interim policy statements. Provisional orders. Taken as a whole they're incoherent. The ones that mention *Bright Hope* place us under conflicting orders to take no action and to save the day at any cost."

"As though we had any idea what 'saving the day' might entail." Eldridge glanced sourly toward the main tactical display. A pale brown orb capped with white, girdled with blue, Jaremi Four hung mockingly before the stars. "It sums up to this: God's on his world and all's wrong in the heavens."

"Captain!" Wachieu shifted nervously on her web. "All was not wrong in the heavens when you spoke, but it is now. A big ship just ramped out of transphotic on the periphery of the Jaremi system. It is not, repeat *not* PeaceForce."

"Condition scarlet!" Eldridge ordered.

"We're already at condition scarlet," Gavisel reminded her.

Eldridge nodded. "Let's see the intruder."

In the main tactical display, the image of Jaremi Four was replaced by the static-laced image of a heavy cargo trawler twenty kilometers long. At her bow, a distended command section bristled with tubes and antennae. A half-klick aft, the propulsion module loomed, domed and immense. Cerenkov radiance flickered from the forward-facing braking drivegates. Behind that stretched a nineteen-kilometer main spine to which had been lashed a menagerie of pods. Tiny in relation to the trawler, each pod was nonetheless a bulbous vastness capable of sustaining over a thousand people.

"That crazy Steward wasn't bluffing," Eldridge breathed. "This has to be his pilgrim trawler."

"Confirmed," Wachieu announced. "Its name is *Damocles,* a modified heavy trawler of Ordhian registry, reportedly carrying forty thousand pilgrims. The ambient electromagnetic noise will preclude my confirming the passenger count until she gets closer."

"Understood." Eldridge clasped six hands behind her back. "Fem Wachieu, continue monitoring the intruder. Fem Gavisel, apprise High Command of our situation." Eldridge didn't need to ask how long before reinforcements might arrive. She knew. *Too long.*

"*Damocles* is closing," Wachieu reported. "Trajectory suggests planned direct insertion into a close parking orbit over Jaremi Four."

"Give me a channel," Eldridge ordered. "Attention, *Damocles;* attention, *Damocles.* This is Captain Laurien Eldridge, commanding the schooner *Bright Hope* of the Galactic Confetory PeaceForce. You have entered a planetary system that is under Enclave protection. Do not proceed."

"This is *Damocles,*" a tinny voice returned. "We will assume a standard parking orbit over planet four."

"Negative. *Damocles,* you are violating the Enclave Statutes. I am authorized to use necessary force."

"The force that would be necessary is our destruction," replied the voice from *Damocles.* "You may have the weaponry for that, but have you the will to exterminate forty thousand civilians?"

Eldridge gestured for Wachieu to cut the comm link. "Fem Gavisel! Full power to gunnery."

"Pardon?" The interjection came simultaneously from Gavisel and Wachieu.

"Whatever weapons this scow was fitted with for the Tuezi encounter, heat 'em up. If they're watching their susceptors, they'll see us charging up." Eldridge lowered her head. "Wachieu, resume the comm link." Louder, she said, "I say again, *Damocles*, you are violating the Enclave Statutes. If you do not come about and keep station on the periphery of the Jaremi system, I will fire." She glanced at a secondary tactical display. *Damocles*'s progress toward Jaremi Four did not slow.

"I must tell you," said the voice from *Damocles*, "we are prepared to die. We will stride the meadows of Jaremi Four beside our god-man or die in the attempt."

I doubt that, Eldridge thought. *Your passengers are fanatics, but you are mercenaries. You intend to survive this.* "Final warning," she called in stentorian tones. "Alter your trajectory at once."

"Impossible," said the voice. "Like the fire we cleave to His Word. Like the fire we will cleave to Him."

"Bluff and counterbluff," Gavisel said *sotto voce*.

Eldridge shook her head. "Power up the Panna drive accumulators. Maybe they'll think they're more weapons."

"What the sfelb!" said Wachieu. Lightnings flashed across the virtual sky: pinks and cyans and oranges, colors not normally part of the bridge's palette. "Captain, I've lost control over the main tactical display."

All eyes snapped to the sky above the windswept plateau. The image of *Damocles* broke up. In its place floated a PeaceForce admiral, puffy-cheeked, with medium brown skin, red hair, and green eyes. His uniform doublet was a riot of medals.

"Admiral Hafen?" Eldridge rasped.

The admiral cocked his head. "Ah, Eldridge. It's been so long. I wish we could meet under less harried circumstances. Look, a quorum of the Privy High Council has contacted me. They're disturbed that you've heated up your weapons and threaten to annihilate forty thousand pilgrims."

"It is a deterrent only," Eldridge explained. "I hope to bluster them out of assuming close orbit."

"I know that," Hafen said sharply. "Nonetheless, the Councilors feel your 'bluster' creates the appearance of pressing guns to the heads of women and children."

"I enforce the Enclave statute," Eldridge replied. "As the Admiral knows, Enclave requires prevention of unauthorized contact between Galactics and protected autochthons regardless of the cost in Galactic lives. In fact, I believe that is the statute's wording."

"It is," Hafen acknowledged. "But *Damocles* hasn't violated Enclave. She threatens to enter an illegal orbit, yes, but that's not contact with the autochthons. In this context, your threat to destroy the ship, bluff or no, is getting horrible saybacks." He flashed Eldridge a mischievous half-smile. "Oh sfelb, I guess they didn't want me to mention that."

Eldridge and Gavisel exchanged weary nods. *The situation hasn't become serious enough to justify ignoring public opinion*, thought Eldridge, *and the public thinks I'm being a bully. Ahh, government-by-sayback.* She forced cordiality into her voice. "Understood, Admiral. Chilling the weapons banks now. *Damocles* will be permitted to assume its parking orbit," Eldridge said. "Permission to speak freely?"

Hafen's gesture confided that protest would be useless. Nonetheless, it was a nod. Eldridge asked, "Have the Privy High Councilors any, ah, strong preferences regarding *Bright Hope*'s next action?"

"I understand, Eldridge. Nobody likes to be micromanaged. But I hope you will understand: the Councilors are under enormous public pressure. Ruth Griszam's identification of Cardinal Semuga has loosed a real plorg storm. Hafen out." The admiral's image vanished from the tactical display.

"Captain!" Wachieu called. "*Damocles* has assumed its parking orbit."

Eldridge crossed three pairs of arms. "Here we are indeed," she proclaimed, quoting the ironic invocation she'd given when *Bright Hope* had arrived at Jaremi Four. "This world that no one is supposed to visit verges on a serious parking problem."

80. Terra—Wasatch Range, Usasector

Alrue Latier leaned forward, meaty elbows on his golden desk. His fingers stroked the bindings of the elegantly bound, oversized fifteen-volume set of The Book of Mormon he displayed there. "We face three mysteries," Latier told Heber Beaman. "One, what is this epidemic of sickness and visions that precedes each of Parek's landfalls, and is he controlling it? Two—"

"Actually, that's three," Beaman said helpfully.

"What are you talking about?"

Beaman's fingers traced figures in the air that held meaning only for him. "Mystery number one is the epidemic of sickness and visions before Parek invades. Mystery number two is whether Parek controls the epidemic and isn't telling us. They're separate problems, it seems to me. Now, as for mystery number three—" Beaman held out his palms.

"Yes?" demanded Latier.

Beaman shrugged. "You didn't say what mystery number three is."

Latier shook his head. "All right, Heber. Mystery number three is, why haven't the sickness and visions struck in Graargy's domain? Everyone but Linka Strasser should be vomiting and walking into trees and seeing ground nymphs in their own excrement by now—and they're not. Why has that tribe alone been spared, assuming that Parek controls the phenomenon?"

"That's mystery number two again."

Latier raised his hands for quiet. "Heber, Heber—when you came to me, penniless, ostracized because you'd tried to live by the old doctrines of polygamy without allowing your plural wives plural husbands in return . . . when you came to me, I took you in."

"I thought you chose me because of my tendency toward precision." Beaman's ferret eyes sparkled. "I'm trying to be precise."

"One can be too precise." Latier tugged at his sweat-stained temple garment. "Now what of the Catholic fleet?"

"No mystery there."

"By the prophecies of Nephi, sing hosanna."

Beaman consulted a pocket modeler. "The man who may be Cardinal Semuga has debarked. So has the Spectator Ruth Griszam, if less voluntarily. Yet one Spectator still sails with the fleet, and his or her cover remains secure. So we can still track the fleet's movements via OmNet. Yesterday, in keeping with Samu's orders, Admiral Spibbert dropped half his land forces at the mouth of a canyon that's at most a week's march from Graargy's domain. The fleet continues toward its planned beach-head at the half-circular bay. It should arrive tomorrow." Beaman shook his head. "Parek's attack down the canal is full of weaknesses, and Spibbert is capitalizing on them. No doubt he aims to trap Parek in a pincers between two infantries."

"By Martin Harris's mortgage!" Latier slammed his meaty hands on the desktop. His tumbler toppled. Pink lemonade soaked the leopard skin blotter. "So matter-of-factly you say they'll skewer Parek like righteous swords through the Lamanites. Time and again we've spoken about taking direct action against these Catholic forces. Now they're dispersing. They'll be harder to kill. Why haven't you acted?"

"You know our options are limited."

"With our primary satellite's heavy manufacturing module dead, we have only one option," Latier agreed darkly. "But if we don't exercise it before they make beach-head, we won't have even that. Now stop this foot-dragging!"

Beaman flattened his palms on his legs. "What you ask is not easy. To kill so many."

Latier snorted. "Autochthons."

"There's one Spectator left."

"And it'll be a pity to lose him—or her," Latier said. "We'll receive no more intelligence as to the fleet's movements. But think, Heber. The fleet's dispersing. Already they've set half their people ashore. Day before yesterday a single strike could have annihilated them all; now the best we can hope for is to kill half of them." Latier stepped around the desk. He sat immediately next to Beaman. "Recall the Book of Mormon patriarchs, Heber. Mormon smote his tens of thousands, as did Nephi, Mosiah, Moroni, and all the rest. At some point each stood in blood up to his knees and kept on swinging a voracious sword. Yet each did so in righteousness."

Beaman stared into Latier's eyes like a Gwilyan brine slug contemplating a spearstick. He said nothing.

" 'And mountains shall cover them, and whirlwinds shall carry them away, and buildings shall fall upon them and crush them to pieces and grind them to powder,' " Latier quoted. " 'And they shall be visited with thunderings, and lightnings, and earthquakes, and all manner of destructions, for the fire of the anger of the Lord shall be kindled against them, and they shall be as stubble, and the day that cometh shall consume them, saith the Lord of Hosts.' The passage concludes: 'I, Nephi, have seen it, and it well nigh consumeth me before the presence of the

Lord; but I must cry unto my God: Thy ways are just.' " Latier edged back. He projected the force of his commitment into Beaman's eyes. "His ways *are* just, Heber.
You must be His agent. Do His work, and do it soon. Remember, the enemy
threatens Parek."

Beaman laughed darkly. "I've never been a mass murderer before."

"Nor have I. But now we will be." Latier grasped Beaman's wrists. "We are
mass murderers. Say it, Heber."

Tonelessly he repeated, "We are mass murderers."

"Be a soldier of the Lord, Heber. May thine arm be strong . . . and *fast.*"

Beaman nodded. His eyes stung. "Remember, First Elder, a PeaceForce
schooner now orbits Jaremi Four. Its susceptors are extremely sensitive." He called
up a quasiperiodic ephemeris. "Our strike must be deadly, but it also must not be
detected. The binary's been very quiet this week. Conditions may not permit the
kind of strike we'd like to mount."

Latier frowned. "Joseph Smith did not quail before unfavorable odds."

Beaman ran knobby fingers through thinning red hair. "True, First Elder. On
the other hand, Joseph Smith died in jail."

"Listen carefully, Heber. Whether or not you think conditions permit it, our
strike *must* fall before the rest of Samu's land forces move ashore, regardless of
risk. Don't disappoint me."

81. Vatican

"Learned doctors," Rybczynsky said grandly. "None can hear us here."

Theologians Sfix Geruda and Xyrel Hjinn exchanged uneasy glances. The
chamber was a walk-through tridee of Michelangelo's *The Creation.* They stood
among cloyingly puffy clouds. God floated overhead, a muscular codger in a
medieval hospital gown. His bulging arm arched downward, concentrating its
energy into a single curling finger. Below reclined Adam, nude and uncomprehending.

"Dreadful, isn't it?" Rybczynsky asked. His tone gave the theologians no clue
how to respond. "A gift from some wealthy donor on a backwater world. The terms
of the gift obliged us to install it on Vatican, but they did not require us to display
it. And so I keep it in this insulated vault within the planet's mantle."

The theologians nodded. Their tentative steps and hunched shoulders
betrayed just how conscious they were of the semimolten rock that surrounded this
chamber and the miles of lithosphere impending above their heads.

Rybczynsky leaned one elbow against a cloud. As always, his simar's pleats were
perfect, his pectoral cross elegantly luminous. "I brought you here to probe with me
an especially puzzling aspect of Parek's, shall we say, ministry. The sickness."

Geruda nodded, stroking his weak chin. "The nausea and visions that weaken
the target peoples before Parek's fleet subdues them."

Rybczynsky nodded. From a nearby cloud rose an immense strategic modeler, essentially a floating table configured for three. "Sit, please."

What choice did they have? The theologians aligned themselves with two of the table's flattened areas. They bent their legs. Polychairs writhed up from the cloud to support them. Rybczynsky, Hjinn, Geruda: each pressed flattened palms to the brushed-metal surface. Their arms became paralyzed; the table's thought engines intercepted the nerve impulses and directed them elsewhere. By willing tiny movements of their arms and hands, they could collaborate in teasing apart elaborate concepts in the workspace above the table's center.

A bubble opened in midair. It suggested exaggerated crystal mountains, tall rough fingers spurting upward like inverted icicles. Two such spires assumed brighter colors. They pressed forward in the image without appearing to change their size. "Here is how far I've progressed on my own," Rybczynsky said. "The spindly peak to your left plots sickness among Southland river tribes whom Parek has conquered. The peak to the right plots the visionary hallucinations. The two phenomena occur simultaneously, but the conjunction between them remains obscure."

Hjinn frowned. At his thought, the twin pinnacles rotated. An adjustment deepened the relief in the tangled landscape at their base. There was little meaning there. "These datascapes are not enough to lead us to a solution."

Geruda arched an eyebrow. He had been exploring the datascapes Rybczynsky had already compiled. They intertwined like columns of backlit type on inter-secting planes of crystal. "Excellency, have you checked each of these data-scapes?"

"Yes."

Hjinn scanned Geruda's display. "Have you cross-referenced them?"

"Not in every permutation."

Hjinn tabbed in filter settings. "In my textual redactions I use certain heuris-tics. Sometimes they lead toward a solution of a problem whose parameters are not entirely understood."

Rybczynsky stared at the n-dimensional polygon Hjinn was building. "Remarkable. This is instinct personified in code."

"Your Excellency is too generous," Hjinn said abstractedly. "It's a long shot."

"What are you sorting against?" asked Geruda.

Hjinn's fingers danced. "On one dimension, His Excellency's existing datas-cape of Parek's intentions. On another, a datascape derived from OmNet, a factor matrix of Parek's capabilities."

"A reverse engineering strategy," Rybczynsky said. "Intriguing."

"Execute," said Hjinn. Immediately two new protuberances surged up beside the original peaks. "And sometimes long shots come in," he whispered. The pair of spires had become a foursome. A glowing relationship bridge sparked between the peaks. Within it red-hot lines coalesced, a throbbing tetrahedron of dependence.

"What's the common point?" Geruda demanded.

"That's strange," Hjinn said vaguely. He exploded the graphic into higher magnifications. "The same thing keeps coming back," he said, baffled.

"What is it?" asked Rybczynsky.

"It seems irrelevant." Hjinn wrinkled his nose. "A survey article on a hallu-cinogen from Terra. What good is that?"

"It looms so bright in the datascape," Rybczynsky observed. "Play it."

Shrugging, Hjinn stabbed an imaginary switch.

"*Claviceps purpurea,*" a dry voice intoned. "A fungus that infects certain grains of ancient Terra, particularly rye or *Secale cereale.* The infection is known as *ergot.* The active ingredient is ergonovine, a component of the intermittently pop-ular folk hallucinogen lysergic acid. From the so-called Middle Ages until approx-imately 1750 A.D. local, many communities in Europe and the North American colonies subsisted on bread and flour made from rye. Ergonovine survived milling and baking, so that humans who consumed foods made from infected rye also suf-fered its effects. Ergot epidemics frequently followed cool wet summers, which encouraged fungus infestation. Consumption of ergoty grain led to convulsions, gangrene, and hallucinations. The symptoms often received mystical interpreta-tions. The Great Awakening, a religious revival that swept the North American colonies between 1720 and 1750 local, is believed to have been triggered by ergot poisoning. Thousands of persons experienced ecstatic visions. Others displayed convulsive behavior so vivid that enthusiasts were called *holy rollers.* Outbreaks largely ended after about 1750 local," the recitation concluded, "after most com-munities largely abandoned rye for wheat, a grain *Claviceps* cannot infect."

A man without Rybczynsky's dignity would have whistled. "I see I did well to bring you here."

Geruda shook his head. "The symptoms seem parallel. But ergot poisoning takes weeks or months to develop. Parek's victims develop symptoms within hours."

"Parek's not using the Terran fungus," Hjinn observed. "The Jaremian analog may work faster or employ a more efficient vector." He manipulated filters. The original peaks in the datascape display faded. Now the modeler's full resources would be trained on finding connections between the two newer peaks. "Let's see what, if anything, connects Parek's intentions and his capabilities."

A blinding bar of light lanced between the two virtual mountaintops.

"Navel lint of Bentito Ynez," Rybczynsky cursed without thinking.

"Judging from its color and smell, it contains a senso clip," Geruda said. "Let's *pov* it."

Suck, rush, wrench.

It was Ruth Griszam's journal from more than three years ago, before Parek's public ministry began, the journal in which Griszam broke into a store room at the old dam to investigate the parcels Parek and Ulf and Chagrin had hidden there. "Is this ever old," Hjinn breathed. "Willim Dultav hasn't even been killed yet."

Clueless, they watched through Ruth's eyes as she inspected the metal vials filled with whitish powder. The redundantly lined vials filled with a dark, granular substance, labeled CAUTION: MOTHER MATTER. The cylinders loaded with clear plastic tubes, each containing the dual-stemmed spike of some Jaremian grain plant, distended by a knobby black mass. It, too, bore a label: RAW MATTER.

✦   ✦   ✦

"A Jaremian grain parasite," Hjinn said when the journal was over.

"Obviously something of great importance to Parek," commented Rybczynsky. "He would later brave a forest fire to reclaim these materials before Ulf and Chagrin led him away from the dam."

Geruda was entering parameters so furiously that his upper arms twitched with the energy of it. In the bubble above the table concepts swirled together like self-assembling jewels. Like searchlights, expert hunt routines crisscrossed it. Points of light shimmered. One zoomed forward and resolved into a datacrawl. "Exhibit one," Geruda declared. "A standard biosummary from the Confetory's initial survey of Jaremi Four. It describes the grain species to which those infected specimens belonged. And yes, there is a native fungus parasite which infests it."

"Biological parasitism on a world other than Terra?" Rybczynsky said, genuinely surprised.

"Indigenous ecosystems are as rich with parasites and symbionts and pathogens and what-have-you as any on Terra," Hjinn chided. "It's just that on other worlds the native flora employ amino acids whose chirality is opposite to that which developed on Terra."

"Chirality?" Rybczynsky echoed.

"Bear with me, I'm passing on biological concepts that are wholly outside my training. When my mind parts from this document I'll need to consult the transcript of this meeting just to see what I said." Hjinn blinked. "Excellency, chirality is a property of amino acids, the building blocks of life. By the rules of chemistry, the carbon chains that compose amino acids could assemble themselves in either of two orientations. Think of a screw with a left-handed thread or one with a right-handed thread."

"I see," said Rybczynsky, not sure he did at all.

"Living things settle on one orientation or the other, and then use it exclusively. Across the Galaxy, indigenous life forms selected the right-handed form. For unknown reasons living things on Terra adopted the left-handed form."

"And became the ancestors of us all." Rybczynsky stroked his cheeks. "That's the reason why on most worlds, humans can eat only plants and animals descended from the food species established by the enigmatic Harvesters at the time human stock was introduced."

"Precisely," Hjinn said. "Left-handed life forms can derive nutrition only from plant and animal tissues of like chirality, and vice versa. Foodstuffs of the opposite chirality are processed in the digestive tract—they are identical from a chemical point of view—but the organism obtains no nourishment from them. The same holds for symbiosis, parasitism, and all the other complex ways living things interact."

"I grasp your point," Rybczynsky said. "We tend to think that parasitism occurs only on Terra, but that simply reflects our human bias."

"Correct, Excellency. Only on Terra is the entire *biota* capable of metabolizing human tissue. On most worlds humans and their food species stand outside the native ecosystems, and so people don't pay the native systems the heed they should." Hjinn rubbed his temples. Plainly manipulating this unfamiliar knowledge was taking its toll. "Nonetheless, on Jaremi Four as on most worlds, right-handed viruses and microbes and fungi can prey only on other right-handed life forms. As far as they're concerned, the humans and their food species aren't even there."

"Wait a minute," Geruda demanded. "We're spending all this time talking about a parasite that infests a grain the Jaremians do not consume?"

"It's indigenous," Hjinn answered. "It has no food value for humans."

"We waste our time, then." Geruda suggested. "If people don't eat this grain, its parasite cannot affect them."

"I've been wondering about that myself," Hjinn said. For a moment he concentrated on the virtual datascape. It turned inside out along several of its dimensions. "Ahh, now I see."

"You do," Rybczynsky parroted.

Hjinn gestured toward the datascape. "What I did was cross-reference this biological knowledge base against Ruth Griszam's observations in the hidden store room. We seem to be dealing with a three-stage refining process. The infected grain plant is called the RAW MATTER. From it is apparently derived that dark granular substance, the so-called MOTHER MATTER. Now, MOTHER MATTER must be highly dangerous to humans, chemically poisonous perhaps, since Parek took the precaution of storing it in those multiply lined vials."

"Then we have the whitish powder," Geruda commented.

"Presumably the end product. It's stored casually, so it must be less virulent. It may even be harmless of itself. When released into the environment, perhaps it infects some other host species. Perhaps it's a byproduct of *that* process that gives rise to the psychotoxin that causes sickness and visions."

Rybczynsky manipulated a few datastructures of his own. "But how is the whitish powder released?" A cascade of sparkles danced across the tabletop display. One metamorphosed into a familiar image. "Consorts of the Virgins," he hissed. "The fans on the forward attack boats!"

"Pardon?" Hjinn gulped.

"Observe." Rybczynsky threw up a flurry of bubbles.

One showed Parek's troopers pouring whitish powder from burlap sacks into the hoppers of the fan assemblies. Another showed a trooper operating a fan, hands and feet on the deadman switches. Next, an aerial *pov* of the boats cruising downriver. Streamers of dust glistened gray-blue as they drifted ahead of the fleet.

Rybczynsky chuckled thinly. "Doctor Hjinn, now I know what you meant about absorbing unfamiliar information. Suddenly I am a meteorologist."

"A meteorologist, Excellency?"

"The means by which Parek disseminates the whitish powder depends on the weather for its effectiveness. It seems that the prevailing winds on all the rivers and canals Parek's fleet has traversed thus far blow downstream. The average wind velocity is slightly faster than the fleet's average cruising speed."

Geruda shook his head. "How can that be?"

Topographic maps and isobar plots erupted above the table. "The river system rises in high marshlands just inland from the coastal bluffs," Rybczynsky explained. "Tropical winds moist from long travel over the Equatorial Sea are forced to overtop those bluffs. In gaining altitude they undergo adiabatic cooling, which triggers condensation, cloud formation, and heavy precipitation. Those processes release substantial heat, but still the air does not recover all the energy it lost bouncing over the cliffs. It remains several degrees cooler, hence denser, than the air further inland. It pours downhill along every canal or river channel."

"Persistent katabatic winds," Geruda breathed.

Hjinn frowned. "Hairs of every Christ, we're all meteorologists now."

"Let's take stock," Rybczynsky declared. "Parek begins with a native grain parasite. In two steps, he processes it into a harmless powder. Thanks to a meteorological coincidence that blesses him with incessant tailwinds, he can spray that powder into fans just a meter across and saturate the whole region he is about to enter."

"Agreed," said Geruda.

"We are left with two mysteries, then," Rybczynsky said. "First, what is the vector species—the species in which the secondary infection occurs, giving rise to the actual psychotoxin? Second, how does that process bridge the chirality barrier, enabling a native parasite with right-handed amino acids to afflict human beings with left-handed ones?"

"I've got it," Hjinn breathed. He stared up at a writhing datastructure whose colors careened into the ultraviolet. "It's *fhlet.*"

"What?" Geruda yelped. "That breadfruit stuff everybody eats in Southland?"

"The same." Hjinn's voice was full of wonder. "Look, it says here that *fhlet* was developed by Jaremian agronomists after the Tuezi strike, just before social order collapsed across Southland. It was a tremendous achievement—listen carefully—'a symbiont uniting the roots and stems of an indigenous plant with the fruiting body of one of the food species the Harvesters had left behind.' "

"Case closed," Rybczynsky declared. "Left-handed and right-handed chiralities in symbiosis. This explains how Parek could derive a psychotoxin effective on humans from an indigenous species that human metabolism would otherwise ignore."

"This explains the success of Parek's southern invasion," Geruda crowed. "The psychotoxin softens the autochthons. When invaders arrive the victims are already delirious and too weak to defend themselves."

"*Fhlet* is a perfect vector," Hjinn added. "It's ubiquitous; most Southerners eat it daily. Further, it's eaten in Northland, too, though not as frequently. Still, Northlanders consume enough *fhlet* that if Parek had encountered the grain parasite during his early years in the north, he would have found it effective enough to reward his trouble in developing it further."

"Already at the dam three years ago, Parek considered the parasite precious enough to conceal it from Willim Dultav," Rybczynsky noted. "We know from recorded statements by Chagrin and others that Parek used the parasite-psychotoxin system to induce visions years before he came to the dam. We know from Parek's recorded discussions with Dultav that Dultav strongly disapproved, and made Parek give it up."

"But Parek didn't give it up, he just stopped using it." Geruda smiled ferociously. "But he prepared a minimal cache of raw materials, which he stored in those trunks and cylinders. Then he found ways to drag those around wherever he went without Dultav's knowing about it."

"Quite," Hjinn said forcefully. "More correlations are coming in on *fhlet.* Recall that Parek forbade his own soldiers to eat *fhlet* while in Southland. Spectators have recorded numerous instances of Parek troopers refusing proffered meals of *fhlet*, sometimes violently, and citing religious justification for so doing. This proves that Parek knows what's going on with the *fhlet*. Oh, look at this! Gentlehoms, we've just solved another riddle that's been frustrating Parek watchers across the Galaxy."

"Which riddle is that?" Rybczynsky demanded.

"Why haven't the autochthons in Graargy's basin developed sickness and visions as Parek's fleet draws near? I've been probing sociological databases. Parek's boats still shoot the white powder downwind. It's still colonizing *fhlet*, still pumping out psychotoxin. The reason Graargy's people don't get sick and see visions is . . . because they aren't eating *fhlet*."

Rybczynsky's jaw dropped. "They're not what?"

"It's all in Linka Strasser's journals. There's an old Southland tradition of observing two week-long partial fasts each year—fasts in the sense that people eat anything *but fhlet*. The anthropologists on the first survey ships thought this fast originated with *fhlet*'s inventors, perhaps with an eye to making sure people would go on eating the stuff. *Fhlet* is appallingly bland. The partial fast may have been intended to rekindle people's appreciation of *fhlet* twice a year by reminding them how inadequate their diet is without it." Hjinn called up half a dozen small datastructures. "Few Southern tribes still keep the tradition. But Graargy's people have enjoyed three generations of continuous leadership, quite a rarity down there. So unlike most Southerners, they still observe the semiannual fast. By happenstance, they're fasting right now, just when Parek is contaminating their *fhlet*."

"No *fhlet* intake, no exposure to the psychotoxin," Rybczynsky said, lifting his hands from the modeling table. "We have done well, learned doctors. Only one puzzle remains. Do our new discoveries bring us closer to determining the identity of Parek's and Ulf's Galactic handlers?"

Geruda twisted datastructures. "Probably not. Parek devised the parasite system—or discovered it, it doesn't matter which—years before he met Ulf, years before either of them acquired Galactic handlers. It is his own."

Rybczynsky frowned. "Yet Parek's method for spreading the powder—those fans—turned out to be so ideally suited to the weather conditions he encountered on the coastal bluffs. Was there not Galactic foresight at work there?"

"The datascape says no," Geruda said. "The fans would have been reasonably effective even if the winds were less favorable."

"I concur," murmured Hjinn. "Every god-man's entitled to one piece of dumb luck. This was Parek's."

Rybczynsky rose. He stepped beneath the pointing hand of Michaelangelo's God. Fastened his slender fingers around the divine wrist and hung from it. It was the most casual pose either Geruda or Hjinn had ever seen the elegant cardinal assume. "So we have learned one thing about Parek's and Ulf's handlers today. Whoever they may be, this parasite system is as much a puzzle to them as it was to us."

"Until today," Geruda chuckled.

"Praise God," Rybczynsky said with deep satisfaction. "When Parek's fleet attacks Graargy's domain, assuming it gets past all those booby traps—when Graargy's people turn out not to be drugged, and mount a serious defense—it will come as a complete surprise, not only to Parek and Ulf, but to both of their Galactic handlers." Rybczynsky raised his glowing pectoral cross to his lips. "The results of *that* should be fascinating to observe."

82.   Jaremi Four—Southern Hemisphere— Half-Circular Bay

"**M**agnificent sight, isn't it, Commodore?" the brigade captain asked.

"Indeed." Friz Labokloer smiled, kaleidoscope to his eye.

"The fleet, I mean."

Labokloer blinked and pocketed the kaleidoscope. "Impressive, I'll say that," he rumbled. To his left the morning sun blazed between rocky summits, filling the strait that led to the sea with white misty brilliance. *Just yesterday we sailed that strait,* Labokloer thought. *We've been so busy ever since, it seems like days ago.* He looked ahead, then to his right. The half-circular bay was huge, ninety kilometers on its longest axis. Except for the strait, it was wholly ringed by slate-gray cliffs tufted with scrubby trees. The cliffs stood forty legs high by the sea; inland, it was more like fifty or sixty. To the north and west, coarse gravel beaches abutted the cliffs. Off those beaches, four hundred ships lay anchored in a surreal arc. The morning sun illuminated them in the act of disgorging some hundred thousand troops and their matériel.

Lord Samu's fleet had made landfall.

"Sorry," Labokloer told the brigade captain. "I guess I'm not in the mood for magnificence."

"Then you've heard no word," the brigade captain said quietly.

Labokloer turned. "What's that mean?"

"Your woman, Commodore. You've heard nothing?"

"Nothing," Labokloer turned back. He contemplated the flagship. It towered a hundred meters offshore, its masts alive with signal flags. The brigade captain stepped beside him. *He's making me talk,* Labokloer thought sourly. *Prying bastard!* Aloud, he said, "My Ruth is nowhere to be found. No one will declare her missing."

"You're a hero of the fleet," the brigade captain said evenly. "Speak to Admiral Spibbert."

"He won't talk to me. I requested an audience with Samu. He shut me out, too." Labokloer chuckled darkly. "Know what? Right now I just want to smite the false god and go home."

He genuinely doesn't know what happened to Ruth, the brigade captain thought. *If she somehow escaped from that sub, she hasn't contacted him.* "I see the commodore is not eager to talk. Very well, to the glory of the god who is to come." Brigade Captain Ambrose Graftig—actually a Galactic from Calluron Five and the last Spectator still attached to the Catholic fleet—trudged down the beach.

He stopped cold. "What's that?" Graftig cried.

Labokloer looked where the brigade captain pointed straight up. At the zenith the sky was still almost night-dark; the shooting star stood out clearly. Slowly it streaked west to east.

For a moment Graftig lost the object in the glow of sunrise. When he spotted it again, it was brighter, irregular in shape, and visibly tumbling.

"Damn, it's going to land in the sea!" Labokloer cried.

Against the glare of sunrise neither man saw the object strike. But they saw a brief flash, whiter than the rosy morning sun. Half a minute later came another flash, softer, greener, lower. For six or eight seconds it lit up the sea beyond the strait from below.

"What the fuck was that?" Graftig demanded.

"An omen, maybe." Labokloer wrapped himself in his arms.

Graftig forced a smile. "It was nothing, Commodore. You'll see." *I hope,* the Spectator said to himself. Peering inside, he queried his satellite for astronomical advisories. Of course there were none. *In twelve hours the bird will start dumping my journal. Maybe someone upstairs will know what the sfelb that was.*

Admiral Oriel Spibbert knew something Labokloer never would: The half-circular bay was more than just Jaremi Four's largest, best-protected harbor. In fact, it had been formed a scant three centuries before, the impact crater from some Tuezi weapon salvo. Which mattered nothing for today's business: offloading the ships, lifting as many troops and as much equipment as possible atop the bluffs. From there the army would march off to smite the false god. *Tomorrow, if all goes well.*

But that would be tomorrow. It was noon, and Spibbert sweltered. The forecastle deck offered no shade against the tropical sun. But Spibbert had to be there. From the bridge he couldn't see the beach where his guardsmen formed ranks for their ride to the clifftop. He leaned over the rail and looked down at the beach. Raising his eyes, Spibbert studied the cliff wall. It was almost invisible now, behind the forest of scaffolds and gantries that had sprung up since morning.

"Signal from the bluffs," singsonged a day officer with field glasses. "The armored wagon lifter is operational."

"Very good, lieutenant," Spibbert said. "What's the count?"

"Fourteen thousand men atop the bluff. Eleven thousand are fully equipped. We're ahead of schedule, Admiral."

Spibbert raised his own glasses. He watched an open-basket elevator lurch up a gantry. A hundred queasy soldiers clung to wooden rails. He angled the glasses downward and to port. Soldiers lined up four abreast before the bucket lift. Every six seconds another bucket would come around. Another quartet of soldiers would climb aboard and begin a tottering ride to the plateau above.

"Admiral! Admiral!" A messenger in tropical fatigues sprinted forward, panting, "the water's vanishing!"

"What? Talk sense."

"The water's vanishing, sir. It is!" With the boldness of desperation the messenger clutched the admiral's sleeve. "Look!"

Spibbert peered down. Below the bow overhang was only gravel. "Are we still at anchor?" he demanded.

"Aye, sir."

"We anchored a hundred meters offshore," Spibbert objected. "The landing parties needed to row ashore in skiffs."

"Not any more," the runner said brightly. "The water's vanishing."

Spibbert looked about. A destroyer lay at anchor off the port beam. To starboard loomed a steamfrigate, its surdecks pregnant with boarding gangways. Neither had drifted. But those craft, too, were beached at the bow. Spibbert knitted his fingers. He scowled at the gantry-studded cliffs. *It's like the tide going out,* he thought. *But Jaremi Four has no moons. Some idiosyncratic behavior of the waters in this enclosed basin?* Whatever the cause, there could be no doubt that the water was receding rapidly.

The sun was low in the western sky when an exhausted sergeant shouldered Graftig into the elevator car. "In you go, brigade captain," he husked. Forty hollow-eyed troopers sat on two decks of wooden benches. Some clung to the lattice of welded metal rods that enclosed them. A near-gale wind was blowing in from the sea.

"Take her up," an officer shouted. A steam motor hissed. There was a jerk. The brief tugging in the stomach, familiar to Graftig but something none of the autochthons had ever felt.

The car was rising quickly.

Framing members blurred past. Beyond them, the car's ascension provided a dramatic "reveal" through irregular gaps in the wind-whipped spray. The bay floor lay barren and dry. Beached ships formed a huge arc, roughly marking the former shoreline. Graftig eyed the dry expanse stretching clear to the cliffs on the opposite side of the bay. Even the strait that led to the Equatorial Sea was an empty channel. *It's all empty.* Dimly Graftig recognized he had a great shot. *Saybacks, think of the saybacks,* he said to rouse himself. *One more high-rated feed and I'll have enough to retire on. And I'm young yet!* The elevator gantry bucked with the force of the wind. Looking eastward, Graftig bobbed his head to compensate. He listened for the *verify* signal. *The bird will release my journal on a twelve-hour delay,* he thought. *OmNet will love this . . . oh, forjeling plorg.*

Maybe it was the gain in height. Maybe it was a shift in the wind that cleared away smoke. Whatever the cause, all at once Graftig could see over the cliffs and out to sea.

What the sfelb, he thought. *At least I know where all that water went.*

Spibbert and Wehrman loped about the flagship's bridge, punching up displays and trying to decide what was happening. Everyone there was Galactic; there were few secrets.

The rumbling began somewhere so deep in the wind that they never really heard it start.

At first there was no direction to it—something felt as much as seen. Wehrman peered forward. He saw nothing amiss. He looked to starboard, then out to sea. Wind rushed through an open window, tangling his hair. "Oriel," Wehrman called woodenly. "Come see this."

Spibbert stepped beside the engineering attaché. He squinted into the dying gale.

"What's that?" Wehrman breathed.

Wehrman's homeworld Frensa Six had no bodies of water bigger than lakes. Spibbert hailed from Ordh, a planet with millennia of seafaring tradition. "You know what happens before a tidal wave?" Spibbert shouted. "After a seaquake or some great impact, the ocean pulls back. Kilometers of seafloor go dry. Bays are sucked clean. The waters pile up near the epicenter. Only hours later does the tsunami roll outward, pressing the air ahead if it."

"They bombed us," Wehrman said hollowly. "That shooting star. When it struck in the ocean, I thought they'd missed. But this is what they'd planned all along."

"'They'?" Spibbert asked sharply. "Who do you mean?" Through the starboard windows he watched gale-driven spray swirl open. It revealed a lowering cliff of water almost forty meters high thundering out of the east. For a moment the setting sun bathed it. Its base spangled like hammered copper, like a surface at once immobile and alive. A kilometer from the cliffs, the sea became too shallow to support the tidal wave. It shattered. Hundreds of thousands of tons of foam overwashed the seaward cliffs. Thundering whitewater rolled across the bay floor, heaving up boulders the size of wagons, reaching the first of the anchored ships, and crushing them or spewing them skyward as a *sturruh* might gallop through dry leaves.

Wehrman was on his knees, praying.

Spibbert thought of joining him but realized there was no point. He felt only an eerie calm. "I'm glad you called me," he yelled. "I'd hate to have missed this."

A screen of froth swept away the bridge.

All around him men screamed. Ambrose Graftig clung to a metal rod, jabbing his head to compensate for the bucking of the elevator car. To the limits of his vision, the half-circle bay was a maelstrom of spray. In its dying the tsunami had swallowed four hundred ships without sign.

Mad water clapped into the cliffs below. Spray leapt through the gridwork of the elevator car floor. *We're above the water,* Graftig caught himself thinking. *Maybe we have a chance.* Then came the sickening lurch. The gantry heeled over, its footers undermined. Welds snapped. The lift car spun free. Holding his eyes perfectly still, Ambrose Graftig watched the clifftop whirl behind the elevator car's cagework. Then water crushed him like the hand of a giant.

The body of Spectator Ambrose Graftig was never recovered.

All along the clifftop plateau campfires dotted the night. Beyond the hills to the north Labokloer watched dim pink aurora dance. *Aurora,* he thought ruefully. *Odds are I'll never see it properly again.* He rolled a *n'dren* back and forth in his hands. It was useless now. The fires weren't bright enough to show the colors.

"You are Friz Labokloer?" An officer circled a stubby tree. He stepped into the firelight and saluted. "The officers chose me by lot to give you a status report."

Confused, Labokloer set down his duffel.

"As you know, the fleet dropped off some eighty thousand soldiers and their equipment at that canyon mouth two days ago. One hundred twenty-two thousand persons remained aboard the fleet when it entered the bay. Many survived the tidal wave. Preliminary counts suggest we are about fifty to fifty-five thousand strong."

"How many equipped for combat?"

"Almost all. Weapons, *sturruh*, wheeled artillery, steamchargers, shells—we got a little of everything up here."

Labokloer slapped his palms onto his knees. "Then we can still pursue the false god."

The officer saluted again. "Aye, sir."

Labokloer struggled to draw an inference. "You say the other officers detailed you to give me this status report."

"Aye, sir."

"Um, why?"

The officer saluted a third time. "Preliminary census suggests that you are the highest ranking officer who survived. You must assume command."

Labokloer's face dropped into his hands. His back and shoulders churned with sobs.

"Sir?" the officer said eventually.

Labokloer looked up. Tears had etched uncertain paths through the dried mud on his face. "Now the god who is to come takes his chisel to me. All that happened today is because of me!"

"I don't understand," the officer stammered.

Labokloer sprang to his feet. "My woman Ruth, it was never right with her. She had too much mysterious knowledge. Too many private agendas. I had her and I took her, but I always knew there was a part of her I could never touch. For weeks I'd considered telling Lord Samu what I feared. Always my courage failed. I threw myself into spiritual exercises. I screamed to the god who is to come and begged him for strength but it never came." Labokloer drew the *n'dren* from its pocket and rotated it between his palms. "The night my Ruth vanished was the last time anyone saw Lord Samu. Angry at my weakness, the god who is to come took them both."

"I'm sure it wasn't—"

Labokloer let out an inarticulate roar. He hurled his *n'dren* into the fire. Its lenses popped from the heat. Labokloer whirled. "You don't know. I know! Ruth was something evil. A spy, maybe a saboteur. And I didn't turn her in! For that, the god who is to come took away Lord Samu—then all the ships and half of us. His final cruel prank is to put me in command of what's left." Labokloer bent over his duffel and tore it open. He withdrew a single object. Then he kicked the duffel into the fire, too.

"Commodore, that's all you possess!" Vetraz croaked.

Labokloer held up a strip of fur; it was his *silish*. "Now *this* is all I possess," Labokloer growled. "Tell the officers I will lead. I will wrap the *silish* around my leg, as in the days when Samu was still teaching us. I will wear no other clothes but these and sleep on bare ground, without bedroll or blanket. I will do these things to purify myself."

The officer stepped back, frightened by the wrath in Labokloer's eyes. "By your command, Lord Labokloer."

"I will do all these things," Labokloer grated. "I will do them so that when we fall on the false god and destroy him, the god who is to come will set us free."

83. The *Bright Hope*

"And to think I scheduled this conference so I could brief *you*." Admiral Yaal Hafen's image ran a hand through his red hair. "Any further news of Panna?"

"Nothing more than what's on the news," Eldridge reported sourly. "Panna's not talking to us anymore."

That morning Panna, a minor celebrity because of her stardrive's success, had called her own Galaxy-wide press conference using one of the drive's telemetry channels. To the astonishment of trillions—not least among them Eldridge, who'd been helpless to stop her—Panna had announced that she was joining a Galaxy-wide hunger strike, adding her prestige to the swell of popular calls for Jaremi Four's removal from Enclave protection. "I do not say whether Vatican overstepped its authority in denying that Arn Parek is the Christ," Panna had declared. "I say that the committed, the fascinated, and the merely curious deserve the chance to visit Jaremi Four and see for themselves."

"Puts you in a delicate situation," Hafen acknowledged. "You sped to Jaremi Four to enforce Enclave. Yet the high-profile passenger who got you there is now an Enclave opponent."

Eldridge nodded. She and Gavisel and Wachieu had gathered in person. Normal practice discouraged command crew members from occupying the same physical location during an alert. For safety's sake, they'd chosen a heavily secured store room deep within the ship and converted it into a temporary meeting chamber. Admiral Hafen's image was slightly grainy, an artifact of the small comm unit they'd brought in with them. *Never mind*, Eldridge thought, *it's contact. Hafen's aides told us to prepare for a lengthy briefing.*

"*Bright Hope*, you're all we've got out there," Hafen began. "A smallish ship. A modest weapons bank, never fully tested. Still, for the immediate future you are the law over Jaremi Four. I thought we owed it to you to let you in on all we know about this Parek character."

"Is that really what this is about, Admiral? Some messianic con-man on a ruined planet?" The distaste in Gavisel's voice was evident.

Hafen smiled. "Ah, the Arkhetil speaks. Yes, Fem Gavisel, this *is* all about Arn Parek. At least, that's where it begins. Our analysts believe we face a clash between veiled offworld masterminds for control of this man some call the new Christ."

"Galactics?" Eldridge breathed.

"Galactics," Hafen confirmed. "Violating Enclave on a scale no one ever anticipated. We suspect who some of them are, but not all. That said, I begin the formal briefing." Image bubbles blossomed over the conference table, depicting significant moments in Parek's ministry: healing Chagrin, reluctantly leading an early village raid, striding the stage at Bihela, pacing the deck of his flagship, interrogating village chieftains. "Fraud, prophet, military leader," Hafen intoned, "lord of a mighty navy salvaged from Jaremi Four's hidden places—is Arn Parek all of these, or none?" The bubbles coalesced into a tridee clip of the old dam. "Here is where Parek's ministry began. Religions can be understood as information parasites—parasites on the minds of their believers. Their spread can be modeled using the tools of epidemiology."

A map of Jaremi Four surged forward. A dot of color began to seethe in North-land, marking the dam's location. "Parekism arose—or, perhaps more accurately, mutated into a form virulent enough to spread rapidly—at the old dam. From there it radiated across the northern continent." Like self-replicating vermilion ants the color patch boiled across the landscape. "More recently it crossed the Equatorial Sea and began its conquest of Southland, too." The map image zoomed out and wrapped into a globe to accommodate the crimson area's voracious growth. "Parekism acquired its new vigor as a result of three mutations in doctrine. Memetic analysis attributes two of them to offworld contacts with Parek himself. There is also a fourth mutation, which we trace to offworld contact with Ulf. Then there's a *fifth* strand of Galactic influence which concerns Parek and Ulf, but has not contacted either of them directly. Detex Officer Wachieu?"

"Yes, Hom Admiral." She hadn't expected him to single her out.

"You're out there, fighting the electromagnetic noise in Jaremi system. I'd like your response to something our analysts have worked out." The map disappeared and was replaced by a graphic of Jaremi Four in space. "Suppose Galactic inter-ests placed a suite of small, illegal satellites in geostationary orbit." In the image, two dozen satellites shimmered on, a tenuous ring girdling the equator. "Suppose three or even four Galactic organizations did the same." Additional satellite rings flashed into place. "Suppose all these birds had been put into orbit before *Bright Hope* arrived. What are the chances you'd detect the satellites?"

"Virtually nil," said Wachieu. "Especially since the polar research station and OmNet already have those orbits littered with legitimate satellites, both operating and moribund."

"That's too bad," Hafen growled. "It means the rest of this very disturbing analysis is probably correct. All right, here we go." Images flashed: Ulf and Parek's small army racked by disease, then suddenly fit again. "The first offworld contact took place here, when Parek miraculously cured his army of venereal disease."

"We don't know that," Gavisel said sharply.

"Very well, a *seemingly* miraculous cure. But the army was cured—after which point Parek's preaching began to reflect elements drawn from the earliest history of Terra's Mormon church."

"Mormons?" Wachieu breathed. "Those old fogies?"

"Don't let the mainstream denomination's present decline mislead you. Early Mormonism had great vitality. If one wanted to control a religious movement on a backwater planet and equip it for cataclysmic growth, one could do worse than borrow from early Mormonism. Now here's a clip I'm certain that none of you has seen." A freeze frame coalesced, a tridee squeezedown from senso: Arn Parek stood on a meter-high platform, cape swirling. White muslin stretched above him, ablaze with sunlight. As for the person whose *pov* it was, he or she was unmistak-ably crawling on hands and knees. "We found this in the most secret files of a Privy High Councilor."

"You subpoenaed the Council?" Eldridge asked.

"Military intelligence stole it. And I'll deny having said that." Hafen gave a self-satisfied chuckle. "Later I'll tell how this image was obtained and what it means. For now, simply note the way Parek receives a guest: wearing a white cape, standing on a platform, and compelling the visitor to approach on hands and knees. The parallel is to an early Mormon figure named Walter Murray Gibson. In the year 1861, Mormon leader Brigham Young sent Gibson on a missionary voyage to Terra's Japan. Traveling by primitive sailing ship, Gibson got as far as Terra's Hawaii. He disobeyed Brigham Young's orders, put down roots in Hawaii, and installed himself as virtual king of one island's Mormon community. In 1864 Young learned how Gibson was abusing his power and excommunicated him. Oddly, Gibson went on to a distinguished second career in politics, serving as Hawaii's Prime Minister from 1882 to 1887 local. Now, what's the point? Simply this: when Gibson was at the height of his Mormon power, he received his visitors *exactly* the way Parek does in this clip—standing over them in a white cape while they approached on hands and knees."

The image disappeared. Hafen sat on an invisible stool, linking his fingers around one of his knees.

"That is offworld strand number one," Hafen summarized, "sustained, direct contact with Arn Parek by someone espousing—or at least exploiting—obscure doctrines of the early Mormon church. Now let's turn to strand number two. Another, independent Galactic agency has had sustained contact with Ulf. Shortly after Mormon influences showed up in Parek's preaching, Ulf's skills as a general mysteriously improved. This second influence didn't just give Ulf strategic pointers. It also provided him with two hundred and eighty-three ships: his and Parek's navy. We believe these ships were *not* found intact in some mothball facility, as Ulf claimed. Instead, they were newly manufactured in accord with the conventions of historic Jaremian naval architecture—then left for Chagrin to find days or minutes after the builders had finished laying down a layer of phony dust."

"Admiral!" Eldridge exclaimed, stunned. "An entire naval fleet, fabricated on the surface of an Enclave planet?"

"Maybe fabricated in orbit, then delivered to the surface. But there's more. We believe that both Parek and Ulf's handlers have remained continually in touch with their respective clients, supplying new ideas and pursuing control over the Parek movement. Consider the way key developments have escalated. Parek proclaimed new doctrines; Ulf came up with the navy. By the time the navy sailed, we suspect Parek's status had fallen so low that Ulf could hold him under house arrest. Somehow Parek charmed his way out. It's unknown how the navy got removed from the Equatorial Sea and injected into the upland river system, but the event apparently restored Parek's sole authority."

"What do we know about Ulf's handler?" Eldridge asked.

Hafen scowled. "Frustratingly, almost nothing. That's all I can say about the second offworld strand. On to the third. We know *just* who this one is: a Galactic institution that never contacted Parek or Ulf directly, yet is deeply involved in their story." Up came a graphic of the papal tiara and keys. "Strand number three is illegal intervention on a massive scale by the Universal Catholic Church, no doubt coordinated directly from the planet Vatican. Ruth Griszam's identification of Cardinal Semuga confirms it."

"*Vatican* built the second navy?" Eldridge gasped.

"That's just part of it," said Hafen. "Remember, today's Church is heir to a strategic tradition of colossal patience and subtlety. The popes always schemed on a time scale of generations. Consider the riddle that confronted Pope Modest the Fourth—and yes, we think it goes that high. Maybe Parek is the Christ, maybe he isn't. To contact him directly would be very risky, and if Parek *is* Christ, blasphemous besides. So instead of seeking to influence Parek directly, Modest apparently opted to raise a huge client force among the Jaremian autochthons. Recruiting probably began before it was decided what the force would be used for.

"Ruth Griszam's more recent journals help us reconstruct Vatican tactics. Her consort Friz Labokloer underwent what we assume was a typical recruitment. He received prophecy scrolls from the sky that brought him sharp gains in wealth and power. We know how they came. In one confidential report, Griszam says she witnessed Labokloer receiving a scroll. It was clearly a Galactic secured courier canister."

"A Spectator saw that, and no action was taken?" Eldridge asked sharply.

"She reported it," Hafen said, "but she couldn't record it—it came during an auroral storm. So the evidence wasn't compelling enough to trigger an inquiry."

"Thousands of minor nobles must've received such prophecies," Eldridge mused.

"But only a handful of them were *pov*ed by Spectators. Ruth Griszam herself met another recipient, a shattered noble from Giwalczor named Ileatz Quareg."

"I *pov*ed that journal," Wachieu said. "Quareg received a prophecy that turned out wrong. It ruined him. That doesn't sound very Galactic."

"Actually, Quareg's fate was the key that enabled our analysts to determine how Vatican raised its army," Hafen said. "How do you convince a large number of strangers you can foretell the future? There's a classic technique, used on every world but Arkhetil. It never fails, and it doesn't require actual foreknowledge of the future. All you need is a pool of prospective victims so large that you can afford to discard half of them with each prediction you make.

"The scam arises frequently in the financial world, so I'll use an example from that arena. Suppose you want to convince, say, seventy-five people to invest heavily in a worthless security. Start with a prospect pool of twelve hundred investors. Send half of them an unsolicited prediction that says security x will increase in value. Send the other half a prediction that x will go down. Then see what happens. If x goes *up*, the six hundred people who got your prediction saying x would go *down* think you're an idiot. Just write them off, and concentrate on the six hundred who got the correct prediction. Send them another forecast. Tell half of them y will go up, half that y will go down. Okay, y goes *down*. Forget the three hundred prospects you told that y would go *up*. The other three hundred—half of one-half of your original prospect pool—have received two correct predictions from you. They're starting to think you're pretty smart. So you send *them* another split prediction, yielding a hundred and fifty prospects who've received three correct predictions. These folks probably imagine you're one hot analyst. Now send *them* one more split prediction. What do you wind up with?"

"Seventy-five people who've received four correct predictions in a row," Eldridge said immediately.

Hafen nodded. "Seventy-five people primed to buy anything you want to sell them, at any price, because they think you're some kind of forjeling genius or psychic—or you speak for the gods. That's how the scam works."

"How the sfelb many potential victims did Vatican start out with?" Gavisel demanded.

"Sixty-four thousand, we think," Hafen said slowly. "They must have sent prophecy scrolls to every petty noble across the far north. Thirty-two thousand were told that such-and-such a battle would go one way. The other thirty-two thousand received the opposite prophecy."

"For thirty-two thousand of them, the prediction was right," said Eldridge.

"And they got another split prophecy—that was the second round," Hafen said. "By the third round, the pope's men were down to sixteen thousand recipients. By the fourth, just eight thousand. Poor old Ileatz Quareg was one of the four thousand suckers who received a false prediction in that round. Now the Vatican planners had a trick up their sleeves. They were Galactics; they knew when energy spikes from Cohller 5114 would strike Jaremi Four. So for their fifth prophecy, they just sent the time when the auroral storm would begin: a 'can't-miss' prediction that didn't lose them a single prospect."

"It's diabolical," Wachieu breathed.

"Probably not the word the pope would use," Hafen said wryly. "So we're left with eight thousand nobles who've received five correct prophecies in a row. Along the way, they'd been taught spiritual disciplines borrowed from a repressive twentieth-century Catholic order called Opus Dei. During the auroral storm that the fifth prophecy scroll predicted, the nobles received a sixth; this was the scroll Ruth Griszam saw Friz Labokloer get. That sixth scroll called the nobles to journey to the nearest of several artificial caves, where over several consecutive nights they all received their marching orders from a man named Samu. We now know Samu was Ato Cardinal Semuga."

"A Cardinal on an Enclave world," Wachieu breathed.

"Giving speeches in caves he had specially excavated for the purpose," Gavisel added. "Does that warm all plorg, or what?"

"By this time," Hafen continued, "Vatican strategists knew how they wished to use the autochthonous army. The pope had declared Parek a false Messiah, so the army would strike at him. Each of those eight thousand petty nobles went back to his domain, raised and equipped an average of twenty-five troops, and journeyed to the launching port." The sky filled with another of Ruth Griszam's images: the Catholic navy as viewed by the bug aboard the rising weather balloon. "Two hundred and eight thousand officers and men—more than double the ninety-five thousand who sailed under Ulf and Parek—sailing in ships presumably built for that purpose by Vatican engineers."

"Of course, those ships are all destroyed now," Eldridge said.

"They served their purpose. They put a hundred and thirty-five thousand troops ashore. Those forces are hunting Parek now."

"Any idea what caused the tidal wave that consumed the fleet?"

"None," said Hafen. "Fem Wachieu, did you track that apparent meteor that landed in the Equatorial Sea a few hours before the tsunami?"

"No," Wachieu replied. "I rolled back the Detex logs, and there is no sign of it. Not that it means anything in all this noise."

Hafen nodded grimly. "In that case, my discussion of the third offworld strand is complete."

A single tridee bubble swelled above the table: Arn Parek—caped and dressed in white—towered once more over a crawling visitor. "I place what I am about to tell you under the very highest secrecy," Hafen said grimly. "The fourth and final strand of offworld influence on Jaremi Four—the one which no longer continues, but which is nonetheless the most shocking—lies at the feet of the Privy High Council itself."

Eldridge gasped. "An Enclave violation by the *Council?*"

"The political ramifications of this discovery are not yet clear," Hafen said without expression. "But here's what you need to know in Jaremi space. Just watch this."

A new bubble opened, another squeezedown from senso.

The Spectator limped in circles before a crumbling amphitheater. "Oh sky gods, through the power of The Word Among Us let me be healed this day! Oh sky gods, this day I would walk like any man!"

The woman who approached him had *staff* written all over her. "Good day, yeoman," she said.

This time, there was no clumsy editing to disguise what the Spectator had said. This time his next words rang out with inescapable clarity.

"I am called Laz Kalistor."

The image froze.

"Yes, *that* Laz Kalistor," Hafen said. "The Spectator who was tortured to death on Jaremi Four and came back not recognizing his own wife. After the tragedy he'd dropped out of sight, until he was tapped by a cabal of Privy High Councilors to be their private spy.

"With one important exception, the journals you are about to see have never been viewed except by the cabalists—and my investigators."

Hafen showed them everything. They saw Kalistor fool the wealthy Jaremian woman into thinking the gods spoke to her. They saw him slip Parek the note that would so entice him. They watched through Kalistor's eyes as he crawled before Parek in the muslin-topped courtyard, and as he showed The Word Among Us how to read through blindfolds and taught him how to firewalk.

"This is an Enclave violation of incalculable scale," Hafen summarized. "Here is what we know about it. When Parek's popularity among Galactics began to blossom, some Privy High Councilors suggested sending an undercover operative to develop influence over the new messiah. The Council could never reach consensus on so radical a strategy. One faction grew impatient with debate; they formed a cabal, secretly recruited Kalistor, and planted him on Jaremi Four."

"Where's Kalistor now?" Eldridge asked.

"Dead," Hafen said. "Eventually the full Council learned what the cabal had done, and ordered the intervention stopped. Kalistor was left in the open, his operation terminated, his mandate whisked away. What finished him? One of his own journals—the first one I played back, the journal from the healing service where he met Parek. He'd made it for the cabal's eyes only, but somehow it got broadcast by OmNet's entertainment division."

"Forjeler in plorg," Eldridge said.

"Kalistor used his Galactic name in that journal," Hafen continued. "Someone tried to edit the sound and cover it up, but it didn't work. It was still possible to reconstruct the Spectator's mouth movements."

"So Parek's Galactic handler *pov*ed this journal," Gavisel speculated.

"Most likely," Hafen agreed. "We know the handler routinely advised Parek to kill Spectators in order to avoid their scrutiny. The handler probably never suspected Kalistor was a spy—just thought of him as one more Spectator angling for a piece of The Word Among Us. We believe Ulf's handler demanded Kalistor's death as well. As for Kalistor himself, his body was never recovered. Does anyone care to *pov* the execution? I thought not."

Eldridge sighed into cupped hands. "It seems unlikely that the journal that cost Kalistor his life just aired by accident."

"I agree, but so far there's no proof. It's still uncertain just how or why that journal made it into general release. Perhaps the cabalists simply withdrew whatever protection they'd placed over Kalistor's material. Some mid-manager at OmNet could just have stumbled on the healing journal and decided to 'cast it for its entertainment value. Or another faction on the Council might have arranged the broadcast deliberately as a blow against the cabalists. Gaps and all, that's all we know about the fourth strand."

"And strand number five?" Eldridge asked.

Hafen invoked bubbles bearing images of vials and trunks and racks of cylinders, of fungus-infested grain, and of attack boats with powerful fans bolted to their foredecks. He told the officers how Parek caused illness and visions to descend upon his victims days before his fleet spewed death into their villages from midriver. "In its own way, this strand is as significant as any of Parek's Galactic influences," Hafen said. "But we believe no Galactic played any role in its development. It seems an authentic innovation by Parek himself."

Eldridge stretched her legs out. "And between this seething cauldron of intrigue and a Galaxy full of religious fanatics stands . . . only *Bright Hope.*"

"That's true for another few weeks, at least. We have a sizable fleet on its way to Jaremi space, but it lacks your speed."

"Admiral Hafen," Gavisel said. "Have your analysts made any predictions?"

"None. Our psych people have thrown up their hands trying to forecast Parek. Not only is he highly creative and intelligent, his confidence has been burnished by something no previous messianic figure ever enjoyed while sane: direct, effective mentoring by his (pardon the expression) god. Time after time, he really *has* stretched out his hand and seen the impossible occur."

"Parek's a first, then," Gavisel said tartly, "a messiah who has no need of faith. He's actually undergone the preposterous experiences every self-styled god-man before him had to imagine, misinterpret, or project into the unreachable past."

An annunciator bleeped by Wachieu. She peered into a small display and looked up, hollow-eyed. "Admiral, I don't suppose there's any possibility of error about that relief fleet being weeks away?"

"Why?"

"Because there's a sizable fleet approaching Jaremi system, and I'd so hoped it was ours." The table lit up with dancing lines and figures. In moments, a remote control station for the ship's Detex had arranged itself at her fingertips. "Here's a first look," she said.

The tactical image was full of static. But there they were: one large vessel and seventy-two escort craft. At ordinary speeds they lay still several days outside Jaremi system. "Not much detail," Eldridge said.

"I know," Wachieu grated. "Forjel this noise. Attempting a forced auto-ident . . . there we are." Her brows drew together. "This doesn't make any sense."

"Fem Wachieu?" Hafen asked gently.

She looked up quizzically. "On forced auto-ident, the flagship announced itself as *Cornucopia*, a manufacturing trawler from someplace called Khoren Four. Other than that, the fleet does not respond to hails."

"Khoren Four?" Admiral Hafen echoed. "Never heard of it."

84. Jaremi Four—Southern Hemisphere— Graargy's Domain

Linka wasn't surprised she noticed the sound of engines first. Of those awaiting full sunrise atop the killing knoll, only she could recognize it. Ever since she'd awakened, she'd been inwardly watching Parek's fleet approach in a series of laterals.

"You've lived among Graargy's people for five years," Neuri Kalistor observed at the previous day's telepresence briefing. *"If most of them die tomorrow, how will you feel?"*

Linka shrugged. *"I'm a Spectator. I observe."*

Today, Neuri had stepped away from her manager's desk. In view of high Galactic interest in the coming battle, she'd added herself to the pool of Spectators flying support overhead. Tramir Duza would've been up there, too, if Ulf hadn't killed him. Cassandra Wiplien floated no-vis at fifty meters, filling the slot Duza would reclaim when he got back from North Polar.

Linka was the only Spectator on the ground. With steady eyes she studied her tribemates for what was probably the last time.

Sweat already moistened the crags of Graargy's face. He scowled over his shoulder at the brightening sky. Sunlight would enter the basin soon. The twice-yearly *fhlet* fast would be over.

Her smile a window on broken teeth, gangly Harapel held out a *fhlet* gourd. Graargy took it.

The mad old tribune Dzettko stood beside the ancient alarm bell. Graargy took from him a short ceremonial blade.

Linka's ex-claspmate Sydeno shuffled and evaded her eyes. *Looks like he hasn't slept well,* Linka thought dourly. *Probably up all night screwing Ixtlaca.* Ixtlaca had drawn no shiny pebble at the last village gathering; she wouldn't be on the killing knoll today. *That may buy her an extra minute before she sees death coming,* Linka thought. She searched her mind for regrets and found none, only readiness for the next posting and an eager curiosity about how today's battle would unfold.

Tsretmak was the first autochthon to hear the distant roaring. "What's that?" he said.

For a moment the others exchanged baffled glances. Then they all heard the engines.

They stared north. The canal above the upper locks lay quiet. A finger's width above it, faint aurora silhouetted inconceivably distant mountains.

"Is it Lormatin?" Harapel breathed.

"Do Lormatin's oarsmen sound like that?" Graargy rumbled. "Tsretmak!" With his free hand he flung his elder son a sheathed sword. "Just in case." Tsretmak gathered a few companions. He led them down the cliff toward the canal along a tortuous route that avoided traps.

Graargy's younger son Jaekdyr climbed a tree. "What do you see?" Graargy demanded.

The dawn's first direct sun rimmed Jaekdyr's hair. "Boats!" he screamed. "More than I can count—coming fast!"

Graargy dropped the *fhlet* and the ceremonial blade. Gripping his staff, he lurched toward the cliff edge. "How do they move?" he breathed.

Close to a hundred small black speedskiffs hurtled down the canal four and five and six abreast. Steam hissed past the seals of oversized engines. In each skiff could be seen perhaps a dozen soldiers, all lashed in place, strapped to seats, or tied down between rails.

Outwardly, Linka gaped like everyone else. With her mind's eye she savored a brilliant *pov* by Wiplien, who'd swept up on the speedskiffs from behind. Matching their pace, she'd hung briefly just a meter above them. She saw the troopers' stubble and smelled their fetid breath. Then Wiplien surged up and ahead. Rotating slowly, she cleared the locks. Still turning, she cut in toward shore and came to rest behind the tribesfolk on the killing knoll, looking over Linka's shoulder as the first skiffs jetted into the locks.

"So fast!" the tribesman Freydiin shouted over the engines' roar. "Still, they must stop."

Graargy smiled grimly. Attackers always stopped.

Linka closed Wiplien's lateral and focused her full attention below. The speedskiffs maxed their throttles. Their bows lifted from the water. Morning sun flashed from the metal plates Parek's fashioners had bolted to their keels. *They're going to shoot out of the lock and drop into the lower basin,* Linka realized. *Perfect strategy for attacking Graargy—it bypasses both the surrounding cliffs and the walkways around the lock itself, the places where booby traps are thickest.*

Wiplien's voice buzzed in Linka's ear. *"I'm airborne. Gook luck."* Linka opened the lateral from Wiplien again. She watched herself shrink and disappear, a dull red glow around her body reminding her that her likeness would be modified when *pov*ed by experients.

The first four skiffs surged into the lock and bounced up onto the lock gates. Corroded railings burst. The skiffs leapt into emptiness. For an instant Linka flicked her gaze to Graargy's astonished face, then back to the canal. The skiffs splashed down, still doing twenty klicks forward. Their sterns plunged beneath the surface. Steam and impetus forced them out. They heeled around through hurricanes of spray, foam streaming from their gunwales. Waterlogged troopers fumbled to unbelt themselves and undog their weapons.

The skiffs bumped ashore near the base of the killing knoll. "They're in!" Graargy shouted.

"It is a judgment," said Dzettko obscurely.

Never while Graargy lived had the basin's security been breached. But he remembered tactics his grandfather had taught him from the days when the traps were less dependable. "Now we drive them out," Graargy cried, twisting at his staff. Curved metal blades snapped from its ends. Other men reached for their staffs, struggling against corrosion and neglect to work their mechanisms.

The second brace of skiffs swept over the lock gate six abreast, trailing sparks and scraps of railing. They disappeared behind towers of spray. When Linka could see them again, they, too, were half capsized, their passengers fighting to unstrap.

Linka leaned forward and peered down. Tsretmak and his companions stepped onto the bank where the first skiffs had beached. The troopers ignored them and went on tugging at their restraints. *They think everyone is sick or mad with visions,* Linka thought. *But they're not.*

Screaming a battle cry, each young man leapt into a skiff and hacked brutally at troopers still tangled in their harnesses.

Another line of skiffs scraped over the gates and splashed into the canal.

Linka stared downward. Two troopers in the first-wave skiffs had unlashed themselves and freed their steamrifles. They stood and fired.

Tsretmak pinwheeled into the canal, staring astonished at the void where his shoulder had been. "Keep firing!" a trooper shouted. Tsretmak's companions fell quickly, shot through the bowels, face, legs.

"My son!" Graargy screamed.

Jaekdyr and two other men rushed forward. They raised bows, nocked arrows, and let them fly. Linka twisted around and looked down. Clutching at arrow shafts, two of Parek's troopers tottered into the already-pink canal water.

"They may have magic boats," Jaekdyr exulted, "but they still die!"

A scraping noise pulled Linka's gaze to the lock. Two skiffs had sideswiped shooting the gate. They came off spinning. One hit the crumbling cement of the opposite bank. She tumbled end-over-end along the shore, throwing up mud and concrete, finally vanishing in a cloud of steam. The other hit the water sideways. Her hull broke up. Shards bolted downcanal like flung stones.

"In the cliffs!" a sergeant roared below. Troopers raised rifles toward the killing knoll. Linka lurched toward a stout trunk that erupted from the knoll's edge. She jammed her back against it. It gave her cover as she watched her companions die. They fell without knowing why. Harapel screamed. She dropped heavily, clutching her belly. Dzettko pitched backward in silence. He had no head. Sculfka, Graargy's senior clasp-mate, collapsed at knoll's edge. Her throat was torn open, her lower jaw a shambles.

Again Jaekdyr ran forward. "Shoot! Shoot!" he cried. His arrows and those of his companions were joined by other arrows from below; a few men down there had scrambled out of hogans or out of the caves carrying their bows. Aboard the skiffs, troopers slumped in harnesses. Some spun into the canal. *Parek's soldiers expected no resistance,* Linka reminded herself.

Surviving troopers aboard the beached first-wave skiffs clambered onto shore, firing wildly. Desperate to evade the arrows, they plunged inland. "Don't go!" a sergeant cried. "Remember your orders!" The sergeant pitched into the water, Jaekdyr's arrow in his neck. Screaming troopers kept deserting their skiffs. They sprinted across the canalside trail.

They lunged into Graargy's traps. Ground lines whisked men high overhead. Threw them into the canal. Impaled them on poisoned stakes. Crushed them beneath logs and boulders.

"Down! Down to battle!" Graargy cried atop the knoll. A handful of men clumped behind him. Graargy gave the body of his beloved senior claspmate a final, silent glance. He plunged down a safe path, yelling like a banshee.

Below, defenders armed with picks and knives and pike poles rushed toward the beaching speedskiffs. Though their weapons were no match for the attackers' rifles, they slaughtered a few score of Parek's troopers before they could unstrap.

A wall of spume filled the basin below the locks. The next skiffs over the gate disappeared in it. *Nothing more to see from up here,* Linka realized. Shells spewed up dust around her. Someone screamed. *Go, go!* She scrambled toward a spot where she could slide into an eroded, trap-free channel well covered by trees. Braking with hands and feet, she caromed down a natural chute caked with loose dirt. Her heels stopped her four meters down. Gravel and clay showered her. She dropped to elbows and knees and rolled onto a ledge. She was hidden by foliage, yet here and there gaps in the leaves allowed her an unobstructed view.

The seventh, then the eighth line of speedskiffs jolted into the canal. Perhaps their commanders saw the tribespeople putting up a fight. Maybe their orders had always been to hang back. Whatever the reason, they did not beach. They lined up midcanal, their marksmen raking the bank with gunfire.

The ninth-wave skiffs carried small howitzers. The gunners were strapped into place behind their weapons. Linka watched the light artillery skiffs leap into the lower basin. They began firing while still hidden behind spray. Linka spoke a nonsense syllable; an implant caused the shells' trajectories to read as unfurling green trails superimposed over her vision in a way her experients would not see. That is why her eyes were already focused downcanal as explosions blossomed across the core of the settlement. Like the footsteps of an invisible giant, detonations pulverized Graargy's hogan and the cave entrance. *How many are trapped inside?* she wondered.

Graargy's primal yell wrenched her attention back to the canal. Skiffs were still beaching before their passengers unstrapped. Through shivering leaves Linka watched Graargy leap aboard one skiff, blade-tipped staff held high. "For Tsretmak!" he snarled. When that skiff was a charnel house of fettered corpses, Graargy leapt into the next. His blade sliced with mad vigor across a sergeant's chest. It was a fatal wound, but in inflicting it Graargy had cut the man's straps. The dying sergeant pulled a steampistol from his sodden doublet and fired.

Graargy pinwheeled overboard in a mist of blood and fur.

A woman screamed. *Close by!* Linka rose to her elbows and peered around branches. It was Blorach. Sydeno'd been trying to help her down from the knoll along a trap-free path. A shell had caught the old scow of a woman in her ample thigh. Sydeno couldn't hang on to her. She tumbled down the cliffside and set off traps. The first ripped flesh but did not break her fall. The second snapped the bones of her left forearm; five meters away Linka heard the crack. The third trap, a buried spike, pierced Blorach through the bowel. The fourth was a ground noose that whisked the riddled body into the sky. Still anchored to the spike, Blorach's intestines paid out like fishline.

The last brace of speedskiffs surged over the gate. Metal chains trailed from their sterns, towing an eight-meter-wide metal plate riding on inflated pontoons. The plate slammed onto the top of the gate. Explosive bolts released the tow chains and ruptured the pontoons.

The skiffs splashed down in the lower basin.

The plate settled heavily onto the gates, its purpose clear. *A ramp to help larger craft shoot the gates.*

A full-size attack boat thundered into the lock. On her deck half a dozen medium artillery pieces bristled under fabric shrouds. She bounced up onto the skidplate and skittered over. For a moment Linka thought she'd cleared the gate too slowly, that she'd hit the water bow-first and go under. But the weight of stern-mounted engines leveled her out. Pancaking into the canal, she scattered what seemed acres of spray.

"Yiii-i-i-i-i!" Close by, a man's voice squealed in falsetto. After exhausting his supply of arrows, Jaekdyr had rushed down the cliff. He'd circled carelessly behind Sydeno and tripped a spring trap. Impaled by half a dozen poisoned spikes, his body rolled down toward the canal. *That's it*, Linka thought. *Graargy, Sculfka, Tsretmak, Jaekdyr—the whole family's gone.*

Troopers marked the spot Jaekdyr'd fallen from. They trained their fire on it. Fusillades tore through the leaves above Linka.

In a lateral from Cassandra Wiplien, Linka watched a second artillery boat move more slowly into the lock. It scraped to a stop atop the skid plate. The first boat had gone over all battened down; this one had gunners already on deck. They opened fire from the top of the lock. Their first shells landed two hundred meters downcanal, by the cave entrance. The net-drying racks became a hail of wood chips. Metal cook tables spun into the air. Bent over almost double, they slapped onto dry earth amid showers of fire and stone.

Linka snapped her awareness back to Wiplien's lateral. More speedskiffs entered the lock, two abreast. They split around either side of the artillery boat and whisked over the gate.

The artillery boat in the lower basin came alive. Gunners squeezed up through deck hatches. They pulled the tarps from their weapons and trained them on targets downstream.

Above, the second boat ceased fire. Her gunners secured their weapons and strapped in. *How long did they practice this?* Linka wondered. The second boat backed out of the lock and stopped. Engines roaring, she surged forward up the ramp and over the gate.

Sydeno had spotted Linka through the foliage and debris. "Linka!" he yelled. He thought her trapped on the ledge. "Linka, *here!*" He edged forward, out of cover. The still-rising sun transfixed the cliff behind him in dappled brilliance.

Below, half a dozen troopers spotted his silhouette. Their guns shouted.

Red fountains bloomed across Sydeno's chest and stomach. For half a second he remained standing, eyes locked on Linka's. Blood bubbled from his lips. He coughed, twisted, and collapsed.

Something whined past Linka's ear. The troopers must have spotted her now. Pain seared her leg like acid! She looked down. *Not a shell.* Anything moving that fast would have triggered her flash-stasis shields. *A forjeling ricochet.* A shale chip six centimeters across protruded from her right leg below the thigh.

She fought for balance and lost.

Dreamily the sky leapt under her. *Traps,* she thought. *They won't trigger my shield either. They'll tear me up.*

Just in time, she dredged the manual shield code from her memory and subvocalized it. Gunshots and screams were suddenly muffled. Linka tumbled, insulated from new pain. Traps exploded about her. Serrated jaws dragged along her shielded leg but fell back. Jagged spikes swung from behind shrubs, bouncing away on contact.

Somehow she'd stopped falling. She lay on her back, sprawled across the canalside trail.

Half a dozen troopers were sprinting straight toward her.

Linka lay exposed. Nowhere to go. *I can't let this many autochthons see my shield work,* she thought. Grimly she subvocalized the code to drop the shields. *I'll have to take their bullets.*

Linka had never been troubled by empathy for her subjects. Perhaps that was why when it erupted unbidden, it struck with such power. Suddenly she grasped exactly how it must feel for the autochthons to face their bleak endings—wounded, helpless, racked with pain, everything they'd ever known torn apart by weapons of incomprehensible power. *If they kill me, I'll come back and spend my bonuses on Calluron Five. But imagine if this was it—if this was all I'd ever had the chance to be, and now even that was to be wrenched away. . . .*

The troopers leapt over her. Firing at survivors downcanal, they sprinted on. *They didn't even notice me.* She didn't expect her limbs to tremble. She didn't expect the acrid moisture that pooled in her eyes.

"Don't just lay there," Wiplien hollered in her ear. *"Take cover."* With part of her awareness Linka scanned the lateral Wiplien was squirting her. The artillery boats were backing up, all but pressing their sterns to the fallen scaffolding in front of the lock gates. Every gun was manned. *"Their battle plan broke down entirely,"* Wiplien told her. *"The plorg-lickers mean to inch down the canal and sanitize everything. They'll sacrifice a lot of their own people to take out the booby traps."* The *pov* snapped off the canal, focused on a dry runoff ditch just to Linka's left. *"Go!"* Wiplien barked.

Linka rolled onto her stomach. The movement worked the shale out of her wound. She felt icy coldness and searing hot pain all at once.

She made herself crawl. She rolled into the ditch on her buttocks. Slapped both hands over the wound. *Forjel, that hurts!* She looked about. The ditch was deep enough for her to sit up without exposing herself. She reached inside her jacket. The knife was still there. Cursing, she cut the right leg off her breeches and examined the wound. *Wide laceration, but not too deep,* she decided. *Not near major blood vessels. Not a critical spot in the muscle.* She pulled off her jacket, ripped off one sleeve and bound the wound. *If I have to, I should be able to walk on this.*

The artillery boats opened fire. Linka sprawled face down. She felt as much as heard the thick *whoomps* of the detonations. She heard fist-sized rocks clattering against nearby surfaces. In some other register she heard screams. She watched Wiplien's lateral: Wiplien circled above the skiffs beached beneath the killing knoll. *Neuri was right,* Linka thought with as much horror as she'd ever felt. *The booby traps spooked them so, they're mowing down their own.* Shells whistled down among the skiffs. Hulls, steamplants, and bodies vaulted flaming into the air. Blazing troopers leapt into fire-sheathed water, or ran pointlessly and then collapsed. Wiplien swooped close to one trooper whose entire upper body was engulfed in flames. The man writhed in a harness he couldn't unbuckle. Her *pov* carried stark impressions of the heat and the stench of charring flesh. The burning trooper snatched up a rifle. He managed somehow, with hands on fire, to stick the barrel in his mouth. He found the trigger. Wiplien jerked to one side to evade the bullet. But she was still essentially looking down into the trooper's skull as his brains burst through the leather helmet.

For a terrible instant Linka could see fire dancing on the skiff's floor through the empty circles of the trooper's eye sockets. She scrunched her eyes shut and closed down all the laterals. Holding her ears, she buried her face in her rumpled jacket.

She never noticed losing control.

The noise and carnage were too much. Racking sobs came on her from nowhere. All at once she felt the absences: *Graargy. Sculfka. Tsretmak, Jaekdyr. Sydeno. Harapel—*

Spectator Linka Strasser had stopped observing the attack. She'd started living it. Terrified inside herself, she shrieked agonized denial at a world that was being pulverized all about her.

Shells pounded the cliffside and the path. Hot gravel rained on her back. The ditch saved her from anything worse. The artillery boats continued past her, creeping downcanal toward what had been the core of the settlement.

Linka lay face down in the ditch sobbing for an interval she was unsure of.

The rifle's muzzle was cold against the back of her neck. It prodded once. Twice. "They don't know what that means," a man grunted. "She thinks you're poking her with a stick." Linka could barely hear him; the relentless bombardment had left her ears ringing. She adjusted her implants and dialed her aural sensitivity back to a useful level.

The man dropped onto his stomach on the ground beside the ditch where Linka lay. He reached down. With his left fist he boxed her ear. With his right hand he pressed a cold knife against her neck. "You understand *this?*" Linka opened puffy eyes. It was a sergeant. Sweat had worn channels through the mud and soot caking his face. His platoon stood behind him. Half a dozen rifles and pistols were trained on her.

Linka swallowed. She searched for her voice. "I won't resist," she croaked. "I'm wounded."

The sergeant gestured. Two troopers squatted on either side of the ditch. They dug fingers into Linka's armpits and dragged her to her feet. Her leg sizzled with pain. She adjusted her implants to minimize it. She peered inside for the *verify* signal and found that she was still recording.

The sergeant scowled at the filthy bandage on her leg. "I've seen worse," he said. He eyed her up and down. She wore muddy canvas breeches; she'd cut the right leg off. Her jacket was still a rumple clutched in her fingers. A narrow strip of dirty fabric crossed her full breasts. Yellowish mud and black dust stood in contrast with the chocolate of her skin. The sergeant leered. "I've definitely seen worse."

Linka glanced about. The path was pocked with still-smoking shell holes. The trees and underbrush along the path were smoldering stubble. Downcanal, black billows twisted skyward, pursued by orange ropes of flame. The buildings all blazed, even the hogan of the blind sewing women.

Further downcanal, the two artillery boats had dropped anchor. They poured shells into the fallen truss bridge. It was already half gone.

Linka was startled to see a dozen other black attack boats at anchor along the bank. Their decks sported diverse gunnery, searchlights, and fans. Troopers thronged their decks. Dozens more rushed along the shoreline, anywhere the artillery had obviously cleared all traps.

With one hand the sergeant lifted Linka's chin. She did not resist. He moved his free hand left, then right, two fingers erect. "Follow my fingers with your eyes," he ordered. He watched how Linka tracked it. "No visions," he said to his men. "No sickness. Why?" To Linka: "Where's your leader?"

Linka shrugged. "Our chief is dead."

"Who succeeds him?"

"You killed his sons, too."

"Who leads?" the sergeant demanded.

"Who's left?"

"You, if you cooperate. Warn us if we're near a trap. Any of us die, so do you." A trooper slapped manacles on Linka's wrists. "Don't hurt her," the sergeant told him. "We'll save her if we can."

I can guess what for, Linka thought with dull resignation.

Later, Linka would review her own journals from that day and be surprised how little she remembered after the initial attack.

The vignettes she recalled were little more than glimpses from a starker canvas. She remembered trudging toward what had once been the settlement's core, and seeing no sign of Graargy's hogan, the cave entrance, or the cooking tables. All she'd recognized was the catch barter from which women used to draw the morning water. Its surface roiled beneath a layer of soot and wood chips like the flank of some lazy creature reluctant to awaken. Charred bodies, mostly those of children, bobbed atop the goo.

She remembered recognizing Ulf and Felegu down by the fallen bridge, which the artillery boats had by then reduced to twisted latticework. Troopers crawled over what was left, brandishing cutting torches. With brute force or improvised cranes, fashioners swung the cut-up pieces onto shore. Ulf wore fatigues and a white leather cape like Parek's. Bird skulls twitched at the end of a chain around his neck as he strode upcanal. "Eleven hundred dead!" he raged at Felegu.

"I have no idea why the people weren't neutralized by the visions; it's worked everywhere else." Felegu squinted at a manifest. "Anyway, though the natives put up a defense, our greatest losses were due to friendly fire. Once it was obvious that the shoreline had to be cleared completely, there was no way to recall the troops already ashore."

Ulf shook his head. "The Word Among Us has decided that conversion is not important here. Our priority is to get the whole fleet over this lock, past this bridge, and over the lock at the other end." Ulf looked downcanal sourly. "Have you seen it?"

Felegu nodded. "Beyond the lower lock? It's a fucking abyss."

"Get the fashioners down there at once," Ulf grated. "All their barges and all their equipment. We'll need a crane capable of lowering every boat."

"How will it work?"

Ulf reached inside his cape. He withdrew a sheaf of foolscap. "Have them build this."

Felegu unfolded a few sheets. Eyed Ulf with one eyebrow raised high. "It's in your hand. But I know you're no fashioner."

"The design comes from the sky god."

"So did the one Parek gave the chancellor of the fashioners two days ago."

Ulf stopped, whirled to face Felegu. "It was the same?"

Felegu shrugged. "Quite different," he said, holding a facsimile of Parek's drawings back out to Ulf.

Ulf scanned the sketches. He smiled grimly. "This'll work, too," he said after a moment. "We'll establish a token garrison here. Who's next in the rotation?"

"Diazlam," Felegu said with what seemed like forced neutrality.

Ulf didn't need to appear neutral. "It'll be good to leave that crazy fuck behind."

Amplify her hearing as she might, that was the most Linka had been able to decipher.

She remembered encountering survivors. There were surprisingly few. *Maybe not so surprising.* The beefy guard Tarbyl sat on a charred log, seemingly uninjured. He was oblivious to his surroundings and talking to himself. She saw Freydiin, too—as far as she knew, aside from herself he was the only person atop the killing knoll who'd survived. He had an arm and a leg set in plaster.

Linka hadn't recognized Ixtlaca at first. An artillery burst had deluged the adolescent with shrapnel and wood chips. From the waist up she was one immense peppered swelling. From the waist down she was uninjured, a fact the half-dozen troopers who'd found her body convulsing amid rubble had not hesitated to take advantage of.

Then more troopers had come by.

Ixtlaca had been brought aboard the medic-boat, but there wasn't much point. By contrast, Linka's sojourn there was actually pleasant. A talkative middle-aged man gave her something sweet to drink. He washed her leg and gently cleaned the wound. He produced a jar of salve. "This comes from a city you never heard of, on a continent whose existence you could never suspect," he said affably. "You'll love it." Even under the care of Galactic doctors, Linka had never known anything as blissful as the relief when the medic daubed on that Northern healing salve.

She remembered sitting on a blasted log. She'd been given a blanket and a bottle of water. She'd swabbed herself down as best she could. By now the afternoon was hot. She lay down with the folded blanket under her head. Spent, she closed her eyes and surrendered to the warmth of the sun.

The rifle barrel prodded her shoulder once. Twice. *Prod, prod. It's all these people know.* "Didn't I tell you it was ordained?" a man whined. "Out of all this death one's been spared who might be suitable."

She opened her eyes. The whining voice belonged to the fanatic Diazlam. Six troopers were with him. Diazlam's grim eyes followed her shape. "She'll do," he said to his men. To Linka, he said, "Get up. Follow."

The assignation, she thought wearily. *I knew it would come.*

Diazlam led her toward the largest of the moored attack boats. Large fans were mounted on the foredeck. View window modules from Parek's old flagship had been bolted above the gunwales. Another window had been fitted into the side of the hull. One reached the deck by means of a wooden stairway whose surface was brightly painted, free of scuffs.

Suddenly she was being *tapped* from every direction.

"Linka!" said Neuri Kalistor breathlessly.

"What they say about your luck is true." That was Cassandra Wiplien, envy unmistakable in her voice.

Bubbles spread across Linka's inner awareness like mushrooms after summer rain. Each of her colleagues was sending images of that particular boat. There was only one exactly like it in Parek's riparian navy.

Linka allowed herself a brief grin. She aimed it skyward toward where she thought Neuri Kalistor might be. *"Maybe I'll buy you guys something with the bonus I'll get for this,"* she subvocalized. *"And maybe not."* She listened for the *verify* signal and opened a comm link. *"Urgent urgent urgent. Be prepared to ramp this into max wide distribution, but do not, I say again, do not go live. Probable subject: Spectator Linka Strasser being debauched by Arn Parek. That's right, The Word Among Us himself."*

85. Jaremi Four—Somewhere

Determined not to show her exhaustion, the young woman mounted her *sturruh*. The carved seat strapped to the creature's back fit her badly. After an hour's riding she'd lose feeling in her legs. No matter. She jabbed the animal's flanks with booted heels. It began to trudge. A poking sensation told her the baby had awakened. She

pulled back the fabric flap so the babe could peer out of the traditional infant carrier that lashed him to her chest over a patched, stained tunic. "Quiet, little basket
of trouble," she cooed. "We leave your mother in the dissolving pit. But you're not
the only one who has lost by that. She was my sister, too."

The woman had always assumed the palsy would take her sister. It had struck
her sister more rapidly than it had struck her; still, all women of their line knew
the risk they faced. Disapprovingly she looked down. She watched her own right
foot turn inward and tremble.

But her sister had not died of the palsy. Contagion in her mouth had claimed
her instead. So the message came: the young woman must make the journey back
over the hills. She must return to the village of her birth and take responsibility for
her sister's newborn child.

The young woman scowled down at the infant. "Two close to you have fallen
since you entered the world," she accused. The babe's grandmother had died first,
when the child was just weeks old. Seven months later his mother died, seared by
infection, raving about the child's destiny. According to tradition, a baby who'd
seen two women die was bad luck. Had she refused to take him, there would have
been no objection, just weary understanding. *Yet here we are, a widow and a child
of tragedy, venturing alone into the cold hills.*

The baby squirmed in the carrier. Grunting almost musically, he grasped at
her breast. "Nothing there for you," the woman said. Her own baby, conceived days
before her man would fall in some skirmish, had died of unknown causes—didn't
they always?—eleven weeks before. Her village had not needed her as a wet nurse;
two other women had just lost children and no more were needed to suckle the village's stock of motherless babes. For two months the young woman's breasts had
been swollen and painful. The distress, and with it her milk, had just subsided
when word came of her sister's death. "No, no," she told the babe, "I have nothing
for you. You'll be very hungry before we reach my village. But there'll be milk
there."

The two days' ride to the village would be a punishing length of time for the
babe to go unfed. But what could be done?

She frowned down at the infant. *They say you're something special,* she
thought. *My sister told me that, before she died. Others told me our mother felt the
same. She thought you had "a peculiar destiny," whatever that is.*

The baby looked vaguely back at her, drool pooling behind his lower lip.

"Not like others?" she said. "I don't know, you seem ordinary enough."

With a start, she realized that the babe's wriggling play had had a purpose.
He'd discovered the flap of her tunic and thrown it aside. Squirming in the infant
carrier, he fastened moist lips over her nipple. "No, no," she laughed, gently
pulling his head away. "I am not my sister. Nothing there for you." Stroking the
child's head, she squinted out at the stern landscape.

The famished babe would not be denied. With firm purpose he evaded her
hand and resumed suckling. "Oh, go ahead," she said tiredly. "Maybe it will distract you." The carrier would hold the child in place without her help. She reached
behind her head and drew braided brown hair over her shoulder. Peering critically,
she groomed the braid, picking away leaf fragments and insects and bits of bark. *I*

hate sleeping outdoors, she thought absently. *I should have let my dead husband's sergeant take me that afternoon. He would've lent me a portable shelter then.* Abruptly her attention was drawn by a familiar warm feeling in her bosom. Astonished, she opened her tunic and looked down.

The babe was sucking happily. She eased his head back. Warm white milk dribbled from his lips. She could see a chalky droplet on her nipple. "Well, I didn't think I had any left," she said bemusedly. "Your trip will be more pleasant than I expected."

For the briefest moment the child met her eyes with what she would later remember as a look of intention, of knowing mischief. Then he returned to his feeding.

I was sure my milk was gone, she thought. *Lucky for him. Lucky for me—I won't have to endure the protests of a hungry babe.* She drew her old maternity jacket's outsized flaps over the infant carrier and swigged tart cider from a canteen. *If I were superstitious like my mother, I might think this a miracle.*

86. Jaremi Four—Southern Hemisphere— Parek's Attack Boat

"Want to see it again?"

Linka Strasser blinked and wrinkled her nose. In the confined space of Parek's compartment below decks she wanted nothing to do with another ball of fire produced from the prophet's palm.

Act like an autochthon, she reminded herself. *Everything astounds you.* "Who—what *are* you?"

He was just as he'd seen in a hundred journals. "I am called The Word Among Us. And you're welcome here."

She fingered the band of stained fabric that restrained her breasts. "You . . . want me to. . . ."

Parek laughed. "In good time, in good time. First you must understand that it is no mere man you confront."

She pursed her lips and said nothing.

"You need another demonstration," Parek said. He reached for her arm. She pulled back. "I will not harm you." Gently he brought her fingers up inside the sleeve of his white silk caftan. "Here, feel my arm. No hard muscles. I'm not a strong man. Keep that in mind." He stepped back from her and extended her right arm fully ahead of her. "Make a fist."

She crumpled the fingers of her right hand. *What the sfelb is he setting me up for?*

Parek moved in front of her slowly, unthreateningly. "I'm going to try to bend your arm. I want you to resist. Squeeze that fist as tight as you can. Use all your strength. Are you ready?"

"Yes," she said uncertainly. She clenched as hard as she could. She felt the muscles beside and above her elbows tense up. "Ready."

"Concentrate," Parek said with cool gentleness. He maneuvered his right shoulder beneath her wrist and lay his forearm across her outstretched arm at the crease of her elbow. He let it linger, let the flesh-to-flesh contact register. He clasped his left hand around his own right wrist. Without apparent effort he pressed down. Linka's arm bent instantly, her muscle tension helpless to prevent it.

He smiled. "See, bending an arm is easy. Think you can bend mine?"

She swallowed hard. "I dare not. . . ."

Parek's laugh hung in the dense air like a glissando. "Try to forget this morning." He looked down at her bandaged bare leg. His concern seemed real. "Are you all right to stand this long?"

Linka wrinkled her nose. "The leg isn't bad. You want me to. . . ."

Parek turned. He pulled up the caftan's generous sleeve to bare his arm. "Bend my arm as I bent yours. I told you, I'm not strong. Bend it if you can."

This is the holy man who's rocked a Galaxy back on its heels? Linka wondered. *Using this hairy old stunt?* She brought her shoulder up under Parek's outstretched arm. *Linka girl,* she told herself, *make him believe you have no idea how you're being had.*

Neuri Kalistor had shown her the unbendable arm trick once. Parek's suggestion that she clench her fist and use all her strength had been designed to beguile her into tensing her biceps. *Under tension the biceps contracts the arm, of course it bent under his gentlest touch!* Glancing over her shoulder, she wasn't surprised to see that Parek hadn't clenched his fist. His palm was open, thumb up, fingers straining toward the far wall of the cabin. *He pressed down into the crease of my elbow,* she thought. *I'll be pressing against his elbow joint from the side. More, by opening his palm and rotating the arm he's that way tensed his triceps. Under tension the triceps keeps the arm extended.*

"Ready," Parek said, mischief in his eyes.

Linka pressed down. Nothing happened. She'd known it wouldn't. She cupped both hands over the side of his elbow and leaned her weight on it. Parek snapped his fingers. He waved his hand, heedless of her weight depending from his outstretched arm.

"This is my power," Parek said after a moment. "I am The Word Among Us."

Linka slowly straightened. She leaned her upper body toward Parek's. Also as she expected, he slid a hand around her waist. It drifted down to cup her left buttock.

"Your power is great," she breathed. Their faces were almost touching. "What about your mercy?"

"What about your desire?" Parek's eyes bespoke generosity and forbidden appetites.

Sweat beaded beside his mouth. She flicked at it with the tip of her tongue.

They kissed harshly, tongues darting. Then they stepped apart. He looked at her, and rested his fingertips on her midriff. He let his hands drop. Languidly he untied the sleeves of her jacket and drew it from around her waist. He rumpled it in his hands and raised it toward his face as though he wanted her scent.

Suddenly she realized he was staring at something.

Something on her jacket.

He looked up at her, eyes wide with disbelief. "The birds," he said. "They twinkle."

It was Linka's turn to stare. With an urgency Parek did nothing to resist, she snatched back her jacket. She found the spot Parek had been concentrating on.

Worked into the detailing of the jacket's lower hem was a small glassy lozenge etched with an ambiguous design. Pearl-gray birds rose in formation. Suddenly they were the sky instead. Where sky had been, birds appeared. And back and forth, in and out. Flicker. Flicker. "You see the birds," she said flatly.

He nodded. His body language had changed altogether. The sexual moment was gone.

Pursing her lips, Linka pulled off her sleeveless shirt and handed it to him. She wore nothing above the waist save two finger-widths of fabric shielding her nipples. He didn't notice. "There are more bird medallions in that garment. Show me how many. Show me where they are."

There were three, one smaller than the iris of her eye. He found them without effort. Inside herself she opened a spare channel and subvocalized an emergency advisory: *"Urgent urgent urgent. Arn Parek can see Escher lozenges!"* She tried to sort out what that meant. *Jaremians can't sense that particular figure-ground illusion, that's why Spectators here all wear it. It's a badge other Galactics can see while the autochthons can't.* The genetic tags the unknown Harvesters had added to each planetary population were robust. Mutation was rare. *Parek an offworlder? Almost impossible.*

Still clutching her shirt, The Word Among Us spoke in a voice free from artifice. "You're like Laz," he said. "You're like Laz Kalistor."

Laz Kalistor! Linka lurched back into a chair. Linka's bumpkin *persona* shattered. *Parek knows of Laz Kalistor? It can't be!* She pushed hard against her knees with her palms. Slowly she let her fingers drop. Let them curl over her kneecaps. *Put the outer self away,* she decided. *Give control to your upper self.* "What do you know of Laz Kalistor?"

"I had him killed."

She blinked and fought to keep her face a blank. "Where?" she asked breathlessly.

"Oh, all over. Chest, neck, abdomen—it was a firing squad."

"No, where were you when it happened?"

"In the north," said Parek. "Across the sea in a city named Bihela. You wouldn't know about that." He thought a moment. "Maybe I shouldn't jump to conclusions about what you wouldn't know."

Oh, Laz, no, she thought. *Why did you thrust yourself into this crucible of a world again?* Aloud, she said, "What became of Laz's body?"

"Ulf had a vision. He chopped the body up and threw the pieces in the fire."

O/N-Two again, she thought, heartsick. "Why'd you have Laz killed?"

"God told me to."

"God," she echoed slowly.

"That's his name," Parek said helplessly. "Oh, he's a sky god, just one of many. One of the nicer ones, of course. But he says his name is just plain God."

"You . . . talk to him?"

"Oh, yes." Parek nodded eagerly. "He comes to me in a glowing cloud. He's about this tall, and he wears—I don't know, it's like a big diaper with symbols on it."

Linka ran fingers through her hair. "Let me understand this. This sky god named God appears before you. The two of you have conversations. And during one of these little encounters, God told you to kill Laz Kalistor."

"That's right," Parek confirmed. "Laz wore twinkle bird medallions."

"The god told you to murder Laz *because* he wore, um, twinkle bird medallions?"

"Of course," Parek said brightly. "Soon the god will tell me to have you killed."

"Oh," she said neutrally. Her eyes darted around the compartment. "Is there anything here to drink?"

Parek smiled. He opened a cabinet and drew out a golden ewer and two goblets. "The god will definitely tell me to order your death."

"You sound sure."

"Oh, no question. Every time I meet someone who wears twinkle birds, he bids me have them killed." Parek hunkered down on a strongbox in order to face her. Lacing his fingers, he leaned forward. She realized she occupied the compartment's only chair. "Sometimes I think God doesn't know I see the medallions," Parek said abstractedly. "I think he doesn't know I understand now that the people he tells me to kill all have the medallions in common." He poured the goblets full. "You'll like this."

"Yes, I did," she said at once. "Another, please." He poured again. Now she sipped. "Have you ever had someone killed *just* because they had the twinkle birds—you know, without the god telling you to first?"

"Sometimes."

Linka fought to remain steady. "Did you do it a few days ago? A village survivor, two settlements up the canal?"

"Yes. Yes I did."

"I see." *That's why he ordered Tramir's death.* "Why don't you have me killed?"

Parek looked her up and down. "Among other things, you intrigue me."

"Then let me ask you something," Linka said hesitantly. "When your god orders my death, will you obey?"

"No," Parek said quietly. "But Ulf has visions of his own."

Linka lowered the goblet. "He does?"

Parek nodded. "Ulf's sponsor is an evil god. She hasn't given me much trouble lately, but. . . ."

"Ulf's god is a she?"

"So Ulf says. She always used to want the twinkle bird people killed, too. As I said, she hasn't done much lately, but you never know. I'll try to keep you out of Ulf's awareness until the fleet moves on."

"Thank you. I think."

"What's your name?" he asked quietly.

"I'm Linka."

"I'm Arn. Look," he said awkwardly, "I'm sorry about killing your people, and everything."

The hatchway opened. Chagrin loped in. Linka tried not to show she recognized him from countless sensos. "You signaled, Word Among Us?" Chagrin asked. His eyes never left Linka.

Parek paused expectantly, holding silent until Chagrin looked toward him. "This is Linka," Parek said.

"Hi," Chagrin murmured.

"Charmed," Linka deadpanned. "My face is up here."

"For reasons of my own I want her untouched and out of sight," Parek ordered. "Have Diazlam build a stockade and put her there."

"As you say, Word Among Us." Chagrin smiled.

"I said *untouched,*" Parek reminded him. "And when I say out of sight, I especially mean out of Ulf's sight."

Chagrin nodded understanding. "It will be as you wish." He turned to Linka and offered her his own tunic. "Here, wear something."

Linka pointed toward her jacket and shirt.

"Wear Chagrin's things," Parek ordered.

She donned Chagrin's sweaty garment and followed him topside and off of Parek's boat.

Chagrin led her aboard another anchored attack boat. He locked her in a cabin belowdecks. "I'll be back to take you to the stockade," he shouted through its dogged-down hatch.

Linka's mind raced. *There was a woman,* she thought. *Very famous case. A Terran Spectator who went Inplanet on Jaremi Four. Never heard from again.* Linka juggled years in her head. *The date of the Spectator's disappearance . . . allow five years for her ovaries to restart . . . compare to Parek's apparent age . . . it fits. So maybe Parek is half-Terran. Maybe he's her child. If so, there was an even chance he'd inherit his mother's ability to detect that figure-ground ambiguity Jaremians can't see.*

Linka dispatched a report summarizing her suspicions. *Not that a thousand people at OmNet won't have drawn the same conclusion already.* Quickly she inspected her financials. What Spectators had come to call the "Parek effect" had visited her with stunning force. *More money than I've earned in all the rest of my career, from a single day's journal. And OmNet's nowhere near done repackaging and remarketing it.* Granted, it had been an outlandish day: at dawn that harrowing assault, butchery beyond anything even Linka'd ever imagined; at mid-morning an emotional breakdown whose full import she was nowhere near ready to confront; in late afternoon, her encounter with the most compelling and mysterious man in the Galaxy—she so very nearly had sex with him, no Spectator had approached that—and then, the numbing revelation of Parek's likely ancestry. *The first major religious leader in years who didn't come from Terra,* Linka thought, *and it turns out he is after all. . . .*

"*Linka, you all right?*" Cassandra Wiplien and Neuri Kalistor *tap*ped her at the same moment. "*That stockade is finished,*" Wiplien said. "*Chagrin is coming to transfer you. When night falls, do you want out?*"

Six hours before, Linka would have given anything to vanish. But now? "*Sfelb, no!*" she answered. "*Thanks anyway.*" She paused, sensing that a connection remained open. "*Neuri?*" she said gently. "*Neuri, is that you?*"

She heard swallowing and muffled sobs.

"*You heard, didn't you?*" Linka whispered.

"*Poor Laz,*" rasped the twice-widowed woman. "*He's not coming back at all this time, is he?*"

In his stifling hot compartment, Parek stared deeply into the Escher lozenges on Linka's shirt and jacket. *Birds become sky. Sky becomes birds. I've seen this before— on my mother, on Laz, and on so many of the people God wanted me to kill.* At a sudden realization, he sat upright. *And on one other. Amazing I hadn't made this connection before!* He poured himself more liqueur. *The other person who always wore the twinkle birds was . . . Ruth Griszam.*

87. Inside the Stardrive of the *Bright Hope*

"T hank you for letting me in."

"I couldn't hold out forever, it's your ship," Annek Panna rasped. "Anyway, my energy flags."

Laurien Eldridge smiled wanly as she lay a small package atop a console. "So it's true," she said sadly. "You're killing yourself."

"No," Panna quavered. "I'm starving myself. The art comes in doing one without the other." Panna lay on a nulgrav hammock in an emergency control room inside the body of her stardrive. "Go on, tell me I look like sfelb." Her skin was gray-beige and lusterless. Unkempt, her hair sprayed out behind her as though it had fallen there before she lay down her head.

"I'm searching for the word," Eldridge said non-committally. "You look . . . sepulchral."

"Mm-hmm."

"You really take no food?"

"Not until Enclave falls. Not until our g—not until those who think Parek their god have the freedom to be with him. Until then—" Her voice cracked. She fell silent and exhaled slowly.

"Annek, I'll be frank. I think you're overestimating how much influence your prestige can bring you. You don't understand how determined they are to keep Jaremi Four under Enclave. They'll wait you out, let you starve. Then what?"

Panna pursed her lips faintly to work up saliva. Even that movement opened scarlet fissures. But she managed to croak, "I will win."

Eldridge drew a thumb along the seam of the package she'd brought. It blinked red and peeled open, revealing packaged survival rations. "Electrolyte supplements. Perfumed waters," Eldridge said. "Guarbeast filet Cortemandaise. Millet spiced with *chuli* powder."

"How cruel of you to tempt me this way." Panna daubed at her bleeding lip with a moist fabric square.

"I need you, Annek," Eldridge said earnestly. "I need the smartest woman on this ship to stop working against me." She reached toward Panna's wrists but thought better of grasping them. "All the time you said you needed a cause."

"I have it now." Panna rolled over, showing Eldridge her back. She tabbed a button; a tridee bubble opened against the cluttered background of instruments and controls.

Eldridge recognized the setting after a moment. It was on Jaremi Four, what had once been Lormatin's domain—the place Tramir Duza had been killed. Two or three skiffs lay at anchor. Near the dock, the Parek garrison had thrown up wooden palisades to form a small compound.

"Look," Panna croaked. "The attack begins. It is always thus."

Artillery belched in the woods atop the surrounding hills. Shells whistled down on the compound. Earth and logs fountained. A wooden guard tower twisted over, shedding planks and troopers. Fireballs corkscrewed inside skirts of debris. On the ground, hapless soldiers scurried. "There are only, what, twenty defenders?" Eldridge said.

"Parek undermans the garrisons he leaves behind," Panna rattled. "But that's not his greatest problem." In the tridee, a dozen more shells struck without hitting anything important. Then one fell among the skiffs. Whitewater leapt. A sundered half hull pirouetted from the spray, vomiting greasy fire. Bodies pinwheeled from it, some thudding onto adjacent skiffs.

A ragtag battle group churned around a bend in the canal—two dozen fighting boats of various sizes. "See that? Those are Parek's own boats. Or, they were. His pursuers take them from the garrisons they've already overrun." Coughing, she fell silent. The lead boats lobbed redundant shells at the compound.

After another minute, the shelling stopped. Three hundred Catholic troops burst from trees at widely scattered points along the hilltop. "So many soldiers," Eldridge commented.

Panna nodded. "Part of the army Admiral Spibbert set ashore in the canyon before he entered that half-circle bay."

Eldridge pursed her lips. "No one could leave behind enough men to defend against this."

"Not true. Parek could man and equip a *few* garrisons to repulse such attacks. But so many?" Panna daubed her lips again. "Garrison after garrison, like pearls dropped along the shoreline, just far enough apart so they can't support one another?" Panna waved a hand dismissively. "Parek was mad to attack down a canal like this. Each new settlement falls before him, but he can't keep what he takes. He can't hold his rear."

The Catholic soldiers overran the compound. They rounded up the half-dozen surviving Parek troopers. Most of them were wounded. A Catholic officer strutted before them. He waggled a silver wand toward the captives. "What's he doing?" Eldridge asked.

"Sprinkling them with holy water. I think it's called last rites." Troopers with swords and machetes pushed around the officer. They hacked the survivors to pieces. "They kill with blades to conserve munitions," Panna rasped.

"They're very close," Eldridge said just to make conversation. "Parek's boats are just two settlements down the canal."

"Soon it'll be three." Panna switched to the journal of a no-vis flier inspecting what had been Graargy's valley. The upper lock was empty; nothing remained in the basin except for the garrison's five skiffs. They lay at anchor near another rude stockade. Patched tarpaulins marked the enslaved survivors' crude shelters. "Parek's moving on," Panna breathed. The no-vis flyer swept past the lower lock and wheeled to look backwards, into the circular abyss beneath the lower lock gates. The gate was encrusted with rigging. Crane arms swung fighting vessels over the lip of the circular abyss. The pit yawned eighty meters deep, three hundred across. Its walls, too, were sheathed with modular cageworks, forming a continuous "ship elevator" from the gates' lip to the plunge pool. Boats descended in chain-and-fabric slings amid huge clouds of steam. The splash pool below was already almost full, hundreds of fighting craft huddled gunwale to gunwale. Engineers were already disassembling some of the huge frameworks. "By the time the attackers reach Graargy's basin, Parek will be gone."

"Does this seem like what a holy man does? Running down a river with vengeance on his heels?"

"Captain," Panna said weakly, "you can believe. Being born Gwilyan doesn't mean you must be faithless forever."

"Annek, please," Eldridge said, frustrated. "I'll ask only once more. Give up this hunger strike."

"Not to be," Panna said, keeping her back turned. "I'm sorry I can't see you to the door."

Panna's fevered eyes watched Eldridge's reflection in a glasteel console faceplate. When she was sure the Captain was gone, she rolled onto her back. *"Music,"* she subvocalized.

The composition that lulled her into contemplation was a strident percussion concerto, all glassy clatter and layered metallic rhythms. She didn't know the composer's name. Nonetheless, she'd listened to the piece half a dozen times a day since she'd joined the hunger strike.

Panna immersed herself in the clashing pulsations. As often happened, she thought she heard behind the harmonics a more primordial chiming:

Clang-*shang-ralang. Clang-shang-ralang. Clang-shang-ralang. Clang-shang-ralang. Clang-shang-ralang.* **Clang**-*shang-ralang.*

88. Jaremi Four—Southern Hemisphere— Graargy's Former Domain

"*W*" *hat do you mean you can't get me out of here?*" Linka Strasser subvocalized.

"*Too many eyes,*" replied Neuri Kalistor, back in her role as section boss. "*Already there are eight hundred Catholic troopers on the ridgetop, peering down here through the trees.*"

Linka tightened her hands on the bars of her cell. "*I'm trapped in this stockade. You've seen the journals. When the Catholics liberate a settlement they start by reducing the stockades to splinters.*"

"*Sorry,*" Kalistor said. Her regret seemed sincere, but of course Linka couldn't be sure. "*Max your shields. Hope for the best. The invasion should begin in less than five minutes. And if worst comes to worst, you'll see Tramir Duza before any of us.*"

"*Right, at North Polar.*"

Kalistor broke the subvocal connection. Linka lay back disconsolately in her tiny cell. Peering through the improvised bars, she was struck by the stillness. The garrison Parek left behind was the smallest number of people she'd ever known to occupy the valley. The noises of cooking and drawing water and tending fires and stretching nets—the increasingly precious exclamations of children at play—for six years these had been the background noise of her life. Now there was only a malignant breeze, strong enough to rustle the trees but too weak to stir the canal.

She watched the soldiers march or putter. *I will probably die today,* Linka thought. *So will they. The difference is, I know it.* Her eyes scanned the bamboo bars of the stockade. *The bars? That's no difference. The soldiers are trapped here, too.*

The experiences of the past few days were sinking in. Wonderingly, Linka observed her own thought processes as an outsider might. *Is Enclave itself the problem?* she mused. *On so many worlds Galactics stand superior, detached. We glean boundless amusement from the agonies of Enclave peoples, but it carries a price: the suffering grinds on, and to have permitted that—to have enjoyed it— coarsens us. We could've remade the autochthons, given them lives of power and ease and confidence beyond their maddest imaginings. Instead we concealed our knowledge, blinkered our moral awareness so thoroughly that we began to think voyeurism was the ethical path—that the wholesome human longing to help was the thing we must resist at all costs.*

Before her inner vision the logic was searing. *Enclave is wrong!* The recognition stunned her. *We thought it compassionate to isolate less advanced societies from more advanced ones. We imagined that so long as we made sure the autochthons' histories unfolded just as they would have if Galactic civilization had never discovered them, we'd do them no harm. We'd see that their development proceeded "authentically." How cruel a word! And how ridiculous. Galactic civilization has found them, that's the brute fact. To pickle the autochthons' ignorance, to fence them off so they'll never develop beyond what we consider anthropologically appropriate for them—that's the real interference. Who are we to decide they can't benefit from the unexpected? Human nature is to communicate, to explore differences, to ogle, trade, screw, exploit, perhaps fight—vanquish or be vanquished, oppress or be oppressed—that is authentically human. Enclave is what's unnatural. If two peoples meet, they've met—and if there's a developmental gap between them the less developed group will never be the same. That's just the way it is. That may be harsh, or sloppy, or unfair, but it's real. It's the way events would play out if our Galactic egos didn't insist that we know better than the cosmos itself how everything ought to work out. To plunge our oars in and think we can make the stream run backwards—that's the most pernicious interference of all.*

Far away, atop the killing knoll, the alarm chime began to clang. "Alert! Alert!" shrilled a voice thinned by distance. Linka rubbed the back of her neck. Her skin was gritty, her hair soaked with sweat. Grimly she issued the subvocal commands that would put her into battle mode.

Kalistor's voice was back in her head. *"We've deciphered the attackers' strategy,"* Neuri Kalistor announced in Linka's head. *"They have five attack boats, old ones of Parek's. Looks like they'll send the boats over the locks with the crews below decks and all the hatches closed. Apparently the lead boats are intended to draw fire and divert the defenders' attention. Meanwhile, the soldiers on the ridgetops will try to neutralize the remaining booby traps and storm the stockade."*

The tocsin rang on. Troopers ran about perplexedly. "Get Lieutenant Diazlam!" one shouted. "He's Brethren, he'll know what to do!"

"I am here!" Diazlam swept past. His white tunic swirled over mud-spattered fatigues. Troopers clustered around him.

Engines thrumming, a quintet of black attack boats filed into the upper lock.

"Courage," Diazlam intoned. "This danger is of the spirit. We must reply to it in spirit."

"Spirit?" cried a junior officer. "We need heavy weapons!" Two sergeants sprinted away to get some.

"Belay that!" Diazlam shouted. "We need no weapons." He strode to the water's edge and raised his arms. His fists clutched an Amulet of Truth. Sunlight glinted on its links. "I'll repulse these invaders in the name of The Word Among Us."

I knew Diazlam was a zealot, Linka thought. *I didn't know he was a crank.*

The attack fleet opened its throttles wide. One after another, the black craft scraped over the upper gate. They slapped down in the lower basin behind columns of foam.

Water lapped. Leaves rustled. Nothing happened.

Diazlam began to chant. "Oh great sky god who speaks to The Word Among Us, hearken to our call."

"Let's get guns," a sergeant cried.

Diazlam whirled, transferring the Amulet to one hand. With the other he pressed a pistol barrel against the sergeant's throat. "Were you asleep during the Miracle of the Ships?" The sergeant shook his head frantically. "Then you know there is nothing the power of The Word Among Us cannot accomplish."

"Great is The Word Among Us," the sergeant stammered.

Diazlam holstered his gun. He watched the attack boats with an expression of peace. Gently he called, "Everyone! Form rows. Join hands." The men exchanged startled glances. "Right now!" Diazlam yelled. "Everyone to me!" Troopers lurched forward and lined up behind him. All but Diazlam himself took others' hands.

Diazlam raised the Amulet high. "By the power of The Word Among Us I expel you!" he shouted. Another dozen men joined the prayer group. "Boatmen, your conquest is frustrated. Return whence you came. Turn your baleful frenzy upon yourselves!"

On the lead boat's foredeck, a hatch opened a few finger widths. Maxing her vision, Linka could make out eyes peering through the gap. The eyes bobbed back and forth; their owner was shaking his head. The hatch lurched shut.

More troopers—the last of them—joined the knot of men praying along the concrete bank. "We are strong in the sky gods of the luminous north," Diazlam railed. "To repel these invaders, to throw them back in terror, we need only the power that streams to us through our master."

Let's see, Linka thought. *Allow time for the lookout to convince the commanding officer that the entire defending garrison really* has *lined up almost unarmed at the water's edge. A little longer to exchange signaled orders among the five boats. . . .*

"We repulse you!" Diazlam cried. "Hear the holy name of The Word Among Us!"

Thirty voices chanted: "Pa-rek. Pa-rek. Pa-rek. Pa-rek! Pa-rek! Pa-rek!"

On each deck three hatches pivoted open. Fifteen Catholic soldiers emerged, each with a grenade launcher on his shoulder.

Linka scarcely needed to duck.

Seven seconds after the first launcher fired, the spot where Diazlam and his men had stood praying was a smoking furrow in the canalside path. All about, pavement shards and boots and helmets and belt buckles and twisted knives rained down. Linka started at a clattering sound overhead. It was the Amulet of Truth, scorched and useless. It had pinwheeled out of the sky onto the latticework of her cell.

Surprised that the boatmen had attacked in advance of their orders, the soldiers above scrambled to deploy their own weapons: great logs seven meters long and a man's height thick, ringed with metal straps, their cores hollowed out and filled with gravel—heavy enough to set off any trap they encountered, too massive for any trap to stop. Twenty such logs lay end to end along the ridgetop. Fighters strained to push them over the edge. *I'm amazed Lormatin never thought of this,* Linka thought. *Sfelb, I'm amazed I never thought of it myself.* Irresistibly, the logs crashed down the hillside in a maelstrom of dust. Ground lines yanked at nothing; spring traps fired spears and barbs through empty air; leghold traps snapped off under the logs' bulk.

Seventeen logs crashed all the way to canalside amid fountains of dirt and metal and leaves. They'd cleared every trap in their path. Eight hundred Catholic soldiers scrambled down behind them waving steamrifles and repeating carbines. But there was nothing for them to kill.

The basin had fallen.

"Say, Neuri?" Linka subvocalized. *"Looks like my trip to North Polar has been*

postponed." She rearranged herself on the bench in her cell and made a leisurely journal of the Catholics consolidating their victory. Commanders organized working parties. Platoons swept for more traps. Squads inventoried the weapons and supplies in the compound's intact storerooms. Work teams boarded the docked skiffs and began converting them for service in the liberation fleet.

The dozen enslaved survivors from Graargy's vanquished colony emerged from beneath their tarpaulins. Tarbyl, their leader, had kept them hidden while there was danger, but now. . . . "We're free! We're free!" Tarbyl shouted. Men and women lumbered toward the nearest Catholic officers, arms wide in gratitude. "You have delivered us!" they shouted, raising their arms in what was simultaneously a celebration of victory and a symbolic embrace. "Hail our liberators!"

The officers drew guns and shouted for sergeants. Sergeants ran up lugging rifles and formed the survivors into two slave labor gangs.

For three hours, Linka was simply ignored.

Then a tall officer appeared at the bars of her cubicle. He had piercing eyes and a scar across his forehead. He said nothing. With crisp hand signals he commanded Linka to stand up, open her tunic, and slowly turn around. She obeyed.

Still silent, the officer marched away. *This is where I came in,* Linka grumbled to herself. *Another forjeling assignation!*

Two more hours passed.

Linka wasn't conscious of having gone to sleep, but the clatter of a baton against wooden bars awakened her. The sky was sunset-ruddy. The silent officer had returned. He had a commander with him.

The commander squinted in at Linka, his right hand behind his back. He flashed his subordinate a neutral glance that seemed to say, *She's everything you said.*

The satellite had broken contact when Linka fell asleep. Hurriedly she resumed recording. The *verify* signal's reassuring hum took less than a second to rebuild. Her bladder burned for release. She shunted the sensation into the background of her awareness.

The officer waved Linka away from the cell door. Two pistol blasts destroyed the lock. The door swung open. The officer jerked his head, clearly a command for Linka to emerge. Smiling wanly, Linka shuffled out of the cell.

As she passed him, he yanked away her tunic. It had only been draped over her shoulders. Linka stood before the commander wearing only what she'd worn at the end of her encounter with Parek: breeches with one leg cut away to the thigh, boots, a bandage, and a two-finger strip of dirty purple cloth across her breasts.

She wore no Escher lozenges. Parek had taken those. Ever since, there'd been so many people around her that not even a no-vis flier had dared bring her replacements.

The commander's lips turned up in a bloodless smile.

"I know what's happening here," Linka said carefully. "I'll cooperate."

"Of course you will," said the commander. His voice was reedy. He brought his right hand from behind his back. It held an elaborate pistol. His smile never changed as he pressed it between her ribs.

And fired.

89. The *Bright Hope*

The command officers had reconvened in their improvised meeting room. Once again Admiral Hafen was telepresent. "The Confetory's foremost advisers, its most powerful computing resources are at our disposal," Hafen began. "Let's see what we can determine about *Bright Hope's* unwanted companions."

"Fem Gavisel, Fem Wachieu," Eldridge began. "You've worked twenty-four hours straight on unraveling this."

"Should've taken an hour and a half," Wachieu groused. "The forjeling binary . . . well, that's just my problem." She darkened the room. "We'll begin with *Damocles.*" A conventional exterior view of the pilgrim trawler crackled into sight above the table. It grew dense with luminous data overlays. "External architecture is normal for a vessel of this type. Forward command section. Half a kilometer further aft, the propulsion section. Behind that, nineteen kilometers of central spine to which are moored thirty cargo pods." Like grapefruits glued to an endless pencil, the immense globes dwarfed the cylindrical spine that connected them. "Once one gets below the surface, the architecture's less standard. Each pod's been lavishly converted to support about thirteen hundred people, for years if need be."

"Thirty pods, thirteen hundred pilgrims—so the total population's just about what Stenoda Gerris claimed," Eldridge said.

Wachieu nodded. "Counting the control crew, the full complement is forty thousand, two hundred forty-nine." She tapped controls. A detailed cutaway of a single cargo pod rushed forward. "Here's an odd feature. Each pod has its own contramagnetic inverter, its own susceptors, J-series comm array, and meta-inertial drive system."

Eldridge nodded. "It's equipped to disengage from the trawler and navigate on its own."

"Within a stellar system, at least," Wachieu agreed. "The command and propulsion sections are also designed to break up. Even the ship's spine can split into five independently mobile segments. Superdreadnoughts and starliners aren't built with that kind of redundancy and independent functionality."

"The control architecture is equally quirky, but in the opposite direction," Gavisel reported. "Despite each segment's sophistication, communication among the subsections is minimal. It's as if the pilgrims in the various pods never talk to each other. Clearly none of them has a voice in running the ship." Schematics flickered past. "Even stranger, *Damocles* has no subsidiary control points. No auxiliary command centers. The *only* place you can fly the ship from is the control room in the command section."

"That's so risky," Hafen said.

"Perhaps," Gavisel answered, "But it's the ultimate security measure when you're hauling forty thousand religious fanatics. There's no scenario under which any coalition of pilgrims can seize control of the ship. They're literally human cargo."

"For the money he spent, Stenoda Gerris could have configured *Damocles* any way he wanted," Eldridge said thoughtfully. "Why *these* features? What do they tell us about the mission profile?"

"No need for reverse engineering," Wachieu said brightly. "We *found* the mission profile."

Hafen nodded slowly. "Your people are first rate, Captain Eldridge."

"Thank you," Eldridge told the admiral. To her officers, she said, "You should be proud."

"Proud, but not happy," Gavisel said darkly. "The *Damocles* control software is the most insidious contingency heuristic I've ever decoded. It's designed to implement a single agenda in response to a surprisingly wide range of inputs—and to do so *absolutely* irrevocably. Suppose *Damocles* is taking heavy punishment from hostile fire, or imagine any situation that the thought engines might read as a grave threat to the trawler's integrity or mission. In such a predicament *Damocles* is programmed at a deep and almost certainly inaccessible level to break up into her component parts and leave orbit."

"The subsections head into space?" Eldridge asked, puzzled.

"They dive for the surface."

"Let me be sure I understand this," Hafen said sharply. "If the trawler's thought engines decide she's deep in crisis, *Damocles* will fragment and her subsections will land."

Gavisel shook his head in strangled little motions. "They don't land, they crash."

"They *crash!*" Eldridge echoed. "It doesn't matter what the command crew does, or what the pilgrims do? The control software just makes its own highly personal decision to splatter *Damocles* all over Jaremi Four, and nothing can stop it?"

"Basically," Gavisel said. A graphics bubble opened: it was a crude animation of the trawler. "Wachieu found this in one of the control software's help files. "Just as Gavisel had described, the ship turned into a swarm of fragments that screamed down independent paths toward the Jaremian surface. "But the subsections don't crash randomly."

"Impact," Eldridge breathed. White plumes erupted in a neat circle, centered on that point that flashed yellow, green, yellow, green.

Gavisel pointed toward the flashing point. "The subsections are programmed to strike in a perfect circle centered on that point," Gavisel explained.

"What's there?" Eldridge asked.

"Not what," Gavisel said. "Who. The point marks the location of Arn Parek."

Hafen and Eldridge exchanged astonished glances.

"*Damocles* has a whole rack of thought engines whose sole task is to track Parek's location using OmNet feeds, dead reckoning, and anything else it can find. If the ship is about to break up, those thought engines transmit the most recent location fix to each of the subsections. Each subsection applies a characteristic offset to Parek's coordinates. Hence the circular distribution of crash sites." Gavisel spread her hands. "The command sequence is as impervious as anything I've ever seen. Once triggered I very much doubt it can be stopped."

No one spoke.

Hafen's question impaled the silence. "Fem Gavisel, the circle around Parek—what's its diameter?"

"Twenty-eight kilometers."

"What's the momentum at impact?"

"Modest." Gavisel tapped controls. "I'm sending you the ballistics data."

Hafen peered at his readouts and conferred with unseen advisors. "Large fragments of debris will survive the crashes."

"I think so," Gavisel said.

"A further computation: unprotected humans within five kilometers of Parek's location will face zero danger from the impacts."

"But they get one plorg-warmer of a show," Eldridge observed.

"But why?" Wachieu demanded. "Why leave major debris in a perfect circle around Parek?"

Hafen looked away briefly. When he returned his attention to *Bright Hope*, his expression was grave. "One of my admiralty lawyers has a disturbing hypothesis. I think we know the crash program's deep purpose." Dataspheres popcorned open above the table. Legal texts boiled across them. "There's an obscure provision in the Admiralty Code, drafted centuries ago when the Enclave Statutes were first passed. The scenario it would govern never occurred, so it had been largely forgotten. But it retains the force of law. What it provides, essentially, is that should a Galactic ship crash onto an Enclave planet, should numerous autochthons witness the crash and survive, and should they inspect the crash site and find wreckage obviously not of their world—in other words, should the secret come out—the planet's Enclave status is suspended at once."

"No matter how primitive the planet's cultures?" Eldridge said slowly.

"No discussion. No appeals. The planet enters the Confetory immediately as no less than a Protectorate. The idea was to limit the emotional toll on autochthons who suddenly realize there's a Confetory out there that's been spying on them all this time."

Eldridge licked the back of her teeth. "If *Damocles* thinks her mission is failing, she breaks up. The pieces rain down all around Parek, leaving substantial wreckage. Enclave is shattered."

"That would seem to be the terminal mission profile," Gavisel said hollowly.

"The pilgrims die," Hafen objected.

Wachieu frowned. "Their sacrifice opens the planet."

"In death, they win," Eldridge breathed. "*Damocles* indeed."

"Fem Gavisel," Hafen interjected after a moment. "Have you any idea how long the software will take to make the decision to crash?"

Gavisel examined his readouts. "The thought engines are programmed to audit their analysis several times before they concede that *Damocles* is fatally compromised. In an ambiguous situation, it might take days. In a more obvious crisis—say, if the trawler were being dismembered by hostile fire—the determination might require as little as fifteen seconds."

Hafen asked soberly, "Could *Bright Hope* fire a single weapons burst that would reduce *Damocles* to particles too small to survive reentry?"

"And kill more than forty thousand people?" Eldridge demanded.

"Were it necessary," Hafen pressed, "could *Bright Hope* do it?"

Eldridge invoked a few datacrawls. *"Damocles* is unshielded. If our little weapons battery functions up to spec, a single full-spasm volley from all tubes should suffice."

"For vacuum's sake," Wachieu demanded, "what are we contemplating?"

"The only thing we can," Gavisel said without inflection.

"Fem Wachieu," Eldridge said. "Preload a firing sequence that will vaporize *Damocles* in one burst. I want that sequence no more than two control inputs away from execution at any time."

"Aye," Wachieu whispered.

"Next point," Hafen said after a moment. "Any sign of large Vatican installations on Jaremi Four?"

"None," Wachieu answered sourly. "But at the miserable resolutions I'm achieving, I could easily be overlooking an underground complex, maybe even a surface facility if it's shielded."

"Any signatures of concealers or displacers?"

"You've got to be kidding," Wachieu said acidly. "Sorry, Admiral."

"So I imagine you've had no luck finding the orbital manufactory we think is there."

Wachieu scowled. "Same needle, bigger haystack."

"As we expected," Hafen said equably. "On to the next item, that fleet from Khoren Four. We've been busy on this end, compiling background. Khoren Four's some miserable little mining world. Two centuries ago it somehow managed not to receive Enclave protection. The whole planet wound up sole property of a clan called Greder. The current owner's Orgena Greder. She controls such a disproportionate share of the planet's wealth that it's unlikely this fleet was assembled without her involvement. And intelligence tells us she's had high-level connections with Vatican."

"Intriguing," Eldridge said. "What's it add up to?"

"We have no idea. Fem Wachieu, sorry to put the pointer on you again, but what have you learned about the approaching fleet?"

"Once again, not much. *Cornucopia*'s a perfectly ordinary manufacturing trawler—no surprises like we found inside *Damocles.*"

"Did your scans reveal anything anomalous?"

Wachieu shrugged. "Every scan reveals something anomalous, Admiral. Are the anomalies meaningful? My analysis says no, but let me squirt your analysts the raw data."

"Received," Hafen said after a moment. "As I said—Eldridge, Gavisel, Wachieu, all of you on *Bright Hope*—the Confetory truly appreciates the extraordinary effort you are . . . well, hello."

"Admiral?" Wachieu asked tonelessly.

"Fem Wachieu, I'm sending you a filter pack configuration one of my thought engines came up with. Reexamine your datascape through it and tell me if you see what I see."

"Working." Wachieu took control of the Detex system and downloaded the filter settings. She then transferred them. "Plorg on a stick," she breathed. "Sorry, Admiral." She stared up at Eldridge. "Trawler *Cornucopia* is flying through her own flux wake. She's not going to Jaremi Four. She's already been there. She is going *back*."

"What about the other ships in the fleet?" Eldridge demanded.

"Of the seventy-three ships in the approaching fleet, only *Cornucopia* is retracing her own path."

Hafen rocked back in an unseen polychair. "So *Cornucopia*'s already been to Jaremi space."

"Something that size was under *Bright Hope*'s nose and we missed her?" Eldridge sputtered.

Hafen shook his head. "As we extrapolate her turnaround point, *Cornucopia* left Jaremi space shortly before your arrival."

Eldridge stood and paced. "What's this mean? Was *Cornucopia* the missing manufactory—did it build Vatican's navy?"

"We think she's too small for that," Hafen said. He paused a moment. "I'm also told that Greder's connections with Vatican were unfriendly. She was essentially thrown offworld by Secretary of State Rybczynsky himself."

"Of course!" Eldridge slapped her hands together. She rushed back behind the conference table. "It has to be—Admiral, I think we've identified Ulf's Galactic handler."

"Greder?" Hafen said blankly.

"You said the Vatican navy was too big to have been manufactured aboard *Cornucopia*. But Parek's navy was smaller."

"Hmm, that might be a fit," Hafen conceded after a moment.

"And if her relations with Vatican are adverse, what would make more sense than for her to provide the *other* navy?"

"My analysts agree," Hafen said. "It's highly probable that *Cornucopia* manufactured and delivered the Parek fleet to the ancient port at Kiewalta."

Eldridge frowned. "Some Enclave planet. Who *hasn't* been down there?"

Hafen started chortling. "Captain Eldridge, I believe we've established Fem Greder's motivation. Three years ago, Greder lobbied unsuccessfully to get a Khorenian chieftain declared an authentic Incarnation of the Cosmic Christ. She spent five hundred and thirty-two billion credits on Vatican before they turned her down."

Wachieu leaned forward. "I think Greder wants control over Parek."

"Why should that appeal to the tyrant of some fourth-rate mining world?" Eldridge asked.

"She knows the benefits an Incarnation can bring," Wachieu explained. "She would've investigated every possible way to wring wealth or fame or influence out of one. That's why she spent half a trillion credits trying to get a confirmed Incarnation sanctioned on her world. And if Greder was spending so freely on Vatican at that time, she may have been among the first to hear rumors that the next Christ was on Jaremi Four."

"The analysts here like it," Hafen declared. "If Fem Greder couldn't have a Christ under her thumb on Khoren Four, why not target the next Christ that comes along?"

Eldridge nodded. "Greder sponsors Ulf. Greder helps Ulf keep the army strong. Parek has to do at least some of what Ulf tells him."

Gavisel rubbed his temples. "This leaves one problem. Why did Greder leave, then come back?"

"What do you mean?" Eldridge asked.

"Assume Greder's motivation was constant all along: she wants a piece of the next Christ. At first she thought the best way to achieve that was to build Ulf a navy, drop it off, and leave. Suddenly she changes her mind. Partway home, she decides the best strategy is to turn around and come back to Jaremi Four, accompanied by every piece of space junk she could order out of Khorenian orbits. What changed?"

"*Damocles*," Wachieu said, sounding haunted. "*Damocles* came to break Enclave. If she succeeded, if Jaremi Four were thrown open, Greder's best shot at influencing developments is to be the first to make a soft landing."

"Legal first contact," Eldridge said. " She'll have a *claim* on the forjeling planet."

90. Terra—Wasatch Range, Usasector

The rail of Alrue Latier's treadmill was like an old-fashioned sailing ship's. Or it would be, if old-fashioned sailing ships had fat platinum rails and coursed from world to world at the breakneck speed of sim. Passing stars seemed to burn tiny reflections into the polished rail. Latier's meaty hands clutched that rail. He looked resolutely to the left and right. He wore his usual symbol-studded muslin jumper. An impossible wind rustled his sandy gray hair.

His zigzag course among the stars brought him close to a representation of each Confetory Memberworld. At each approach, bubbles opened depicting the protests, riots, mass crucifixions, epidemics of suicide, public renunciations of material wealth, civil wars, or peaceful festivals—whatever the form might be in which "Parek fever" had most luridly manifested itself on that planet.

At least, that was what the experients of Latier's devotional tridee 'cast would see. The reality was more prosaic. In actuality, Latier clasped the rail for dear life as his gimbal-mounted treadmill bobbed and pitched two meters above the studio floor. Banks of remote-controlled lights flickered and waggled and shifted colors to create interactive lighting effects. Tridee pickups feinted to and fro on flexible stalks, creating a visceral sense of movement which the background plate of shifting celestial objects would amplify.

Ferret-eyed, Heber Beaman stood in the studio, beside the gimbal rig, silently relaying subvocal commands between Latier and the tridee artists in the communications center.

"On Rikub," Latier intoned, "Parekians have set fire to a lakeful of sparkling whiskey. On Nikkeldepayn, other Parekians are leading arenas full of the faithful on multiple-day public drunks. On Ghyrel Two, sons of the powerful seafaring families are scuttling their ships in mid-ocean. More than two dozen Memberworlds have been disrupted by riots, even civil war. On Kfardasz and Gheltt, disorder has toppled the established governments. Across the Galaxy mountebanks heal in Parek's name. Yea, the mighty are confounded as they struggle to adjust to the presence among us of the One Mighty and Strong." The last conspicuous planet passed astern of his tousled hair as Latier stared grimly ahead. "All this hope and rage and uplift and pain is centered on a single world, of course—a world unimaginably far away across the great star-strewn pinwheel of our Galaxy."

"On my cue, look thirty degrees up, ten o'clock," Beaman subvocalized. *"Now. Peer earnestly . . . earnestly . . . now light up your face, your hopes are answered. Eyes back to the rubes."*

Just as Latier looked back into the pickups, his face beaming, the object he'd apparently been watching swam into view astern. A dun-colored orb, its equator was girdled in blue. "Jaremi Four," Latier proclaimed. "Where even now the current Incarnation of Christ flees from sinister pursuers." The pickup pressed in close to Latier's sweaty face. "Of course, we can do nothing directly to help Arn Parek. He's on an Enclave world, after all, and in any event the path of a Christ's life belongs only to God. But you can give your spiritual support, as I do. In fact, you can give your spiritual support most powerfully by simply giving to me.

"There's so much to do, homs and fems, so many missions to launch—truth be told, so many bills to be paid. I have some ships in mothballs on Minga Four that I could stand to—" Latier struggled to keep his face calm as Beaman subvocalized shouted warnings. "Well, never mind that, soldiers of Christ. Just reach for those credit chits and let the old Prophet, Seer, and Revelator see how much you love Parek. Any day now he may give his life for you. Why not let Alrue know what *you* can give?"

91. Inside the Stardrive of the *Bright Hope*

Annek Panna sat up on the nulgrav hammock. Her mind brimmed with confidence. An overpowering urgency shone through her. Time to act, she thought. Time to end the charade. The starving inventor saw her future with pellucid clarity.

The same clarity with which, at the height of her reverie, she had beheld Arn Parek.

Clang-shang-ralang, the harmonics had chimed. *Clang-shang-ralang. Clang-shang-ralang.* **Clang**-*shang-ralang.* Had she imagined it, or were those tones really implied in the textured densities of the recorded percussion concerto that spangled in her ears? Had she imagined the swirling mists before her eyes that sparkled and whirled and coalesced into that compelling face?

Close-cropped hair in front. A shaven triangle, downward-pointing, leading the observer to his smoldering eyes. Such eyes! A lustrous scar across one cheek. Full hair flowing in torrents from the back of his head.

Chords had rained in her ears, pitched and pitchless, muffled and sharp. The ringing clatter splashed her. Sonic textures overlapped. *Bamboo chimes.* Fluttered. *Tom-toms in dialogue.* Crashed in opposition. *Tiered curtains of glockenspiels.* Surged in concord. *Wood blocks and glasteel bells.* And the rhythms. *The rhythms.* In that cacophony had she imagined the contours of his voice? "Annek," Parek had said, his tone hypnotic. "I don't know you. But I fathom your devotion. I sense your capability."

He'd looked up at her imploringly. Was that blood rimming his eyes, advancing down his cheeks like two meandering fingers?

"I hear you, Word Among Us," she'd said in a clear voice. *I haven't sounded so strong in weeks.*

"Save me," Parek had implored her. "Only you can save me." The pixels composing his face had swirled and whirled over each other. They recombined into an image of Jaremi Four. Then they compounded again into a rough image of the Galaxy, With its central disk and spreading, circling arms.

Shrill percussives had rippled. Clangor had swept through Panna's brain.

"Save me," he had implored.

"Anything for you," she'd whispered.

His neediness had risen viscously inside her and outside, too. It pressed wet and heavy against her hands, her hips, her chest. She'd savored it. "Only you," he told her countless times. "You are the special one. Save. Save. Save. You are the special one. Save. Save. Save. Save. Save."

Clang-shang-ralang. Clang-shang-ralang. Clang-shang-ralang. Clang-shang-ralang. **Clang**-*shang-ralang.*

On the console beside her hammock still lay the food pouches Eldridge had left. Groaning, Panna sat up. She took a liter carafe of water. *A sip only*, she told herself. She pulled out container after container of contraband foodstuffs. In short order the night table and the floating comm console were covered with packaged foods. She went over and over the plan that had come together in her mind. She turned it this was and that, tore it inside out the way she liked to dissect engineering solutions.

She could find no flaw. Resolution had begun to form like an ice crystal imposing its structure on liquid water's soft lattice. The sense of mission she felt, the impression of belonging, filled holes she'd never fully acknowledged noticing in herself. *Now is my time*, she thought with implacable joy.

Panna allowed herself a whole mouthful of water. She raised a glittering cylinder and contemplated its label. *Guarbeast filet Cortemandaise, eh?* she thought. *Why not? Something tells me I'll be needing my strength after all.*

92. Terra, Jaremi Four

"An urgent pastoral message from His Holiness, The Holy Father of the Universal Catholic Church, bishop of Rome, vicar of Jesus Christ, successor of the prince of the apostles, supreme pontiff—"

Alois Cardinal Rybczynsky muted the announcement. He frowned at the sky. Thick clouds flickered. Whitecaps raked Lake Albano a hundred and thirty meters below. Valets scurried his luncheon inside. Castel Gandolfo had been the summer residence of Terran popes. Like many church properties abandoned when the Holy See moved to Vatican, it had been purchased by private speculators who leased to a succession of influential clerics. Rybczynsky was the fourth cardinal to call Castel Gandolfo home when church business called him back to the motherworld. He would not be the last to abandon his beloved *terrazzo* for the former papal apartment at the approach of a peninsular storm.

Scowling, Rybczynsky settled into a velvet wing chair. A monk flipped on the tridee in there. Modest IV's familiar visage swam together in midair: the golden miter, the virtual *pallium*, the grandfatherly smile. "To be a Catholic is to embrace many mysteries. God is three, yet one. That is a mystery which the faithful cannot understand, yet believe. The Eucharist is truly transformed at the moment of its consecration, yet to the senses it remains bread and wine. Another mystery which the faithful simply believe without comprehending.

"Not long ago We spoke to the Galaxy and proclaimed *ex cathedra*—that is, infallibly—that Arn Parek is not the Cosmic Christ." Modest leaned forward, startlingly close to the tridee pickup. "We come before you today to make another infallible pronouncement, informed by prayer and weighted with the full teaching authority of the Church. Arn Parek *is* the newest Incarnation of the Cosmic Christ." He raised two fingers in a gesture of benediction. "The faithful will not understand, but believe."

Rybczynsky savored a mouthful of turbot seasoned with contraband Jaremian *skhaar*—a peace offering from Semuga, back when Semuga had still cared about maintaining the appearance of peace between them. In the tridee, the pope seemed awkward as he turned to open a meterwide patristic tome. *The theology Modest must present is daunting*, Rybczynsky thought, *the more so because he hopes to convince the general public. If Modest can't present his case with supreme confidence, his gambit will fail.*

The Pope spread his palms above the ancient book's illuminated leaves. He looked up, eyes weirdly asparkle. "Perhaps too often Mother Church emphasizes the teachings that various Christian communities hold in common. Doing so risks losing sight of the faith's diversity. In fact, authorities disagree as to how the Cosmic Christ takes on flesh. As late as the time of Saint Augustine, Terran Christians who revered the Gospel of Matthew could still believe that the Cosmic Christ first entered Jesus at the moment he was baptized by John the Baptizer. 'Thou art my beloved son, in thee I am well pleased,' God the Father says in the earliest versions of this Terran Gospel: 'This day I have begotten thee.'"

Straight out of the Ebionite and Manichaean heresies, Rybczynsky thought uncomfortably. *Then again, it's also straight out of the Letter to the Hebrews.*

"Apotheosis," Modest said as if sharing a secret. "The elevation of a human vessel to godhead. The essence of Incarnation. Theologians and the faithful wonder: What does it mean? When does it occur? I pose another question. Need the Church insist on a single answer? Does it not disparage Our Lord's creative authority to insist that there can be only one way?"

Modest's voice rings with assurance, Rybczynsky thought approvingly. *That assurance is beginning to enter his posture also.*

"On Kfardasz," Modest lectured, "Scripture says the mother and father of that world's Christ knew their destinies for fifteen years before they met. On Vyrdis Ten, the man the Cosmic Christ chose as His vessel did not understand his status until late middle age, by which time His putrefying body had already sloughed off an arm and a leg. The Christ of Wikkel Four announced Himself aloud at the age of two—a necessity, since this particular Incarnation would end just three years later in a still-unexplained playground accident. On Frensa Six, Christ entered a profoundly insane man of forty who died—by his own hand, some say—still denying His Godhead."

The pickup pressed closer. Choral music sounded gently. "Mother Church has directed holy men and experts of every stripe to study developments on Jaremi Four. Formerly they agreed that Arn Parek was not a Christ. Later developments have caused them to reverse that decision." Modest clapped the palm of his free hand against his chest. "We, Ourself, concur in this."

Rybczynsky sipped astringent Ghelttian wine. *This just may work,* he thought.

"There are two ways one might interpret such a reversal," Modest said affably. "The less credible solution is to imagine that Holy Mother Church has contradicted herself in response to some venal motive. True, abbeys and cathedrals and monasteries have been lost to schism or violence. Catholics across the Galaxy have suffered because of popular impatience with Our refusal to proclaim Parek's Godhead. But Ours is a church militant, no stranger to persecution on some of the very worlds over which She now exerts blithe dominion. Though Her pews and coffers lay empty, though every hand turned against Her, Mother Church would ever cleave to truth."

Rybczynsky couldn't help smiling. *He almost makes me believe that.*

Modest smiled. "The more reasonable interpretation is that Parek's early ministry, despite its many, um, unusual aspects, was Our Lord's means of preparing the man Parek to receive an Incarnation which has but recently occurred. Months ago We spoke infallibly when We said that Arn Parek was not the Christ. Today We speak infallibly when We say that He is." Modest spread his palms. He beamed the tridee pickup a smile that might convert a roomful of Gwilyans. "Glory be to God the author of all blessed mysteries—not the least of which is that He has selected as the current vessel of Christ His Son this blood-soaked prophet on Jaremi Four."

"Heresy! Transparen' falsehood!" Ato Cardinal Semuga raged. His hand tensed once more around the autochthonous woman's neck. The skin was starting to cool. "Holy Father, you disgrace yourse'f!" Semuga levered his pale nude bulk toward the foot of the soma disk. His elbow slipped in blood that had pooled atop the silken sheets.

"Other accusations have been leveled against Holy Mother Church," the pope said with an air of wounded innocence. "Some say high-ranking Catholic agents violated Enclave. Some say Church emissaries raised an army, then a navy to smite Him whom We now acknowledge as the Christ. We assure you now that all such charges are baseless."

Roaring, Semuga seized an empty brandy bottle and smashed it redundantly against the woman's body. "Baseless, Mod'st?" Semuga slurred. "Unfound'd, you say?" He hurled the bottle toward the terrace doors. They whistled open. The bottle shattered outside.

Cursing, he waddled toward the terrace and stared outside. His hands left crimson prints on the pink crystal walls. "I buil' you a city!" he raged. Rows of towers and cranes and manufactories loomed purple-gray in the Vatican Island twilight. "No one served you as I did!" He lurched back toward the sleeping platform. He rolled the dead strumpet onto the floor.

Modest-in-the-tridee stood. He waggled a single upturned finger. "And if there *were* activities in Jaremi Four's vicinity," the pope continued winsomely, "operations not authorized by Mother Church, but perhaps inspired by Her interests, informed by sympathy with Her desires—surely such operations, if they existed, would have been intended solely to authenticate and protect this Incarnation."

"Parek's the fals' god!" Semuga snorted. He slapped an autobar. A fresh brandy bottle appeared. Fingers clumsy with anger tore at its seal. Snarling, he hurled the bottle into the main chamber. Glass and liquid scattered.

"An open one!" The autobar obliged.

The pontiff crossed his arms, a pose better suited to some angry pugilist than to the Vicar of the Prince of Peace. "In the name of the Universal Catholic Church," Modest intoned, "in the name of the Cardinals and Bishops assembled, indeed in the name of God Himself, We say: Enclave must fall! We demand in righteous majesty that the Privy High Council withdraw Enclave protection from Jaremi Four. A Galaxy of pilgrims must no longer be denied. *Enclave must fall!*"

Semuga rested his pockmarked buttocks on the edge of the soma disk. Swigged deeply. Frowned. Waved the bottle toward the pontiff's still-smiling visage. "You have pros'ituted your Church on th' altar of public opin'on," Semuga slurred. "You b'smirch yourse'f by proclaiming false Parek th' Christ. *Chamberl'n!*" he shouted at the air.

"Y-yes, Most Eminent Lord?" a tinny voice replied.

"I need another woman," Semuga said. He looked down. The strumpet's mouth was shattered. He'd stoved in her skull above the left ear. Blood matted her hair. "This 'un fell down."

"Sorry, Excellency," came the chamberlain's voice after an awkward silence. "That was the last one."

"We're *out?*" Semuga brayed.

"Unfortunately so, Eminence. I'm told a submarine swims here with fresh, pleasing specimens from Southland."

"It better swim fas'," Semuga said drunkenly.

"We expect it the day after tomorrow."

Semuga grunted. He filled his mouth with brandy. "Y'watchin' this?" he demanded of the air. "It's horrib'e. Forjelin' pope's betrayin' us all."

93. Jaremi Four—Vatican Island

*S*o this is North Polar, Linka Strasser thought. *I didn't think I'd ache this much.*

She forced her head up. The first object she recognized was an institutional sink. Its glassy-metallic finish, the absence of physical controls, marked it as Galactic.

But the room smelled of nature and sunlight and jungle flowers. To the left of the sink was a slit in the wall, a meter and a half wide by twenty centimeters high. It seemed unglazed. *An open window at North Polar?* Outside, trees wafted gently on a zephyr. *Tropical species,* she thought.

Which was when raised her head—and realized she hadn't come back to life at all.

She still wore the muddy breeches, the right leg cut off hip-high. A filthy bandage still covered the thigh wound. Above the waist she wore only the two-finger-wide fabric band. Grime clung to her full breasts, here imprisoning flecks of dirt or woody debris, there scraped clean by the erratic paths of long-dried sweat. Her right nipple had sprung free of the band.

Dirt and salt itched beneath the waistband of her breeches. The skin between her fourth and fifth ribs on the right-hand side hurt like sfelb.

I'm not dead.

Muffled voices sounded outside. She notched up her hearing. "D'you look in there?" asked a man with a deep guttural voice.

"Oh yeah," drawled a tenor voice. "I like the . . . well, you know."

Frowning, Linka stuffed her errant nipple back under the fabric. Her mind reached for the satellite. No response.

She was cut off.

Where the sfelb am I? Linka thought. She tried to sit up. Her side hurt. She lay down and resolved to keep listening to the guards.

"What a shape on her," leered the baritone. "Isn't often you see one of those native women that's cute enough for a Galactic to—" His lusty chortle choked off.

"You know, she probably wouldn't mind," said Tenor. "These autochthons—I hear they screw anytime they want to."

Baritone gasped.

Tenor sounded mortified. "Um, I think I'll confess right after I go off duty."

"I would," Baritone agreed gravely.

This is definitely not North Polar, thought Linka. She tried again to rise. This time she pushed past the initial discomfort. She rolled off a Galactic standard soma cot. Her ribs ached, but she could stand. She realized her boots were gone. She checked beneath the bandage. Of the wound in her thigh there remained only a shallow, almost painless scar. *That Northern healing balm is wonderful stuff.*

Again she strove to contact her bird. She could almost feel her signal bouncing back at her. It was as if she were trapped under a bowl. *What kind of bowl blocks— sfelb, reflects—delta-band?*

There was a scraping sound. Tenor was twisting the ball of his foot back and forth on a concrete floor layered with grit. "Wow," he said at last. His tone suggested he was in awe of his own baseness.

"Wow," Baritone agreed. "I don't believe you said that."

Tenor became defensive. "We both knew what we were talking about."

"Well, maybe. But thinking it's one thing. Coming right out and saying it in plain words—" Baritone trailed off. He started mumbling what sounded like a prayer.

There was a mirror over the sink. Linka inspected herself. On her right side, three fingers beneath the breast, glistened a tiny, closed cut. *Sliver gun,* she thought. *That commander only shot me with a sleeper dart. So where did I wake up?*

She peered through the window slot. Her cell was fifteen or twenty stories up in a building that was part of some plainly Galactic installation.

"What are you doing?" Baritone outside asked sharply.

"Just adjusting my holster," replied Tenor.

"Careful! What if the gun goes off? You'd find yourself standing before the Cosmic Christ with that lust on your soul."

"Oh yeah," Tenor breathed. "Forjeler."

Baritone whistled. "Wow, with that lust on your soul *and* that profanity."

Lukewarm water caressed Linka's cheeks. It felt glorious. She raised cupped hands from the sink and splashed her face again. She swept her hands to either side over the sink. Warm air rushed from an unseen wall vent. *Standard Galactic autosink,* she thought. *Just like home.* She watched the water drain. It formed no vortex, it just drained straight down.

"Say," asked Tenor, "think you could cover for me?"

"You want to sneak away *now?*"

"Shift doesn't change for four hours. My soul's sullied now."

"Oh, for—" Baritone stifled laughter.

"I need to confess," Tenor said sharply.

Baritone snorted. "You'll live."

"What if I don't?" Tenor demanded, his voice edging close to genuine terror.

Footsteps clattered outside. "Sister Barkela!" Baritone said with the air of one snapping to attention.

"And where were *you* about to go?" demanded a harsh female voice.

"Nowhere, Sister," quaked Tenor. "I just forgot something."

The compartment door's red border flickered green. Linka whirled. The barred door slid into the wall with a muted sigh. Two guards flanked the new opening. Linka supposed Baritone was the weathered man openly staring at her, Tenor the gangly youngster averting his eyes. Obviously, neither was Jaremian.

The woman who bustled between the guards was bulky and double-chinned. She was clad in a shapeless robe of scratchy black fabric that somehow emphasized the fleshiness of her hips and upper arms. Her face was vaguely asymmetrical, spattered with angry violet-brown moles studded with hairs. She was black-skinned, but also plainly no Jaremian.

Then the pain washed through her. It flamed beneath her skin and seared her joints.

Linka wailed. She dropped to her knees.

As abruptly as the suffering had consumed her, it ended.

The heavy woman held out one hand. She had a tiny remote between her thumb and forefinger.

Negative reinforcement apparatus, Linka thought breathlessly. *Definitely Galactic.*

"I made that pain," the hag growled. "I make it happen." The agony scoured at Linka again, just for a moment. "I make it stop. Understand?"

Gasping, Linka could only nod.

"Get up," the woman barked. She watched Linka rise, and then looked her up and down. "Do what you're told and I won't do that again."

"I understand," Linka husked.

"I am called Barkela. Sister Barkela Mary Halv'ekral. Who are you?"

"I am a Galactic and a Spectator!" Linka almost shouted. But she didn't. Instead she dropped her eyes. "My name is Linka," she said as abjectly as she could.

"Welcome, Linka," rumbled Barkela, her voice devoid of hospitality. "You are in a strange place. You will see strange things. Speak when spoken to, do what I say, and I won't have to—" she waggled the remote. "Now come."

The cloaked harridan led Linka down a corridor whose floor and ceiling glowed softly. Comm units, touchpanels, and similar Galactic devices protruded from the walls. Linka scuttled behind, her mind racing. *My Escher lozenges are gone. They think I'm an autochthon. Yet here I am in some Galactic installation and they don't care how much offworld technology I see!* Once more she tried to link with her bird. The silence was palpable.

The lavchamber was tiled in gray plasteel from floor to ceiling. A dozen shower stalls were arranged around a central core, surrounded by benches. The hag waved Linka toward a stall. "This will clean you up," she growled. "Come on, strip and get in."

A Jaremian wouldn't understand what the stalls are for, Linka thought. She turned toward Barkela, compliant fingers in the waistband of her breeches, vacant confusion on her face.

"Stupid primitives," Barkela muttered. She glared at Linka, said slowly, "Take off your clothes." Up came the remote. "Do it!"

Linka tore off her breeches and tossed them on the floor. She managed a suitably autochthonous yelp of astonishment when the floor swallowed them. Barkela brandished the remote again. Linka worked the breast band over her head. Hesitantly she held it out. She dropped it, wide-eyed, and watched the floor consume it.

"Into the stall," Barkela ordered, settling onto a bench.

Faltering as long as she dared, Linka turned. She stepped hesitantly into the stall. A thick mist of warm water leapt from its walls. She affected a scream, tried not to show how eager she really was to cleanse herself.

"That's right," Barkela said. "Now get clean. Just stand there, rub yourself all over."

Linka took a deep breath. It was a Galactic shower; microsurfactants in the water cut mud and grime without suds. She clawed fingers through her hair and scrubbed with gusto—and not just for the pleasure of being clean. *They didn't take time to bathe me. They're making me do it. So they probably haven't bothered to implant that negative reinforcement unit. Likely it's just a micromodule stuck on my skin somewhere. They won't expect me to recognize it—maybe I can yank it off.*

Rough hands smacked over her breasts. Thumbs shoved at her nipples. "What the—" Linka whirled. Lost her balance. Her back slapped against the shower stall wall.

Barkela, naked, pressed her weight against Linka's shoulder. She fastened full lips over one of Linka's nipples and slid a hand into her pubic hair. *Oh, I don't forjeling believe this,* Linka thought. She stared out into the lavchamber. No one was around. Barkela's robe and some burlap jockstraplike garment lay on the bench.

Next to them lay the remote. Barkela had left it outside.

Linka twisted and brought her shoulder against Barkela's collarbone. Raising a knee, she planted her thigh against the larger woman's hip. She pushed hard. "No!" she shouted. *Cuss like an autochthon,* she reminded herself. "What the fuck are you doing?"

Barkela staggered back against the sidewall. Adipose made a near-lunar landscape of her hips and belly. Her knees looked like sculpted cheese. Hard nipples bulged from pendulous breasts enveloped with brown-gray stretch marks. Roaring, she said, "You want the pain?" as she surged forward. She grabbed Linka's wrists and clapped Linka's hands beneath Barkela's drooping breasts. "Come on, knead. You know how you like someone to do it to you."

"No," Linka hissed.

"I'll bring the pain."

Linka glanced toward the remote on the bench. "Not without that."

Barkela blinked. "You're a smart one." She pushed herself against Linka and tried to kiss her. Linka's back pressed to the wall. Water streamed around her shoulder blades. "Come on, you autochthons screw on a whim," Barkela husked. "Men, women, it doesn't matter; I've seen the sensos, I know."

"I don't want this," Linka snarled. She brought a knee up, hard. Barkela staggered back against the opposite wall. Linka edged toward the stall door. She would get to the remote before Barkela could. Linka locked eyes with the hag. She demanded, "Do your superiors know you do this?"

"God forjel you!" Barkela hissed, wild-eyed. She pulled back her arm.

Linka braced for a punch in the face. But it never came.

Barkela stood immobile, face contorted with rage, fist trembling in mid-air.

She's unwilling to hit me, Linka realized. *Or she's been forbidden to. Why?* Crossing her arms over her breasts, Linka edged another half-step toward the door. *Time to take the reins here.* "Others here are scared even to think about sex," Linka said coldly. "What makes you different?"

Barkela dropped her fist. "I'm a nun. Do you know what that is?"

Play the autochthon, Linka reminded herself, hiding astonishment. "Um, no."

"A nun's a woman who's given her life to the Universal Catholic Church," Barkela said thickly. "Nuns don't marry. They don't have sex."

Linka spread her hands. "What the fuck do you call this?"

"You don't understand," said Barkela. To Linka's amazement, the misshapen woman began to sob. "I can't help myself. It isn't my fault."

For vacuum's sake, Linka thought. She stood there wearing only spray, helpless to decide what to do next.

The nun looked up. Her tears had been replaced by anger. "For thousands of years the Church treated its women like refuse," she seethed. "First on Terra, then everywhere. Eventually the male religious of the Galaxy revolted against celibacy. The Fourteenth Vatican Council gave them an outlet, the *Codex Pederasticus.*"

An autochthon wouldn't understand any of this, Linka thought. *This nun must feel safe to vent this way—to speak so openly of Galactic affairs before a Jaremian. I guess I know what happens to women in my situation after . . . after whomever-it-may-be gets done with them.*

"Ritual pederasty was great for the priests and monks," Barkela railed. "Think the Council made any such provision for *women* religious? Think those dried-up old Cardinals would recognize we have physical needs, too?" Barkela touched a control surface. The water shut off. They were instantly dry. "Priests and monks still aren't supposed to screw, you understand." Barkela squeezed past Linka. Their breasts grazed. "Not with women. Nothing that might seem, well—conjugal."

Linka strode toward the bench. She got there before Barkela and snatched the remote.

Barkela shrugged and sat down. She swept her own robe and undergarment onto the floor. They disappeared.

So much for getting her dressed, Linka thought. Having few other options, she crossed her arms and listened.

"Can't have male religious screwing adult women like laymen do, oh no," Barkela continued. "But the further you depart from that standard, the more acceptable it becomes—for men, anyway. Homosexuality—man on man, you know? That's better than a man and a woman because it closes off the possibility of reproduction." She laughed bitterly. "Homosexuality with a child? That's best of all. It satisfies lust, while least resembling the forbidden conjugal love. But do you suppose they allow women religious even that?" Barkela stood slowly. "You don't understand a thing I've said."

If only you knew. "A little. But why vent your desires on me? I'm no child."

"So? I'm not a priest. Life is imperfect." Barkela pulled Linka against her. She kissed her neck, pawed her breasts and buttocks. The women spilled onto the floor.

Linka wriggled free. Barkela lunged again, only to take the heel of Linka's hand below her left eye. Barkela fell back, clutching her cheek.

Linka scrambled to her feet.

Barkela looked up at her with murder in her eyes.

Linka hurled the remote across the room. It struck the wall and shattered. "Look," Linka hissed, "I know why I'm here."

"You do?" Barkela brayed, slowly standing. "Ignorant savage, you think you understand anything?"

"I know I was brought here to be somebody's toy. But not yours."

Barkela's eyes widened.

Linka smiled. "Let's see how much I understand. I have to do what you say when people are watching. But when we're alone, and you're trying to make me do something you're not supposed to be doing either—" Linka shrugged. "You can't beat me. You can't starve me. You can't do anything to me that might reduce my ability to please whoever it is I've been brought here for."

Barkela settled back onto the bench. She stared darkly at the floor. "You'll say nothing of this."

Linka nodded. "And you'll keep your fucking hands off me." She gestured toward the shattered remote. "And no more games with that."

"Very well." Barkela rose, stepped toward the lavchamber wall. A half-dozen religious medallions and a vial of holy water hung from a tiny hook, each on its own chain. Barkela gathered the chains and put them over her head. She tapped a featureless spot on the wall. A locker whirred open. Linka barely remembered to act surprised.

Barkela drew out a fresh habit, then a short burlap frock. She threw the frock to Linka.

I'll remember you, Sister Barkela, Linka thought coldly.

"Ruth!?" Linka subvocally shouted. Across the broad refectory, Ruth Griszam dropped her omnitensil into her consommé. Flustered, she made apologies to the monks and *monsignori* with whom she'd been dining. *"Sorry I yelled,"* Linka said in a more ordinary tone. *"I couldn't reach my satellite. I didn't know if my implants were working at all."*

Ruth's dark hair had been cut short. She wore a tooled leather jerkin over a doublet of some wet-looking synthetic fabric. She sat in an upholstered chair at a long marble table. Before her were arranged fine obsidian bowls and plates, platinum tumblers, and crystal chalices. Friars and priests were her luncheon companions. She allowed herself a moment's eye contact with Linka across the refectory's central aisle. *"Your implants are working, all right,"* she affirmed.

Linka wore the simple burlap frock Barkela had given her two hours before. She sat on a long bench before a rough-hewn wooden table. The simple metal platter before her bore unseasoned *fhlet* and fish. A cloudy glass mug contained warm milk that half a dozen would have to share. Linka's companions were autochthonous slaves, monks under punishment, and nuns in scratchy habits. *"What are you doing here?"* Linka asked.

"What are you *doing over there?"* Ruth replied.

"I lost my Escher lozenges. They think I'm an autochthon," Linka replied. Grimly she looked across the table. Barkela had taken the seat opposite her. The nun's moles writhed as she chewed *fhlet* with her mouth open. She saw Linka watching her. Barkela winked, the gesture twisted by the bruise under her left eye. *Oh well,* Linka thought, *at least I know she has no idea I'm having this silent conversation. "How did you get here?"* Linka asked Ruth.

"Didn't you see?"

"I know those Catholic troopers took you off Semuga's flagship. The piscine sub took you away."

"Well, it brought me here," Ruth explained. *"I've been here—I don't know, three weeks? They treat me well. Regally, in fact. But they've kept me out of touch. I get nobody but these forjeling religious to talk to, distinguished as some of them are. What's your story?"*

"Parek conquered Graargy's basin. I met him."

"Parek?"

"He took my Escher lozenges."

"What?" Ruth demanded.

"He sees them. Did you know?"

"No, never," said Ruth, sounding shaken.

"Well, he does," Linka said grimly. *"His navy had barely escaped beyond the lower lock when a Catholic detachment overran the basin. An officer slivergunned me and I woke up here."*

"When?"

"This morning," Linka replied. *"Then they herded me in here for lunch. I looked across the room and there you were."*

"Um, hi." Ruth said it gingerly.

"Hi," Linka answered in an neutral tone. Uneasy, she looked about the refectory. Swiss Guards in traditional costumes stood at each corner of the pentagonal chamber. They carried halberds but wore disintos. The sidewalls were colonnades defined by vertical marble slabs. Above, reproduction tapestries hung from cedar beams under stained-glass clerestory windows. Three or four hundred people were eating there. None was aware of the subvocal conversation occurring in their midst.

"Linka, are they treating you all right?" Ruth sounded genuinely concerned.

Linka glanced dourly toward Barkela. *"Don't ask. What is this place?"*

"The biggest Enclave violation you've ever imagined," Ruth answered. *"It's an enormous base Cardinal Semuga built on an island in the Equatorial Sea. Eighteen or twenty thousand Galactics, mostly religious, live here."*

"Nobody knows about it?" Linka demanded.

"It's behind all kinds of shielding, including a screenfield that blocks delta-band. We can't talk to our satellites. But we can talk to each other like this, implant to implant."

"So you haven't reported any of this."

"Couldn't," Ruth said. *"I'm incommunicado. Now so are you."*

The common mug came by. Linka reached for it, slurped some milk. It tasted brackish. *"If we're near the equator, why do the antennas point toward the horizon?"*

"I gather there's also an orbiting platform," Ruth explained, *"disguised as an asteroid or something, in an eccentric south polar orbit. Presumably the arrays are aimed at that."*

"So what do we do?" Linka said quietly.

"You're the senior Spectator," Ruth said archly. *"If I were you, I'd tell them who the sfelb you are."*

"They know who you are, and it doesn't sound like they give you much maneuvering room," Linka objected.

"Maybe I'd better tell you what you're here for," Ruth said after a long moment. *"Semuga and the pope have fallen out. Semuga erected this installation for the pur-*

pose of eliminating Parek, and now I understand Pope Modest has declared Parek a true Incarnation of Christ."

"Now Parek is the Christ? You're plorging me."

"Wish I was. Even before the papal address, Semuga'd spent days in a rage, holed up in his suite, eating, drinking—going through a long succession of autochthons."

"Boys?"

"Women," Ruth said with an edge in her tone. "And when I say he goes through them, I don't mean he gets bored and sends them back. At least eleven autochthonous women reported to his suite in the last week. None returned."

"Don't tell me, let me guess," Linka shot back. "I'm next."

"I don't know about next. But he'll get to you."

Linka stabbed her eatstick into a square of *fhlet* and popped it in her mouth. She pondered her next move. *If I tell them who I am, I'll be safe from Semuga.* She peeped over at Barkela. The homely nun was swiping at fish she'd dropped on her habit. *Imagine what'll happen to you, Sister, when they learn you tried to rape a Spectator. Then again, I may have more freedom of action if they go on thinking I'm an autochthon.*

"If you reveal yourself, I'll vouch for you," Ruth promised.

"One more thing I need to know before I decide. Have you learned anything about the screenfield equipment?"

"A fair amount," Ruth said. "Using my implants I can sometimes interface with the island's thought engines. I don't think they know I'm doing it. Once, I managed to interrogate the unit that generates the antidelta-band screenfield. There's a narrow band of frequencies it lets through. If I can contact my bird on one of those channels, I've developed a command sequence that the bird can retransmit at higher power. I think it'll fool their thought engines into dropping the screenfields for a few minutes."

Linka whistled inwardly. "Plorg, woman, you've made good use of your time. This command sequence of yours—will it work?"

"Can't be sure," Ruth answered grimly. "To test it would be to tip my hand. They'd develop countermeasures and I'd never get to actually use it for anything. So when I decide to use it, that'll also be its first test."

"That may be soon," Linka said after a moment. She risked a direct glance across the refectory. "Ruth, can you trust me?"

Ruth risked a direct glance back. "For what?"

"Will you send that sequence on my signal," Linka demanded, "then stand aside and let me have the Mode?"

"Meaning I defeat their screens and you get to file a journal."

"That's right," Linka said flatly.

"You're senior. Is that your order?"

"No, I'm asking you."

"Why?"

"Under the circumstances, I feel I owe you that choice."

Ruth savored fine Ghyrelian wine. "What if I say yes, Linka?"

"Then I stay in deep cover."

"If I can't punch through to my bird, or if my command sequence doesn't work, you'll be one more mangled autochthon under Semuga's bed."

Linka swigged more tainted milk. She arched an eyebrow in Ruth's direction. *"I knew there'd have to be something in it for you."*

The two Spectators locked eyes across the refectory. Once before, Linka Strasser had given Ruth Griszam orders—orders designed to destroy Ruth's career. *If Linka's onto something that hot,* Ruth thought, *she's asking me for one more career sacrifice—this time a voluntary one.* The monsignor next to her made a joke. Ruth laughed, replied in kind without having any idea what she'd said. *Of course, last time Linka tried to ruin me, she sent me to that dam and made me the richest Spectator in the history of OmNet. What the plorg, she's taking most of the risk.*

"All right," Ruth subvocalized reluctantly. *"But, Linka?"*

"Yeah."

"This better be forjeling good."

94. The *Bright Hope*

"*D*amocles is transmitting on every band," Lynn Wachieu rasped. "They say they're going to the surface."

"Let's hear it." Laurien Eldridge crossed two pairs of arms. With the last she tugged absently at her uniform. *Soon I must order forty thousand deaths.*

The *Damocles* spokesperson's voice crackled in the air. "Men and women of the Galactic Confetory! On behalf of our pilgrims—and, for that matter, on behalf of God—we acknowledge our joy at the courageous words of Pope Modest the Fourth."

Eldridge went cold inside.

"Few aboard *Damocles* are Catholic. All the same, we embrace the Catholic leader's call for an end to Enclave. For us, waiting for the Privy High Council to do as the pope asks is not enough. We feel called to the peerless and terrible honor of striking the first blow."

"Captain!" Wachieu called. "Priority communication from High Command."

"Put it through," Eldridge ordered.

A tridee bubble rattled open before Eldridge. It was Admiral Hafen. "Enclave must stand, Captain Eldridge. I'm calling to confirm: you are authorized at the highest levels. Destroy *Damocles* the instant she begins to break orbit."

"Understood, Admiral." Somewhere behind her simulated goddess body, Eldridge felt her human mouth go stone dry. "Fem Wachieu," she made herself say.

"Captain." Wachieu crouched stiffly on her web.

"Load the firing sequence. Send the trigger to my console here."

"Aye, Captain," Wachieu called, her voice buoyant with relief. It would be Eldridge's hand, not hers, that tabbed the fatal control.

An instrument panel flowed up under Eldridge's hands. When it was time to fire *Bright Hope*'s weapons bank, Eldridge alone would perform the act. *Forty thousand pilgrims,* she thought direly, *most of them helpless dupes.*

"In a few moments we will initiate atmospheric entry," the spokesperson proclaimed. "Soon we shall stride beside the Cosmic Christ in his new flesh—the flesh of The Word Among Us. Like the fire, we join His Word made flesh."

There was a brief crackle as the audio switched over. "We've been hearing an official spokesperson," Wachieu explained. "This will be actual bridge traffic, the mercenary command crew at work."

"Prepare for de-orbital braking," said a crisp professional voice.

"Contramagnetic shunts nominal," reported another voice.

"They're charging the braking drivegates," Wachieu reported. "They'll fire a retro pulse in ten seconds."

Eldridge had never felt so solitary—so powerless; despite the destructive power at her fingertips, she was powerless to create any positive outcome.

"Nine," Wachieu called.

"Go ahead, Captain," Gavisel said urgently.

"Inertial compensators optimized to mission profile simulators," droned the *Damocles* bridge voice.

"Seven . . . six . . ."

On the comm channel, something clattered. "Don't do this!" a young man's voice cried.

"Four . . . three . . ."

The audio crackled. "What are you doing?" the bridge voice rasped. "Arrest him!"

Dissension on the Damocles *bridge?* Eldridge thought.

"Stay back!" That was the younger man, desperation flaring in his tone.

"Now!" Wachieu called. The blue glare of Cerenkov radiation shimmered to life in the propulsion section's forward drivegates. "*Damocles* is bleeding off velocity."

On the comm channel, the bridge voice was full of fear. "You know what you have there?"

"Yes," the young man's voice rang with manic confidence. "I know exactly what I have, and I say we will not violate Enclave today."

"Captain," Gavisel hissed, "you must fire!"

Damocles's drivegates went dark. "Braking has discontinued!" Wachieu shouted.

Eldridge pulled back her firing finger. "Holding fire. Holding fire. Status!"

"Gunnery secure," Gavisel called.

Over the comm channel they heard the younger voice pronounce a single, strangled monosyllable: "Oops." They heard something metal hit the deck and then a spraying sound.

Wachieu's web was surrounded by virtual instruments. "I've lost audio from the *Damocles* bridge," she reported. "The trawler has assumed a lower orbit, but it's stable. Her drive buses are going cold. Stand by, stand by . . . Captain!" Wachieu's voice was thick with amazement. "They're all dead."

Eldridge gasped. "The pilgrims?"

"No, the control crew. No life signs in the command section. I'm reading only bodies."

The tactical display flickered. "I reconstructed this from Wachieu's Detex data," Gavisel announced. It was a crude 3-D schematic of the *Damocles* bridge. Vaguely human-shaped smudges marked the thermal signatures of thirty mercenaries. Other body signatures could be seen dimly on levels below.

A smudge representing a young officer stood on top of a console, brandishing a small metal cylinder. The others had abandoned their stations. They surrounded the young man in concentric knots.

"What's in his hand?" Eldridge said.

"Some sort of biowar device," said Gavisel. "Here, I can play back the action synchronized to the audio we received."

"I know exactly what I have," the young officer said fuzzily, "and I say we will not violate Enclave today."

Bitterness evident in his body language, an onlooker made a chopping gesture in the direction of the drive control stations. *The captain,* Eldridge realized. *He's capitulating, ordering the braking to stop.* Three smudges hastened to their stations to carry out the command.

"At the last minute, one officer refused to be party to an Enclave violation," Eldridge said admiringly. "A mercenary with a conscience."

"But a clumsy mercenary," Gavisel cautioned.

"Oops." The cylinder dropped from the young man's hand. With his other hand he tried to catch it, but to no avail. The others scattered. There was a spraying sound. All went still.

A moment later the distant smudges representing crewmembers on other levels were still, too.

Wachieu poked at controls with her spider legs. "I'm into their enviro system," she reported. "I've got its thought engines analyzing the biowar agent." Breathless seconds passed. "It says it's GDX."

"What's GDX?" Eldridge demanded.

Gavisel called up a covey of datacrawls. "Plorg for dinner, it's a highly advanced antipersonnel agent. Instantly fatal to all mammals. Penetrates any filter system or protective clothing until the end of a preset active period, usually seven days."

"No one's at the controls of *Damocles,*" Eldridge protested. "We need to get somebody in there."

"This GDX uses a substrate capable of quantum tunneling. You could open the *Damocles* bridge to space and send the boarding party in wearing vacsuits. It would still get them."

"There has to be a way."

"Negative," Gavisel replied. "This is just the sort of situation GDX was designed for. Its purpose is to sterilize a modest area and deny its use to all combatants for a fixed period." Angrily, Gavisel shut down her datacrawls. "It's state of the art, it's ours, and there is no countermeasure."

Eldridge crossed all her arms. She sat down on a pedestal that surged up from the bridge floor to meet her. "Situation review. *Damocles* has no auxiliary control centers. Her control architecture is so well protected that we cannot hope to seize control from elsewhere on the trawler, much less from here."

"Correct," Gavisel said grimly. "Wachieu can penetrate tangential systems like enviro. But we can't get anywhere near the nav modules."

"So *Damocles* cannot be flown except from her bridge. But everyone on the bridge is dead. Moreover, the bridge is full of GDX. No one can go there for seven days. Summing up, we have forty thousand pilgrims just sitting in a can. There's no hand on the tiller, and that's how things are going to remain until the GDX goes dormant."

Gavisel and Wachieu nodded their assent.

Eldridge rose and paced. "Fem Gavisel, Fem Wachieu. Speculate, if you will, on the probability that at some point during the next seven days, the *Damocles* control software will realize that its control crew is dead, panic, and execute that crash program."

"Oh, sfelb," Gavisel whispered. She scanned a bevy of readouts. "I don't believe we have enough information to calculate that probability."

Eldridge stood. "I didn't think so. Fem Wachieu, reload that firing sequence. We must stand ready to annihilate *Damocles* at the first hint that the crash program has begun."

95. Jaremi Four—Vatican Island

"**W**ant to see it again?"

Linka Strasser blinked. In the vast uterine space of the apartment, the fireball Ato Cardinal Semuga had produced from his palm seemed trivial.

Sister Barkela had shambled into Linka's cell an hour before. "Don't worry, I can't take you now," Barkela growled. "You belong to a holy man."

"I'm sick of holy men," Linka had complained, yawning.

Barkela led Linka to a chamber filled with flower scents and soft blue-white brilliance. There three younger nuns bathed, perfumed, and camisoled her. Barkela kept her distance, and the young nuns stuck to business. When they were finished Linka admired herself in a mirror. *Not bad,* she decided. *If Semuga's been getting typical Southland women, he'll think I'm something special. He'd better; I'm counting on that to keep me alive.* Linka bent one knee. Her right leg protruded through the slit in her emerald-mesh skirt. The scar was gone. She took a deep breath and watched her bust swell between tufted strips of aquamarine fabric. Her ribs had stopped hurting.

She turned to Sister Barkela and flashed the nun a paradoxical, inviting smile. *This is the best you'll ever see me look, and you can't touch. Sorry, bitch.* She released a long-held breath and said, "I guess I'm as ready as I get."

"If only you knew," Barkela said opaquely. She led Linka into a tiny platinum upchute capsule. Barkela kept her hands clasped inside her habit during the slow upward ride.

"I feel like I'm rising," Linka said, blinking. *No Jaremian knows about upchutes.*

"You're going to the top," Barkela said, nodding. With a hiss Linka felt, rather than heard, the car stopped. That was when Barkela groped Linka's crotch. Linka jumped back. The nun withdrew the hand. She turned to regard Linka with a surprisingly gentle expression. "I only wish I'd gotten to know you better."

Linka sneered. "You'd know my hands around your ugly neck."

"Such spirit." Barkela smiled thinly. "You'll need it."

It occurred to Linka that Sister Barkela genuinely did not expect her to come back from whatever awaited her at the top of the upchute shaft.

The nun drew her vial of holy water from beneath her habit. She waved it at Linka in a vague sign of the cross. "Go with God," Barkela said as she thumbed the door control.

Linka had stepped alone into the crystal womb of Semuga's apartment.

Semuga's private suite had been hollowed out of a single huge synthetic pink topaz, after the style of Vatican Center's grand halls. The furniture was of gold and diamond and platinum, damask and silk and precious-metal cloth, all extravagantly decorated. An irregular table of sheet diamond floated at the center of the main room. It supported a thirty-centimeter-tall statue hewn from solid sapphire. *Another Greneil,* Linka thought. *Good reproduction, too.* To her left, a wide doorway yawned onto an outdoor terrace. Late afternoon sun parched neighboring structures. To her right, two curved steps led up to a circular chamber dominated by an outsized soma disk. The bedchamber's wraparound windows were partly opacified.

Another rose of fire bloomed from Semuga's palm.

Act like an autochthon, she reminded herself. *You've never seen such tricks. Sfelb, you've never seen a white man.* "Who—what are you?" she breathed.

He lurched toward her, jiggling beneath an earth-colored caftan dotted with dried sauces. "I am called Samu. You are welcome here." He wore a cardinal's sapphire ring. He stared openly at Linka, black eyes glistening amid the cushions of his cheeks. His breath stunk of liquor.

"Oh, my captains did not exaggerate," he purred. "They truly have outdone themselves."

Semuga reached out. He rested a porcine fingertip against Linka's neck. The chubby finger slowly traced its way onto her shoulder, then over her collar bone. Veering toward the center, it followed the plunge of her garment's neckline and stopped between her breasts.

Linka forced herself not to flinch.

Semuga's head drifted downward. He stopped with his nose a hand's width from the cleavage. He drew a breath and smiled. "Eucalyptus. They know I like that."

Linka fingered the waistband of her emerald skirt. "You . . . want me to. . . ."

Semuga straightened. He laughed. "In time. The others? I just took them. Some, I hit." He grinned. The effect was grotesque. "You seem different. What's your name?"

"Linka."

He took her right hand, raised it, kissed it lingeringly. His lips were greasy. "You must understand something," he said over her knuckles. "You confront no mere man."

She pursed her lips and said nothing.

Gently he led her before a full-length mirror. It was framed in lathe-turned diamond sections and rare sculpted woods. He extended her right arm fully ahead of her. "Now make a fist."

No, Linka thought in dull astonishment. *First fire from the palms, now the unbendable arm stunt? What, is this the fake holy man's program of the week for seducing autochthonous hicks?*

Of course, Semuga bent her arm with ease. They reversed positions. She cupped both hands over the side of his elbow. His flesh was hot and spongy. Of course, she couldn't bend his arm. As she tried to hang from it, Semuga waved his hand. He snapped his fingers. "You see?" he said after a moment. "That is my power."

She straightened. He slid a flabby hand around her waist, and then down over her right buttock—just as Parek had. Realization struck her: *He probably* poved *my encounter with Parek. He's copying it because it's easier than thinking of something original. Of course, he has no idea he's with the same woman!* "Your power is great," she breathed aloud. Their faces were almost touching. A sharp brandy smell hung between them. "What about your mercy?"

Semuga shrugged. "I haven't hit you yet." His free hand plopped against her ribs. It rose. Soft fingers slicked toward the underside of her left breast. "What about your desire?" His eyes bespoke forbidden appetites without end.

Sweat beaded beside his mouth. She flicked at it with the tip of her tongue. *Not sweat,* she realized, wrinkling her face. *Dried pastry icing.*

"Never mind desire," Semuga growled. "Just remember my power." Like a ship striking a pier his lips billowed over her mouth. His tongue, rough and sour, dueled with hers. He moiled her breasts. After a moment, they stepped apart.

Semuga rested his fingertips on her bare midriff before letting his hands drop. He fumbled with a clasp; with a glassy rustle her skirt slid to the floor. Her camisole split open at his touch and came away in his hands. She remembered to act surprised. Semuga came away holding the halves of her camisole. He raised the tufted aquamarine fabric toward his face as though he wanted her scent.

She realized he was staring at something.

He blinked. Slowly he shook his head. "Great God in heaven," he rasped at last, "just look at those tits."

Swallowing hard, she stepped toward the soma disk. Semuga nodded.

They climbed two steps into the circular bedchamber. Keeping his eyes on her, he backed toward an autobar. She remembered to seem startled when it spat out a tumbler of brandy. "You are so beautiful, Linka," he husked. "Does your passion match your beauty? If so, rest assured I will not harm you."

She forced herself to smile. "What—what do you want?"

He downed the brandy. Then he touched a thumb to the neckband of his caftan. It sloughed away.

His skin was blister-white and riven by stretch marks. Spider veins reticulated everywhere. His teats drooped, flaccid, onto a swag belly lightly dusted with graying fuzz. Below the belly, skin bunched like stacked ropes of pudding. Ragged gray pubic hair framed a tiny scrotum—*so small*—as if it were retreating from the rest of his bulk.

The penis was erect, purple with excitement.

"What do I want?" Semuga chuckled. He pushed Linka back onto the soma disk. He fell atop her, his tongue slathering her breasts.

"I can't breathe!" she shrieked. Without a word he realigned his mass and went back to his slurping. *"Ruth!"* Linka screamed subvocally. *"Ruth, if you're ready to try bringing those shields down, do it **now!**"*

Linka's inner awareness sparkled with Ruth Griszam's consciousness. *"What the sfelb is going on?"* Ruth demanded.

"Transmit now, ask questions later, okay?"

"I'm tuning onto one of the frequency bands the island's screenfields should pass," Ruth reported. *"Transmitting."*

Carrying his weight on knees and hips, Semuga reached out. He squeezed Linka's breasts painfully. *"Well?"* Linka voicelessly demanded.

"Yes," Ruth hissed. *"My bird acknowledged. It's uploading the command sequence."* Linka tried to ignore what Semuga was doing. His head rolled between her tits. *"The bird is retransmitting the command sequence at full power,"* said Ruth. *"Hold on!"*

She gasped as Semuga crawled upward. He clapped his hands to her shoulders. His mouth covered her chin. It was soppy with drool. She felt a prodding between her legs. His cratered buttocks shuddered. *"Oh sfelb,"* Linka thought, *"he wants. . . ."*

"It's in!" Ruth shouted.

Semuga slammed inside Linka. She yelped.

"You liking this?" Semuga gasped.

She clutched his hands in hers. With thumb and forefinger, she rotated his ring so she could see it clearly in the corner of her eye.

"Vacuum's sake, it worked," Ruth exulted. *"The antidelta-band screenfield is down!"*

Linka's inner awareness took on depth and texture. *Ready* signals sounded from the satellite one by one. *"Thank you, Ruth,"* Linka husked subvocally. *"Now get the sfelb out of my way."*

"All yours, Spectator."

Linka subvocalized the nonsense syllable that would put her into Mode. Her cheeks started to tingle. The implants that recorded neural traffic between her vestibular system and her parietal cortices flickered on.

Semuga's thrusts, his hideous shouts of pleasure, were accelerating. *You're not coming until I'm ready,* Linka thought. She pressed her heels against Semuga's vast buttocks to lessen the vehemence of his thrusts. It didn't work. She reared up with her head and kissed him savagely. That broke his rhythm. He slapped moist hands to her breasts, probed her mouth with his tongue. "Oh yes," he growled. "A little breather."

Linka's transceiver implant made contact with the satellite. It beamed back
sync information. Alternate regions of Linka's brain assumed expanded control of
her muscles. Nerve shunts routed routine somesthetic information beneath conscious awareness. Her sensory acuity heightened, which she regretted when
Semuga resumed his movements inside her. An artificial hormone reset her olfactory bulbs. She smelled the brandy on his breath all over again.

She listened for the *verify* signal and then subvocalized the start command.
Suck, rush, wrench! Automatically she suppressed the "senso shudder" that otherwise would cause her eyes to dance.

Spectator Linka Strasser was recording.

Shifting his weight, Semuga fell into another blissful rhythm. Linka stared over
at his cardinal's ring. *"Flash flash flash!"* she called on the captioning channel.
*"Maximum urgency, maximum news value! Go live! Go live! Go live! This is Linka
Strasser, documenting the biggest forjeling Enclave violation you've ever imagined."*

Her eyes turreted from Semuga's ring to his shuddering bulk. With each thrust
of his hips he drew a racking breath. She looked him up and down, watching
bloated skin flap on his arms, legs, and chest as he rocked. She took his head in
his her hands and kissed him again. With a thumb she levered one of his eyes open
and stared into it with her own.

Semuga was close to climax. *Time to turn the tables,* she decided. With a
colossal effort, she suppressed the reflexive mental inhibition that stopped her eyes
from dancing. *I'm so used to restraining the shudder. It goes against all my training
to let it show.* After a moment, her irises began to twitch violently. She looked like
some unpromising documentarian in her second year at Academy.

Because Linka's face was so close to his, Semuga couldn't quite decide what
he was seeing. Still immersed in his pleasure, he raised his shoulders and lifted his
head.

He focused.

He gaped.

A second or two later, his dick stopped moving.

Senso shudder didn't look like epilepsy. It didn't look like a convulsive disorder. It looked only like itself, an unmistakable signature that could only be displayed by someone who'd been specially trained and modified, an unmistakable
signature that could only be displayed by a Galactic.

Semuga stared down, open-mouthed.

Linka grinned up ferally. "Most Eminent Lord," she said with mock formality.
"We should be more thoroughly introduced. I told you my name was Linka. I'm
Linka *Strasser,* OmNet's senior Spectator on Jaremi Four. And I believe you are Ato
Cardinal Semuga, a high-ranking prelate of the Universal Catholic Church and in
my opinion, a lousy lover. On behalf of the billions of experients across the Galaxy
now *pov*ing this in real time . . . good daypart, Excellency!"

96. Terra—Wasatch Range, Usasector

"**I** know about the navy that pursues me," said the tridee simulacrum of Arn Parek. "But you say another force moves straight towards me from the opposite direction?"

"The navy behind you is the half of the enemy force that set ashore weeks ago." Alrue Latier draped upon the railing of the performer's treadmill in his studio. His temple garments were dark with sweat. "The other half landed further south, then doubled back overland. Their plan was always to trap you between the two battalions."

"You say this is inevitable," mused Parek.

"Full as bleak as that," Latier sighed in a voice shorn of hope.

"I've never seen this approaching force. Ulf's forward scouts say nothing of it. How do I know it exists?"

Latier bristled. "Because I tell you! I am your god named God! When has my counsel misled you?"

The tiny figure of Parek looked up with scorn. "If what you tell me today is true, everything you've ordained since the Miracle of the Ships has been a terrible mistake."

"You doubt me?" Latier thundered.

Parek frowned. "Once I was in awe of your power. Now I learn it's insufficient to deliver me."

"*Fire,*" Latier subvocalized. In his control room, the sim artists writhed in their waldoes.

Parek blinked at the three-dimensional ring of flame projected around Latier's floating presence. He blinked, but nothing more. "If only you had such a fire I could cast at my enemies," he said coldly.

"Cry unto your god named God," Latier paraphrased desperately. "Let your heart be full, drawn out into prayer for your welfare, and also for the welfare of those who are around you."

Parek unrolled a parchment map across the tiny table in his private chamber below decks. "Very well, I'll cry out to you," Parek mocked. "But no despair, please. Rather than assume the situation is impossible, let's search for solutions together."

"*And it came to pass that I began to be old,*" Latier quoted somberly on the command channel. "*Quickly! Bring me in closer.*" The *pov* shimmered forward until Latier could see the map clearly.

Parek's fingers swept over it with authority. "We're approximately here. If we don't stop to convert the next village, it will take us two days to reach this confluence." His hand circled an area where the canal became a meandering river. It split in two in the midst of a flood plain. "Can we reach this spot before our enemies fall on us?"

"*Well?*" Latier demanded subvocally.

Heber Beaman punched variables into his modeler. He leaned toward the control room audio pickup. "He can do it. He'll have a day to dig in, then both enemy battalions will reach him at about the same time."

"Yea and behold," Latier declared. "You can reach that spot with one day to spare before the forces of darkness come against you."

Parek nodded. "See, the land is wider between the valley walls there. There'll be room to maneuver. And *here*"—his finger stabbed at some ambiguous markings—"here's a ruined city where Ulf can establish defenses. The navy that's pursued me will have to abandon its boats and rig for land warfare. Finally, this confluence gives us access to three river channels. Perhaps one of them will not fall under enemy control. I can use it for my retreat, if necessary."

"Surely you'll need to retreat," Latier groaned.

"Not necessarily," Parek said speculatively. Latier's *pov* swung upward from the table. Parek locked eyes with his god as one would when facing an equal. "I must have your permission to speak of something. Something of which you once forbade me to speak."

"What do we have to lose? I mean, speak as you must."

"You've disapproved when I enhanced my message with devices of my own invention," Parek said carefully. "Back in Northland when I used that plant matter to feign my own death. Most recently, when I admitted that my men had been spreading the same plant matter as a mirage dust ahead of the fleet."

Beaman cringed inwardly. During that session Parek had been dumbfounded to learn his god simply had no idea what he'd been so busy doing. It had marked the beginning of Latier's fall from majesty in Parek's eyes.

"The dust is a refined product," Parek explained. "It only disorients people and triggers hallucinations after it falls on *fhlet*. That dust is refined from something called *mother matter*. Mother matter's highly toxic; during the sea voyage I had to replace three chemists who mishandled it." Parek drew an empty mortar shell from a cabinet. He rotated it in his hands. "If my fashioners load shells with raw mother matter, the mortarmen can rain them down among our enemies."

"Ahh," said Latier with renewed energy. "You shall send forth mighty winds, yea, your shafts in the whirlwind, yea, and your hail and mighty storm shall beat upon them. And we shall drag them down to the gulf of misery and endless wo. Behold, they must unavoidably perish."

Parek eyed Latier quizzically, as one might regard a child who'd said two and two are five. "Hardly, not at the concentrations we'll be able to achieve. But they'll lie around crazed, vomiting, unable to attack until the mother matter runs out."

"Verily," Latier mumbled. "But can't you send your troops among them to smite them in their weakness?"

"Of course not," Parek snapped. "The mother matter would overcome them, too. I can't render my own troops immune. Unless, oh great god, you could send me impervious suits they could wear into battle so they will neither breathe nor touch the mother matter? Perhaps, oh, eight to ten thousand such suits?"

Latier clasped his hands behind his back, if only to keep from doing something more embarrassing with them. "Behold," he harrumphed at last, "'tis not well to presume too highly of one's god."

"I thought not." After a moment Parek asked, "Perhaps I should confess to you how long the supply of raw mother matter will last."

"That would benefit your escutcheon, yes."

"There's enough to hold off the enemy for three or four days, no more. It cannot be replenished. So when the mother matter runs out, I must be ready with a military thrust to defeat my opponents . . . or some spiritual demonstration that can sap their will to harm me. Either that, or I'll need to have made my escape with the bulk of my forces."

"That would seem to cover the options, yes," Latier said uncertainly.

Parek pulled up a chair. He plopped down with one leg propped on the map table, the other bent at the knee, fingers laced across it. He looked at his god with an expression of mocking expectancy. "So, oh great and powerful god named God . . . which?"

Latier blinked. "Which what?"

"Which strategy? Attack my enemies? Befuddle them? Escape? Which is it to be? And how? I await your counsel."

"Any ideas?" Latier hissed over the command channel.

Beaman scowled at his modeler for a few seconds. *"Stall, First Elder,"* he shot back.

Latier raised his chin. "It is written: 'And also ye yourselves will succor those that stand in need of your succor.' "

Parek nodded gravely. "In other words, I'm on my own."

"Ye of little faith," Latier chided. "Look to your heart. When the time is meet, yea, it shall come to pass that you will see what I have written there."

"That's more like it," Beaman commented on the command channel.

"At your time of privation ye must look to your soul. To your own faith and hope. For there lies the way of elevation over your enemies," Latier proclaimed with growing confidence. "We will speak again when circumstances demand that you drink from the cup of my wisdom."

"Understood, oh first among sky gods," Parek said doubtfully. "Till then, Ulf and Chagrin and I will try to think of something."

97. Jaremi Four—Vatican Island

"You know, Cardinal," Linka said brightly, "many Terrans still call this the missionary position." Semuga blinked at the sudden chill between his thighs as she withdrew herself from around his softening penis.

Linka jammed her elbows into the mattress. She pushed out from under the dumbfounded Cardinal. Rolling off the soma disk, she padded down the steps and paused nude before the full-length mirror. "Yes," she narrated, "this is Linka Strasser—a Terran, a Spectator, and very much an adult woman, fresh from undergoing sexual assault on an Enclave planet at the hands of a Galactic cleric who'd once sworn to reserve his passion for little boys." Linka wondered what the experients would actually see. The Spectator's likeness was usually suppressed. But now her body, her sexuality were critical story elements. *Later I'll have to call down a checking journal and see how the editors dealt with this. Now, I have a little reporting to do.*

The topaz floor was cool and oily against her bare feet. "Here on the Enclave world of Jaremi Four, Cardinal Semuga has built himself a haven that recalls the ostentatious galleries of planet Vatican. Note the crystalline walls, this floating diamond-sheet table—this Greneil reproduction." She lifted the sapphire statuette from the kidney-shaped table.

"Careful with that!" Semuga sputtered. He rolled onto his back, his torso waggling like marmalade in a tornado.

"What, this knockoff? Oops." Smiling absently, she dropped the statue. It snapped into three pieces. The fragments skidded spinning across unyielding topaz.

She wasn't prepared for the intensity of Semuga's dismay.

"That . . . wasn't a reproduction, was it?" Linka breathed. She took a moment to compose herself—and also to call down the dossier on Semuga she'd been unable to access before. "Well, gentle experients, if you've ever wondered what it feels like to break a genuine Valatu Brouhkin ve Greneil worth, oh, several billion credits, commit this journal to wafer and you can enjoy the feeling again and again. Title, title, where's his title? Oh, here it is. Now let's see what *else* the Pontifical Councilor for Arcane Works has spent his Church's treasure on."

The balcony doors hissed open at her approach. Plasteel simmered hot against her soles. The late afternoon sun cast dry heat against her skin. "Great mother of stars," Linka said quietly. If the installation had looked ponderous from the window of her cell, from Semuga's oviform terrace it seemed vast. Looking east, she stared through canyons of labored architecture ablaze with orange light. Beyond the buildings gleamed shield cones, airpushers, and antennae. Beyond *them* the rainforest hulked verdant and mysterious. With Spectator control she panned west. Golden highlights skimmed founding docks, manufactories, warehouses, assembly buildings. An incongruous stone steeple topped by a holo of the papal tiara and keys.

"Turn around, Fem Strasser."

She did.

Semuga had waddled downstairs. He'd tugged on his caftan. From a hidden drawer in the dressing table he'd brought up a Galactic needler.

Linka thought of ramping her implants into battle mode. She decided she didn't need to. Instead she strode back into the apartment, straight toward Semuga.

Someone was pounding at the upchute door. It was locked. Its borders flashed crimson.

"Stop right there!" Semuga screeched at Linka. "How dare you violate my privacy like this?"

"Cardinal!" Linka snorted. "Violate your *privacy?* You've been caught in profound sexual misconduct, not to mention an Enclave infringement of mind-numbing proportions. To that roster of—what's the word?—oh yes, *sins,* you propose to add the cold-blooded murder of a Confetory citizen. An act that, might I remind you, will be witnessed in the first person by trillions. And you whinny about your privacy." She had drawn within an arm's length of Semuga. "Let's see what *you* dare, Cardinal." She furled the fingers of one hand over the needler. His trembling fingers parted. It was her weapon now. "As I thought."

Semuga stepped backward. He glanced toward his comm annunciator. The blinking lights on its face resembled a city under bombardment. Everyone was trying to reach him.

The pounding at the upchute door grew louder.

"Go ahead, use the comm box," Linka told him. "Call the engineers. You know, the ones struggling right now to overcome the signal that made the screen-field fall. Tell them to stop."

"What?" Semuga whispered.

"Order them to discontinue their efforts to restore the antidelta-band screen-field." Linka jammed the needler into his belly. "Don't forget, there's a PeaceForce schooner above us. *Bright Hope*'s captain knows where we are. If the screens pop back up and nobody knows my fate, what might Captain Eldridge do?"

Semuga blinked back tears.

"Give the order," Linka hissed.

Semuga thumbed the comm annunicator. "Excellency!" a thin voice shouted. "We've been trying to—"

"I know, a screenfield went down," Semuga snapped. "Cease all attempts to restore it."

"Excellency, you can't mean—"

"Leave it down," Semuga screamed. "That's an order!"

"Now the door," Linka ordered coolly.

"What? Oh, of course." Into the air he commanded, "Upchute unlock."

The portal twisted open. Ruth Griszam burst into the apartment. She wore a calf-length open surcoat over gray leather pants and a platinum-weave blouse. Images flickered on half a dozen Escher lozenges worked into the ensemble.

She pressed a Galactic blaster against the ear of the tonsured engineer who stumbled before her. Clearly the gun had originally been his.

For the first time in more than six years, Ruth Griszam and Linka Strasser stood within five meters of each other.

"Forjeling plorg, Linka," Ruth groaned. "Put something on."

Linka glanced toward the pieces of her camisole on the sleeping room steps.

"Oh here, take this." Switching her blaster from hand to hand, Ruth shrugged off her surcoat. *"You all right?"* Ruth subvocalized urgently.

"It wasn't fun. But revenge is cathartic." Linka tied half the camisole around her hips. She donned the surcoat. "Well?" she asked aloud.

"A forjeling fashion plate, you are." Ruth nodded toward Semuga. "Daypart, Cardinal."

"This isn't right," Semuga blubbered. "You're a proper Spectator, Fem Griszam, you wear Escher patches. Why didn't she?"

"When I was wearing what your nuns provided, Excellency?" Linka demanded, aiming the needler at him again. "Or when you tore off even that?"

Mustering composure, Semuga leaned toward Linka. "Posture as you will, Spectator. I saw your passion."

"That kiss with my eyes open? I was documenting your iris print."

"Hey, Linka!" Ruth called. She pressed her blaster a little harder against the engineer's temple. "Want to see their control room?"

Semuga's eyes snapped wide. They seemed to say, *No, not that.*

Linka's narrow smile said, *Oh, yes, that.*

Semuga led them down a broad avenue and across a square that boasted an enormous outdoor Greneil, then to—and *through*—the steps of the virtual Amiens cathedral. Along the way, Linka made him order a passing nun to give up her work boots.

The security chamber beneath the cathedral was all brushed plasteel, and cold white lumipanels. Flummoxed guards in gray body armor stood about impotently, their weapons on the floor.

"It's below us," the engineer bleated when Ruth twisted the gun behind his ear. Semuga gave him a sulfurous look.

"Now, Cardinal," Linka hissed. "Show us your control room."

Dourly Semuga waddled to the center of the room. A series of large disks were inscribed into the brushed-metal floor. Semuga stepped onto one of them. Reluctantly, he gestured for Linka, Ruth, and the hostage engineer to join him. He thumbed an ID pad on a nearby control stalk. The disk beneath them flashed. All at once it was the luminous circle of a downchute. They dropped slowly through the floor.

Softly he began to recite: "Be you accursed of God the Father, who created humankind; accursed of God the Sons, who suffered for humankind; accursed of the Holy Spirit which cometh in baptism; accursed of the Holy Virgin Mary and all the known and unknown mothers of God; accursed of St. Michael, the receiver of blessed souls; accursed of the angels and archangels, the princes and powers, and all the hosts of heaven. . . ."

The downchute lowered the four past a safety catwalk and into the metallic vastness of the subterranean control hall. Walls of instrumentation slanting inward as they rose, it yawned sixty meters long and fifteen wide.

"Mind if I log on, too?" Ruth asked Linka.

"Go ahead. Can't have too many eyes on this."

Semuga's imprecation continued: "Be you accursed of the wonder-working band of saints and martyrs and confessors whose good works have been pleasing to God; accursed of all the holy virgins who have shunned their worlds for the loves of the Christs; accursed of all the saints, beloved of God, from the beginning even unto the end of the worlds. . . ."

"What's he prattling about?" Ruth subvocalized to Linka.

"Cursed be you wherever you be, at home or abroad, in the road or in the path, or in the wood, or in the water, or in the church."

"The bird's thought engines say it's a slight update of the 'Curse of Ernulphus,' " Linka replied. *"Terran, quite medieval. I'm being excommunicated."*

"Sfelb, Linka," Ruth said silently, *"I didn't know you'd been communicated."*

"Be you accursed in living and dying, eating, drinking, fasting or athirst, slumbering, sleeping, waking, walking, standing, sitting, lying, working, idling—"

Cadets and nuns and monks and priests stared up from their consoles. Swiss Guards on their floating watch platforms dropped their halberds and clutched the disintos on their hips. Linka prodded Semuga's belly with the needler. "Back off!" Semuga shouted to the nearest guard, interrupting his cursing. "Take no action, any of you!"

Linka glanced down toward the technicians. "If they turn anything off, I'll kill you, Cardinal. I want to see it all."

"Step away from your controls!" Semuga shouted. "Touch nothing. That is my command!" He fastened stony eyes once more on Linka. "Um, let you be accursed in all the forces of your body. Let you be accursed outside and inside; accursed in your hair and accursed in your brain; accursed in the crown of your head, in your temples, in your ears, in your brows, in your eyes . . ."

"Look at all this equipment. You could run a war from here," Linka subvocalized.

Ruth nodded. *"Can't imagine what else you'd need all this to run."*

". . . in your jaws, in your nostrils, in your front teeth, in your back teeth, in your lips, in your throat, in your shoulders, in your upper arms, in your lower arms . . ."

"That's low enough," Linka ordered Semuga. They were five meters above the gallery floor. "Make the disk drift over toward the end. Slow walking speed."

The chutedisk floated them over scores of consoles. Behind one instrument cluster, a display panel four meters wide showed dozens of images. *Must be from that space platform of theirs,* Linka realized. "Nice orbital data," she told Semuga. "From your asteroid?" *Wow,* she thought, *I didn't think he could blanch any further.*

". . . in your breast, in your heart, in your stomach and liver, in your kidneys, in your loins, in your hips, in your private parts—oh, yes, in your private parts . . ."

The *tap* carried enormous power. Linka and Ruth both flinched when it surged into their awarenesses. *"Fem Strasser! Fem Griszam! Neuri Kalistor here."*

"Daypart, Fem Kalistor," Linka replied. *"Somehow a message from our section boss is unsurprising just now."*

Kalistor's voice crackled with enthusiasm. *"I want to congratulate you both on the superb job you're doing."*

Ruth swallowed. *"So far I've kidnapped a Kfardaszian engineer and Linka's bagged a high official of the Universal Catholic Church. You want more?"*

Kalistor guffawed. *"I know you're in an extraordinary situation, taking extraordinary actions. Neither of you signed on to enforce Enclave from the hip. First, let me tell you your saybacks are astronomical. This is pulling better than our last few Parek 'casts!"*

"Maybe I'll get as rich as you," Linka quipped to Ruth on a private channel.

"Second," Kalistor chattered, *"no-vis flyer support is on the way. It'll take a couple minutes, since you're in the middle of the ocean. But it's coming. Third, I thought you'd like to know that your 'cast is being poved at the very highest levels."*

"Oh?" said Ruth.

"The Privy High Council interrupted an executive session to pov this plorg. The

Councilors are all sitting with their mouths open." Ruth and Linka exchanged astonished glances. Kalistor continued, *"The Council has deputized you both. As extraordinary legates of the PeaceForce you are authorized to use necessary force against anyone, Jaremian or Galactic, who might prevent you from continuing to document this Enclave violation. Kalistor out."*

"Forjeling plorg," Ruth breathed aloud. *"In spite of everything, Linka, it seems we make an effective team."*

". . . in your feet, in your toes, and in your nails. Let you be accursed in every joint of your body."

The disk was passing over an outsized, ring-shaped control console. Inside it a central round table was scattered with wafers, datasheets, a few stale pastries. In the hole at its center leaned an overstuffed command chair, its stained cushions bowed deeply in the middle. "Yours?" she asked Semuga.

Semuga scowled at her. "Let there be no health in you, from the crown of your head to the sole of your foot."

"Yeah," Linka chuckled. "I gathered that."

"Cursed be you in your coming in, and in your going out," Semuga continued. "Be you accursed at home, and homeless elsewhere. Let you strain out your bowels and die the death of heretics."

The next *tap* came quickly. *"Greetings, Spectators. This is Laurien Eldridge, commanding* Bright Hope."

"What did they do, publish our access codes?" Ruth jibed on the private channel.

Linka shrugged bemusedly. *"Hello, Captain. I believe we're doing your work down here."*

"And I thank you for that. Your discoveries resolve numerous mysteries. I wanted you to know that although I'm awaiting exact orders from the Privy High Council, I anticipate dispatching a small impoundment squadron and an investigative team shortly. Until then, carry on."

The downchute settled onto the gallery floor next to a cluster of tactical modeling consoles. "I'll give you one thing," Linka told Semuga. "You Vatican types don't think small."

Ruth nodded severely. "They never have."

Semuga raised his hands. He pressed his thumbs to his forefingers as if snuffing out twin candles. "May the Christs, the Sons of the Living God, curse you throughout the Galaxy, and may Heaven with all its Virtues rise up against you to your everlasting damnation. In the name of the Holy, Catholic and Universal Church, I pronounce *anathema* on you, worlds without end, amen."

Linka's stepped off the chutedisk. "Your curse doesn't impress me, Cardinal." With Spectator sureness she swept her gaze past the staring technicians, along the gallery's immense sloping walls, and up to the ceiling grid. "We've been deputized as extraordinary legates of the PeaceForce," she shouted. "You're all under arrest!"

For the first time in—what, weeks?—she felt at peace with herself.

She flashed Ruth a manic grin. "Effective team indeed," she said. "What do you think, Ruth? I'd say we have matters pretty well under control here."

98. The *Bright Hope*

"Those Spectators didn't deserve me lying to them," Laurien Eldridge complained.

"The decision was out of your hands," Gavisel reminded her.

"Too much has been out of my hands," Eldridge grumbled.

The tactical display showed Vatican Island, exposed to all eyes since Ruth Griszam had brought down its concealers. Verdant and volcanic, it was a roughly T-shaped island surrounded by barrier reefs, thirty-two kilometers across its widest point. The junction of the *T* formed a natural harbor. Its shore bristled with jetties, piers, docks, and submerged guide rails. Ranked avenues paralleled the primary harbor, studded with improbably colored buildings. Like pastel cancer, the city encrusted a bit less than a tenth of the island's surface area.

Minutes had passed since Linka Strasser's astonishing journal began. Yet already an outraged Galaxy had settled upon its response. "Sir," Eldridge grumbled to Admiral Hafen on a private channel, "I still believe this course of action is precipitous."

"I agree. But it was a political decision not a military one. All we can do is execute it."

Bright Hope had her orders. She was to fire a single, intimidating warning shot at Vatican Island, then launch such scouts and flitters as she had in an attempt to take control of the illegal facility.

Hafen had squirted Eldridge an orbital view of the island. An orange ring lit up, two-thirds the size of the island itself, centered on the city. To its east, the ring overlay what appeared to be unsullied rain forest. To westward, the ring arched out to sea. "A circular pattern of fire, radius twenty kilometers, will create maximum visual and auditory impact with minimum danger to personnel and structures," Hafen had said. "The Vatican installation is compact. Beyond it the island is undeveloped and uninhabited. A twenty-klick circle centered on that replica of Amiens Cathedral crosses only rain forest, barren lava flows, and a parcel of ocean well removed from the Catholics' principal piscine sub routes."

"Intensity?" Eldridge demanded.

"Force three," Hafen replied. "The Catholics will think the planet is erupting all around them."

Eldridge had consulted her modelers. "To achieve force three over that radius, we'll need to push our single weapons bank to one hundred forty percent."

Hafen nodded. "Do it."

Eldridge swung close to Hafen's ear. "The weapons bank may burn out. Then if *Damocles* starts its crash program, we'd be unable to destroy it."

"It's out of our reach, Laurien," Hafen whispered back. "The decision's been taken at the very highest level."

"A quorum of Privy High Councilors could review it."

Hafen shook his head. "I said the *highest* level, Laurien. The Councilors didn't vote their will. They're doing what the people demand."

"Government-by-sayback," Eldridge said bitterly.

Hafen shrugged. "Linka Strasser's journal hit like a thunderbolt. Before she was out of Semuga's apartment, people across the Galaxy were boiling with fury. Strasser's journal was the final, incontrovertible evidence of Vatican's Enclave violation. People feel stupid they didn't demand action months earlier."

Eldridge scowled. "So the Councilors take this dangerous step because the polls tell them they have to."

"Now you understand." Hafen addressed Eldridge in a voice that commanded obedience. "Fire when ready, Captain."

"Fem Wachieu!" Eldridge yelled sourly. "Primary telemetry, please."

Five bubbles opened in the virtual sky: The straight-down vista of the island from *Bright Hope*'s own Detex system. Linka's more personal *pov*, a sweaty closeup of Semuga in despair. Ruth's squeezed-down *pov*, panning the Vatican Island control hall for what seemed the thirtieth time. The *pov*s of two no-vis fliers who'd just arrived on station over the *faux* Amiens Cathedral.

"Fem Gavisel," Eldridge called again. "As preset. Full battery, twenty-klick ring pattern, one-four-zero percent. Aim to straddle. Fire!"

The flanging sound of *Bright Hope*'s guns could be heard all over the ship. "Volleys away," Gavisel called redundantly.

The no-vis flyers' twin bubbles simply snapped off. Ruth Griszam's and Linka Strasser's feeds flashed white, then orange. Then their bubbles went black. The channels stayed open, but there was nothing in them.

Alarms began to warble. "Damage control to the gunnery bay! Damage control to the gunnery bay!" a tinny voice called.

"Auto fire suppression just triggered in the gunnery bay," Wachieu singsonged. "I'd say our little spliced-on weapons bank has burned itself out."

"What the sfelb—" Gavisel muttered.

When the visual-from orbit rebuilt itself, it was clear to everyone that something had gone terribly wrong.

A perfect circle of fire branded the island's landscape. To the east, it blazed from the rain forest. In places it spilled off the island's eastern shore, marked by towers of ocean spray just now scattering. To the west, the circle fell almost entirely on land.

The volley had struck fully ten kilometers east of its intended position.

Eldridge leaned closer to the virtual image, straining to see detail. When she succeeded, she felt hollow inside. The ring of fire's western edge seethed right *through* the Vatican complex.

"Gavisel," Eldridge croaked. "Belay the occupation force."

"Zooming in on the city," Wachieu reported. Secondary explosions bloomed across the blasted cityscape. Twenty-story towers lay in wreckage.

"I want a report!" Eldridge barked.

"The volley struck ten kilometers east-southeast of its mark," Gavisel said. "The city we meant to miss took a direct hit."

"Captain, the island seems to have shifted!" Wachieu called. "Detex now shows it ten point zero zero four eight kilometers north-northwest of its previous position."

"Surely you're not suggesting that the island *moved?*"

"Oh, no, Fem Captain."

"Then, um, Lynn, what *are* you suggesting?"

Wachieu paced her web. "Stand by, I'm reviewing the previous Detex images," she reported. "Oh, plorg in sfelb. . . ."

"What is it?" Eldridge barked.

"There's a faint harmonic in the island's signature. So faint it would escape cursory analysis, as it escaped mine. The island didn't only have concealers, it had displacers, too—and they were still on."

"*Displacers?*" Eldridge barked.

"They shifted the island's apparent position ten klicks south-southeast off its true position," Wachieu said. "It fooled all our susceptors."

"If we'd *tried* to hit them, we would've missed," Gavisel said hollowly.

Eldridge scowled. "Fem Gavisel, have the impoundment force stand down. Have the quartermaster refit the ships for rescue duty and send them down to the city." *This isn't real,* Eldridge thought. *I'm going to turn a corner, or give an order, or get an idea, and all at once I'll realize that this is just some daydream gone wrong.* Even as she formulated the thought, she knew how pitiable it was.

"Concealers *and* displacers," Gavisel said in disbelief. "Heavy technology for a civilian installation."

"Forjeling plorg," Eldridge whispered, "what *didn't* the pope's men bring onto Jaremi Four?"

Gavisel gave an appalled chuckle. "Obviously, they didn't bring shields."

99. Jaremi Four—Vatican Island

Linka awoke screaming, not that she could hear it. Her ears rang like a gong some lunatic had pitch-shifted to dog-whistle heights. She couldn't press palms to her ears hard enough to lessen the pain in her head. *I think my eardrums are ruptured.* She scanned her autonomic monitors. Yes, that was it.

She made adjustments. The pain sluiced away. Backup auditory implants crackled to life. *What the sfelb.* . . . Linka pushed up onto her elbows. New pain blazed. Her entire right side was bruised. Nothing important broken, she determined; she minimized those pangs, too. She glanced about. *Semuga's control hall,* she realized, *or what's left of it.*

The trapezoidal control gallery slumped at the center, its back broken. A two-meter chasm had opened in the floor. Half the objects attached to the gallery's ceiling had crashed down, crushing banks of instruments here, people there. Fires and electrical arcs were the primary sources of light. Far above, the chutedisk apertures in the gallery ceiling had popped open. A malignant glow stammered through their circular openings.

In the basement of her awareness, the *verify* signal resumed. Spectator Linka Strasser was back in touch with her bird.

She heard a moan and whirled. *Ruth!*

Ruth tried to push herself out from under her tonsured hostage. It was unclear which nearby fallen object had struck him. But his chest was stoved in. Stubs of mangled grillwork protruded from it. Blood blackened his clothing.

In death, Ruth's hostage had saved her life.

Ruth started screaming.

"It's your eardrums," Linka shouted over a priority subvocal channel. *"Ramp them down. Hear with your echolocators."* Relief washed Ruth's features. "All right," Linka said aloud. "Any bones broken?" Ruth introspected. She shook her head. "Let's get you up." Linka straddled the dead hostage. She scooped hands into his bloody armpits. He was heavy; she sucked air through her mouth as she hefted his body. Smoke and dust scratched at her throat.

Ruth staggered upright.

"You recording?" Linka asked.

Ruth nodded. "What happened?"

Linka maxed her vision. She spotted only a dozen survivors. Some crawled from beneath consoles. Others had simply awakened in spots that remained free of debris while neighboring areas were buried. All held their ears and howled with pain. *We've all lost our eardrums,* Linka realized. *But only Ruth and I carry the implants to do something about it.*

Brown water rushed up through the breach in the floor. The turbulent pool rose while Ruth watched. "We're below the water table here," she shouted. "It'll flood in a hurry." The rising pool lapped at the base of a control console. The console erupted in a blue-white detonation. It became a fountain of sparks. When the radiance died, half its instruments had burst.

"What in—" Linka breathed.

"Look," Ruth cried. A handful of meters away, a wounded Swiss Guard stumbled downgrade. He splashed into the water. His limbs went rigid. His body fell forward stiffly. "That water's electrically hot!" Ruth shouted. "There must be ruptured cables down there."

"The power systems are damaged so badly their safety breakers can't trip," Linka speculated.

Ruth stared through thickening smoke toward the nearest sidewall. The floor had become a ramp; the sidewall lay twelve meters away, four meters above them. "Are there exits?" she asked.

"Never mind," Linka shouted. She pointed toward the opposite end of the gallery. The far sidewall buckled with a contralto moan. Spray hissed around seams. Then whole panels spewed free. Whitewater scattered consoles and shelving and bodies and debris before it. The air it pushed ahead of it was minty. It carried a saltwater tang. "Water table my ass!" Linka cried. "The harbor's coming in!"

"Must go up," Ruth shouted.

Linka scanned the ceiling. "Tapes! There should be tapes." Any large underground chamber built by Galactics would be equipped with rescue tapes. The tough strips of self-luminous polymer, five centimeters wide by a single molecule thick, were designed to pay out from overhead dispensers when power failed.

"There!" Linka yelled. Ruth followed her around a fallen airpusher. Five or six of the diaphanous tapes swayed from side to side, each ending in a stirruplike loop.

Linka grabbed one. It felt bigger and rougher in her hand than it actually was, a helpful bioadhesion effect. The stirrup loop swelled shut around Linka's right boot. Monomolecular straps peeled away from the tape between the stirrup and her hand to swing around her waist.

Automatically, a mechanical winch in the dispenser overhead began hauling the tape back in.

Linka lofted toward the ceiling, twirling slowly. Ruth boarded an adjacent tape.

This is one forjeling surreal image, Linka thought. A few meters away Ruth ascended. At various distances other survivors, too, rode tapes toward the ceiling. Below, electrified water had wholly covered the floor. Blue-green arcs flickered in it. The only people alive below were those who'd found some large, nonconductive fallen object to clamber onto.

"Look!" Ruth cried, pointing.

Semuga was alive. He'd made it onto the roof of a fallen walkway. He staggered, meaty hands clasping his ears. His caftan was black with blood. His own? Someone else's? Linka couldn't tell. Another survivor already occupied the walkway roof: a nun cradling a broken forearm. Where she clutched it, bony stubs protruded from mangled tissue.

A single rescue tape fluttered over the fallen catwalk. The nun was almost to it.

Semuga tottered behind her. He backhanded her broken arm. She doubled over, howling. Semuga lurched past her. He planted a foot in the stirrup. The waist straps needed two tries to tighten around him.

"That plorg-warming son of a bitch," Linka hissed.

Semuga winched clear just as water overtopped the walkway roof. It lapped at the nun's bare ankles. Fingers rigid, she spasmed off into deeper water. She writhed a good ten seconds before going under.

Linka captured a memorable image: Semuga rising, silhouetted before a wave of fire that swept the wall behind him, shedding tresses of sparks.

"He's going to make it," Ruth shouted.

"No he won't!"

Ruth looked where Linka was pointing. Maxing her vision, Ruth could distinguish the rescue tape dispenser hauling Semuga up: a fist-sized gray box anchored to the ceiling. A crimson telltale flickered on it. Soon the dispenser's entire underside flickered red.

Unable to bear Semuga's weight, the winch had burned out.

Linka's head snapped down with impossible precision. Her eyes found Semuga just as he realized he was no longer rising. His eyes saucered. Cursing, he clasped both hands around the tape and tried to pull himself up. Even if he'd been capable of it, he couldn't have. With the tape dispenser powered down, the straps around his waist wouldn't open.

Terrified, Semuga stared up at Linka.

She blew him a kiss and turned her back.

A few catwalks still crisscrossed the narrow gallery ceiling. The tapes lofted them alongside one. Linka touched it gingerly. She didn't get a shock. Ruth clambered on after her. Ruth stared up through downchute openings. Linka panned the gallery one last time.

The control hall was two-thirds full of water. Where Semuga had dangled, she saw no one.

The women clambered into what had been the security chamber. Now it was a twisted jumble of plasteel panels and shattered lumipanels. To the left, debris flickered with the light of an unseen fire. Fifteen body-armored guards had been stationed here. Now she could identify charred traces of only six. A smell like cooking meat hinted at what had happened to the others. *Whatever did this was enormously powerful.*

The *tap* was unexpected. *"Fem Strasser? Fem Griszam? This is Eldridge, commanding* Bright Hope. *Glad you're all right."*

"Don't know if that's the term I'd use," Linka answered. *"Any idea what happened to us?"*

"Unfortunately, yes," Eldridge answered. *"It was our warning shot."*

Linka and Ruth exchanged astonished glances. "Bright Hope, *this is Griszam. Consider us warned."*

"A tragic error," Eldridge explained. *"The island had displacers. Our straddling volley struck you square on."*

"Ruth!" Linka shouted aloud. Rounding a fallen pilaster, she'd spotted the tunnel to the outside. "It's collapsing! Run!" Linka yelled. Ruth sprinted in, Linka a single step behind.

They emerged into air orange with blowing embers. In every direction highrise buildings lay in ruins or flames. A monsignor in singed vestments staggered past shouting out prayers, clasping blistered hands over his eyes. He lurched toward a smoking cavity in the pavement and vanished. After a moment his shrieks ceased to echo. "It's like Minga Four down here," Linka shouted.

The virtual cathedral was gone. Fire belched from a crater ringed with fallen lintels. "Disruptor beam struck right here," Ruth cried. "No wonder so many in the control hall lost their hearing."

Uncertainly, Linka nodded in the direction opposite the harbor. In the next block, one of Semuga's gaudy personnel carriers lay on its side, surrounded by dead footmen. "Keep recording," Linka said dully. "It'll help rescuers know where to look."

By the time the Spectators had wandered even half a block inland, most of the wounded they encountered could hear. A few approached Ruth and Linka to ask after some friend or coworker, only to retreat, aghast, when they saw the womens' Escher lozenges.

High-pitched screams sounded over the whine of twisting metal. Linka snapped her attention a block away. "What the sfelb?"

At first she thought it was an external fire escape. After a moment, she realized with horror that it was the central staircase of a twelve-story dormitory. Half the building had already collapsed. Its core stairs stood exposed to the open air, choked with evacuees.

Children!

They were boys between the ages of seven and twelve, more than a hundred of them.

"Why don't they use downchutes?" Ruth asked.

"No power," Linka said.

"Why so many children?"

Linka scowled. "Must be the priests' harem."

Choked with boys, the stairway was wobbling free of the building. There was nothing the children could do, nothing Linka or Ruth could do, either, but watch the staircase wrench free. Amid a hail of sundered fastenings it twisted, spewing boys like a dog shaking off water. With a roaring clatter stairplates and girders and small bodies pancaked unseen behind a burning religious goods shop. A fountain of dust boiled up, acknowledging the collapse.

Linka ran into the debris-choked avenue, blinking back tears. She would have sprinted to the spot where the stairway had fallen and tried to help.

If she hadn't been stopped by a familiar voice.

"Linka—" the sound trailed off into a strangled croak. "Linka," it came again. "Help me."

Linka looked down. It was Sister Barkela.

Scour marks on the pavement told the story. The personnel carrier that lay overturned twenty meters away had lost power and scraped along the roadway. The elaborately sculpted flagpole it sheared off had fallen on Barkela, crushing her midsection.

Blood trickled from the nun's misshapen lips. "I'm dying, Linka." Barkela rattled. "Help me." Ardently she stared to her left. Her fingers strained toward some object just beyond their reach.

Her holy water vial, Linka realized. The impact had flung it from around her neck. Amazingly, it hadn't broken.

"Please, Linka! I need it to go to heaven." Barkela coughed. Red specks appeared among the moles on her chin. "You don't understand, but—"

"I understand more than you think," Linka said maliciously. She straddled the dying nun. "My name's Linka Strasser. The one from OmNet."

Barkela's mouth twisted into a perfect, tiny *o.*

Linka sidestepped. She brought a booted foot between Barkela's hand and the holy water.

Tears welled from the nun's eyes. "Please," rattled Barkela.

"I don't want you to go to heaven," Linka hissed. With a kick she sent the vial flying. It shattered against an upturned curbstone, dampening a circle of pavement barely the size of a fist. Barkela's face went slack. *Hope I have the terminology right,* Linka thought. Aloud, she hissed, "Go . . . to . . . hell!"

Barkela's features contorted into the starkest display of terror Linka had ever seen. The nun seemed to be watching her future gel before her: epochless despair, agony beyond measure, fire and sulfur, heat and choking fumes, melancholy and sterile rage, forever and ever world without end amen. Barkela's lips trembled open in a wordless howl. Her eyes stared *past* Linka, bottomless with misery and fright.

Linka was surprised by the strength of her own sudden impulse to look over her shoulder and make sure no demons were coming.

Abruptly she realized the gravity of what she'd done. *I told Barkela go to hell,*

Galactic Rapture

and she believes I guaranteed her place there. It's all prosaic reality for her: my kicking her holy water away cut her off from perpetual bliss. Simple as that. She's certain that endless pain and terror await her—she expects them now, as literally as you expect the sting to follow a slap across your face. And I'm the reason why.

Linka stepped away from Barkela. Wordlessly she glided toward the curbstone. Squatting painfully, she dampened her fingers in the spilled holy water, intending at least to moisten Barkela's forehead with it.

"Don't bother." Ruth squatted beside the nun, one hand against her flabby neck where a pulse had been. Barkela's eyes were sightless, the mouth locked in a final simper of dread. "She's gone."

Jamming her hands in the surcoat's big pockets, Linka turned her back on Ruth and the corpse.

Ruth rose slowly. "Someday," she said after a long moment, "you must tell me what this was about."

Linka whirled, suddenly furious. "It's about ignorance, forjel it! It's about people wasting their lives chasing payoffs that don't exist, passing by the good things right in front of them." All at once, the rage contorting her features collapsed into woe. "Dying terrified of phantoms a child shouldn't have to believe in."

"Excuse me." Kalistor's *tap* was gentle but insistent. *"Eldridge's relief forces are coming. If you're still here when they arrive they'll detain you for debriefing."*

Ruth glanced at Linka. She brushed dirt from her own arms. *"Maybe we could use a good debriefing."*

Kalistor's tone was tentative. *"I know you've been through a lot. But the ultimate battle between Parek's forces and the Catholic armies is about to begin."*

"Don't tell me," Ruth said acidly. *"It would be good for the saybacks to have it covered by the Spectator who discovered Parek."*

"Not to mention the Galaxy's favorite Southern Hemisphere war correspondent," Linka chimed in.

"I had a high-sounding speech ready about the documentarian's obligation in the face of historic events, but I guess we're beyond that," Kalistor said tiredly. *"Shall I tell you about the bonus?"*

She told them.

Ruth and Linka exchanged astonished glances. The bonus Kalistor named might make them the richest women on Terra.

"I guess I can soldier on a little further," Ruth breathed. *"After all this, I don't think I'd mind watching Parek die."*

"I'm spent," Linka said exhaustedly, *"but what the sfelb. Count me in, too. But how do we get there?"*

"Maybe you didn't know," Kalistor said. *"Two no-vis flyers had arrived on station over Vatican Island just before* Bright Hope *opened fire. We're almost certain they're dead, but their no-vis gear and flight packs may be intact. You know how heavily that equipment is armored."*

"Understood." Ruth logged off. Linka did the same.

Hands on hips, the women blinked at each other through swirling smoke in the middle of an avenue choked with shambling wounded. Ruth shrugged. "In the middle of all this, we have to find two specific bodies. Forjeling great."

"Quiet," Linka said. "I'm trying to remember something I haven't used since my Academy days." Without optimism she spoke a nonsense syllable. She spun as if orienting to a sound Ruth couldn't hear. "The packs are intact." She pointed past the children's dormitory. "This way."

Ruth subvocalized the control syllable Linka had said aloud for her benefit. *Oh yes, the* crash beacon *command.* She, too, heard the crisply directional beep superimposed on her hearing. When she faced in the direction Linka was running, she felt a nonexistent wind at her back.

She pushed past two blood-spattered *monsigniori* and sprinted after Linka.

"Should be right around this corner," Linka said. "What the sfelb—"

The moment she turned the corner, Ruth knew what Linka meant. The beeps whose direction they had been so sure of now came from everywhere. The illusory breeze struck her face one moment, her back the next. "What's this?"

"The bodies must be close together. Interference between their two beacons could muddy the spatial resolution." Linka stepped around a fallen cornice. She stopped dead. "I don't think we'll need the beacons any more."

It had been an artisan's shop, devoted to the repair of reliquaries and similar rarities of the church. Its roof was gone. Linka stood staring at its front window: glasteel whose contramagnetic moment had been altered—say, by a disruptor bolt landing nearby—tended to craze in an odd but predictable way. It would retain the outline of anything that crashed through it. The shop window had two perfect human silhouettes punched out of it. "Look at the angle. Has to be the Spectators." Struggling with the shop door, Linka glanced back at Ruth. "Remember the *forced reveal* command?"

"I do." Half-smiling, she raised her blaster. "And I know a great *open the door* command."

Linka skipped backward.

The blaster shot stripped the shop door from its frame. Ignoring a rain of fine debris, Ruth stepped over it into the shop. Sidestepping an overturned kiosk displaying fragments of Terra's True Cross, she subvocalized the priority command to ramp down the fliers' no-vis generators.

"Oh, forjel," Linka breathed. The fliers lay side by side, face down amid the debris of a shattered work table. Their bodies were deeply charred.

Tramir Duza's head lay at an unnatural angle. The landing had snapped his neck. "Sfelb, he's dead again," Linka groaned.

"You knew him?" Ruth said quietly.

"Part of my team down here. Tramir couldn't have been back from North Polar more than a day."

Cassandra Wiplien was impaled in a dozen places on a tray of upright inscribing tools. "Cassandra worked support for me once," Ruth said. "Knew her plorg, she did."

"Let's make some room," Linka grated. A reliquary cradling a finger bone from the leprous Christ of Vyrdis Ten—doubly remarkable because by the time of his Incarnation, this Christ no longer had fingers—shattered on the floor. Ruth heaved away a five-sided case containing a corroded energy pack from the True Suicide

Weapon of the Christ of Frensa Six. An ornate platinum ark bearing the True Sand
Box Shovel of the Christ of Wikkel Four tumbled to the floor. Now there was space
to lever Duza and Wiplien's legs onto the table, to begin the grim task of harvesting
the corpses' no-vis belts and flight packs.

"This fits somehow," Ruth said sourly.

"Pardon?"

"Last time I covered Parek, my final act was to rifle a body. This time, that's
how I begin."

One piece of Spectator equipment remained on both bodies: their locator beacons. Linka spoke a command that maxed their output.

"Their power won't last long that way," Ruth warned.

"But they'll be found." Linka doffed Ruth's surcoat. She fastened the no-vis
belt around her waist. "Tramir and Cassandra are the only stiffs on this island who
didn't break the law coming here. It's only fair that they get taken to North Polar
first." She jammed the flight pack into its container on her no-vis belt. She grimaced.

Ruth eyed Linka's bare frame with concern. "That's an awful contusion. Break
any ribs?"

"Probably." Squinting against pain, Linka tugged the surcoat back on. "Let's
get the sfelb out of here."

100. Jaremi Four—Somewhere

"**U**p! Up!" chided the messenger.

"What now?" The young woman stirred reluctantly. Her ribs ached from spasmodic crying. She felt spent.

Above the waistband of the messenger's saronglike skirt, her flaccid abdomen
was tracked with shallow scars. "They want you again."

"Sentencing, so soon?" The young woman heaved her legs over the edge of the
sleeping frame.

"The elders didn't say." The messenger edged toward the chamber door.
"What they did say was hurry."

The young woman reached into a moss-caked bowl. "Now I must scurry to my
own banishment?" She splashed putrid water onto her face. "Let's go."

The screech sounded like the call of some animal. Both women spun toward
it.

It was the babe.

He'd awakened in his cage. The left side of his face was swollen, the white of
the eye shot through with red. Seeing his new mother preparing to leave, he
reached toward her between irregular bars of decaying wire. Even though it was she
who'd beaten him, his loyalty was undaunted.

Snarling, the young woman hurled the water bowl at the cage. It shattered and sprayed the babe with dirty water. The child backed away, howling, clutching one hand.

"Suffer, intruder," the young woman hissed.

The messenger scowled. "He's a baby."

"A devil baby," said the young woman. "He saw his grandmother die, then his mother." Shaking her head, the young woman followed the messenger outside. "Let's go see if now he's killed me."

Decades—centuries?—before, the immense oil storage tank had pitched over on its side. At least, so the elders said. Its sludge-crusted skin curved high overhead, carpeted with mold and fungi. Within, the light of countless torches revealed a maze of catwalks, platforms, wood stairways, and huts perched on scaffolds that receded into the tank interior. Candles flickered in some of the windows. Men and women huddled around them making the best use of their feeble precious light.

The young woman followed the messenger between two slumping shanties. They came to an ancient circular stairway made of neither wood nor scraps; ages ago it had been hewn from metal by artisans whose skills no one now remembered. "Go on," said the messenger.

"I know the way," the young woman said sourly. She worked her way upward in dizzy circles, panting in the fetid air. The circular stairway ended at a giddy platform. Silent guardsmen flanked a plain wooden staircase. Clutching herself, the young woman trudged toward it.

The stairway continued up through a jagged-edged breach in the tank's wall.

Puffing, the young woman emerged into evening air. Below, thatched roofs undulated around the fallen tank. Other tanks and vessels stood silhouetted against the blackening sky like the fingers of dying giants. Some were wide and squatty. Others rose tall and slender. The thinnest were ringed with twisted ladders and platforms overhung with tainted vines. The elders said the fallen tank had once stood upright like its companions. If so, it had been the proudest of them all. *How could they know that?* she wondered. *I shouldn't mock the elders,* she reminded herself. *They know something I don't. They know my fate.*

Now she could see the wood and thatch and metal of the elders' compound. Though it was almost night, the compound's windows were dark.

She followed the wooden stairs through the structure's ceiling and into the antechamber. "Hello?" she whispered.

"Ah, there you are!" The Elder of the Soil wore his best ceremonial robes. His tone was jovial, his smile bizarrely congenial. He held out a gleaming drinking bowl. "Come, drink," he said gently.

She took the drinking bowl with trembling fingers. "Is this poison?" she croaked.

Laughing, the elder pressed scrawny fingers against the bowl's lip. He tilted it toward her mouth. The bittersweet flavor of ceremonial liquor assaulted her. She spat, then swallowed lustily. *Usually I get a few drops during the sun festival,* she thought in confusion. *He's given me a war hero's draught.*

All at once the Elder of the Soil recognized the source of her puzzlement. "Ah, I see no one told you," he said gently. "Come, follow me. You and your adopted boy, you're heroes now."

Heroes? Bewildered, she followed the Soil Elder deeper into the elders' compound. Widely spaced candles cast barely enough light for her to see her way. "Why so dark?" she finally dared ask.

"So your eyes can adjust. You'll see."

They entered the darkened council chamber. "She's here!" called the Soil Elder. The young woman's astonishment deepened as two dozen pairs of hands slapped against hips and walls and railings in respectful applause.

"Come," said the Soil Elder. Festively costumed men and women stood in a circle three deep around a marble tabletop on which a single gray candle burned. The settlement's entire leadership was gawking at it.

It occurred to the young woman that she'd never seen a candle burn so serenely. Its flame was a piercing yellow-white. It didn't flicker. It emitted no smoke. Though half consumed, its sides were uncluttered by drippings.

"This is one of the candles you made yesterday," the Elder of the Soil explained. "It was lighted immediately after you left these chambers." She stared into the tiny, dazzling flame without understanding. "It's burned continuously ever since," he continued.

"Since midmorning?" she whispered. "That's impossible."

"Precisely," said the Highest Elder. He was old beyond imagining, stoop-shouldered, almost hairless.

"But how—" she stammered.

"We hope you'll tell us." It was the Elder of the Chandlers. He wore a gown made from tiny panels of glazed hardened wax. "Please, tell us all what happened."

She stepped back. "Mighty Elder, you know better than anyone what happened."

The elder smiled. "Tell us what you remember."

She stared into two dozen pairs of welcoming, delighted eyes. "I was in the dipping shanty with the other women married into Clan Aurora. I had the babe with me. My dead sister's child, you know. The shift steward said it was all right."

"Yes, yes," said the Elder of the Chandlers. "Explain what happened. Remember that you are speaking to many who do not know candlemaking."

The young woman composed her thoughts as best she could. "We take big open frames and tie lengths of yarn to them. They will be the wicks. We rub them with fat till they're shiny and hang down perfectly straight. Then we lower them into a cauldron of molten tallow. After a short time, we lift them out and let them drip. Then we dip them again. We repeat this a few dozen times, and the result is a batch of candles."

"And this morning?" demanded the Elder of the Glowing Ooze. "What happened this morning?"

"My back was bothering me. I couldn't keep the babe lashed to my shoulders. I tethered him on the countertop, well away from the cauldron. The Compounding Mistress had come by a few minutes before to test the tallow. She'd added a few drops of resin."

"Resin?" asked the Elder of Manufactories.

"Made from *skraggel* fat through a rather elaborate process," explained the Elder of the Chandlers. "A small quantity added to the tallow makes for candles that break less easily and burn longer."

Silence descended. "I don't know what happened. Perhaps the Compounding Mistress forgot . . . I mean. . . ."

"Speak your mind," said the Elder of the Soil tenderly. "No one's on indictment here."

"I suppose the Compounding Mistress forgot she'd left the bowl of resin on the countertop. There was some problem with the wicking yarn and she was called away suddenly. We were about to lower our candles for the final dipping when someone screamed. My sister's babe had gotten out of his tether. I snatched him just before he fell into the tallow. But he upset the resin bowl."

"The resin went into the tallow cauldron?" said the Elder of Manufactories. "A whole bowl?"

"About two-thirds full," the young woman whispered.

"Two days' supply," breathed the Elder of the Compounders. "Into the last dipping of a single batch."

"I screamed out what had happened. No one knew what to do. The shift steward said go ahead, dip the candles the final time. As soon as we pulled the frame up we knew something was wrong. They were shiny and the color was wrong."

"Not wrong," breathed the Elder of the Chandlers. "Just different."

"But it is not tradition!" the young woman stammered.

The Elder of the Chandlers pulled an ancient glass disk from his pouch. He squinted through it at the candle flame. "No, not tradition," he said pensively. "It's . . . better."

"Better. . .?" The young woman touched dirty fingers to her lips. The Elder of the Soil guided her beside the Elder of the Chandlers. She gaped as he gave her a convex glass to look through. "It makes everything bigger," she gasped.

The Elder of the Chandlers chuckled. "The better to see what your miracle candle is doing. See why it doesn't drip?"

"The outermost layer doesn't burn as fast as the rest of the candle," she said after a minute's hushed scrutiny. "It remains a little higher and makes a kind of lip."

The Elder of the Chandlers nodded. "The lip holds the molten tallow back. Instead of running down the sides, it stays beneath the flame until it is burned away. So the candle burns longer."

"How much longer?" she said tonelessly.

"As long as three traditional candles, maybe four."

"Brighter, less smoke, no dripping, lasts longer," wheezed the Highest Elder. Seized by a sudden coughing fit, he leaned back against a litter. But even the hacking could not erase his smile. "Think what this could mean."

The Eldress of Refectories stepped forward, tapping a scarred finger alongside her good eye. "Legend says the ancients could read and learn any time they wanted, day or night, without regard for the cost of light."

The Elder of Manufactories nodded. "More time to think, to plan, to teach the young."

"Wealth now squandered on candles freed up to pursue other, more important projects," breathed the Eldress of Tannery.

"Light to grow food at night," mused the Eldress of Farms.

The Elder of the Soil stepped forward. "Perhaps the first step back to those ancient days of power and wonder."

"Fuck all that," growled the Highest Elder. "Imagine what these candles will bring in trade!"

The Elder of the Chandlers cupped his hands around the candle's unmoving flame. "And now we know the secret. Dip the body of the candle using regular tallow, then finish with a resin-rich outer layer."

The Eldress of the Tannery gave the young woman a toothless smile. "That impish babe of your sister's," she said. "Truly he is a miracle child."

The Matriarch of Clan Aurora tapped her walking stick on the floor for attention. "Nor is this his first miracle." She leered toward the young woman. "You told me when you brought him here, he made your milk run again."

The young woman fought back laughter. "That was nothing. I hadn't given suck since my own baby died. I mustn't have been as dry as I thought I was."

"You're over-modest," chided Matriarch Aurora.

"A miracle child," voices murmured.

Clutching his staff, the Highest Elder wavered to his feet again. "Surely this babe from beyond the hills is no ordinary child. From this moment forward let him no longer be treated as one."

"Let us go to him," whined the Elder of the Clouds.

"Let us go," voices chanted. "Let us go to honor the miracle child!" Suddenly the young woman found herself lifted atop shoulders—*atop the shoulders of our hereditary leaders! No war captain has ever known such honor!*—and bustled from the chamber at the crest of a idolatrous human surge.

No one even bothered staying behind to time the dripless candle's burn.

They're going to find the babe as I left him, she realized. *Beaten and caged. Shit, I hope I didn't hurt him too bad when I threw that bowl at him.*

101.   Jaremi Four—Southern Hemisphere— Parek's Ruins

T he Spectator had approached Parek's fleet in broad daylight, crawling along the riverbank for more than a kilometer. He begged to join. Touched by the man's audacity, Ulf attached the Spectator to a crack Brethren platoon as bodyservant to the platoon's commanding sergeant.

Now that Spectator stood atop a dusty ridge. Forty meters below, at the foot of a muddy slope, Parek's boats had tied up in a broad cove, gunwale to gunwale, like pickets in a fence. Soldiers labored like so many insects, hauling weapons and matériel off the boats, arranging them in staging areas ashore. Here, the ancient canal gave up its walls and became a river, widened by the waters tumbling down the muddy slope from a channel high above.

Jagged with decay, an ancient city slumped uphill, thick with overgrowth. It had been a ruin for centuries already when the Tuezi struck. Now Parek's fashioners prepared it for what might be their leader's last stand. Gaudily uniformed Brethren and fashioners with backpacks full of tools explored the ruin's central feature, a crumbling empty stone cistern twenty meters around. Already they had identified the magazine where they would store their spare munitions. Even as laborers wrestled shells and powder down into the cistern, fashioners tended to its concealment. Woodworkers assembled a portable stage over it, typical of the stages Parek favored for revival meetings.

Behind the city rose a steep escarpment. There was a waterfall ten meters wide; below it, buttermilk rapids tumbled toward the river.

A stone bastion jutted out of the hillside, its edges softened by centuries. Mortarmen struggled to set up the army's artillery along its crest. Between its height advantage and its commanding view of the river, that position would enable Parek's gunners to shell oncoming boats long before enemy snipers could threaten them.

The Spectator whirled. A lanky black figure in white leather approached. Flanking him was a hawk-nosed commando in stained fatigues and a gaunt assassin in a tropical caftan. The trio was surrounded by Brethren. The Spectator maxed his hearing. "Behold," Parek was proclaiming, "our arms shall be mighty in the sight of the gods. Our swords shall rain sore destruction upon our enemies."

The Brethren commander blinked. "We have to use swords?"

"No, no," said Parek. "We'll use all we possess. And we will win. Spread the word. We shall follow the skygod's counsel and we shall not fail."

Parek's entourage had inched along the bastion, scrutinizing each detail of the preparations. Now it drew near the Spectator. Parek's hypnotic eyes came to rest on his. "You," Parek called. "Serving boy. Come here."

Haltingly the Spectator stepped forward, playing the autochthon. "I am honored," he stammered.

Parek didn't answer. His eyes flicked toward the Spectator's sleeve, his breast and his belt buckle. "You twinkle," Parek said coldly. In a lightning move, the prophet reached behind him. He snatched the pistol from Chagrin's holster and fired.

The Spectator fell back onto gravel. His hands clutched uselessly at a fist-sized hole in his stomach. Parek's second shot ruptured his skull like a *bohtti* sprout. The third shattered his jaw. Teeth rained like spilled coins.

Parek put a fourth round into the dead man's crotch, then handed Chagrin back his weapon. "Ulf," he said darkly. "Tell the mortarmen to move their artillery off the ancient wall."

"That's the best place for it!" Ulf objected.

"Move it to the second-best place," Parek said firmly. He pointed toward the pulped Spectator. "He saw us placing guns up there. So the enemy god has seen it, too. Depend on it, that ridge will be bombarded before the enemy draws near our range."

102. Jaremi Four—Three Kilometers Above the Equatorial Sea

"Sfelb on shale," Linka hissed. "That asshole Spectator went in there wearing Escher lozenges, didn't he? Didn't he *pov* my journals? Didn't he know Parek would see them?"

"You know what happened," Ruth said coldly. "A Spectator who goes deliberately among autochthons without lozenges violates the Enclave statutes."

"Forjel Enclave," Linka spat.

"Forjel it all," Ruth replied. Of one mind, they closed all their bubbles. They focused on the reality before them. Three klicks below, the Equatorial Sea was slate blue. The sky was ruddy ahead, cerulean above. The setting sun floated higher than it had on Vatican Island. At their flight packs' top speed, Ruth and Linka were gaining on the sunset.

Ruth's hand on Linka's came as a surprise. Linka's impulse was to draw her hand back. The look in Ruth's eyes convinced her not to. "I never got to ask," Ruth asked levelly. "I couldn't *pov* any of your stuff on the island. How'd it go for you?"

"Forjel it," Linka husked. "There's no such thing as an even fight on Jaremi Four. Just one lopsided slaughter after another. Watching them is one thing—"

"I know."

"During Parek's attack, for the first time I knew how it felt to be doomed and helpless." Linka's eyes softened, as though she'd recognized a truth whose simplicity surprised her. "That's how it must've felt for all those invaders who challenged Graargy's dam and got swallowed up," she brooded.

Ruth nodded. "How was it on the island?"

"You had it fine," Linka said crossly. "Lunch with the VIPs. Witty company. Regular velvet bondage."

"I asked how it was for you."

"I was sex chattel."

Ruth's eyes narrowed. "That nun. . . ."

"And Semuga. Though I think I can call it even with him."

Ruth tightened her grip on Linka's hand. "If it makes any difference, I stopped being angry with you long ago. You know, for banishing me up north."

Linka pulled her hand away. "Sure," she said edgily, "it worked out well enough for you."

The two women flew on, unspeaking.

Three klicks northwest of them, a piscine sub broke the surface. Ruth thought of logging on and breaking over toward it, but she decided not to. *Everybody knows this sea is full of Vatican subs. No need to cover this one. I'm needed offline, right where I am.*

Linka had seen the sub, too. She knew what Ruth's decision not to overfly it meant. She stammered, "Ruth, I'm sorry."

"It's too late for that," Ruth said gently. Her tone spoke not of bitterness but rather forgiveness.

"Guess it's too late for a lot of things," Linka replied. She turned her face toward Ruth. "Past time to let go."

Kilometers of sea slipped beneath them while they talked out the incident that had made them enemies six years before. Ruth, then a novice Spectator, had been appalled when Linka had let Laz Kalistor die so horribly. After the tribal chief Kaahel had presided over Kalistor's torture, dismemberment, and burning; after Laz's ill-advised revivification from a years-old sample-and-scan; after the collapse of his marriage to Neuri Kalistor—after all of that, the wrathful "widow" had taken Ruth aside. Ruth was new and green; Neuri had no trouble persuading her to take the risk of filing a critical report. Despite Ruth's low seniority, OmNet brass leapt to act on her complaint; Linka's overly scrupulous reticence had sparked controversy in all the wrong forums.

Linka had lost a year back on Terra as an all-too-leisurely tribunal ground on.

Finally exonerated and reinstalled as senior Spectator on Jaremi Four, Linka had abused her authority to assign Ruth a shabby posting: the old dam in soft Northland, far from Southland with its violence and lucrative saybacks. Little happened up north. No Spectator had attained fame or wealth there.

Until Ruth met Arn Parek.

"You're not who you were then," Linka said quietly. "Neither am I. Today I sure as sfelb abandoned caution. Bang, right into the center of the action. I don't like the results, but you've got to admit I made the story change."

"You couldn't know *Bright Hope* would hit the city."

"But that's the point, isn't it?" Linka demanded. "I couldn't predict the consequences, yet I acted anyway. Doesn't that make me partly responsible for the carnage?"

"It certainly does not," Ruth bristled.

"I'm not so sure."

"I'm sure of one thing. You'd better turn around."

Linka spun and yelped.

The medical bark was wedge-shaped, about seventy meters across—and directly in front of them.

Below the stern thrusters, the hull clamshelled open. The entry lock bore a flickering OmNet logo.

The woman who awaited them had olive-gold skin, thin black bangs, and a polychromatic crystal sparkled in the V of her uniform jumper's neckline. "Fem Kalistor?" Linka said in surprise.

"Daypart," Neuri Kalistor's manner was cordial but rushed. "You have no idea how difficult it was to free up a hospital ship. They're all wanted on Vatican Island." She guided Ruth and Linka through narrow hallways bathed in antiseptic light. "Auto diagnose," she commanded the walls. To Ruth and Linka, "I didn't want you two moving on to the final conflict without getting you fixed up."

Linka shrugged. "The gesture's appreciated, but I don't really think—"

"If you dialed your pain sensibility back to normal, you wouldn't be *able* to think," Kalistor snapped. She consulted a wrist readout. "Linka, you have three broken ribs and related blunt force trauma throughout your right upper quadrant. You and Ruth both have punctured eardrums. You're both covered with minor cuts and burns." Kalistor bustled them into an infirmary. White-clad medical personnel lay the Spectators on surgical tables. "We're going to hover here, over the ocean where no autochthons can see us, and get you both some high-speed surgery."

Linka awoke. She peered at the chronodisplay. Two hours had elapsed since she'd lain on that surgical table. Now she lay on a soma cot wearing a short white robe. She swung her legs onto the floor. She took a deep breath, then another. Her ribs were free of pain. She hummed a tune. *Hearing's back to normal.* She examined her arms and legs. *The cuts, the burns, the dirt under the nails . . . all gone.* There was a unique feeling in all her movements. *Being clean,* she realized. *I haven't been really, deeply clean in weeks.*

She left the recovery cubicle and padded down the hallway. "Fem Strasser!" Kalistor called from a cramped wardroom. Linka maneuvered herself onto a bench. She faced Kalistor cautiously across a servotable. "Feeling better?" Kalistor asked.

Linka shrugged. "I suppose."

Kalistor eyed her quizzically.

Linka couldn't stay angry. She stretched out her arms and laughed with the intensity of nervous release. "What the sfelb, I feel *great!*"

Trays rose from twin apertures in the table surface. "Kobe steak, roasted leeks, and brown rice with *chuli,*" said Kalistor. "That was your favorite at the Academy."

"Still is." Linka impaled a cube of rare meat on her prodstick, popped it into her mouth. She gave herself over to savoring it. "Superb, I have to admit it," she said after swallowing. She locked eyes with Kalistor. Hot salty water lined the lids. "Oh, look, Neuri, I have to say something."

Kalistor's features softened. "No, I have to tell *you* something."

They opened their mouths at the same moment and dissolved into laughter. When Linka opened her eyes again, they were hugging. "Peace," Linka husked into the other woman's hair, wondering if Neuri'd catch the reference.

"For eternity," whispered Kalistor, a catch in her voice.

"Forjel it, Neuri, I'm so s—"

The section boss held up her hand. "I won't apologize to you, you don't apologize to me. It's just over."

Ignoring happy tears, Linka reveled in another mouthful of steak.

"You know, it isn't you. Or me."

"I know," Linka said with real hostility. "It's Enclave."

Kalistor arched an eyebrow. "You *have* been through some plorg."

"Doesn't matter," Linka said tonelessly. "The system will grind on."

"Maybe not. You and Ruth are going to be household words. Maybe you can press for change." Kalistor's face darkened. "Laz died again, you know."

Linka nodded. "Parek told me."

Kalistor nodded wistfully. "Some sordid Council intrigue." She raised one hand. Her spearstick tumbled from finger to finger, rolling across her hand as if alive—one of the simpler sleight-of-hand effects Laz had taught her during their years together. "They sent him to teach Parek magic."

"You're plorging me."

"You know, he never left another sample-and-scan? It would've been the same

Laz as climbed out of the soup last time. Too young, too unbruised for him and me to click." She picked at her guarbeast Cortemandaise. "For some reason, they commed me and asked whether I wanted them to bring him back again. I said no. I thought he'd suffered enough." Blinking furiously, she raised a glass of Rikubian whiskey. Linka had one, too, though she hadn't noticed it on her tray before.

Neuri Kalistor managed a certain grandeur in tone as she toasted, "Here's to Laz. His pain is finally over."

"To Laz," Linka said, fighting sobs. They hugged again.

After a moment Linka asked, "Where's Ruth?"

"Still in surgery."

"She was less badly hurt than I was."

"Remember when I told you and Ruth to get off the island before the Confetory debriefed you?"

"Sure."

"Well, they caught up with us anyway. With Ruth, that is. The message went from the Privy High Council to President Silbertak, then straight to me."

"What do I have to do?"

"It's not you they want," Kalistor said. "You just go cover the final battle and receive that bonus we discussed. They want Ruth because of her previous experience with Parek. She's in surgery for the installation of several new, special-purpose implants. Then she'll embark on an extraordinary mission."

"Can you tell me what her mission is?"

"Sorry, I can't."

Linka half-smiled. "Too bad for Ruth. She'll miss out on her bonus."

"Despite its sensitivity, her mission should be brief. She may catch up to you before the battle's over. Anyway, what the Council's paying her for the extraordinary mission is fifteen times the bonus for covering the final battle." Kalistor flashed Linka a mischievous look. "Looks like you'll have to settle for being the *second* richest woman on Terra."

103. The *Bright Hope*—Stardrive Bay Eight

Annek Panna had never felt so serene, so calmly certain of her next move.

The guard had not challenged her. Why should he?

The corpse-slender physicist climbed a short ladder. She pressed her thumb to an identipad. An overhead hatch irised open. A gentle tractor field pulled her body up through it.

Laughing gently, she hauled herself into the nulgrav zone at the stardrive's axial center. It was like a womb. Tugging gently at metafiber conduits, she wafted forward. She recognized every module on the tubular wall. *Para-quantized flux diverter. Multiplexed harmonic phase lens.* This was her creation. She'd reasoned out its physics, scaled it up to size, supervised every phase of its assembly. She felt sanctioned and affirmed here, surrounded by the manifest handiwork of her own mind, the only mind she felt she'd ever truly understood.

Until *his.*

The tunnel split. Panna floated down the left-hand fork. Auxiliary control apparatus glowed like the eyes of friends who'd waited for someone too long into the night.

As confident as I've always felt in this place, even here I could never silence all my doubts. Did creating this drive really mean something? Was it was part of some genuine destiny for me? Just make-work? Barren self-diversion?

She'd moved beyond all that now.

Annek Panna possessed the purpose she'd so ached for.

The tunnel opened into a cylindrical chamber studded with control arrays. At its top was a circular hatch. She was accustomed to precision, but the way her fingers danced across control tabs—the grace and economy with which she slid aside the security covers, even in nulgrav—surprised even her.

But of course she knew with ice-calm agitation every act she would next perform. Her life was integrated now. Like syrup, conviction bubbled up from outside her— from beyond her. It had congealed into an amicable new floor for the arena of her emotions, a rising surface that interred her old doubts like unmourned shipwrecks.

I never guessed it could be like this. But now I know. I belong!

She floated through an elaborate airlock. *The core command pod.* She tapped in a passcode; the lock screwed shut behind her. Air bladders inflated around the edges of its doors. All around the chamber, red lights twinkled into green. Dormant dataspheres came alight. Ventilators hummed.

The core command pod had switched over to its own power and enviro. It was connected to *Bright Hope* only by data links.

As it was an experimental installation, the Panna drive was not one with *Bright Hope* in the almost organic way of the ship's other primary systems. There hadn't been time to connect it properly. Further, there'd been concern that some error flashing between the cruiser's thought engines might prod the stardrive's untested control intelligence into some dangerous failure mode. At its deepest levels, then, the Panna drive lay grandly isolated from *Bright Hope*'s command matrix. There were things one could only direct the Panna drive to do from the core command pod. There were instructions it could receive from nowhere else aboard *Bright Hope,* instructions it could hurl into *Bright Hope*'s command matrix that could be originated nowhere else, instructions that would be rejected from anywhere else— even from *Bright Hope*'s own bridge and command crew.

From the core command pod deep within the stardrive, not only the drive but *Bright Hope* herself lay vincible, open to Panna's manipulations.

Parek knew that, Panna thought. *That's why he chose me. That's why he came to me in my secret misery and bestowed on me the most prodigious of all his gifts.* She swam toward the primary console and pressed her thumb to its corner. Covers within covers slid open, baring the stardrive's most intimate control interfaces. Bliss rose in her. It seemed to press joyously against her fingertips, her skull. She felt delight so unconditional that she couldn't declare it stridently enough to bleed off the pressure of it before she burst.

Iamsofortunate, she thought in a rush. *Ofallthecountlesstrillions onlyIknowthe-truth.Only Iamofthedestiny,onlyIwill playtherolethat opentheportalsto anunimaginable future.*

The primary console whirred open. It surrendered up a curved panel studded with tiny mechanical switches, hard-wired jumpers Panna had crafted with her own hands. Resolutely, she set about rearranging the connections, defeating safety interlocks, and folding power flows back on themselves in ways she never would have dared before. "In visions he came to me," Panna singsonged to herself. "Parek. Word Among Us. Cosmic Christ. He calls me to save him. My destiny is to rescue him from the Vatican assassins so redemption can move forward. I realize now: *this* is the challenge I spent my life preparing for."

"Nav systems active," a mechanical voice droned.

"Propulsion active," purred another.

"Eject sequence primed," buzzed a third. "Ready to receive emergency escape command."

As a routine safety precaution, the core command pod had the capability of blowing itself free of the stardrive, rocketing Panna to safety in the event of some disaster during the drive's testing.

When the drive had been fitted into *Bright Hope*'s hull, Panna made certain the ejection channel retained clear access to space. She hadn't made an issue of it; it was just routine good practice to sacrifice no safety mechanism unnecessarily. Even then, she'd wondered whether Captain Eldridge knew that *Bright Hope*'s new drive harbored a nucleus capable of independent flight.

Why must Bright Hope *die? Panna asked herself. So she will no longer stand between Parek and his worshipers. So no one will notice me flying to be the first by his side.*

"Checklist," she said to the pod.

A datacrawl snapped on above her left eye. It followed her head movements, always maintaining its position in her visual field. *"Bright Hope, Bright Hope,"* she said urgently. "This is a direct emergency override. All shipboard systems, on demand. Direct control access. All safeties, override. All life protocols, override."

Parek. Word Among Us. Cosmic Christ, Panna thought. *Parek. Word Among Us. Cosmic Christ.*

"Monitor all," Panna ordered. More crawls and tridee bubbles germinated around her: *Bright Hope*'s system status readouts and security-camera images of various shipboard compartments and chambers.

She consulted her checklist. Her cadence was rapid, precise, and unemotional. "Power transmission subsystems J-delta-eight through B-tango nine one six, forced burnout now. Execute."

The number-three tridee bubble brightened. Sheets of energy crashed between the supercooled vanes of *Bright Hope*'s primary power core. The bubble went white, then black.

Bubble number two imaged *Bright Hope*'s primary docking bay. A thirty-passenger maintenance scow floated on a colloidal slipfield. The slipfield winked out. Five techs who'd been standing on the scow's underside tumbled to the bay floor. The scouter lumbered forward with some forgotten intrinsic momentum. It heeled over in a shower of pipes and girders and flame.

Even in the control module she could feel *Bright Hope* shuddering. *I order vital subsystems to override their safety mechanisms and destroy themselves—and they obey.*

"Control anticipator loops echo echo five one nine through foxtrot zed eight nine six," she recited. "Induced refractive failure in three, two, one . . . execute. Security override networks five one nine eight delta tau through eight two seven seven foxtrot beta, phase-congruent overload in three, two, one . . . execute."

Parek. Word Among Us. Cosmic Christ. Parek. Word Among Us. Cosmic Christ. Parek. Word Among Us. Cosmic Christ.

Panna surveyed her work with a grim satisfaction. In eighty seconds her beloved stardrive would turn on itself, spasming an intolerable overload through *Bright Hope*'s main systems. She slid back an access cover and settled into the acceleration couch hidden behind it. "This is Panna," she said crisply. "I say, eject."

"Please say again," whirred a machine voice.

"This is Panna. I say, eject."

Straps launched themselves across Panna's chest and hips and knees. Cushions inflated down each side of the couch. She closed her eyes. "For you, Word Among Us!"

The eject charges slammed her like a bagful of mercury landing on her chest. The roar was overwhelming. Even in the acceleration couch she felt painful jerking.

It isn't supposed to be like this.

The first thing she saw was Jaremi Four, glowing dun and blue through the small porthole that now looked out into space. Next she saw stars, and then the planet's limb swept up again. *Sliding by way too fast.* Stars. Planet. Stars.

Panna shook her head. *The pod's spinning,* she realized. She jerked her head right and left. Two-thirds of her readouts were dark. The console to her left lay at a peculiar angle. *What went wrong?* To her right, a flickering tactical schematic held the answer. Over and over it played an animation of the command pod blasting out of the stardrive. The ejection channel hadn't been clear after all. A twist of scaffolding, debris from one of the explosions Panna had touched off, had surged across it. When the pod struck the scaffolding it left a third of its mass behind. It careened away spinning.

Something exploded down below Panna. She saw magenta lightning dance across the tiny porthole. With a squeal that submerged into the roar of escaping air, hull plates yawned apart beside her. Where instruments and hull plates had been, she saw stars.

All sound ended. *It's so cold.*

Pain burst like fire in Panna's chest, her head, then everywhere. Her lungs sprawled outward under their own internal pressure. Her sinuses boiled, her eardrums ruptured. Gaseous bubbles precipitated out of her blood and lymph, bursting capillaries throughout her body.

Of course, well before that process reached its conclusion, Annek Panna had ceased attending to it. She had expired in agony so profound that she never finished composing her final mental prayer of love to Parek.

104. Jaremi Four—Somewhere

So quickly, everything had changed.

The young woman lifted the Highest Elder's hand from her breast. She stood beside the bed. The night wind tickled her nipples. She studied the naked sleeping patriarch's bare body: the hollows of his inner thighs, the sags and wrinkles, the hair shot through with silver. Despite his lameness and chronic cough, the Highest Elder had proven an enthusiastic lover. If he took too long to finish, such was the price of joining the Highest Elder's household.

On warm nights the old chief liked to sleep under the aurora. His bed perched atop the roof of the elders' compound, sheltered only by a gauzy canopy. A score of meters below, thatch-roofed hovels spread in all directions around the fallen refinery tank. The young woman could see candle flames flickering in windows. Inside, found-glass chimneys flanked the principal walkways.

So quickly everything changed. She tugged on a fabric wrap and padded down a wood-and-rope staircase into the room that had just been refitted as the babe's nursery. Four women nodded as the young woman neared the crib. *Strange child,* she thought. *First you were a burden. Now, suddenly, you catapult me into wealth and respect.* The child lay on his stomach, face turned to one side. *You don't understand a bit of it, do you? No more than I understand what you are.*

"A sign!" a man bellowed below.

The young woman edged toward the other stairway, the one that led down from the nursery to the council chamber. She peered down. It was the Elder of the Soil who was shouting. "Let me pass, I tell you! The Highest Elder won't want to sleep through this!"

"What's so important, Soil Elder?" she demanded with hauteur befitting the Highest Elder's new consort. "Do you know the time?"

The Soil Elder rushed upstairs. He grabbed her wrist. "Take your child!" he hissed. "He must be a part of this."

Confused, she edged toward the crib. The Soil Elder let her scoop up the babe. Pressing the babe to her breast in the crook of one elbow, she rushed after him onto the roof.

"Look!" the Soil Elder cried, pointing out into the sky.

She looked. "I see . . . something," she said doubtfully.

There was no mistaking the pinkish flashes, tiny though they were. They were not stars. They were not aurora.

"You asked for a sign, Highest Elder," stammered the Elder of the Soil. "Get up and see!"

The Highest Elder rose too quickly from the bed. He clung to the Soil Elder's arm until the coughing passed. "I made love to this woman and I didn't die," he chortled. "I need a sign beyond that?"

"Look at the sky!" insisted the Elder of the Soil.

The Highest Elder looked up. His mouth drifted open. Sidling toward the young woman, he clasped her free hand in a hot, papery grip.

In the sky, where the pink flashes had danced, now there flickered a tiny yellow cloud. From its center, glowing just visibly brighter, a point of orange-white light emerged.

The light wobbled and continued to brighten. Abruptly it spewed forth a star pattern, five or six bits of glowing material. They leapt from the central spot in all directions, leaving glowing trails. The central spot calved the same way again and again.

"Surely this is the sign," the Highest Elder breathed. He fastened rheumy eyes on the babe. "Surely this child shall lead us." Releasing the young woman's hand, he limped to the bedside table. An ancient bell waited there, suspended above the table by a wooden post. Drawing a mallet from the fabric pouch below the tabletop, the Highest Elder sounded the bell three times. He paused and then sounded the bell three times again.

Bells began to sound across the settlement. The Highest Elder's tocsin would be repeated across the ancient refinery, until all the people had awakened to see the portent in the sky.

The central spot had grown into a disk of fire, an entity in its own right. "Behold," cried the Matriarch of Clan Aurora as she bustled onto the roof. "It's as the holy madmen promised."

"Yes," agreed the Highest Elder. "The night ignites to greet the child."

Can this really be happening? the young woman mused. *My sister's child, born to such misfortune, a tool of the gods? His destiny and mine—is that what's being written on the sky?* She stared at the glowing spot. She thought she could see its edges rippling now. There could be no doubt. It *was* getting closer.

For a fleeting instant she thought it might be coming too close. *That's insane,* she thought. Hurling uncertainty from her mind, she extending both arms, presenting the babe to the cosmic messenger.

The young woman never had time to shut her eyes nor to try shielding the babe. The blast front annihilated them all before anyone heard its roar.

The chunk of Panna's pod that had made it to the surface was unrecognizable. A twisted clump of superhardened plasteel just a meter and a half across. It could never have given any Jaremian knowledge dangerous to Enclave.

It would have been wholly unremarkable but for its velocity.

Traveling at an angle of about twenty degrees relative to the surface, the core command pod fragment surged into the half-buried oil refinery at seventy times the local speed of sound. It pierced one holding tank, then another, and finally a third. It plunged into barren soil that boiled away before it like a hapless flock. Below ground the chunk, now plasma, perforated two more long-hidden tanks. Those stunning impacts reliquefied long-congealed lubricant and solvent stocks and ran them through with cores of fire.

The resulting blast and explosions scoured the valley. The night coruscated with white-hot fire that left nothing behind.

When the next day's sun scowled down, there was only a crater. No hint remained that human beings had ever lived or worked or wielded tools at the place where for centuries the shattered refinery had stood.

Of the babe, nothing further was ever, ever heard.

105.   Jaremi Four—Southern Hemisphere—
Parek's Ruins

"**I** don't fucking believe it," said Ulf, lowering his field glasses. "They shelled the shit out of the bastion, all the high walls, and our ships."

"Freakish accuracy," Commander Akkad Felegu agreed. "How'd they aim so exactly while this place was still over the horizon to them?"

"It's as I said," Parek announced, rising from the marble desk Ulf had made him hide under. "If the people with the twinkle birds see something, our enemies see it, too."

Ulf dug out his improvised ear plugs. "Good thing the guns weren't there any more."

Parek peered through a viewing slit. Below, at the base of the muddy slope, the ships of Parek's riparian navy had been lashed together in quiltwork arrays. The shelling had left them all aflame. "My navy," Parek said, sounding strangled.

"You were also right about not stationing defenders aboard the ships," Ulf said grimly.

"Green flare!" cried Felegu. "Enemy navy sighted to the east." A minute later he called, "Red flare. Enemy army sighted to the west."

"They surround us," Ulf breathed.

Parek whirled toward Ulf. "All the officers know the plan?"

Ulf nodded. "Hold fire until the enemy draws close—until you give the order."

"Look there!" an adjutant shouted. The first ships of the enemy fleet were visible through a break in the trees.

Ulf raised his 'scope. "Conversion ships—they look like ours!"

"Our own ships, come to destroy us," Parek whispered. He edged toward the door. "Ulf, Felegu, I need time alone."

Ulf grasped on Parek's wrist. "Stay here. Only this bunker is safe."

Parek gestured with his free hand toward the guarded door. "But I need to—"

"No!" Ulf's snarl was guttural, even primitive. "We stay."

Parek shrugged. He sat down.

"Their amphibious craft are about to land," Felegu called. "Permission to fire?"

Parek stepped to the leftmost window again. Enemy soldiers and wagons and banners and siege engines could be seen among the trees. To his right, the navy advanced, the forward landing craft lowering their boarding platforms. "Tell the men to lock and load."

Ulf nodded to Felegu. Felegu barked to his adjutants. Men scrambled into the open to waggle semaphores. Throughout the ruined city, soldiers scrambled out of low places. They trundled racks of mortars out from under sagging porches, hauled cannon out of basements, and pulled leafy branches away from emplacements on the backsides of hills. They wrapped their hands around the shells marked for first use, shells which contained not only explosive, but also a charge of mother matter.

Gunners chambered their loads. Mortarmen held their shells above the throats of their weapons.

"Open fire," Parek barked. Felegu gestured outside. A trooper fired an ancient flare pistol.

The mortarmen and gunners let fly.

Explosions puffed among the landing craft. Waterspouts rained steaming chestnut mud among men and their weapons. A gray-brown haze blanketed the river. Parek and Ulf and Felegu whirled their scopes and field glasses toward the west.

Among the massing army, shells tossed up showers of dirt and rock, cutting down handfuls of men. Translucent sheaths of beige dust swirled from the impact points. They drifted on the river breezes, back among the attacking multitudes.

This was not the whitish, refined end-product powder Parek's men used to blow out ahead of the fleet. This was mother matter. As airborne dust, whether breathed or absorbed through the skin, its chemical makeup caused immediate hallucinations, nausea, paralysis, or, depending on the victim, spasmodic purposeless action.

It was as irresistible as fire or the wind.

Men clutching live grenade launchers, men with hands clasped to throttles or gripping the reins of *sturruh* teams, men tending their fire carts—all lost contact with their surroundings. They convulsed and fell; they flung their limbs in all directions, struggling to escape onrushing demons of fancy. They leapt unseeing into fiery water or staggered over embankments into the wheels of onrushing wagons.

The mother matter had claimed their minds.

On the river, metal screeched. One landing craft, its helmsman convulsing, had turned sharply to port, impaling a companion craft. Another boat, its engines mistakenly set to all ahead flank, churned toward Parek's lashed flaming ships. Three, four, five more collisions occurred between the close-spaced attacking boats. Fire belched across the deck of one transport. Burning soldiers scurried about uselessly.

Parek and Ulf stared toward the west. Soldiers were running and dropping to their knees. Parek watched one involuntary racer stumble toward a bonfire. Two mates tried to stop him. His momentum pitched the trio into the flames. Felegu watched a man buckle, his face idyllic as a siege engine's mammoth wheel pulped his legs. *Sturruh* surged and bolted. Battle wagons spilled out their occupants, flipping on their sides as frantic steeds hauled them over tree roots or through hairpin turns. Ulf watched a wheeled gun lurch into a fire. Orange tongues leapt among the ammunition boxes lashed to its frame.

The detonation was immense. Bodies spurted skyward, flanked by gouts of earth and clouds of shattered wood. The roar rammed at their ears. For a few moments after it subsided, Ulf and Parek and Felegu couldn't hear their own triumphant screams. "It works!" Parek hooted. "It works! The mother matter fucking works!"

Ulf stepped backward. He regarded his prophet suspiciously. "Of course it does, Word Among Us."

"Felegu," Parek commanded. "Signal the mother matter gunners to hold their fire. Give the command for conventional weapons."

"By your command," Felegu shouted exultantly. He barked to his adjutants. Men scrambled back into the open to waggle semaphores. Throughout the ruined city, marksmen sprinted to the steaming ramparts. Gunners shifted their positions. Half a dozen long-gun crews pushed their weapons out of concealment.

Explosives and incendiaries rained onto the disarray of attacking craft to the east, into the woods to the west. Riflemen sent invaders pitching from siege engine platforms. They cut them down on the bridges of offensive boats.

After a minute, Parek's marksmen realized no one was shooting back at them. They climbed into the open and poured deadly fire into ships eight and ten and twelve rows to the rear.

"Order the gunners to lob mother matter into the enemy's rear," Ulf commanded.

More semaphores. Explosions ceased to raven the enemy front, which in any event was now almost wholly aflame. From the bunker, Ulf and Parek couldn't see the mother matter shells detonating a kilometer and more deep in the western woods. Through gaps in the trees they *could* see gray-brown mist enveloping distant boats. Their formations wavered and broke down. Boats collided; some capsized.

To the west, scattered fireballs whirled above the tree line.

Parek sprinted toward the bunker door. Pursued by Ulf and Felegu and a dozen officers, he bounded up two flights of stone stairs and emerged onto a roof. The others followed.

To the west, the forest was alive with fire. To the east, the river was a random hell of flaming hulls drifting into one another. Beyond, ships beached themselves or circled. Far to the rear, ships surged in full reverse. Incendiary shells vomited fire across their decks.

"Die, attacking *skraggel!*" Parek screamed. "Fall before the mighty swords of the true army of destiny! We cut you down like the unclean ones, like the hideous Gadiantons of old, squalid minions of that secret society condemned of the highest gods for their insidious secret works!"

Ulf and his officers exchanged puzzled looks. "Secret works?" an adjutant asked Felegu. "Is that like our secret names?"

"Don't mention them," Felegu hissed. "They're a secret."

"Have the gunners hold fire," Parek cried. "When the enemy forces re-form, give them the mother matter again."

Felegu squinted into the smoke. "You think they'll re-form?"

"Count on it," Parek said tiredly. "They're too numerous; we've killed at most a tenth of them. They'll be back. And they'll be more cautious about throttles and open fires when they attack again."

"This wasn't victory, then," Ulf said hollowly.

Parek shook his head. "We've bought time, nothing more. We can keep confounding them and picking them off until the mother matter runs out."

"And then?" Felegu demanded.

"There will still be thousands of them left. Four, five days from today will come the final reckoning."

Ulf swallowed and edged away. "I'll be right back."

"Hold!" Parek barked. "You must stay here. See how quickly they recover." He dropped his hands and clasped them before his loins. "You stay here. *I* will go below for a while."

"No!" Ulf drew his pistol. He stared down at it as though it had leapt unbidden from its holster. Scowling, he leveled the weapon at Parek's chest. "You will not leave us now."

Slack-jawed, the other officers exchanged dire glances. Hands crept toward sidearms but stopped in indecision.

Parek met Ulf's desperate eyes with a mischievous smirk. He began to laugh, thinly at first, and then he roared with it. Palms spread, he inched toward his High Commander. Gently Parek reached out and touched the wrist of Ulf's gun hand. "Enough subterfuge, enough dishonesty," he said quietly. "We both know what must happen now."

Hesitantly, Ulf holstered his pistol.

"We'll both go," Parek said gently. "Run to your inmost command center, friend. Call your sky-nymphs. For my part I'll summon my god named God. Later we'll come together and compare their advice."

Ulf swallowed and took a deep breath. Straightening his back, he saluted his prophet fist-on-chest. "By your command," he husked. "My apologies."

"No need," Parek replied with an air of brittle hope. "At this juncture, we need all the miracles we can get, no matter where they come from."

106. Vatican

Cardinal Rybczynsky looked up hollow-eyed. He'd just *poved* the latest senso from Jaremi Four. Papal Prefect Wleti Krammonz knew the clip had affected Rybczynsky deeply, for the elegant cleric had failed to brush at the crease in his simar that formed while he'd sat, arms crossed, lost in the senso.

"It was carnage," Rybczynsky murmured. "I was in the man's mind, even as he lost it, even as his ship sailed into fire." The patrician cardinal began to shudder. To control the shivering took several attempts. "Did any of the Spectators survive?"

Krammonz scowled. He stroked his white beard. "There were three Spectators aboard our naval detachment. The land force hosted but one. Of course, they'd all maneuvered their way to the front. I don't believe any were recovered."

"That other Spectator showed us where Ulf had placed his artillery," Rybczynsky said perplexedly. "We sent word to our proxy forces to shell there, and they did."

"Something told Parek to move the guns," Krammonz said quietly. "Perhaps a miracle, if he's the Christ."

"Yes," Rybczynsky rumbled. "Our sending word to the native gunners, telling them where to shell, merely casts Parek's divinity into sharper relief."

"It's come to that?" Krammonz sighed. "We proclaim him a fighting Christ, then judge his godhead by the quality of his tactics?"

"It has to be that way," Rybczynsky whispered hauntedly. "Otherwise—"

"Otherwise, we have betrayed the Son of Man." Nodding sadly, Krammonz held his hand over the senso player. The wafer leapt from the device and slapped into his palm. Krammonz held the wafer out to Rybczynsky. "This is a matter of state. You are the Secretary of State."

Rybczynsky shook his head, an exquisite movement. "Waking His Holiness at this hour—that is a concern for the Prefect of the Papal Household."

Krammonz's hand began to tremble.

"I am a Cardinal," Rybczynsky said without expression. *"Bishop* Krammonz, I order you to wake His Holiness and show him what Parek has done to our proxy forces."

Krammonz nodded hopelessly. "May God be with us."

"God *is* with us, Wleti. That is the problem."

107. Jaremi Four—Southern Hemisphere— Parek's Ruins

"T oday was a victory," Parek sobbed. "But we cannot win in the end."

"What do you propose to do about that?" the god named God demanded. Alrue Latier's image floated, tiny and luminous, in the dank root cellar Parek had chosen as his meditation space.

"What do *I* propose?" Parek asked bitterly. "You're the god here. I hit them with the mother matter. Each time the enemy charges it will kill more of them— but never enough. When the mother matter runs out, the enemy will have enough men for one more charge, and that charge will succeed. Perhaps it is my destiny to die here."

"You've already played that card," Latier drawled. "Try to think more positively."

"I don't mean faking death for a few hours, the way I used to," Parek objected. "I mean actually dying. Maybe that's what I'm meant for. To fall gloriously, to inspire future generations with the nobility of my last words." He smiled thinly. "Maybe even my second-to-last words."

"Those don't have to be too noble. You'd be amazed how much mileage you can get from 'Father, Father, why have you forsaken me?' Trust me, Arn, martyrdom is not for you."

"That's the word I was trying to remember," Parek exulted. "I'll be a martyr. My memory will burn as a beacon."

"Or they'll forget you in two weeks and a day. Forget dying. Think of a way out."

"You think of that! Getting out of this will take a miracle, and I'm fresh out."

Parek threw his back against the wall. He blinked back tears. "One bright dawn I'll stand atop the highest parapet. I'll stand before all their gunners and spread my legs and arms, the way I did for the Miracle of the Ships. Before anyone can shoot at me, I'll jump. No last words. No homily at the brink of death. Just the silent eloquence of my plunge."

"Forjeler on plorg," Latier raged, "that is to say, um, *fucking shit!* Quit planning to die, Arn. You want to achieve immortality through death? You don't know the first thing about it."

"I don't?" Parek turned back toward his sky god.

Latier spoke with slow crispness. "Let me tell you what it takes to play that role, what the recognized man-gods had to go through. First you have to die, not beautifully, not gloriously, but in hideous snarling agony. It usually takes hours. Then they wrap you in shrouds and put you in a tomb. You lay there and decompose. Three days pass, then some followers come to your tomb. And you're gone."

"That's it?" Parek asked, dumbfounded.

"No one's even present to record your return to life. Kind of a significant event, don't you think? No one sees it. Those who chronicle it are so befuddled by the events they *do* record that they can't even agree who went to the tomb, or what they saw there. One chronicler says there was one angel, another says two. The others didn't notice. *Angels,* luminous messengers of the Almighty, and half the writers couldn't be bothered to notice them! All they agree on is that the tomb was empty."

"Inscrutable," Parek breathed.

"Maybe so, but that's typical of what it takes to do this death-and-resurrection thing properly. First the torment, the prolonged decay, then the ambiguity—are you ready to go through all that?"

"Um, I suppose not."

"Then stop whining." Latier's projected figure gazed up at Parek, arms akimbo. He smiled thinly. "I'm sorry. I'm sure much of what I said meant nothing to you. Search for the meaning. Strive to encompass it. Then call me. You know, when you think of something. Everlasting welfare unto you."

Parek folded up on himself. The irregular pebbles dotting the floor of the shaft dug into his thighs and buttocks. *It's worse than Dultav predicted. It's not that my followers use me like a* bohtti *sprout. Now my god abandons me.*

Parek wrapped himself in quivering arms. He began to cry.

108. The *Bright Hope*

Eldridge, Gavisel, Wachieu, and a half-dozen other officers had crowded into the improvised conference room. Glowtubes furnished the light. Field packs vented oxygen into the chamber's hot, damp air. "Okay, how bad is it?" Edridge demanded.

"Literally everything but orbital maintenance and base enviro's been down for the past three hours," Arla Gavisel said. Her uniform was dark with sweat, shiny with spilled lubricants. "No comm, no detex, no thought engines, no tactical displays. They should all start coming back on over the next hour, except long-range comm. It'll be at least three days before we can talk to High Command."

"The weapons bank was destroyed earlier, when we fired on Vatican Island." Wachieu reported.

"Primary docking bay's badly damaged," reported Sergeant-at-Arms Will Bickel. "Looks like a maintenance scow blew up. The only scouts or fighters we'll be able to deploy are those that can launch and redock using their own power and guidance. Ship's power core is damaged, but we can restart it at thirty percent capacity or so. We shouldn't need more than that, because the stardrive is completely destroyed."

Gasps sounded around the conference table. "Let's keep our heads, people." Eldridge shot Bickel a critical look. "Define 'completely destroyed.'"

"Blown to sfelb," Bickel rasped. "Pieces of the axial assembly are all over the drive bay. The core's completely gone, like it spewed out of the ship."

"All the simulations we've been able to run on portable equipment suggest that the anomaly began in the stardrive," Gavisel reported.

"'Anomaly,' now there's a weasel word," Eldridge quipped. "Any sign of Panna?"

"Can't find her anywhere," said Bickel.

"Well, it could be worse. Our stardrive's gone, but we were supposed to keep station here anyway until reinforcements joined us. More disturbing is the fact that we can't see and we can't shoot."

Crackling sounded overhead. "Internal comm is now available, capacity fifty percent."

Wachieu and another officer wrestled a portable control interface onto the table. "If comm's up, we can get this auxiliary control station online." She dropped onto a stool and slapped her hands onto the control surface. Geometric forms lit up and began to dance. Wachieu cradled her face into the hood of an old-fashioned one-person viewing scope. "Damage control has part of the Detex back online."

After the applause came a frightened silence. "Where's *Damocles?*" Eldridge asked at last.

"Scanning . . . scanning. . . ."

Eldridge's hands were fists. She willed her fingers to unclench.

"*Damocles* remains in orbit, as ugly as ever," Wachieu called out. "No activity."

People clapped. They whistled. They hugged. What Eldridge didn't need to remind anyone was that if *Damocles* had used *Bright Hope*'s blind interval to trigger its crash program—even if the trawler hove into view just now beginning to break up—there'd have been nothing they could do. Enclave would fall.

"Oh, sfelb," Wachieu breathed. She stabbed furiously at controls, face in the viewing hood, saying nothing.

Eldridge cleared her throat. "Under the circumstances, Fem Wachieu, 'Oh, sfelb' must be considered an inadequate report."

Wachieu looked up sheepishly. "Of course, Captain. This just took a little analyzing. The orbital dynamics thought engines are back online; they say we have a problem. While we've been blind, *Damocles* drifted into a collision course with one of the small moonlets that orbits Jaremi Four."

"How small a moonlet?" Gavisel demanded.

"Big enough," Wachieu sighed. "Tens of kilometers in diameter. *Damocles* will hit it head on. Prognosis: devastation. Time to impact: five hours nine minutes."

"Sooner or later the thought engines on *Damocles* will predict the collision, too," Gavisel grated. "They'll initiate the suicide program."

"Any idea when?" Eldridge asked.

"None. You know that."

"Captain!" Wachieu's voice boomed. "Danger may be averted."

"Explain."

"The moonlet's firing thrusters," Wachieu said matter-of-factly. "They're not terribly powerful, but they're enough to get the moonlet out of the trawler's way in time."

Some of the officers cheered. Others exchanged astonished stares. "Fem Wachieu," Gavisel queried. "Where you come from, is it normal for moonlets to, well, just start firing thrusters?"

"Sure," she said abstractedly. "Gwilya space is full of mansions and resorts and science stations built into asteroids and—" She looked up from her viewing hood. "Hmm. Guess it's kind of strange around an Enclave world." She buried her face in the hood again. "Scanning moonlet at full power—or as close to it as I can get."

The officers crowded around Wachieu's primitive control station. Eldridge thought of calling them back to their seats—no one but Wachieu could see anything useful. *But what's the point of that?* she realized.

"Plorg on a stick," Wachieu hissed. "Improved report to follow shortly." Her fingers leapt convulsively over the control surface. "The moonlet's been extensively modified inside. I read a substantial power plant. Generous manufacturing spaces. Launch facilities. Sfelb, it's completely hollow."

"Any life signs?" Eldridge demanded.

Wachieu punched in filters. "A small crew. Fifteen or twenty adults. Odd, they're all male."

"I think I know who they are," Eldridge rumbled. "Fem Wachieu, do we have any external comm?"

"Fifteen minutes," Wachieu said.

"Very well," Eldridge said, a plan coming together in her head. "Wachieu, as soon as you get external comm, call OmNet. Raise that section boss, what's her name?"

"Neuri Kalistor," Wachieu supplied.

"Yeah, comm her. Tell her to send us, oh, half a dozen Spectators up on a shuttle, crash priority. That will put us back in touch with the Galaxy—and in touch with developments on the surface—while long-range comm is still down. Then beam a forced auto-ident to that moonlet. I predict that when you do, you'll get back an icon of the Papal tiara and keys."

109. Jaremi Four—Southern Hemisphere— Parek's Ruins

"God and goddess, life and death, initiator and destroyer," Ulf recited.

"Yeah, yeah," Orgena Greder bristled. Juxtaposed with her voice were ringing bells, keening prairie winds, and crystal shards propelled by gusts across marble. "What do you want now?"

Desperation had driven Ulf to clarity. "I want a way out."

The general and the miniature goddess faced each other across the stuffy dankness of Ulf's bedchamber. The goddess planted her hands on her hips. "For whom?"

"For us all." Ulf leaned back. He sucked at his teeth. "If that's impossible, a way out for me alone."

"I see."

"We inflicted great casualties today." Ulf paced. "But Parek thinks his magic mulch will run out before we can get them all."

"You believe him?"

"This time."

"Where's Parek now?"

"Talking with *his* sky god."

"Do you know anything more about Parek's god?"

"No." Ulf scratched his chin with the knuckles of his left hand. "Why don't you know about him? You're both gods."

"There's more to it than that." The goddess picked at lint on her right breast. "All right, Ulf, how do you see the situation?"

Ulf blinked. *She was a lot more fucking helpful in the past.* "This can end three ways. If nothing is done, they kill us all. Or Parek will find a way out. Or I will. Whoever gets out commands from then on."

"I agree. Well, let's examine this tactically. To your west, a hostile army lines the banks and prevents escape by boat. To your east is the enemy navy. To the north, atop the ridge, a little past the crest, the river that feeds that waterfall is navigable. Could you escape that way, and put days between you and the enemy forces while they waste time reducing the fortifications you've already abandoned?"

"You're saying make the ruins look like we're still here. Then we just sneak out the back, up onto the ridge."

"All of you that matter. Leave half the garrison behind, if that will cost the enemy more time."

Ulf pursed his lips. "We build rafts or something, and escape up the north channel."

"See any reason why it shouldn't work?"

"Only if Parek gets some other damn fool idea from his god."

"If he does, you must keep him from acting on it."

Ulf nodded grimly. He drew an obsidian dagger. Turning it in his hands, he contemplated the dance of reflections on its curves.

110. The *Bright Hope*

"Papal tiara and keys, all right," Wachieu chuckled. "The moonlet is the missing piece of Vatican's illegal infrastructure."

Eldridge smiled. "How's it doing getting out of the way of *Damocles?*"

"As long as it continues firing thrusters at current rate, there'll be no collision."

"Where are those Spectators?"

Gavisel checked another data matrix. "OmNet's launching a shuttle from North Polar Station now. They'll be here in twenty-one minutes."

"Tell the shuttle to divert to the moonlet," Eldridge ordered. "Sergeant Bickel, round up some security personnel. Take some kind of scouter out and rendezvous with the moonlet. Don't open the airlock until the Spectators arrive. Have them start recording—not for our use, but their regular OmNet feed. As soon as they're in Mode, Sergeant, you will raid the moonlet and arrest the occupants."

"Good idea," Gavisel said. "Let the Galaxy see that even half-crippled, we're continuing to enforce Enclave."

"My thoughts exactly," Eldridge agreed. "But let's not rest yet. Fem Gavisel, please see that the docking bay is restored to the best order possible. When that GDX on the *Damocles* bridge goes dormant—assuming there still *is* a *Damocles* then—I want to get as many engineers in there as we can and try to disable that suicide program."

111. Jaremi Four—Southern Hemisphere— Parek's Ruins

Assuredly Parek struck out into blue-black darkness. As he'd ordered, fewer than a dozen Brethren escorted him. He wore his white leathers—surely not for comfort, the night was humid—but rather so that any who whispered about his departure from the ruined city would say he looked suitably godlike.

If the people he'd sworn to secrecy kept faith, it would be nearly morning before Ulf even knew he'd left. *Surely Felegu won't talk,* Parek thought with grim satisfaction. *When I read his ammunition manifest through a blindfold, I thought he was going to faint dead away.*

Having memorized the ruins, Parek needed little light to follow the terraces as high as they traced, even to strike into the hills just behind the ruined city. Unpredictable light came from the flashes of the mortars as they lofted fresh doses of mother matter into enemy positions. *Which they can do only through tomorrow,* Parek thought grimly. As he climbed, he could see irregular orange glows on the eastern and western horizons: the signatures of fires accidentally kindled by attackers in the thrall of the mother matter.

An angled finger of rock lanced skyward before them. "Stop," Parek told the Brethren captain. "I go alone now."

"You must be protected," the captain stammered.

Parek jerked a thumb toward the promontory. "No one goes up there but sky gods."

"Who'll carry your fire things?" the captain demanded.

Parek smiled. "I will. Stay here with your men. See to it that I'm not disturbed."

The one in three grade commanded attention, but was not truly difficult, not even with the fire pack slung between his shoulders under his cape.

The higher Parek climbed, the more he could see of the fires ravaging both enemy fronts. *Perhaps I'll wear them down,* Parek hoped. *Perhaps when the mother matter runs out, none of them will be left. But I know that will not be.*

Sheened with sweat, Parek sat in a notch of clefted granite at the top of the rock. *Day after day I hoped and prayed for some answer. Apparently my god named God has nurtured the same forlorn hope,* Parek chuckled cynically; *the hope that I would find an answer.*

"I'm out of days," he said aloud. "Tonight's when I must find a way to beat them—or baffle them—*and* get Ulf back under my thumb."

He shrugged off the fire pack and built a bonfire. He leaned back on his elbows and threw his head skyward. *Let the Brethren watch me. Let them see me transfigured by this fire, staring at the sky. Maybe when I come down with whatever desperate idea occurs to me up here, someone will be impressed enough to do what I say.* His eyes followed the swirling ascent of sparks. *Once I thought myself a god, or I thought gods worked through me. Now I worry only about finessing the next crisis, so I can live on—for what? For some bright new day of conquest and glory? Surely I am past believing that.*

He wished there were aurora tonight. But the sky was like the underside of a black hammock, pierced only irregularly by bashful stars.

"Arn?"

"Huh?" Parek looked up. The voice had sounded—not close, but not distant. It seemed to transcend mere directionality. Still, it was familiar.

"Arn, do you hear me?"

"Who asks?" Parek demanded of the night.

"Look up."

Expecting nothing, Parek raised his face. His eyes saucered.

A woman shimmered into visibility twenty meters above him. She didn't drop into sight; she became visible at a location where she hadn't been before.

She wore white also. Her left hand rested on one of the tiny boxes attached to her belt. Her right hand caressed the other. She seemed to glow orange by the fire-light below her. Parek recognized gentle curls of brown-black hair framing auburn skin. She had full lips and compelling dark eyes. Now he could pick out the enameled lozenges sewn into her cuffs and waistband. Sky, birds. Birds, sky. "I never dreamed you'd make this so easy," she said.

"What?"

"Finding you. I came ready to sneak my way in, or shoot my way in. Instead—"
She chuckled. "Out in plain sight on top of a rock, you are."

Parek glanced below. The Brethren had seen the floating fluttering woman.
The captain had all he could do to keep half his men from charging uphill and the
other half from running.

Parek turned back toward his descending visitor. "Hello, Ruth."

Ruth Griszam touched down a bodylength away. She wore blousy silk culottes
gathered at the ankles, a loose-fitting blouse, its full sleeves tucked into white
canvas wrist straps studded with Escher lozenges, and a belt of the same material.
On her shoulders were epaulets, flat canvas panels clinging to slender straps of
silk. From neck to toes she wore white.

Parek stood. He bowed gallantly to the Spectator he hadn't seen in more than
two years. "Are you well?"

"I didn't fall." She seemed as touched by his concern as she was clearly
unaware that he hadn't asked that question. "I fly," she explained, continuing on
her tangent. "That is, I can now." She pointed to two of the boxes at her belt. "This
makes me invisible, or visible again, as I choose. This one lets me fly. Don't question, soon enough you'll understand. May I sit?"

Parek nodded. They sat facing each other, upwind of the bonfire. "I didn't
bring anything to drink," he said inadequately.

"It's not like you expected me." She peered within. The *verify* tone hummed
confidently. Her inner awareness called up another data channel. The saybacks
were literally beyond the capacities of the standard survey instruments.

She forced her attention outward, then back to him.

"So much has happened since the dam," he began.

"Ships up a cliffside," she agreed. "Long, futile river warfare." She nodded,
acknowledging Parek's stare of surprise. "I know about much of it, despite the care
you and Ulf took to dispose of people like me." She managed to say that without
sounding accusing.

He nodded. "You know much."

She glanced around the promontory. "Aren't you worried, alone in the open up
here? With such a bright fire? The enemy might see you."

"The enemy's not seeing much right now. What matters is what *I* see."

She nodded. "This is the sort of place you used to come to when you wanted a
vision."

He nodded sadly. "Tonight I need one."

Ruth leaned forward. "What do you see?"

"Nothing."

"One thing?" she echoed.

"What," he asked more loudly, "the gods gave you flight, but took away your ears?"

"Long story," Ruth said sheepishly. "But I will appreciate your speaking up.
So, your visions come to nothing."

He raised his palms, stared into them. "I can find no way out," he husked. "I
wait for the deepest still of night and stare upward, or I stare within myself. No
matter which, I see nothing. Nothing ahead, nothing beyond."

"You're in a fix," she agreed. "What happens now?"

"Perhaps my answer has come." He reached out and took her wrist in his left hand. With two fingers of his right, he caressed the Escher lozenge in her wristband. "You know I see the birds twinkle."

Ruth nodded. "I know."

"Did you know that at the dam?"

"Not then."

"Still remember Willim Dultav?"

"Always."

Parek's smile was wistful. "Sometimes Willim would say something wise and you'd start thinking he was another one like you, like my mother. I could tell." His mouth hinted at a grin, nothing more. "You'd start *hoping* he was one of you. No?"

"Yes," she admitted, blinking rapidly.

"You'd just keep angling your twinkle birds into his sight, trying so hard to see if Willim noticed them. Each time you did, I wanted to jump up and shout, 'Me! I'm the one! I see them!'" He released her arm. "I didn't dare."

She arched an eyebrow. "Now you'd dare anything."

"That was true once. But my options are closing."

She pulled back her hand. "Such despair hardly becomes one to whom gods speak."

"My god's out of ideas. So, apparently, is Ulf's goddess. You know a goddess visits Ulf?"

"That was recognized, eventually."

"Well, she's no more help than my god named God." Parek pursed his lips. He stared down at the bonfire. With the piezo stick, he pushed a half-burned strip of wood toward the fire's center. "You know, being the figurehead of an invading army gives you time to think. Maybe too much." His lips twisted in a half-smile that reminded Ruth of Dultav. "Once I thought religion was just my material to work with. I didn't care what was true, I didn't care whether it meant anything, it was just a tool for manipulating people. Later, I came to think that religion was real, but that I was the holy one it was all about."

"That's where your mind was back at the dam."

He nodded. "And for years since. Lately, on the river, I've probed into myself. I've tried to gaze—you know, out there. In there." He chuckled at the inadequacy of his words. *"Down* there. Wherever that 'there' is where we root our deepest yearnings."

She nodded and eyed him expectantly.

"And you know what?" Parek said sourly. "There's nothing there. It's empty. No reasons, no purposes, no higher existence. Just clatter."

Gnawing doubt, she thought. *Could be promising ground for the seed I came here to plant—assuming I get the chance to plant it.* Aloud, she said, "So the mysteries remain."

Parek frowned sourly. "Mysteries are things whose answers are unknown. You expect they *have* answers, you just don't know what they are. The questions I was asking were different. They don't *have* answers. Eventually I came to realize the problem lay with my questions. What is the soul? What is true religion? What is the code *outside* our world that prescribes how we ought to live *inside* it? Such questions seem important. But you know the hidden truth? They mean nothing." Parek shook his head. "All this time the philosophers, the moralists, the mystics— they've all been posing the wrong questions."

She hugged her knees. "Care to pose any of the right questions?"

"They'll be more prosaic."

"Good."

He took her wrist again and stared at the birds. "Who are you, Ruth? What are you? Who—what—was that woman Lika?"

"You mean Linka," Ruth corrected. "Linka Strasser. I was just with her."

He blinked, briefly surprised. "Of course you'd know each other."

"We are not what we seem."

Parek guffawed. "That much is clear."

"What is there to fear?" she echoed, puzzled.

"No, no. I said, 'That much is *clear.*'" His grip tightened. "Did you—did either of you know my mother?"

Ruth swallowed. "Only by reputation. What do you remember about her?"

"She was beautiful," Parek said abstractedly. "She always seemed full of regrets, as if she'd given up something so precious she could never bear to talk about it. I always knew she'd chosen everything about herself. She loved to challenge me with questions—to get me playing with ideas I now recognize were too profound to share with a small child. I suppose she ruined me for the companionship of others my age." He shook his head and contemplated the fire. "I was always different. Even as a child I made no friends, just followers. That was all right with her. She seemed to know there was something about us both that didn't fit."

"I see."

Parek clasped his fingers together. "She died when I was six or seven, before she could've told me what she was, or why she'd chosen the life she did. So when I ask you to tell me about my mother, I guess what I'm really asking is: Who, at least by inheritance, am I?"

She smiled. "You have the right questions." She pulled her wrist away from him. "And I have all the answers."

She showed him her palms. With a tiny whirring, their skin irised back.

"What the fuck," Parek hissed.

Firelight glinted on mirror-bright metal disks, one set into the palm of each of Ruth's hands. Infinitesimal lines whorled the disks' surfaces, scribing out impossible trefoil mazes.

Parek thought he'd never seen anything so beautiful.

"The people I work for have made a very special decision," Ruth explained. "Special? Unprecedented. They've made me more machine than woman, for a while anyway, so I can give you every answer you've ever dreamed of, answers to questions you don't even know how to frame yet, but you will."

Parek's brow folded. Wonder gave way to caution. "How can you know what my questions are? Can you even imagine them?"

"Who is Arn Parek?" she asked gently. "Who is your god? Who's Ulf's goddess? What's the aurora? What are those points of light that the night sky hints at when the aurora sleeps? Why am I the way I am, and why did I come into your life? Why do you see the flickering pictures in my clothing and others don't? What was the precious thing your mother gave up?" She half-smiled. "How'm I doing?"

He clasped her wrists urgently. "Tell me."

"There is risk."

"Tell me," he hissed.

She stood, bending so he could maintain his grip on her wrists. "Kneel," she commanded.

He moved forward onto his knees.

"Slowly. As though you are Chagrin. And I am you."

Parek understood the reference at once. Without hesitation he pressed her palms against his cheeks.

"Higher," she urged.

He moved her hands to his temples. The disks tingled against his skin.

"Before we begin," Ruth said formally, "I am obliged to make an announcement that will mean nothing to you. What I do, I do by special authorization of the Privy High Council of the Galactic Confetory."

"You're right," Parek admitted. "That meant nothing."

"It will." She seated the palm disks tight.

"I'm ready," he said calmly.

You think so? Aloud, she said, "Open your mind. In all the Galaxy no one in your position has been shown what you are about to see."

Ruth peeked within, to make sure she was still transmitting three-by-three greens—and to make sure she hadn't received any last-moment messages commanding her to stop. She returned her primary awareness behind her eyes. Parek's face was peaceful and expectant. His eyes were closed.

She subvocalized the command. Specialized thought engines implanted in her body sparked to life. Neural susceptors examined Parek's brain activity. Biofrequency transponders synchronized to its principal rhythms. Software constructs of inconceivable sophistication reached into Parek's mind and began rearranging its connections.

Parek went stiff. His mouth opened as though he wanted to groan or scream. He did neither.

He couldn't.

Ruth kept her hands to his temples.

Scarcely believing the process she'd set in motion, she watched the torrent flow. Woven among Ruth's neurons and sinews was an advanced deep-brain high-speed didactic imposer. Top neuro wranglers, psychometricians, historians, and teachers had collaborated and programmed the system within her for a single purpose: to transmit into the brain of Arn Parek, in the briefest possible nonlethal time, a comprehensive understanding of the way everything was.

Everything.

The Galaxy and its countless peoples. The Memberworlds. The Affiliates. The Protectorates. The Enclave worlds. The Harvesters. The Tuezi. The tangled reasons why Jaremi Four was as it was. The Spectator system and Ruth's place in it. Linka's place in it. Laz Kalistor's place in it.

Parek's mother's place in it.

The dazzling science and art and power and wealth of Galactic civilization. All the things his mother had left behind when she'd disappeared among the autochthons of Jaremi Four—all the things she'd abandoned to bring Arn Parek into being.

The mind-numbing understanding that although humans attached the label *home* to some forty-two thousand worlds, only one was the cradle in which all their lines had originated, that life had sprung from nonlife only there—an audacious act of bootstrapping whose traces lay everywhere upon the homeworld, whose like was discernible nowhere else. Among the jewels of Galactic science was the relatively recent discovery of the world Terra. Senso had come from there, as had Ruth Griszam, Linka Strasser, and Parek's mother.

As had the most fulfilling and powerful religions Galactic civilization had seen. Into Parek's mind deluged all the religions human beings had cloven to since history began. The reasons for each one's power. The reasons why so many Galactics found them wanting. The reasons why, even so, few Galactics ever matured to the point of discarding a one of them.

Overarching it all, the ultimate impossibility: the knowledge that for Galactics, more often than not, death was at most a temporary inconvenience.

The connection sputtered out. A force like magnetic repulsion pushed Ruth's palms from Parek's head.

He tumbled onto his back. He lay immobile, knees drawn up, eyes open. After a moment he began to gasp.

Ruth glanced below. The Brethren were frantic. They could see their prophet laying atop the rocky finger. He must look dead to them. Yet they saw the heavenly messenger—surely she must be that, hadn't she dropped out of the sky?—tenderly watching The Word Among Us. They dared not charge. They dared not call. *I have enough armaments built into me to hold off a platoon. For these guys, a cold stare should do.*

Ruth glanced toward Parek's prostrate form. *Dear messiah*, she thought, *I'm sorry. Wiser heads than mine—at least, I hope they are—decided you should not go on brandishing your vast power without understanding the stakes. Now you have a lot of integrating to do.* She knelt down and drew his eyelids closed. Then she hunkered down beside the bonfire. To watch. To wait.

112. Vatican

Cardinal Rybczynsky felt Krammonz's mental *nudge* deep in his consciousness. Reluctantly he shut off the senso player. Suck, rush, wrench. His Vatican Center apartment reintegrated in his awareness: Angled walls of cold, precise crystal glowing white from internal illumination; severe glass-and-metal tables devoid of ornament; stiff-backed wooden chairs sculpted in rectangles reflecting the Golden

Mean, their arms and seats padded in dour taupe brocade. Rybczynsky sat in a silver-and-black sling chair at the center of the room. The scarlet of his simar was the only blush of color.

Krammonz was there. He was self-effacing and quietly efficient. Beside him stood the Cardinal-President of the Council for Devout Protocol. "God be with you, Cardinal," Rybczynsky said tersely. "Obviously your maneuvers at law did not succeed."

Devout Protocol nodded. "What happens on Jaremi Four?" he asked urgently.

"Parek lies there," Rybczynsky said with a shrug. "His condition has not changed for forty minutes now."

"And the Holy Father?" Devout Protocol asked.

Rybczynsky glanced toward Krammonz. "His Holiness has abandoned his schedule for the day," the Prefect of the Papal Household reported. "He reclines in his most private chamber, just watching the senso."

"Never has the prolonged study of a man sleeping generated such high saybacks," Rybczynsky said wryly.

Devout Protocol gestured helplessly. "Perhaps the Holy Father will wish to hear my report."

"His Holiness drove *me* from his chambers, not twenty minutes ago," Krammonz reported. "He said no visitors."

Rybczynsky gestured toward the straight-backed chairs. "Have a seat, brother Cardinal. Report to me what has happened. I shall inform the pontiff as promptly as circumstances permit."

Krammonz scuttled away, holding the door as a dozen servitors marched in bearing two bottles of Callurian wine and traysful of tulip goblets.

Devout Protocol let wine linger bitter on his tongue before he spoke. "You *pov*ed Ruth Griszam performing the didactic imposition upon Parek. So you know our effort to secure an injunction against her doing so was unsuccessful."

"Indeed." Rybczynsky drained the two-centimeter pool of wine in his goblet. He set the empty glass aside; busy hands whisked it away and replaced it with another tulip glass charged with another single swallow of wine. "Speak frankly, Ocal. Did our petition ever have a chance?"

"Never. From the moment the sim-gavel sounded, it was clear the Justiciaries held the Church in low regard in this matter. The presiding Justiciary cocked his eyes toward me and said, 'I trust the esteemed Vatican counsel is not here to accuse another party of violating the Enclave Statutes.' The remark elicited general laughter."

"Laughter? From sitting Justiciaries?"

Devout Protocol nodded. "Then another Justiciary asked me whether I'd been informed that one of my moonlets was missing." He raised his goblet, scowled at the tiny puddle of wine it contained. "May I have a full glass, please?" he asked the servitor captain.

"But the benefice," the man whispered.

"The benefice will not suffer," Devout Protocol said. "I intend to drink heavily today." With a smile he took the full glass from the servant, drained three-quarters of it in one gulp, and emptied it with the second. "Thank you," he told the servant.

"You may resume pouring driblets. Now, where was I? The Confetory's counsel launched into her opening statement, stressing that in authorizing such unprecedented disclosures of knowledge to an autochthon of an Enclave World, the Privy High Council had explicitly waived the Enclave Statues with regard to Arn Parek."

"Surely that was expected," Rybczynsky sighed.

"Of course. I proceeded to argue from the platform on which we had all agreed—that the Universal Catholic Church, a revered and potent social institution, stood to suffer terrible damage if the Confetory should tamper with the mind of a man who may be the present vessel of the Cosmic Christ."

"How did the Confetory counsel respond?"

"She said that if Parek is in fact the Son of God, then according to the Church's own doctrine Parek is omniscient in virtue of his Godhead. It follows that no imposition of knowledge could add to or alter the totality of knowledge he already possesses, thus no damage could result. On the other hand, she said rather too archly, if Parek is not the Son of God—and I quote her *verbatim* here—'if, for example, there is no God; or if he exists, but is not the sort of deity who goes around having sons; or if he exists and begets sons, but the Church has erred in identifying Hom Parek as one of them—if any of *those* things are true, then Arn Parek is just another autochthon. He stands in no special relationship to the Universal Catholic Church, nor the Church to him.' She concluded that no one can know Parek to be the Son of God except by faith. 'And therefore it follows that the Universal Catholic Church has no standing to bring an action against the Privy High Council in any matter regarding Arn Parek.' With that, she moved for dismissal."

"Which I assume was granted," Rybczynsky said tonelessly.

"On the spot. Servitor, another full glass, if you will."

"For myself also," Rybczynsky said sourly. "We never expected the court challenge to succeed. Still, it was a gambit we had to play, and I believe you rendered it as capably as anyone could. And now—what is the time?"

"Eight-nineteen in the evening." Devout Protocol glanced at a skylight. The sky's green algae had gone muddy brown with the last glimmerings of sunset. In a few minutes it would turn gray-green by reflected light from the planet's unbroken urban carpet.

"My brother in the Christs, would you see to the distribution of a most urgent invitation?" Rybczynsky asked.

"Of course."

"In light of developments, the Holy Father will convene an emergency meeting at dawn."

Devout Protocol nodded. "Such is the pontiff's wish?"

"It will be when I explain it to him. He will want everyone, and I mean *everyone*, there: all the high curia officers, the theologians Geruda and Hjinn, whomever else is onplanet, and even Y'Braga, too."

"Y'Braga? You wish the Jesuit General brought from detention?"

Rybczynsky nodded serely. "His previous offenses notwithstanding, Y'Braga is a wily strategist. God willing, he may ferret out some solution that eludes the rest of us."

Devout Protocol smiled ironically. "Scraping bottom, I see."

Rybczynsky shrugged. "Scraping bottom? I turn over the barrel. Go with the Christs, Ocal. At dawn bring me all the minds I asked for."

Devout Protocol stood, bowed smartly. "I'll see myself out."

"Thank you." Rybczynsky stood and smoothed the creases of his simar. He downed a last swallow of wine, hurried back to the silver-and-black sling chair, and thumbed the senso player back on.

Suck, rush, wrench.

113. Jaremi Four—Southern Hemisphere— The Promontory

Ruth Griszam pulled another length of wood from Parek's fire pack and arranged it atop the coals. She spun when when Parek groaned. She polled his vitals. *He's awake,* she realized. *He's watching me. But he wants me to think he's still out.* She fixed her gaze on his eyes. Gradually one side of her mouth twitched into a half-smile.

Parek couldn't keep from laughing. He raised his head. "Good daypart, Fem Griszam. That is how you, um, *Galactics* say it, no?"

She swallowed. "Yes. Yes it is."

Groaning, he sat up. He pressed his hands to his head. "Fucking shit, Ruth. Or should I say *forjeler?* Is this all true?"

"Every bit."

"So you're from—from—" he said as his finger waggled toward the sky, "—up there. Not like a sky god, but literally, physically . . . up there. Out there. Hundreds or thousands of. . . ." He searched for the word. "Hundreds or thousands of *light years* from here."

"That's right."

"As I sit here, on this world, under this sky, people like me in numbers beyond imagining stand beneath the skies of thousands of worlds."

Ruth nodded. "No small fraction of them watching—I mean, *poving*—our talk."

"You came from one of those worlds. Linka did, too, and so did Laz Kalistor." His eyes grew wide. "That serving boy I killed days ago."

"It's all right," she said. "He lives again."

Parek thought a moment. "Oh, they came for his body by night—what's the word?—*no-vis,* and took him to your—your city beneath the polar sea."

"Exactly."

"Laz Kalistor didn't live again," Parek said darkly. "Now I know why Ulf's goddess wanted Ulf to lop his head off and burn it in the fire." He stared at his feet again. "Millions of people on thousands of worlds just heard me say that."

"More or less," Ruth confirmed. "Actually, it's *trillions* of people, a number I don't imagine you use much here."

"Millions. Billions. Trillions," Parek said softly. "A lot of people."

"What? You want to let the people . . . let the people do what?"

He tapped a finger beside his ear. He spoke more loudly. "I said a *lot* of people, Ruth." He drew up his knees and clasped his arms around them. "You came from one of those planets."

"Terra," Ruth supplied. "Where humanity began."

"Linka came from Terra, too," Parek reasoned.

"Yes."

"And so did—so did my mother." Parek's eyes danced in his head, as though he were watching a diagram of the correspondences assemble before him. "My mother was Terran, a *Spectator* like you and Linka."

"With one important difference. She never came back."

"Who was my father?"

"Unknown," Ruth said. "Someone from here."

Parek nodded darkly. "An *autochthon.*" He rocked back and forth, inwardly watching new bubbles of knowledge float into place. "It was an even chance, then, whether I would inherit her ability to see the birds twinkle."

"That's right."

"You Terrans can see them, but we—we *Jaremians* cannot."

"Most humans can distinguish that particular figure-ground ambiguity," Ruth explained. "Essentially, it's *only* Jaremians who can't. That's how the Harvesters marked the human stock they deposited here. So now Spectators from any other world can come to Jaremi Four, live among you, and always identify each other without making themselves conspicuous."

"Well, I'll be dipped in plorg," Parek breathed.

"Where do you want to be shipped?" Ruth asked baffledly.

Parek chuckled. "All that technology they packed into your body, and you can't fucking hear." He guffawed. "I find incredible complexity within you: All that equipment. Half a dozen things inside you with the gift of independent thought, all but aware of their own existence. You're not a person, Ruth, you're a colony. Yet the people who did all that to you can't make your ears work?"

Ruth shrugged. "Just before they decided to send me here, I was on an island. The base where other off-worlders manufactured your enemies' fleet."

"The . . . *Universal Catholic Church,*" Parek said.

"Exactly. The island was fired upon from orbit. Focus on that, it'll make sense to you in a moment. My eardrums ruptured. I would've been deaf but for the implants that are part of every field Spectator's standard equipment. Afterward, the medics rushed the process of restoring my hearing." She chuckled. "They were in a hurry to start packing me full of equipment."

"What about the, um, *implants* you used to hear on the island?"

"The surgeons took them out. They needed the space for some of the new stuff. So when you address the Galaxy through me, please speak loudly and clearly."

Parek laughed. He looked Ruth in the eye. "Hello, Galaxy."

He understands, she thought with wary exultation. *He isn't just parroting information, he truly understands this whole absurd situation. Not that I should have expected less from him.*

"Hello, Galaxy," Parek repeated. "Everlasting welfare unto you."

"Isn't that what you usually say to people before you annihilate them?"

Parek drew up the corners of his mouth to laugh. All at once his smile collapsed. His eyes grew hard. Astonishment became repugnance, repugnance became rage. His sides began to shudder. *They warned me he might become volatile*, Ruth thought. Aloud, she said, "Talk to me, Arn. What connection did you make?"

"You knew," Parek sobbed, his face buried on his knees. "You knew."

She leaned forward. "So few? What did you say?"

He uncoiled and leapt to this feet. Through gritted teeth he shouted, "You knew! You knew! You did nothing! You watched it all die!"

She rose to a squat. "I hear you. But I don't understand."

Parek waved one hand. "Not you personally. I'm looking back three hundred years, when fire rained from the skies onto Southland and spread ruin everywhere. You call it a Tuezi, a machine from some unknown place and time. It appeared over my world and annihilated millions, snuffed out civilizations, and set into action all the cascades of ruin that later condemned Ulf and Chagrin and countless others to stunted futures. It warped their personalities." He whirled, gathering his threadbare cape before the bonfire could ignite it. "No one from your Confetory was there when the Tuezi struck. But they found Jaremi Four not long afterward. The damage was still mitigable. Sparks of civilization could've been blown back to full flame. Instead, from the sanctity of, what's the word, *orbit*, the first explorers just watched Jaremian civilization stumble into its grave." He strode toward her. She stood. He grabbed her tunic, tears streaming down his face. "Do you deny it?"

After an endless moment, she said, "No. But look into yourself. Look into the record. You'll see how difficult that decision was, how much it cost everyone involved."

Grimly Parek nodded. "Yes. I see that. Everyone connected with that decision felt sullied by it. And they admitted it, too." He laughed darkly. "They admitted it sixty years later, when they were old and safely dictating their memoirs. Or they took the guilt to their grave, leaving their children or grandchildren to write some high-toned essay and atone for it without consequence." He shoved her back and strode to a far corner of the rock, at most two bodylengths away. "Your precursors from the oh-so-righteous Galactic Confetory could've fixed everything with a single stroke!" He lurched back toward her and put forth clenched hands, the knuckles mere centimeters from her. "With no investment greater than making the decision to do it, your forbears could have descended among the still-intact societies of the North and taught the powerful how to set everything right."

Tenderly she wrapped her fingers over his hands. "You've seen everything. You've seen the Enclave Statutes and the hard experience they were based on."

"What I see can't be right," Parek grated. "Forty-two thousand inhabited worlds—forty-two thousand *worlds*—and you keep forty thousand of them . . . like this, locked out of your culture, trapped in squalor and ignorance? Doesn't that strike you perverse . . . no, of course it wouldn't. It's all you've ever known."

Ruth could say nothing. She could do nothing, save fight back tears.

"At the dam, I'd watch your mouth twist when Ulf and Chagrin spoke of prowling through the woods and stealing food from helpless old men, men they'd doubtless killed in snarling agony. Yet behind your Spectator detachment, you always knew: all the pain Ulf and Chagrin had suffered, all the pain they dealt, could've been prevented by a humane action your forbears refused to carry out on *principle!*"

Ruth slid to her knees. She looked up at Parek. "All you say is true," she croaked. "Arn, you know why I came. You know how unprecedented this all is. For just one moment, put history aside. You and I are here now. The enemy surrounds you. For the first time in your life, you know everything that depends on your decisions—not just on Jaremi Four, but all across a Galaxy that has irrationally decided that you ordain the course of trillions of lives. Please concentrate on that. What will you do?"

He wrapped his arms about himself. "I will stay the course."

"What?" she demanded.

"I spoke clearly," he said, annoyed.

"I heard you," she all but stammered. "But how can you—"

Angrily he swept his arms left and right. "Here is the reality I knew before you came! Ships on my right, siege engines on my left. Hundreds of thousands of troops who'll outlast my mother matter and surge down to kill me. I was close to despair. Then you came. Now? So what if everything on Jaremi is turning to shit, I mean plorg; there are trillions—think of that, *trillions!*—across the scattered skies for whom my life has transcendent meaning."

Mother of stars, Ruth thought, *it's all going wrong.*

Parek spread his arms. "If not for me, if not for the people of Jaremi Four, then for the Galactics, I must persevere. They're my people, too. I'll be the bridge between my tiny world and all those above who tolerated our suffering for so long."

Slowly, Ruth stood. She gathered into her mind the command codes for the weapons systems that had been built into her. *If he won't surrender, my orders are to kill him.*

"This time I know what you're thinking," he told her. "Perhaps while I was in your head I saw more than you were meant to show me." He held forth his palms. "Don't do it! Without me, who will restrain Ulf? He'll plunder this world to no purpose."

She extended her right arm as though her fingers were weapons. *Actually the blast will emerge from just below my wrist, but the principle's the same.* "He'll be stopped here," she countered aloud. "It's over for you both."

"Most likely," Parek admitted. "But suppose Ulf gets away. What if by some mischance I die and he wins? He'll surge forth again, this time under the banner of Parek the martyr. I serve Ulf's cruel agenda best dead. As a living prophet, I can be his foil and proclaim unwelcome new doctrines."

For a few seconds they locked eyes, his hands raised, her arm extended, slowly circling the bonfire. *Is this how it ends?* she thought? *After three years of blood and subterfuge and conquest, it ends with me flying down and toasting him with a ravisher bolt? Isn't that somehow profoundly unsatisfactory?* She watched his eyes over the knuckles of her raised hand. She could read nothing in them.

When Neuri Kalistor's voice crackled in Ruth's mind, it made her jump. *"Don't kill him,"* ordered Kalistor. *"The Privy High Council finds his argument sufficiently convincing to warrant keeping him alive. I say again, do not kill Parek."*

Ruth lowered her arm. "You convinced them," she said coldly.

Parek squatted. He shook his head. Whatever relief he felt at saving his own life, it was overwhelmed by amazement. *My argument changed minds up there— out there—in the vast Galaxy.* "You doubt your choices, too," he beamed. "We're not so different."

Ruth shrugged. "Just because I didn't kill you doesn't mean I'm diffident."

Parek laughed convulsively. *"Different*, Ruth, different. I said we're not so different." Looking into the sky, he shouted, "Can't someone up there fix her ears?"

Ruth couldn't help laughing herself. She found a rock outcrop convenient for sitting on and did so. "No," she said at last. "I guess we aren't so different."

Parek laced his fingers. He stared hollowly into the night. "If we are not so different—if even you Galactics are not like gods—then there *is* nothing beyond, is there? Nothing higher?"

"No."

"Intellect and emotion, matter and energy," Parek continued. "Those categories alone exhaust all that there is?"

"Yes."

"But what about the certainty people feel that something more exists—that there's something 'ultimate,' that from time to time men and women *do* experience it? If no such thing exists, what causes that feeling?"

"Run with this, Ruth," crackled Kalistor. *"The analysts like where it's leading."*

"Big question, Arn," Ruth began. "Where does subjective religious experience come from? Most likely, from systematic cognitive errors. Human brains were never designed to apprehend a cold, complex world of impersonal causes. The neural firmware—there's a word you'll recognize, give it a minute—was shaped by hundreds of thousands of years of hunting and gathering on Terra. Knowing the world as it really is was never a design priority."

"Evolution, Ruth," he reminded her archly. "The brain was never *designed* at all. People respond to stimuli, religious stimuli included, using mechanisms the brain just happened to acquire through evolution."

"You're right," Ruth chuckled. "Sometimes even people who understand evolution stumble into talking about 'design.' It's verbal shorthand."

"No, it's sloppy thinking. I, of all people, should know the difference." Parek paced around the fire. "You know, Willim used to make a point like this, though he didn't have this vocabulary of evolution in which to express it. A cognitive system that's predisposed to make outlandish mistakes will repeat those mistakes endlessly, and be reinforced for doing so, *if* errors of that sort coincidentally incline people to do the right thing in everyday situations." He hunkered down beside her. He smelled of leather and sweat. "If anthropomorphizing nature, or being too quick to defer to authority, helped early humans find food and get mates and avoid getting killed, then after thousands of years it would be those errors, not the power to perceive reality correctly, that evolution conserved."

"On the right trail, you are," Ruth agreed.

"If there's nothing beyond," he mused, "then each of us is alone—alone, but free."

She wrapped herself up in her arms. "There's something they teach us about freedom at the Spectator Academy. In some ways no one in the Galaxy's more free than a Spectator in deep cover. None of your peers knows your real nature. None of the Galactics who *pov* your work give a plorg how you treat the autochthons. That kind of power and autonomy. . . ."

"That kind of solitude," Parek added.

"Yes, the solitude, too. Take them together and they can lead a field Spectator deeply astray. As a sort of intellectual vaccine, at Academy they had us memorize a reflection on freedom by a man named Robert Green Ingersoll. He lived a few centuries before the Confetory discovered Terra."

"An early outspoken critic of religion," Parek recalled. He looked up, vaguely surprised. "Amazing what that device of yours has crammed into my head."

Ruth chuckled. "Here's the quotation. Try to overlook the ornate diction, it was characteristic of the period. The meanings of anachronistic terms should come to you after a few moments; you've absorbed enough background to figure them out."

He leaned toward her and lay a hand on her shoulder, cupping the epaulet there.

"Ingersoll on freedom," Ruth announced. She began to declaim in a voice that was quiet, but limned with grandeur: " 'When I became convinced that the Universe is natural, that all the ghosts and gods are myths, there entered into my brain, into my soul, into every drop of my blood, the sense, the feeling, the joy of freedom. The walls of my prison crumbled and fell, the dungeon was flooded with light and all the bolts, and bars, and manacles became dust. I was no longer a servant, a serf or a slave. There was for me no master in all the wide world—not even in infinite space. I was free—free to think, to express my thoughts—free to live to my own ideal—free to live for myself and those I loved—free to use all my faculties, all my senses—free to spread imagination's wings—free to investigate, to guess and dream and hope—free to judge and determine for myself—free to reject all ignorant and cruel creeds . . . free from the fear of eternal pain—free from the winged monsters of the night—free from devils, ghosts and gods.' " Caught in the majesty of the words, she stood.

His hand slipped from her shoulder. He held it against himself as though concealing something precious; Ruth noticed nothing.

" 'For the first time I was free,' " she intoned. " 'There were no prohibited places in all the realms of thought—no air, no space, where fancy could not spread her painted wings—no chains for my limbs—no lashes for my back—no fires for my flesh—no master's frown or threat—no following another's steps—no need to bow, or cringe, or crawl, or utter lying words. I was free. I stood erect and fearlessly, joyously, faced all worlds.' "

Parek swallowed. "This man Ingersoll said that before his people traveled in space?"

"Almost a century before the most primitive space travel."

He nodded gingerly. "To fearlessly, joyously, face all worlds. That's what I must do."

Time to conclude this, Ruth thought. "Exactly, Arn. Face all worlds—Jaremi Four, the worlds of the Galaxy—and admit your fraud. Clean your breast of it before you lead anyone else to ruin."

He raised empty palms to her. "You ask me to abdicate everything I am."

"A lie? Is that really all you are?" She extended her hands. "You need be neither the herald, nor the messenger, nor the tool of forces that don't exist. You understand that now," she said urgently. "The Galaxy watches through my eyes. Hold my hands. Look into my eyes. And say what you know you must say."

" 'Say the words,' Parek sneered. "Now it's as though *you* are Chagrin." He pulled his hands free. "Don't you see, Ruth? If there are no gods, no realm beyond—if there truly is no greater standard to guide my actions—then what goal can be higher for me than satisfying my new audience in the skies? Trillions of them want me to be *their* Word Among Us."

"But you're not," she hissed. "You'll destroy yourself trying. Why make that sacrifice for Galactics? We're not gods either."

Sucking his teeth, Parek turned to stare into the fire-dotted night. "You'll do."

"You're not getting away with that," Ruth snapped. She stepped between Parek and the bonfire. "We Galactics are just people. We're no different from Jaremians. We just have more powerful tools. You know how some Southerners thought your soldiers were gods because they have steamskiffs and rifles and that plorg-licking mold. . . ."

Parek's mouth tightened. "You know about that."

"We know everything," Ruth breathed.

"Then you *are* gods!" he exulted. He glided around her and settled into his notch in the rock with the air of a king flouncing before his court.

Ruth followed. She stood a bodylength from him, scowling, fists on her hips.

He chuckled. "I toy with you, Ruth. I know what you are and what you aren't."

"Then tell the Galaxy what *you* are, Arn Parek."

"You mean tell them what I'm *not*," Parek said levelly. "Sorry, Ruth. You think you love truth so much. You think I've lost touch with truth. Yet I have a hard truth for you." He sprang to his feet. "Do you know that my mother matter runs out tomorrow, that then I'll be helpless before these encircling armies? I know that. That's my truth. I must decide tonight what I will do." He crept around her. "Based on what I could sense of the religious preoccupations of Galactic culture during my brief tour through your mind—and upon some hints my dubious 'sky god' may not know he dropped—I think I know what I must do. I'll tell you and see what you think."

Ruth edged toward him. Her mouth was suddenly stale.

All at once Parek understood the purpose of her oddly symmetrical gait. *Smooth, fluid movement for the trillions who watch through her eyes. I should have guessed it long ago.* "Tell me, Ruth. Do you think my admirers among the stars would be impressed . . . if I rose from the dead?"

"You can't mean that," she blurted, aghast.

"Judging by your response, it's *exactly* what I mean."

"Rising from the dead won't impress Galactics," Ruth lied desperately. "We do it all the time."

Parek smiled. "*We* don't." He raised his right fist. "*Attention!* Homs and fems of the Galactic Confetory! I, Arn Parek, The Word Among Us, beloved of the sky gods, shout this proclamation for all my followers amid the worlds. Tomorrow morning, I shall die and rise again!"

Ruth's tears welled up again. *Forjel what it does to the visuals,* she thought angrily. *What does it matter? We've lost.*

"Ruth?" Parek said gently.

"Yes?"

"There's something else I probably wasn't supposed to see while I was in your head."

"What?"

"The miniature stunner hidden beneath the epaulet on your left shoulder. The one for emergencies, the only weapon you carry that isn't woven in among your body tissues." He lunged forward extending his left arm. She chopped at his wrist. No matter, the stunner'd been in his *right* hand. He pressed it against her neck and fired. At such close range there was nothing her implants could do to resist its effect. *He'd known that,* she thought with ebbing wonder.

She smelled ozone. Cold suction claimed her awareness. The last thing her experients *pov*ed was Parek's chest rushing toward her.

Then obscurity.

114.   Jaremi Four—Southern Hemisphere— Parek's Ruins

Dawn gave way to gray humid morning. With trembling hands Ulf gripped the stone balustrade outside the command bunker. He stared down the muddy slope. "High Commander!" Felegu stumbled around the corner, braking from an all-out run. "The last of the mother matter has been fired."

Ulf pursed his lips. "Just now?"

"Minutes ago."

Ulf clasped his hands behind him. He continued staring at the river. "That's all you have to tell me?"

Felegu swallowed. "Yes, High Commander. No sign of The Word Among Us."

Ulf whirled. "It's your fault, Felegu. Letting him go out last night with an escort of less than a dozen Brethren!"

"He ordered it," Felegu stammered.

Ulf sighed. With defeat so close, anger so readily gave way to resignation. "Any of them awake?"

"No. They're still as we found them." At first light, a patrol had found the guards who'd accompanied Parek to the promontory. They'd lain scattered across a rocky heath, as if felled while on the march. They weren't dead. They bore no wounds, nor did they seem poisoned. Breathing, body temperature, the handful of indicators Ulf's medics knew how to measure—all were buoyantly normal. Yet sleep had an adhesive grip on them.

"No one can wake them?" Ulf demanded.

"No," said Felegu. "We've tried everything."

Ulf turned slowly, thumbs jammed in the waistband of his stained fatigue pants. "Have you placed one of their forearms across the edge of a table and broken it?"

Felegu's eyes saucered. "Of course n—"

Ulf interrupted, "Have you sliced somebody's scrotum open and pulled out the balls with metal hooks?"

"High Commander! Our own men? Brethren?"

"Have you tried fire?" Ulf asked slowly. His hands came forward as though he meant to shake Felegu. Felegu edged back; Ulf's hands circled, palms up, into a gesture of false comradeship. "There, see? You *haven't* tried everything."

Felegu dropped his eyes. "No, High Commander. You want the Brethren awakened at any cost."

Ulf nodded. His voice was feral. "At least one of them. One of the foot soldiers, I mean. I don't care how loud he's screaming, as long as he can say what happened to Parek. And I need that *now.*"

Eyes still wide, Felegu saluted fist-on-chest. He melted back around the corner.

"Don't maim the captain!" Ulf cried after him.

A figure stirred in deep shadows. He was tall and gaunt and had haunted eyes. "Remind me not to go to sleep on you," Chagrin said archly, stepping from behind a slumping column. His death's-head face lifted in bitter laughter. "Parek's fuckin' left you, you know that? The Word Among Us fuckin' ran away. Left you to lose his final battle."

"Maybe he did run away," Ulf mused. "Then again, maybe he wandered too far from the ruins and the enemy got him. Maybe after the mother matter wears off, they'll send a messenger with demands. And maybe Parek has some scheme. Maybe he'll bide his time and come back."

"Bide his time!" Chagrin snorted. "We spent four days shooting off all the mother matter we'll ever have. All that time, we were waiting for him to think of something. Even for *you* to think of something." Chagrin brought up his right hand, two fingers and thumb slowly closing together. He stared at the place where they met. "Now time's all gone, and we're still right here."

Ulf turned back toward the river, palms pressing on stone. "I wish I knew what happened to Parek. Then I'd know what to do."

Chagrin's laughter was bitter and derisive, not at all private.

Ulf stared outward. Once before he'd brought together a band of doubting officers. Once before he'd made plans to wrest the power from Parek, to step out of the murk of revelation, to act in ways shaped solely by the logic of war. *It's so late now. Even if I'd started planning days ago, what could I hope for? To get away with a few trusted officers, a couple of hundred troops?* He twisted his mouth into something like a smile. *Compared to how I'll wind up if I do nothing, that's not so bad.*

Off to the east, a blossom of fire rolled up, searing orange against the morning's gray. The mother matter still hadn't worn off. Attackers were still staggering about knocking boxes of ammo into their campfires. The *whoomp* reached him just as the fireball twisted in on itself and broke up.

Doesn't matter what Parek does, Ulf thought grimly. *I know what I have to do. And there isn't much time.*

115.   Jaremi Four—Southern Hemisphere— West of Parek's Ruins

Something ropy twitched in Linka Strasser's soup. She didn't care. *If I feel that way, how must it feel—the hunger of the ones who endured these five days of nausea and retching without Spectator implants?* She blinked inwardly, surprised again by empathy.

"Think it's over?" someone asked behind her.

"Nobody knows what it was, so how the fuck c'n they know it's over?" another voice slurred. "All I know's, this is first time in days I wanna eat."

"The curse is lifted! The curse is lifted!" shouted a limping officer. Two troopers trudged past, kerchiefs over their noses and mouths. They carried a corpse. Its skin was soot-black, alternately gathered in folds or stretched drum-tight. The body lay rigid, posed like a boxer—legs bent, arms raised, hands clenched. *Limbs contract like that when heat coagulates the muscles,* Linka recalled automatically. *Poor bastard must have pitched into a fire.*

"You there!" called an officer to someone Linka couldn't see. "Up here, get your chow, then back to firefighting." Idly she sipped acrid soup. *The mother matter bombardment ended three hours ago,* she thought. *The stronger among us are functioning almost normally. Another three hours, four at the outside, and this army will be ready to mobilize again.*

Out of the corner of her eye she noticed a man's eyes on her. Once strong, the man was scrawny now. His ill-patched rags were flecked with vomit, as was the mold-flecked bandoleer he wore over one shoulder pocked with sores. His skin shone from filth pounded in deep. One of his upper legs had ballooned. Swollen skin lapped over on itself, almost concealing a festering trench occupied by what had once been a *silish. Forjeler, that's Friz Labokloer,* she thought. *Or what's left of him.*

"You look strong enough," Labokloer said. "And your body armor's in fair shape."

Struggling against deep tiredness, a junior officer trudged past Labokloer. He handed Linka a small fabric pouch. She looked up to ask Labokloer what this was all about. But he'd already staggered on, seeking new troops to review.

The pouch contained the one item missing from her own body armor: a hood to go over her head. It was clean, crisply quilted, incongruously well made. *Where'd they get these? They must've been made on Vatican Island. Labokloer's hoarded them until now. Until the final battle.*

Another officer swayed toward her. He wore a fresh bandage over what must have been a very old cut in his chest. Dried blood spread like a brownish delta down his shirt below it. Strapped to his back was an immense fabric-walled box. "Whatever. If Lord Labokloer thinks you can fight, I'm supposed to give you a gun." He turned his back to her. "Take just one." The backpack was open. A couple of dozen steam pistols were arranged in crisp rows. The guns were clean and shiny. Obviously they had never been used before.

They were also fully charged.

She thrust the pistol into one of her holsters. "Why pistols?" she asked.

"It's going to be close quarters," the weapons master predicted. "But you know what? We're going to kill the false god slowly. I yearn to hear him scream." The man turned to face her. He flashed her a sinister smile. "When you hear drums beating—*boom* boom boom, *boom* boom boom—come to the tall mound by the river for muster." Not waiting for acknowledgment, he staggered after Labokloer and his armorer.

Linka set the fabric armor hood on a fallen tree trunk. *What the sfelb, I'll fight,* she thought. *At least I don't have to screw anyone.*

116. Jaremi Four—Southern Hemisphere— The Promontory

"*G*ood daypart, Ruth."

"*Um, which one?*" she subvocalized groggily. Her right leg had gone to sleep folded under her. Her implants rushed the job of restoring circulation. Sensation.

"*Morning.*" Neuri Kalistor's voice was solicitous. "*Late morning. We've been tap*ping *like crazy. You were out eight and a half hours.*"

"*I can tell.*" No one was in sight. She tugged off her culottes and sighed with relief as her bladder emptied. "*I guess that didn't go too well.*"

"*As far as I know, the Council's satisfied with the outcome.*"

"*I gave Parek the idea of rising from the dead, then he shot me with my own stunner. Not exactly what I'd call a stellar perf—oh, forjeler!*"

"*What?*"

Ruth stood. She patted her belt and surveyed the rocky expanse about her. "*My flight pack. That cute little no-vis generator. They're gone, too.*"

"*Did Parek take them?*"

"*I wouldn't know,*" she said sourly, pulling her culottes back on. "*But it seems foolish to assume they were taken by anyone else.*" Inventorying herself, she poked a finger under her left epaulet, where the little fabric-wrapped stunner had been. In its place was a wad of paper. She unwrapped it and gaped. "*It's from Parek. The bastard left me a note.*"

She willed herself fully into Mode and showed the Galaxy the note.

It said: "MAIN STAGE. CENTER OF THE RUINS. HURRY."

"*If I were you, I'd hurry,*" Kalistor said.

"*Oh, forjel it again!*"

"*What now?*"

"*I stashed my peasant clothes in the top of a tree a dozen kilometers from here. I can't get back there without the flight pack. I'll have to march into the ruined city in this white getup.*"

✦ ✦ ✦

"This is Ruth Griszam reporting," she commented after the Brethren captain had shown her to her reserved seat. *"As I drew near the ruins, I encountered two soldiers. By their uniforms I recognized them as Brethren—members of Parek's elite guard corps. They looked up at me and said to each other, 'The woman in white.' They'd been told to expect me. I've just received a VIP's escort through Ulf and Parek's encampment. They showed me to a seat high in a gantry, overlooking an improvised stage built atop an ancient cistern. Apparently Parek wants me to have a good view of whatever will happen here.*

"The camp is tense this morning. To either side, the enemy organizes for battle. Everyone here knows it. Still, aside from a handful of guards on the ramparts, most people are here, at the center of the ruins, crowded around the stage four tiers high in improvised bleachers. The people were called here for a major announcement. The announcement is to be made by Ulf; Parek's nowhere in sight. Judging by the conversations I've overhead, most people here think he's gone. Many believe their prophet deserted them just before the final battle—a battle which most people here realize, with unusual clarity and resignation, they are almost certain to lose."

With Spectator grace Ruth panned her vision across the stage. Ulf stood behind a boxy dais. He wore pale green fatigues. He exchanged whispers with a group of heavily armed officers who'd lined up behind a background flat made of Jaremian bamboo. While they spoke, soldiers carried on another four-meter-wide bamboo panel. They set it up just behind the officers, sandwiching them between two opaque screens. Obviously the officers' role was to lurk in hiding, right there on stage.

Which could only mean that the person they meant to hide from had not yet arrived.

Parek?

"No one but Parek could have told those Brethren to expect a woman in white at the perimeter. I doubt he's as absent as his followers seem to think." Ruth spared a moment to glance within. The *verify* signal was three-by-three greens. She checked her saybacks and looked again. Never before had so large a fraction of all the Galaxy's trillions of humans dropped what they were doing to watch a single 'cast at one time.

She checked her financials. Credits were pouring into her account at a rate that she felt sure would make the most jaundiced Galactic blanch. *Never mind its effect on a hick Terran like me,* she thought wryly. Adding to the sense of unreality was the realization that all this wealth would remain hers. Kalistor'd found the idea of Parek having the capacity for invisible flight so unnerving, she'd insisted on calling back all the no-vis flyers who'd been lurking around the ruins.

The biggest story in living memory and she was the *only* Spectator covering it. *Don't look the wrong way,* she warned herself as she fastened a couple of bugs to the scaffolding around her.

"May I have your attention?" The amplified voice—Chagrin's—boomed like a god's. Thousands of soldiers and techs fell silent.

To say nothing of the white-clad Spectator occupying the best seat in the house.

Unseen drums rolled. Ulf strode from behind the stage-right tower. He, too, had donned white. He wore bleached fatigues, an almost comically broad white leather belt, festooned with utility pouches; hastily whitewashed boots; and a cape of ecru silk that displayed only faint stains and water marks. He clutched another microphone. "Everlasting welfare unto you all," he growled.

Ulf's steely eyes prowled the audience. He squinted toward Ruth. *Does he recognize me?* she thought. *No, he just wonders what a woman in clean white garments is doing way up here.* She felt an inward chill. *How profoundly Parek must understand senso technology! He knew to seat me far enough from the stage that Ulf or Chagrin couldn't identify me—yet not so far that I couldn't enhance my vision and see them just fine.* She tightened her lips. *What's Parek going to do with my flight pack and no-vis and stunner?*

"I called this assembly," Ulf said harshly. "Parek is gone. No one has seen him."

Urgent murmuring swelled into a rush of nervous talk.

"But we are not abandoned!" Ulf thundered. "The Word Among Us may be gone, but his spiritual might has passed to me!" Drums rolled. Cymbals collided. But the tone of the crowd was decidedly skeptical.

"Here," Ulf brayed. "I'll show you!" He held the mike close. His voice rumbled deep and buttery: "I want each of you to think of a number. Don't speak, just think of it in your mind. And here is the number I want you to think of. Did you know we are going to *live* through today? Did you know we are going to prevail? I want you all to think of that. And I want you to think of how many decades—yes, how many *tens of years*—you plan to live on after today. How many decades? Choose a number between one and nine. Don't be greedy!"

That quip sparked nervous laughter. *He's drawing them in,* Ruth thought.

"Don't talk about your number, don't tell it to anyone. Just think of it in your head. Remember it. Now, has everyone picked a number?" Ulf paced the stage. If Jaremians had known the animal, they might have recognized the Terran rooster in his strut. "All right. Here comes the next step. I want you to take the number you chose and multiply it by four."

Conversation rustled. Ruth scanned the crowd. By and large, common soldiers were squinting and counting on their fingers. Among the officers, some had pulled out writing sticks. Others did the reckoning in their head. After they'd finished, they exchanged smug glances among themselves.

"Has everyone finished multiplying?" Ulf asked. "Be sure to remember the result. You don't need to remember it long, not like your original number. Just long enough to use it again. Now, I want you take the number you just figured and multiply it again. I want you to multiply it by . . . twenty-five."

Soldiers' mouths dropped open. Officers hunted in their pockets for paper. Excited dialogue foamed across the amphitheater.

"I know what he's doing," Kalistor buzzed excitedly in Ruth's inner awareness, *"but forjeled if I know why. This is one of those number tricks where you pick a number and multiply it by a hundred. Ulf asked them to multiply their original numbers first by four, then by twenty-five."*

"There's your hundred," Ruth silently agreed.

"Usually the next thing is to fool people into calculating their ages. You have

them add a specific number to the total, then subtract the year they were born. When it's all done, if the audience has done the arithmetic correctly, they wind up with a three-digit number. The two rightmost figures show their age, and the leftmost figure is the number they picked at the beginning of the trick."

"*Cute,*" Ruth whispered. "*But with* this *crowd?*"

Ulf paced, clearly disturbed by how long people were taking to multiply their previous number by twenty-five. "All right," he blared, "who's done?"

Fewer than a tenth of the audience raised hands. They were officers mostly, except among the artillery platoons, where more than half of the troops had completed the calculation.

"If you haven't gotten an answer yet, just get close to someone who has." Ulf wiped his free hand across his brow. "Those of you who've followed this far, get ready. Birthdays—does everyone understand about birthdays? I know we come from all over Northland. Does everyone pay attention to the anniversary of the day you were born?" Most people nodded. "All right," Ulf said with growing nervousness. "Stay with me here. If you've already had your birthday this year, take the number you multiplied last and add, um, two hundred and four. If you haven't had your birthday yet *this year,* add two hundred and three. Everyone understand?"

Thousands of hands scratched thousands of heads. Thousands of shoulders shrugged. Thousands of heads turned, exchanging thousands of looks of perplexity with thousands of neighbors.

"That's two hundred and four if you've had your birthday. Two hundred and three if you haven't." He strutted left and right. "Add it. Just add it!" His fingers worried at the microphone, sending thunderous rubbing sounds across the amphitheater. "All right, now we're going to subtract. And what I want you to subtract is *the year you were born.*" He surveyed confused faces. "Come on," he urged. "Say it out loud. When were you born?" He pointed. "You! Yes, you, with the bandoleer. When were *you* born?"

"In the fourth year of the reign of the third Lord of Cranh," the man stammered.

"Oh." Ulf blurted it as though he'd been kicked in the chest. "Um, you. Wagon master. When were you born?"

"The year twelve thousand six hundred and six."

"That many?" Ulf croaked. "That many years since—what?"

"Since the skygods first caused water to plunge over Nyagalipek Falls," the wagon master said brightly. "So our priests teach back home."

"Who else?" Ulf asked too fast. "Who else can sing out when they were born?"

"Eighteenth year of Thane Gucredd's regency," shouted someone.

"Two hands of years after the great fire on the plains," offered another.

"The year the aurora covered the sky from north to south for a whole week."

"A hundred and eight years after the Third *Fhlet* Blight."

"I'm twenty-eight, but my people don't attach names or numbers to the years."

"I was found by the roadside as a toddler. I don't even know my age for sure."

Slowly Chagrin stepped toward Ulf. He cupped his hand over the head of his own microphone. With the other hand he shielded Ulf's. Feedback whistled briefly, a sound most in the audience had never heard. Idle conversation stopped.

Ruth gave the command to max her hearing but remembered she no longer carried that subsystem. She subvocalized the *lipread and sound* command. Chagrin's words sounded in an eerie synthesized voice. "Forget it," he was saying. "Most of them can't do the figures. And they all count years different. I told you your goddess was slipping when she came up with this."

Ulf nodded grimly. Chagrin set his microphone on a forward corner of the dais. As he loped offstage the audience's murmuring resumed.

"All right," Ulf said sharply. "All right," he said again, with a different emphasis. The talking stilled. "We'll go no further. Your faith is so strong you don't *need* this miracle today." This time the crowd erupted into a low roar. Hostility, doubt, disappointment—all were palpable in its tone. Ulf stared outward, his face slack with defeat. All at once his eyes narrowed. His mouth twisted into a half-smile.

Ulf held his microphone forward. He cupped his hand over its screen, as he had seen Chagrin do. In tiny increments he pulled his hand away.

The curve of his hand formed a natural amplifier that concentrated the PA system's background hum into the mike. The feedback began as an alto groan. It gathered strength, spread across the audio spectrum, and then hurled itself into the amphitheater as a high-pitched drone of seemingly infinite power.

With a flourish, Ulf raised his free hand. The howling ceased.

The amphitheater was silent.

Grinning like a predator, Ulf lowered his hand over the mike again. He moved his palm up and down. He clenched and loosened the fingers. Inside ten seconds he'd made it clear to everyone that his hand controlled the merciless screech that clawed at their eardrums and tickled the roots of their teeth.

Ulf knew he'd won the crowd back. In a single movement he pulled his free hand away from the microphone. He swept it to his lips. "Aaaarn Paaaaarek," he almost groaned, drawing out the vowels. "Parek abandoned us. He left us between the hammer and anvil of our twin enemies. But that doesn't matter. I, too, hear from the gods. They taught me this!" He cupped the mike again and assailed their ears. "See, I've spent hours with the beautiful Host Nymph and her wise Mistress," he crooned when the shrieking had died. "'They taught me much." With swelling confidence Ulf stepped up onto the dais. The bamboo screen concealing Ulf's loyal officers formed a backdrop behind him.

Someone had put a wooden lectern on the dais. Ulf leaned his forearms on it. The gesture seemed at once folksy and threatening. "It's a bitter thing, but Arn Parek has lost favor with the gods. Even now he's abandoned us. In rage and in shame he shambles about, out there somewhere, stumbling through thorn bushes, wading through fouled waters. He's trying to escape. But he can't escape from his guilt and failure. Parek interpreted the gods falsely, and that's how we wound up in this predicament today."

Ulf circled the lectern. He snapped into a commanding stance. "Here is what we shall do. Here is what the skygods ordained. At the end of this service, we will split into three detachments, one large one and two small ones. The large detachment will steal through the woods and approach the attacking army's position. On signal, you all leap from the trees shouting and firing your weapons. As soon as the enemy notices you, run back toward the ruins. At the same time, one of the smaller detachments will draw near the spot where the attacking navy is moored. They'll lob a few shells into the forward boats, then run back here. The third detachment will stay in the ruins under my personal command. And this is how it will be. The enemy will chase the first two detachments toward the hulks of our moored, burned-out fleet. When they do, my own detachment will cut them down. So command the gods!"

Ulf paused. He gauged the tone of the murmuring. It was fearful and suspicious.

"High Commander!" an artillery officer shouted.

"Speak."

"How do we know you will stay in the ruins and fight?"

Ulf raised his mike. He poised a cupped hand beside his face. "You must have faith," he intoned. At once he dropped his free hand and made the feedback again.

"High Commander! High Commander!" This time the voice belonged to Felegu. The loyal commander stood by his seat a few rows back from the stage. "I ask a question that I'm sure is on everyone's mind, and I ask only so you may make this part of our situation completely clear." He spread his hands out, palm up. "How do we *know* The Word Among Us has deserted us?"

Ulf circled behind the lectern once more. Leaning on its canted surface, he said gruffly, "Do you see him here? Does anyone see him? Of course not! I am your leader now."

Ulf emitted a harsh yelp and lurched forward. The lectern's legs collapsed. Ulf pitched off the dais onto the stage, the lectern shattering beneath him. He still had the mike; his moans rang out through the speakers.

Another sound echoed. It was the hollow drag of metal over wood.

"Look!" a hundred voices shouted.

Of its own volition, the wireless microphone Chagrin had left behind dragged itself across the dais. Now it rose. It swept through empty air to a height where someone's mouth could have been.

If there'd been someone there.

"Away with you, Ulf," announced a familiar voice.

At the middle of the dais the air began to shimmer. All at once a figure in white dimpled into view.

It was Parek.

"I am always with you," he boomed into the mike. His other hand gradually withdrew from his belt, from a small fabric-wrapped box clipped there.

Well, Ruth thought wanly, *we know what he did with the no-vis generator.*

The crowd erupted. They were yelling, stamping feet, slapping thighs, and—once everyone had stood up, which took only seconds—slapping the backs of their own chairs. *Jaremian applause.* The ovation thundered for two or three minutes.

"They're applauding all across the Galaxy," Kalistor buzzed in her ear. *"It's forjeling uncanny."*

Parek stepped to the edge of the dais. Grandly he surveyed the crowd. "I am The Word Among Us. I will always be with you." He scowled down at his fallen general. "But, Ulf—you know what? I'm getting sick of having *you* with *me.*"

Ulf struggled to one knee. He blinked up at the prophet. "But what were you—"

"*Silence!*" Parek addressed the astonished crowd in clear commanding tones. "My sky god—the king of all the sky gods, the god who is alone named God—*my* sky god sent a messenger to me last night." For just an instant he glanced toward Ruth. He half-smiled, a mannerism that had always been uniquely Willim Dultav's.

This is exactly where he wanted me, Ruth realized hollowly. *He's playing to my Galactic experients.*

"God's messenger gave me the power of invisibility. The power to induce deep, dreamless sleep. Of those, invisibility has been the greater boon." His tone retreated to a conversational register. "As The Word Among Us, when I move about the camp I tend to be shown only the things people want me to see. Armed with invisibility, I could pass where I wished among the people. I could learn the truth." His eyes scanned the crowd. "That's just what I did. I listened to your fears, your pains, your concerns for survival, and perhaps—just perhaps—victory." He looked down at Ulf. His face clouded with rage. "The gift of invisibility meant that I could also shadow you."

Ulf's eyes widened.

"Invisible, I watched you conspire against me," Parek hissed. "You planned to depose me today if I returned."

"That's not true!" Ulf stammered.

Parek stepped back. He looked over his shoulder at the bamboo background flat. "Your word is empty, Ulf. Even now your loyal assassins hide behind that piece of scenery, lying in wait in case I should appear. Of course, they didn't expect me to appear out of the air already standing on this platform. Such is the power of invisibility." His free hand fumbled in a tunic pocket. It came up clutching a little silken rectangle.

My stunner, Ruth realized.

"Now behold my power to cause sleep."

The mike picked up a trilling hum as the stunner fired. The flat began to wobble. It collapsed. Half a dozen unconscious assassins tumbled to the stage amid a clatter of bamboo rods.

"Pa-**rek!** Pa-**rek!** Pa-**rek!**" the chant resumed. Ruth stood. She drifted forward, toward the edge of the scaffold-mounted platform on which she sat. The subtle movement caused her *pov* of the audience to blossom just as its cheers and foot-stamping and chair-slapping reached the peak of frenzy.

Parek held up his hands for silence. Eyes wide with anger, he hurled his words at Ulf. "You're a traitor! You plotted against me and against these people." He looked toward the crowd. "Don't do as Ulf ordered. All that running through the woods and teasing the enemy? You'll be mowed down. And Ulf *won't* stay up here and fight. He'll run away up the north channel and let you all die. That's what he plans. I heard him say it."

Ulf had risen to both knees. With his arms folded around himself, he rocked back and forth.

Parek addressed him once more. "But out of all the ways that you've betrayed me, one in particular fills me with rage. I went to the infirmary, Ulf. I was there when the most loyal and trusted members of my personal guard—my favorites among all the Brethren—awoke from the sleep I had imposed on them."

So that's what happened, Ruth thought. *After he stunned me, he must have climbed down from the promontory, led his guards somewhere out of the way, and stunned them, too. That way he could go no-vis and disappear, and nobody'd know what happened.*

"As each foot soldier awoke, he started to scream in pain," Parek growled. "There's been no shortage of agony during this campaign. But the shrieks I heard from them!" Parek shook splay-fingered hands. "While they were *sleeping,* Ulf. You broke their bones, castrated them, and held torches to their skin. They knew nothing. They just woke up and found their bodies ruined." Parek bent low. He hurled words at his former general. "Why . . . did you . . . do that . . . to them?"

Painfully, Ulf brought up his mike. "I feared for your safety, Word Among Us! I had to know what happened to you."

Parek stood. He gestured toward Ulf's stunned loyalists lying on the stage. "The sleep I impose is so deep that nothing can awaken the sleeper until the ordained interval passes." He fastened accusing eyes on Ulf. "My beloved protectors. You maimed them all for nothing."

"Not all," Ulf croaked. "The foot soldiers, yes. But I ordered that the Brethren captain not be hurt."

Parek's eyes narrowed. He spoke with eerie control. "Don't you know, Ulf? As you did it to the least of my Brethren, you did it to me."

Ulf jerked a steampistol from under his outsized belt. "Enough," he rasped. "You're the false prophet of a false god. This ends now."

"Not like you think," cried an unamplified voice.

With a blunt *thump* Ulf's chest exploded. People in the first rows shrank from a rain of blood, bone, flecks of tissue, and scraps of leather. Ulf tottered backward, his head and neck lolling from what remained of his left shoulder. The jagged wound had hollowed him almost to the diaphragm. He thudded to the stage on his back. The head bounced once. It came to rest with Ulf's unseeing eyes gaping into the amphitheater.

Parek stared down at the corpse, oblivious to the red spatters dotting his chest and face and hair.

Chagrin stepped from behind the tower at stage left. He carried a steamrifle, mist still pouring from its barrel.

Four steps brought Chagrin to Parek's feet. He sat on the edge of the dais and lay the rifle across his lap. With his right hand he drew a knife. He began to cut a notch. "Sorry, lord," he said matter-of-factly.

"Pa-**rek**! Pa-**rek**! Pa-**rek**!" roared the audience.

Parek squatted. Slowly, he reached out and cupped his fingers over Chagrin's knife hand. He lifted it. A vague look of wonder crossed his features. "Once, you pressed this finger against a trigger and cast me into chains," Parek said into the microphone. "Today you have set me free."

"Pa-**rek**! Pa-**rek**! Pa-**rek**! Pa-**rek**!"

Parek rose to his feet. He shouted, "Hear me!" The audience fell silent. "I've flirted with death before. This day, indeed before the sun rises to mark noon, I shall die in earnest." He held up both hands to forestall any reaction. "Before the after-noon is past I will rise again and set our enemies to rout. Then shall we see who is truly of the gods."

Soldiers, sailors, gunners, techs, fashioners, cooks, camp followers—all surged to their feet. "**Pa-REK! Pa-REK! Pa-REK! Pa-REK! Pa-REK! Pa-REK!**"

Arms high in a victory pose, Arn Parek accepted the adulation of his followers. He lifted his face and locked eyes at a distance with the woman in white who stood amid scaffoldwork on the edge of a small raised platform.

Ruth didn't feel Parek was looking into her eyes. Rather, he was looking *through* them, using her as the vessel of vicarious contact with a Galaxy of new wor-shippers.

Parek blinked. He shifted his weight. He was looking at Ruth Griszam now.

"Ruth," he mouthed silently.

He affected Dultav's half-smile again. And winked.

117. The Trawler *Damocles*—Command Section

"It's got to be fifty degrees Celsius in here," Sergeant Will Bickel breathed.

"Here's the reason why," called a software tech.

The body of a *Damocles* control crew member lay sprawled across the main enviro console. "He must have fallen on it as he died," Bickel grunted. "Jammed a thermostat forward." With armored hands Bickel tugged at the distended corpse. "Oh, foreling sfelb."

In the heat the cadaver had putrefied rapidly. It was swollen all over, the face bloated to double its proper size. Blistered skin parted from the tissue beneath like a wrinkled overliner. Black distended eyeballs thrust forward. The nose had inflated and puckered all along its underside. It almost collided with the lips: glossy, distended, as as bumpy as if they contained tiny pearls. The mouth was a grotesque upward-pointing triangle, tongue protruding black and swollen. Long-dried fluids trailed from nose and mouth. Beneath this runoff the skin of the man's chin had cracked open.

"Dead, all right," Bickel whispered.

Exosuited security personnel slapped nulgravs onto the body. *Bright Hope*'s entire security force had been detailed to collect the hideously decomposed bodies of the trawler's command crew, load them into a cargo bay, and pitch them into space.

"They have our work, we have ours," Gavisel snapped. At the center of the bridge stood a shiny black-glass pyramid about a meter high. "That's the central interface with the trawler's thought engines. The crash program's in there some-where. We may not have long to find it." She removed her gloves. "Though the GDX is dormant now, we'll probably want to keep the helmets on."

Gloves off, eyes closed, the software techs laid their hands against the glass pyramid. It responded to their touch, dancing with lines and boxes and patterns of light.

"My job's over," Bickel said. "With your permission, Hom Gavisel, I'll go back to the scouter and monitor comm traffic."

"Why not join us, Will?" asked Gavisel. "Another channel of input here would speed our work."

"I'm no software wonk."

"No need to be."

Bickel approached the pyramid and sat down. He removed his gloves and touched his fingers to the glass.

Suck, rush, wrench.

The reality shift felt like a boundary surface moving front-to-back through his head.

All at once, though still aware of his continued presence on the *Damocles* bridge, Bickel was principally conscious of a huge tangle of spaghetti, or wires, or flexible tubes—or snakes. He sensed Gavisel and the techs around him, but couldn't see what they were doing.

"At this level of virtual abstraction, you don't need to understand what the data structures do," said Gavisel. "Just treat them as tangled cables you need to separate from one another."

With growing confidence Bickel began teasing apart the tangled skeins of data before him. "What *am* I doing now?" he asked.

"We've just begun," said one of the software techs. "Right now we're overcoming outer-layer passcodes, shunting susceptor channels into dummy pathways that will keep the thought engines from monitoring our actions—things like that."

Bickel nodded. He fell silent as he lurched into the rhythm of the work. Deftly he unsnarled the braided channels. Though he could see only the twisted tubes that he himself prised apart, he was somehow aware that because of his effort, the work of the others was proceeding faster. "Fem Gavisel?" he asked after a few minutes. "How'll we know when we're done?"

"When we find the fundamental command kernel. At some point we'll pull away the last sim cable or pipe and find ourselves looking at a long, slender shiny metal cylinder."

"Like a drive shaft."

"Yes, much like a drive shaft."

"And that's where we'll find the suicide program?"

"That's right."

Bickel settled back into his work. "So we keep unbraiding till we're done."

"Unless the suicide program executes first," said a software tech. "Remember, we have no idea what algorithm drives the final decision to trigger it. We could set it off by accident, or it could simply happen to execute at the same time it would have if we weren't here."

"Now there's a happy thought," Gavisel said irritably.

118. Terra—Wasatch Range, Usasector

W hen the rusty jaws of Galactic justice finally closed on Alrue Latier, this was the way of it: Unable to finish writing a complication *lookatme* string in the hubbub of the tridee control room, Heber Beaman had grabbed the largest portable modeler Latier's ministry owned. Retreating to a disused storage room beneath the studio, he could find the quiet and privacy he needed, and a place where, quite by accident, he would be out of sight when the authorities came.

Releasing air from his puffed cheeks, Beaman scanned the report of his final debugging run. *Hardest thing I ever wrote,* he thought. *I hope I finished it in time.* His fingers skittered over the modeler's surface. Half a dozen tridee bubbles opened above his worktable. Beaman was back in touch; with relief, he saw that Latier was still delivering the preamble of what was to be a lengthy sermon on the topic of Parek's coming final battle. As scheduled, the eighteen-minute opening harangue ended with a tridee clip of imprisoned New Restorationist missionaries leading Minganese children in an illegal Parek worship service. Beaman buzzed Latier on the subvocal channel. "The *lookatme* is finally done, First Elder."

"And not a moment too soon," Latier's voice crackled back. *"Will it do everything we discussed?"*

"And more besides," Beaman gloated. "When you give the command, every tridee watcher and senso experient in the Galaxy who's been following the live coverage from Jaremi Four—which is to say, most of them—will receive your 'cast instead. Once it's in place, talk fast—I doubt it will hold for more than eighty or ninety seconds."

Which was when Beaman first noticed the rooftop intruder alarms.

Unaware, Latier resumed his preachment. "Like Moroni, who before he became an angel and a messenger of God found his destiny as a mighty warrior, Arn Parek soon will try his mettle in this, his final struggle. And what are the faithful to think, what are we to hope on this terrible day? 'Now behold,' quoth the prophet, 'this giveth my soul sorrow; nevertheless my soul hath joy in my son.' The Son of the Living God draws close to his decisive test. He faces his ultimate challenge, as did the prophets and the holy men in Zarahemla of old."

"By the weapons of Corianton!" Beaman whispered. A security bubble revealed armored police streaming down the access stairs from the roof. Not your usual shabby Terran Zone gumshoes, either: there were Galactic constables and commandos, armor buffed and gleaming. *"Trouble, First Elder,"* Beaman advised. *"Whatever happens, keep preaching."*

He seized control of building systems. Fire doors rumbled down, isolating the control room from the rooftop stairs, the studio from the control room. *These guys will defeat the doors in minutes,* Beaman realized, *but I'll take all the minutes I can get.*

"The worldly think Parek will fall." Latier's gray eyes glittered like agates. "I believe Parek will triumph. In that I have my faith. As it is written in Third Nephi,

'And if it so be that they will not believe these things, then shall the greater things be withheld from them, unto their condemnation.' "

The security system thrust a new bubble into Beaman's sphere of vision. He gaped: three dozen more constables lurked *outside* the building on floating sky-barges. Black-armored civil engineers levered one of the five-meter panoramic windowpanes out of the wall. *It's been years since a Galactic raid on this scale occurred anywhere on Terra,* Beaman thought with mounting fear.

Constables streamed into the sitting area. They sprinted toward the control room. Beaman's gaze flicked to another bubble: a commando technician backed away from the fire door at the bottom of the rooftop stairs as it sighed open, its software seals defeated. Cops poured into the control room from two directions, their weapons snapping from aim point to aim point with liquid precision. They'd already started arresting the affectational colorists and meta-modelers; busting the sim artists would take longer, because first it would be necessary to extricate them from their waldoes.

Hands a blur above the portable modeler, Beaman seized control of the ongoing tridee 'cast. He locked the studio equipment into a mode where it would follow Latier's movements automatically while continuing to matte him into a generic space background.

"Heber?" Latier demanded subvocally while continuing to harangue his listeners. *"What in sfelb's going on?"*

"It's a raid, First Elder. You're going to be on your own for a little while. I've assigned the lookatme *string to the second round red button on the rail of your treadmill. You can trigger it at will."*

"A raid?" Latier spluttered.

"We've discussed this contingency, First Elder."

Latier chuckled subvocally. *"Wasn't quite how we planned to use your* lookatme, *was it?"*

Desperately, Beaman scanned eventuality tables. *"No, but it'll probably work this way, too. Concentrate on sounding confident. Just don't wait too long to fire the* lookatme. *Got to go."* The portable modeler was a meter on a side; Beaman slid it, still operating, into a vanisher valise the size of his fist.

Tapping in a passcode, Beaman jumped onto an upchute. It whisked him up into Latier's office, with its golden finials, crimson damask, white leopard-skin, and soft light leaping from marble sconces to wash an alabaster ceiling.

And constables everywhere.

Atop the ornate gold-leafed desk were the fifteen books of the Book of Mormon, separately and extravagantly bound.

Almost fifteen; the second-to-last volume was missing.

"Look at this!" Beaman raged at the nearest constable. "You call yourself guardians of justice? If you want a Book of Mormon, we give them away free downstairs."

"We landed on the roof," a constable protested. "We haven't been downstairs."

"One of you flatfoots is going to take his booty home and get a big surprise," Beaman raved, stabbing a hand toward the broken set. "These aren't whole Books of Mormon. Each volume contains just *one* of the component books."

A constable in a bright red exoskeleton hustled into the room. "Hey, isn't that

Heber Beaman?" Two blue-armored flunkies whirled. They seized Beaman by each arm and jerked him forward toward Red Exoskeleton.

"Are you in charge here?" Beaman demanded as haughtily as he could.

"Yes, I'm the High Investigator. Heber Beaman, you're under arrest for complicity in a gross violation of the Enclave Statutes."

"And you're going to pay for this damage," Beaman shouted.

Red Exoskeleton stepped back into the control room. The blue-armored flunkies followed, carrying Beaman between them.

In the control room, Latier's tridee crew had already been formed into a ragged line flanked by blaster-wielding troopers. Constables flurried about slipping restraint tapes around wrists, taking iris scans, and muttering data into wrist recorders. One of the sim artists had slipped free; she ran around and around her console, deputies always missing her by inches. Finally a lieutenant in green armor stepped over. Reaching into a vanisher compartment in his armor, he produced the missing book from Latier's desk, which he used to swat the fleeing sim artist over the back of the head. She sprawled on the floor, unconscious.

"Hmm," the lieutenant said as he read the book's spine. "The Book of Ether."

In the studio, Latier leaned as far forward over his treadmill railing as he dared. He grabbed the closest tridee pickup and twisted it to face the communications center window. *This is no tax evasion arrest!* he thought.

He stared down. The second of five red buttons recessed into his platform railing was blinking furiously—the button that would trigger Beaman's *lookatme* string, the button that would give him the eyes and ears of the Galaxy, once, for less than a minute and a half.

"Like the hated Lamanites, mine enemies mass and swarm," Latier shouted. "I am sore oppressed. But I fear not, for the mighty arm of the Lord has bared itself in the cause of my defense."

The door between his studio and the control room door vaporized in a hail of blaster fire.

"Well, maybe I fear somewhat."

"Idiot!" Latier could hear Beaman yelling at the constables. "Why not just defeat the fire-alarm software like you did coming down the rooftop stairs?"

"We're on tridee now," Red Exoskeleton cried. Armored constables followed him into the studio four abreast.

No time like the present, Latier thought. He jammed his fat thumb onto the blinking red button. He smiled as the *ready* tone sounded in his ear.

Beaman's *lookatme* had succeeded. Whether they wanted to or not, a staggering majority of the Galaxy's tridee and senso users were now watching that scene, hearing whatever Latier might choose to say. *You'll get one chance, First Elder,* Beaman thought as the flunkies wound him with full-body restraining tape. *Do it just right and you may yet emerge the victor.*

"Pardon the intrusion, homs and fems," Latier called solicitously. "This is Alrue Latier, Prophet, Seer, and Revelator of the Church of Jesus Christ of Latter-day Saints, New Restoration. I've interrupted your viewing of the preparations for Arn Parek's final battle into order to share with *you* unprecedented truths about Arn Parek, The Word Among Us and the holy Son of God. That is, I will share those truths, the very truths God ordained, if the constables down below will permit me. Will they? That decision, gentle *povers*, lies with you.

"If you'd like to hear these truths, please use your polling devices right now. You know where you keep them. Pick them up and vote *yes* if you'd like me to be allowed to continue."

Constables and operatives and commandos and enforcers surrounded the base of Latier's treadmill. Red Exoskeleton marched forward, drawing a scroll from a pocket in the wrist of his armor. "Alrue Latier," his amplified voice blared, "I arrest you on charges of conspiracy to violate the Enclave Statutes, forbidden communication with quarantined autochthons, conspiracy to commit mass murder by means of an artificially induced tidal wave, directing the murder and bodily destruction of deep-cover Spectators, gross obstruction of justice, and—" He was silent for five seconds, then ten. He then hissed, *"What?"*

Latier smiled down. "I gather by your tone that government-by-sayback has worked its magic."

Red Exoskeleton snorted disgustedly. "The people spoke. We're ordered to pause while you make your case." He rolled up the indictment and tucked it back into his armor. "We are *not* leaving."

"Thank you, homs and fems," Latier gushed to his vastly swollen audience. "Now, the reason most of you *might* hear my life-changing report about The Word Among Us—remember, I said you *might* hear it—is a special *lookatme* string prepared by my associates. Even now, OmNet techs are laboring to defeat it, after which you'll be returned to your regular programming. If you'd like OmNet to stop trying to neutralize the *lookatme*, please use your polling devices now."

Confident that a curious Galaxy would grant his second request as affably as it had his first, Latier launched into an indulgent monologue. "You see these troopers, massed like the legions of old, like the besiegers of Antiparah, like those who vexed the holy stand of Rameumptom. Why have they come in their multitudes? Why have they swarmed my humble tower, stormed the inmost fastnesses of my place of refuge, mine own most private abode? They're here to accuse me of great crimes." He leaned forward. "And I affirm by Almighty God that all the things they are here to accuse me of are true."

Latier pointed an accusing finger at Red Exoskeleton. "The man in the lobster suit here wishes to tell you that as Almighty God commanded me, I disobeyed the laws of men and opened a path of contact to the Incarnation of God's Son on Jaremi Four, so that the Cosmic Christ might command the full resources of His most holy New Restoration. And I say to you, the man in the lobster suit is also here to tell you that I did coach The Word Among Us, and did share with him the holy doctrines of God's restored church, for such was the way Almighty ordained so that during this Incarnation His Son might wend his way toward spiritual maturity."

Latier waved hefty clenched fists toward the studio ceiling. "Now behold, the man in the lobster suit has come here to say unto you that when the agents of a dark and oppressive tyranny endowed the crafty Ulf with an entire navy—a navy built entirely by unknown Galactics, a thumping transgression of the Enclave Statutes next to which my own violations stand as the tarnished coins of the iniquitous alongside the gleaming tithes of the just—um, where was I?"

"Dark and oppressive tyranny," Red Exoskeleton supplied. "Navy built by Galactics."

"Thank you. It came to pass that when the hideous forces of the Whore of Babylon, the great and abominable Church of Vatican, raised an entire *army* among the Jaremian autochthons—the strongest army raised on the tortured face of Jaremi Four since before the Tuezi performed all manner of abominations thereon—when, thereafter, Unholy Mother Church compounded her perversity by endowing that fetid army with yet *another* navy—and when *that* navy lay ensconced in the half-circular bay, girding to spew a fatal thrust inland, toward the very throat of the Son of God—then, the man in the lobster suit will tell you, I stretched forth *both* my hands and dropped the Judgment of the Lord down upon them. Powie! And I stretch forth—oh, never mind, you get the idea. *Yea.* It is all as mine enemies say.

"For behold, I caused one of mine own illegal satellites to drop one of its con-tramagnetic inverters into the briny vastness of Jaremi Four's Equatorial Sea. And it penetrated therein, sinking deep into the bosom of the waters, wherein it deto-nated according to the commandments that bound it, for behold, my minions had devised it to explode with passing great power. And it came to pass that the waters drew back, and clustered without the half-circular bay. And I say to you that the iniquitous Vatican ships became beached, and behold, they lay upon the draining sands like, well, like iniquitous Vatican ships out of water, for gosh sake. And there-upon, it came to pass that the waters did mount up into towers of rage like unto the very banners and cimeters and battle standards and other tall things of the heavenly hosts. And the waters crashed down, crushing the remains of the iniquitous Vatican ships into fragments tinier than the fibers from which are woven the cart ropes of the sinners in all their brutish flagrancy. Which is to say, they were trashed, annihilated, wiped out, utterly forjeling *destroyed.*" He shrugged and smiled innocently. "What can I say but *yea? Yea,* 'twas me. Mine own doing, none other."

Latier raised his head. He folded his hands. "The man in the lobster suit will also tell you that on certain occasions I arranged for Spectators employed by OmNet to come to untimely—sometimes, permanent—ends, so as to prevent their covering Arn Parek's ministry in improper ways." He looked sheepish. "You guessed it. *Yea* again. But, hey." He spread his hands, palms up, and alternately raised and lowered them in a balancing motion. "On the one side, the Son of God. On the other"—he scrunched his face up—"one more journalist. Land o' Goshen, what would *you* do?"

Latier flashed a cherubic smile. "I say unto you, the man in the lobster suit is here to say unto you that I did all these things. And I tell you why not? For it was given to me by Almighty God to be the vessel by which His Son should be saved from the schemings of those *other* Galactics, those with their armies and their ships and their swollen budgets and their islands and their factory ships and their huge orbiting manufactories. With my humble small satellite network and my unas-suming unilateral tridee link to The Word Among Us, it came to pass that I con-founded them all. How could that be? Behold, I say unto you: only because such was God's plan for the deliverance and final victory of His Son."

Latier leaned over the railing. He yanked a tridee pickup around and pointed it toward Red Exoskeleton. "What about it, man in the lobster suit?"

"I prefer to be called High Investigator."

"As you wish, High Investigator. Please tell the Galaxy: Are the charges against me as I described?"

The investigator unrolled the indictment once more. "On my copy, they're much shorter. But, yes, Hom Latier, the charges are substantially as you say."

"Call me Alrue," Latier said cheerily. He twisted the pickup back on himself and raised his eyebrows. "It's all true, fems and homs. It really happened! Behold, I did conspire to violate the Enclave Statutes, to participate in the passage into manhood of God's Son, and to smite the wicked on His behalf whenever the Almighty so ordained." He blinked into the pickup, his eyes limpid as a cow's. "Should I be arrested for that? Is that . . . fair?" He spread his palms in a gesture of benediction. "If you'd like them to leave me alone, please use your polling devices now."

Struggling to keep his expression neutral, Beaman glanced from constable to constable, straining to read body language through their armor.

Little effort was required to interpret Red Exoskeleton's posture. He touched a finger to his helmet over his ear. He tore the helmet off and hurled it across the studio. "I swear, I'm gonna give up my commission. Let 'em go. Let 'em all go."

"What?" a dozen metallic voices demanded.

The tridee techs' wrist restraint tapes vanished.

"Government by forjeling sayback," Red Exoskeleton spat. "They believe him. Can you imagine the people believe him? They voted him a plorg-warming pardon."

The restraint tapes confining Beaman's body unwound and turned to vapor.

"What about due process?" a blue-suited deputy objected.

"Too many people *pov*ing," Red Exoskeleton rasped. "Because of the huge number that voted, the decision can't be overridden, not even by the Privy High Council." Red Exoskeleton picked up his helmet. He cradled it under his arm. "Stand down, everyone. Officers, constables, deputies, enforcers, commandos! Full retreat!"

"Leave quietly, please," Latier called, wiping his cheeks. "We're doing a 'cast here."

Beaman's waldo artists and metamodelers and affectational colorists sprinted back into the control center.

"Heat 'em up," cried the head metamodeler, his fingers dancing over controls. "Give me something happy. Blue sky, bright backlit clouds. Big organ chords. A couple tabernacles of vocal. Golden backlight on the First Elder!"

"Mother of stars," said a returning colorist, eyeing someone else's display. "Have you seen these saybacks?"

"Must be one of the most-watched 'casts in history," a tech breathed.

"Hop smartly, people," Beaman called. "This is victory!"

On the studio treadmill, Alrue Latier swallowed. His gaze flickered toward a monitor: The effects had come together. He seemed to stand upon a slowly revolving, endlessly growing marble pylon that rose perpetually into rain-cleansed skies. Luminous clouds wheeled about him. Angels and cherubim peeked from behind them. Celestial musics swelled.

"In for the closeup," Beaman breathed to his crew.

"Thank you! Thank you!" cried Latier to the Galaxy. "Thank you for believing. You know, don't you, that we all need to believe! We do. Yes, we do. We're all human beings, despite those fundamental differences the Whore of Babylon keeps striving to disguise. And deep in our hearts, we all need to believe. What's the truth of the secular world, anyway? A shifting chimera."

"Push in on me and plorg-wrap the angels," Latier barked over the subvocal command channel. *"Colorists, give me maximum humble and sincere. Brothers and sisters, it's time to pay for the repairs!"*

"I shall tell you about the truth I believe in," proclaimed Latier with swelling confidence. "I believe that the Lord has just now set me a table in the very presence of my enemies. Yes indeed, those enemies were right here, like a smelly old host of Lamanites. Behold, I defied them, and I won the victory. They're gone and I prevail, having supped mightily at the table which the Almighty ordained." He patted his stomach. "Mm, it was good, too." He leered toward the pickup. "But you know what? It was an expensive meal, and I'll need your help in picking up the tab. I need your Terran dollars and, most of all, your Galactic specie. Show me your faith by giving what matters most: your money. Come to think of it, there's still time to support my mission to Minga Four. You know, we haven't talked about that in such a very long time. Those Minganese are still suffering, bless their hearts, and I've still got one or two small ships impounded down th—I mean, on the surface doing the Lord's work. You can testify your faith by calling my processing center. . . ."

119. Vatican

The early afternoon sky shimmered in pistachio swirls. Pope Modest the Fourth dropped his eyes from the overarching skylight. "We face perhaps the most unique and frightening juncture in the long history of the Universal Catholic Church," he intoned, "and by 'we,' valued advisors, We mean all of us." Modest looked down from his broad dais. Nine leading men of the church occupied damasked seats around an immense, flat-topped ring of amethyst. At the pontiff's right hand sat Alois Cardinal Rybczynsky: pallid and severe, resplendent in crimson watered-silk choir dress. To Rybczynsky's right sat the Dean of the Stewards, his body tense within the brocaded green cassock of his order. Next was the Cardinal-President of the Council for Devout Protocol, resplendent in archaic *magna cappa.* Then came Fram Galbior, father of the equilibrational calculus, in a high-necked gray brocaded cassock draped with a single midnight-blue sash. To Galbior's right sat the Cardinal-Prefect of the Congregation for Institutes of Consecrated Life and Societies of Apostolic Life, his tiny body afloat in a sea of silk and jewels. Past him, the Cardinal-Prefect of the Congregation for the Evangelization of the Worlds fumbled with a pectoral cross hewn from a single immense diamond. Aresino Y'Braga,

Father General of the Society of Jesus, sat on a straight-backed chair. Among these grandly accoutered churchmen, his plain black cassock was a subdued indictment.

"Steward Galbior?" the pontiff called.

Galbior stood. "Your Holiness."

"We must know one thing this day. Is Arn Parek the Christ?" the pope demanded.

"Yes," Galbior proclaimed stridently.

Modest steepled his fingers. He began to smile.

Galbior nodded stiffly. "You have declared it the infallible teaching of the Church."

Modest stopped smiling. "Yes, Hom Galbior, We infallibly proclaimed Parek the true Christ. But before that, We had infallibly proclaimed that Parek was *not* the Christ."

"Had Your Holiness asked the question then, I would have answered *no.*"

Modest closed his eyes. "The doubters, the mockers—they say faith found too suddenly makes a man stupid. We begin to think they are right."

"Holiness?" Galbior whispered. He glanced around the huge table, marking Rybczynsky's stoic smirk and Y'Braga's look of muted censure. To Galbior's right, the theologians Sfix Geruda and Xyrel Hjinn stifled titters.

"We wish to address Galbior the mathematician," rumbled the pope. "Ignore what We have taught about Parek. And remember it is your Pontiff who commands that."

"As you wish, Holiness."

So, Hom Galbior, what do *your equations* say? Is Parek the Christ?"

Galbior tugged nervously at his sash. "My equations say Parek could be the Christ, to be sure. But so could any Jaremian male under age thirty-three. So, still, could any male child who may be conceived during the next three years."

"That would suggest the odds *against* Parek's being the Christ are several hundred million to one."

"Three hundred million, two hundred thousand, six hundred and ninety-seven to one," Galbior said brightly. "Of course, that is only the counsel of my computations. It is nothing compared with the revealed truths of Holy Mother Church."

The Pope's voice cracked as he said, "Then your mathematics says Parek is probably not the Christ."

"No, Holiness! The issue is simply indeterminate. You recall that here I work at the ragged edge of my equations' resolution. That resolution will improve with future Incarnations."

"There's a source of comfort," Y'Braga piped up.

"Esteemed Father General," said Galbior icily. "Out of all the places the Galaxy contains, my equilibrational calculus identified Jaremi Four as the site of the next Incarnation. Of the truth of that there is no doubt. Then, out of all history, my calculus identified a band of no more than thirty-six years during which this Cosmic Christ can have taken on flesh."

Y'Braga chuckled. "With your proud calculus you imagine you can read the mind of God. This may yet bring Mother Church to disgrace and ruin."

Rybczynsky watched the Jesuit superior through narrowed eyes. *Y'Braga is right. What he doesn't mention is that if the Parek affair brings the Church to her knees, Y'Braga's Jesuits will be able to say that all this happened over their objec-tions. They'll surge back into favor.*

Stiffly, Y'Braga rose to his feet. "Four years ago, Steward Galbior could not say for certain whose flesh the Cosmic Christ would assume. Today he still cannot. How has Holy Mother Church responded to this ambiguity? Clumsily, at best. While Your Holiness was at first convinced that Parek was not the Christ, Cardinal Rybczynsky set into motion an elaborate series of intrigues. Through the agency of Cardinal Semuga, God have mercy on him, a vast illegal infrastructure was created across Jaremi Four. An outlaw army was raised among its autochthons. The army was transformed into a navy, which then went to sea to smite Parek, whom we all still thought the false Christ.

"Only then, when we no longer had any way of calling the navy back, was it suddenly decided that no, Parek *is* the Christ. Now the tatters of that confusion threaten to consume us." Y'Braga crossed his arms. Coldly his eyes tracked from Rybczynsky to the pontiff. "The sin of this is easy to determine. It is pride. Your Holiness, Eminent Cardinal-Secretary of State—you and others made the error of imagining that after managing His Son's Incarnations altogether competently for countless millennia, God the Father suddenly required our assistance."

"General, *sit down!*" Devout Protocol roared.

"No," the pope said gently. "Surely at this time of crisis We must hear all sides, whether couched in respectful tones or not. Father General, I can only reply by noting that the circumstances of this Incarnation are unique." He gestured toward Galbior. "God has vouchsafed to us the means to predict—even if not as precisely as We might prefer—the time and place of this Incarnation. This is the *first* time a self-consciously Christian institution has been allowed such knowledge. Of course it is also the first time a Christian institution has possessed the Galactic scope to participate directly in an Incarnation narrative."

"Because the Church can thrust Herself into the unfolding of this particular Incarnation, She *should*—is that your contention, Modest?" Y'Braga riposted. "For centuries we have stood firm against arguments of this character when advanced to defend uses of technology contrary to Scripture. On what grounds can you presume to justify this conduct?"

Modest spread his palms. Krammonz set a chalice before him bearing a single swallow of Appenine spring water. Modest swigged. He then spoke thoughtfully. "Surely God's Church has not grown so rapidly . . . encircled a Galaxy in Her loving arms . . . deciphered the footprints of so many Christs—surely all that has not occurred without being part of some divine plan. Mother Church was given riches and power because She is called to a great work. Has it not always been so?"

Y'Braga settled back into his chair. "In that there is truth. Holy Mother Church has grown at a rate She has not experienced since She forged the Donation of Constantine. Still, it remains unclear how it follows from *that* that the Almighty is unwilling—or unable—to send His Son on a simple errand without our help."

"Help?" Geruda said abruptly. "If Parek is the new Christ, we are no help to Him. In hours, perhaps minutes, we shall destroy Him."

The Dean of the Stewards raised a cautioning hand. "It is not *we* who will do that."

"It will be done by the force we raised," Evangelization of the Worlds said grimly. "After Semuga, the whole Galaxy knows our role in it."

"Deniability is no longer among our options," Rybczynsky agreed.

"What *are* our options, then?" Modest demanded.

With a thin smile Y'Braga drew a physical scroll from the sleeve of his black cassock. Theatrically he unrolled it. "In the twelfth century of Terra, a bishop named Dietrich von Nieheim was battling heresy. He set down the grim options that are open to a man of God in desperate times." In a resounding voice Y'Braga read: " 'When the existence of the Church is threatened, she is released from the commandments of morality. With unity as the end, the use of every means is sanctified, even cunning, treachery, violence, simony, prison, death.' " With his face neutral, Y'Braga locked eyes with the pope. His practiced hands seemed to roll and hide the scroll on their own volition.

"General Y'Braga?" Devout Protocol asked.

Y'Braga smiled aridly. "Yes, Excellency?"

"What is 'simony'?"

Y'Braga consulted his wrist display. "The buying and selling of ecclesiastical offices or pardons."

"You want us to pay someone to forgive the Church?"

"If only it could be that easy," Y'Braga said painedly.

"Treachery . . . violence," Kwaede recited.

"Prison," continued Evangelization of the Worlds.

"Death," Geruda concluded.

Institutes of Consecrated Life shrugged. "Sfelb, we've tried all those."

Y'Braga nodded. "Of Bishop Nieheim's options, the only one we haven't explored sufficiently is cunning."

Rybczynsky bristled. "I beg to differ!"

"Ahh, Alois," Y'Braga said with uncharacteristic familiarity. "You and Semuga showed cunning when you sent down your scrolls and predicted auroral storms. But that was tactical cunning. I envision something more sublime. Call it strategic cunning, perhaps even theological cunning."

"Go on, Father General," said the pope.

Y'Braga rose. He approached a lonely pillar near the center of the room. The Egyptian obelisk was said to have been the last object the Apostle Peter beheld as he was crucified upside down at the hands of the Emperor Nero. Everyone knew the story had no scriptural warrant, appearing only in an apocryphal *Acts of Peter* purged from the canon by an early church council. Yet for centuries the obelisk had dominated a square in the old Vatican City, and when Roman Church became Universal Church, some prelate had seen fit to bring the obelisk to planet Vatican and place it near the center of this confidential conference chamber. "As you've said, Holiness, the circumstances of this Incarnation are in some ways unique," Y'Braga mused. "Still, there are abiding elements which form a part of every genuine Incarnation. Think of Sfem Brogradus, Hezho Dhebbuniad, Judas Iscariot, Fons Maguffin."

"Fons who?" Hjinn interjected.

"Fons Maguffin," the Dean of the Stewards supplied. "When the child Christ of Wikkel Four died on the playground, Fons Maguffin was pushing the swing."

"In every Incarnation there is a Betrayer," Y'Braga explained. "Someone who sets into motion the events that end in the death of Our Lord. Someone whose action, driven by base motives, forces the Christ to overcome his human half's reluctance to accept the coming Passion. The Betrayer is almost universally reviled. Yet without these figures, Christ's saving resurrections would never occur."

"I don't believe We have ever thought of it that way," the pope breathed.

"No, Holiness, but others have. From time to time Betrayers *have* been revered by certain Christian communities. Learned doctors?"

Hjinn and Geruda tapped queries into their modelers. "On Terra, Gnostic sects such as the Cainanates and the Ophites venerated Judas Iscariot," Hjinn reported.

"On Kfardasz," Geruda added, "members of a long-lived heresy esteemed Vebla Rasz Gomaystek more highly than the local Christ, whom she had betrayed. They felt Gomaystek was a more perfect sacrifice because as a suicide, she remained in hell forever while the Christ left hell after three days."

Hjinn nodded. "On Ordh a long-lived heretical community revered the Ordhian Betrayer, one Scabillax Veuth, who turned the Ordhian Christ over to the authorities only because he thought the Christ would defend himself with miracles and reveal Himself as a worldly messianic leader. Only when it was clear that the scheme had horribly backfired, Ordhian scriptures say, did Veuth take his own life."

"Thank you, learned doctors," Y'Braga wheezed. "Holiness, esteemed colleagues, that is the counsel of cunning which I offer today. As the pontiff has observed, the Incarnation on Jaremi Four is already unique in many ways. It will be unique in at least one more. *It will be the first Incarnation in which Christ's own Church will play the role of Judas Iscariot.* Like it or not, before the day is out we will be the agents of Arn Parek's death. We will be Fons Maguffin. We will be Scabillax Veuth. We must search the Galaxy's Christian traditions in search of minority doctrines in which the Betrayer is honored rather than vilified. Only thus can we hope to introduce one *more* unique element to this Incarnation narrative—to make this the first Incarnation in which the Betrayer is not driven to guilty self-destruction."

Evangelization of the Worlds locked eyes with the Dean of the Stewards. Devout Protocol scanned the faces of Hjinn and Geruda. Rybczynsky and Institutes of Consecrated Life exchanged calculating glances.

After a moment, they all turned to the pope. Grimly, almost as one, they nodded.

"We are agreed, then," whispered Modest. He, too, polled the participants' eyes. He lingered longest on the Dean of the Stewards. Of them all, he had the most to lose by Y'Braga's triumph.

The Dean fingered the gems in his elegant sash. "I can add nothing to this."

So quickly the tides turn, Rybczynsky thought.

"We, too, concur," announced the pope. "General Y'Braga's path is the only one open to us." Modest lifted the gem-studded golden pectoral cross from his snow-white simar. He kissed it. "Learned doctors, I shall need an encyclical—ideally, one I can deliver while Parek yet lives."

"That could be only minutes, Holiness. By your leave." Hjinn scrambled to his feet. Geruda followed. Their trains of servitors followed them out of the chamber.

"Holiness," Y'Braga said unctuously, leaning against the Petrine obelisk. "Perhaps now is the time to discuss the terms for rehabilitating the Society of Jesus."

120. Jaremi Four—Southern Hemisphere— Parek's Ruins

F or more than two hours Brethren captains had led the people in chanting and song. At intervals nervous lookouts would scramble into the amphitheater, announcing that enemy forces were creeping downriver or advancing out of the forest. Always the captains said the same thing. "The Word Among Us commanded: This battle shall not be won on the ramparts. We'll win it here."

"Pa-rek! Pa-rek!" the people would cheer. Tens of thousands of exhausted believers surrounded the central stage.

Perched on the edge of her platform two-thirds of the way up the highest scaffold, Ruth Griszam shook her head. She'd been scanning laterals from Linka Strasser and other Spectators among the approaching forces. *Parek cuts this too close,* she thought. *He won't have time to feign a death and resurrection before the enemy strikes. Or is he planning to feign death?* She frowned, thinking uneasily of all the munitions stored in the cistern beneath the stage.

She looked up as bell lyres pealed. *Clang-shang-ralang.* **Clang**-*shang-ralang. Clang-shang-ralang.* "The time is now!" shouted Chagrin, striding onstage in white leather, wireless mike to his lips.

Up went the cry. "Pa-rek! Pa-rek! Pa-REK! Pa-REK!"

"Silence!" Chagrin called. "In His name, silence!" The tiered throngs fell still. For the first time Ruth could recall, Chagrin spoke without notes. "We've seen The Word Among Us work many miracles. The Miracle of the Ships, there was a big one. One time I even found The Word Among Us dead. I watched life stream back through him as he returned from an errand among the skygods. But *this.* . . ." Chagrin chuckled. "Nothing that's come before can prepare you for what you're about to see. Before our eyes The Word Among Us will die and rise again. He'll come in glory and power to slay our enemies. He'll lay them flat like the grasses of autumn. Soldiers of the skygods . . . seekers after a restored civilization . . . I give you The Word Among Us!"

Bell lyres clanged. Voices screamed. Feet stomped. Hands slapped.

Out from behind the wooden tower that served as the stage-right proscenium strode Arn Parek. He wore a sleeveless high-necked tunic of white leather. It was assembled from overlapping vertical panels, giving it the look of stylized armor. The garment ended above his knees. On his feet were thick-soled sandals. Narrow white leather straps crisscrossed his calves, vanishing below his knees into white fabric garters decorated with wildflowers. A white leather skullcap concealed the short-cropped hair of his scalp with its shaven triangle. In the front, the cap reached almost to his eyebrows; at the back it flared to let his full black mane escape down his shoulders.

"Pa-REK! Pa-REK! Pa-REK! Pa-REK!" shrieked the crowd.

Clang-shang-ralang. Clang-shang-ralang. Clang-shang-ralang, jangled the bell lyres.

Arms held high, head turreting slowly, Parek marched forward. He seemed to make eye contact with every person in the house. With a wry expression he stepped over Ulf's assassins, who still slept in a scatter of bamboo center stage. He continued downstage. Slowly, grandly, he peeled off his skullcap.

At once parallel rivulets of blood began to trace their way out of his scalp, through the patterned stubble on his forehead, and down his face.

It was as though he wore an invisible crown of thorns.

Arms held high, Parek turned left and right, showing his worshippers his blood-striped face. *The scalp bleeds easily,* Ruth thought. *He probably made half a dozen small cuts before he donned that skullcap, then relied on its pressure to hold the blood back until he was ready.* Among the crowd, voices buzzed. People looked from neighbor to neighbor, barking questions. *Jaremian religion contains no exact analog to the crown of thorns,* Ruth thought. *The autochthons find the image of Parek drenched in blood dramatic, but it has no deeper associations for them.* She followed Parek with her eyes as he mopped his brow with his fingers. He swept his arm, flinging blood like rain into the first few rows. People scrambled for the precious droplets. *This symbol is intended for just one person here,* Ruth realized coldly. *Me. Me, and for the Galaxy watching through my eyes.*

Part of Ruth's consciousness peered within to monitor the attackers' progress. Wary of booby traps that weren't there, Labokloer's advance troops crept slowly across the burned-out hulks of Ulf and Parek's fleet. Still, in minutes they'd be on the muddy slope, just one long dangerous sprint from the ruins. *It'll be close,* Ruth thought. *Does Parek even care what his own people see? Does he care any longer what happens to them? Or is everything from here on out solely for Galactic consumption?*

"Time is short," Parek intoned as if he'd read Ruth's mind. He stepped a manlength upstage. His face shone like crimson glass. "Chagrin!" he called. "Bring the device."

Ruth caught her breath as Chagrin and three Brethren wheeled a bizarre contraption onto the stage. It bore marks of having been crafted on the spur of the moment. Yet its nature could not be mistaken. Not by a Galactic, anyway.

The outsized wooden *T* had been hewn from two stout wooden beams. Each was half a meter thick. The upright stood as high as a man's shoulder blades. Near its base a tangle of ropes and chains and leather straps depended from two fat rusty eyebolts. A similar arrangement sprouted from just above the beam's midpoint. As for the crossbar, it stretched broader than the span of a man's extended arms. Near each end dangled more eyebolts, more ropes, more chains and straps. The whole assemblage rode on a wheeled cart made from metal rods that seemed too slender to bear this nightmare burden. *Maybe the beams are hollow inside,* Ruth thought. *But why bother doing that?*

"Here," intoned Parek. Chagrin and his Brethren wheeled the device to the spot the prophet indicated. They set ponderous brakes.

Action in one bubble diverted Ruth's attention. The bulk of Labokloer's troops had streamed out of the woods less than five hundred meters from the perimeter of the ruined city. A skeleton force of Parek troopers defended the ramparts. They opened fire with steamrifles and light artillery. Attackers fell here and there all across the broad advancing battle line. But there were only a handful of snipers and thousands of *them*. Hundreds of enemy rifles drew beads on the ramparts. Steam spurted from their barrels. The rampart crest seemed to go soft with spewing dust and pebbles and rocks. Bodies whirled and fell.

That nest of troopers would defend no more.

A second later, the cracks of massed rifle fire reached the amphitheater. Parek's faithful were too riveted to the stage to pay attention.

Parek strode along the stage lip, pointing into the audience. "Volunteers!" he cried. "You, and you, and you, and you!" Two soldiers, a fashioner, and a cook's assistant sprinted onto the stage, their hearts on fire with the honor of having been selected. Moving economically, Chagrin showed each man where to stand. One near each end of the crossbar. One on either side of the upright.

Fidgeting with something in the shoulder of his tunic, Parek backed toward the rude wooden cross.

"The Word Among Us needs silence!" Chagrin barked.

The bell lyres stopped. The chanting and stamping and slapping stopped.

In another bubble, Ruth watched the first of the attacking navy's troop carriers scrape ashore. Drunk on adrenaline, soldiers dashed onto carbonized ground, their eyes and gunbarrels a-flit in search of opponents they never found.

Another transport surged ashore, then another and another.

Parek backed against his cross. "Lock me in," he commanded the volunteers. "Tie the ropes around my feet, my waist, and around my wrists. Then the leather straps. Lash up the chains. Lock them tight."

One more bubble: Sheltered by a deep cleft in a rock overlooking the embankment, three defenders with automatic rifles opened fire on the soldiers debarking from landing craft. A score fell; three score more scattered or fell in the water. An artillery boat roared forward, her engines howling, bow rising from the froth. Her howitzers belched. Fountains of fire and dust leapt from the rock face above and below the defenders. Finally a shell found their hiding place. Flame, gas, and gravel vomited forward, incinerating the snipers as it collapsed their hidey hole.

Another bubble: Labokloer ran along his line like a crazy man, waving his troops forward. At brigade strength, Catholic infantry began to march up the muddy slope toward the ruins, fifty abreast.

"Am I completely confined, gentlemen?" Parek demanded. The four volunteers nodded. He was triply confined with ropes and leather and chain at each wrist, his waist, and his feet.

"Take your seats," barked Chagrin, hustling the star-struck volunteers offstage.

Parek stood in front of the fallen assassins, lashed to his cross, his face slick with blood.

"All is ready, Word Among Us," Chagrin intoned.

Parek nodded. He tried to move. Chains glinted, rope and leather tightened. He was immobilized.

Eyes blazing, Chagrin backed toward stage right, trying not to react to the rifle and artillery fire now sounding continuously in the middle distance. With much squeaking and rumbling, fashioners pushed in wheeled scaffolds from either side of the stage. They met several manlengths behind Parek. The planks across their top formed a continuous catwalk, spanning the stage some three meters in the air. Fashioners wheeled bamboo staircases up against the scaffolds. Wordlessly, Brethren officers mounted the stairs. They sprinted across the catwalk.

There was a moment of perfect silence. Downstage, Parek writhed on his cross. Behind him, three dozen gaudily armored officers stood side by side atop the scaffolds, feet spread, arms akimbo. Ruth used the moment to check her saybacks. *Four thousand trillion people are poving this,* she thought, awestruck. The Galaxy had laid down almost all its business to *pov* through her. She thought she could feel its weight.

Artillery thundered nearby. "Hear that?" Parek cried. *"They* think those sounds mean our doom. Now behold as I step to the very threshold of death . . . and leap across it . . . thus to accomplish our deliverance!"

Clang-*shang-ralang. Clang-shang-ralang. Clang-shang-ralang. Clang-shang-ralang. Clang-shang-ralang.* **Clang**-*shang-ralang.*

Parek writhed against his bonds. Ruth noticed that he had so far managed to work one foot free of the rope and the chains, though not yet free of the leather strap.

Another bubble: the Spectator was a foot soldier scrambling off the embankment and into the first tier of relic structures. Boots kicked down doors. Gun barrels, then soldiers darted into dark empty rooms. "Where the sfelb is everyone?" a sergeant barked.

Parek's left foot pulled free of its last restraint. While most people were staring at that, Parek jerked his head to the side. Ruth hadn't noticed the stiff little tube protruding above the left shoulder of his leather tunic. Parek took its end into his mouth. He bit down.

In one corner of Ruth's awareness, telemetry cascaded. A Galactic nulgrav generator had whirred alive.

Hers.

"Pa-*rek.* Pa-*rek.* Pa-*rek.* Pa-*rek.* Pa-*rek.* Pa-*rek.*"

Parek and his heavy cross began to stir. In a sudden movement, they lurched a hand's width out of the cart and into the air.

The chanting stopped. The chiming stopped. The crucified Parek floated gracefully a manheight, then two, above the stage.

Parek's most clever, Ruth thought. *He managed to rig a bite controller and interface it to my nulgrav unit. He must have had it built into . . . what? The cross? His leather suit?* Ruth stood. Smoothly she sidled as far to her right as her platform would allow, adding the power of slow lateral movement to what was already an incredible image.

"Freedom!" Parek cried. After the levitation, it seemed almost anticlimactic when he withdrew his left hand from a now-useless jumble of ropes and leather and chains. He brought his hand to his throat and peeled away a vertical strip from his armorlike tunic. It revealed a tall narrow compartment sunk into the layered garment, extending from just below his Adam's apple to just above the fetters still binding his waist. The compartment was at most a fingerlength deep. But it offered space enough to contain Ruth's stolen nulgrav generator—and also a long combat knife with an ornately decorated golden handle.

Parek pulled out the knife. He held it high, twisting it slowly. His eyes darted around the vast chamber, seemingly aglow against the blood-soaked blackness of his skin. For a burning moment those eyes looked straight into Ruth's. He seemed to wink at her.

"I am The Word Among Us!" Parek shrieked. "I am the Ancient of Days, the One Mighty and Strong! See me die for you!"

His face betrayed no expression as he
drew
the
blade
straight
across
his
throat.

Ruth caught a glimpse of the jagged wound. *If he faked that, I'll be forjeled if I can see how.*

Parek's head bobbed forward. It would be Ruth's last image of him.

Just then, an enemy mortar shell dropped from the sky. It crashed through the stage and exploded among the munitions clustered in the cistern.

The stage vanished with an intolerable roar.

Ruth threw herself back from the lip of her platform. Shrapnel whanged against its stamped iron underside. Hastily Ruth subvocalized the command sequence for battle mode. While her implants retuned, she clutched swaying scaffolding and listened to debris clatter like evil rain.

After the stage explosion, the attackers knew just where their quarry was.

Mortar shells thudded down among the surviving onlookers. Smoke retched upward. Bodies and scraps of planks spun into the air.

Enemy infantry surged into view, pumping shells into the amphitheater.

The air was brown with smoke—orange or red when explosions roared. Ruth clambered down the pitching scaffold, searching desperately for Parek. *Probably vaporized,* she thought. She glanced where the stage had been. The forward half was gone, the cistern an open maelstrom of fire and smoke below it. Amazingly, the big explosion had not killed the Brethren officers on their catwalk. The scaffolding had been too far upstage. But the blast had weakened its supports. With an eerie grace the Brethren's catwalk collapsed. Guardsmen tumbled screaming into the flames.

There's a caption for you, Ruth thought with wry cruelty, *Brethren in cistern.*

Below, hand-to-hand combat had broken out. Attackers on the amphitheater's rim fired indiscriminately into the tumult, dropping friend and foe alike. Ruth looked about feverishly, vision maxed. *I still can't see Parek.* One of her bugs still

functioned, high above; Ruth fed its output into a tactical modeler. Its display rippled open in her interior awareness. A bright green line stuttered through the
image, marking a high-probability escape route that would open in two . . . one. . . .

Now! Ruth let go the scaffold. She dropped several bodylengths into a gap that
suddenly opened in the carpet of struggling bodies. Her flash stasis field triggered
briefly, breaking her fall. Simultaneously watching the scene before her and the
jagged path in her tactical display, Ruth lurched through the swirling mob. The
modeler had done its usual acute job of reading metapatterns in crowd movements.
More than once Ruth felt a stab of unreality as she plunged toward some knot of
wrestling soldiers only to watch it roll aside or tumble open before her. Once, twice,
distant snipers' shells struck her. Her stasis field caught the rounds. In all this
bedlam, no one would notice.

Whenever she could, she scanned the air and the ground for Parek. She set
one detector module to seek her stolen nulgrav's distinctive power signature. It
found nothing.

Ruth had drawn near the rim of the amphitheater. In the tactical display, her
bright green course jinked around a pillar and cut hard left. With unthinking confidence she threw herself in that direction. She collided with an enemy soldier and
pitched onto her back. The attacker dropped atop her, knees pinning Ruth's forearms. The soldier's face was invisible behind puffy fabric armor. Through its slim
eyeslits nothing could be seen.

A steampistol pushed hard into Ruth's neck. *Direct contact,* Ruth thought forlornly. *My shields won't protect me.* All at once, it occurred to Ruth that the soldier
should have killed her by now. *What the sfelb is . . . ohhh.*

Among the dozen-odd bubbles still flickering in her interior awareness, one
returned a picture of Ruth. Her likeness was shrouded in red, showing that the
equipment had recognized her Galactic Escher lozenges. *The soldier kneeling over
me is a Spectator.*

"Daypart, Linka," Ruth rasped.

Linka Strasser reached up with her free hand. She tugged the body armor up
off her head. "Hi," she said, withdrawing the pistol. "Nice mess we helped start,
huh? Let's get the sfelb out of here."

Ruth started off in one direction, Linka in another. "Running a modeler, I am,"
Ruth called. "From a bug overhead."

"Then you steer." Linka clutched Ruth's wrist. The women dodged among victims and combatants, skirted columns of fire, and ducked raining debris. The
amphitheater was a charnel house of slaughter now.

They squeezed through a stone archway just before a mortar shell brought a
manheight of stones down upon it.

Up the escarpment, perhaps upon the promontory, they might have a chance.

121. The Trawler *Damocles*—Command Section

T he synthesized voice rang harshly across the Damocles bridge. "CRASH SEQUENCE, BEGIN. CRASH SEQUENCE, BEGIN." Will Bickel and the five software techs locked eyes briefly with Arla Gavisel.

Gavisel tongued her comm link. "Come in, *Bright Hope.*"

"Eldridge here."

"Captain, is *Damocles* doing anything unusual?"

"No. Why?"

"Bridge annunciators say the crash sequence has started."

"I know why," Eldridge said. "Arn Parek just died."

"Oh, plorg." Gavisel eyed each of team members in turn. "I can't order you to stay a little longer, but we know how *Damocles* is supposed to break up. The process takes several minutes, and the control section won't split off until all the cargo pods have jettisoned. I'd suggest we keep working until the trawler starts ejecting pods. We might find the command kernel first."

"That little drive shaft thing?" Bickel said.

Gavisel nodded. She asked the lead software tech, "Any idea how long we have to go?"

"None."

"Forty thousand lives ride on this," Gavisel husked. "We have to try." The techs returned their fingers to the black glass of the control pyramid. Bars and patterns of light danced around their fingertips. Gavisel and Bickel, too, returned their hands to the cold smooth surface and surrendered themselves to reverie.

Gavisel was uncertain how long she'd spent staring into the jumble of virtual conduits, solving knots of fractal dimension, prising away layers of tendrils representing alarm programs disconnected, intrusion sensors neutralized, booby traps turned back on themselves. The call from *Bright Hope* came just as she felt the deck rumble.

"The restraining pins that hold *Damocles*'s sections together just pulled back. Eject thrusters are preheating."

"Understood." Gavisel locked eyes with the lead software tech. "Time for you to go."

The tech smiled. "We can cut it closer than this."

Gavisel smiled. "Suit yourselves." Seven minds returned to the quest for the suicide program. Gavisel's virtual gaze tracked along the path of a sinuous blue tube as it laced over and ducked behind a major cluster of conduits. *There*, she thought. *I can tug it there and pull the whole section free.* Her intuition had been correct. Steady pressure against one ninety-degree loop pulled the blue tube free of its companions. A tangle of concealing structures pulled loose and floated off into problem space.

"That felt like a breakthrough," breathed a software tech.

"Everyone, focus on that section the X.O. opened up," barked the lead tech.

For the first time they had the impression of working at some depth. If they had no idea how much virtual spaghetti lay before them, at least the sidewalls were rising above them, a marker of their downward progress.

Deep, deep below them, something flashed red.

Bass rumbling slapped at their chests. The bridge seemed to jerk to one side.

"The eject sequence is underway," Wachieu's voice crackled. "Six pods are away." The overhead lights switched from white to red. Somewhere beyond the floor, turbines were spooling up.

The next voice from *Bright Hope* was Captain Eldridge's. "Time to leave, Arla."

Gavisel stood. "Sergeant Bickel, escort the techs back to the scouter. Plot an immediate return to *Bright Hope*. Beware flying debris."

The software techs didn't need to hear that twice. They double-timed down the corridor toward the embarkation lock. Bickel followed them for two strides before he stopped short and turned around.

Gavisel had resumed her seat before the interface pyramid. Her hands were pressed to its glossy blackness.

"Fem Gavisel!" Bickel cried.

"You have your orders, Sergeant," Gavisel said tonelessly, eyes still closed. "Get the techs on the scouter and out of here."

"What about you?" Bickel yelled.

"Forty thousand lives," Gavisel shouted back.

"Without the techs? In a couple minutes? You can't save them."

"Probably not," Gavisel said softly. "But if there's the smallest chance. . . ."

Bickel opened his mouth, but there was nothing more he could say.

"You distract me, Sergeant," Gavisel said with a touch of anger. "*Move!*"

Gavisel commanded herself to hurtle forward, deeper into the endless matrix of protective software. Banks of piping and glowing tubes and colorful helices peeled away before the relentless pressure of her awareness.

"Scouter is safely away," Wachieu's voice echoed distantly. "*Damocles* has now shed thirty-five of her seventy-four component sections."

The air around Gavisel filled with flashing light and hooting alarms. *Not much time left,* she thought. Her virtual path was blocked by a luminous orange thread. It traced a tortuous path like a hedge maze through nested quiltworks of tubing. *If I can work that thread loose, this whole complex of tubing will come away.* She stared at the thread, visualizing its path with a rich complexity her brain could only achieve while communing with a powerful thought engine. *There? Might as well try it.* She focused intention on the spot he'd chosen.

And tugged.

The thread gave and shuddered. Like an animal stirring in its sleep, the quilted tubing snapped into a new configuration. *Forjeler!* The thread was *more* tightly packed now, its insinuations fractally more devious. *Wrong place to pull,* Gavisel realized hollowly.

Suddenly two white arrows flickered into place at unlikely points on the thread. "You pull there," Will Bickel ordered. "I'll twist here."

Gavisel opened her eyes. "Sergeant, I gave you an order!"

Bickel shrugged, hands on the pyramid. "I got the techs onto the scouter and tabbed a safe course into the autopilot. You never said I had to go."

Briefly Gavisel locked eyes with the loyal sergeant-at-arms.

"There's no time," Bickel said gruffly.

Gavisel went back in. Bickel joined her. Gavisel pulled. Bickel twisted. The thread came free. Thousands of tubes broke away, spinning past them into emptiness or vaporizing in cascades of multicolored sparks.

Their awarenesses leapt forward and then down. "See that drive shaft thing?" Bickel asked.

After they had dived a seeming kilometer or two, a surface at last came into sight. Gavisel's heart sank. It was just more hoses and conduits and neon. "Keep going," she said grimly. "It could be just past this layer."

It wasn't. Nor was the narrow metallic cylinder that would represent the fundamental command kernel behind the next tangle they unraveled, or the next, or the next. Suddenly Gavisel found she could no longer concentrate; the howling of alarm horns in the bridge was too insistent.

The final module of the *Damocles* command section—the module containing the bridge—blasted free of the trawler's spine. Jerky acceleration thrust Gavisel and Bickel away from the pyramid. They slammed painfully into bulkheads several meters away.

Gavisel wondered what ejection had felt like for the pilgrims in the pods.

The pyramid lay uphill now, a stiff grade, at least forty percent. She dragged herself back up along the wall, clutching conduits and display screen shrouds and instrument rack handles. Bickel followed, panting. They passed a viewport. *Damocles* was completely dismembered—irregular chunks of the command section, the propulsion section, and the spine floated in formation amid the globular cargo pods.

Gavisel all but fell onto the interface pyramid. She shoved her mind into it. For a split second she saw the mocking, limitless confusion of tubes. Then the metaphor puffed away. The control program was shutting itself down.

Gavisel's *being-thereness* shuddered back to the bridge. The pyramid's faces were alive with indicators, all of them red. One by one they winked out. "P R O G R A M . . . C O M P L E T E," an annunciator squawked.

Engines howled. The gravity horizon began to shift again. "I think we're going in!" Bickel managed to say.

Gavisel came to amid a tangle of piping. Nothing virtual about it; sudden deceleration when the bridge module broke orbit had hurled her against a circuitry cabinet far down the central corridor. Gavisel tried to sit up. Several broken bones announced themselves. She howled with the pain.

"You too?" Bickel groaned, somewhere to Gavisel's left.

Gavisel forced her eyes open against agony. It was as if the bridge's central corridor had been set on end. A good ten or twelve meters straight up, the pyramid was lifeless, dusty black.

"I'm over here," Bickel croaked. He lay next to Gavisel, spattered with blood, his body all mixed in with a shattered console.

Something howled ear-splittingly.

From outside.

Gavisel managed to peer out a viewport. The limb of Jaremi Four shuddered and bucked. They were already so close that the planet had no apparent curvature. As Gavisel watched, the surface blinked and finally disappeared behind the angry glow of ionized superheated air. *That roaring—it's atmosphere rushing past.*

"Told you we were going in," Bickel gasped.

There was an immense clatter. Massive impacts cascaded down the hull from front to rear. *Something of genuine size tore loose outside.* With the final, sharpest concussion, Gavisel thought she saw a structural member buckle above her.

To her own surprise, Gavisel thought of praying. Not of doing it, not really— just of the subject. *Arkhetils tell a joke about an Ordhian on the brink of death who dies unsaved because he can't decide which of his three dozen gods to pray to first.* Gavisel reflected on her life: the Parek affair, government-by-sayback, the calamity of Vatican Island, the hundreds of thousands of meaningless tragedies this whole sorry fiasco had wrought among the autochthons. *Ineptitude, fanaticism, misplaced fidelity, cruel happenstance. Those brought me here; they're all that thrust any of us into this web of dilemmas,* she realized. *Which god to pray to? Why one of them?* He smiled knowingly. *No power that would plan things this way deserves my respect. And no power that would just let it happen is worth my time.*

"Fem Gavisel?" Bickel croaked. "I just wanted to say I'm sorry."

"For what?"

"The pyramid. The crash program," Bickel said. When his voice worked now, there was bubbling behind it. "All those pilgrims."

Gavisel blinked to clear her eyes of tears. "We tried, Sergeant."

"We failed." Bickel coughed up blood. He lay still for a minute. Gavisel watched the last of the control displays wink out overhead. "You know what I mean, Fem Gavisel," Bickel gurgled. "In the pyramid. The control interface. We never—" He coughed wetly. "We never got the shaft."

Gavisel looked up. With a calmness whose source she didn't fully understand, she watched the chamber above them twist. The module was breaking up. "I don't know, sergeant," Gavisel husked with what she was fairly sure would be her last breath. "I wouldn't be so sure about that."

122.   Jaremi Four—Southern Hemisphere— The Promontory

Linka and Ruth squinted down from the promontory rock. Peering north, they could see onto the tablelands that stretched away from the top of the cliffs. The north channel glistened. Near the cliff edge it formed rapids; half a klick inland, the river widened and slowed. There, two large motorized rafts, all that remained of Ulf's escape plan, were tied up. Staring south, the Spectators looked down the escarpment toward the burning hulk that was Parek's ruined city, down the muddy slope to the shoreline battleground.

With Ulf and Parek both apparently dead, command fell to Chagrin. He was doing a surprisingly good job of harassing the victorious Catholic forces. With clever use of sharpshooters he kept them off guard, unable to advance above the city. That made it possible for survivors from the city to sneak away through trenches and behind the cover of rocks and trees. They gathered among the scree at the foot of the cliffs, clustering near easily climbed routes to the crest.

"He's going to do it," Ruth hissed. "Son of a bitch, Linka, Chagrin's going to get several hundred people up those cliffs and up to that north channel."

Kalistor's voice hissed in their ears. *"Fem Strasser, Fem Griszam. Thought you'd like to know that the saybacks are holding. People are staying glued to this. Maybe they expect Parek to rise from the dead."* Kalistor's laughter broke off suddenly. When she spoke again, she was shouting at someone on her end. *"What the sfelb? What? Oh, forjel. Open the channel, give me everybody."* Kalistor pitched her voice down. Slowly, deliberately, she called, *"All Spectators. Attention all Spectators in and around the battle zone. Maximum alert. All previous assignments are belayed. Red alert, red alert! Go airborne, go airborne, go airborne!"*

"*Airborne?*" Ruth cried.

"Right now!" Kalistor replied. *"Brace for impact from orbit!"*

Linka stood. She armed her nulgrav and no-vis systems with two quick stabs of her thumbs.

Ruth stood, too. She reached for her belt. It was empty.

"Oh yeah," Linka said. "Your gear was on loan to the son of God. Hang on." Linka threw her arms around Ruth. Ruth clutched back. Linka subvocalized command syllables. Snapping invisible, the two Spectators shot into the air.

Ruth stared down at the receding landscape, Linka's hair whipping at her eyes. Chagrin's survivors had crested the cliffs; partway down the muddy slope, the attackers' disrupted columns were re-forming. Below that, the ruins were just a blot of fire. Below even that, Catholic troops were still marching out of the woods and sprinting off of the last of the landing craft.

"Colleague reveal," Linka was hissing at her. "Do it."

Ruth subvocalized the command. Suddenly she realized the skies were crowded.

More than a dozen no-vis Spectators surrounded them in midair, a kilometer up. A supply captain drifted near Ruth and Linka, rummaging in the bulging pockets of her quartermaster's jumper. "The moment you lost contact with Parek, Fem Kalistor scrambled every Spectator on Jaremi Four toward the battle zone," she explained without being asked. She held up compact no-vis and nulgrav units. She primed them and slipped them onto Ruth's belt. "All right, Fem Griszam, you can fly free now."

Ruth whispered her thanks to Linka and pulled away. She scanned the landscape. Ruth glanced straight up and stared. "What the sfelb is that?" she shouted.

"The sword of Damocles," Kalistor said. *"The trawler broke up and the pieces are thundering in. I'm told by Bright Hope that the pieces will crash in a circle of twenty-eight kilometers' radius centered on your current location."* Linka followed

Ruth's gaze toward the zenith. Even in daylight, the approaching wreckage formed a brilliant blotch of light. As they watched, it began to separate into separate coruscating points.

"Twenty-eight kilometers?" Ruth snapped. "What am I doing up here?" She dived and leveled out just six meters above the ridgetop. Angling downhill, she swept slowly above the main attacker column as it finally approached the cliffs. She was *poving* the soldier's faces as they noticed the specter in the sky. Mouths dropped. Eyes goggled. Men looked frantically about. Some lost step with one another. Once again, the column's cohesion broke down.

Ruth doubled back toward the cliffs. For effect, she buzzed the broad milky waterfall, then popped straight up. She rotated slowly above the clifftop, hanging meters above the surviving Parek forces. Some had clambered aboard the two rafts. Others hiked along the bank in a dense column. They, too, were just noticing the spreading mirage over their heads.

Ruth twisted and looked skyward. The points of light with their luminous trails had visibly diverged. Checking her tacticals, she turned gracefully on her long axis and sidled closer to where she knew the lead raft was. Her *pov* swept down from the sky—down, down—into a tight facial closeup of Chagrin staring at the splendor in the air. *Perfectly timed,* she exulted.

Impossibly wide-eyed, Chagrin raised his hands to heaven. Tears trickled through the grime on his cheeks. "We're here, Lord," Chagrin shouted to the sky. "Right here. See? I saved all these people for you."

"Ruth, I'm in awe of that shot," Kalistor said over a private channel. *"But now get back with the others for assignment. I mean now."* Kalistor clicked onto the channel all the Spectators could hear. *"Homs and fems, I'd appreciate your closest possible coverage of this crash. Crashes, actually. I'm told they'll be seventy-four simultaneous impacts. I have suggested postings for each of you. Try not to miss anything."*

Ruth rejoined the other Spectators. Simultaneously they downloaded the distribution assignments Kalistor had prepared. Ruth and two others stayed hovering one klick above the ruins; the rest jetted off in every direction.

Ruth lay on her back in the air, staring straight up.

Like an octopus unfurling its tentacles the contrails spread across the sky. Seventy-four yellow-white trails crept, then raced from the zenith, tracing jagged spokes across the wheel of the sky. Further—further—further—Ruth had to choose a single contrail. Her eyes followed it as it raced toward the horizon—as it struck.

The flash was blinding.

Linka floated above the scrubby forest perhaps a klick east and two klicks north of a predicted impact site. A pod screamed down sheathed in fire. While it was still in midair, she captured a split-second image of its roundness dimpling, crumpling, spewing away into a hail of fragments. The pieces hit the ground, blooming into a miasma of white. Accelerating, Linka followed the shock front's headlong gouge across the surface. For two, three kilometers, debris raced forward, seemingly in pursuit of its own vapor plume. It spat up trees, rocks, ancient twisted girders, the stones of forgotten buildings.

✦ ✦ ✦

Ruth's body hung vertical now. She panned off the impact she'd been *pov*ing and commenced a twenty degree-per-second rotation. All across her a gargantuan new forest rose: mushroom shrouds of topsoil and debris. Every five degrees another such spreading tower lanced the sky.

Ruth polled some of the other Spectator's *pov*s. One had jetted up to an altitude of fifteen klicks or so. The view from there didn't even seem real. The distribution of crash sites was perfect—seventy-four plumes of dust and fire described a twenty-eight-klick circle with Parek's ruins at its center. Meanwhile, Linka was executing a close fly-by of what remained of the pod whose crash she'd watched. As close as she dared, anyway. There was little to see—mostly fire and steam and settling curtains of superheated dirt. But one could make out twisted irregular shapes, the remains of structural members and a contramagnetic inverter and a docking bay. They were artifacts of substantial size which hundreds, perhaps thousands, of Jaremians would start exploring as soon as the fires cooled.

Reclining in an orbiting command ship, Neuri Kalistor gave herself over to bitterness. *The end of Enclave on Jaremi Four,* she thought. *Dear Laz, now the cause for which Linka Strasser sacrificed you has come to nothing.*

"Fem Kalistor?" a director said hesitantly. "Ready for your commentary."

"Oh?" she rearranged herself in her sling chair. "Kalistor commentary, begin in three . . . two . . . Just over forty thousand Ordhian pilgrims died in this choreographed destruction. Forty thousand lives—for what? If they could still speak, some of those pilgrims might have an answer for us. Their answer might be tinged with Pyrrhic irony, now that Arn Parek seems to have died without a trace, but it would be an answer all the same. These pilgrims committed their lives to lifting Enclave here; and whatever else one might say, or want to say, about today's debacle, it is undeniably the end of Enclave on Jaremi Four."

123. Vatican

The Pontiff's footsteps tapped hollow down the gold-floored corridor. Sweaty ovals darkened Pope Modest's white simar under the arms, down the sternum, and at the small of the back. He'd opened his garment at the neck. Three valets scuttled away carrying the alb, surplice, chasuble, and miter he'd already thrown to the marble floor as he burst out of the studio. Now the pope hastened down a darkened hallway, flanked by Rybczynsky and Krammonz. "We ask you, Alois, Wleti—has ever any Pontiff been so undone by his timing?"

"Holiness," Rybczynsky said consolingly, "there was no way to know Parek's apparent death would occur in the middle of your Judas speech."

"Do we know what it did to the saybacks?" Modest demanded.

"I'm sure it decimated them, Holiness," admitted Krammonz. "But you were heard by those who truly mattered: the ecclesiastical specialists, the Vatican watchers, and the rest of the opinion makers who will *pov* your speech or a digest of it before they compose their screeds tomorrow."

With the wordless hush of a cooing boychoir, the double doors of the pope's private library sighed open.

"Mothers of God!" Krammonz exclaimed.

"Security to the guest library," Rybczynsky breathed into the audio pickup. "Emergency, level three."

Krammonz, Rybczynsky, and the pope edged into the library. They stared toward the crystal ceiling and up at the gray-robed figure whose body hung by a scarlet sash from an Orhizan-crystal chandelier. Rybczynsky fastened long fingers around the hanged man's wrist. "Quite dead," he said redundantly.

"There's something in his other hand," ventured Krammonz.

Rybczynsky frowned. "It's a wafer."

"He hanged himself before taking communion?" the pope demanded.

"A data wafer, Holiness." Krammonz tugged the wafer free of digits bloated and purple with pooling blood. He handed the wafer to Rybczynsky, who slid it into a nearby data reader.

Krammonz and the pontiff crowded in to see the display. "What?" Krammonz breathed.

"I think it's Latin," Rybczynsky said in wonderment.

Krammonz shook his head. "Damnable neotraditionalists."

Half a dozen Swiss guards bustled into the room. Rybczynsky gave them quiet instructions. Silently they set about cutting the body down. Rybczynsky scowled at the screen.

"Latin," the pope complained. "Who reads that stuff anymore?"

"Hjinn reads Latin," Rybczynsky muttered.

"Get him in here."

"Quite the prose stylist," the theologian Xyrel Hjinn said admiringly, scanning the Latin text in the data reader's display. Swiss Guards bustled past with the body. He cringed. As he read on, his lower lip drooped lower and lower. He lay down the machine. "Holiness," Hjinn said in hushed tones, "I should prepare a careful translation and present it to you in the morning. In confidence."

"Why?"

"It's sensitive. One might even say, explosive."

"No matter," Modest said tiredly. "We will hear it straight out."

Hjinn's chin trembled. "Holiness, I don't know if—"

"Translate it now," the pope bristled. He fastened angry eyes on Hjinn. "We will hear it out loud."

"As you command." Hjinn picked up the reader. He glanced about. When he was certain none but Rybczynsky and Krammonz could overhear, he began to read:

" 'These last three years have been difficult ones for the Confetory and for Holy Mother Church, times filled with discord and embarrassment,' " Hjinn translated. " 'For many of these tragedies, it is widely acknowledged that I bear at least partial responsibility. This night I watched Arn Parek court death on a bastardized cross. At the same time I watched my Pontiff rush to claim for his Church the mantle of the Betrayer. I can only imagine the dead, the wounded—the churches, even cities, scarred by unrest—that will greet tomorrow's dawn. I feel I am to blame and I can stomach no more.

" 'Father General Y'Braga was right: In daring to predict the next Incarnation we have led ourselves into the sin of pride. But long before that sin besmirched the Church, it surged in my breast. I dared to imagine my limited intellect could unravel the plan of God.

" 'Errors like mine have a long history, if not a proud one. On the Church's homeworld, in the nineteenth century local, astronomers were astounded to find that the distances of Sol's planets from their star followed a numerical sequence. If memory serves—and in matters of this sort I'm cursed by a memory that's little short of eidetic—the planetary distances corresponded to a formula in which one took the progression *zero, three, six, twelve, twenty-four, forty-eight, ninety-six, one hundred ninety-two and three hundred eighty-four,* added four to each, then divided by ten. The correspondence turned out to be genuine, but meaningless; while the distribution of planetary distances indeed reflected that peculiar numerical sequence, the sequence had no relation to the processes that had caused the planets to occupy those particular orbits. To use a phrase we numbermongers are often too eager to avoid, it was just a coincidence.

" 'At about the same time, *circa* 1864 local, a gullible archaeoastronomer named Piazzi Smyth began to ruminate on Terra's famed Pyramid of Cheops. Dividing the length of its base by the width of an arbitrarily chosen stone, he got the exact number of days in the Terran year. Multiplying the height by a suitable exponent, he derived the distance between Terra and Sol. Dividing the perimeter by twice the height, he obtained a remarkably close approximation of *pi.* For centuries thereafter charlatans, mountebanks, and the deluded subjected random pyramidal dimensions to ever more sophisticated calculations. Often they obtained amazing values: the Planck constant, the magnetic moment of the electron, the half-life of sundry radioactives measured in oscillations of the element cesium, the contramagnetic integral, and so on. Time after time, they mistook correspondence for causation. Time after time, some numerical relation was invested with meaning it never deserved.

" 'A century later, it was fashionable among both Christians and Jews to subject various editions of Scripture to lavish mathematical processing. Self-proclaimed savants would stare up from their thought engines and claim they'd found future events foretold. They would even claim to detect the unambiguous signature of the Almighty Himself in the texts.

" 'Errors of this character are seductive. I do not make that point to lessen my shame. I say it to illustrate *why* it's so easy to forget the quiet skeptical counsel of common sense in situations like this. Just because the numbers work—just because the calculations are elegant—doesn't mean the numbers have any referent in the real world.

" 'When I believed in nothing, when I was a rash child who thought I could tear free the secrets of the universe entire if only I would calculate carefully enough—well, in those days I brought something impressive into the world. It was my good fortune to give humanity its first real weapon against the Tuezi, a tool that's served us well from that day forward.

" 'Much later, when I believed in far too many things, when I was a rash old man who thought I could snatch the secrets of God himself with my numbers, I found another wondrous coincidence. The equilibrational calculus that predicted the Tuezi also corresponded to the past Incarnations of Christ. In my pride I imagined I could predict the next one.

" 'Many have made use of my calculations. Many have abused them. And many—oh, how very many!—have been pulled into the fetid maelstrom of the Parek affair. Christ and God and Holy Mother Church have been cruelly mocked, most often at the Church's own hands. As this day ends, I find myself unable to imagine how a genuine God could tolerate such treatment at the hands of His creations. The mere fact that I go on living makes clear to me that nothing in religion can be true! Were there a God, were there truly Christs, surely they would smite me for the disgrace I have caused to be heaped upon their holy names.

" 'Too late, I realize the nature of my error. Like the astronomers, like the pyramid mystics, like countless others, I forgot to check my abstractions against reality. Did the beliefs through which I sifted my numbers for meaning actually mean anything in and of themselves? I know now, they did not.

" 'I write this to express the depth of my misery and my contrition. I can never truly atone for the devastation I've helped unleash. I deserve only to die a suicide—the sin for which no forgiveness is possible. Even that's not punishment enough. But it is all that remains within my power.

" 'Holy Father, when they ask you what became of me, I pray you will have the courage to share my words. In my faithful pride—my prideful faith—I forgot the most important difference between the calculations of my rash childhood and the calculations of my rash old age.' " Hjinn stared at the display a moment. He swallowed and pressed ahead with his translation. " 'Though the Tuezi are real, the Cosmic Christ is not. And now I go to meet my maker. I shall make that journey, even though I now believe it an engagement at which only I will appear.

" 'In days past I might have signed *Yours in Christ*. This day I sign:

" '*Yours in cold reality,*

" 'Fram Galbior.' "

124. The *Bright Hope*

T he improvised conference room had been turned into a full-fledged auxiliary control center. It was hot, crowded with people, thick with jumper cables and jury-rigged panels hanging open. Rushed back to life and jetted into orbit from North Polar the instant they'd lumbered out of the tanks, Spectators Tramir Duza and Cassandra Wiplien sat at a horseshoe-shaped table. Half a dozen small tridee projectors around the horseshoe threw up minimal tactical displays. Beside each

Spectator hulked a field delta-band transceiver from which thick cables ran into retrofitted wall jacks. The wall jacks, in turn, connected to external antennae whose usual client subsystems were still down. Other Spectators held stations elsewhere on *Bright Hope* or on the Vatican moonlet, which security personnel from *Bright Hope* were still exploring. Thus did the Spectators OmNet had lent the PeaceForce keep *Bright Hope* more or less in contact with the Galaxy.

Laurien Eldridge hunched over a portable tactical modeler. Lynn Wachieu slouched in an unpowered command chair, monitoring a handful of working consoles. Other officers milled about, intent on their various tasks.

No one wanted to make the first comment on the crew's—on *Bright Hope's*—shared failure.

An indicator's flashing caught Wachieu's eyes. "Captain, *Cornucopia* is making a transmission. All bands."

"Put it on," Eldridge said leadenly.

"On three," Wiplien replied. A new bubble spun open in midair.

Greder stood among huddled instruments. Her gray-brown body armor dully reflected unseen spotlights. "I am Orgena Greder, owner of Khoren Four and as such a recognized head of state. As provided by the Admiralty Code, I announce my world's intention to claim, annex, attach, bind, and colonize the former Enclave world of Jaremi Four. Our flagship, the factory trawler *Cornucopia*, now lies a short distance outside Jaremi space. We proceed at once to the surface to cement and administer our claim." The image winked out.

"How long before they touch down?" Eldridge asked Wachieu.

"Three hours."

"Incoming comm from High Command," Duza called. "It's an Admiral Hafen."

Hafen's ruddy-haired, green-eyed visage flickered into a large new bubble. "You heard that, *Bright Hope?*"

"Certainly did," Eldridge breathed. "Admiral, can Greder do what she says, just walk in and claim the planet?"

Hafen crossed his arms. "She's a head of state, and *Cornucopia* certainly enables her to set down on the surface. So yes, she can *make* the claim. It may not survive legal review. But the Khorenians will have achieved first contact all the same, which will position them to command an extortionate buyout from the Confetory. In addition, they'll no doubt retain preferential mercantile rights, and with them the power to shape the planet's economic development. Given what we know about Fem Greder, this would be just about the cruelest way the Jaremians could enter Galactic life."

Eldridge shrugged. *"Bright Hope* can neither move nor shoot. What can be done?"

Hafen smiled grimly. "You can claim Jaremi Four directly for the Confetory by making first contact before the Khorenians arrive."

"What, send a blue-ribbon delegation down on a scouter?"

"Has to be a capital ship," Hafen husked. "First contact protocols are strict and hallowed by millennia of tradition. If we send a scouter and Greder lands *Cornucopia*, first contact is hers."

"I remind the Admiral that the only capital ship in the area is a pile of junk," Eldridge said gently.

Hafen nodded. "For how long?"

Eldridge gestured for the admiral's patience. She and Wachieu tapped inputs into their modelers. "If damage control gives top priority to restoring inertial maneuvering, we probably can get *Bright Hope* onto the surface ahead of *Cornucopia*. We'll be half blind, in contact with High Command only through the Spectators. As we are disarmed, we'll be helpless if *Cornucopia* elects to make a shooting war of it. But I do believe we'll get there first."

"Then this order should come as no surprise, Captain Eldridge." Hafen snapped her an Academy salute. "Get there first."

Ninety minutes later, the conference room was an immense farm of auxiliary control consoles. Most of them were dark. "Status, please," Eldridge breathed.

"Inertial navigation should come online in two minutes," Wachieu reported.

"Spectator Duza is 'casting three-by-three greens from *Bright Hope*'s smallest and fastest scoutship, as you ordered, Captain," Wiplien stated.

Eldridge pressed her hands together. "I said it before, so I'll say it now. Here we are. The difference is, this time we're not staying."

Eldridge nodded. She scanned the room. One by one, previously dormant inertial navigation consoles flickered alight. "Just in time, Damage Control," she announced. "Thanks for a job well done."

"Standing by," Wachieu prompted.

"Launch the scouter."

"Here's Hom Duza's *pov,*" Wiplien called. A bubble opened above her table, showing *Bright Hope* as viewed through a scoutship viewport. Her hull was charred and buckled in a hundred places.

"Spectator Duza here," a voice crackled. "You weren't kidding, Captain Eldridge, this scoutship is *fast*. So far, no problems maintaining the subdelta band link."

Eldridge nodded. "Stand by to go live on my signal, Spectator. You're our secret weapon."

"Our only weapon," Wachieu breathed.

"Power up the drive accumulators," Eldridge called.

"Accumulating," called a tech.

"*Cornucopia's* increased her thrust," Wachieu called.

"Greder must've seen us powering up," Wiplien said. "She just made a broadcast saying they've maxed their engines. She now predicts *Cornucopia* landfall in thirty-one minutes."

"Almost an hour earlier," Eldridge breathed. She smiled toward Wachieu. "And within ninety seconds of your prediction, Lynn. Okay, people, stand by. From here on out we follow Plan C." She planted balled hands on her hips. "Wachieu, scan Hom Duza's scoutship if you would. Hom Duza, activate the scout's concealers."

"Done," Duza's voice crackled.

"They're working," Wachieu reported. "I can no longer see the scoutship with such Detex as I have."

"Hopefully, neither can *Cornucopia,*" Eldridge said anxiously. She splayed her fingers over the helm console. Light spattered across its face. She felt thrumming in her feet as the engine prewarmers maxed.

"Ready for inertial deceleration," Wachieu sing-songed.

"Course laid in, navigationals are hot," chanted another officer.

"Our estimated time of touchdown is twenty-two minutes ahead of *Cornucopia*'s,*" Wachieu called out. "*Cornucopia*'s throttles are maxed; she can't put on any additional speed."

"Retro-ing out of orbit," Eldridge said abstractedly. In Duza's lateral they could see the drivegates pulse white and purple all along *Bright Hope*'s dorsal centerline. There'd been neither time nor power to tune the inertials precisely. Everyone felt a sidewise tug at their shins and in their chests.

"*Cornucopia* is hailing," Wiplien reported.

"I'll just bet she is." Eldridge wiped sweat from her face. "Let's see her."

Tridee player number five cast up an image of Greder. "We see her," Wiplien said. "She can't see us. She only hears us."

"*Bright Hope, Bright Hope,*" Greder called. "Explain your drive activity."

"We go to make first contact with the Jaremians," Eldridge said levelly.

"Jaremi Four is ours," Greder snapped.

Eldridge smiled thinly. "Not yet. Consult your copy of the Admiralty Code."

Greder's face vanished. "She's signed off," Wiplien said.

"*Cornucopia*'s heating up her guns," Wachieu called.

"Analysis of her armaments?"

Wachieu scowled at her displays. "Enough to reduce what's left of *Bright Hope* to neutrons."

Eldridge turned slowly, locking eyes with each person in the improvised control center. "This is just what we expected," she reminded them. "Let's stay calm and work the plan."

"*Cornucopia*'s hailing again, Captain," Wiplien cried.

"Also as expected," said Eldridge, beginning to smile. "Let's see her."

"Resume your orbit, *Bright Hope,*" Greder said imperiously. She gazed at something in her hand. "I have my copy of the Admiralty Code right here. I invoke section delta nine gamma dot four: We have already declared an approach vector crossing the orbitals over Jaremi Four. Your movement poses a collision hazard."

Eldridge knew the regulation. A craft facing a collision hazard could make limited use of its weapons to clear a preannounced flight path. *I've got to give her credit for trying.* She gestured for Wiplien to cut the audio link to Greder. Aloud, she said "Spectator Duza, come in, please."

"Duza here."

"Go live, Spectator. I say again, go live." Eldridge turned toward Wiplien. "When you have Duza's channel assignment, squirt it to my console."

"Understood, Captain."

"Now reopen my audio link to Greder." Eldridge spoke rapidly, almost breathlessly. "Apologies for the technical difficulties, Fem Greder."

"That's Tyrant Greder, if you don't mind."

"As you wish. I respectfully challenge your reading of the Admiralty Code.

What governs in this situation is actually Section epsilon five two zed dot—um, it's in there somewhere. Military craft may operate outside conventions of navigational courtesy in critical situations."

"This is not a critical situation," Greder replied in a mocking tone.

"You have made it so, Tyrant Greder. You energized *Cornucopia*'s weapons. I ask your intentions."

"I say for the last time, *Bright Hope*, resume your orbit."

"And I'll say this once, Tyrant Greder. Before you act, monitor OmNet." Eldridge glanced at her console. "Check out channel four-one-G dot six-two-three." Eldridge gave Wiplien a hand signal.

"All right, Tramir," Wiplien subvocalized. *"Start talking."*

Tramir Duza began his commentary. "Here is the schooner *Bright Hope*, horribly damaged. Her desperate crew has patched her back together just enough to attempt a surface landing, the only act that can save the people of Jaremi Four from a nightmare of Khorenian exploitation."

Eldridge watched Greder's face look away. Her eyes widened as she realized that somewhere in the emptiness, *Bright Hope* had placed an untouchable witness. She barked garbled orders to unseen crewpeople.

"Bright Hope is running first in the race for the surface," Duza continued. If *Cornucopia* should be the first to touch down, it will be only because the tyrant of Khoren Four opened fire on *Bright Hope*. Remember, though she's a military craft, *Bright Hope* is defenseless, weaponless, shieldless, almost blind, and barely able to move."

"Mother of stars," Eldridge muttered. "Call us incompetent while you're at it."

"Though they mean well, *Bright Hope*'s crew is wholly out of their element here," Duza went on. "Overwhelmed, incapable of responding to the clustered crises within and without, the crew does its hapless best. Now even their survival is out of their hands, beyond their power to influence. Only Tyrant Greder's forbearance has the power to preserve them—"

Eldridge muted Duza's audio.

Thirty seconds passed. A minute. Greder's look of harried frustration spoke volumes.

"They can't find the scouter," Wachieu breathed. "Weapons are no longer charging. Plorg on a stick, she's heating up her metainertials." Wachieu called in amazement. "*Cornucopia* is calling in her support ships, ordering them to dock in preparation for. . . ." Wachieu scowled and pressed a finger to each ear. She brought her hands away and pumped her fists into the air. "Confirmed! Greder has ordered the small ships of her fleet to dock with *Cornucopia* in preparation for a high-speed return to Khoren Four."

Eldridge smiled. "She'll find a police cordon awaiting her."

The auxiliary control room erupted into a spree of cheering.

"All right, people," Eldridge called. "There is now no question that *Bright Hope* will reach the surface of Jaremi Four. There remains, however, substantial uncertainty as to how hard. Let's give this our full concentration and make this a landing we all walk away from."

125. Jaremi Four—Southern Hemisphere

Ruth and Linka swept no-vis above the knotted armies. They struck out in opposite directions. Ruth overflew the Catholic infantry. For the third time that day, its formation had collapsed on the muddy slope. Men were laying down their guns. They dropped to their knees and wailed in prayer. "Look!" cried one. "Look in the east!"

"Is it a star?"

A kilometer further inland, Linka drifted directly above Chagrin. She heard him order his two rafts back to the north channel's shore. His gaunt eyes turning skyward, Chagrin mumbled over and over: "Parek spoke of this. It's Zion of old, returning from the realm of the sky gods." He leapt from his raft the moment it beached and started running back toward the crestline, his followers clustering behind him.

Nearer shore, Ruth swooped toward a familiar figure. Like a twisted hermit Friz Labokloer pushed through the ranks, ever uphill, favoring his horribly swollen leg. "Do you see it!" he ranted. "It's the fruit of our Work! The vessel by which civilization will be returned to us!"

What do you know, Ruth thought. *For what may be the first time in his life, Friz Labokloer got something right.*

With empty hands Catholic soldiers shambled uphill. Facing them, Chagrin's refugees gathered in unarmed clusters at the cliff's crest. Some scrambled down rocky channels, angling toward the attackers. Hostility was the last thing on anyone's mind. *There are some things in whose presence one simply feels the need to join with others,* thought Linka. *Any others. Even those who moments before were deadly enemies.*

Still airborne, Linka leaned her head back. She let her feet swing up. Like the autochthons, she surrendered herself to the awe of gawking into the afternoon sky.

Bright Hope looked like a falling city, descending among the smoke columns that still rose from the trawler's impact sites. Slowly, grandly she twisted on her long axis. Scouters and tugs and flitters and workboats swarmed her hull in layers. The vessels that could, fired off colorful lighting effects out into the Jaremian atmosphere.

Bright Hope was no more than ten klicks up. Inertial drivegates flickered in a circular array at her stern. Vast pitted hatches stuttered open. Articulated landing feet skulked into daylight, looking as if one could reach out and shake hands with them. *An illusion,* Linka recognized, *driven by the fact that each foot assembly is the size of a small building.*

Ruth Griszam bobbed up beside her. "Hey Linka, check this out."

Linka followed Ruth's eyes uphill, then down.

Though neither of them knew it, Labokloer and Chagrin were wandering straight toward one another.

"See you down there," Linka said, twisting away. She arched skyward, looping back to the ground among the soldiers at the cliff top.

Ruth hurled herself downhill, toward the river where Parek's shattered fleet still bobbed. She landed among the Catholic soldiers on the muddy bank. *Everyone around me is staring at the sky.* She just snapped visible among the slack-jawed troopers. No one noticed her. She pushed uphill on foot. Men stood where they were, their bodies almost limp; squeezing forward between them was not difficult. In a bubble, she saw that Linka had done essentially the same thing. Having popped into view behind a knot of Chagrin's troops, she was now pushing downslope.

When Linka overtook Chagrin he was walking with open hands raised to the sky, tears rushing down his cheeks. Linka tugged at his leather tunic. "A great day, First Disciple," she called.

It took Chagrin a moment to look at her. Recognition took longer yet. "Lina?"

"Linka."

At last Chagrin remembered where he had last seen her—locked in a cell beside the canal in Graargy's valley, helpless to flee the irresistible Catholic pursuit force bearing down on them. "What the fuck are you doing here?"

When Ruth overtook Labokloer, she lay a hand on his bare arm. The last time she'd touched him there, muscle had billowed. Now he felt scrawny and dry as crumbling papier-mâché. "Friz, look at me."

"Ruth? *Ruth!*" He threw his arms around her. He smelled like a canyon full of dead *sturruh.* "This is the wonderful! This is the wonderful!" His breath was like an unharvested field of *chuli* moldering under the next spring's sun. He stepped back. He stared at her face, her body, her soiled but still-elegant silk costume. "How did you—how can you—" Blinking back tears, he clamped her wrist and led her uphill at a trot, waving with his free hand at the sky. "Who cares how you got here. You're here. The right place. The right time."

Bright Hope hung a kilometer above ground, poised to land on a low bluff about five klicks to the east. Though she'd lost altitude, she seemed taller than ever. *What a forjeling mess,* Linka thought, scanning the charred pits and twisted components that peppered the schooner's hull. Gray smoke leapt from the land below. *Bright Hope* hovered, burning away a forest with the power of her thrusters.

Flitters and scouters whirled less than a thousand meters overhead, some lower. A workboat whistled past no more than a hundred meters above their head. Panes of color washed its terraced sides. Countless troopers scattered. Labokloer stood firm. He smiled. He sobbed. "This is what we fought for," he told Ruth. "This is what Lord Samu promised."

"Commodore Labokloer!" Linka called. Ruth and Labokloer turned. Linka and Chagrin stepped before them. Fighting a sense of irony, Linka made historic introductions. "Commodore Friz Labokloer, commanding the army of Samu. Meet Chagrin, First Disciple of the army of Parek."

After hesitating a moment, the two commanders clasped hands.

"The war is over," Labokloer said forcefully. "Its purpose was to burn away our blemishes."

Chagrin bobbed his head up and down. "Oh, you mean like on our escutcheons."

"Um, yes," Labokloer said uncertainly. "The great stone mason chipped away at us from the inside. Today we are ready for him."

"I've seen him, you know."

Labokloer blinked. "Who?"

"The god named God."

"The God who is to come?"

"Yeah, him."

"You can't be serious."

Chagrin smiled. "I saw him only once. Sort of by accident. You know, it's funny." He gestured toward *Bright Hope*, descending again amid a column of smoke and fire-suppressant mist. "His holy city is so beautiful it makes your eyes hurt, but God himself—" Chagrin shrugged. "He's kind of this clumsy rustic guy. Only wears one rumpled-up sheet."

Of course, Ruth realized eventually. *Latier. . . .*

"Holy shit, *Ruth!*" Chagrin's hands leapt out to clasp Ruth's shoulders. "Ruth Griszam! Haven't seen you since the dam!" Perplexity inched across his deep-set eyes. "Shit, woman, how did you—hey!" All smiles, he pushed Linka forward. "Ruth, you gotta meet Lina."

"Oh," Ruth said vaguely, "we've met."

The small craft had broken from their looping orbits. They mustered now in two lines, hovering above the river, facing downstream. Some of the Catholic troops had gotten the message; they, too, were gathering in ranks along the riverbank and preparing to march to the east toward the towering apparition that was *Bright Hope*.

"I know you," Labokloer told Linka cautiously.

Linka smiled. "You approved of my body armor."

"If you say so. So you know Ruth—" Labokloer squinted toward Ruth and looked her up and down.

Chagrin did the same. "Holy fuck," he breathed.

Incredulous, Labokloer looked up from Ruth's body and over toward *Bright Hope*. His voice was almost inaudible. "By the skygods, Ruth. Do you have—have something to do with *that?*"

"Friz, I don't know what you're talking about," Ruth said innocently.

Linka caught Ruth's eye. Eyebrows high, lips atwist, Linka's fingers were stabbing toward her own belt, then toward Ruth's.

Ruth looked down. She realized her nulgrav wasn't completely shut off. She was floating perhaps a hand's width above the ground.

"For vacuum's sake," she snorted before collapsing into laughter. A moment later, she raised her head. She smiled broadly and clasped one hand on Labokloer's shoulder, the other on Chagrin's. "Friz, Chagrin, listen." She tilted her head downslope and past the ruins toward the river. "Your people are about to begin an adventure like you've never imagined. They need leaders."

Labokloer scowled. "After this battle, I planned to lay down the burdens of leading."

Chagrin nodded. "Anyway, what's to lead?" He nodded toward the lines of small craft whose paths the columns of soldiers now followed. "Everybody knows where to go. The leader's just the guy in front."

Ruth shook her head. "Look, both of you. This is going to sound strange, but your . . . your *world* needs you." She jerked her head again toward the massing armies. "Your people march east, toward the—toward *it*. If you hurry, you can still get in front."

Buffalo, N.Y., and Amsterdam; Berlin; Boulder, Colo.; Brussels; Cincinnati, Oh.; Chicago; Denver; Detroit; Erie, Pa.; Geneva, N.Y.; Himrod, N.Y.; Houston; Independence, Mo.; Kitchener, Ont.; Los Angeles; Oslo; New York; Palmyra, N.Y.; Philadelphia; Salt Lake City; San Francisco; Sidney, Oh.; Toronto; Washington, D.C.; Watkins Glen, N.Y., June 1991/January 1999

Glossary

affectational colorist An artist/technician who manipulates sensory imagery and various subsensory channels in order to enhance the persuasive or emotional effect of a *tridee* or *senso* program.

antecedent sample A sample of one's body tissues removed and banked prior to some activity which might result in death. Usually accompanied by a brainstate scan. See *O/N-two; sample-and-scan.*

authochthon Inhabitant native to a planet. On an *Enclave* planet, autochthons are to be protected—at any cost—from learning about the Galactic *Confetory* or about the true nature of the *Spectators* in their midst.

auto-ident A communications signal beamed from a military spacecraft with appropriate clearances. It causes the target vessel to beam back basic information about its name, registry, and mission.

being-thereness The completely engrossing sensation of somesthetic presence—a complete *sensorium*—characteristic of viewing *senso.*

benefice

(Universal Catholic Church) The right of certain Cardinals and other high-ranking prelates to sell objects used in the discharge of their office as a means of helping to pay their expenses.

bird

Slang term used by *Spectators* to refer to the orbiting satellites which receive their raw transmissions, record their *senso* journals, and serve as their node to Galactic civilization.

bubble

An artificial zone, typically spherical, in which a tridee recording or three-dimensional data stream is typically viewed. A conventional tridee bubble is projected into midair and viewed with the ordinary senses. Various artificial enhancements, such as *Spectator* implants or mental communion with properly enhanced creatures or *thought engines,* permit humans to experience "virtual" bubbles as overlays of conventional awareness.

bubbleprint

A flat *bubble;* a virtual circular zone within which two-dimensional information such as datacrawls may be experienced.

bug

A small, self-contained remote monitoring device used by field *Spectators,* usually disguised to look natural when scattered about or secreted within clothing. The bug returns a full-bandwidth, multisensory image at slightly better than *tridee* resolution, which can be used in place of a Spectator's own sphere of awareness *(pov).* Bugs are often used by Spectators to provide additional viewpoints of fast-unfolding action, or to monitor activities in the Spectator's vicinity.

checking journal

A recording of a senso broadcast as actually distributed to *experients* (the audience), requested for review purposes by the Spectator who recorded it. Used to check recording quality and the effects of any alterations made by machine and human editors. See *journal.*

chute

A Galactic device for moving between floors or levels in a building. It appears as a faintly luminous disk, which supports the person or persons standing on it and permits vertical passage from level to level.

concealer

A contramagnetic energy field that renders the user invisible to vision or various types of *susceptors.* Alternatively, a device which generates such a field to protect a single person, a ship, a city, or an island. See also *displacer.*

Confetory   The Galactic empire or confederation. A centuries-old, gen-
                             erally peaceful political coalition that binds together some
                             42,000 planets inhabited by humans. Fewer than twenty full
                             "Memberworlds" produce most of the wealth, fund most
                             Confetory activities, and exercise legislative authority. The
                             vast majority of planets have a status subordinate to that of
                             the full members. Affiliate, Protectorate, or *Enclave* planets
                             enjoy progressively lower status and more restricted access
                             to the Confetory's cultures and technologies.

consubstantiality   *(Universal Catholic Church)* Theological doctrine based on
                             acceptance of mitochondrial evidence suggesting that
                             human life evolved only once—on Terra—and was then
                             physically exported to other worlds (see *Harvesters*). Con-
                             trasts with earlier, now largely discredited doctrines which
                             held that the humans of various planets resulted from sep-
                             arate acts of divine creation.

contramagnetic   A physical force parallel (or more properly, correlative) to
                             the weak nuclear force. Mediated by *transphotic* particles,
                             contramagnetic force is immune to the universal speed
                             limit, c. The principal applications of contramagnetic force
                             is for faster-than-light interstellar propulsion and real-time
                             communication over unlimited distances.

Cosmic Christ   *(Universal Catholic Church)* The Son of God as instantiated
                             in a recognized *Incarnation* on a particular planet. Church
                             doctrine holds that the Cosmic Christ is successively
                             embodied on one planet after another, across the Galaxy.

datascape   An abstract visual representation of causal relationships
                             between phenomena, presented by a *strategic modeler* or
                             similar device. Has the appearance of a schematic land-
                             scape with imaginary mountains, valleys, and bridges map-
                             ping casual links between the phenomena under study.

deep cover   An assignment in which a *Spectator* joins an *autochthonous*
                             community and lives among its members as one of them.
                             Secretly the *Spectator* records the community's affairs.
                             OmNet then massages these *journals* and releases them to
                             the Galaxy as *senso* entertainment programming.

Detex   Generic term for the battery of *susceptors* used by spacecraft
                             to navigate, determine spatial conditions, and monitor dis-
                             tant events.

disinto   Weapon which liberates subatomic bonds within its target,
                             utterly annihilating it. In practice, always combined with a

force field projector which confines and filters the very high energies released. Available in sizes from pistols to immense, ship-mounted guns capable of annihilating other ships or large natural features.

displacer

A contramagnetic energy field that causes vision or various *susceptors* to see the user at a position significantly shifted from the user's actual location. Makes people miss when they shoot at you. Alternatively, a device which generates such a field to protect a single person, a ship, a city, or an island. See also *concealer*.

echo

Later replay of a *Spectator*'s journal into the awareness of the same *Spectator* who recorded it, usually for purposes of review.

Enclave

The policy, established under the famed Enclave Statutes, under which peoples judged too primitive to tolerate awareness of the Galactic Confetory are quarantined from most intercourse with Galactic civilization. Mere knowledge of the Confetory's existence might damage the self-image and warp the development of *autochthonous* peoples. Of the Galaxy's forty-two thousand inhabited planets, forty thousand lie under Enclave. These worlds are never to be assimilated into Galactic culture, but rather allowed to develop or destroy themselves as they will. Carefully screened scientists and *Spectators* working *deep cover* are the only Galactics routinely permitted to permeate the Enclave barrier.

equilibrational calculus

Computational discipline developed by the math prodigy Fram Galbior. Enables highly reliable prediction of the spatial and temporal coordinates at which a *Tuezi* will appear. Experimentally applied to solve other seemingly intractable problems involving distribution of repetitive phenomena in time and space.

experient

One who *pov*s, views, or experiences a *senso* program.

fashioner

An *autochthon* on the planet Jaremi Four who is skilled as a craftsman, fabricator, smith or engineer.

fhlet

Bland, pulpy fruit ubiquitous on Jaremi Four. *Fhlet* was bred by Jaremian biologists after Jaremi Four was ravaged by a Tuezi strike, but before civilization collapsed altogether. A rare hybrid between a native Jaremian plant and a food plant of Terran origin (see *Harvesters*), *fhlet* grows vigorously and is nutritious for humans.

flier A *Spectator* equipped with a flight module. This small belt-mounted device modifies local gravity and permits a skilled wearer to hover or fly long distances. A *Spectator* working *support* typically wears a *no-vis* generator and a flight module, and is therefore called a *no-vis flyer.*

GDX Biological warfare agent, instantly fatal to mammals. Capable of quantum tunneling, it penetrates any protective clothing or filtering apparatus. An area contaminated by GDX cannot be entered until the end of the substance's virulence period, usually seven days.

gero-mentor An older person who serves as a teacher, exemplar, or role model to the young, especially in *procreant cliques* or other organized child-rearing systems. See also *ward captain.*

glasteel Basic transparent engineering material, used for numerous applications up to and including spacecraft viewports.

Harvesters Unknown alien entities. No artifact, fossil, or other trace of their existence was ever found. But mitochrondrial evidence makes clear that about eighty thousand years ago, *someone* visited Terra, took specimens of protohumans and various food species, and seeded them on some 42,000 other planets about the Galaxy. Whether the Harvesters are related in any way to the unknown aliens who construct and dispatch the *Tuezi* is unknown.

Incarnation (*Universal Catholic Church*) Officially sanctioned embodiment of the *Cosmic Christ,* as sanctioned by the *Universal Catholic Church*

inverter The power plant in which *contramagnetic* energy is generated and controlled.

journal The raw *senso* recording dumped from the satellite's buffer onto Net just before the *Spectator* goes out of *Mode.*

lateral Relaying of one *Spectator*'s current awareness or recent journal to the awareness of another *Spectator,* often through a *bubble* in the receiving *Spectator*'s awareness.

mode An altered state of consciousness, mediated by biogenetic implants, which puts a *Spectator* fully in touch with an orbiting satellite (or *bird*). When one establishes this link ("goes into *Mode*") one enters *polyphasic consciousness,* a state in which the Spectator's ability to experience multiple images and/or perform multiple simultaneous tasks is heightened. The resulting *subdelta band* link offers extremely generous bandwidth. While in *Mode*, a Spectator can upload his or her entire *sensorium* or receive and *pov* previously recorded sensoria, such as *senso* recorded by another *Spectator* or a recorded *journal* of one's own work. At the same time one may send or receive up to a dozen channels of tridee, experienced inside *bubbles* that float in one's awareness in front of the one's *sensorium*. At the same time, one may also send and receive multiple channels of data.

modeler, strategic   See *strategic modeler.*

no-vis   Invisible. On an *Enclave* planet, *Spectators* who work *support* are issued a *no-vis* generator, a compact device that attaches to one's belt and renders one invisible when desired.

no-vis flyer   On an *Enclave* planet, a *Spectator* who works *support* is equipped with a *no-vis* generator and a *nulgrav* unit. The no-vis flyer can travel at high speed, or monitor developments from close quarters without being noticed by the *autochthons*.

nulgrav   Gravity-neutralizing device, especially a small module, often belt-mounted, that permits a *no-vis flyer* or other specialized operative to fly within an atmosphere without resort to *chutes*, aerial platforms, or other flight-capable apparatus.

O/N-two   "Obliterated, Not Recoverable, or Not Sampleable." If a Galactic dies under circumstances where the body is utterly destroyed, cannot be recovered, and timely sampling of cadaver tissues is impossible, death is irreversible unless one has previously banked tissue samples (see *Sample-and-Scan*). Even then, one revives with memories intact only up to the time when the *antecedent sample* was taken, recalling nothing between the time of sampling and the time of death.

OmNet   An immense interworld monopoly that owns and controls senso technology, and programs the senso programming throughout the Galactic Confetory. Based on Terra, it is the human homeworld's second largest source of export revenue (see *Universal Catholic Church*).

outer self   The local, *autochthonous* identity affected by a *Spectator* for the purpose of a *deep cover* assignment.

plasteel   Basic engineering material, widely used throughout the Galactic *Confetory.*

polyphasic consciousness The many layered awareness experienced by a *Spectator* who is fully in *Mode*. The *Spectator* may simultaneously, and discretely, experience his or her immediate sensations; one or more tridee playbacks, in *bubbles;* any number of datacrawls in two-dimensional *bubbleprints;* and even full-*senso echoes* or *laterals,* usually at a reduced level of resolution. Underneath it all chatters a channel of "housekeeping" information, most importantly the *verify* signal.

posting Actual sending of a *journal* by the *Spectator* who recorded it. At their option, *deep cover* Spectators may elect to transmit their feeds in real time, or they may direct their assigned satellites to hold the recordings for a selected interval, later transmitting them to *OmNet.*

pov The recording *Spectator*'s sensory field *(sensorium),* point of view, and *being-thereness* as experienced by another (an *experient)* in the course of viewing a senso.

procreant clique In most, though not all, Galactic societies, the preferred means of low-level social organization. Rapidly supplanting the conventional family on Terra, whose inhabitants were understandably startled to discover that the family was merely a local aberration. Children are raised in cohorts or *wards* under the supervision of *ward captains* or *gero-mentors.*

ravisher Weapon that encapsulates, then incinerates its victim. At low power, one side effect of the ravisher field is the preservation and enhancement of human consciousness. Death by ravisher pistol is thus considered the most exquisitely agonizing way in which a human being can die.

sample-and-scan A process in which a Galactic's body tissue is sampled and one's brainstate recorded, often before embarking on some dangerous mission or assignment. If one is rendered *O/N-Two,* precluding revival from one's bodily remains, one can be restored from the sample-and-scan, albeit only with the memories one possessed at the time of scanning. See *antecedent sample.*

saybackers Public opinion pollsters.

saybacks Early returns; comments from experients. Similar in function to overnight Nielsens. Also, public opinion polls; the results of such polling.

senso An entertainment technology in which the user (or *experient)* loses awareness of his or her own sensory awareness, experiencing instead the complete *sensorium* of another person. A person trained and equipped to create senso programming is called a *Spectator*.

sensorium The *Spectator* or *experient*'s complete sensory field: vision (including depth), binaural sound, taste, smell, tactile impressions, and somesthetics. When an experient *pov*s a senso, the experient's awareness of his or her own *sensorium* is overwritten by the recorded *sensorium* of the *Spectator*.

sim Technology that creates simulated settings in which the *experient* enjoys the sensation of free movement and interaction with the nonexistent surroundings. More casually, any technology that creates awareness of nonexistent "realities" for purpose of data display, communication, or entertainment.

Spectator A human who by dint of specialized training and biogenetic implants is able to record his or her complete *sensorium* in a way that may be experienced, or *pov*ed, by others. Employed by *OmNet*, Spectators function as human cameras. Assignments range from overt news-gathering to *deep cover* documentary work among *autochthon*s on *Enclave* planets.

squeezedown To adapt a *senso* journal or other program for presentation in a lower resolution format such as *tridee* or twodee.

squirt To send a defined data stream to a particular recipient. *Spectators* often squirt portions of their journals to one another when they desire others' opinions about their situation.

steward Religious order within the *Universal Catholic Church*, dedicated to defending the teachings and prestige of the pope. Unlike the Society of Jesus ("Jesuits"), previously famed as "the pope's Men," the Stewards accept lay persons *and* ordained clergy into their membership, by invitation only.

strategic modeler A specialized thought engine optimized for complex "what-if" problems in logistics, military strategy, or estimating the most likely causes of historical events. Available units range from pocket size to desk-sized units designed to accommodate multiple operators.

subdelta band A band of *transphotic* frequencies reserved for broad-bandwidth communications between *OmNet Spectators* and the geostationary satellites which record their *journals* and monitor their biogenetic implant systems. *Subdelta band* communication is among the most reliable, robust, and noise-immune communications links known to Galactic technology.

support An assignment in which a *Spectator* is stationed on an *Enclave* planet to meet special needs *deep cover* Spectators may have. *Support* personnel are typically issued a *no-vis* generator and a flight module; may also be called a *no-vis flyer*. Typical *support* tasks include aerial reconnaissance; "backup" or aerial coverage of a complex event such as a battle; recovery of a dead Spectator and transport of his or her body to a base station for attempted revival; and assassination, for example when an *autochthon* is about to discover forbidden knowledge about *Enclave* or the *Confetory*.

susceptor Sensor. Any remote sensing system. On a spacecraft, *susceptors* constitute the suite of remote-sensing equipment that make up the ship's *Detex* system.

tap A subjective prodding sensation, an attention signal used to alert a *Spectator* to urgent incoming communication or important information from a *bug*.

thought engine An artificial device optimized for image processing, data manipulation, trend detection, automatic control applications, or any/all of the above.

transphotic An energy band above (or more properly, oblique to) the electromagnetic spectrum. Unknown to Terran technology until the Galactic *Confetory* made contact with Terra. Transphotic radiation propagates instantaneously without regard for distance, making possible real-time communication across the Galaxy.

trendrider A human who by dint of specialized training and a symbiotic relationship with a specially designed *thought engine* is able to analyze and interpret highly complex social and political trends. Also known as *wonk*s.

tridee Mass communications technology which produces a three-dimensional, partly multisensory experience. The image floats within a physical viewing space or *bubble* whose borders the viewer can still apprehend by looking away from it. Largely supplanted by *senso* as a primary entertainment medium; still widely used as a communications and information-gathering medium. Tridee broadcasts require far less comm bandwidth than senso, and permit the *experient* to remain aware of surrounding events. Often used to view *senso* journals at reduced resolution (see *squeezedown*).

Tuezi

Gigantic robotic spaceship/weapons platform. Manufactured by unknown entities, employing technologies unknown to the Galactic *Confetory*, a Tuezi simply pops into existence at a random time and location in the Galaxy. Left to its (considerable) devices, it will raise impenetrable shields, head for the nearest solar system, ravage or destroy most of the planets encountered there, and finally self-destruct. Tuezi (the word is irregular, and may be either singular or plural) have only one known vulnerability: For about a fiftieth of a second after they "appear" they are powered down and unshielded.

Universal Catholic Church

Name assumed by the Roman Catholic Church after it concentrated its missionary work on worlds other than Terra, especially after transferring its headquarters from Vatican City of Terra to the planet Vatican. Vatican is Terra's first sovereign planetary territory outside Sol system; the Universal Catholic Church is Terra's largest source of export revenue, followed by the senso monopoly *OmNet*.

upper self

The *Spectator*'s true *persona* as a Galactic and a citizen of the *Confetory*.

vanisher valise

An item of luggage which uses *transphotic* energy to collapse spatial gradients in its interior. By this means objects of great volume or weight can be stored and carried in smaller, lighter containers. Further, objects contained inside the valise cannot be detected by common forms of noninvasive inspection.

verify signal

A tone heard at the basement level of a *Spectator*'s *polyphasic consciousness* from the satellite or other system that is recording one's *journal*. Confirms that one's signal is being received.

wafer

Data storage device.

ward captain

An adult who has formal responsibility for—and command authority over—a specific troupe of children in a *procreant clique* or other regimented child-rearing system.

winkies

Jaremian-speak for "pilot lights." Used to show the readiness of steam-powered weapons.

wonk

See *trendrider*.

the characters

First Name	Surname	Homeworld	Description
Rikhard	Allihern	Zbaghiel Three	Commander, Jaremi Four research station
Nevrol	Andervek	Terra	Spectator
Ul' Fze	B'Khraa	Khoren Four	Native chieftain; Orgena Greder's candidate Christ
	Babe	Jaremi Four	Newborn child
Heber	Beaman	Terra	Assistant to Alrue Latier
Will	Bickel	Zbaghiel Three	Sergeant at Arms, schooner *Bright Hope*
	Blaupek	Jaremi Four	Subject of Graargy; allegedly murdered by Yelmir
	Blorach	Jaremi Four	Subject of Graargy; widow of Blaupek
Sfem	Brogradus	Minga Four	Betrayer of that planet's recognized Christ
Valatu	Brouhkin ve Greneil	Ordh	Recently deceased artist collected by Ato Cardinal Semuga
Vitold	Byrtoldi	Terra	Pope Modest IV's real name
	Chagrin	Jaremi Four	Parek's second convert and trusted confidant

	Coblasta	Minga Four	"Straightener of the Way" who, according to legend, prefigured the religious leader later endorsed as that planet's authentic Incarnation of Christ
	Compounding Mistress	Jaremi Four	Autochthonous leader; guild supervisor for candle making in refugee community
	Congregation for the Evangelization of the Worlds	Terra	Cardinal, Universal Catholic Church
	Dean of the Stewards	Ordh	Leader of a religious order
Hezho	Dhebbuniad	Scalbulia Eight	Betrayer of that planet's recognized Christ
	Diazlam	Jaremi Four	Overly devout officer in Parek's army
Tramir	Duza	Gheltt	Spectator
Moreyn	Dorga	Braciax Omicron	Chief scientist, Jaremi Four research station
Willim	Dultav	Jaremi Four	Jaremi Four autochthon; onetime professor; partner of Arn Parek
	Dzettko	Jaremi Four	Jaremi Four autochthon; subject of Graargy; tribal tribune
Highest	Elder	Jaremi Four	Jaremi Four autochthon; supreme tribal leader
	Elder of the Chandlers	Jaremi Four	Jaremi Four autochthon; tribal leader
	Elder of the Clouds	Jaremi Four	Jaremi Four autochthon; tribal leader
	Elder of the Compounders	Jaremi Four	Jaremi Four autochthon; tribal leader
	Elder of the Fashioners	Jaremi Four	Jaremi Four autochthon; tribal leader
	Elder of the Glowing Ooze	Jaremi Four	Jaremi Four autochthon; tribal leader
	Elder of the Soil	Jaremi Four	Jaremi Four autochthon; tribal leader
	Eldress of Refectory	Jaremi Four	Jaremi Four autochthon; tribal leader
	Eldress of Tannery	Jaremi Four	Jaremi Four autochthon; tribal leader
	Eldress of the Farms	Jaremi Four	Jaremi Four autochthon; tribal leader
Laurien	Eldridge	Gwilya	Captain, schooner Bright Hope

Akkad	Felegu	Jaremi Four	Jaremi Four autochthon; commander in Ulf's army
	Freydiin	Jaremi Four	Jaremi Four autochthon; subject of Graargy; husband of Verina
Fram	Galbior	Guerecht Six	Famed mathematician
Arla	Gavisel	Arkhetil	Executive Officer, schooner *Bright Hope*
Stenoda	Gerris	Ordh	Shipping magnate, convert to Parekism
Sfix	Geruda	Terra	Theologian, Universal Catholic Church
Vebla Rasz	Gomaystek	Kfardasz	Betrayer of that planet's recognized Christ
	Graargy	Jaremi Four	Jaremi Four autochthon; chief of Southern Hemisphere settlement
Ambrose	Graftig	Calluron Five	Spectator assigned to Samu's fleet
Orgena	Greder	Khoren Four	Industrialist, tyrant
Ruth	Griszam	Terra	Spectator
Yaal	Hafen	Guerecht Six	Admiral of the PeaceForce
Barkela	Halv'ekral	Gonsephinone Four	Nun assigned to Vatican Island
Bei	Hanllei	Khoren Four	Assistant to Orgena Greder
	Harapel	Jaremi Four	Jaremi Four autochthon; subject of Graargy; accuser of Yelmir
Fzel	Harisjen	Jaremi Four	Soldier in Parek's army
Xyrel	Hjinn	Ordh	Theologian, Universal Catholic Church
Marnen	Incavo	Nikkeldepayn	Tainted detective
	Ixtlaca	Jaremi Four	Jaremi Four autochthon; subject of Graargy; adolescent female
	Jaekdyr	Jaremi Four	Jaremi Four autochthon; younger son of Graargy and Sculfka
	Jerl	Jaremi Four	Jaremi Four autochthon; northern hemisphere resident; father of deformed child
	John XXV (Pope)	Terra	Dissolved the Jesuit order for second time in 2088 (Clement XIV did so the first time in 1773)
	Kaahel	Jaremi Four	Jaremi Four autochthon; Southern Hemisphere chieftain; killer of Laz Kalistor
Laz	Kalistor	Orhiza Three	Spectator

Neuri Kalistor	Orhiza Three	Spectator
Friz Labokloer	Jaremi Four	Jaremi Four autochthon; petty Northern Hemisphere lord
Alrue Latier	Terra	Mormon New Restoration televangelist
Lormatin	Jaremi Four	Jaremi Four autochthon; southern hemisphere chieftain; rival to Graargy
Fons Maguffin	Wikkel Four	Betrayer of that planet's recognized Christ
Matriarch of Clan Aurora	Jaremi Four	Jaremi Four autochthon; tribal leader
Meryam Mayishimu	Ordh	Journalist
Messenger	Jaremi Four	Jaremi Four autochthon; minion of the Highest Elder
Midwife	Jaremi Four	Jaremi Four autochthon
Modest IV	Terra	Pope, Universal Catholic Church
Young Mother	Jaremi Four	Jaremi Four autochthon; mother of the babe
Muldowa	Jaremi Four	Jaremi Four autochthon; subject of Graargy
Annek Panna	Gwilya	Scientist; inventor of stardrive installed aboard schooner *Bright Hope*
Arn Parek	Jaremi Four	Jaremi Four autochthon; self-styled messiah
Pius XV (Pope)	Terra	Ratified the *Codex Pederasticus* which institutionalized pederasty and the keeping of young boys in harems by Universal Catholic priests
Prefect, Congregation of Institutes for Consecrated Life and Societies of Apostolic Life	Terra	Cardinal, Universal Catholic Church
Prefect of the Papal Household	Kfardasz	Wleti Krammonz, Bishop, Universal Catholic Church
President, Council for Devout Protocol	Ghyrel Two	Cardinal of the Universal Catholic Church
Laerl Q'Flehg	Calluron Five	Spectator briefly attached to Ulf's army
Ileatz Quareg	Jaremi Four	Jaremi Four autochthon; noble who

			received erroneous prophecy
Alois	Rybczynsky	Terra	Cardinal; Vatican Secretary of State
	Sculfka	Jaremi Four	Wife of Graargy
	Selwaga	Jaremi Four	Subject of Graargy; lame woman
Ato	Semuga	Terra	Cardinal; Pontifical Councilor for Arcane Works
Ged	Silbertak	Terra	President of OmNet
Oriel	Spibbert	Ordh	Rear Admiral; C.O. of flagship; deacon; Semuga aide
Linka	Strasser	Terra	Spectator
	Sydeno	Jaremi Four	Jaremi Four autochthon; subject of Graargy; Linka's native lover
	Tarbyl	Jaremi Four	Jaremi Four autochthon; subject of Graargy; sentry
	Tarklan	Jaremi Four	Jaremi Four autochthon; itinerant minstrel
Giela	Tregsna	Jaremi Four	Jaremi Four autochthon; wealthy woman drawn to Parek cult by Laz Kalistor
	Tsretmak	Jaremi Four	Jaremi Four autochthon; elder son of Graargy and Sculfka
	Ulf	Jaremi Four	Jaremi Four autochthon; Parek's first convert and general
	Verina	Jaremi Four	Jaremi Four autochthon; subject of Graargy; pregnant woman
Scabillax	Veuth	Ordh	Betrayer of that planet's recognized Christ
Lynn	Wachieu	Ordh	Detex officer, schooner *Bright Hope*
Garren	Wehrman	Frensa Six	Ato Cardinal Semuga's engineering attaché
	Weldaey	Jaremi Four	Jaremi Four autochthon; subject of Graargy; dies of bowel obstruction
Cassandra	Wiplien	Terra	Spectator; no-vis flier assigned to southern hemisphere of Jaremi Four
Haggard	Woman	Jaremi Four	Jaremi Four autochthon; palsied mother of Young Mother
Young	Woman	Jaremi Four	Jaremi Four autochthon; sister of Young Mother
Aresino	Y'Braga	Ordh	Father General, Society of Jesus

Lor	Ye'Uhz	Parctantis Two	Enclave Compliance Officer, Jaremi Four research station
	Yelmir	Jaremi Four	Jaremi Four autochthon; subject of Graargy; falsely accused of murder
Bentito	Ynez	Buerala Six	"Straightener of the Way" who, according to legend, prefigured the religious leader later endorsed as that planet's authentic Incarnation of Christ